M000158716

DINOSAUR

THE NEW WORLD SERIES | BOOK ONE

Stephen Llewelyn

Published by Fossil Rock Publishing 2020

ISBNs:

978-1-8380235-0-8 paperback
978-1-8380235-1-5 ebook

For Sally, thank you.

The author also wishes to acknowledge:

Mum and *Dad*, thanks for encouraging my latest crazy idea.
Special thanks to *Nick, Karl, Melanie* and *Linda*, who gave so much of their time when they didn't have to, cheers guys.
Also, to a friend I sadly never met, I would like to thank *Hannah Armstrong*, who sketched the beautiful Giganotosaurus skull titling chapter 6. One of her many friends told me that she loved dinosaurs so much she even made up a few of her own. In this series I invented a new dinosaur called Mayor Dougli Salvator, who shows great courage – I dedicate him to you, Hannah.

…And last but by no means least, to everyone who reads this book, thank you.
The crew of the USS *New World* will return soon in

THE NEW WORLD SERIES | BOOK TWO | REVENGE.

No dinosaurs were harmed during the making of this book.

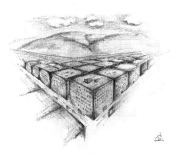

Chapter 1 | I'll leave you in hell

"Do you wish us to acquire the item, sir?"

The old man sat motionless behind his extravagantly carved desk, staring dispassionately at the academics. It was obvious that the balding, middle-aged man standing before him was desperately trying not to wring his hands. The woman, younger and clearly of sterner material, returned his gaze without emotion. The old man enjoyed the fear in the scientist's demeanour. He let him sweat a moment longer before shaking his head. "No, Doctor. Simply knowing of the artefact's existence is enough – for now. I authorise your project and whatever assets you require." He raised a wry eyebrow. "We *are* attempting to save the human race after all, are we not?"

"Yes, sir," replied the petitioner, experimenting briefly with tucking his hands into the pockets of his lab coat but removing them at once, hoping the action had not been perceived as slovenly or disrespectful.

The old man scrutinised him once more, coldly feline. He wondered whether it would be more expedient to simply replace him immediately, or wait to see if he could pull himself together once the process began. His master's approval given, the fellow appeared more nervous than before.

The woman spoke for the first time, interrupting his musings. A flash of annoyance crossed his face but she continued undeterred.

"We are two years away from a working prototype, sir – 2112 at the earliest. All of our tests so far have destroyed the drives completely."

He eyed her for a moment. Still, she held his gaze. Eventually he nodded slowly. "Very well, Doctors. In that case, I had better not keep you." Slight pressure on a sensor in the arm of his chair made it rotate away from them and towards the view over the remnant rainforest around his fortress. The meeting was over.

He watched with satisfaction as the scientists bowed before leaving, reflected in the curved glass of the window wall. After the door closed behind them, he waved a hand over another sensor in the chair's arm to activate an intercom link to his personal aide.

"*Yes, sir?*" The woman's response was immediate, her voice projected from sound plates artfully concealed within the exquisitely carved jet wall panelling. The panels were inlaid with gold etching, the sound, perfectly balanced to centre upon him, wherever he happened to be within his large study and inner sanctum. The vastly expensive electronics removed any trace of echo or destructive interference. He could eavesdrop on locations all over the world from here, with equal clarity. However, the source of this particular voice happened to be in the next room.

"I wish to see my granddaughter, tell her to book a few days vacation. I will expect her tomorrow," he stated, peremptorily.

"*Yes, sir. Is there anything else I can do for you?*"

The old man considered. "Yes. Get me a full report on the boy, I wish to check his progress. That will be all."

"*At once, si—*" He closed the connection mid salutation, continuing his survey of one of the last surviving pockets of the natural world; and it was all *his*.

He nodded contentedly. A human being, unprotected, would be lucky to survive even an hour out there now. The creeping, crawling creatures of the forest became more aggressive each year. It was almost as though they sensed their environment being taken from them and nature had programmed them to fight back, turning normally dangerous creatures murderous. It certainly deterred visitors. Mother Nature abhorred weakness. "…As do I," the old man completed the thought aloud. "All is as it should be."

He considered the full ramifications of the project he had just set in motion for a moment longer and then leaned forward slightly. Placing an elbow on the arm of his chair, he cradled his chin with a thumb and forefinger. Frowning in concentration, his thoughts turned towards *the boy*.

AD2112 – England

It was a milestone in the life of Tim Norris. Recently turned sixteen, he was leaving school today. However his mind was, as it often was, somewhere else, because in just a few days he would also be leaving Earth.

"Am I interrupting your daydream, Mr Norris?" his teacher broke into his reverie.

Startled, Tim rallied quickly. "No more than usual, Miss."

Some of his classmates sniggered and Mrs Montgomery smiled indulgently at the young man. "This is the last time I'm going to be able to say this to you – pay attention!"

"And for the last time, yes, Miss," he replied, returning her smile. He liked Mrs Montgomery, which made her fairly anomalous to his general schooling experience. Regardless, he leaned back toward his window sill, the one against which he had propped himself for the past four years, and slipped right back into Tim-world. Taking a deep breath of recycled air, he could taste metal as he gazed out over the concrete and the smog, pondering the many *little* steps mankind had taken over the last forty years, all leading up to the voyage he was about to make. *Yes, it's for the best,* he thought.

Over the last eighteen months, Tim's adoptive mother, Dr Patricia Norris, had fought tooth and nail to secure a place for them both on the next Life Pod Mission to Mars. Her dedication, driven by poverty and the need to provide a future for her son, had eventually been rewarded. As the date of their departure drew near – just a few more days now – the relief and gratitude he felt left him almost lightheaded. His teacher knew they were going. Tim had told no one.

The media hype was intensifying towards a crescendo. Even the often cynical Mrs Montgomery had not been entirely immune. The school leavers' lessons had officially ended, so the teacher used her remaining hours with them to fill the large screen, built into the glass wall at the front of the classroom, with images, statistics and footage relating to the Mars Programme. "I know it began a little before your time," she said, "but I'm sure you're all aware that human beings have maintained a presence on Mars since early 2095." She pointed at a simplified map of Mars as an indicator appeared on the screen, drawing the class's attention.

"During the last seventeen years, four small townships of modular, interconnected Life Pods have grown up, managing the planet's atmospheric conversion to eventually support complex life.

"The fifty year terraforming programme is being led by NASA, working alongside international partners in Germany, New Zealand, Australia, Italy, Japan, India, and of course us, here in Britain.

"Now, as we all know – because the news feeds talk of little else these days – the mining and resource industries of the mid to late 21st century took massive leaps forward. They had to, as they were driven ever on by the combined pressures of scarcity and commercial requirement. It is perhaps ironic that this 'rape of the Earth' as it was, and still is, seen by many, brought about and drove the very technology which now provides hope for Mars – the hope of resurrection from a frozen, celestial grave."

Tim could feel his excitement growing, his tummy aflutter with butterflies as he felt escape drawing within his grasp. Technically, he was now part of the Mars Programme, so he knew all this stuff anyway; had been following it long before their opportunity knocked, in fact. As head of the microbiology department, his mother would be a senior member of the mission. He was immensely proud of this, of course, but most importantly, it would give him first-hand access to knowledge and information. No more piecing together fact fragments, bagpiped through the media news wringer. He could not wait to fully immerse himself.

Back in 2072, just a few short decades before he was born, mankind had stepped into a larger universe after the first ever successful manipulation of a wormhole. It had changed everything.

As if following his thoughts, Mrs Montgomery called up an image of the world-famous wormhole drive system on the screen.

"After several false starts," she continued, "NASA, with wonderfully American belief and vision, in conjunction with internationally drained brains, managed to send a probe through an artificial wormhole all the way to the Oort Cloud – all within an infinitely small fraction of a second, real-time.

"The project scientists worried and waited for several days for a return signal. Needless to say, the probe's message finally reached Earth and a massive party at NASA ensued! Indeed, the asset's secondary mission, to scan a segment of the Oort Cloud, seems to have disappeared into the trashcan of history. All anyone remembers is this—," she turned back to face the class, "that was the day science fiction became reality. And once the hangovers had been Alka-Seltzered away—" a few of the teenagers giggled dutifully, "they got back down to work. Further probe missions followed this astonishing breakthrough. Suddenly, our solar system was being explored within timeframes previously believed impossible. Crucially, these latter models were capable of piloting themselves back in the same way. Within a few short years of these successes, the Mars colonisation programme went from conception to birth to growth."

Tim's head buzzed as the history drew him in, crystallising the moment. Peripherally, he watched the clock creep closer to the final bell which, as far as he was concerned, could not come quickly enough. He fully expected his classmates to cheer or dissolve into tears, promising each other that, "Of course we will stay in touch and always be best friends." He was already on Mars in his mind.

His attention drifted again as he looked around his contemporaries, wondering if he might miss any of them. He noticed that the boy in front of him, a minor bully named McGovan, had dropped his smog mask again. He never secured it properly to his bag and had to be called back almost daily by the teacher, to retrieve it. Maybe the extra smog he inhaled explained why he was so stupid? Tim could not help smirking as McGovan kicked the respirator under his desk without noticing. Surreptitiously, Tim nudged it just a little further out of sight with his own foot. While enjoying this tiny triumph, it occurred to him that he understood the millions-of-years-dead more than the living, always had.

His focus switched to the girl, the one all the lads chased after. Her name was Trixie and against all school rules she had several tattoos. Being neither sporty nor in any way cool, Tim had never caught her notice. Other than the occasional withering remark, he could not remember her ever speaking to him. Yep, they were all a whole 'nother country, these people.

5

At least he always had the past. In a very real sense it was his future too. It was his life. Palaeontology was an obsession shared with, and nurtured by, his adoptive father and a tool of rebellion against conformity for Tim. He revelled in a whole universe that none of *them* understood.

Recent events focused his latest fantasy on the chance discovery of a fossil on Mars. What a splash that would make: 'Evidence of complex life from another world, locked in stone since before Mars lost its oceans and most of its atmosphere, 2.9 *billion* years ago!' He could already hear the headlines. That would probably put him right up there with Darwin. All that attention...

He shuddered. Maybe not.

His gaze was drawn towards the factory where his father had worked – until the accident. He could see it clearly from his twentieth floor window. Ted Norris had been the only father he had ever known and he would never forget that awful day. His emotions threatened to overwhelm him, so he tore his eyes away from that hated building and suppressed them, as he had learned to do.

Realigning his thoughts, he returned to the present and the extraordinary opportunity he had been handed. "Bring it on!" he said out loud, startling the young man next to him out of his own daydream.

Distracted by past sorrows and future prospects, he had completely lost track of time and when the final bell rang it took him by surprise.

In a surreal moment, this classroom full of freshly minted adults looked from one to another as if unsure what to do, or how to feel. Gradually a ragged cheer erupted, closely followed by some tears. Tim wished a few people well as he waited for the room to clear. Eventually he was alone with Mrs Montgomery.

"Thank you for not telling anyone, Miss," he said.

Seated on a raised dais at the front of the classroom, she looked down from her desk with a mixture of pride and sadness. "I think it would have been nice to let your classmates know you're going to Mars, Tim. You'll soon be famous after all."

Tim shrugged, shyly. "I don't want to be. I've spent years trying to stay off the radar of the bullies and 'popular' types. I'd hate to blow all that hard work on my last day."

"I expected the school to be overrun with press this afternoon – that would have let your cat out of the bag, eh?" Her eyes glistened as she studied him.

"I daresay, but there are bound to be loads of rich kids about to become part of this programme. I'm sure they'll all be more interesting than me," he chuckled. "Anyway, I'm glad they didn't come."

Montgomery sighed. "Tim, you should have more faith in yourself. Your mum, Patricia was brilliant too – an extraordinary mind. She didn't believe in herself enough either, but it appears she managed to overcome that particular obstacle in the end. Look what she's achieved now!"

"You taught my mum?"

"Taught your— how old do you think I am?!" She shook her head, adding witheringly, "Don't answer that. No, we were here at the same time, although she was a couple of years below me. Some of our older teachers taught her, though. They'll be over the moon when word gets around of her success."

"She's still broke, Miss."

"Ha! – A transitional drawback. She's on track now, and deserves everything she's won – after all she's been through. However, I think you might even surpass her." She stepped down, placing a hand on his shoulder. "I've got high hopes for you, Tim."

"My report matrices would seem to disagree," Tim could not help noting.

"Your *report cards* have always said the same thing: A brilliant mind – won't push himself!"

Tim shrugged again. "I just do what I do, Miss."

Montgomery gave him a look of exasperation, but she could never remain cross with Tim for long; she had never acquired the knack. Softening to a kindly smile, she gazed at this young man, grown up in her care, quite possibly for the last time as she said, "Please keep in touch, will you? Our list of successful alumni is pretty thin in this place. It will be a joy to follow your life on Mars. I hope it will inspire some of these other kids to do well themselves, too. What do you say?"

A hunted expression crossed Tim's face. "Erm..."

An hour later, Patricia welcomed Tim home to their housing cell – four boxy rooms within a block of hundreds of cells, similar to hundreds of thousands of other blocks all over the planet. "How was it, sweetheart?" she asked sympathetically, remembering her own last day at school.

"It was fine, glad it's over really," he replied bravely.

"Were there any reporters?"

"No, Mrs Montgomery was expecting them, but none came." Seeing his mother's look of disappointment he added, "I'm relieved, really. I didn't want to be grilled and photographed. You know me. Honestly, Mum, it's *fine*."

"Never mind, that's their loss. Maybe they'll take more interest when yours are among the very first exam results communicated to Mars for the public record. Well, the time's here at last. Still sure you want to do this?" she asked, referring to their rapidly approaching departure.

Tim nodded enthusiastically. "Oh yeah! You know, Mum, I just want to say thanks."

Patricia was slightly thrown by this bolt from the blue. "For what?" she asked cautiously.

"For working so hard to get us this placement – I know how tough it's been, the hundred hour weeks and going without to keep up the payments for my education," he grinned cheekily. "Of course, I'd always suspected you *might* be a genius. Nice to have some proof at last, though!"

She cuffed him playfully and pulled him to her, amazed at how much she had to look up at him these days.

Tim hugged her back, a *very* rare event since the teens had struck. "It's all gonna be OK now, Mum, isn't it?" he asked quietly into her shoulder.

She squeezed her eyes closed against a tear. "I promise," was all she could manage, hiding in the hug.

Cape Canaveral – USA

Across the world, it happened to be a milestone in the life of James Douglas, too. At fifty years old, he was certainly not leaving school, but he was about to leave Earth in a few days – again.

The significance of the briefing scheduled for that morning could not have been foreseen. Although otherwise routine, it was actually to be his last and, unlike previous mission briefings, was in no way preparatory for what was to come.

Douglas was a Scotsman harking from Hawick, in the borders. His position within NASA carried authority and respect in measure, but having just awoken, he sat on the side of his bed as all men everywhere. He rubbed his face a bit, mussed his hair a bit, yawned a bit and finally stood, stretching.

He walked into the bathroom and splashed a little water on his face, dispelling the last vestiges of the dreadful hours. Looking in the mirror, he continued to greet the day just like billions of other men around the world, with a shave, a shower and a… well, et cetera.

Fifteen minutes later he was clad in a crisp, freshly ironed uniform and reaching for one of his dress jackets from the hanger. He smiled slightly, proudly buffing his captain's insignia. The patch on the sleeve gave him a moment's pause. It was sewn onto the upper left arm, deep blue with a diagonal white cross stitched into the motif.

Douglas allowed his mind to travel home for a few moments, before donning the jacket, lingering on a past life flying for the RAF. He had few regrets. Picking up his officer's hat, he gave it a jaunty little tap into place and checked his appearance one last time in the mirror. Content that his shirt was tucked in, his tie straight, he made for the door.

Suitably suited, booted and *abluted*, he left his quarters to catch one of the run-about buses, ever zipping around Canaveral Space Port and Airbase.

He arrived at mission control in minutes and waded through the security treacle, a necessary misery of modernity. It seemed there was always someone who needed to be kept at arm's length. For the Canaveral security staff, if it was not terrorists, it was activists and if not activists, then tourists. Slowly Douglas *proceeded*.

Construction work meant that staff and military personnel were temporarily forced to wait in line with everyone else to enter the complex. Inching towards his scheduled appointment and trying to remain patient, Douglas noticed one of his oldest friends further back in the queue.

He had known Captain Arnold Bessel most of his life. He caught Bessel's eye, making a forward motion with his hand then miming a drink – meaning after the meeting they were both to attend.

Bessel grinned, replying with a thumbs-up gesture. While distracted, he was hit from behind by a giant suitcase with a large 'I heart New York' sticker on the side. Bessel straightened his hat, turning to give the impatient tourist an earful.

Douglas turned away too, his shoulders rocking with laughter.

After a few moments his thoughts returned to the appointment ahead. These briefings were a fact of life for men like Douglas and Bessel, but as with every humdrum thing we humans take for granted in our daily routines, there comes a time when we do something for the last time. It is rare that we recognise these little milestones. James did not realise either.

One week later – Canaveral Space Port

Launch day. The last Life Pod to leave for Mars saw Canaveral awash with families, well-wishers, spectators and press. All the passengers and many of the crew waited in the departure lounge. Most of the colonists attempted to steady their nerves, hoping to make good first impressions upon people with whom they might possibly spend the rest of their lives on Mars – population 5106.

Theirs was not merely the last Pod, but the last *factory* Pod to leave as part of the first wave of colonisation and would boost the total, permanent Martian population up to 5208.

Tim stayed close to his mother, observing the diversity of his fellow pioneers. He spotted a few other teenagers among the group and speculated nervously on whether this was a good thing.

The group were very much multinational and doubtless there would be all sorts of adjustments to make, for everyone. Tim wondered whether all of them realised this yet. The good old English language appeared to be providing a reliable *lingua franca*, allowing respectable levels of communication among all parties. However, he could not help noting that the Americans and the Australians, whilst each speaking their own perfectly understandable version of English, seemed to have some difficulty in understanding one another. He had filed their dialect mashing under 'possibly entertaining' when he spotted a lad who seemed to wear a near constant grin of amusement. He also wore a New Zealand shirt and appeared to be about Tim's age.

The other teenaged male among the group, perhaps slightly older than Tim, appeared subdued, as did the pretty girl who stood beside him. She was maybe three or four years the young man's junior. He assumed them to be American, although he had only heard the older male in their party, probably the father, speak.

He caught his breath when he spotted his other contemporary. Forget Trixie, there had been no girls like *that* at his school – he would have noticed.

Patricia caught him gawking and prodded him mischievously. "Nervous?" she asked.

"Er…" Tim's voice croaked. He cleared his throat, pulling himself together. "No, no, of course not, Mum. You?"

Slightly embarrassed, he willed himself to stop staring at the stunning blonde and stared up in admiration at the USS *New World* instead. This was the ship that would carry them to their new home. The day may have been grey but to Tim's eager eyes she stood magnificent on the strip, despite the hellscape background; a technological marvel waiting patiently to whisk them away to lives very different from the ones they had known.

There were five ships in the fleet, all built specifically to carry the Pods and matériel to Mars. Tim had read everything he could find about them and now, standing before the *New World*, he could clearly appreciate her skeletal design; see how she, and her sister ships, carried their loads, or Pods, depending on the requirement, under their bellies for easy release and take-off. The *New World* was the first of the fleet to be constructed and she was Tim's favourite. He was overjoyed when he discovered she was to be his transport. He knew her specifications by heart – 550 metres, bow to stern, she was as capable in atmosphere as she was in space, allowing total flexibility and utility. Yet despite her size, she carried a permanent crew complement of just thirteen. Best of all, the USS *New World* was under the command of Captain James Douglas, a man Tim very much hoped to meet.

Seated on his bridge, Captain Douglas turned to his first officer. "Open the boarding ramps, Jill. Please supervise the arrivals."

Commander Jill Baines acknowledged the order. "Let's hope they're better housetrained than the last lot."

The captain's mouth twitched at the corners as he raised an eyebrow. "Book and cover, Jill, book and cover. Let's not judge."

Baines saluted and left the bridge. She took her time as she strolled through the ship. This would be the last trip they would make to Mars and back for a while, unless some kind of disaster struck the colony. The *New World*'s next assignment was transporting construction materials and equipment for the planned, brand new from scratch, moon citadel. The project carried the grandiose title of 'New Rome' but most of the British engineers involved called it '*Moonton* Keynes' and the name had stuck.

She was the first person ever to be born on the moon – more specifically moon base *New Florida*, in 2071. Her family still lived there, so naturally, spaceflight was in her blood.

With no reason to suppose that this launch would be any different from the many she had undertaken, she sighed contentedly, grateful to be staying with Captain Douglas and, if that were not enough, she would soon be able to spend some quality time with Mum and Dad, too. Her future looked exciting and positive as she entered the embarkation area of the Life Pod.

The *New World*'s two-man security complement ushered people aboard, checking everyone over slowly and methodically. The Mars Pod had its own security team, who were helping to expedite things, but they came largely under the jurisdiction of ship's security for the extent of the voyage. Baines waited patiently until most of the 102 boarders were seated and strapping in for take-off.

Sergeant John Jackson called for the last few stragglers to get themselves situated.

All of the ships had mixed nationality crews, as befitted a shared endeavour. However, both security operatives aboard the *New World* happened to be ex British Army. The second was Private Dewi Jones, a Welshman from Gwynedd. Baines watched people drift almost subconsciously out of his way. Jones rarely spoke, but being the size of a brick shed, he rarely needed to.

Jackson was already at full volume. "I am Sergeant John Jackson, known to my friends as 'The Sarge' and as you will all hope to keep my friendship," he added menacingly, "you may also call me Sarge."

Baines' eyes twinkled with amusement. The cockney bruiser enjoyed presenting all the charm of a scrapyard dog, but she was not fooled by the rough edges.

He continued, "THESE ARE MY TEN COMMANDMENTS – HEED THEM *WELL*! Number one, you are free to move about all non-secured areas of the Mars Pod as you will, but you will not, for any reason, set foot aboard the *New World* unless expressly ordered to do so by myself or a senior officer, is that clear?"

A disgruntled mumble chuntered around the room.

"IS THAT CLEAR?"

"*Yes, Sarge.*" A more spirited response, along with several giggles of embarrassment, followed.

"Number two, public areas, passageways and corridors will be kept unobstructed at *all* times and no luggage, equipment or litter will be tolerated in these locations! How you people conduct yourselves when we dump you on Mars is up to you, but whilst *your* home is attached to *my* home IT WILL BE A TIDY HOME!"

This drew another murmur of mostly good-natured assent. Baines tuned out, having heard this speech many times over the last few years as they ferried people and plant to Mars. She chatted quietly with Mary Hutchins, purveyor of all things treat related, standing next to her trolley of delights.

"IS EVERYONE CLEAR ON ALL THAT?" The Sarge barked loudly, wrapping up his barrage of dos and don'ts.

Another, *"Yes, Sarge,"* staggered through the assembly.

"Any-questions?-No?-Good!" he closed suddenly. "I'll hand you over to Commander Baines for a few words," and without warning she was on. The Sarge strode to the front of the room and stood to attention behind her, wearing just the ghost of a smirk.

"Erm..." said Baines, caught off guard. "Thank you, Sarge. *Thank you very much,*" she added out of the corner of her mouth.

The Sarge merely saluted smartly, still eyes-front.

"Hello everyone," she continued. "After takeoff, some refreshments will be served by our local gal, from sunny Florida, Crewman Mary Hutchins here. She is the New World's janitor and cook and is therefore quite possibly the most indispensable member of our little crew!" She gestured to Mary, who was bobbing about to the side, waving to any newcomers who caught her eye.

There were a few polite chuckles as several people returned Mary's waves.

"You will not find anyone more committed to the wellbeing of this ship, or its passengers and crew," she added kindly. "Captain Douglas will be along to formally greet you all once we have broken orbit and laid in our course. He will also explain what you may expect when we jump through a wormhole. I don't believe any of our passengers have experienced this before, so I'm sure it will be very exciting. But for now, I welcome you aboard the USS *New World* and look forward to getting to know all of you over the next three days of our voyage together. Thank you."

Once sure everyone and everything was safely stowed and secured, Commander Baines made her way back to the bridge in preparation for takeoff.

"Well, what are they like?" asked Douglas as she slipped back into her seat.

"Still cowering from The Sarge's 'ten commandments' so it's too early to say for sure," she answered, strapping herself in.

"Ah, good old Sarge," Douglas remarked, as he activated the ship-wide PA. "Welcome aboard everyone, this is Captain James Douglas speaking.

Please make one final check that luggage is secured and all seatbelts are fastened. We lift off in three minutes – Douglas out."

Within the next minute all crew reports came in 'green for launch' and at the appointed hour the ship took off vertically with little drama, achieving orbit a few minutes later.

Jim Miller was a senior member of the Mars Mission staff and this earned him a window seat for what promised to be an extraordinary view as they left the Earth behind. In his typical fashion, he gave up this remarkable privilege in favour of his daughter, and the apple of his eye.

Sixteen year old Rose tucked a lock of blonde hair behind her ear and watched the airstrip recede as the *New World* climbed, blurring the details into minutiae. Once within the cloud layer there was little to see for a few moments until the *New World* burst, Pegasus like, through the top of the clouds into perfect azure nothingness, lit by brilliant sunlight. There was very little Earth left, just the vaporous envelope above which allowed everything to work and above that, the deepening void.

Rose hunkered down in her seat, reliving all the attention she had so recently received as a Mars colonist. The massive publicity which naturally whirled around the first Pod mission to 'the new world' had gradually petered away for subsequent departures. She had been too young to remember the early launches, but to offer perspective, her father had pointed out that it is quite often more advantageous to be last than second. He was always telling her things like that, but as it turned out, he had been right. The media frenzy had indeed fully revived and redoubled for the last Pod of the initial wave to depart for Mars. The very Pod in which Rose now sat, holding her father's hand and looking out at the first stars pricking through the blue.

It was all so beautiful – exciting too. So why did she have this persistent, nagging doubt?

Her parents had had a blistering argument about the Mars Mission a few weeks ago – her mother, Lara, had won. She had not been privy to their second conversation, the pivotal moment where Lara had changed her mind and made up theirs for them, sealing all their fates. Rarely do teenagers consider what their parents have to do out in the world while they are in school; a necessary safety mechanism, allowing them one last hurrah before their turn comes. Rose had simply believed the subject closed until her last day in lower secondary education, where it became apparent that she had been mistaken.

Leaving school is normally a wrench, a sea-change, in any young person's life, but Rose had barely noticed it amidst the uproar. Much more than her last day of school, it had been the day where she glimpsed her future, just moments before it hit the headlines… and now she was on a space ship travelling to another world.

Out of her window, the blue sky above gave her a feeling of ever-increasing depth. It was strangely like looking *down*, into a perfectly clear, fathomless lake. Within moments the *New World* made the transition to space and, with the last wisps of atmosphere behind them, their ride went from smooth to serene. Passengers began unbuckling their safety harnesses and mingling once more. Lara left her seat without a word and began prowling among the other colonists.

Probably checking out what they're worth, Rose thought uncharitably. She kept her father's hand, preventing him from leaving his seat to follow her.

"Dad?"

"Yes, sweetheart?"

"Did you know that Mum forgot to tell me she'd changed her mind about leaving for Mars?"

"Eh?" Jim was clearly honestly shocked. "But I left you a message? You know, when I had to leave, to be processed by NASA?"

"Uh-huh. She forgot to pass it on and with all her pressing concerns, like shopping and ordering new outfits for us, she forgot she'd *forgot*. You know she always deletes everything from the house computer so it doesn't get too complicated for her. I actually found out when I arrived at school for my last day and was mobbed by the press."

"Wow, I'm really sorry, darling. When I didn't hear from you I just thought you were on board with all this and simply busy preparing," Jim answered quietly, looking perplexed.

"Don't worry, Dad." Rose squeezed his hand. "It *is* exciting and we're here now, so let's just see. How did you change Mum's mind to let us join this mission, anyway?" she added tactfully, despite knowing who had really made the decision.

"Well, I didn't exactly. Later, on the evening I told you both about all this, your mum went out with—"

"—Barbara? And her friend Barbara told Lara she'd be famous?"

Jim looked surprised. "Erm… I'm not sure it was exactly like that, but how did you know?"

"Because she believes everything Barbara tells her. For God's sake, Dad, Barbara spends even more on shoes than Lara does." Rose rarely thought of her mother as Mum. "*Of course* she takes her opinions as gospel!"

Jim did his best to look disapproving. "Please don't call La— Mum, by her Christian name."

When Lara got together with Barbara, it rarely worked out well for Jim. He lapsed into a brooding silence for a while, wondering whether Mars would be far enough to escape the reach of Barbara's influence. He hoped his family would make new friends now, good friends, or at least ones who would have a less deleterious effect on his marriage.

With the Millers' attention firmly focused on their future, the enormity of Lara's change of heart and what it would mean for their family was obscured; a happy accident of linear time – with the result held back to be produced suddenly, from the bottom of the deck, when they least expected it.

Rose was watching her mother move among the passengers, a predator in heels and bling, when a nebulous feeling of dread descended upon her. At that moment she would have given anything to know the future, even if that divination showed that the future would soon be the very least of her problems. This whole affair had made her nervous when it was her father's idea, but now Lara had signed off on it, she feared disaster. Stealing a furtive glance up at Jim as they sat quietly together, she was pleased to see his face light up. As he caught his first view of space, the schoolboy glint in his eye, always at odds with the perfect suits and perfect haircuts Lara chose for him, sparkled to life.

Poor Dad, she thought, *the man who has everything but chose the trophy wife from hell.* "Do you think this new life will change us?" The thought surprised her and she gave it voice without censor. "*Dad?*"

Jim, startled out of his trance, looked down at his daughter. "Where did *that* come from?" he asked, eyes full of amusement and the love he held for her. "If it does, I say we let it change us for the better, eh?"

His expression became more serious. "Look, sweetheart, there's something I've been meaning to tell you. It's the main reason I accepted this position, actually."

Rose listened, piqued.

"When the terraforming is complete, all the people involved in the project will be granted prime real estate on Mars. We're talking ocean views and eventually fresh air and wonderful wildlife – a lifestyle we can't even dream about on Earth anymore. I'll probably be knocking on a bit by then, but I want this future for you and if you decide to have a family of your own, for them too. It may take time but if there's one thing I want to give you, darling, this is it – a true future of health and happiness." Jim paused for a moment. "I love you," he added, seriously.

Douglas sat comfortably in his captain's chair and relished the view unfolding before him through the forward view ports. No matter how many times he saw it, the sudden explosion of light and colour that was the Milky Way always took his breath away.

Second officer and helmsman, Lieutenant Sandip Singh, laid in a course to Mars and activated the autopilot. Like Captain Douglas, he too was an air force man. Before joining NASA and the Mars fleet six years earlier, he had served eight years in the Indian military, a serious power in the latter half of the 21st century, as India rose to dominance as the second richest nation on Earth, locked in a cold war with China over resources.

"Course calculated and laid in, Captain. Autopilot engaged," he said, turning to Douglas.

"Thank you, Lieutenant. Good to see that Cambridge education wasnae wasted."

"Certainly wasn't, Captain – that's where I perfected my awesome fast bowl!"

"Aye, Ah know, Ah saw ye take three wickets in that friendly a few months ago."

"You're welcome to join me for a game in my holograph room, Captain."

"Ah wouldnae stand a chance, Sandy. Now maybe if you programmed a nice links course with a sea view, Ah could get behind that?"

"You know I struggle with golf, Captain. I just can't get the hang of the bat!"

Douglas chuckled.

Singh turned back to his readouts. "We will reach our cruising speed of 50,000 kilometres per hour in a little over two minutes and reach our 1,800,000 kilometre, minimum safe distance from Earth in approximately thirty-six hours, sir."

Douglas nodded. "Very good, Lieutenant. Right, Ah suppose Ah'd better go and meet our guests."

Commander Baines looked up from her console. "Enjoy yourself, Captain, we'll be here, glued to the monitors for the next thirty-six hours if you need us."

"OK, Commander, you have the bridge," he replied. "Ah'll try not to wake ye up when Ah get back."

Singh chuckled and watched the captain leave before returning to his calculations. He always rechecked them one last time before fully handing over to the computer. Once satisfied, his mind drifted back to his NASA accommodation, the place he was calling home for a while, and his cat.

Her name was Fang and he wondered whether he should have let her out, but it was a hell-hole outside. It was always the same when he had to leave her. At least this was only a short mission, nothing to worry about... and yet he always did.

Leaving the automatic cat food dispenser set for three days, he simply accepted that upon his homecoming the litter tray might hum a little. He lived in fear of a delayed return. If he let her out and the mission dragged, he might lose her. If he kept her in, she might make a mess or run out of food. He sighed, the agonies of the cat father.

"Do you think the captain might let me bring Fang onboard, Commander?" he asked. "*Commander?*"

Baines had disappeared stealthily into the small galley off the bridge; he could hear the coffee machine. Singh sighed again and returned to his worrying.

Post-takeoff checks complete, the ship, her crew and passengers settled into the quiet wait of space travel, the hours drifting by. Just one man's heart pounded as he made his way to the forward bank of escape pods. Now they were underway, security would be lax until they were on final approach to Mars. This created an ideal opportunity for the saboteur. He lifted a floor plate in front of the entrance hatch to *Lifeboat 1* and very carefully extracted a component. Once removed, it would render the escape capsule effectively useless, but it would provide him with all the power he needed.

"I'm hiding again!" Henry 'Hank' Burnstein Jnr muttered to himself, fuming. The walls and door were a bleak, utilitarian grey, every surface so very *wipeable*. His nerves were frayed indeed if the cleanability of the walls was upsetting him too. He waited stolidly for his tummy to settle, and for his bowels to perform to the accompaniment of plumbing.

The young man raked his fingers through his hair in agitation. Less than two days ago he had been all fired up for a skiing holiday at the new, million-dollars-a-day resort near the top of Mount Everest. Now he was flying through the stars in a giant tin can, whilst hiding *in* the can.

As soon as the *New World* broke orbit, Hank had jumped out of his seat to get away from his father. It was not like there was anything to see,

Hank Burnstein Snr had taken the window seat as his right. Offering it to anyone else would simply never have occurred to him.

Now Hank Jnr's cubicle rang with the gentle *splosh* of solitude as he sat in the last remnant of everyman's castle, barely surviving in the reduced circumstances of an overpopulated world. At least the gates were barred; if only he had something to read.

He clenched his fists. Unfortunately, his stomach, which was only ever a problem when his father was around, did likewise. Memories of his life ending, and a very uncertain new one beginning, resurfaced.

The day before yesterday, he had been completely oblivious to this new future on Mars. Recently turned eighteen, he had left his school for the last time, fully expecting to be drummed into a position within his father's multi-trillion-dollar corporation which sold something or other, *tout suite*, whether he wanted it or not, but what actually happened had shaken him to the core.

He had tried to get his mother to take a stand but as always, there was no help there. He guessed she had lived in fear of his father, and his lawyers, for so long that she had no fight left.

"There's nothing I can do, son, nothing but be here," she had said, "and I promise I will always be here. You and Clarissa *are* my reason, Hank, and I will never leave you or your sister alone, whatever happens to me." The brave smile for her boy's benefit caused a tear to escape down her cheek and broke Hank's heart.

His father had paid every trainer and teacher he ever had to drill him with the knowledge that he would achieve something important and should be proud he belonged to the greatest nation on Earth. Grudgingly, he had to admit that without the US space programme, humanity might simply be looking at its end in pretty short order, this much was true. He was proud of his country, they had achieved so much, but men like his father made him wonder if they had a future.

The world's population, almost fifty billion now, was many, many times more than the planet could sustain, he knew. Virtually every problem human society faced stemmed from it. He had read somewhere that the net population growth was close to a quarter of a million people a day, *a century ago*. It was simply outrageous now and the world could not cope. Men like Burnstein Snr had always seen this as a fantastic opportunity for profit – of course, that was before he had jumped onto the 'saving the planet' bandwagon.

Now, his father kept repeating over and over again: "The Mars Mission is the last and best chance to preserve our civilisation and God bless the US of A!" Hank could hear the booming voice ringing in his ears even now, nuancing the death knell for his own plans. He knew it was all hot air from a buffalo's backside! His father would *only* permit God to bless America *if* he had blessed Burnstein Senior's bank accounts first. There was clearly money in this Mars venture and it looked like their lives on Earth were being offered in sacrifice, to balance the payment.

Hank's anger subsided a little, causing him to realise that he had been finished for a while now, so he flushed and washed his hands. Splashing water onto his face, he looked with bloodshot eyes at someone he hardly knew in the mirror, had never been allowed to know. "One day…" he promised the stranger. A single tear brimmed but did not fall. He wiped it with a finger; it was like saying goodbye to boyhood.

However, some lessons can never be completely unlearned, so he washed his face thoroughly, for the sake of appearances. It was time to lower the drawbridge and rejoin the world, or at least the *New World*. He had heard there was a bar somewhere aboard this crate. Maybe there would be a pool table or something…

In the bar and restaurant, so new that no one had yet given it a name, four teenagers sat at different tables wondering who would make the first move.

Woodsey looked out of a portside window. He marvelled, not only at the stars, but also the endless nebulae visible without the obscuring haze of atmosphere. It was hard to believe he was here. Everything had happened so quickly. His dad's position had become available, been offered and been accepted. Before he knew it, he was suddenly on his way to begin a new life on another world, quicker than the death of a Christmas hit.

He grinned at his own reflection in the window as he sipped a cold beer; it was good to be sixteen at last. With a bottle in his right hand, he lovingly stroked the short, fluffy, blond beard he was trying to grow, with his left. Outside, the unadulterated starscape gripped him. "What a view," he mumbled to himself, with a single shake of his head. "This would humble a lesser man."

In his heart of hearts, of course, he realised this was no small thing – such a momentous event, in fact, that he wondered if his mother was watching, if she was still with them somehow. Dr Thomas Wood's invitation to join the Mars Programme had certainly been spookily unlooked for.

Woodsey now understood that the offer had actually landed some weeks ago. His dad simply chose to wait until his last day of school was over before telling him, not wanting to load his plate with any further concerns.

They were here because his father was an exceptional engineer, with PhDs in mathematics and structural engineering from Victoria University in Wellington, New Zealand. Woodsey knew his dad hoped he would follow in his footsteps and become an engineer too, one day. He certainly had the mathematical aptitude, but Woodsey preferred to wait and see what called to him.

Thoughts of home...

"Mum." The word came out as little more than a breath. Woodsey had lost his mother, Sarah, almost thirteen years ago. He tried not to think too deeply about that. Despite living with the ghost of her loss, his father had poured a huge commitment into his upbringing since. They never really talked about it, but Woodsey knew it was there. Being so young when his mother passed, he always thought of her as a hole in his life, rather than an ache.

"The stuff you think about when you're leaving your home planet behind," he muttered ruefully. His ancestry traced back to Richard Wood, who had arrived in New Zealand during the 1840s as part of the early mass immigration and now the Wood family appeared set to become colonists all over again. He breathed in deeply through his nose and out slowly through his mouth. Everything aboard the Pod seemed to have that 'new car' smell. He liked it.

He sat up straight, coming back to the now with a wry smile. The southern hemisphere must have seemed like a *long* way from Southern England to Richard Wood in the early nineteenth century. What would his ancestor have made of the 225 million kilometre average distance between Plymouth and Mars?

Woodsey chuckled at the thought, suddenly feeling the need for a little companionship, maybe even a few laughs. The bar around him was almost empty, so he glanced around at the other teens once more, before standing and theatrically clearing his throat. "Hi, I'm Woodsey and I'd like to welcome you to Woodsey Hour!" He caught their attention and continued, "For one hour only, *you* get to buy *me* drinks in exchange for me listening to you droning on about your boring lives and how you came to be here!

"Woodsey makes no promises to stay awake through the whole hour, nor that he'll remain if drinks are not forthcoming. Your statutory rights will not be taken into consideration. Come on down!"

Tim Norris and Hank Burnstein Jnr grinned at one another, nodded and approached the young New Zealander with hands outstretched. A quick round of introductions ensued and Hank called over to the bar for more drinks.

Rose Miller studiously examined her tablet, ignoring the trio. She was writing endless messages to *friends* on her network, blogging a brag about how marvellous space travel was, what with all the stars and stuff, and how only the very cream of the top of the most exclusive set was here with her.

Although she would not be able to send the messages until their arrival on Mars, it had been her intention to use the journey to work up an account that would make the people back home seethe with envy. Yet somehow, now she stopped to think about it, it felt like going through the motions of an old life. Did it really matter if her friends from school were jealous? She would probably never see most of them again anyway.

Deep, confusing thoughts stirred. After a few moments' introspection, Rose realised that pondering her future was once again proving an uncomfortable exercise. What made matters worse was that she had just caught up on the latest download from a radical, teen-news feed she followed, called 'The Social Metronome'. Suddenly, she could not help looking askance at these three strangers hanging around in the bar. Also the barman – did he have a squint?

The article read: "*Today! As many as seventy-five percent of us suffer from some form of mental illness, a figure which has only increased by five percent in the last hundred years, so that must mean it's stable!!! Since our holding company was almost bankrupted by a lawsuit last year, following an article where we called a boy an idiot for hitting a snake with a stick, to see what would happen, our lawyers have forbidden us from naming any examples – but you all know who you are, don't you? Deep down? Really? So! The world may have gone mad, but somehow* humanity *is still hanging on by a big, fat twenty-five percent! That's almost a third people! Hooray for the humans!!!*

[Footnote: *Unfortunately, the dramatic increase in population during the last century means that, statistically, you are now much more likely to be murdered by someone that you do not know. In summary: watch yourself – it's all gone bonkers...*]"[1]

Rose was appalled by this latest social trend. However, born beautiful, popular and rich, one-upmanship provided her with a comfort of sorts, so she returned to mulling over her explanation of just how *select* her travelling companions truly were. As her hands hesitated over the keypad, a shout echoed across the mostly empty room.

"Hey! Who's the Sheila?"

Rose fixed the uncouth youth with a glare intended to spit him alive.

"How did *you three* get accepted on this trip?" she asked snootily.

"By pure ability, lady! I take it you're a paid seat? Daddy rich is he? Slip NASA a few beer tokens and she'll be right? Eh?" Woodsey retorted.

---

[1] The editor of The Social Metronome, a man named Fasto Legardo, was well known for spending more time in court than at his keyboard – also for sailing dangerously close to the wind with his topics, choice of reporters and irreverent editorial style. While he described his version of the news as 'edgy', his detractors maintained that he simply traded on the age-old truth that the less acceptable the material, the more kids would want to know it – if the subject were really nasty, they might even trouble to read about it. The backbone of his defence, during his latest appointment with His Majesty's bench, was a claim that his publications "encouraged literacy in young people" because of this. Legardo was also famous for spearheading the campaign to reintroduce swearwords (also known as curse words) back into the dictionary on the grounds that: "Removing them in Common Era 2029 led to the drastic 'disencouragisation' of many young children from wanting to learn to read, and anyway, removing them has not made them go away – it has not even reduced their use. It has simply led to them being misspelt on social media." He also rebutted the argument that four-letter-words were now considered three-letter-words simply because people have grown lazier.

"My father happens to be a genius at, at… science!" she blurted, suddenly realising that she did not really know what Daddy did do, only that what Daddy did do was dull – or so Lara had always told her. The three lads collapsed into laughter and Rose strode angrily toward the exit; she had never known such treatment.

"That went well," Tim noted.

"Shhh, shhh," said Woodsey. "I can see I need to teach you boys a thing or two about the fairer sex."

"Oh, this should be good," said Tim.

"No, no worries mate, you see women are like little birds – little birds in the bush," Woodsey explained. "If you go in loud and rough, they fly away—"

"What, like shouting, 'Hey! Who's the Sheila'?" mocked Hank.

"Dude, that was a *blind*," the New Zealander expanded. "I was flushing her out so she could be corralled this way. Then before she knows it," he closed his hand to a grasping fist, "she's mine."

Tim laughed and Hank prompted, "Well go on then, go and close the gate before she bolts."

"Alright, I will!" Woodsey stood up purposefully and marched quickly after Rose. He caught up with her just as she reached the threshold to the corridor. She stepped back inside for a moment allowing the doors to close again. Hank and Tim could not hear what they said, but Rose's face reddened and she looked furious. She suddenly turned her nose up and stormed out.

Woodsey looked very sheepish as he wandered back to them. He sat down heavily.

Tim, already giggling, asked, "Well?"

"I'd rather not talk about it."

Hank laughed loudly.

"Well, why don't you show us how it's done then? Genius!" Woodsey laid down the gauntlet.

"*Right*," replied Hank. "So I can look stoopid too? I think I'll pass."

Woodsey turned to Tim.

"Don't look at me!" he answered. "The last time a girl spoke to me was about two months ago, and that was in the queue at a coffee stand."

Woodsey scratched his chin, studying Tim with curiosity. "So what did she say, dude?"

Tim looked away bashfully. "Will you get off my foot," he answered in a small voice.

After a couple of heartbeats, Hank threw his head back and laughed and laughed until the tears streamed down his face.

When he eventually recovered, he admitted quietly, "Actually, it's me who's the paid seat. My dad put 200 billion dollars into this programme because he wants to sell condos on Mars or somethin', after the place is terraformed and the land stakes are divvied up that is. He thinks he'll increase his money exponentially. I suppose he's right, he usually is... I guess." He tailed off.

"And how did you come to be here, Tim?" Woodsey asked.

"My Mum's a microbiologist – a very, very good one. I'm riding her coattails," he answered, with a small, self-deprecating smile. "She worked so hard for this. I owe her everything."

Woodsey glanced between them, giving both an appraising look – the princeling and the pauper, with himself somewhere in the middle. "Well it doesn't matter *how* you made it," he said, "only *that* you made it!"

"What about you?" Tim asked in return.

"Ah, me old man's a structural engineer, a pretty good one too."

"He'd need to be to get on this crew," said Hank. "Unless he just happened to have a few billion to spread around," he finished darkly.

"Don't get on with the old man, then?" asked Woodsey, perceptively.

"What can I tell ya? I only found out I was going to live on Mars a couple of days ago. I wasn't asked, or even told, about it. No choice – bang! Thanks, Dad."

Woodsey whistled softly.

"I hardly know anything about what we're doing on Mars, other than slogans and the broad strokes," continued Hank. "You guys have parents who are scientists, what can you tell me?"

"Well, to tell you the truth," replied Woodsey, "my dad was one of the last people to be employed by the project, so I don't know a huge amount myself, other than what's in the news feeds and the bits I've picked up on the ship."

They both looked at Tim, who reddened.

"I know a *bit* about it," he confessed awkwardly. "My mum worked so hard to get us here, I thought the least I could do was take an interest. To be honest though, our efforts on Mars are fascinating. Would you like a bedtime story?" Tim ostentatiously checked the level in his almost empty bottle.

"*Subtle*," Woodsey noted. He grinned appreciatively and ordered another round.

The bartender brought three bottles over to the young men.

"Well?" asked the New Zealander. "There's your payment. Where's my story?"

Tim lubricated his throat and began. "The first stage was simple in principle but required a gargantuan, not to mention astonishingly complex and expensive, effort to bring about. It involved kick-starting the static, and partially frozen, core with a planet-wide series of huge explosions. These detonations were created by ordinance being drilled deep into the planet to begin a super-enormous chain reaction, igniting the core and getting it spinning again."

"Nukes?" asked Hank.

"*Big* ones," agreed Tim. "A decade later, Mars began to stabilise. After the planet-wide shockwave and hundreds of massive volcanic eruptions, the magnetosphere began to re-establish itself. The magnetosphere's an essential element of the planet's natural defences from the sun and other bodies spinning around the solar system.

"Phase two saw the construction of carbon dioxide plants on the surface of Mars to belch out greenhouse gases, further augmenting the effects of volcanicity in the atmosphere. What the scientists wanted to do was trap heat and bind it to the planet, until a constant and reliable atmospheric temperature could be maintained.

"All this effort and work was designed to replicate the beginnings of our own world," Tim paused for thought there. "I suppose I should say *Earth* now, as our *own world* will soon be *Mars*." He stopped with his bottle halfway to his mouth. "Have you considered that, I mean really thought about it?"

The three took a moment to let Tim's point sink in.

Eventually Woodsey spoke. "D'ya know you talk like a textbook, dude?"

Hank snorted his beer and Tim laughed in spite of himself. "*You* asked for a story. I'm sorry – did you want Three Little Pigs?"

"Little Red Riding Hood, if you can manage it, mate?"

"You can have Little Red Planet, if you'll shut up for a minute!"

Hank laughed again. "Please, go on, Tim. I need to know this stuff if I'm gonna be stuck there."

"Anyway," Tim continued, "this all needed to be manufactured within a timeframe which could benefit us – mankind, that is. It's a pretty extraordinary achievement. Can't help thinking that it would never have happened if we weren't faced with our end in the fairly short term, or at least the end of the comfortable civilisation we've all learned to enjoy. Just goes to show how close to the edge we must really be for even elected officials to pile this sort of money into a science project."

"I *was* feeling a little low but, wow! All better now," Hank remarked sardonically. "Do you do parties?"

Now Woodsey laughed too.

"Well, I'll sort you a 'happy ever after' if you'll let me tell it!" Tim rejoindered, playing into the banter and enjoying the attention from these new friends. Not really used to anyone actually being interested in what he knew, he was discovering he liked it.

"There is a silver lining to this rather noxious cloud, or there will be when we get to phase three in a few years time. That is, seeding Mars with bacterial and eventually plant and animal life, in theory. That's where my mum comes in. We should be able to transplant life from home, hopefully before we kill it all off!"

Woodsey wet a finger and held it up in the air, looking around in feigned puzzlement.

"What is it?" asked Tim.

"Ah, nothing. Just thought I felt rain. Must be your silver lining has slipped again."

"I can't help it if we've annihilated the natural world, can I?" asked Tim reasonably. From the very first moment he saw Woodsey, before the launch, he had observed that the New Zealander rarely stopped grinning. Woodsey added a very overtly indolent wink too, just in case Tim failed to notice that he was being mocked.

"Hurry up," said Hank. "They'll be closing!"

"OK, where was I?" Tim muttered.

"When your mum gets to third base," Woodsey reminded him, helpfully.

Hank snorted again and, caught in the throes of a coughing fit, now had beer streaming down his nose. Eventually he managed to wheeze, "He said *phase three*, third base means—"

Woodsey and Tim stared at him quizzically.

The young American cleared his throat. "Erm… something else," he finished weakly.

"Alright, alright," said Tim, holding his hands up. "As it happened, Mars wasn't quite as dead as some of our scientists suspected. Deep core drilling revealed that many of the ice seams still contained some photosynthetic bacteria. These microorganisms have proved themselves to be extraordinarily adaptive. You see, hardwired into their genomes is the ability to survive freezing for millions of years, eons in fact, in the thin layer under the glaciers where ice rubs against stone. Similar systems exist in the polar regions of Earth. This pulverised rock acts like a fertiliser for these microbes that are waiting, dormant, for the chance to photosynthesise again.

"My mum leads a team of biologists, who will study these microorganisms to see how they act and react with Earth born genomes. She hopes that when Mars has a much warmer, largely carbon dioxide atmosphere, much of the ice will become liquid water once more, releasing these tiny miracles – as she calls them – in their trillions. This should allow them to go to work using photosynthesis to absorb the carbon and give out oxygen. As this process begins to replicate, Mars should slowly come back to life – metaphorically, at least.

"Seeding life from Earth is kind of like a Noah's Ark approach. It was planned around the construction of four settlements, as I'm sure you know. Three of the four townships were completed a while back. Only the fourth and final one is still missing one of its factory Pods. As you've probably guessed, that's what we're sitting in."

"The pub?" asked Woodsey, fatuously.

Tim ignored him, speaking to Hank instead. "The townships have full manufacturing capability – as well as pubs – for the building and proliferation of the atmospheric processing plants which will continue to produce greenhouse gases all over Mars. Obviously, this process will largely be carried out using locally mined material. That's why we've got such a large mining and construction contingent on board. I expect Woodsey's dad is part of that team?"

Woodsey nodded affirmative.

Tim continued. "Other essentials will be bulk transported from Earth via ships like the *New World*. Their design makes them ideal because, my, what big eyes you have and they all lived happily ever after."

"Eh?" asked Hank and Woodsey, together.

"Just checking you were still listening," said Tim, archly. He raised his drink to toast, "Here's to new worlds and new mates."

The three young men chinked bottles together.

"Cheers," said Tim and Hank together.

"To Woodsey," said Woodsey simultaneously, making the others laugh again, "and to new brews. I need another drink after that load, dude!"

"You liked it?" asked Tim.

"It was a hell of a story, mate. Pithy," the New Zealander added sarcastically. "Shame about the pigs, though."

"Eh?"

"S'right. When we get to Mars, I'm calling dibs on the house made of bricks in case there are any big bad space monsters there. We've all seen the movies!"

They continued to laugh until a thought struck Tim. "Ooh, talking of monsters, I've got a movie I made when I was at school which you might think is cool. It's got blood and guts – the lot!" He pulled his personal comm from a pocket and folded the screen out to the size of a small monitor, standing it in the middle of the table.

"Is there any nudity?" asked Woodsey.

"Erm…" Tim looked up, searching for the answer. "Technically, yes," he replied, truthfully. "However, I'm guessing you're thinking of a different *kind* of movie."

Wrapped up in their own little world, the three teenagers turned in surprise when a man in his early forties approached them bearing a tray full of bottled beers. "G'day lads, I thought I might find you in here."

"Dad!" Woodsey cried, pulling up another seat. "Good of you to open the gate with your knee. I'd better take those cold ones off your hands!"

Setting everyone up with a couple of bottles, he dropped the tray on an empty table.

Thomas nodded to the teenagers as he took the proffered seat. "Just thought I'd see how you were getting on. I've only got time for a quick stubby. You gonna introduce me to your mates?"

"Sweet as. Pity you missed the recital."

"Recital?"

"Yeah. Lads, this is me dad. Dad, these are me mates, Chapter and Verse. They go on a bit and one of 'em has a tendency to leak beer from the nostrils. And on that note, fellas, I need to go and powder m' nose. Tim, you'd better hold that movie, unless you wanna pipe it through to the dunny?"

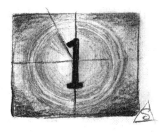

Chapter 2 | Disaster

Almost a day after launch, the engineering team had largely settled into their routines with the stresses of preparing the ship and taking off behind them. In between takeoff, the wormhole jump and landing, they usually hoped for long periods of 'low excitement'. On this occasion one of them remained on edge.

There were four engineers aboard the *New World*, headed by Chief Engineer Lieutenant Hiro Nassaki. Sensing movement out of the corner of his eye, he looked up from his console momentarily, just in time to see his second in command slip away, looking almost shifty.

Hiro shook his head. Tokyo born and bred, he would be the first to admit that although he could get by in Japanese and English, he only really spoke *machine* fluently. Indeed, he could compel the most sophisticated shuttlecraft to 'handshake' electronically with a lowly toaster, but people... they were just so *unknowable*. Technically, Hiro's shift had ended a couple of hours ago, but the position he held was no mere job to the chief. He knew he was a first rate engineer and wore his love affair for the *New World* on his sleeve, but until recently had never considered people skills particularly important – a deficit which placed him at a disadvantage when recruiting his engineering team a few years ago, after a reshuffle. It was the primary reason he had ended up with the second in command nobody else in the fleet wanted.

Despite his blind spot where people were concerned, Hiro was not an unkind man and often stewed over just what to do with Lieutenant

Geoff Lloyd. He had tried to befriend him several times, but it had never gone well.

Lloyd had a reputation among the crew for being embittered and almost wholly unlikeable, but Hiro simply saw him as an imposition. Yet he seemed to be stuck in this binary struggle with the man. He knew Captain Douglas would offer support if he needed it, but asking would feel like failure, somehow. He sighed, staring at the door through which the impossible man had made his exit a moment ago. "What's he up to?" he muttered to himself. It was times like this he wished his father were still alive – he always knew how to handle people.

He lapsed into thought. *Lloyd has been passed over for advancement several times, even since I was promoted chief engineer – and quite rightly so, in my opinion – could that be his problem? Jealousy?*

Conversely, Hiro's relationship with the other engineers, Crewmen Georgio and Mario Baccini, was quite different. The young twins from Pompeii were almost identical, which led to occasional misunderstandings, but crucially, they 'got' Lieutenant Nassaki's hands-on way of working. Being roughly of an age, the three fostered a healthy competitiveness which Hiro encouraged. His experience was not exhaustive, but he found that it made for an efficient department – despite *Old Man Lloyd* dropping the occasional spanner in the works.

However, just lately Lloyd had seemed even more irascible than usual. As a man who only ever dreamed of being an engineer, Hiro did not always understand the desires of others. All he knew for sure was that his overtures of friendship had continually failed. Forced to admit that making friends was perhaps not really his forte, he had recently decided to try stealth – something about which he knew even less. In his innocence, it never occurred to him that, when dealing with human beings, small acts can have cumulative consequences; and by issuing Lloyd with tasks all over the ship, always carefully away from his own theatre of works, he was compounding a fracture which far transcended a mere generational gap.

Second Lieutenant Geoff Lloyd made his way along the corridor on a personal errand, heading away from engineering for now. He was both anxious about something new and annoyed about something old. As he stopped by his locker, hoping to retrieve his precision socket set, his annoyance dialled up another notch.

Gasping in frustration, he balled his fists. "Those damned kids have been taking my tools again! How the hell do they always break my encryptions?!" he exploded, violently slamming the locker door.

"Second engineer!" he spat angrily to himself. "I should be in charge of this ship – at very least, chief engineer! Instead I have to play subordinate to a kid who still has wet ink on his diplomas! As for the others, I know more about the ship, leadership and hardship than all of them put together – including that damned Scotsman who's three years my junior! Nearly thirty years a lieutenant. Thirty damned years!

"I've put everything into this job, it even cost me my relationship with Audrey and none of it was my fault. I could have been married and happy if it wasn't for the benighted nepotism within NASA! I could have... I could've..." His rant ended abruptly, his rage honing to a cutting edge.

It's time I made a change, time I taught these people a lesson, he brooded silently, *and today's as good a day as any.*

Crewmen Georgio and Mario Baccini ran advance system checks on the wormhole drive. It would not be needed until tomorrow, but Mario, whose responsibility it was, liked to run tests well in advance, so that any problems could be flagged up and fixed before the captain ordered a jump.

Today was important to the brothers. This would be the last trip the *New World* would make to Mars for a while and still they considered their options with no decision in sight. They could stay on for the moon mission or look to ply their talents elsewhere. Unwilling to be parted, they were equally unwilling to agree about it.

"Hey, Mario, if we don't decide soon, we're just going to have to stay here and that's all there is to it," stated Georgio in English. The Baccinis often conversed in English, even when alone, to improve their skills.

"Yeah, *yeah*," replied Mario. "I'll think about it later. Of more immediate concern, did you return Geoff's socket set?"

Georgio's brows knitted. "Oops," he muttered.

"Ha! He'll go *pazzo*!" laughed Mario.

"Geoff Lloyd dampens my *bonhomie* not at all," replied Georgio, snootily. "Besides, he won't if you don't tell him. I forgot about it – is no big deal."

"I'd put it back now if I were you. I thought he was going to have a seizure the last time you borrowed something from him without asking."

"But he always says *no*," said Georgio, with frustration.

"Well, I'm just saying…" Mario sniggered at the silly situation Georgio had gotten himself into. It was commonplace for one or other of the twins to be in Lloyd's bad books; they were that sort, and so was he.

"He *always* blames me," continued Georgio, plaintively.

"It always *is* you!" bit back Mario.

"What! Why don't you remind me about the time you put his dirty laundry in the air vent next to his work station?"

"Hey, it stank, man!"

"So what, you thought a couple of days of having warm air passed over it would help?"

"He located them – eventually."

"He went *loco*, you mean! I thought he was going to see the captain for sure that time. I'm positive he would've too, if he'd known which of us did it. But don't worry *fratello*, I would have helped you pack your belongings, maybe even played you a few sad songs before waving you off, that type of thing. HEY!" Georgio cried out as an empty food carton whizzed overhead. "I thought you never allowed food around the wormhole drive?"

Mario looked scandalised. "*You* brought that in here!"

"*Me*?!"

"*You*! Look Georgie, *I'm* going to go to the captain if you keep leaving your crap in my work space. OK? He'll kick you off the ship and you'll have to go back to correcting that *plodding* thesis you slapped together on temporal mechanics!"

Georgio blustered for a moment. "Plodding? It was more widely regarded than that *derivative* work you hashed up about wormholes. Hey, and what do you mean by *correcting*?"

"Derivative?!" sputtered Mario. "My thesis got us our jobs."

"Oh *please*," Georgio replied witheringly. "You press a few buttons here and there, give the drive housing a bit of a polish in between jumps and drink filthy NASA coffee. I'm surprised you haven't shined the casing away!"

Mario laughed at his brother's insults, despite himself.

"Mary, the janitor, could do your job," continued Georgio, laughing himself now, "in between cleaning the refectory and making drinks for all the crew! I do all the real work with Hiro. And FYI, that food carton was *yours*. I saw you walk past the bin with it on the way here, in one of your little 'fetishist' daydreams, probably."

Seeing his moment, Georgio launched it back across the room.

Mario went down.

"Mario...?"

A pained voice came from the floor behind a work station. "You gotta me in the plums, *idiota*!"

Late that night, the hatch leading into the wormhole drive section of engineering slid open. The doors made very little noise and the man stepped inside, equally quietly.

The whole engineering deck was deserted, its crew either on a rest cycle or running systems checks elsewhere on the ship. Subsequently, the wormhole drive was also left unattended.

The man checked the system's status – all of Baccini's diagnostics seemed to have been completed with no faults logged. *Good*, thought the saboteur, *even the fastidious Mario is unlikely to check on his beloved wormhole drive again until it powers down after the jump.* He opened the drive casing and planted the device he had constructed, knowing exactly where to place it for effect. Once satisfied, he closed the housing and left.

He knew the device was much more powerful than it needed to be, but he had been afraid of being caught with it – he did not like handling it either.

Sweat ran down his face and neck. "Sod it! It'll do. Now, get a grip," he told himself, wiping his brow with a sleeve.

He had everything worked out, escape and all. It was risky but if timed correctly, he would make Earth orbit within three days, carrying the sad news of a disaster. *Lifeboat 7* would be slower than the *New World* and more cramped, but he was being paid a *lot* of money, so these were small matters.

He paused to look carefully around a corner, having already confused the surveillance system in this area. However, you could never fully factor for passersby. Content the coast was clear, he propped up his justifications and vacated the area, silencing his conscience as he tried to regulate his breathing.

The USS *New World* was now a day and a half out from Earth and on a heading straight for Mars. Her crew busied themselves, preparing to make their jump through a wormhole.

Due to the relative infancy of the technology, the stipulated minimum distance of 1,800,000 kilometres was an agreed safety margin. Few of the scientists involved with its development could agree with any surety what gravitic effects a planetary body might have on a forming wormhole.

Captain Douglas gave the passengers his usual thirty-minute warning, asking them to make their way back to the embarkation area, a multi-functional space and in some ways the heart of the Pod. At any time, it could be an auditorium for shows, lectures or gatherings, but most importantly, with over a hundred secure, tiered seats, it made an ideal passenger seating platform while the ship underwent manoeuvres.

Passengers entered in small groups, taking their seats over the next twenty minutes or so. The atmosphere was electric and naturally, excited chatter made everyone louder than everyone else. Apart from the new life on the new world which awaited them, this would also be their first wormhole jump.

Within minutes of taking his seat, Tim Norris became fast friends with a four-legged passenger named Reiver, a beautiful, long-haired border collie who happened to own a human called Dr Natalie Pearson.

Natalie was a young zoologist, consulting for the team of geneticists who would one day make Mars home for Terran invertebrates and eventually larger animals. Tim and Natalie rattled away happily, lost in the wondrous story of life on Earth, with occasional interruptions for attention from Reiver. Tim stroked the collie's head. Dogs always know an animal-lover and the border collie had latched onto him at once, amongst so many. At that moment, Reiver hooked a paw over the top of the expanded screen on Tim's personal comm and pulled it down – it was stealing his attention.

"Reiver, no boy," said Natalie.

That did it; his mistress was ignoring him too now, in favour of this glowing thing that made strange noises. He slapped his paw down harder, speaking an indignant, husky, "Chuff!"

"Reiver, sit down!" Natalie snapped crossly.

The collie's ears flattened to his head. *Oops*, he may have gone too far. He tilted his head to one side and laid it on Natalie's lap, staring up at her with a look of innocence so timeless that it may have predated Eve's apple.

Tim burst out laughing.

[PLAY]

Branches rustle and swish, a whiplash making it all but impossible to see ahead. Just outside the forest canopy, bellows of fear and anger cross the plain. The sudden daylight is dazzling and the ground, four metres below, begins to move by much more quickly – it is time to run, it is time to hunt.

The approach makes the reek of fear in the air almost tangible as the Mapusaurus pack close, jostling and shoving one another, claws grasping in excitement. From the centre of the charge, nothing can be seen but the flexing of powerful hind legs and angry tails through the dust. Surrounded by fourteen killers, some as large as Tyrannosaurus Rex, the view of the quarry is almost nonexistent. After a 200 metre sprint, the enormous, plodding Argentinasaurus herd cast panicked shadows over the hunting pride. The Mapusaurs scatter, tearing between their prey, separating them and attacking opportunistically until a victim is singled out.

From their relatively small heads to the ends of their massive tails, the oldest Argentinasaurs are easily forty metres long, their giant necks contributing almost half that length. At eighty tons or more, even the largest of the Mapusaurs give them a wide berth, instinct and experience telling them that a strike from those twelve-metre-long tails, weighing as much as twenty tons, would be devastating. The technique, honed over millennia, is to separate the young or infirm before focusing their efforts, and sure enough, the Mapusaurs soon split an adolescent from the herd. The terrified creature whips its tail and rises up on its hind legs to stamp at the hunters as they come near. Even this smaller quarry is ten metres long, and weighing around fifteen tons, can kill by clumsy, terrified flailing alone.

Undaunted, the hunters attack from several directions – hit and fade, hit and fade. The terrible, serrated teeth of the Mapusaurs slice the flesh of their prey causing wickedly jagged lacerations. They cannot kill such a giant animal outright, but know that it will eventually succumb to blood loss and shock. Soon this huge and magnificent force of nature will be carrion; food for the pack and those who will follow down the chain.

Fear goes to work, weakening the creature still further as it falls onto its front knees, crying mournfully for help, for a mother it has never known to save it from this horrific fate. The largest of the Argentinasaurs are unaffected either by its plight or the general chaos around them. So vast that fear is a forgotten memory, these ground-shaking sauropod dinosaurs simply continue their business of felling trees and stripping the branches of their bounty.

Suddenly having all the time in the world, the Mapusaurs focus their attention on the weakening sub-adult. They run around the terrified creature, hind legs pumping, tails keeping them balanced through every tight turn and instinctively choreographed manoeuvre.

One adventurous adolescent is so caught up in the excitement of the hunt that he fails to notice the shadow which falls across him and the force of the tail-whip smashes his one-ton body instantly. The youth lands ten metres from where he was struck, a pulped slab of soggy flesh and shattered bone. Before the motion of this deadly game of bat and ball is fully spent, or the young life even fully extinguished, a giant Mapusaurus bull picks up the broken remains in its jaws and slopes off to feast on his own, in peace, the flicks of his tail an earnest warning to any who would barter for a share.

The shadow over the pack's chosen prey grows, as a second, mid-sized Argentinasaurus cow swings her tail threateningly, in the path of the hunters. Despite losing a lot of blood, the injuries are not fatal and the wounded sauropod gets back to its feet, hiding among the females who instinctually answered its call. None of the individuals are its mother, it is simply understood that they all are.

Slowly the giants return to the herd as a new battle commences over the corpse of the dead Mapusaurus. For a pack this size, it is merely a snack, but the giant herbivores can never outpace their predators, so there will always be tomorrow.

The lucky Argentinasaurus takes one last look behind at the squabbling carnivores as it limps away.
[PAUSE]

"You made that film yourself?" Natalie asked breathlessly, clearly moved by the young dinosaur's plight.

"Yes," Tim answered, hoping his pride was not too obvious. "It was a project for traditional animation class. You don't think some of the subtitles were a bit much?"

"No way! I hope you got an 'A'? It's awesome, I actually felt like I was running with the pack at one point."

Tim cringed awkwardly. "Thanks. I played it to the guys last night in the bar, and they asked me that. Well, when I say 'they' I mean Hank and Woodsey's dad. Woodsey said that baby dinosaurs weren't the kind of naked chicks he was into."

Natalie laughed until Tim confessed, "Actually, I got a 'B'."

"You're kidding?" Natalie was genuinely surprised after watching such a life-like video. "How did your teacher justify that?"

"Well, I decided to create a movie showing an attack on a herd of Argentinasaurus by a pack of Mapusaurus, as you saw, but the assignment technically called for a short film showing the preparation or cooking of a meal. I got bored, I got sidetracked – I got a 'B'. Of course, I argued that this was exactly what my film *did* portray, if you needed a meal in the time of the dinosaurs, anyway. But despite my best arguments, *Cretaceous Cookery* just didn't go over very well with my teacher. Still, I didn't mind really," he smiled ruefully. "My classmates did some quite difficult work, making virtual pastries rise and such, but guess whose film everybody wanted to see *again!*"

Natalie grinned at the young man. "I'm not surprised. I was almost in tears at one point. I would never have forgiven you if the young sauropod had died."

Reiver whined. He scented a change in the crowd's mood and feeling left out, jumped onto the arm of the seat between them, shoving his nose into Tim's face whilst losing traction with his hind legs and sliding back, gracelessly, into Natalie's lap. Flailing to stop him from falling, she was rewarded with a lick which covered her nose and left eye as Reiver settled into a cradled, upside-down position across her chest. All she could smell was her beloved pet's last meal... it could have been worse, a lot worse.

Panting happily, the collie was indifferent while everyone else stopped whatever they were doing to listen, as a second announcement from the bridge echoed around the cavernous space.

"Creating a stable wormhole in T minus two minutes," the captain's voice boomed over the public address system. Previous journeys had demonstrated that the volume at this stage needed to be dialled higher than usual, to compensate for the natural excitement among the passengers. *"We will follow the wormhole, exiting 1.8 million kilometres from Mars. Please make sure all luggage is secure and all safety harnesses are fastened – captain out."*

Most of the passengers' belongings had long been secured in their quarters, but there was still a shuffle as everyone gave bags and belts one last check.

The captain's voice soon sounded again, unnaturally loud this time, as the passengers fell into silent anticipation. *"We're about to jump and will arrive near Mars straight away. There will be no perception of time for us in the wormhole. Please remain seated and calm."*

The official part of his message relayed, he continued with more of his natural warmth. *"We've done this many times and there's nothing to fear, we'll be back in real-space before you know it – Douglas out."*

The tiered seats of embarkation faced a large, curved screen, some sixteen metres wide by nine high. When it lit up to show the view from a camera set into the nose of the ship, an audible gasp travelled around the auditorium. Mars, their destination, could be seen in the centre of the display as a slightly reddish dot among the heavens.

Stars...

The universe viewed from Earth is as through cellophane. The only way to truly see space is from space. No metaphor can truly carry the majesty. It must be seen, it must be experienced and Tim was agog.

Glancing back down at his comm, he scrolled back to an unfinished document.

So this is what freedom feels like. Part of me feels selfish, like I've left everyone in hell... [SAVE]

He copied this first entry of the voyage to his private diary. Not wishing to miss a thing for the next few minutes, he folded his tablet back down to the size of a personal comm once more and slipped it into a pocket. He was glad he chose that moment to look up. Grinning, he considered his change in fortunes. *Whatever* came next, he would embrace it, would make it his own – he had to.

Everyone was strapped into their seats for the last, anxious seconds. Natalie held on tightly to Reiver, hardly seeming to even breathe as she studied the view-screen. In the top left corner, a giant number '10' appeared, frozen in place. Presently, the countdown commenced and people began calling out, with others joining in like the countdown to new-years. Suddenly everyone in the place was roaring, "4! – 3! – 2! – 1! Yeaaah!"

Space appeared to distort slightly, followed by a huge *BANG* from somewhere aft, but very definitely within the ship. The *New World* rocked once.

Neither Tim, nor any of his fellow travellers had ever voyaged through a wormhole before, so the distortion and far-off bang was unsettling but not instantly terrifying. However, as klaxons and warning lights came to life all around them, someone panicked and like dye in water, its spread through the group was fast and absolute.

The view-screen still showed space in front of the ship, but anyone keeping their wits amongst the chaos erupting around them would have seen the distortion replaced by stars which were... *different.*

Few noticed, as panic continued to rip through the passengers like a second wave of the explosion.

Major Ford White, an ex-US marine in command of Pod security, uncoupled his belt and jumped out of his seat calling his ten-strong team about him. Quickly, he charged his people with restoring order. White's composure was a balm of sorts and they soon began re-seating the passengers while he strode calmly but purposefully over to a comms panel to call the bridge.

Although Tim travelled with his mother, for some reason which made no sense to him, their allocated seats were in different rows. He could not imagine why some soulless official would split them up for such a life changing event and subsequently, he was left all alone in a crowd, gaping. Even Reiver had bolted, but worse… Mars was gone too.

"I am cursed," he muttered.

Mere seconds after Captain Douglas instructed Lieutenant Singh to engage the wormhole drive – calmly anticipating the usual ripple of distortion across space, through the viewport – the bridge crew were shocked by an explosion from somewhere behind them.

Douglas and Commander Baines gripped the arms of their command seats, sharing a split-second look of astonishment. "What the…?" they said in unison before years of training immediately reasserted and they got down to business.

Baines scrolled through the ship's systems on her touch screen, looking for the cause of the explosion, while Douglas demanded reports from all departments.

She arrived at an answer just as a call came back from engineering reporting the complete destruction of the wormhole drive. "*It's taken part of the hull with it and she's venting atmosphere.*" The voice sounded very young and very distraught.

"Seal the hatches!" the captain bellowed. There was no time to consider anyone's feelings at this point.

"We're on it, Captain." This second voice was unmistakably that of the chief engineer, Hiro Nassaki, and gradually the rumble felt throughout the ship quieted, eventually stopping altogether. *"The breach is sealed but we've taken heavy damage to the hull. It's difficult to ascertain the full extent of it yet. The wormhole drive is a smoking hole in a room that's mostly gone, sir."*

Douglas let out a breath that he had not realised he was holding. "Secure everything you can, Chief. Do you have casualties?"

Hiro paused. When he eventually spoke again, his voice cracked a little. *"Mostly cuts and bruises, but we've lost Mario, sir."*

"Oh, God no," said Douglas quietly. "Is Georgio OK?"

Hiro spoke quietly, clearly trying not to be overheard. *"Physically OK, sir, but I think he's in shock."*

"What about Lloyd?"

"He's not here, sir. I don't know his condition."

Douglas ordered Lieutenant Singh to get a medical team down to engineering, stat. "Hang on Hiro, Dr Flannigan and his team are en route and Ah'll be doon maself as soon as Ah can leave the bridge – Douglas out."

As he signed off, Baines gave him a fearful look. "Did I hear Mario...?"

Douglas nodded. "Commander, can you get down to embarkation, please? Those people are likely to be frantic and will need calming. Lieutenant, hold our position here. Ah'm heading for engineering, and Lieutenant..."

Singh looked around from his console. "Yes, sir?"

Douglas pointedly looked out of the viewport. "Try and work out where here is, there's a good fellow."

Singh looked stunned, but nodded and bent to his task. Douglas turned to see Commander Baines already leaving the bridge, summoning the *New World*'s security team to meet her in embarkation.

"Chin up, everybody," he said. "Ah'll be in engineering." *Or what's left of it*, he added in the privacy of his own mind.

As the captain left, Lieutenant Singh answered the frantic buzzing from the comm system. "Bridge," he stated.

A surprisingly calm, American voice responded. *"This is Major Ford White speaking from embarkation. Things are mostly under control here, but folks are very concerned. We could really use a sitrep if possible."*

Singh checked his read-outs. "Yes, sir," he replied, "this is Lieutenant Singh. The ship has sustained damage to engineering. We suspect some kind of malfunction leading to an explosion at the moment and are working to bring things back online as quickly as possible. There should be no immediate threat to safety. Commander Baines is on her way down to you with our own security team to help calm the situation and the captain has left for engineering. More as we get it, Major, please stand by."

"Thank you, Lieutenant – White out."

Presently, Baines entered embarkation at the head of a trio with The Sarge and Private Jones. Quickly assessing the situation, she nodded her approval of White's efforts to restore calm.

"Good job, Major," she said, approaching him. "I thought it would be worse in here, thank you."

White nodded acknowledgement. "Is it bad, Commander?"

"Bad enough, Ford," she replied, bleakly. "Better get our game faces on for the passengers, though."

She stepped up onto the small dais in front of the huge view-screen, turning to address a century of frightened faces. The crowd were getting restless as Baines held up her hands for a quiet which was not forthcoming.

"SILENCE!" bellowed Sergeant John Jackson. "SHUT UP AND LISTEN TO THE OFFICER'S REPORT!"

Like a bucket of cold water, his command snapped the passengers out of their agitation and the auditorium fell still at last.

Commander Baines toggled the microphone concealed within the dais so that she could speak calmly and be heard by all, without the need to raise her voice. Taking a deep breath to centre herself, she began, "There has been an incident in engineering—"

"An *incident?*" several of her nervous audience spoke out in shock and disbelief.

"An explosion," she corrected herself. Clearly there was only so much sugar that she would be able to coat this with. "Damage control crews led by Captain Douglas are working on the problem as we speak and there is no immediate danger to your safety, or the ship."

"*Immediate* danger?" a booming male voice with an American accent cut across her. "What the hell does that mean?"

Baines cursed under her breath for that slip. Composing herself, she tried again.

"Please try to remain calm, sir. I simply mean that the ship is still flying, our engines are all in the green and life support is unaffected. At the moment it seems we've been fortunate."

"*Seems...*" said the same man, raising an eyebrow.

Baines grimaced slightly, feeling as if she was on trial. "Ship's systems are optimal. All we know for sure at this stage is that there was a problem with the wormhole drive.

"I also have to report, with great sadness, that one of the *New World*'s engineers, twenty-five-year-old Mario Baccini, was killed in the blast and another of our engineers is currently missing. A search is underway for the missing man but we remain hopeful that he'll be found safe. Unfortunately, Mr Baccini was our foremost expert on the wormhole drive, so it may take us a little while to work out exactly what has happened."

Before Baines had chance to add anything further, the American called out again. "How far are we from Mars?"

Damn, she thought, *there goes any hoping of fielding* that *one later.* "We're unsure of our coordinates at the moment, sir. The problem has necessitated a reboot of many ship's systems, but we'll keep you all informed as we know more."

"Phuff!" her antagonist scoffed.

"I'm sorry, Mr...?"

"Burnstein, Hank Burnstein."

"I'm sorry, Mr Burnstein. We have to ask you all to remain patient for now. The crew are working as hard as they can to find answers for us all, so that we can either continue our journey or return to Earth."

A barrage of questions flew from all quarters, forcing Baines to raise her voice.

"We will keep you appraised as we know more. *Please*, I must urge you to remain calm and be patient. Now, I'm sure you will understand that I have critical duties. Major White will liaise with the bridge throughout the next few hours as more news becomes available. Thank you, ladies and gentlemen."

With that she stepped down and walked past the Major, making for the exit.

"Oh, thanks for that," he said sardonically.

"Sorry, Ford," Baines replied quietly, as she passed. "We'll try and let you know as much as we can, as soon as we can. Hopefully, I can get the man in the big chair to come down then. I think they might eat me alive if I try and stall again."

White smiled lopsidedly. "Until later, Commander."

Baines flipped a casual salute as she strode towards The Sarge, standing near the exit. "Sarge, post the door. Ensure all the passengers remain in one place and see if you can ask Mary to organise some refreshments for everyone."

"Yes, ma'am," The Sarge saluted as Baines left.

Douglas was full of trepidation as he approached engineering. He hailed the bridge.

"*Singh here, sir,*" the response came back immediately.

"Sandy, can you stop these wretched klaxons and flashing lights? They're making *me* anxious."

The noise stopped and the lights lowered in their intensity.

"*Better, sir?*"

Douglas nodded. "Much. Thank you, Lieutenant." However, the sight which greeted him as he stepped into engineering made his heart sink. The hatch through to wormhole drive control was sealed but much fire and smoke damage was evident across the whole bulkhead, along with some twisting to the hatch itself.

"We were lucky, Captain."

Douglas turned, surprised to find his chief engineer, Lieutenant Nassaki, standing right behind him, also eyeing the damage.

"How so?" asked Douglas.

"The hatch is twisted but we got it to seal," explained Hiro, smoke staining his uniform and a smudge of grease across his brow. "If it hadn't made a full connection we'd have lost the whole of engineering and been left a dead duck in space, sir. Poor Mario wasn't so lucky though."

Douglas noticed Mario's twin brother, Georgio, slumped in a corner with his head in his hands. A wave of sadness washed over him as he studied the young man, who hardly seemed to move or even breathe. Lieutenant David Flannigan, the ship's doctor, knelt by his side and spoke quietly, but he gave no response.

Another man stood next to doctor and patient. Justin Smyth, the ship's nurse, caught the captain's eye and shook his head sadly.

Flannigan stood a little stiffly, and noticing Douglas, came over. "Bad business, James," he said without preamble.

"How is he?" asked Douglas.

Flannigan glanced back to where the young man sat, still unmoving. "Physically he's fine, a couple of minor contusions, but psychologically..." he shrugged. "It's been a shock, James, time will tell."

"Where's Dr Schultz?" Douglas asked.

"I sent her down to embarkation, in case anyone needed a Band-Aid or a hand held," Flannigan drawled.

Douglas looked at him in surprise.

Flannigan took his meaning. "I know, I know, but she would have been even *less* popular down here. This man has *really* suffered. The civvies can make do with Heidi. She is a brilliant doctor and surgeon. Anyhow, it'll be character building for them. At the very least they'll think twice before calling by sickbay for no good reason."

Douglas raised an eyebrow. "Aye, her detachment brings a whole new meaning to the word 'surgical'. Let's hope they survive Flight Officer Schultz's tender care," he commented wryly.

"Well I'm damned certain they won't complain about her looks," answered Flannigan.

"Hmm," replied Douglas, considering. "It's when she looks back at ye you're in trouble." He glanced towards Crewman Baccini, still crumpled in the corner, and any humour left him completely. "Ah'd be grateful if you'd take care of young Mr Baccini personally, Dave. He's going to need our support. Alright if Ah talk to him?"

"Yes, in fact it may be that what he really needs is to get back on the horse. He can grieve later in his own time, at his own speed. Play it by ear, James."

The two men nodded to one another and went their separate ways.

Douglas approached to kneel beside the anguished young man. "Georgio?" he enquired gently. "Georgie?"

With enormous effort of will, the engineer lifted his head to look up, bleary eyed. "He's gone, Captain. Mario…" he tailed off, choked.

"Ah'm so, *so* sorry my friend," replied Douglas kindly, "but Ah need you now. All the souls on this ship need you. Do you think you can help me?"

Georgio roughly batted the tears from his face and nodded as resolutely as he could manage. "I'll do my best, Captain – Mario would expect me to get this ship home."

Douglas smiled sadly, patting the engineer supportively on the shoulder. "Thank you, Georgie," he said.

Getting to his feet, he offered a hand to pull the younger man up after him and calling Hiro over to them, faced both engineers.

"Has anyone heard from Geoff?" he asked.

Hiro shook his head. "No one's seen Lieutenant Lloyd for a while, sir. I put a call out just before the jump but didn't get a response. As all systems were primed and we were about to open a wormhole, I…" he faltered, suddenly realising that an irritating breakdown in communication may have signified something more. "Should I have stopped the ship, Captain?"

Douglas took measure of the two – apparently all that remained of his four-man engineering staff. *How young they are to have to deal with all this loss and calamity*, he thought, but quickly brushed it aside. These were some of the best engineers NASA could buy and as he put a hand on each of their shoulders, he poured his faith into them.

"Maybe, but let's move on from that for now. We're in the S-H-one-T here, boys. We need to know exactly what happened and what state we're in to continue our journey." He was encouraged to see Hiro and Georgio straighten, the engineer's pride sparking to life in their eyes.

Surprisingly, it was Georgio who spoke first. "Captain, I suggest we send an EVA team out to check the external damage and if possible, get into wormhole drive control to see what happened."

Douglas nodded his assent. He was about to speak when Hiro added, "Among the Pod passengers there's a Captain Gleeson, I spoke to him in the restaurant last night. It was late and we were the only ones in there, so we shared a table. Gleeson is an Australian army explosives expert, seconded to the mining team on a five year tour. I suggest we get him suited up as part of the EVA team, sir."

Douglas stared at the chief for a moment and blinked.

"Sir?" Hiro enquired, hesitantly.

"Explosives expert?" asked Douglas. "Hiro, what are ye telling me?"

Hiro hesitated, glancing at Georgio next to him. "The wormhole drive didn't blow itself up, sir," he said flatly.

Georgio looked at him sharply, also catching the chief's meaning. "Hiro?" he asked.

Hiro looked from his junior to his captain and sighed. "Gentlemen, Mario treated that drive like a baby. There's no way I'm ever going to believe that he messed things up or sabotaged it." Focusing on Douglas, he continued, "The only other explanation is a bomb, sir."

Douglas rocked back slightly as the enormity of this revelation hit him. "But we checked the ship rigorously prior to take-off, both before and after the passengers boarded, as policy. Ah don't see how...?" He tailed off, slumping a little as a second stark realisation struck, full-force. "You're telling me that we have a saboteur, or even a terrorist *on board*, as part of this mission?"

"That would be my guess, Captain," agreed Hiro.

"You're saying he was murdered?" Georgio blurted out, the strain in his voice obvious. "Someone killed Mario *on purpose*?"

Douglas straightened up – the ship's captain again. He squeezed the young man's shoulder in an attempt to reassure. "We don't know anything for certain yet, but if that is indeed what happened, we'll find who did it and they will pay! That Ah promise ye. If we're going to do this, Ah need ye to stay focused, Georgie, huh?"

The Italian stiffened, eyes cold with sudden anger. "I'll get the EVA suits checked out, sir, and will be ready for your team at airlock one in thirty minutes." Saluting, he turned and left.

Douglas and Nassaki watched him go with a mixture of sympathy and respect.

"Ah think you'll need to head the team, Hiro. You OK with that? It may be..." he searched for the best words but gave up and just spoke his mind. "It may be that whatever is *left* of Mario is in that room."

"I know, sir. No choice, it has to be me. I can't put Georgio in there." He nodded to the captain and left to prepare.

Douglas opened a channel to Commander Baines on his personal comm.

"*Baines here, sir.*" The response came back in a heartbeat.

"Jill, Ah need you down in engineering. Bring The Sarge and Jones with you. Also, can you ask Major White to spare us two trusted men from his security detail as well?"

"*Sir?*"

"That's the order, Commander."

"*On the double, sir.*"

Within a few minutes Douglas heard running, booted feet on deck plates and Baines entered engineering at the head of a four-man security detail.

Douglas nodded to her before speaking to Sergeant Jackson. "Sarge, secure this room. No one saving myself, the commander, Lieutenant Nassaki or Crewman Baccini is to enter."

A question crossed Jackson's face.

Douglas saw it. "Sarge?"

"And Lieutenant Lloyd, sir?" he asked.

Douglas stared The Sarge in the eye. "Only the four names Ah just gave you, Sergeant."

With the blank eyes-front of the professional soldier, The Sarge saluted. "Yessir!"

"Also, Ah've another duty for ye, Sarge. Get Jones and one of Major White's men to find Lieutenant Lloyd and bring him to the bridge. There are some questions which need answers. Organise Nurse Smyth to go along with them too, just in case he's been injured."

He looked at Private Dewi Jones directly. "Private, when you find Lieutenant Lloyd, make sure he knows that his immediate presence is required on the bridge and *that* is an order from the captain. Tell him Ah'll brook no poncing about, and you can use those exact words, is that clear?"

Jones nodded. "Understood, sir."

"I'll call Smyth back from the infirmary to join you," The Sarge added. "Stay as a three-man team, don't split up and remember, he's an officer and a gentleman until we're told otherwise."

"Yes, Sarge," replied Jones and the two men left quickly.

Douglas and Baines also left engineering, making their way back to the bridge. The captain brought his first officer up to speed on what little he knew and what he further suspected.

"Get a three-man EVA team to join Hiro at airlock one, please Jill, and make sure an Aussie captain named Gleeson is among them. He's our main man on explosives, apparently."

"Yes, sir," replied Baines. "I'll see you back on the bridge when I'm done."

Douglas was suddenly alone with his ship. He knew her every nook and corner like the back of his hand, yet she was somehow changed, subtly but intrinsically. She had been violated and as her captain, Douglas felt it like a physical hurt. He could not help feeling that it was like visiting one of the *New World*'s sister ships, where everything was familiar, but not the same at all.

"Och, damn it!" he raged, storming down the empty corridor. "It's not even been half an hour!"

Suited-up for vacuum, Lieutenant Nassaki led his four-man team outside the ship. Leaving airlock one, they travelled some thirty metres along the outer hull to wormhole drive control. It was not hard to find. A black rent had been opened along the side of the *New World*, the edges all torn metal and ceramic, blown outwards by the force of the blast.

The extra vehicular activity suits the team wore were equipped with thrusters to provide manoeuvrability and to prevent anyone from drifting. However, Hiro could not help dutifully drawing everyone's attention to the many external anchor points where an EV work detail might tie on to the hull for safety. This did impede their rate of travel.

"Bladdy 'ell Nasso," Gleeson felt the need to comment. "I'd have brought me bladdy camera if I'd known we were going sightseeing!"

Hiro frowned. "Drifting in space is not like getting lost in the bush, you know. Hypoxia trumps alligators every time!"

"Crocodiles, mate. Lead on…" said Gleeson, gesturing through the rip in the hull.

The team pulled themselves into the ship. Bringing up the rear was a geneticist named Wright and another of Major White's security team, Drummond. Together, they would inspect the area as a crime scene, searching for any remnant DNA or traces of explosive from the damaged surfaces.

Wright was a leader in the field of DNA manipulation and was part of the team whose job it was to research the viability of Earth-based life on the Red Planet.

Drummond, a recent addition to the NASA Security Force[2], had previously been a detective in Detroit, America.

The four men moved further into the damaged drive room. Hiro's engineer's eye immediately saw just how lucky they were to have successfully sealed the bulkhead. The wrist and helmet lamps on their suits threw shadows around wildly, adding to the horror of the scene. Hiro cast about with dismay – the area had been decimated. He sighed deeply and opened a channel.

"*Bridge here,*" Lieutenant Singh answered.

"Are you receiving pictures from our head cams, Sandip?" asked Hiro.

"*Clear as a bell, Hiro – picture and audio, recording. We'll be able to run spectroscopic analysis on the hull damage and markings upon your return.*"

"I think this is blood," Hiro's voice wavered a little.

Douglas's voice cut into the conversation. "*Just inspect and record, Chief. We can analyse later when you're all back inboard.*"

"Yes, Captain, sorry. The damage is extensive. The tear down our hull must be two metres high and seven metres long. I don't think we can fully repair it without setting down, but of course that will present another problem. Entering atmosphere with a hole in the ship will be detrimental to our aerodynamics, to say the least, sir."

"*Will it be within tolerances for a landing, Chief?*" asked Douglas.

---

[2]   NASASEC: founded in AD2105 with a specific brief to counter the ever-mounting threat posed by terrorism to space-going traffic.

"I can't answer that yet, Captain. I'll take measurements now and when I get back inboard I'll be able to run a few simulations. Please stand by, Captain…"

Gleeson was beckoning the engineer to him. "Nasso, can you take a look at this? Am I right in thinking that the mountings here, used to fix the wormhole drive in place?" The Australian was pointing at some badly slagged, heavy duty, steel brackets.

"Yes, there *were* four of them," Hiro replied, sadly.

"I'm taking samples of this scorch residue," continued Gleeson. "I can't be sure without analysis, but I think this is some kind of plastic explosive. There's traces of metals too, possibly some kind of detonation device. My first impression is that this was surgical. The bloke was no drongo mate, he clearly didn't want the ship to go down from this. Maybe he had an escape plan in mind, Captain?"

"*If this was only meant to scupper our trip to Mars,*" Douglas replied over the comm channel, "*it would only be a temporary set-back, newsworthy, but not catastrophic. Had it not been for the brutal murder of a brilliant young man, it would have simply meant a week in space-dock and another few cents on the income tax. Are we missing something?*"

"Captain, this is Wright speaking. There are definitely DNA markers here, around the bomb area and in the room generally. Most of them probably belong to the engineering staff, but we may have something. I'll know more when I get to my lab and compare what we've got with the crew and passenger records. Of course," he concluded with a sigh, "it may be too badly damaged to tell us much."

"*Thank you, Dr Wright. Let me know what you turn up,*" said Douglas. "*Drummond, what does your copper's eye tell you, anything?*"

"Well, Captain," the American answered, "I can't add anything that these tech guys haven't already told you but my *hunch* is that you were on the right track when you questioned the motive. If all this was only meant to stall the ship, then there must be a second part to the plan.

"Obviously, we've seen plenty of cracker-boxes over the years who wanted to blow 'emselves up to make a point, but if the guy who died did this, then his plan was unlikely to do much harm other than taking himself out… no, that just doesn't track – no finale.

"So, if we assume the bomber had reason to stall us, then it follows that he might have another goal before leaving the ship. Whether that's sabotage, theft or some other criminality, I can't say.

"Either way, this distraction could buy him all the time he needs to do whatever he has to do and escape, under the cover of the chaos he's created. If this *was* a terrorist attack, getting away may not be part of his plan, of course. But I still recommend we get security to all escape pods and the shuttle bay ASAP anyway, Captain, just in case."

Back on the bridge, Douglas massaged his temples, exhaling to relieve the pressure in his head. "Damn it, you're right, thank you, Drummond. We cannae take any chances – Lieutenant Singh, get Major White on the line please – Hiro, wrap it up down there and get your team back inside. Douglas out."

Within seconds Major White answered the comm. *"How can I help you, Captain?"*

"Ford, we may have another emergency on our hands. Can you leave two good men guarding the passengers and lead the rest to the bow and aft escape pods? Check for any loiterers, the bomber may not be finished with us."

"Bomber?" White broke in, quietly.

"Aye, 'fraid so. Once you've secured the escape pod docks, please leave two men to guard them and begin a full sweep through the ship looking for anyone out of bounds. Do you have any explosive-sensing equipment in your stores?"

"We do, Captain, please stand by."

Douglas could hear White barking orders to his security team as he transferred the channel to his personal communicator.

"OK, we're en route, Captain. I've sent two officers to the aft escape pods and two more up to the pods at the bow. I'm proceeding with another man to our equipment cache to get the sensors you requested."

"Thank you, Major. We're spread pretty thinly, so Lieutenant Singh and I will make our way to the shuttle bay. Between us we should have all escape pods, engineering, embarkation, bridge and the shuttle bay covered. Start your sweep immediately upon retrieving your equipment.

Commander Baines will seal the bridge and remain in control up here to liaise and direct our efforts – Douglas out."

Closing the channel, he strode across the bridge to a locked cabinet. Keying his access code, he broke out three stunning pistols. Giving Baines and Singh a weapon each, he tucked the third into his belt.

"Lock the door, Commander, and be damned sure before you open it. See if Jones has found Lloyd yet. If he hasn't, route him to join White's scanning team. We've got a lot of ship to cover and, if we're right about all this, there may not be much time."

Baines nodded acknowledgement. "Watch your backs, guys. I'll monitor you, every step."

Douglas ran full tilt towards the shuttle bay with the younger man barrelling after him. They found it deserted. The captain opened the shuttle's passenger hatch and stepped aboard.

Singh took up a position outside, facing the entrance to the bay.

Once more using his captains' access codes, Douglas locked down the shuttle's controls, keying them a final time to confirm his instructions before running back to where Singh waited. "Naebody's nicking ma damned shuttle!" he spat, dead-locking the hatch from outside.

Grinning acknowledgement, Singh asked, "Where next, Captain?"

Douglas thought for a second. "We have to find Lloyd – he's a piece that just won't fit into this puzzle. Ah need him found, if only to rule him out."

"Do you think it could be him, Captain? I know he's not the most popular chap on the ship, but all this?" The Indian Lieutenant shook his head, scarcely able to believe such a thing of a fellow officer.

"Ah know, Sandip, Ah know," agreed Douglas, sadly. "But we should try not to jump to conclusions yet."

"We know one thing, sir."

Something in the younger man's voice made Douglas stop. "Is this more bad news, Lieutenant?"

Singh nodded uncomfortably. "I'm sorry to drop this on you with everything else, Captain. So here's the good news first: I know where we are and we're still in our own solar system."

"And the bad news?" asked Douglas.

"The bad news is that Mars and Earth aren't where we left them, sir."

When Douglas did not respond, but merely frowned with confusion, Singh continued.

"What I mean, sir, is that Mars is on a completely different orbit around the sun, hundreds of millions of kilometres away. This is almost an order of magnitude further from Earth than *we* have ever known. The Earth, miraculously, is currently only about four days' travel away at our maximum speed. However, that will change with its orbital velocity around the sun, so we'll need to start back within twenty-four hours to keep the advantage. Thing is, sir," he paused, shaking his head in exasperation, "well, that's not the damnedest thing in all this."

"It gets worse?" Douglas raised an eyebrow, always a sign that his temper was fraying.

The younger man rubbed a hand down his face as if to revive himself. "The stars, the local objects, *everything* is different, sir. Whilst everyone has been busy with what I believe we will soon come to think of as 'the smaller crisis', I've found a *far* bigger one.

"The only way I could plot the stars and make sense of their positions was to extrapolate for Doppler shift, sir. It turns out that what we now see out of the window, are the stars as they *were…*" Singh paused, allowing the captain to absorb this information. He looked more anxious than Douglas had ever seen him.

"I'm struggling to believe this myself, sir, but there's no way to break it gently, so here goes: We departed from Earth on Thursday, yes? Well now it's about 99.2 million years before we left."

Silence bloomed…

"I think it's a Tuesday, but I might be wrong about that."

Douglas let go a single, involuntary bark of laughter which died as quickly as it had lived. "Seriously?" he asked.

"Seriously, sir," replied Singh. He suddenly looked stricken. Closing his eyes, he put his head in his hands. "*Damn it*! I knew I should have put the bloody cat out!" he cried, wretchedly. "Oh, Fang. I'm sorry."

The captain leaned back slightly, drumming his fingers on a nearby surface. After a few moments he shook his head. "No, Ah'm going to have to get back to you on all this," he said and sprinted away.

"Captain?" Singh shouted after him, in surprise.

"Get back to the bridge," Douglas shouted over his shoulder, "and make damned sure you know what you're talking about before we have to break *this* news, Lieutenant – *damned sure*!" He disappeared round a corner leaving Sandip alone with his mouth open. He closed it and ran for the bridge.

Private Dewi Jones, Nurse Smyth and Pete Davies, a member of Major White's security force, waited outside the doors to the bridge with a disorientated and ever disgruntled Lieutenant Geoff Lloyd. Surprised to find the bridge locked down, Jones pushed the communication button.

Commander Baines' face appeared on the small screen to the side of the door.

"Commander," began the Welshman, "we have Lieutenant Lloyd here as per captain's orders, isn't.it."

"Understood, Private," she replied. "Please stand by while I comm the captain for further instructions."

Captain Douglas was combing the ship with Major White's sensor team looking for further explosives when the commander hailed him. The EVA team had also joined the search and together they were making progress. "Och, Ah wondered why we'd no' met up with Jones," he replied.

"When I contacted Jones' team," Baines explained, *"he'd just come across Lloyd, slumped in a corridor. I told him to continue with his original instructions and to bring the lieutenant here, to the bridge, sir. You know... in case he disappeared again. He looks like he's had a beating."*

"Good call, Commander. Has Jones hit him?" Douglas asked, mildly surprised.

"I don't believe so, sir, he's still breathing. Looks like he may have lost an argument with a bulkhead, though."

"Has he," Douglas responded stonily. "We've searched the *New World* top to bottom. Ah'm sending the teams on to search the Pod now – starting with the reactor core. Ah'll make my way to you. Put Lloyd in the meeting room off the bridge and keep Jones' team with him at all times. There are just too many imponderables at the moment – Douglas out."

The scanning team hit pay-dirt almost immediately upon entering the Pod's reactor room. Their equipment began beeping frantically and White placed a hand on the shoulder of one of his men. "Paolo, go down to embarkation and find the engineers who look after the core. Bring them back here on the double!"

The man saluted and ran from the room.

White toggled his communicator. "This is Major White to Captain Douglas."

"Douglas here," came a slightly breathless reply. *"What do you have for me?"*

"We've found a device, Captain. Gleeson is looking at it now but I've sent for the core engineers too, just in case we mess with something we shouldn't. Gleeson doesn't think it's doing anything, but the countdown could be silent or perhaps waiting for a signal from a hand remote."

"So it's possible our man has a remote detonator in his possession? Thank you, Major, that's helpful. Ah'm about to have a wee chat with our missing engineer, maybe he can fill in a few blanks. Please keep me informed."

"Do you want Gleeson to try and deactivate the device, Captain?" asked White.

"Does he think he can?"

"After he's checked with the reactor core guys, yes, he thinks so."

"OK," replied Douglas. *"If he thinks it's worth a shot. We may have no time to waste but Major, Ah've one order for Captain Gleeson and it is vital that he obeys it to the letter."*

"What's that, Captain?" asked White.

"Don't balls it up!"

Commander Baines stood as the captain entered the bridge. Lieutenant Singh was completely engrossed in a screen full of impossible equations and did not look up.

"Lloyd's in there with Jones' team, sir," she said. "I sent Justin back to the med-bay to pick up some painkillers for him."

"Let's hope for his sake they have time to take effect," said Douglas, deadpan, as he strode towards the meeting room.

"Captain?" enquired the commander.

He stopped and turned. "Put it this way, Jill, if Lloyd gives me the wrong answers, he's going to get some very bad news," he said, menacingly.

Tim, Hank Jnr and Woodsey sat in three adjoining seats excitedly discussing the turn of events. Reiver repeatedly brought them a rope toy, dropping it hopefully on each lap in turn, until the young humans worked out what to do. His long coat rippled like black silk as he moved under the bright white lights overhead.

"Did you notice the viewscreen before they killed the feed?" Tim asked his new friends.

"Well, I saw it go all wibbly," said Woodsey, "then it went back to stars."

"I thought the display jumped," said Hank, "but I guess that was just the explosion, then all hell broke loose, so I'm not really sure what I saw next."

Tim nodded sagely. "Yes, I think you're right, Hank. Although my guess is that it wasn't the picture that jumped, but the ship."

Woodsey frowned. "Are you saying that we entered the wormhole after all?"

"If we did," Tim replied, "then it clearly didn't take us where it was meant to."

Hank looked concerned. "Why do you say that?" he asked.

"Well, if we were still near home or had arrived near Mars, that commander woman would have been only too keen to tell us so. Just to stop us all from flapping like big girls," replied Tim.

"Hey, I don't flap," said Woodsey, trying to look stern.

"Is that a fact?" Tim mocked. "You were sat just two rows in front of me, remember? For a minute I thought that someone had strapped a rather large, gaudily dressed, flightless bird to a theatre seat!"

A raucous laugh burst out of Hank.

The New Zealander glared at him. "Lucky you had your titanium strides on mate, or we'd still be mopping out the aisles after the way you jumped!"

"Hey!" Hank retorted, still laughing and struggling to get his words out. "I wasn't allowed to jump in such close proximity to my dad – might have creased his half-million-dollar suit!"

Tim looked at him in surprise. "Didn't your old man jump out of his skin like the rest of us?"

Hank sobered slightly. "He wouldn't show himself up. He'd say, 'If you're taken by surprise, only jump on the inside' or somethin' tough like that," he replied, giving an impression of his overbearing father.

"Well I reckon even 'Captain America' had a few new stripes under his star after that bang!" added Woodsey.

"HAHAHA!" The three lads buckled with laughter again.

"You know," said Tim, as the amusement subsided, "this could be really serious, like life and death serious."

"Your point?" asked Woodsey.

"Well," Tim continued thoughtfully, "it just goes to show how crap our lives were before, if this is fun – speaking for myself anyway."

"That's pretty pessimistic, dude," said Woodsey.

"Well, I have to offset your overwhelming optimism," Tim smiled wanly.

However, the thought did give them pause.

Hank nodded slowly, considering Tim's words before saying, "When are they gonna tell us anything? I'll just be happy to get the hell outta this room. It seems like hours and nothin' at all is happenin'!"

Captain Gleeson opened the bomb's casing with a precision screwdriver and a pair of tweezers. Removing the lid, he was relieved to see a very simple, if sneaky, little detonator; a device which relied on stealth rather than any micro-electronic genius.

Taking a pair of electrical snips from his tool case, he cut a couple of cables and removed the detonator from the explosive with one economical and entirely undramatic gesture. Dropping the entire assembly into a bag, he sealed it for forensic testing and got to his feet, handing it to Rick Drummond.

"There you go, constable," he grinned at the detective. "See what the lab rats make of that."

Drummond nodded, accepting the bag with an appreciative nod.

"Is that it?" asked Major White.

The Australian looked at him askance. "You were hoping for more?" he asked eventually. "Fair go. Still got another pair of pants that need road testin' have ya?"

Ford White and several others chuckled. "You gotta admit it, Bruce, it looks a lot more impressive in the movies," he ribbed the Australian.

"Actually, the name's not Bruce," said Gleeson and then gritted his teeth, immediately regretting drawing attention to this fact.

"Are you sure?" asked one of the engineers.

"Of course I'm bladdy sure!"

"But all Australians are called Bruce!"

"Har har."

"Not all of them," said an engineer from New Zealand called Burton. "Only the women, I think the blokes are called Sheila."

Gleeson fixed his tormentor with a stare. "I wouldn't expect a bladdy Kiwi to know much about being a bloke and still less about women!"

Burton laughed and the mirth spread relief, as they all took a breath.

"So what is it then?" Major White tried again.

"What's what?" asked Gleeson.

"Your name!" shouted several people at once.

Gleeson tugged at his collar and looked uncomfortable. "It's ...er... it's E...s P...l."

"Come again?" asked Hiro, enjoying payback for the Australian's badgering of his safety talk along the ship's hull.

"It's Elvis *bladdy* Percival Gleeson, OK?"

A roar of laughter echoed down the corridor, causing the guards manning the doorway outside embarkation to turn in surprise.

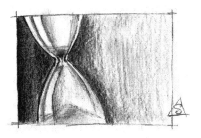

Chapter 3 | Revelation?

"Jill, get the computer to scan Lloyd's vitals while Ah grill him, Ah want to know if he's lying t' me."

"Yes, Captain."

Baines fed the parameters into the computer as Douglas strode into the meeting room, trying unsuccessfully to control his agitation. He carried a list in his head: a crewman dead, his ship heavily damaged and they were all lost who knew when. He was angry, very angry.

A rather dishevelled Lieutenant Geoffrey Lloyd sat at the large table in the centre of the room. He was slumped in his seat with a lump on his head and dried blood on his face. Two security operatives levelled stun rifles at him. Nurse Smyth rejoined them, looking concerned.

The captain acknowledged the younger man. "If he needs a horse-pill, give it to him now," he said abruptly.

Smyth shook his head. "Dr Flannigan told me not to give him anything until he's checked him out. He suggests this should be soon, Captain."

Douglas pulled up a chair, sitting across the table from Lloyd. He stared intently at the man for a full minute. Lloyd, still looking rather dazed, did not seem overly perturbed by the scrutiny, so Douglas piled straight in.

"Lieutenant, there was an explosion that seriously damaged our ship a couple of hours ago, killing one of our crewmates – know anything about it?"

Lloyd struggled to focus for a moment, tried to speak, coughed and tried again. "I was running final checks before we entered the wormhole. I was knocked out..." he said blearily.

"Surely your engineering checks should have kept you in engineering, not hovering around the escape pods where Private Jones' team found you?" Douglas asked roughly.

"*My* duties take me to every corner of the ship, Captain," Lloyd replied, some of the usual asperity returning to his voice as he continued with deliberate contempt. "That *very young* officer *you* chose for chief engineer sends me all over the place tidying up after him!"

Douglas felt his dislike for the man raise another notch. "Lieutenant Nassaki is Chief because he's an extraordinary engineer. He's also your direct superior and you will speak about him, and my other officers, with respect in my presence – is that clear?"

Lloyd wore the expression of someone who had swallowed a wasp. "Yes, sir," he answered, completely without sincerity.

Douglas hailed Chief Nassaki over an open channel, "Chief?"

"*Nassaki here, sir?*"

"Chief, did you order Lieutenant Lloyd to check the escape pods prior to our jump?"

"*No, sir,*" Hiro replied.

Gotcha! thought Douglas.

"*I ordered him to do that yesterday and he told me it had been completed, sir.*"

Damn! Douglas stared at Lloyd for a moment. "Well?"

Lloyd seemed to lose focus, taking a moment to return. "I can't remember... There was something... I..." He trailed off again, confused once more.

Justin, the ship's nurse, spoke quietly, "Sir, I really think he should see Dr Flannigan now."

Douglas considered for the briefest instant before shaking his head. "In a minute," he said, turning back to Lloyd. "That explosion killed Crewman Mario Baccini. What have you got to say about *that*?"

"Killed..." Lloyd rubbed his head. "I don't know about any... Killed?" He fell forward, catching himself at the last instant.

"*Captain...?*" The nurse did his best to disapprove as politely as possible.

Douglas held up his hand. "One last question, Lieutenant. Chief Nassaki put out a call for you to return to your station just prior to the jump – why did ye no' answer?"

"I must have knocked my comm off in my pocket when I—" Lloyd slumped onto the table, his answer incomplete.

"*Captain*, please?" Justin prompted, urgently now.

"Och alright, take him down to sickbay but Ah want him under guard around the clock." He looked at Jones. "Help Smyth get him down there, Jones. You're to stay and take the first watch. Ask The Sarge to work out a rota with Major White. He's not to be left alone for a second, clear?"

"Yes, sir," replied Jones, helping the male nurse lift Lloyd to his feet. Between them, they hauled him away.

Douglas turned to the security officer seconded from Major White's force. Reading the nametag on his chest he said, "Thank you for your help, Davies. You can get back to your squad."

"Sir," Davies saluted and left.

Douglas summoned Commander Baines into the meeting room. "Did we get anything from his readings?" he asked, waving her to a seat.

"Not much – a jolt when you said we'd been damaged and we'd lost someone, but anyone might have been shocked by that news. We got another spike when he alleged that he had been running final checks. He may have been lying. The rest of the conversation though..." She shrugged helplessly. "His vitals were up and down like a yoyo. He's probably got a concussion. It's impossible to say for sure whether he's confused, lying or both, Captain."

"So we've got nothing then?" asked Douglas, angrily.

"Even if we had, he didn't know we were scanning him, so it wouldn't have been admissible in court."

"*What* court?"

Baines opened her hands apologetically. "Fair enough, but that aside for a moment, all we can be sure of is that he seems to have been the only one out in the corridors during class."

Douglas nodded. "Have you spoken to Sandip?"

"You mean have I heard the bombshell? Yes. After that he buried himself in calculations and I could barely get a word out of him."

"Ah don't suppose, by some miracle, he's found that he was wrong?" Douglas tried hopefully.

Baines shook her head. "Sorry."

"What the hell am Ah going to tell those people, Jill? This was supposed to be a taxi run!"

"Not your fault."

"Ah'm Captain, *everything's* my fault."

"James," she leaned over and squeezed his arm, "we'll get through this. Together, just like always." She gave him a lopsided grin and Douglas smiled in spite of himself.

"So stop being a grumpy auld sod and feeling sorry for yeself, is that it?"

"I would never say that, Captain," Baines replied with a chuckle. They shared a comradely moment, as they tried to push back the growing fear of their situation.

Captain Douglas and Commander Baines entered embarkation together, striding straight up onto the dais. Baines stood to the left and just behind Douglas.

All the passengers and crew were gathered in anticipation of the captain's address. He took a moment to study the faces before him and nodding, more to himself than anyone else, he began.

"Welcome, everyone. This is what we know so far: We have been damaged by a bomb placed in wormhole drive control at some point *after* we left Earth orbit."

Shocked murmurings filled the auditorium. The captain held his hands up for calm and the crowd, desperate for news, quieted quickly, hushing one another.

"We've not yet been able to ascertain who's responsible for this atrocity. Some of you have been working on the forensics we've collected, so we remain hopeful that the culprit or culprits will be found soon."

Douglas looked around again, trying to gauge the mood in the room. "It's entirely possible, even likely, that the perpetrator is still hiding among us."

This time, the swell of concern took far longer to die away. Some passengers looked angry, some afraid, many both.

The captain raised his hands and waited for silence again, fully understanding their fear and agitation. "It is vital we remain vigilant at all times. We are *all* in danger as long as this person or these persons are free upon our ship. As you've already heard, one of our engineers, Crewman Mario Baccini, was tragically killed by the blast – murdered!" He banged his fist on the console.

"Now Ah'm telling ye, we *will* find who did this! However, Ah'm pleased to report that the saboteur has not had it all their own way."

Douglas summoned Gleeson up onto the dais.

"A couple of hours ago, a very brave and completely successful attempt was made to disarm a second bomb discovered attached to the Pod's reactor core. Some of you may already know Captain Gleeson here. He's an explosives expert working with our miners – he's also the man who quite possibly saved all of our lives today and Ah would like you all to join me in giving him a very grateful round of applause for his courage and commitment."

Douglas stood back and applauded with everyone else before stepping forward to the mike once more. "Very workmanlike, Captain, thank you." He leaned over to Gleeson and spoke quietly. "Don't worry, we havenae the time for a speech today," he winked.

"That's a relief," said Gleeson, and meant it. He was already red to the roots as he stepped back down.

"Now, back to business," the captain continued. "The ship is in good health apart from the wormhole drive and we're in no danger at the moment. We are of course running rigorous checks to every system and therefore we'll not be moving for at least twenty-four hours. So, settle in, people. The good news is Earth's only four days' travel away. Once we're sure we can engage the engines again safely, we'll be on our way.

Also, please remember that we have plenty of provisions, so there's no need for alarm."

OK, Douglas thought, *Ah've bought a little time, on with the next.*

"Ah require all department heads to talk with your teams and collate any and all possible information which may help with our situation. Once you've spoken with your people, Ah'll expect you to join me and my senior staff in the bridge meeting room two hours from now. We will then examine what you've found and consider our options. A public forum will be convened tomorrow to discuss the matter further. Thank you."

Douglas walked away quickly with Baines in tow.

"Always leave 'em wanting more, eh, Captain?" she commented, once they were back in the corridor.

He raised a wry eyebrow, pointing a thumb back the way they had come. "Ah don't have to tell them anything Ah don't want to. That's one of the perks of being captain. You can stay and answer their questions though, if you want to, Commander?"

"No, sir," she said, raising a snappy little salute. "That's one of the perks of *not* being captain!"

Douglas snorted, wagging an admonishing finger. "You'll get your chance."

They walked in silence for a little while, each lost in their private thoughts.

"Actually, James, when you consider the new reality, maybe not. We may be all we have – forever. Still, seeing as I have the *only* boss, and therefore the *best* boss in the universe, who am I to complain? Oh…" Baines pulled up suddenly outside the doors to the bridge.

"What is it?" asked Douglas.

"I've just realised that I must have the *worst* boss in the universe too."

Douglas aimed a mocking backhand at his first officer, who dutifully ducked underneath to enter the bridge.

"Now do me a kindness, will ye, Jill?" he asked. "As Mary's being run ragged looking after the passengers, make one of those special coffees for the auld man. Actually, scratch that, Ah'll have a cup of Earl Grey please – Ah could do with a little taste of home right now and Northumberland's close enough for a borderer like me." He rubbed tiredness from his eyes. They were all coming down from the adrenaline of the last few hours.

"We've bought ourselves a couple of hours to work out how we're going to tell these people about the BIG, big problem, and you're not getting out of that conversation, Commander."

Baines squeezed his shoulder warmly as he sat and went off to prepare a 'Captain's Special' in the bone china set he kept specifically for his northern beverage.

Ship time still respected Pacific Time and it was late in the afternoon as department heads began arriving on the bridge. They were greeted by Crewman Mary Hutchins, drafted once more to keep the gathering fed and watered. Despite the tension of their situation, Mary was still jolly, ever trying to put people at ease. Even on their usual trips, she always managed to offset the strangeness of the passengers' new surroundings with her down-to-earth friendliness. However, continuing to do so under their current circumstances marked the true strength of her character.

Douglas watched with admiration. *No matter where she is or what's going on, she's still Mary*, he thought. *With one or two exceptions this is a hell of a crew.* He allowed himself a brief moment of pride to count his blessings before studying his notes one last time, ahead of the meeting.

Last to enter was Lieutenant Flannigan, the ship's doctor. Douglas nodded a sombre greeting. "Still favouring that left knee, Dave?"

Flannigan shrugged. "It'll need another new one sooner or later," he replied. "I knew my days of running around battlefields fixing up a bunch o' crazy green berets were coming to an end when I hit forty, but when I got my knee shot out, it was time to get the cheque."

He made light of it but Douglas was deeply respectful of Flannigan's highly decorated US army career. The USS *New World* would normally have required only a medic, but given the importance of the mission and the average size of the passenger contingent, policy called for a medical complement of three for all Mars carriers, comprising a doctor, a junior doctor and a nurse.

"Still," continued Flannigan, "that's all ancient history now."

"Aye, seven years you've been on ma staff for our journeys to Mars, Davey, and Ah've never been more grateful for it than today," stated Douglas, seriously. "Ah'm sorry Ah couldnae give you a heads up before this meeting, but when Ah ordered you to bring sickbay up to the highest state of readiness, Ah wasnae joking."

A shadow passed over Flannigan's normally cheerful face.

Douglas sat at the head of the long conference table, facing five people seated along either side. "Right, is this everyone?" he asked through the hubbub, calling them all to order.

"Yes, Captain," replied Major White from Douglas' far left, "although there was another guy who demanded he be included in this meeting."

"*Demanded*, did he?" Douglas enquired in sweetly Scottish tones. "And who might that have been?"

"A guy named Burnstein. Apparently he paid for half of this Pod, or so he claims. He said that no decisions could possibly be made without consulting him first, and tried to bully his way past the guards."

"Oh, I remember *him*," said Baines. "What happened, Ford?"

"Well, your security sergeant asked him to 'calm down, there's a good little chap'. Burnstein lost his shorts at that point, so The Sarge laid him out because he was upsetting people." He grinned as he recalled the episode. "It was beautiful to behold. Is Jackson a boxer?"

"Only on a Saturday night," Douglas quipped.

White chuckled, gesturing towards Flannigan. "Anyhow, when Burnstein came to, the doc here was called, but told me that—"

"Unfortunately, I was way too busy in sickbay," Flannigan interrupted, his cheerful demeanour returning. "After I was told what happened, I sent Dr Schultz back down there, Captain."

"You were really laughing," said White, looking puzzled.

The crew of the *New World* shared a knowing look. Baines spoke up, "Dr Heidi Schultz is brilliant, but not exactly known for her patience or tolerance, her gentleness, sympathy... I could go on. Burnstein will have something to cry about now. He was probably better off with The Sarge."

"I see," White nodded understanding. "Some of the kids are already calling him 'Captain America'." This comment drew a few sniggers from individuals who had already sampled Mr Burnstein's company.

"Anyway," said Douglas, "we'd better get down to business. Burnstein may be the richest man aboard but no amount of money will help us at the moment. Let's start with introductions: James Douglas, captain of the USS *New World*, as Ah'm sure you know." He pointed to himself before leaning forward to introduce his senior staff up the table. "This is Commander Jill Baines, my first officer; Lieutenant Sandip Singh, my second officer and ship's pilot; Lieutenant Hiro Nassaki, my chief engineer; Lieutenant David Flannigan, my chief medical officer and Major Ford White Ah already know."

Glancing up the table to White he added, "And by the way, we're very grateful for your help over the last few hours." He gave the Major a nod of gratitude before sitting back.

"So that's the military," he concluded. "Forgive me, Ah don't know the Pod science team so, beginning with the lady to my far right, Ah'd be grateful if you could introduce yourselves, please."

"Hi. Dr Samantha Portree, USA. I'm chief engineer of the mining and construction team."

"Thank you, Doctor," said Douglas, nodding to the man sitting to her right.

"Another Sam," he said. "I'm Dr Sam Burton, New Zealand, chief of operations for the Pod. I'm responsible for resource allocation, maintenance and repairs, that sort of thing."

"Doctor," Douglas nodded again.

The next man introduced himself. "Dr Satnam Patel from India. Astrophysicist by trade, but on this mission I head up the environmental team controlling the greenhouse gas producing factory machines and other mechanical elements of our terra-forming efforts."

"Thank you, Dr Patel." Douglas looked to the woman to Patel's right.

"Dr Patricia Norris, England. My field is microbiology and I've been given charge of the team who will be seeding Mars with life." She looked directly at Douglas. "I work closely with Dr Wright, who I believe you already know, Captain – the DNA specialist?"

"Indeed Ah do, Doctor. Do Ah understand correctly that you will be working together to forensically examine the material we've collected from the bomb sites?"

"Yes, Captain," Patricia replied.

"And last, but by no means least?" Douglas prompted the last man with a smile.

He returned it and introduced himself. "Dr Jim Miller, England. I'm a chemist and manufacturer and lead the team who will be working on turning the material Dr Portree mines for us into more greenhouse-factory machines, tools and well, anything else the mission and Dr Patel's team may require, hopefully." He gestured appreciatively toward the American woman seated at the other end of the table.

"Thank you, Doctors. Just being in the room with such a heady group makes me feel more positive about what we face," Douglas acknowledged respectfully. "Now, before we get started, do we have a list or at least an idea of the other skills we may have at our disposal amongst the passengers? Ah must apologise here, but we were only meant to be a taxi service to Mars and weren't required to know each individual on the roll or their assets and skill sets. All that was organised by the brass hats back at NASA and there simply hasn't been an opportunity for us to examine the roster."

Everyone pooled their knowledge, offering what they knew of their fellow passengers.

"Do we have anything useful amongst the paid seats?" asked Douglas, at last, using the colloquial slang term for anyone who got to Mars via financial investment, rather than as part of the science team. "Sorry to be blunt, but we need to cut straight to it," he added, softening his question a little.

"Well, we've got Mr Burnstein," offered Major White.

"Yes, at least there's him," added Baines, drily.

"He's got a half-million-dollar suit…" White moderated reasonably.

"Fancy," she replied.

"I was talking to a man earlier called Derek Bond, who really wanted me to call him 'Del'," said Chief Nassaki, looking perplexed.

When no further information followed, Baines prompted the engineer. "And…?"

"Oh," Hiro continued, "erm, well, he said he was some kind of 'preeminent philosopher' apparently."

"No terra-forming expedition should leave home without one of those," Baines muttered.

"If he's rich, I suppose he can afford to philosophise all day," continued Hiro, unfazed. "I think he might be an idiot," he finished, innocently matter-of-fact.

Baines snorted her coffee and began to cough as she tried not to laugh.

Douglas sighed gently. "Remember, we've talked about people skills, Hiro?"

Baines got her control back, taking another drink to ease her throat.

"Sorry, Captain," said the engineer, "but he kept following me around. In the end I had to tell him to go away."

"And what did 'Del the philosopher' say to that?" Singh asked, fascinated.

The engineer looked slightly confused. "He said, *why?*"

Baines coughed again, slapping her chest as she fought for breath. "Stop it!" she pleaded, choking and laughing at once.

The engineer appeared completely bewildered by the jocularity his statement seemed to draw, which in turn drew a few smiles of endearment around the table.

"I was talking to a Catholic priest before the explosion," said Patricia Norris. "Maybe a chat with some of the crew would make them feel a little better?" she hazarded.

"Is he a scientist, also?" asked Douglas.

"Actually, he is a she," she replied. "No, she's on a 'paid-for' ticket."

Douglas looked impressed. "A priest could afford to be here?"

"Thinking about a change in vocation, Captain?" asked Baines, innocently.

"Ah wouldnae have a prayer," he winked.

"Actually, it's all paid for by the Church," continued Patricia. "Apparently they want representation on Mars, so they sent Mother Sarah. I have to say, she seems lovely."

"The *Catholic* Church has sent a *woman* priest to *Mars?*" asked Baines. "That's pretty progressive."

"Being *seen* to be progressive sounds about right," commented Burton darkly. "Fire and brimstone is all out of fashion these days. The modern Church is all about apology and capitulation."

A few eyebrows rose.

"Sorry, my father was a fair-weather believer," he explained. "A hand-wringer," he finished weakly.

People in the group cleared their throats and shuffled uncomfortably.

"I think there are a couple of historians on board," Jim Miller chipped in brightly, speaking into the embarrassed silence, "and I even spoke to a spiritualist medium! Good for staying in touch with where we've been perhaps, but of limited help where we find ourselves now, I expect."

"There's a retired chap who used to be a high flying psychiatrist," said Patel. "Or did he say psychologist?" he added, frowning.

"He could be useful in the long-term," commented Singh, thinking aloud.

"Long-term?" asked Jim Miller.

"Ahh," said Captain Douglas, eyeing Singh. "That would be the sound of the cat escaping from the bag."

Singh winced. "Sorry, Captain."

"No, it doesn't matter, Sandy," eased Douglas. "We've been collating and fact-finding, but ultimately this was always what this meeting was going to be about."

Samantha Portree leaned over and looked down the table. "This is the *other* bad news, isn't it, Captain?"

"I take it this is about the stars being shifted?" added Patel for good measure.

Douglas was impressed. "Well, we weren't going to be able to keep much from you guys for long," he said. "Sandip, tell them what we know."

Lieutenant Singh seemed to take a moment to gather his thoughts, when suddenly he blurted, "We're 99.2 million years in the past!"

A short silence greeted this statement, followed by an elongated silence just ahead of a protracted one.

"Thank God you broke that gently," Satnam Patel said eventually, speaking in rich, accented tones to his fellow countryman. "I might have panicked otherwise."

"Say what!?" Flannigan burst out, absolutely flabbergasted.

Douglas gave Singh a look which asked, *Seriously?* He cleared his throat. "Sorry folks, but that *is* pretty much the size of it. Sorry, Dave. Now you see why Ah needed sickbay on high alert."

Flannigan appeared thunderstruck but nodded slowly. "I think I'll let my ears do the talking for a while, James," he muttered.

Douglas' expression softened. "Good man. It seems that the explo—"

"It's a Tuesday... I think," Singh mitigated quietly.

Douglas glared at him once more, drumming his fingers a couple of times on the table. "As Ah was saying," he continued, "the explosion at the moment the wormhole formed seems to have had an unexpected and rather serious effect."

"I feared it was so," admitted Patel.

"You'd already worked it out?" asked Douglas. "That's very impressive, Doctor."

"Just guesses and surmises, Captain, whilst desperately hoping I was wrong."

"Can you shed any light on this?" pressed Douglas. "Can we reverse it?"

"You mean recreate the effects of the explosion and return back? Unlikely, Captain, but we should gather every bit of data we can from the locus where the wormhole briefly existed in space. Hopefully, we can correlate it with the information gathered from the explosion site. With time, research and experimentation we may be able to calculate the effect on the wormhole and recreate it in some way, but I must stress," Patel looked around the gathered professionals, "the chances of being able to exactly recreate the 'incident' which sent us here are extremely poor. At this stage, I would have to say negligible."

"Well, use whatever resources you need to collate your information, Doctor," replied Douglas. "We'll only get one chance at it."

Patel nodded acknowledgement, while scribbling a few notes to his electronic pad.

"Are we really only four days from Earth, Captain?" asked Dr Portree.

"We are, Doctor, more or less. Perhaps more like four and a half days now, as we've been drifting without power for a while. We've told no lies but we thought it better to hold a *small* meeting before completely spilling the beans to the larger group, if you follow me? Ah'm guessing we're all pretty shaken up by this news, so who knows what effect it might have on the people down in the Pod?

"We need some kind of plan or strategy, something for them to cling to and work towards or we'll have a total collapse on our hands if we're not careful."

Nods of agreement followed his conclusion, everyone looking thoughtful and anxious.

Major White leaned forward. "I take it we have no choice but to go back to Earth? No point in sticking around here?"

"Unless anyone here can give me a better idea," said Douglas, looking around the table. "Ah cannae see what else we can do. It's the only place we can breathe outside this ship after all."

"Forgive my lack of a scientific background, but when we get back to Earth aren't we gonna find it full of dinosaurs and who knows what else?" asked White.

They took a moment to process as the reality of his statement dawned.

"Does *anyone* know what we can expect?" asked Douglas, eventually. "Not just the flora and fauna, either. What about the climate?"

The people around the table looked from one to another in growing concern.

"I guess NASA didn't think we'd need a palaeontologist," commented Samantha Portree, sheepishly.

Patricia Norris raised her hand. "I may have some answers for you, Captain."

Douglas looked relieved. "Thank you, Doctor. What can you tell us?"

"Not me, my sixteen year old son, Tim," she answered.

Douglas looked unrelieved. "Your... *son*?" he asked weakly, trying to remain polite.

Norris smiled indulgently at him. "I know what you're thinking, Captain, but you would genuinely struggle to find anyone more knowledgeable about Earth's history in any museum or university across the world. I'm not just saying that as a proud mother. It's his passion, along with his lifelong love of animals."

Douglas exchanged glances with his senior staff.

Baines shrugged. "Maybe we should get him up here, Captain, if he can give us a heads-up before we try and land? Any knowledge would help us at this stage. I don't wanna be a T Rex tuckbox!"

Hiro snorted. "Imagine a T Rex's lunchbox! Do you think it would have a sticker of a human on the side?" He chortled to himself, oblivious to the stares he received. Engineers rarely have time for the whole appropriate/inappropriate thing and Hiro was a one-man case study in that regard.

"That's precisely it, Captain," added Norris. "I mean… not, not the lunchbox thing, but Tim. He will be able to give you a good idea of what types of animals and plants we're likely to encounter wherever we put down. He's got an encyclopaedic knowledge of this type of thing, along with untold terabytes of information on his personal storage drives."

Douglas clicked the communicator built into the table. "This is Douglas to Sergeant Jackson."

"*Jackson here, sir!*" The barked response was immediate.

"Sarge, can you organise for Mr Timothy Norris to be escorted to the bridge, please? He's Dr Norris' son. Tell him that Dr Norris thinks he may have some information which might help us."

"*Right away, sir.*"

Jim Miller put his head in his hands, exhaling a huge sigh.

"Are you OK, Doctor?" asked Douglas, concerned.

Miller looked up. "I'm sorry everyone, it's just that I expected to be manufacturing parts for our terraforming machinery on Mars by this time tomorrow. Now I'm on my way back to Earth and about to be given a talk about which *dinosaurs* I can eat and which ones I need to avoid. My reality's on shuffle!"

Nervous agreement greeted his assessment.

"Ah'm sorry, people," said Douglas. "Ah really am, but we simply don't have the luxury of an adjustment period. We need to plan and go. When we land, we will be faced with challenges that no human being has ever experienced.

"However, Ah've got every confidence in the people here and elsewhere on this vessel. We have some of the most brilliant and brave that mankind has to offer! And Ah refuse to believe that we will lose ground to a bunch o' animals, however big they are."

Douglas looked to his second officer. "Sandip, from the scans you've taken of Earth, have you calculated our best approach vector, using the least amount of fuel?" For the benefit of the others he added, "Although our power-core is nuclear, our thrusters are still chemical rockets, so saving as much fuel as possible is vital if we mean to, or need to, take off again." He checked back with Singh. "Where is our best landing opportunity, Lieutenant?"

"I've calculated that the coordinates providing the leanest burn times," replied Singh, checking his notes, "are in Patagonia, South America – or what *will be* South America one day."

Naturally, the scientists began tentatively discussing the merits of this course of action, when the door chime sounded.

"Come," said Douglas, clearly, above the chatter.

The Sarge strode up to the table with a nervous looking teenager edging into the room behind him.

"Mr Norris as ordered, Captain."

"Thanks, Sarge."

Jackson saluted and left.

"Thank you for joining us, Mr Norris," Douglas welcomed the young man, warmly. "Mary, would you be kind enough to organise another chair for our guest, please?"

Tim watched Mary open an adjoining door, which turned out to be a storage cupboard, and return to him smiling kindly. "I'll put you next to your mum."

"Thanks," he replied, sitting down a little more heavily than he intended.

"Please relax, Mr Norris," said the captain, sympathetically. "Do you mind if Ah call you Tim?"

"No, er... that's fine, er... Captain," the young man answered nervously.

Patricia also smiled at her son, crowning his anguish by squeezing his hand in the sort of motherly way calculated to embarrass any *almost*-man to the point where he questions whether he wants to live long enough to make it all the way. He moved his hand off the table immediately, his face stop-light red.

"Tim," continued Douglas, oblivious to the young man's agony, "we'll have a full, open session tomorrow, in which everyone may take part. However, for today Ah have to ask you to keep everything you hear in this room absolutely secret. Can you do that?"

"Yes, Cap—," Tim's voice croaked. Clearing his throat he tried again. "Er... yes, Captain."

"Thank you," Douglas continued. "As you already know, an explosion has destroyed the wormhole drive, but more than that, it affected the wormhole which was created. Instead of propelling us through space to near-Mars, it left us where we were but..." He stalled out, studying the youth in front of him. Douglas hated having to inflict something so horrifying on the lad, but what choice did he have? Sighing heavily, he tried again.

"Basically, Tim, the damaged wormhole sent us back in time."

He awaited the young man's reaction.

Tim merely frowned, leaning forward slightly. "How far back in time?"

"Well, that's why you're here, not to put too fine a point on it," continued Douglas encouragingly. "Your mother has told us that you have an exceptional knowledge of Earth's history."

Tim leaned further forward, completely piqued. "How far back?" he asked again.

Douglas rubbed a hand across his jaw, feeling the beginnings of stubble. "The better part of 100 million years, give or take," he answered quietly.

He expected a meltdown and leaned forward himself, in a consoling manner.

"Look Tim, it's all—"

"WHOA!" shouted Tim. "Awesome!"

"—going to be alri— *What?*" asked Douglas, dumbfounded.

"Seriously?" asked Tim, ecstatic.

"Erm..." Douglas looked to Patricia for help, but she was looking at her son with an expression somewhere between exasperation and pride.

Baines leaned back, putting her hands behind her head, grinning. "Hands up guys, who feels like a big girl's blouse now?"

Most of the other adults in the room chuckled or smiled, shaking their heads ruefully.

"The kid took it better than I did," said Major White, giving Tim a nod of respect.

"So how can *I* help?" asked Tim, glancing around the group with interest.

"You're probably the only person on the ship with any idea of what we'll find when we get home," Patricia answered her son.

"Actually, you're probably the only person in the universe," Singh added – to his mind, helpfully. "No one else will exist for about 98 million years."

Baines leaned over and fixed Singh with a look. "You're on a roll today, Sandy. I was afraid you might say something inappropriate for a minute there."

Singh looked sorry, again.

"We need to know what you know, Tim," Douglas soldiered on, pulling himself together. "As much as possible, anyway. For example, where would likely be the safest place to set up a base?"

Tim took a few moments to think.

"At this point in time, near the end of the Albian Stage of the Cretaceous Period of the Mesozoic Era, if memory serves, there are dinosaurs, other large reptiles and amphibians on virtually every land mass. There are extraordinarily dangerous animals in every ocean."

He pondered some more.

"I suppose near the poles might be a little safer, if only because the animals there, so far as we know, tended not to grow so huge."

"But wouldn't living on an ice-field make it more difficult for us to live and gather resources?" asked Jim Miller.

"The poles only ice over during the winter months in this period," Tim countered. "As far as we've been able to ascertain, anyway. However, you may still run across one ton predators even at the poles, descendants of Allosaurus, for example. Even early Tyrannosaurs in the north – God help anyone running into one of those."

"Would it be any safer back home?" asked Douglas.

"You mean Britain, Captain? Historically our wildlife has been a little more manageable, true, but we are a long way back, Captain. There wer—, sorry, *are* some real terrors around in this period."

Tim took a pull from the mug of tea Mary had set before him, to calm his nerves. He grimaced. *What the hell is this slop?* His expression made his thoughts plain, the realisation increasing his self-consciousness still further.

"Erm," he spluttered, "Baryonyx, for instance, was a very dangerous predator of the Mid-Cretaceous. The very *first* dinosaur known to science, in fact, was found in Britain – a ten-metre-long killer named Megalosaurus.

We also have one of the earliest ancestors of the infamous Tyrannosaur line back home, too. Proceratosaurus and Megalosaurus were more than sixty million years further back in time than where we seem to be, though, so there's a good chance they've really upped their game by 'now'. Of course, that's if you can even *find* Britain in the post-Pangaean break-up."

Tim realised he was rambling and stopped. "Our own time has seen nature decimated, but at this stage, life on Earth knows no bounds and we'll get to see it all again," he finished, almost breathless in his anticipation.

"Er… yes," Douglas acknowledged, fervently wishing *he* could feel so positive about it all.

"So we're not looking for Albion in Albian then?" Baines quipped. "Eh? Eh?"

Douglas gave her a look, one of his succinct ones.

"Sorry, Captain," she mumbled.

"We'd do well to stay away from North Africa," Tim continued, almost to himself, trotting across a prehistoric globe in his mind. "Hmm… China would be lethal too." Another moment of reflection and he added, "We should also try to avoid Patagonia—" just as Lieutenant Singh blurted, "But we need to land in Patagonia!"

Everyone looked at Singh.

"What's Pangaean?" he asked.

Before Tim could explain, Baines groaned, putting her head down on the table and covering it with her hands.

Chapter 4 | The Council of Del Bond

James Douglas, Captain of the USS *New World*, sat alone in his quarters, legs hanging over the side of his bunk. He rubbed his eyes to dispel sleep from his mind after a lousy night. Proper sleep had eluded him, despite his utter exhaustion. Twenty-three hours had passed since the explosion. *Not even a day*, he thought numbly.

Today he faced a meeting with the entire ship's complement and this gave him cause for concern. He knew very little of these people and could only guess how they would react.

His first meeting, with the small group of Mars Mission department heads the previous evening, had gone about as well as he could have hoped. At least no one freaked out. The scientists seemed to cope with their predicament well enough, even trying to offer constructive help where possible. However, their meeting had revealed one undeniable and uncomfortable truth: the only person on board with any real answers was a kid a few weeks out of school.

Douglas did not hold the lad's age against him, he was clearly exceptional, but how would the rest of the crew and passengers respond to this? He was fairly sure of the military contingent; they would respect his rank as captain. However, the civvies, especially the paid seats, might be bad news. He – they – could not afford a free-for-all right now. If they went round the houses trying out every ridiculous idea about 'how we should all live together' they would, in very short order, find themselves as extinct as… the dinosaur? Wow, he would really have to wrap his head around that one.

His comm chimed. "Douglas," he answered automatically.

"Morning, Captain," said Baines. *"Sorry, did I wake you?"*

"No, Ah was already up. Morning, Jill, what can Ah do for ye?"

"Hiro has finished the ship-wide checks ahead of schedule," she reported. *"He says that, as far as he can tell, we're good to go."*

"My God, does the man no' sleep?" remarked Douglas, his voice cracking with tiredness.

Baines chuckled. *"I think he just plugs into a socket for a couple of hours here and there, you know how he is. He wants to know if we can power up the engines for a short hop to shake everything down?"*

"OK, Commander, but not 'til Ah get to the bridge. Ah'll need five minutes, so make sure he waits. Ah dinnae wish to be bounced off a wall and swallow ma toothbrush! Douglas out."

"Good morning," Douglas greeted, taking his command chair. Once seated comfortably, he sniffed the air. There was definitely something aromatic wafting about his bridge. He looked around to query his first officer, only to find her patiently proffering a mug of his favourite coffee.

"How did ye know?" he asked rhetorically, accepting the beverage. He took a slurp of the drink and grimaced. "Whoa, that's a wee bit strong!" he said hoarsely.

"I know. I gave myself the same sentence. Can't have any droopy eyelids today, Captain," Baines answered. "I expect you slept about as well as I did, possibly not even that well?"

"Och. Ah'll never sleep again if Ah doon this coffee," Douglas chuntered to himself, forcing down another gulp. "Thank you," he wheezed.

Baines smiled at him.

"What?" he asked.

She leaned in close, speaking quietly, "I love the way you sound more Scottish when you're tired or cross, it's very sweet."

Douglas snorted in spite of himself. "Has Hiro found a way to warp us back to the 22nd century yet?"

"Unfortunately not, but he has sent another request to try a short jump towards Earth, Captain." She arched an eyebrow. "Anyone would think he had to be somewhere. He recommends a quick burn up to speed and then coast whilst he runs more checks. On another subject, Hiro also reported back about the simulations he ran last night before bed. Despite the bomb damage, we should be able to – his words – put down on the planet, *with care*."

"We'll be in for a bumpy ride then, eh, Sandip?" asked Douglas.

"Quite probably, Captain," replied the pilot.

"So, shall I order him to begin his engine tests and move the ship?" asked Baines.

"Yes. Tell him we're ready when he is," replied Douglas. "Ah feel so wired now, Ah could get out and push – this coffee doth murder sleep!"

"The Scottish play, Captain?" asked Baines.

"Aye, ma favourite," he winked.

"I think we're all going to have to roll up our ravelled sleeves today," she muttered.

"*Very good*, Commander," complimented Douglas.

"Hmm, let's hope so, James."

"Aye," he sighed. "Still, it *will* feel good to be moving again."

After a short dialogue between the bridge and engineering, Douglas announced the impending manoeuvre across the PA. The engines powered up smoothly, propelling the *New World* on her four day journey back towards the old world – the very old world.

Baines was in her quarters freshening up, ready for the general meeting with all passengers and crew, when her comm chimed.

"*Commander – Sarge. Sorry to disturb you, but there seems to be a large, well-attended council going on in embarkation. This is well ahead of the meeting scheduled for 1500 hours. Some geezer calling himself Del*

Bond appears to be chairing it, ma'am. It's getting a bit rowdy, shall I break it up?"

"No, I'd better see what's going on first. We don't want people any more upset than they are already. Just keep it contained. I'm on my way." Baines clicked off the comm, leaving her quarters at a fast walk.

She came upon The Sarge, Jones and a couple of the major's security team outside embarkation, watching the proceedings obliquely through an open hatch from the corridor.

"Any idea what this is about, gentlemen?" she asked.

"I'm not really sure, ma'am," Sergeant Jackson replied with a shrug. "That Del bloke seems to be firing everybody up to get answers about what's going on and when anyone says anything he asks them why they need answers at all? Why *do* humans need to know things? Some people are getting pretty cheesed off and when they say so, he just asks them why they're angry? What is anger, does it help? Do we need anger? That type of thing.

"Someone said, 'Yes, we would have never survived as a species without fight or flight' to which he said..."

"*Why?*" Baines interrupted.

"Oh, did you hear the discussion, Commander?" asked The Sarge.

"No," Baines laughed, "but I did try to read a philosophy book once. It seems that to be a philosopher you have think about impossible scenarios that no one else would waste time on. After twenty pages I considered handing it into a charity shop but in the end I recycled it, deciding that the charity had enough problems without driving their customers crazy!"

The Sarge nodded. "Some of the people in there are getting quite agitated, Commander. I think most of them only came down early to get a good seat. They weren't expecting this. They're wound up enough already without this little Herbert upsetting them even more."

"Yes, I suppose we'd better remove him from the podium before someone throws a chair at him."

They looked at one another; neither moved. The moment dragged.

Jackson looked at her quizzically. "Maybe we could afford to lose one chair?"

Baines snorted. "Come on, Sarge."

He nodded to his men who fell in behind them.

The commander listened to the proceedings for a little while, to gain a measure of what was taking place. The passengers appeared to be split into factions. Some were ignoring the arguments altogether, others were trying unsuccessfully to talk sense into Del Bond. Another group were on their feet hurling abuse at the philosopher for wasting their time and upsetting everyone further, fairly stating that their situation was worrying enough as it was.

His response was calm and infuriating.

"Why do we get upset? What is upset? How do we know that we are feeling upset? Is it real? How do we know anything is real?"

Naturally, this did very little to quiet his gainsayers. However a small gaggle of young children were clearly having the time of their lives, shouting, "Why? Why? Why?"

Baines made her way to the front of the auditorium with the intention of supplanting Bond. She passed a couple, the woman sobbing into the man's shoulder. He fixed her with a glare. "Is this your idea of a warm-up band, Commander? What the hell is going on?"

There was anger in the air and she could feel it rising. The security team knew they had to prevent the situation from escalating and immediately set about restoring order.

Presently, the captain arrived to give the speech he had been so dreading. He was rather taken aback by the riot which appeared to be in full swing.

"If we ever need to sacrifice anyone to appease the dinosaurs, Ah choose that man!" Douglas shouted. The afternoon had passed into early evening and he was once more addressing his senior staff and group leaders in the meeting room.

"I think that was King Kong, sir," offered Lieutenant Singh.

"Huh, the offer's still on the table!" replied Douglas, sourly.

"Once we'd removed Bond and calmed everyone down, it didn't go too badly, sir," Baines added, encouragingly.

"Ah wouldnae call it a success, Commander. Just because discussing the terrifying insanity of our situation was deemed preferable to continuing a debate with that man. How the hell did it degenerate into that, that riot? What was he even doing up there?"

Douglas could see that no one had any answers so he took a deep breath and let it out slowly, to calm his anger before continuing.

"We have a little over three and a half days until we land on Earth. In that time we need to develop rotas for everyone and build teams, possibly even break up some teams for a more balanced skills allocation." He counted on his fingers, "In no particular order, we'll need to set up a defensible base and source fresh water. We'll have to find a way to feed ourselves – we've excellent seed stocks, but who knows what dangers we'll face trying to plant them. Also, Ah'm pretty sure we'll have to refit our vehicles for life on Earth so we can send out survey and reconnaissance teams to map our new surroundings and search for natural resources."

Douglas paused to glance around the faces at the table. "Comments and suggestions please," he concluded.

Dr Patel leaned forward saying, "We have reasonable stores of components but only limited supplies of bulk material. We have the capability to manufacture, of course, but will need to mine for iron ore, aluminium, various silicas, et cetera for building, precious metals and other elements and minerals for circuitry, plus anything else we may need – if we can find them.

"Plastics and ceramics are going to be in very short supply at first. As the captain stated, we will need to adapt our plant and machinery, certainly, but we may also need to build new vehicles – not to mention the farming equipment we will need for the long-term. Otherwise we will all spend our every waking second in the fields just to feed ourselves, like peasants from the pas—" He stopped himself, shaking his head. "From the future, I mean. Some people may welcome a fresh start in the open air, but food production is only part of our survival strategy. And survival is what we are talking about here, my friends. Even with our technology, humanity has never faced such dangers as those which await us on prehistoric Earth.

"Our numbers are also against us. There will inevitably be losses but we are so few we can't afford to lose anyone."

"I could probably stretch to doing without Del Bond," Baines commented, bitterly.

"Seconded," said Douglas.

"If he can use a shovel, we need him, Commander," Patel answered seriously.

The other department heads nodded in tune with the astrophysicist's appraisal.

"Dr Patel, have you been speaking with young Mr Norris?" asked Major White.

"I have, Major, and our conversation was at once enlightening and frightening."

White nodded, "I agree. I know I'm a military man, so forgive me if this seems predictable, but we're gonna need more and better weapons than we currently have."

Douglas turned to White. "What sort of arsenal are you carrying, Ford?"

"Not much more than a few hand weapons, stunners and crowd control, Captain. According to Mr Norris, we're looking at some seriously heavy game – hundred ton, forty metre long herd animals, not to mention eight ton, fifteen metre long predators, to name but a few. Tim says there are some pack killers alive in this time that are even bigger than T Rex!" He held up his hands, placating, "But don't worry, he also assured me that T Rex was probably still more dangerous and luckily he's not due for another 30 million years."

"Oh, that's alright then," said Baines, flatly.

"Precisely," said White. "The kid's knowledge is going to be crucial to our survival though."

"There may be one or two other things we should discuss before we do *anything*." Dr Patricia Norris joined the conversation. "I don't want to sound like our friend Derek Bond but there are some rather big philosophical, or at least ethical, questions we need to ask ourselves. Questions about how we proceed as a people – more importantly as a people out of time."

Douglas groaned. "You're talking about disrupting the timeline, aren't you, Doctor?" he asked. "And we'll go with ethical shall we? Ah've had enough philosophy for one day!"

Norris nodded agreement. "Just for starters, before we even think about how we're going to live, do we assume that the timeline has already been disrupted by our presence here? Which leads to the question: do we start again now, as humanity's last and perhaps only chance, or do we touch the Earth lightly, hoping the future will continue along the same path and we are simply forgotten?"

"Looking at our own time, isn't it clear that we made a hell of a mess of things?" put in Dr Jim Miller, the chemist. "Whatever we do here, it's hard to believe we could make things worse."

"But we could make things never have happened at all," Singh noted, cryptically.

They pondered for a moment, in silence.

"I know that Dr Patel's team have begun to think about how a return may be possible, however unlikely," said Baines. She paused and spread her hands on the table. "Firstly, shouldn't we agree, or not, as to whether getting home is our primary goal – after survival of course – surely we could cause all manner of changes to the timeline just by trying, if we're poking around with time travel?"

Another silence…

"So, what, do we take a vote, the eleven of us here?" asked Samantha Portree. "And in doing so are we setting ourselves up as some kind of government?"

"Oh my God," said Douglas. "We'll have landed before we've even decided what to call ourselves if we're not careful, let alone how we define our responsibilities. Ah think we're going to have to grab the bull by the horns on many issues here, and quickly."

"Don't you mean the Triceratops, Captain?" asked Baines, innocently.

"Thank you, Commander," he glowered. "Firstly, we need to elect *somebody*, or a *panel* of somebodies, to take charge. This clearly needs to happen before we talk any further."

"Well, you're the senior man here, Captain," White stated.

"No," said Douglas flatly. "Ah'll remain in charge of this ship but that does not empower me to control a mostly civilian population."

"Maybe we should elect a triumvirate then," offered Jim Miller. "Then there will always be checks and balances on the very top level decisions made, but without too many opinions in the way, yes?"

There were a few nods of approval.

"It worked for Caesar, Pompey and Crassus after all," he continued hopefully, gesturing over his shoulder with a thumb, "back in Rome."

"But were many Romans happy with that situation I wonder?" asked Patricia Norris, looking mildly concerned. She frowned as a memory surfaced. "And didn't that all end in a bloodbath across several continents, after the triumvirate was destabilised by the untimely death of Crassus?"

"That's settled then," said Baines. "As long as we don't elect anyone named Crassus, we're good, yeah? You see, we just need to use our heads. A little bit of application," she added, tapping her temple with her index finger.

"Yes, but use them for thinking, presumably, not as props in a play," retorted Patricia Norris, unable to resist.

"Look," Douglas brought his hand down palm first onto the table with a slap. "If Ah could just bring you forward twenty-three centuries for a minute," he growled acerbically and then stopped, looking thoughtful for a second, "...whilst dragging you back 992 thousand centuries into the past," he added, for the sake of both clarity and his chief engineer's OCD. "If we are going to suggest this, it needs to be a decision ratified by a *majority vote*. We need everyone back in embarkation again, so we can put this to the whole complement and proceed from there."

"How?" asked Patricia Norris, simply. "Do we choose candidates and ask people to vote? Or do we ask them to suggest people or even themselves perhaps?"

"Do we want anyone in charge who *wants* to be in charge?" asked Sam Burton. "That's never gone brilliantly before has it? Back home or in Rome," he added for good measure.

Again, more silence as they pondered.

"We'll just have to see what 'the people' say," stated Portree.

The atmosphere in embarkation was charged once more, despite the lateness of the hour. Most were still in the dark regarding the larger crisis facing them, 'philosophical differences' having derailed the meeting to fully reveal their situation. All they knew was that they were headed back to Earth after surviving a terrorist attack.

Captain Douglas stood on the dais once more, studying the worried faces in the crowd. *Ah'll be glad when Ah can kick this responsibility upstairs to someone else*, he thought darkly.

"Hello and thank you, everyone, for attending. We find ourselves in a crisis…"

Douglas explained about the bomb in the wormhole drive and its effects upon the wormhole as it formed. He explained all they knew and where it had led them, to a surprisingly silent crowd. Whether this was due to the need for news or just shock, he could not tell. His tale of the last thirty hours disappeared into a silent vacuum.

No reaction…

Any second now the tidal wave of panic will come, he thought, but what actually happened surprised him.

Hank Burnstein Snr stood and called loudly over the heads of the seated passengers, "As I have experience in running corporations employing millions of people, and I practically paid for this Pod, I should be the new president until we get back to our right time and place."

Douglas' prophesied tidal wave arrived at last, but it was less of panic than of angry incredulity as the silence erupted to the sound of a hundred people, all chuntering their disapproval at once.

Another male voice travelled clearly over the drone. "Bladdy 'ell, it's the new Messiah!"

Some of the people sitting around Captain Gleeson broke into appreciative, if nervous, laughter.

"Order! Order people, please!" yelled Douglas into the storm.

"SHUT UUUUP!" bellowed Sergeant Jackson and the room quietened by several notches.

"Thank you for your input, Mr Burnstein, we'll take that under advisement," Douglas went on. "However, Mr Burnstein does have a point. We do need to elect some sort of governing body to make the necessary decisions which will allow us to work as a cohesive unit – if we are to survive the coming months – and we need to do this quickly."

"When you say unit, are you really saying military?" someone asked out. The voice was American and female.

"No!" Douglas stated firmly. "Forgive this auld RAF man for his turn of phrase," he added more gently. "We are not suggesting a military state, nor any kind of *autocracy*," he added, glaring meaningfully at Burnstein.

"What *are* you suggesting, Captain?" the same woman asked reasonably.

This time Douglas pinpointed the voice to a woman dressed as a priest, dog collar and all.

"It's Mother Sarah, isn't it?" he asked gently.

"Yes, Captain," replied Sarah, looking pleasantly surprised.

"What we're suggesting," continued Douglas, "is a triumvirate elected by all of us here and that everyone cast three votes, one for each individual we believe should lead us. The three chosen will have the right to accept or refuse, but should they accept, they will be the panel of three – simple and, hopefully, effective."

"What if the three chosen by the numbers suit no one?" asked Mother Sarah again.

"That may be so, and we're not suggesting that this be set in stone, but *if* this works and the people chosen are acceptable to the majority of us, then we can at least proceed. Make no mistake that we have a he— er, an awful lot to plan and organise, Mother Sarah."

The priest smiled at his slip and attempt at courtesy, nodding her agreement.

"Does anyone else have any suggestions or issues with this idea before we proceed?" Douglas asked.

"It's a good principle, Captain," another male American voice called from the crowd. "But I've been thinking, wouldn't it make more sense to choose some candidates and for us all to vote on *them*? Or maybe the first vote could be simply to name the candidates? Then we could take a second vote to select our final three out of the, say, top ten named?"

This suggestion seemed to garner much approval throughout the assembly; its source was chief medical officer, Dave Flannigan.

Douglas smiled his appreciation. "That sounds wise – and popular it seems," he added, looking around the nodding heads in the auditorium. "Thanks, Dave. We'll—"

"Who's going to be allowed to vote?" Another voice interrupted him.

Douglas recognised the voice and singled out the face of young Tim Norris.

"That's another fair point," he conceded. "Ah recommend the age of majority is set at sixteen years. Does anyone else have anything to say on this point?"

Someone shouted out that it should be twenty-one, eighteen at the very least, as these young people did not have enough life experience to be able to make these kind of decisions and another free-for-all developed where no clear voice could be heard. Douglas appealed for calm, to little avail. So, putting a finger in his left ear, he gave The Sarge a small, foppish wave to signal that another call for order was required.

"SHUT UP!" Jackson obliged.

"Thank you," said Douglas to the room at large. "Ah agree, sixteen years *is* young but, in my opinion, not *too* young. We are in very unusual circumstances and if sixteen is old enough to marry, have a family and go off to war in normal times, then surely it's old enough for our purposes in the here and now?"

This point was generally accepted but with a few complaints.

"Shall we say sixteen to vote then, people?"

Overwhelmingly the response came back "YES!" and so the motion carried. In the privacy of his own mind Douglas thought that this 'first principles of democracy' approach was going to take so long that if they were not careful they might crash into the Earth before deciding anything. He had to increase momentum and foreshorten these little niceties of civilisation if they were to survive even landing, let alone *living* on ancient Earth.

"The first vote will basically be 'names in a hat' for candidates. We'll each choose three people from the crew and passenger roster who we feel would do a good job of leading us. As the passenger lists for the Mars mission were established some time ago, we assume that most of you have a fair knowledge of your fellows' files. As leadership is an absolute prerequisite, Ah put forward that we set the bar at twenty-five years and over for candidates."

Douglas singled out Tim Norris in the crowd again, giving him the merest ghost of a wink.

"This is not to say that we don't have some brilliant younger people on board, who have skills and knowledge essential to our survival. This is simply a *command readiness* decision.

"So please think hard on whom you would like to vote for and we'll reconvene in two hours. Ah'm sorry it's not much, but it's all the time we can afford at the moment.

"We'll set up a box at the front here, into which each voter may drop their three choices. After that we'll simply call out the names and set up a public tally on the screen behind me, so that everyone can see the count and witness the full process. Is this acceptable to us all?" Douglas asked in conclusion.

"YES!" the vast majority responded.

"No!" Burnstein called out, but the captain affected not to hear him.

Douglas and Baines made their way back to the bridge after the conference. The time was 2030 hours and as the evening strolled away, so did they, their pace leisurely after the panic and rush of the last couple of days.

"That was well done, Captain," said the commander, genuinely. "Although, I was slightly disappointed you didn't lead with: Friends, Romans, countrymen – after our staff meeting."

Douglas looked down at her. "That's kind of you to say – *Jillia*," he said with a glint in his eye.

"You're welcome, Jamesius."

Douglas stopped, looking back the way they had come. "But what if they all vote Burnstein?"

"Weeell," Baines replied slowly, "in that event, I guess we'll have to pin a 'Kick me!' poster on your back."

They both laughed, feeling a little lighter simply because they were doing something, rather than having things done to them. In that spirit they continued onto the bridge, hoping for a couple of hours' peace to shuffle through candidate files.

Lieutenant Singh, still at his post, stood when the two senior officers entered. "Captain, Commander," he nodded respectfully.

"Everything OK, Sandy?" Baines asked, taking her seat.

"Everything's fine with the ship, Commander. Hiro reports the engines checked out perfectly and all systems are working well. He's also cut all power to wormhole drive control and reinforced the damaged bulkheads to further secure the area." His initial report discharged, Singh suddenly looked uncomfortable.

"Is there something else?" asked Douglas.

"Yes, Captain. Another message came in just after you left for the conference. This one's a little more... difficult."

"Difficult?"

"Yes, sir. Lieutenant Lloyd is now fully recovered from his concussion, with a clean bill of health, and Dr Flannigan has two questions. He asks: a) What is he to do with him and, b) When will you get your damned soldiers out of his sickbay, sir?"

Douglas and Baines looked at one another.

"You know I'd almost forgotten... with everything," said Baines, tailing off as thoughts of the young and ever-smiling Mario Baccini flooded her mind, unbidden. By the look on Douglas' face, she judged he was having similar recollections.

"Sandip, tell the doctor to stand by, he'll have my decision directly." He nodded for Baines to join him in the meeting room off the bridge.

Douglas waited for the door to seal behind them.

"We havenae a damned thing on the man!" he blurted angrily. "Ah'm glad Dave didn't bring that up during our meeting or at the conference, but what *should* we do with Lloyd?"

Baines nodded but remained in thought a moment longer. "Do you think he did it, Captain?" she asked eventually.

Douglas sighed. "Ah don't know," he admitted. "Yes. Well, probably – maybe? If Ah'm honest, part of me wants it to be true because of the way Lloyd makes me feel. Ah'm genuinely concerned that it's colouring my judgement on this one, Jill. What do you think?"

"I think he's our man, but it's just a feeling. His motive is hidden from us and we can't put the smoking gun in his hand... yet," she said. "The trouble as I see it is this: locking somebody up on a suspicion could get us into hot water, even here. We have to be careful what precedents we set – possibly now more than ever."

"Agreed," said Douglas and then reflected a moment. "Or perhaps not."

"Captain?"

"Ah hear ye, Jill, but we have a responsibility to provide safety and a chance for life to every soul aboard. This isn't the early 21st century. We cannae afford a terrorist, even an unproven one, the chance to run freely around this ship – this last piece of our world – unchecked and wreaking havoc. He's an engineer for God's sake, who knows what he might get up to next?"

"I'm with you, James, honestly, but we're trying to give birth to a new democracy down there whilst discussing human rights contraventions up here? Whichever way you choose to jump I'm with you, you know that, one hundred percent. All I'm saying is, this needs to be handled with care and either way I think there will be fallout," she concluded seriously.

"You're right," admitted Douglas, "Ah can see that. This could be used against us down the line, but my way we *live* to carry the can for what we've done. This is it, Jill, the entire human universe in a bottle. If we make the wrong decision it could cost us everything – *everything*! So what Ah'm saying is, Ah cannae afford to be lenient. Ah need him made safe."

Baines nodded thoughtfully. "So, we chuck him in the brig?"

"That's all we *can* do for now, but we keep a lid on this until the voting is finished and we have our governing body. Later, we can spin it that he's in the brig *pro tem*, pending the completion of our investigations. That ought to keep the bleeding hearts off our backs for a wee while at least, whilst hopefully buying us the time we need to land this bird safely, before we face the next task. What do you think?" he asked finally.

"What if the investigations turn up nothing? There's always the possibility that we're wrong and the real bomber is down there," she gestured, "waiting to vote."

Douglas adjusted his collar uncomfortably as he considered. "Let's build one bridge at a time, eh?" he said at last. "More than ever now, we cannae guess what tomorrow is going to bring us."

"So why *second* guess ourselves today?" Baines agreed, tiredly. "You're right. We might get hit by a bus."

"Not anymore," he replied, deadpan.

Baines chuckled at that. "The lesser of two evils it is then. I'll get The Sarge to escort the priso— to escort *Lieutenant Lloyd* to the brig, in order to help us with our enquiries."

Two hours later, almost the full complement of the *New World* assembled once more in the embarkation lounge. Only Lieutenant Geoff Lloyd was left furious and impotent in his cell, under the impassive stare of Private Paolo, a member of White's security contingent.

The major visited Paolo, following the first meeting, to explain the developments in embarkation. Shortly after, he left with Paolo's proxy votes and Lloyd's remonstrations ringing in his ears.

Douglas invited the people to vote for their preferred candidates by dropping their slips into the box on the stage at the front of the auditorium. Once all slips were in, they were removed one at a time and the nominees transferred to the large overhead screen. A tally of votes slowly grew against each name.

Douglas watched morosely as the tally next to his reached ever higher, leaving all others behind. *Damn*, he thought.

When complete, the list showed twenty-one candidates. The eleven at the bottom of the list were congratulated warmly on their nominations before being deleted, leaving the ten highest scorers for the final vote.

Douglas was dismayed to find himself by far the most popular. With a sigh he climbed back onto the dais. "Thank you, everyone. Now we select from the top ten candidates here and the three with the most votes are *it*."

He stepped down allowing everyone, including himself, to scribble their preferred choices. Once again, people walked forward through the aisles in ones and twos, posting them into the box.

Captain Gleeson could not help feeling anxious. He was astounded to find that he had accrued eighteen votes in the first round, putting him in the upper middle of the herd. Defusing that bomb and saving the ship probably had something to do with it, he surmised sourly. The problem, as he saw it, was that he was much happier 'sticking it to the man'. He most certainly did not want to *be* 'the man'. He exchanged a look of unspoken commiseration with Douglas.

Even more worrying, Burnstein had seventeen votes and Gleeson stewed over this too. *Some people really do just need to be told what to do and where to sit by someone with absolutely no doubts about their right to be in charge*, he thought darkly.

Forty minutes passed before all the votes were in. The names appeared on the board again with a tally growing alongside each.

After the untimely death of Mario Baccini, there were one hundred and fourteen people aboard the *New World*. Excluding Lieutenant Lloyd, who had not been *invited* to vote, and the five younger children, this meant there were 324 votes cast. The table of candidates reordered itself automatically as the last vote was counted:

106 votes – James Douglas, Captain

48 votes – Satnam Patel, Doctor

42 votes – Jill Baines, Commander

29 votes – Sarah Fellows, Mother

28 votes – Ford White, Major

28 votes – Patricia Norris, Doctor

The last four positions shared the remaining 43 votes with more than half of them for Hank Burnstein Snr.

Douglas looked up at the screen with consternation. Absolutely everyone on the ship had voted for him except for Lloyd, the five younger children, himself and one other – probably Burnstein. *The man's not a complete ass then*, he thought as he climbed the dais for a final time, to address the waiting crowd.

"Thank you, everyone, for taking part in this vote. However Ah must say that as a military man still holding a commission, Ah don't believe Ah should be a member of a civilian governmental institution, however small and fledgling it may be. Ah must suggest that my place be reconsidered."

This was met by a gale of noes, so he tried a different tack.

"If that is indeed the opinion of the majority, then may Ah suggest Commander Baines take my place on the council of three as the military representative? She is clearly popular with you all from the votes cast. This would leave myself as senior officer in charge of the ship only, and thus prevent too much power being delivered into any one pair of hands?"

To his great relief, this actually prompted some approval; even a few yeses could be heard. He dared hope that he might yet escape his predicament when Baines stood and spoke before the assembly.

"Actually, Captain, I believe I should stand down."

Douglas' heart sank.

She continued, "I agree that we do not want a council weighted towards the military, but it is also crucial – now more than ever – that there is no confusion in the chain of command and responsibility. If I was part of a governing body telling the military what to do it could muddy the waters aboard ship."

She looked from face to face in the crowd.

"I thank you all for considering my candidacy and the Captain for his confidence in me. However, I think I speak for us all when I say that we need the best and most experienced leadership we can get right now," she turned back to Douglas, "and that has to be Captain Douglas."

She smiled a sad apology towards the captain as she sat back down.

Douglas tried to smile too, but looked rather like he had bitten into a nettle sandwich.

"OK, if it is the will of the majority," he began again, "Ah accept." As an afterthought he added, "Thank you."

Glancing back up at the screen to find the next names, he searched the crowd for Dr Patel. "Ah also call on Dr Satnam Patel. Will you serve, sir?"

Patel stood and bowed slightly. "I will, thank you," he said simply, sitting back down. His demeanour was less than ecstatic too, which raised Douglas' spirits slightly.

"As Commander Baines has stepped down, that leaves Mother Sarah in the next place." Douglas looked to where the priest had been seated earlier and found her once more. "Will you serve, ma'am?"

Mother Sarah stood to acknowledge him. "I will, and I'll do my very best for you all. I know we have people from many faiths and belief structures here so I say, respectfully: may God bless us and protect us all in the difficult days ahead." She too, bowed slightly before retaking her seat.

Many religions were indeed represented by the people in the crowd, but most appreciated the sentiment behind her words, even the atheists.

For Douglas there was just one more thing to ask. "Before we proceed, does anyone wish to speak on what has transpired here? Is everyone happy with this result?"

"No!" exclaimed Hank Burnstein Snr, jumping to his feet. "I've chaired bigger *board meetings* than this gathering! It's a farce, damnit! Who here has more experience o' runnin' things than I do?!"

"You mean 'I have'," shouted Gleeson unashamedly, in his deep Australian accent. "Why don't you put a bladdy sock in it, Burno!" he added, his colour rising. "We need folks in charge who know how to do stuff, not just how to pay some other poor bagger to do it and then stiff them on the payment!"

Burnstein went puce, but Gleeson continued unabashed.

"Besides, being proficient at firing people after a quarterly review won't be worth squat when T Rex is biting the arse out o' your favourite shorts, mate!"

Douglas covered the lower half of his face with his hand, his shoulders rocking as he fought for self-control. Catching Patel's eye, he saw that he too was fighting to keep a straight face and despite their best efforts, they both snorted with laughter.

Turning away from the crowd for decency's sake, Douglas looked to Commander Baines for support, but she was grinning, so he gave up. He turned around fully, until he felt he could trust himself once more.

After taking a moment, he raised his arms for calm. The room was full of laughter and jeering. *Well*, he thought privately, *we're probably the first government in human history to start off with a huge round of laughter, at least there's that – let's just hope we don't turn into a bad joke like so many before us.* Waiting for the hubbub to die down, he spoke once more.

"Thank you, everyone. The votes are cast and in accordance with the principles of democracy, we must now proceed along this course. Let loyalty, diligence and honour be the glue which binds us because we're alone now, people, and it's the duty of each of us to work together, to the best of our abilities. Our very survival depends upon it."

A few seconds passed as the assembly processed the gravity of his words.

"OK, if anyone has any comments or wishes to raise any further points, please put them in writing and ask one of the security team to deliver your notes to the bridge, " he added. "Ah would also just like to ask if the department heads who attended our previous discussions would be kind enough to join us in the bridge meeting room at 0800 hours, please? We've a lot to go through.

"Now, it's already past midnight and so on that note, we thank you again for taking part and wish you all goodnight."

As people began to shuffle, he called across to his fellow councillors.

"Mother Sarah and Dr Patel, would you accompany me, please?"

With that, Douglas strode out, Patel and Fellows following behind to begin a whole new epoch in human civilisation, in more ways than one.

The brand new triumvirate sat around the table in silence whilst Mary Hutchins, burning the midnight oil, poured them drinks.

"I'm ever so glad it's you guys," she said. "I'll just get you some cookies, then I'll leave you to talk."

Douglas smiled warmly at her. "Thank you, Mary," he said. "Ah havenae had the time to ask how you're holding up with all this. Most people on this ship knew they were turning their backs on the world – although this is a little more drastic than anyone could have guessed, Ah'm sure – but you were expecting to be home in a few days. How are you?"

The ship's cook, janitor and dogsbody stopped her fussing for a moment. Looking across the table to the captain, her face crumpled slightly.

Douglas got up from his seat and walked around to her, putting a comforting arm about her shoulder. "Ah'm so sorry about all this, Mary," he said gently.

"It's not your fault, Captain," she sniffed. "I'm just worried about my mum. Her health's not bad, thank the Lord, but she's alone and getting on in years. I do as much as I can for her, around my shifts. I'm just worried that if I never get back, there'll be no one to take care of her. My sister is never around, you see? Her career takes her all over the world." She wiped a tear away.

"Ah'll never give up trying to find us a way home, Mary. None of us will," said Douglas, looking to Mother Sarah and Dr Patel for support.

"Of course not," agreed Patel, kindly.

"If you ever need to talk, my door's always open, Mary," added Sarah.

"You're such good people, I couldn't ask for any more," replied Hutchins. Choked with emotion, she took a shuddering breath and smiled bravely. "Now, about those cookies."

She broke open a packet from her trolley and piled them onto a saucer in the centre of the table. "Bless you all," she said as she left them, following her trolley out of the room.

As the door sealed behind her, the three were alone for the first time, but despite the enormity of all they had to discuss, none of them could find a single thing to say.

Mother Sarah shook her head, smiling ruefully at their condition. "Let's use this moment of silence," she said, putting her hands together as if to pray, "to eat a chocolate cookie," she finished quickly, her hand darting out to retrieve the largest from the saucer.

The two men chuckled with both humour and relief, before following suit.

"Well, it seems we've proven that deep time is real, we're now part of it. Are you OK with that, Mother Sarah?" asked Douglas, with genuine concern.

After scrabbling for a way to break the ice, he realised as soon as the words left his possession that they were astonishingly tactless. He winced slightly.

"Please, just Sarah will do," she said before he could apologise. Noting Douglas' discomfort, she grinned mischievously. "You mean am I going to fall apart because of a crisis of faith?"

"Er... no, of course not, Ah mean..." the captain stuttered through his embarrassment.

Sarah let him off the hook with her laughter.

"Don't worry, Captain," she replied. "If you believe that God is eternal, as I do, then what's a few million years here or there? The Earth towards which we are headed may not be ours, but it's still His and He will find us – I truly believe that. The real question is: Who would want to be lost here, alone and in such peril without Him? Not me!"

She smiled again, infecting the others. "Thank you for your concern, Captain, but I will do my best to remain in the real world for you," she patted his hand across the table, "*whenever* that is."

Douglas smiled back. "Sorry," he said, still a little embarrassed. He could feel a respect growing for Mother Sarah that he had not expected. *Religion aside,* he thought, *she may provide a useful perspective for the future.*

"Captain," Patel interrupted Douglas' thoughts. "Based on the points we touched upon before recessing to elect a new leadership, I have put together a mental list of priorities for us. Although not exhaustive, I hope this will provide a framework for our thinking. I know it's already very late and we'll discuss the details in conference tomorrow, but one thing I thought we should put into effect immediately, before we even get back to Earth, is rationing. I have no doubt that growing and catching food will present us with significant challenges – even collecting water is likely to be extraordinarily dangerous. Watering holes in India and Africa can be the most deadly of places. One can only imagine what they will be like in the Cretaceous Period!"

"Ah wholeheartedly agree, Doctor. I'll speak to Sam Burton and the Pod's quartermaster first thing in the morning," said Douglas. "That is, if we're all agreed?" He looked to Sarah for confirmation.

"Indeed, Captain," she answered thoughtfully.

"Are you OK, Sarah?" asked Douglas.

"I am, Captain, thank you. I'm sorry. I was just thinking about what that colourful Australian guy said – about T Rex biting the rear out of our pants? It seems regrettable but inevitable that many among us will see this as a military threat. If I'm honest, I can't really argue with that assessment." She turned to Patel. "When this conversation comes along, Doctor, would it be possible to have a plan in place to make weapons that warn first? Maybe make a bang or something? Leaving 'kill' as a last resort? I know we're in a crisis here and I don't want to be too heavy-handed about the sanctity of life and all God's creatures, and so on, but we do also – if I understood the Captain's talk correctly – have to consider ways to achieve a 'low impact' presence when we land.

"I'm no scientist, but I'm guessing that our usual 'Uncle Sam approach' of shooting and blowing everything up may affect this – could even alter the timeline itself...?" She let the question hang.

Patel nodded. "I believe you are right, Sarah. In fact, we have already discussed this, albeit briefly, and I've been thinking along similar lines. When I have the details worked out I'll lay my ideas before you both."

"Thank you, Doctor. May I call you Satnam?" asked Sarah.

"By all means."

"And please call me James," Douglas invited his co-governors.

Patel took a deep draught from his mug. He lapsed into silence for a moment, studying the half-eaten cookie in his hand intently.

"You look a million miles away, Satnam," prompted Sarah, kindly.

"Forgive me," said Patel. "I was just considering this biscuit. Have you ever really thought about what a small treat like this represents? I fear our soft, pampered lives are," he sighed, giving Sarah a half smile, "what is the phrase you Americans use, coming to a middle?"

Douglas nodded solemnly.

"We are indeed incredibly fortunate that our Pod is one of the manufacturing units," continued Patel. "Things would be far worse otherwise. The odds may still be stacked against us, but I would say that without the Pod and its equipment, we would have virtually *no* chance of surviving the Cretaceous world at all. The reptiles rule the Earth absolutely and there is no room for man, at least not in our minuscule numbers. Like most of the creatures with which we'll be sharing our world, we'll have to eat whatever we can get for a time.

"Or perhaps I should say, *their* world – interlopers that we are."

"Interlopers?" Sarah repeated the word as a query. "Perhaps. We're certainly people out of time. Clearly, for us aboard this ship, Earth was always meant to be our 'forever home'. Leaving's not an option now. Let's hope she won't reject us, and that brings me onto the question of how we should live when we get back."

The two men gave her a questioning look.

"I guess what I'm getting at," she pressed on, "is how do we go forward as a people?"

"What are you suggesting, Sarah?" asked Douglas.

"Well, as you know, I only found out what has happened to us a few hours ago, but whilst we took that two hour recess to choose candidates, I wandered around and talked to folks. It seems to me that people are already discussing our impact on the timeline. I suppose that when you have a shipload of scientists they will inevitably jump ahead to the big questions whilst the rest of us are still wondering what's for dinner!

"It seems that *camps* are emerging on how we should proceed. As far as I can tell, some folks are saying that as soon as we land, the timeline will be irrevocably disrupted and every single thing we do after that will only make the changes bigger and more wide-ranging. They're basically saying that the future we know may no longer happen, so we may as well start to colonise as if this is *it*, humanity's last, and possibly *only*, stand. There may never be a human race after us now. Someone even started to theorise about how we could devise a way of surviving the asteroid impact at the end of the Cretaceous. You know, the one that helped bring about the extinction of the dinosaurs, thirty-two million years from now – scientists!" She chuckled, good-naturedly.

"Another camp is suggesting we live as 'lightly' as possible. They're talking about a pastoral, harmonious existence alongside nature, even if those lives are short. They believe this will minimise the damage, allowing time and evolution to take their natural course, and hopefully, everything to play out as it should."

She drained her cup.

"Others were talking about devoting all our efforts and resources into getting back to our own time, simply taking whatever we want along the way to make this happen. Ironically, this group didn't seem to consider that, if we undertook this approach and actually managed to get back to 2112, would it be *our* 2112, if we messed things up in the past? Still, it's *a* point of view I suppose – I noticed that you were shaking your head there, Satnam?"

"Yes, sorry," said Patel. "I just think it is very unlikely that we will be able to 'get back' as you put it, but I hope I'm wrong. Please, continue Sarah, forgive me."

Sarah took a moment to absorb his words.

"Well interestingly, a splinter group from this last set were talking about rebuilding the wormhole drive and using it to get to another planet altogether. Apparently there are several 'Earth-like' planets in our computer's database, all relatively close, galactically speaking. These folks thought that one of those might be a safer option, when compared to living in the age of the dinosaur. They also suggested that the shorter the time we stayed on Earth, the less damage we could do. Of course, if these planets are Earth-like, who knows what could be living on *them*?" She raised her eyebrows.

"The last group I came across thought we should stay on the ship and were actually calculating ways to continue living aboard the *New World*. They thought it might be possible for our society to survive for centuries with strict population control and maintenance. We would simply trip down to Earth from orbit to get what we need now and again, like going shopping, using the shuttles and lifeboats we have on board."

She looked at the two men.

"Well, that's what folks are saying. What do you think, gentlemen?"

"Thank you, Sarah," said Douglas. "That's some really useful insight Ah may have missed altogether." He pinched the bridge of his nose and sighed, feeling impossibly tired.

"Now Ah'm wondering, how can we possibly make these kinds of decisions? Deciding a way forward for the 115—" he stopped, a haunted look in his eye, "for the *114* souls aboard this ship is big enough all on its own. But we could be deciding the fate of humanity itself here. Not to mention the untold billions of species that will rise and fall over the next 100 million years, every one affecting the world in a billion tiny ways. Anything we do, however small, could change or even *erase* everything!"

He spread his hands on the table, eyeing his fellow councillors seriously.

"This feels like playing God to me and Ah dinnae feel qualified! Perhaps that last group have it right and we shouldnae even land?"

Patel looked very uncomfortable and, for the first time, unsure of his own mind. Mother Sarah, however, merely smiled slightly. She reached across the table and took both men's hands in her own.

"You know I believe that God is with us, it goes with the job," she said lightly, "but we must all have faith, gentlemen – faith in ourselves. We have to make these calls so that the men, women and children aboard this ship get a chance to live.

"I know you may not agree with this, you may even think me foolish for saying it, but for myself, I think that Jesus Christ was always meant to be born and always *will* be born. No matter how weak we are as individuals, I believe our destiny to be less flimsy than we might imagine.

"We should also have faith in our companions – our companions in peril, if you will. Just look at how much we've achieved already. In a whirlwind we've gone from a terrible act of evil intent and a brutal murder to a new democracy with the hope of survival.

"Furthermore, just look at the people's choices! What started as a vague numbers game led to our companions choosing *us* to lead them – a scientist for knowledge and intelligence, a priest for comfort and conscience and a soldier for protection and action – still think we're alone? Was this really all just blind luck or coincidence?" she asked, smiling broadly now. "Humanity, our destiny and our beautiful world will survive, gentlemen, as will we."

Chapter 5 | The New World Order

Three weeks earlier and 99.2 million years later – Patagonia

The old man watched the rainclouds move in over his forest. There was a storm coming. It was almost as if the weather was tracking his mood. He was incandescent, but as ever, he served his fury cold.

How dare they disrupt my plans! He scathed in silence, alone in his study. *Two years of planning and they change the rota just before launch. Someone has tipped them off and when I find that someone, I will ensure that it takes* them *two agonising years to die*!

He quirked a sickly smile, pleased with the sentence he contemplated. Now he just needed to find an offender to whom he could apply it. Getting out of his seat, he turned his back on the storm outside and began to pace. "This can be no coincidence," he muttered, shaking his head. After a few passes he stopped suddenly in his tracks. "Yes. *Her*. It has to be! Some misguided revenge for the necessary purification I ordered – she forced me to order! *Yes*, Elizabeth, of course."

He strode purposefully back to his seat, sending out a call for his aide.

"How can I help you, sir?" Her response was prompt as always.

"Has Lieutenant Hemmings left for her special assignment with the fleet yet?"

"Yes, sir. Three days ago, sir."

"I want her recalled – right now!"

"I'll get onto our contacts in the Middle East immediately, sir, but if she has already taken her station she will have gone deep undercover and will observe the comms blackout you ordered, sir."

"Then don't waste any more time!"

"Yes, sir."

The comm link closed and the old man stood once more in front of the huge, curved window which filled an entire wall of his study. He clasped his hands behind his back and glared out over his private remnant of the rainforest.

Just moments later, the intercom beeped again. He waved a hand over the arm of his seat to answer it. "Yes?" he snapped peremptorily.

"I'm sorry, sir, but she's already taken her post and will no longer be contactable." The aide's anxiety was obvious. *"I'm very sorry, sir. Sir?"*

Taking a deep breath, he forced his rage to subside. He could not afford distractions now.

"Sir?" the aide asked again.

"Do we have the new Mars Mission personnel lists yet?" He spoke very slowly, enunciating every syllable as though he had a grudge against them.

"I'll check, sir. Please stand by..." Thirty seconds passed. *"Yes, sir. The information has just been received from our contact at NASA. I'm sending it to your terminal now, sir."*

He sat and spun the chair to face his desk. A keyboard glowed to life within the surface and a screen rose from the back of the desk automatically. He glanced down the list quickly, scanning to see if it contained any assets he could use.

"Is there anything else I can do for you, sir?"

"Yes, send a secure copy to my granddaughter and tell her I need to see her straight away, tomorrow at the latest."

"Of course, si—"

He cut the link. Still glowering over the new list, he slammed his fist down on the desk. "Damn!"

Surrey – England

The tube ran under almost all of Britain, even offshore. Jim Miller's wealth, derived from successful businesses in the chemicals industry, provided *gold class* travel permits for his family. Rose Miller was about to make her usual tube journey home from school, her gold card placing her in a queue very much shorter than the one endured by most. The endless lines of un-notables, who spent much of their 'leisure time' travelling between work and sleep each day, watched morosely as she and her immaculately turned-out friends boarded their car.

High speed tube cars made the journey to her stop virtually instantaneous. She said goodbye to her classmates and disembarked. The platform was at the end of her street in Surrey, just a short walk from her family home. Trains stopped every few minutes, continually disgorging drove upon drove of masked strangers – all eager to step back into a controlled environment where the recycled air was filtered and they would be safe from the violent unpredictability of the weather.

Rose was no exception and she left the busy station quickly.

The overwhelming majority of people now lived in the giant concrete cubes which covered most of the world's landmass not given over to industry or industrial agriculture, each packed with hundreds of housing cells. By contrast, Rose's family owned a 1995 three-bed, semi-detached house. Built over a century ago in the old-fashioned street layouts, the property came with a garage, front *and* rear gardens – fully landscaped with synthetic lawns and plants – and was about as decadent upper middle class as it was possible to get in 2112.

The white picket gate opened automatically for her and she dragged her feet to the front door. The heads-up display inside her latest model, lilac, *'Lady Breathe'* smog mask automatically called up a retina scan as she neared the building. With a sharp look down and left, she confirmed the action and a small hatch opened in the door for her thumbprint. Her personal comm, linked via the mask, provided her code to their home security system and the door swung open. She stepped in and blinked through the menus to disable the poisonous gasses 'app' as the door closed behind her.

"Welcome home, Rose!" said a friendly, enthusiastic voice.

She rolled her eyes as she removed her smog mask. That stupid application on the house computer needed deleting. It was so cheesy and she hated it. Not only did it log when she was late back, it also announced her arrival, *when she was late back*. One of the boys in her class had already disabled his for those exact reasons. She sloped off to her room, making a note to ask him how he did it, in the morning.

It was a warm, stifling evening in July, which promised to be no different from so many others; but when Rose's father returned home from the office looking pensive a few hours later, she sensed *possibilities.* He brought with him, to his mind, the nuts and bolts for a very different future for them all – just how different, he had not the faintest idea at that point. Unusually subdued throughout dinner, he eventually raised the subject of the Mars Mission with his family. He explained how the threat of terrorism had forced a personnel reshuffle close to the deadline, leading to new positions becoming available.

Rose had the feeling of a wave curling overhead, almost feeling the need to duck before it crashed. Lara did not seem particularly interested and so, risking chronic indigestion, Jim dropped his bombshell at the table.

"Because of my background in advanced chemistry, NASA have offered me – us, really – a place on the Mars Mission. It came in a couple of months ago but I wasn't sure how to… I mean, it's a big decision and now time's caught us up and…" He tailed off.

Fearing the sudden pregnant pause might birth a monster, he quickly plunged into further explanation of the socio-political situation behind the reasoning for the changes. Unfortunately, this passed Rose by as she zoned out, struck almost insensible by the thought of leaving everything behind. Her favourite dessert went virtually untouched as Jim confessed his hopes, dreams and concerns to his family. After his words ran out, there remained only the smell of warm chocolate in the air for a long moment.

During the course of the row which followed, Lara rejected the idea out of hand, at volume.

Jim was a man petrified of his wife's displeasure, had been for as long as Rose could remember. He usually just agreed with Lara – that he was very lucky to be able to afford her – and once again it seemed his latest 'big plan' had not begun well for him.

Rose's shock at her father's announcement ebbed slightly, leaving her with mixed feelings about the prospect offered. She was not sure, but it felt like something new was stirring within her; a chance for adventure, perhaps? Her life had always seemed as if drawn along a golden thread, but this… terraforming, space travel – who knew where *this* could lead her?

Lara was naturally mortified.

"Lara, darling," Jim placated, "we'll be giving birth to a new planet, a new world. Not to mention we'll be well and truly in the history books."

It did not seem to be working for him; at least, not at first.

Lara's response was blunt. "Whoever heard of anyone who mattered being in history books? Who even reads that stuff anymore?! And how can *I* stay fashionable on Mars? Really Jim, you're such an idiot! You just tell them to keep their job in, in, whatever it is – or I'm leaving you!"

Rose always cringed when her mother trotted out that tired old line. However, the devil inside her always wondered whether the same trick might actually work for her one day. She had mixed feelings about that too. Would she want a man who always caved in? It usually worked on Dad, though.

Even as she was considering it, this time proved no exception.

"OK, sweetheart, I'll refuse it tomorrow."

"Huh, see that you do!"

The opportunity to join the Mars Programme may have ended right there for the Millers, but for an unexpected change in their fortunes triggered by Lara's night out with her friend Barbara.

Three weeks later, Jim walked along the corridor leading to his family's suite of rooms within the Life Pod, pondering whether Barbara – a woman that, for his wife's sake, he had sincerely tried not to loathe – had not turned out to be the best friend he had ever had. She had nudged Lara into making the decision he wanted and in the process cut herself from Jim's life altogether.

He felt excited, happy even. Of course, intellectually he understood that they were lost millions of years in the past and faced a disconnected and very uncertain future, but these were *abstractions – so* important that they did not really matter. In the right-here and right-now, all he knew was that these people *needed* him and he had a purpose. His old life had been full of people who wanted things from him, certainly, but if not him, then they would have surely got those things from someone else. Not so here. Suddenly, he felt *alive* and could not wait to see his family to hold them and tell them how great that felt.

Keying his access code, he walked into their apartment whistling cheerfully but was forced to duck as a flying cup exploded against the door, closing quietly behind him. The 'hello' died on his lips.

"I can't believe you got us lost on the other side of the universe!" Lara Miller screamed at her husband.

"Wha—" he tried.

"Don't give me that!" Lara snapped.

"But—"

"You told me we'd be in the history books! Famous, you said!" she continued, throwing a small makeup bag at him which, after a clumsy juggle, he was able to catch. "Who will ever hear about us now?"

"Well—"

"Don't try and get out of it!" she bellowed. "I want to go home! It seems like forever since I saw a shop—"

"It was only four days ago…"

"—and I want to know what you're going to do about getting us back! What?!"

"Erm… nothing, darling. Look, we haven't moved across the universe," Jim tried, gently. "We've been thrown back in time—"

"What difference does it make? Don't try and confuse me with your scientific gibberish! I want to go back to Earth right now!"

Jim opened his mouth and closed it again, deciding on a different tack. "We'll be back on Earth very soon, sweetheart, any day now," he tried.

"Promise?"

"Promise." Jim was a man who firmly believed in clearing one hurdle at a time as far as his wife was concerned.

Lara seemed to calm a little. "I knew I shouldn't have let you talk me into this!"

"But you called me from your club with Barbara and insisted that we accept—"

The volcano erupted again. "DON'T YOU *DARE* BLAME ME FOR THIS!"

"No, darling, I wouldn't, of course you're right—"

"I wish you'd come on your own so that you could be lost in space or time or whatever, and I could have stayed with my friends, the people who really cared about me. You've *never* cared about me!" she snapped again.

The usual waterworks came on cue, and Jim fell for it, like always. He tried to comfort the centre of his world, which only led to another overreaction. Lara stormed out of the room and Jim was about to run after her, following in the well-rehearsed steps to the familiar dance, when Rose caught her father by the arm.

"Dad, please stay and talk with me," she said.

"I will, sweetheart, as soon as I've made sure your mum is OK," he answered, but Rose refused to let go.

"She *is* OK, Dad. Don't go after her, it doesn't do any good. She's been working herself up to this all day. I knew you were going to get it when you got back." Rose gave her father a sideways look. "You know she's bonkers, right?"

"Eh?" was Jim's lightning riposte. He stopped trying to pull away, noticing something different about his daughter, something about the way she was scrutinising him.

"Now, now, sweetheart," he said at last, sitting down next to her and trying to pull himself together. "That's no way to talk about Mum. So, what did you want to talk about?" He looked nervously at the door through which his wife had departed, clearly desperate to run after her.

Rose's brow furrowed. "Dad, I've been thinking, after everything that's happened and the fact that most people are saying there's no way back for us... well, everything's changed and I've realised that I'm worthless here."

"*Darling,*" Jim comforted, "of course you're not worthless."

"No, Dad, in a very real sense I am. I have no skills to help me, or anyone, with what's coming next." She shook her head sadly. "I don't know what to do." Her voice shook and she gulped tearfully.

"When I was at school everyone wanted to fit in with me, because I was rich and pretty and popular. None of that matters anymore. The other kids on the mission all seem to be really clever and making friends but all I could think to do was write down how I was going to brag about what we're doing, to the people back at home."

Her tears came in earnest now and Jim moved to hold his daughter in his arms. "There, there, it's OK. You'll always be the most important person in the world to me," he assured her.

"No!" she said, pushing him away slightly. "You've always given me the 'daddy's little princess' speech and let me get away with everything for as long as I can remember and now I'm useless. Like her!" She pointed at the door through which her mother had departed.

Jim was speechless. He had never seen this before.

"You've always done everything for us, Dad," she continued, hammering her points home. "You let us spend all your money without ever getting cross, no matter how much we yelled at you or took you for granted and now..." Temporarily out of words, she sniffed and wiped her eyes. "We need to change. *I* need you to teach me, please."

Jim sat back, taking a deep breath. "I never wanted to get cross with either of you because you're everything to me," he said with bewilderment. "Have I somehow done you harm?"

"Without meaning to, I think you have," Rose sniffed again, "and your kindness has ruined Lara!"

"That's Mum, sweetie."

"Huh! When it suits her! Did you know she makes me call her *Lara* when we're out shopping so that people, particularly the men, think we're sisters? Or used to, I should say."

Jim looked a little discomforted. "Well, we all like to feel young and attractive."

"No, no, *no*! Dad, stop it! Stop making excuses for her! You remember when we voted for the councillors? She voted for the captain and that Gleeson man who stopped the bomb going off – because she thinks he's a hunk and *sooo* brave. The final vote she cast for some other bloke who was giving her the glad eye, when we were in embarkation!

"I asked her why she didn't vote for you, Dad, and do you know what she said?"

Jim shook his head, looking crestfallen.

"She said – and I quote – 'Oh I didn't think about him, silly me'."

"Well, it was a shock," he replied in a small voice. "I'm sure your mum was as confused and upset as the rest of us and it probably just didn't occur to her..." He tailed off, all too aware of how pathetic this sounded.

"*Dad*, she didn't *think* about you, the man who does everything for her and always has! Well, it's all changed now and this family needs a shake-up. We need *you*, Dad. You're the only one of us who is worth anything to these people and I need you to teach me. Also, I don't know anything about the natural world. Is there someone you know, through your contacts, who can train me on how to do things? *Outsidey* type things?" she finished hopefully.

Jim smiled. Her courage added an ache to the sorrow he was feeling inside.

"Well, I'm sure one of Major White's security people will be able to teach you a thing or two about survival outdoors and I understand that Captain Gleeson is something of a master at bushcraft… as well as being a hunk," he muttered sourly. "However, I would suggest you start by making friends with young Tim Norris, Dr Norris' son. He's a little shy, or at least he seems so, with us *old-timers*. I reckon he'd be glad of a friend in you. Tim knows a great deal about this period of Earth's history. I'm sure he'd be delighted to tell you all about it, although I doubt he's had much attention from girls and certainly not ones as pretty as you, so go easy on him."

This brought a smile to Rose's face and Jim held his daughter close to hide the hurt in his eyes.

"I love you, Rosie."

"I love you too, Daddy."

Lieutenant Geoff Lloyd looked up sharply as Commander Jill Baines strode into the brig. Nodding to the security operative guarding their prisoner, she walked to the centre of the room and stood directly in front of the bars to Lloyd's cell.

"It's about time!" he bit out. "I demand to be let out of here immediately!"

"Let the wind out of it, Lloyd," she retorted. "You're going to answer some questions about the murder of Mario Baccini."

"I already told Douglas I don't know anything about that," he answered crossly.

"That's *Captain* Douglas to you, or have you decided you like it in here, or something?" she asked with ill humour.

Lloyd seethed in silence.

"We now have incriminating evidence back from the bomb site putting you in the frame, Lieutenant. I want you to tell me why you tried to destroy your own ship, your colleagues and all of these innocent people?"

"*Colleagues*," Lloyd mocked. "You haven't got a shred of evidence against me for any of this!"

"Why would you say *that*?" asked Baines, her face a mask of puzzlement. "I have a file full of evidence in my hand and you're already in jail – you're an engineer, surely you can bolt those two circumstances together and make them run?"

Lloyd looked uncertain for an instant and then smiled nastily. "You're just bluffing. Never kid a kidder, Commander."

Baines pulled up a chair and sat down, thumbing through the file.

"Firstly," she said, casually. "Perhaps you can explain to me why your DNA was found on the wormhole drive mountings, or what was left of them?"

"*Engineer*?" Lloyd answered in a sarcastically questioning, sing-song voice. "I don't doubt that I've touched everything in engineering at some point!"

"Yes," continued Baines, unperturbed, "but can you explain why *only* your DNA was found on the remnant fixings and none of Mr Baccini's? He was, after all, the man in charge of the wormhole drive, was he not? Despite what the explosion did to him, he left not a trace on what little remains of the drive chassis. Odd that, don't you think?"

Lloyd sat back. "No idea, please *do* enlighten me," he said, crossing his legs and making himself comfortable.

Disgust settled on the commander's face as she leaned forward.

"We know well how fastidious Mario was in the cleaning of his equipment. If anyone so much as left a coffee cup in the WHD room they would be in danger of having it bounced off the back of their head! So it *almost* looks like you were the very last person to touch the drive before it exploded? Even the man who was murdered hadn't touched it before it blew," she stated, again with affected puzzlement.

Her expression hardened. "You'd better start cooperating or things might get very bad, very quickly, for you!" she added menacingly. "A brilliant and kind young man has been brutally murdered and I think you know something about it."

"Brilliant? Huh!" Lloyd scoffed. "He was just a mediocrity like the rest of this crew. No great loss."

"There are a few things you need to know – *Geoff*!" She spat his name.

"Like what?" he sneered.

"Like the fact that the law you think will protect you and pander to your every little tantrum and whim is all gone," she confided with satisfaction.

"What *are* you talking about?"

The commander smiled again. "That bomb, the one you can't remember anything about, has sent us all back 99.2 million years into the past. That's right, let *that* sink in!"

"You're raving, woman!" he snapped, arrogantly.

"When we get back to Earth in a few days you may find yourself cast out and alone in a world full of flesh-eating monsters, if you don't start talking pretty sharpish!"

"You wouldn't dare!" Lloyd shouted, getting to his feet. "I know my rights. You can't do anything to me without a fair trial and there *is* no death penalty, so don't try and scare me with your ridiculous stories."

Baines merely smiled as she leaned back in her seat, taking her ease in response to Lloyd's obvious distress.

Lloyd sat once more. "I don't believe you," he mumbled sulkily. "It's just one more conspiracy to get me out of the way. Everyone knows I'm the most competent and experienced officer on this crew. If it wasn't for all the nepotism and playing golf with 'people like us' that everybody does at NASA, I'd be captain of the *New World* – and I'd run things properly, I can tell you. Then you'd see a 'new world order'!"

Baines continued to smile. Unfazed, she ignored his outburst. "No more law, nor trials, nor due process. If I don't like what you tell me – *you're* out! And there's more," she leaned forward again, grinning savagely. "I've been swotting up on middle Cretaceous South America – which is where we're going to have to put down, by the way, thanks to you. As I understand it, an adult Giganotosaurus or Mapusaurus could easily swallow a man whole, but please don't let that scare you too badly. I have it on very good authority that the smaller predators are likely to be even more dangerous to us. They can apparently run at speeds of up to seventy or eighty kilometres per hour and have serrated teeth and terrible killing claws on each foot."

She shook her head with mocking sadness. "Oh, I doubt they will give much consideration to your *rights*, Geoff."

"I've told you I don't know anything," he repeated, brittlely.

"OK. Let's leave the scene of the crime for a minute. Tell me, why were you hanging around the escape pods when everyone else was either in embarkation or at their stations? See if you can remember anything about that," Baines asked sarcastically.

"I've already told Doug—the captain, I was asked by Nassaki to run some checks—"

"Those checks were for the day before," she interjected, disdainfully. "You had no reason to be there. No legitimate duty at least." She gave him a hard stare. "You set the first bomb to stop the ship, creating havoc, so you could make your escape via a lifeboat just before the second bomb went off in the Pod reactor core. What was your plan? Huh? Get home after a few days discomfort, looking a bit dishevelled and then go bleating to everyone about the *tragedy* you'd miraculously survived? What next? Get pensioned out on compassionate grounds due to the 'terrible trauma' you'd suffered?

"And finally, of course, you're free to collect a fat payment for your handiwork from some terrorist organisation or other, soon after. How am I doing so far?"

Lloyd looked away. "You haven't got a scrap of evidence to support *any* of that." He rounded on her once more, adding, "And if I was trying to escape and blow the ship up, why didn't I have the detonator on me then, eh?" He sat back, a victorious grin on his face.

Baines placed her elbow on the arm of the chair and rested her chin upon the back of her hand, scrutinising him. Eventually she asked, "Who said anything about a detonator?"

Dr Thomas Wood sat in his office pondering the task before him. A frantic drive was underway to adapt all of the Pod's vehicles for life on Earth and, as part of the construction and mining team's contribution, Dr Samantha Portree asked Thomas to throw the full weight of his engineering expertise behind the effort. His specific brief: Design and modify lightweight structural reinforcement for their plant and machinery.

The vehicles and equipment were designed to cope with very little external atmospheric pressure and the lower gravity of Mars. Upon their return, some would be heavy and perhaps underpowered when subjected to the greater atmosphere and gravity of Earth.

Balancing the machines for equal internal/external pressure was a small matter. The greatest problem they faced was adapting them to withstand the potentially huge shock loads which might be thrown against them by enormous, and in some cases vicious Cretaceous creatures.

Thomas massaged his temples as he struggled with the enormity of their predicament. Not really sure what they would face, once on the ground, he was just grateful for a knotty engineering problem with a ludicrous deadline to distract him from his other worries.

At least his son seemed to be coping well and even making some interesting friends by all accounts. *That lad falls on his feet no matter what*, he thought proudly.

The memory of his first conversation about joining the mission with Christian, known to everyone else as Woodsey, resurfaced. *What a mess. How could I have been so stupid as to bring my boy into this fiasco?* He felt that he had really screwed up, but what made it worse was the fact that his son did not seem to blame him at all.

Thomas sat back and stretched. Despite his guilt, a genuine smile of warmth spread across his face as he recalled Christian's last day of school; it turned out to be their last day of normality, too...

Thomas returned home from work early. The Woods' property was near the top of a lane which wended its way up a small hill. From this vantage point, he watched his son's group of friends divide and divide further as they passed various homes, eventually becoming a band of one.

His heart nearly burst with pride – his boy's last day of school. He was a man now. Drifting away from the window, Thomas gazed longingly at a portrait of his departed wife. "Where have the years gone?" he asked her. Lifting the picture from the mantle, he held it to his chest and closed his eyes. He was in danger of being overwhelmed by his feelings, so he returned the picture to its position on the shelf, smiling bravely. "Today's no day for sorrows, is it?"

There was a slam and several bumps and scrapes as Woodsey entered the house. He dragged his bag into the lounge, seeming to knock into everything along the way and was momentarily surprised to find Thomas home early.

"Hey, Dad, you skiving?" he greeted, casually dropping his school gear on the sofa and pulling his comm from a pocket to begin scrolling in one easy motion.

Thomas chuckled. "Nah, I just didn't want you to have to come back to an empty house after your last day. I remember how it is, saying 'see ya' to your mates for the last time."

"They only live down the road, Dad."

"You'll be surprised, mate," replied Thomas, a glint in his eye. "How'd it go, anyway?" He suspected his son might be upset, or perhaps a little nervous of the big wide world opening up before him.

"Cool, yeah," Woodsey acknowledged, bored.

Thomas eyed his son with a mixture of respect and amusement. Most kids live for the day they will leave school but upon realising the dream, get all maudlin for the place. Not his son. "Thanks for that *detailed* description. Anything in particular stand out for ya?"

"Nah, yeah. Well, you know."

"*Right,*" Thomas acknowledged, grudgingly letting go any hope of getting a breakdown of his son's last day. "That was a fascinatingly monosyllabic description, thank you. I can only imagine that your English essays were a highly anticipated source of delight, enveloping your teacher's evenings in warm glow."

"Yeah, well you know, English was never my thing," Woodsey spoke distractedly, dutifully filling the gap in the conversation whilst waiting for his dad to continue or give up. Either would have allowed him to carry on scanning the social media feeds open on his comm.

"Yes, I *well* remember your last report, in which your English teacher described your attitude and aptitude for the subject. I also remember having to look up the word 'contabescent'. Anyway, I've got a *small* piece of news myself, as it happens."

Thomas knew he was throwing good irony after bad, so he simply laid the NASA proposal before his son and waited for the fallout. When it did not arrive, he tried a different tack to provoke reaction.

"After the initial surprise, I re-read the communication and our comfortable, predictable future seemed to judder like a locomotive at a set of points, ya know? Naturally, I was in two minds. We have a good life here in New Zealand. Our home and my work are in one of the few beautiful places left on Earth – how many of us can say that these days? It's hard to see a reason for leaving when so many have so much less. What do *you* think, son?" he asked, realising he was rambling.

After a long moment, Woodsey finally asked, "So, I've just left school and now you want me to leave the planet, is that it?"

"Erm…" Thomas tried, not sure which way the teenaged psyche might jump with this news.

"OK, cool." Woodsey eventually let him off the hook with a shrug. "Why not? Let's see what's there."

"That's *it*?" his father sidled cautiously.

"Yeah, course." To Woodsey's way of thinking, it just made sense to bend and sway with the world. Getting riled was for losers. Of course, this was *big* news, but he would never have blown his cool by admitting as much to the old man. Instead, he teased his father by casually adding, "Yeah – sounds great."

Thomas' response was not so slick. "Well, erm… we'll need to go and spend some time at NASA first, you OK with that? I don't want to leave you here alone, son. Ya see?"

"Yeah, she'll be right."

"Well, erm…," parents have always repeated themselves, "is there anything you want to ask me about it?"

Woodsey considered for a moment before providing his answer as two questions. "Can we have a party?" he asked firstly.

Thomas rubbed a hand down his face, feigning strained patience but secretly hiding a smile, as he always did. "I suppose so," he agreed, mildly exasperated.

"Also, Dad, well, it's about my allowance."

Thomas' eyebrows shot up. "Your *allowance*?"

Parents often repeat other people's words too. "Yeah, nah," Woodsey continued down the home run, all youth and hope. "I assume this big NASA number comes with a raise?"

Alone in his office, Thomas laughed out loud at the memory. Anxiety about their situation notwithstanding, his son often had this effect on him – it was just one of the reasons he loved him so dearly. Which reminded him, Christian was in fact meant to be helping him with this work. Where *had* he got to?

Almost as if summoned by thought, his son strode into the shared offices of the construction and mining department's technical arm just moments later, chatting animatedly with another young man Thomas recognised.

He remembered Tim from their first meeting in the bar soon after leaving Earth, but more lately knew him as Tim Norris, Dr Norris' son – unofficially known as 'The Dinosaur Kid' by the senior staff.

"You remember Tim, Dad?" asked Woodsey. "I thought he might be able to help you."

"I certainly wouldn't turn help away," replied Thomas.

"Tim's got some animated footage showing the kinds of creatures that'll be trying to rip open your vehicles like food containers," confided Woodsey with a wink.

"That's a comforting way to put it," Thomas acknowledged. "I'd be interested to see them, though."

"Good to see you again, Dr Woodsey," said Tim, offering his hand.

"You too, Tim," Thomas replied, taking the proffered hand, "and it's 'Wood' by the way, regardless of what my son likes to call himself." He chuckled lightly at the young man's slip. "Please just call me Thomas or Tom, I'm not precious. We're all in this together after all."

Tim smiled back, reddening. "Sorry," he said, playfully punching a cackling Woodsey on the arm.

"Hey, he was three sheets to the wind last time he saw you, Dad, remember?" Woodsey added helpfully. "I'm surprised he remembered you at all."

Tim nodded sarcastically at his friend whilst unfolding his comm to the size of a small personal computer. He placed it on the desk, the fold lines quickly disappearing as the screen lit up. "Maybe you could play with some building blocks over there in the corner, while I work with your dad?"

Both Woods laughed.

"Right, these are obviously 'best guess' indications of the animals' structure, size and movement," said Tim, making inverted comma bunnies in the air, to emphasise his point. "I also have some three-dimensional mathematical models, which might be more down your street, Dr W— er, Thomas. Compiled with the aid of palaeontologists and anatomists, they've been used to calculate how powerful the creatures were, theoretically, and how much force they could bring to bear."

The three men grouped around the small screen.

"That sounds ideal," said Thomas.

The scientists, engineers and construction personnel worked around the clock preparing their equipment for the USS *New World*'s return to Earth. For her part, Mother Sarah made endless rounds of the ship, tirelessly propping up the crew and passengers' morale, offering support and encouragement, or even just a kind word here and there. Douglas commented that she was probably the first non-wartime official in history to do that *after* she had been elected.

However, the only person to seek *her* out during that time had spiritual problems of a different sort.

Sarah's door chimed. Not recognising the stranger, she invited the young woman to take a seat in her lounge. Offering a drink, she began, "Forgive me, but I don't know everyone's name yet, Miss...?"

"Mawar," the visitor replied, "Rebecca Mawar, but most folks call me Beck."

"It's good to speak to a fellow American," replied Sarah with a welcoming smile. "Where are you from, Beck?"

"LA."

"Kansas," said Sarah.

Beck nodded. "Mother Sarah, I'm sorry to call on you like this but I just don't know who else I can tell."

"It's fine, really, Beck. My door's always open, day or night, if you ever need to talk."

"Someone to talk to…" Beck mumbled, almost to herself.

To Sarah, it appeared that the young woman tuned out for a moment, as though lost in memory.

"I don't know if you'll understand what I'm about to tell you," she elaborated, "but you're the only other spiritual person on the ship that I know of."

Beck looked down into her cup for a long moment, visibly struggling to pull herself together. Sarah could clearly see that her guest was distraught about something. "What is it, child?" she asked, leaning closer.

"I'm a spiritualist medium," Beck stated.

Sarah sat back slightly. Although not sure what to expect, this was certainly a surprise. Rallying quickly, she asked, "We've got all kinds o' folks on this ship, Beck. What's troubling ya?"

"I know the Church frowns upon people like myself – what we do," replied Beck. "I find that endlessly ironic, as most people think that we *both* talk to imaginary friends," she added archly.

"The Church has always enjoyed a good frown," Sarah responded encouragingly, smiling at the truth of the statement. "I can give you a really good one if it'll help?"

Beck laughed a small, fragile laugh which dislodged a tear. "I hoped I would like you, Mother Sarah, and I do."

"Please, just Sarah will do, we're not in church."

"Sarah," Beck repeated. "I have, almost by accident really, made a good deal of money from helping people with my gifts. That's how I could afford to be here. People used to come from all over the world for my readings or to appear on my network show. I've always been guided by spirit, more precisely by my spirit guides. I have several, we all have. Some take the form of people, others animals and they guide us through our lives – even if we don't realise we're being guided."

She looked intently at Sarah.

"It's hard to explain but, look, have you ever braked for a blind corner for no reason, only to find something in the way that would have hurt you, if you hadn't slowed right up? Or have you made a choice that seemed crazy, but worked out real well? We usually say something like, wow! That was lucky! These are often the situations where one of our guides steps up and holds our hand at a crucial moment."

Sarah nodded, thoughtful. "I believe that God guides us in the ways you describe," she said at last.

"Do the two beliefs have to be mutually exclusive?" asked Beck, seriously. "Wouldn't God show us things in a way that we'd understand?

"But I didn't come to you to debate theology or spirituality, Sarah. I came to tell the only person on the ship who I thought might understand, what has happened."

She took out a tissue, wiping her eyes.

"All my life I've been able to see the spirits, my own personal guides and family passed on, but also other spirits. There were many watching over the people on this ship when we took off. In fact I was relieved and exhilarated when I realised that they were still with us, even after we left Earth. They're truly amazing!" She smiled at the memory.

"That must have been a great comfort," said Sarah, kindly. "I believe that no matter how far we run or *when*, God will always find His children."

"Do you really think so?" asked Beck, earnestly and urgently. "I need you to understand that, ever since I was a very young child, I've never truly been alone."

"It's a great gift that God has given you, Beck."

The young woman nodded, absently. "Then we entered the wormhole, the explosion occurred and everything went wrong. I thought that, with all the stress and the panic, maybe we were just a little off kilter, but things haven't righted themselves." She began to cry.

Mother Sarah moved to sit next her unusual guest, trying to ease her distress with a comforting arm around the shoulders. "What is it, my dear? You can tell me."

"Sarah," Beck sobbed, "they're all gone!"

An hour later, Mother Sarah sat with Douglas and Patel in the meeting room. Commander Baines, having paused the recording of her interview with Lieutenant Lloyd, stood to face them from the far end of the conference table.

"Clearly he tripped himself up there," she said, "or so I thought, but his attitude is so awful it's hard to tell if he's the 'bad guy' or just a completely unlikeable one. What came next I just couldn't believe, but I'll let you judge for yourselves."

She restarted the footage.

"Who said anything about a detonator?" continued the Baines on screen.

Lloyd visibly twitched. "Don't bombs usually require one?" he countered.

"Not necessarily, some have timers. How did you know we were looking for a remote detonator?" pushed Baines.

"Lucky guess," Lloyd answered flippantly, settling back, his composure in place once more. "You need to start questioning the other people with access to the engineering systems of this ship."

"What's that supposed to mean?" asked Baines.

"There were four people with access to the engineering systems in that area, not to mention the bridge crew. For all I know, *you* could have placed the bomb."

"Oh, please," Baines retorted witheringly. "I've heard some desperate stories from people caught out in my time, but that takes the cake!"

"Relax, Commander, I don't seriously think it was you. I wouldn't credit you with the intelligence to be able to pull this off," he added nastily. "But I would look more closely at the affiliations and agendas of the other engineers on board before throwing your accusations around."

Baines audibly sighed. "What are you talking about now?" she asked, bored.

"Young Mr Nassaki has some very colourful associates back home, for example." He leaned forward and stared. "They certainly might have given him the motive. He has just about enough ability, I'd wager, and he certainly had the opportunity. He's forever sending me all over the ship away from his work area – his way of making sure that no one with any serious knowhow ever sees what he's up to."

He leered spitefully. "Have you never wondered why he has me running left and right doing this demeaning task or that, when *I* should be handling the most intricate and vital systems?"

Baines leaned forward slightly. Stroking her chin, she spoke thoughtfully. "You're right, now I come to think of it, why would he do that?"

Lloyd sat back, pleased with himself.

"No, wait," she continued. "I think I understand now."

"Finally seen the truth, have you? As to why I've been sidelined all this time?" Lloyd asked, hopefully.

"Indeed, I think I have. Could it be because the chief is up to some nefarious business aboard the *New World*?" she asked anxiously.

Lloyd nodded excitedly.

"*Or*," she added thoughtfully, "is it because Hiro thinks you're an incompetent, arrogant, interfering halfwit that he really can't trust with anything more critical than making sure that the toilets only flush *after* you've waved your hand?"

Lloyd glared defiantly. "Just ask young Hiro about Sargo Lemelisk if you don't believe what I'm telling you. Then you might want to check *his* quarters instead of victimising me!"

Baines stopped the recording, turning back to the council of three.

"After that he clammed up and wouldn't say any more."

"Who's that he's referring to?" asked Douglas.

"At the moment I don't know, there wasn't time to find out before this meeting." She looked at him directly. "I didn't think I should get anyone else to look into it, Captain."

Douglas nodded. "Aye, but make it a priority, Commander." He turned to his fellow councillors. "For myself, Ah wouldnae put any stock in Chief Engineer Nassaki being involved with this."

"Would you have expected it from Lloyd?" asked Mother Sarah.

"Well, no – at least, nothing this bad," admitted Douglas, "but the man is an unpleasant fellow."

"And Hiro is a nice fellow?" Sarah asked again.

"Well, yes but that's not why—" Douglas tried but Sarah interrupted him.

"We can't afford any favour, Captain. Until this is resolved it may be necessary to suspend the chief's duties perhaps?" she suggested with a hardness he had not suspected in her.

"But we've never needed him more!" retorted Douglas, anxiously.

"That *would* make it the ideal time to strike at us, don't you think?" suggested Patel, quietly.

Douglas opened his mouth to speak and then closed it again.

"But we're in a totally unknown situation," tried Baines. "No one could have foreseen what has happened to us."

"And if we were dealing with a purely financial reason for destroying this ship that may be an end to it, Commander," Patel responded. "But we know that terrorists come in two main flavours: the seekers of power and the seekers of glory. The second can be far more unpredictable, as they often wish to die for their cause."

This brought a thoughtful silence down upon them.

Eventually Douglas broke it. "If we turn against each other," he said, looking hard at the other three people in turn, "then whoever *was* responsible for all this won't need bombs. We'll tear ourselves apart."

This brought an *uncomfortable* silence down upon them.

"I refuse to believe that Hiro had a hand in this," said Baines.

"That goes for me too," agreed Douglas, belligerently, "but clearly it has raised a question that requires an answer. Sargo – what was the name?"

"Lemelisk," supplied Baines.

"Right," said Douglas, standing. "Jill, please give my apologies to the department heads, but the meeting scheduled for," he checked his antique wristwatch, "ten minutes' time will have to be put back to *one hour* and ten minutes' time."

"Captain, may I ask where you're going?" asked Baines.

"To interrupt an incredibly busy man who is working to save our ship and our lives just to ask him a load of almost certainly pointless questions!" he snapped and strode from the room.

"I hope I didn't upset the Captain?" Sarah asked Baines.

"No, I think it's the situation that's upsetting him. He also has a lot of respect for Hiro, but by the same token he can't afford to take any chances with our lives. I just hope he gets the right answers," she added thoughtfully.

Douglas met Hiro at airlock one. Georgio Baccini was in the process of helping the chief out of his space suit as he approached.

Hiro smiled at the captain. "Hello, sir," he greeted. "That ought to help a little."

Douglas had lost touch with the engineer's schedule. Realising he had no idea what the younger man was referring to, he asked, "What have you done? Sorry, Hiro, Ah've been tied up."

"I've cut all of the rough edges away from that gash in our side, sir. There *was* a memo," he said gently. Cutting and welding equipment was being dragged into the corridor by two Pod engineers seconded to Hiro's team since the sad loss of Mario, and Lloyd, of course.

"I was worried about further tearing under the extreme pressure of atmospheric entry and didn't want to risk more of the hull being ripped away or fire damaged. I've also welded a curved plate coated in silica ceramics at the front of the hole, oriented to improve our aerodynamics, sir. We keep a good stock in the hold in case we lose some of our re-entry protection tiles."

Douglas was impressed. "Will that ease our re-entry, Chief?"

"Hopefully, sir. It's not like I can test it in a wind tunnel or anything, but theoretically it should deflect much of the atmospheric resistance, and with a little luck, the heat, around the tear in our side rather than into it. Bit like a spoiler on the cab of a truck. I'm confident it will help us to get down in one piece, sir, so I can repair her properly on the ground." He shook his head, adding, "Doubt it will be a smooth ride, though. Actually, I was rather fortunate, Captain – twice."

"Why, what happened?" Douglas asked with concern.

"Well, working on a vessel moving at 50,000 kph has its risks, even in vacuum. Obviously, I too was moving at the same speed as the ship but when relocating my tether I accidentally pushed off too hard and began to drift. I just about recovered myself and managed to lock on before I zipped off into space, never to be seen again," he confessed with a grin, but he was clearly shaken by his experience.

"What about your suit thrusters? Were you no' able to manoeuvre yourself back into position?"

"No, sir. I didn't realise at the time, but whilst removing the sharp edges I must have snagged the fuel line in my suit. The tanks are very small and I was probably trailing a tiny stream of hypergolic fuel all over the place."

"And after that, you still managed to weld that heat deflector in place?" remarked Douglas.

"Yes, sir, that was when I was lucky for the second time. I believed the thrusters to have malfunctioned, I didn't know about the ruptured line. If the leaking fuel had come into contact with the high energy electrons at the weld seam, I would have gone up like a bomb – further damaging the ship!"

Douglas' expression softened as he tried to hide his amusement at the chief's skewed priorities.

"Nevertheless, I completed my task," the engineer stated proudly. "Was there something you needed to see me about, sir?"

Feeling awkward, Douglas quickly reached a decision. "No, it's OK, Hiro. Ah just thought Ah'd come and see how you were getting on."

Embarrassed, he changed the subject. "How are *you* feeling today, Georgio?" he asked instead. "Sorry Ah've no' been able to check in on ye."

The young engineer looked up from unbuckling Hiro's air tanks. "I'm OK, Captain. Thank you," he answered quietly. "There's talk about the ship regarding Lieutenant Lloyd, sir?"

Douglas sighed. "Aye, but despite our efforts we *still* don't know anything for sure. His DNA was found around the wormhole drive, but as a senior engineer on this ship, that's hardly proof. He was hanging around the escape pods when it all hit the fan, but again, he stated that he was meant to check on them but was a day late in doing so – despite telling his immediate superior that the work had been completed." He nodded at Hiro. "He was also injured in that event. We haven't found any trace of the detonation device and nothing linking him to it. Basically, it's all circumstantial. We've no hard evidence at all."

"So we need to give him the benefit of the doubt for now then?" asked Georgio.

"Ah'm finding that difficult, after everything that's happened to us and with how much danger we're still in," replied Douglas.

"But if there *is* nothing linking him, then are we holding him in the brig simply because we don't like him, sir?"

For a second time, Douglas felt awkward. "You think we should release him? *You*, of all people? Wasn't Lloyd always horrible to you and Mario?" he asked, rather surprised.

Georgio Baccini looked at the captain keenly before agreeing with a nod. "He's not a very nice man, and forgive me for speaking ill of a superior officer, but I don't think he's a very good man either. That doesn't mean he's a murderer or a terrorist though, sir. I want more than anything to find my brother's killer, but I know Mario would not want the wrong man to pay the price for it, Captain, especially now. We've all lost and need each other so much."

Douglas smiled sadly.

"You are a very good man, Georgio Baccini, and Ah'm very proud to serve with you. No decisions will be made either way until after we've landed safely, then we can look at everything again in meticulous detail. Ah won't let this turn into a witch hunt, Georgie, Ah promise, and Ah'll take on board what you've said."

Hiro was out of his spacesuit now and Douglas waited until both men were standing, facing him. He felt ashamed for even having a moment's doubt about Chief Nassaki. Reaching out, he grasped each of them by the upper arm.

"Ah know the *New World* couldn't be in better hands, gentlemen, thank you." He threw them a quick salute, turned on his heel and strode away.

Douglas entered a bridge where everything seemed so *normal*. For the first time, in what seemed like a long time, there was calm – klaxon free, non-running-around-shouting, honest-to-goodness, calm. Baines worked at a console in silence, while Singh plotted minor course corrections at the helm as he synchronised the ship with the Earth's movement around the sun.

The *New World*'s captain took a moment to burn this peaceful image into his mind, because who knew what they were heading into next. This was the way it had been, just a few short days ago and he could not help grieving for the loss.

"Are we on course, Sandip?" he asked.

Singh looked up from his console. "Aye, sir," he replied. "Less than two days until touchdown. Lieutenant Nassaki has just reported successful alteration to the outer-bulkhead of the ship—"

"Ah know," Douglas interrupted. "Ah've just seen him."

At this Baines looked up, caught the captain's eye and motioned towards the meeting room. She closed her screen down and they walked through together.

"How'd it go with the chief?" she asked as the door closed.

"It didn't," Douglas admitted, "but before we get into that, there's something Ah need you to know. Something that was brought up earlier but Ah couldn't comment on it at the time."

Baines gave him a questioning look, but kept her silence.

"In the meeting with Sarah and Satnam, you said that we're in a totally unknown situation," he said.

She nodded.

"Well, that's pretty inarguable," he continued, "but you also stated that no one could have foreseen what's happened to us."

Now Baines looked at him askance. "Where's this going, James?" she asked quietly.

Douglas nodded too, understanding her apprehension.

"This information is quite old now, although no one below the rank of captain was meant to be told." He exhaled sharply, somewhere between an exasperated snort and a sigh. "As we're all that's left now, Ah need you to know, just in case anything happens to me or it has some bearing on our future."

He looked at her intently. "Some years ago, a paleobotanical project was funded by a university in North America, Ah forget which one – may have been Princeton. Anyway, the students came across something quite remarkable whilst digging amber deposits. They were working in, wait for it, South America," he said sardonically, "and very close to where we are proposing to put down."

"Found what exactly?" asked Baines, completely rapt.

"Well, that's the bizarre thing because amongst all the insects, seeds and general natural debris, one piece of amber contained something manmade. Do Ah need to tell you how old the seam was that they were digging?" he asked.

"99.2-ish by any chance?" asked Baines.

"Hole in one," agreed Douglas. "Circa 100 million years ago was the verdict. What they found was a ring-pull from a tin can locked in a lump of amber and because of the preservation they were able to scrape samples from the back of the tiny piece of metal. They believe it was, of all things, a beer can!"

"Wasn't Australian beer, was it?" asked Baines, in horrible fascination.

Douglas smiled. "Let's not jump to conclusions. Needless to say the whole complement were silenced and treated to a little chat at governmental level. Not one word was to get out on pain of imprisonment in a very dark hole, never to be seen again."

"They didn't feel that freedom of speech and of the press was in our best interests then?" asked Baines.

"Not so much," he replied. "Obviously, many of the shadier elements within the US government were all over this in a heartbeat, in case it represented a threat to national security or, more importantly, in case there was anything in it they could use – what with talk of time travel being bandied about.

"This information eventually found its way to the senior staff at NASA and someone, up on high, reasoned that if anyone was likely to cause a cock-up that ended by sending people back in time, it was likely to be us with our shiny new wormhole ships." He shook his head ruefully. "Ah guess it was a fair cop, eh?"

"So you're thinking that the ring-pull off the beer can was, or will be, down to us?" asked Baines, struggling to take in this latest twist.

"Well," Douglas posed the question, "how likely is it that this has happened twice, and both parties just happened to be sent back to the same time and place?"

Baines had to bow to the logic of this. "Part of me is hoping someone else *has* been there first, so that this isn't on us! So do we need to talk to people about littering or…?" She tailed off, more than a little confounded.

"Don't know," Douglas admitted. "Haven't even thought about it for years. Not everything deemed 'top secret' seems of any particular use to us plodding foot-soldiers to be honest with you.

"Ah suppose it should have come to me earlier when we worked out where we were, but it didn't. It was just a fascinating conundrum long forgotten about, until you struck a chord with what you said earlier, about this situation being unforeseeable. Ah didnae want to mention it in company and none of this may even be relevant to anything. Ah just think it's likely, probable even, that that artefact will be left somewhere on ancient Earth by this crew. Just log the information in case it becomes useful later."

"So NASA and the US government knew that this was a distinctly possible outcome to our mission to Mars?" she asked in disbelief.

"No one knew anything for sure, as far as Ah could tell," said Douglas. "Everyone was baffled by it. We were simply the most likely people to cause it, so the captains were all told as a precaution. Would it have made any difference if everyone *had* known? We still need Mars. Earth is still sickly and overcrowded. We had to press on regardless and act on our best information and intentions."

Baines thought for a moment. "Yeah, I suppose you're right, there would've been no other choice. At least the Mars Programme is well under way and the last Pod, which we have, will be replaced soon enough for them, I'm sure."

"Exactly," said Douglas. "So now you know. File it away – at least it looks like we survive the landing anyway!"

Baines was still thoughtful. "True. Alright, that's food for thought for another day," she said, at last. "Back to the now, and at the risk of a second bout of indigestion, what *did* happen with Hiro?"

Douglas explained how Hiro had spent the last perilous hours and how he had almost been twice lost to them.

"Ah just couldnae bring myself to ask him, Jill," he said, his native Scottish dialect becoming more pronounced with his emotions. "The guy had just risked his life again for us, so that he could give the ship the best possible chance of landing safely. How could Ah accuse him of sabotaging the mission and murdering the brother o' the man he was working with?"

A flicker of emotion crossed Baines' face. "How is Georgio?" she asked.

"Georgio, my God!" Douglas exclaimed. "Ye'll never guess what he asked me to do. He asked me to release Lloyd if there is nae direct evidence against him! The man's a saint! And Ah was there to accuse the other man, who could have just been killed trying to save us, of being a traitor. Ah couldnae do it, Ah just couldnae!"

"And are you? Going to release him, I mean?"

Douglas took a deep breath and puffed out his cheeks slowly. "No," he said flatly, tying down his anxieties. "Ah cannae take the chance, not until we've landed safely and we can put things in place. All Ah know for sure is that this *transference* of guilt Lloyd is trying to get us to buy into is not working for me. Hiro is worth ten of him – a hundred, in fact!"

Baines looked concerned, chewing her lip, as she was prone to do when worried.

"What?" asked Douglas, with a sinking feeling in his heart.

"I looked up Sargo Lemelisk," she said.

"And?"

"He's a known terrorist and," Baines looked Douglas in the eye, "it turns out there may be a link with Hiro after all, James."

Chapter 6 | The Dinosaur Kid

Dr Thomas Wood whistled softly. "They're really that big? Hang on a second." He waved a hand over his desk, causing a keyboard to light up within the glass top. After typing a short prompt, the large monitor built into the laminated glass wall of the office also lit up and began searching for Tim's comm. Within seconds, the devices synced and the dinosaur suddenly filled much of the wall. Thomas moved closer to study the detail.

"Ah, that's better," said Tim. "Actually, there may have been much bigger animals than we know. The examples you see here are reconstructed from semi complete fossil remains, representing some of the largest sauropod dinosaurs known to have lived in South America during the late Albian Stage of the Mid-Cretaceous.

Some Titanosaurs, Argentinosaurus for example, could have grown up to forty metres in length with an estimated weight of eighty tons in life, possibly more. They could have stood easily nine or even ten metres tall at the hip, too.

"Interestingly enough, or should I say *worryingly* enough, the largest and most complete individual found so far was not even a full adult, so who knows how big they could get? Scientists have been unable to agree on that one. I suppose we'll find out soon enough though, eh?"

"A comforting thought. I assume by the comparative smallness of the head and the lumbering posture that these were herbivores?" asked Thomas.

"Correct," Tim replied. "But there are hints in the fossil record of similar animals much larger even than these. For example, Amphicoelias

Fragmillius – only a single vertebra of that animal was ever found, but its vertebra was 2.7 metres tall!"

Despite his workload, Thomas was fascinated. "And how does that compare with our friend, Argentinosaurus here?"

"The comparable vertebra belonging to Argentinosaurus was about 1.5 metres tall," Tim supplied, with obvious relish. "*Yes*," he continued, noting their expressions and nodding slightly, "Amphicoelias scales up to an animal some sixty metres in length and is what's known as a mega-sauropod. Although this animal was probably of lighter build proportionally than Argentinosaurus, the sheer size of the animal would have probably weighed it in at well over a hundred tons."

"Were they of the same family or *genus*, is it?" asked Woodsey.

"Not exactly," answered Tim, "although they were both part of the generic sauropod family of dinosaurs – you know, the long neck, long tail types – Argentinosaurus was a Titanosaur, as I said. They were massively built eating machines able pick from the treetops fifteen or even twenty metres up, all the way down to the ground, left and right and swallow any vegetation they came across, whole – and they ate a lot! It's believed that most sauropods let the bacteria in their guts break down the tough plant fibres during the digestive process, so they could shovel it in at a prodigious rate, without the need to waste time chewing. It's likely they even swallowed stones to act in tandem with their enormous stomach muscles, like a grinding mill for tough plant stems, et cetera.

"Back to your question, the Amphicoelias Fragmillius is believed to be of the Diplodocid family, like the much more famous Diplodocus. Although spectacularly huge animals, they were lighter in frame than the Titanosaurs. A Diplodocus of similar or even greater length than Argentinosaurus would probably weigh no more than 20 tons. As luck would have it, one of the ways in which sauropod dinosaurs can be identified is via their vertebrae. This single piece of evidence is far from the whole story, but it does at least make some kind of basic comparable supposition possible."

"Twenty tons, is that all?" mocked Woodsey. "So are we going to see any diet-dippies out there?"

"Diplodocids, or their progeny possibly, but not Diplodocus – as far as we know they've been extinct since the end of the Jurassic Period. That's about forty-odd million years before *when* we find ourselves now. The Jurassic Period ended about 145 million years ago in our own timeline," Tim added for clarification.

"I would say I'm reasonably qualified as a mathematician—" began Thomas, modestly.

"I'll say," Woodsey butted in. "You've got so many letters after your name, it has the consonant consistency of a Welsh shopping list!"

"—but the numbers you're reeling off are quite extraordinary. The mathematics involved in calculating how they carried their weight and how they moved must be completely engrossing. The *forces* at work…" Thomas ran out of words, shaking his head ruefully. "Mother Nature, the greatest engineer of all!" he said at last. "This would be incredibly intriguing if we weren't stuck here and about to start trying to live next door to these awesome creatures."

Tim frowned, staring at Woodsey.

"How do you know what Welsh looks like – shopping list or otherwise?" he asked.

"The evening we left Earth, I went to the gym to try it out and Private Jones was in there. I asked how he got so big and he showed me the workout charts he'd drawn up." It was Woodsey's turn to frown. "They didn't look like words, but Dewi assured me they were."

"Oh," said Tim.

"I'm more surprised by 'consonant consistency'," remarked Thomas, drily. "I thought you were expecting to flunk English? Or is it simply that Mr Norris here is having a positive effect on you?" He turned back to Tim, smirking at his son's look of annoyance. "OK, you've shown me the biggest, now show me the baddest. Somehow I've got to remake these trucks and diggers so that their cabs, at least, can take a smack from these guys."

Tim bent over the computer to call up Giganotosaurus Carolinii, Mapusaurus Roseae and Irritator Challengeri.

"In the late Albian, early Cenomanian stages of the middle Cretaceous," Tim began, "the supercontinent of Pangaea – which literally means entire Earth, and included most of the world's land mass during the early Mesozoic Era – was well on the way to dividing into the continents we're familiar with.

"The world in front of us still looks quite different from the one we left behind, but there are recognisable features beginning to emerge, like the Atlantic Ocean for instance – although 'ocean' may be too grand a title for the sea that exists in this period.

"Very simply, Pangaea split into Gondwana in the south and Laurasia in the north throughout the Jurassic Period. The Gondwana where Lieutenant Singh wants to land is made up of what will be South America, Africa, Antarctica, India and Australia. Subsequently, Laurasia is where we'll find what will be North America, Europe and Asia one day – excluding India, naturally.

"We believe that by the middle Cretaceous, Gondwana too was split or splitting up, leaving South America disconnected. This means that the animals there share common ancestry with other creatures but have been alone long enough to begin evolving separately. However, and I can't stress this strongly enough, this is *all* conjecture – highly sophisticated and well researched by some extraordinary minds over the last few centuries, but conjecture nonetheless."

"So what you're saying is we *may* find these animals there when we land?" asked Thomas.

"Partly, yes," Tim turned to face the engineer, "but, as I've already briefed the council, there are likely to be huge gaps in our knowledge. We may even find a land bridge still extant between Gondwana and Laurasia, with animals passing to and fro that we didn't even know of. It's less likely, but the fossil record is just too *incomplete*, too *fragmentary*, for us to be sure of anything. We may also be out on our dating information."

"I had the same problem when we moved to the States," Woodsey interrupted, nodding sagely. "I met this one girl and she had a... well, never mind," he said, remembering that his father was standing next to him.

"*No matter how sophisticated,*" Tim emphasised, talking over his friend, "our carbon dating technology, we have limited fossils in the record, so any dating can only really be a guide at best. Sometimes even the geology can make accurate dating difficult. Sandstones, for example, can be difficult and notoriously expensive to date.

"Also, who can say how long a species has lived or will live? All we can do is use the fossil record, correlating as best we can against known systems from our own time. Or at least that was all we could do until now," he added, with satisfaction, considering the opportunity before them.

"Anyway, what I mean is, there must be thousands of species we've never found any signs of amongst the larger fauna, alone."

"Do you remember those 'grab a granny' nights you used to go to in Wellington, Dad?" interjected Woodsey, nudging his father boisterously as he grinned at Tim. "He could teach you a thing or two about carbon dating!"

Dr Wood grabbed Mr Wood roughly around the neck, tousling his hair.

"Aaah, Dad!" Woodsey protested in a muffled voice. "You're messing my hair up!"

"You mean it was meant to look like that?" asked Thomas, grinning. "I thought you'd left your hairbrush back in New Zealand, mate."

Father released son and the three men bantered as the teenager checked his 'do' in the reflective glass of the office wall.

"Perhaps we could get back to the end of the world crisis we're facing? If that's OK with you, Woodsey?" Tim asked innocently. "My point, I think, was that science has made some astounding discoveries over the last three centuries but we still don't fully understand our planet or the creatures that live upon it in AD2112, so what chance do we have at accuracy in 99,200,000BC? We just don't know."

"You're a real comfort to me, d'you know that?" chided Woodsey. "So what *do* we know? Who are *these* guys you've pulled up?"

"Giganotosaurus and Mapusaurus lived, as far as we can tell, in South America more or less contemporaneously, roughly… well, *now* I suppose."

Tim called up animations of the beasts running side by side.

"Giganotosaurus is one of the biggest flesh-eating dinosaurs that have ever been discovered. At around fifteen metres long they may possibly have weighed as much as eight to ten tons.

"About a century ago people interested in palaeontology, or dinosaurs anyway, went through a phase of trying to 'out T Rex the T Rex' and this guy was a contender. Of course, calmer heads, less interested in sensationalism, thought that the largest of breed were probably fairly comparable in size. As we've only found a few dozens of individuals, from even the best-known species, we're far from knowing the full story, especially if they vary as much as say, dogs or humans.

"Tyrannosaurus Rex seems to have had a much larger brain, likely providing it with stronger senses and faster reflexes, as well as greater intelligence – or at least *instinct*. The encephalization quotient, or EQ scale, estimates the size of brain to body mass of T Rex at around 2.4. To put that in context, our EQ is around 7.5 – alright 0.6 for Woodsey."

"Hey!"

"A dog is around 1.2, although I think Reiver might weigh in at an 8.0 – don't ever think you can outwit him by hiding his rope toy, you will merely look foolish. T Rex has about the same EQ as a chimpanzee. Now, consider that for moment...

"T Rex also had one of the most extraordinary olfactory systems in the fossil record, excellent hearing and binocular vision equal, at least, to that of an eagle. Binocular vision, like our own, is essential for three-dimensional depth perception. Indeed, it is possible that Tyrannosaurs had the best eyesight of any terrestrial animal, ever. All those characteristics would have made those animals lethal hunters – or fighters, for that matter. Although, it's doubtful that any predators, from any period, set out to find the strongest adversaries they could. Chances are that, like lions for example, they would have preyed on the old, the young and the weak. There is certainly a lot of fossil evidence to suggest this, and it makes sense, because injury can prove fatal to any carnivore living wild.

"If you were a Tyrannosaur's prey, standing still would *not* have saved you! All those senses, allied to the possible intelligence of a higher primate, would have been a devastating combination. I don't think throwing him a banana would have helped either!

"When compared to Carcharodontosaurs – the family Giganotosaurus belongs to – the Tyrannosaurs must have been extremely formidable. Or will be twenty-odd million years from now and thirty million, before we see a Rex. The Tyrannosaurs had a much bigger and more 'general purpose' set of crushing and cutting teeth, with a bite maybe three times more powerful than Big Gee. Its skull was a lot broader and much more solidly built in terms of bone mass. Crucially, and we believe this to be an exclusively Tyrannosaur trait, the nasal bones were fused to give the skull immense strength, and perhaps adding to the evidence that they were built to tackle struggling prey that were very much alive!

"Luckily for us we won't meet any Tyrannosaurs," Tim paused, thoughtfully. "Actually, that might not be strictly true. Their lineage may well go back further than we first believed – well into the Jurassic. There's evidence suggesting so, although that far back they wouldn't necessarily be obviously recognisable as Tyrannosaurs. Thinking about it, their early lineage might also give them wider continental dispersal than we thought, too. Only merest hints have been found. They *could be* in Patagonia."

Tim had a faraway look in his eye as he imagined finding new species of, hitherto unknown to science, Tyrannosaurs. He stroked the wispy teenaged whiskers on his jaw contemplatively.

"Ahem," Woodsey barged into his thoughts. "Remember us?"

"What? Oh yes, well, let's just go with, we shouldn't see any *advanced* Tyrannosaurs – *hopefully*. You never know, Dr Patel might find a way for us to jump forward in time skipping past the late Cretaceous altogether," Tim added, grinning.

"Yeah, right! You'd love to see one really though, wouldn't you?" asked Woodsey, accusingly.

"Ah, well… OK, busted," Tim admitted ruefully, turning back to the screen. "Tantalising evidence has been found to suggest that Mapusaurus, also a Carcharodontosaur and slightly smaller cousin to Giganotosaurus, may have been a pack hunter. I may have put the mighty Tyrannosaur on a bit of a pedestal just now, and perhaps deservedly so, but for the love of God, don't underestimate the Carcharodontosaur. They were huge apex predators, dominating the southern hemisphere for many tens of millions of years. When we meet them, they will be more terrifying than anything man has experienced before, at least terrestrially.

There is one thing that we should all know about these large theropod animals before we set foot outside the ship. It has to do with the middle toe on each hind foot. Basically, the metacarpal is fused, literally squashed, between the two outer metacarpals."

"Wow! I'm glad you let me in on that!" Woodsey acknowledged, mordantly.

Tom Wood, realising just how important anything relating to a structure built to carry heavy loads might be, waved his son down. "Go on, Tim."

Tim nodded. "It's a feature known as 'the arctometatarsalian condition' and is usually associated with – and you'll see why I think this is important now – fast running. This arrangement removes practically all the movement between the bones. When we run, our metacarpals move within our foot and this costs us energy. Now this is significant – many of the predators we will face down there on the planet will likely be fast, yes, but they will also be very *efficient* runners, good for the long haul. It is entirely likely that these predatory dinosaurs I've shown you, could outrun even the fastest human over the hundred metres, but worse – far worse – they'll be able to keep up that speed, possibly for a few miles."

He looked at Woodsey. "*Now* are you glad I let you in on that?" he asked, dryly.

"I think 'glad' might be a little strong, mate," Woodsey accepted, paling slightly.

"Giganotosaurus and Mapusaurus may *both* have been social – who knows? Maybe we'll find out?"

"*Social?*" asked Woodsey. "I find it hard to imagine them streaming social media or sharing a cup of tea and a bit of a dance."

"I don't mean they messaged one another, you numpty!" Tim shot back, laughing.

"Do you remember the Bookface Centenary?" Woodsey rambled on, "When they unveiled that they would henceforth be known as Holoface because most of their users didn't know what a book was anymore, leading to 'serious concerns' that this made them less *social*? Remember? They were raked in the press with that headline: HOW THE HOLO WILL FOLLOW! Well it's... well it's nothing like that actually, sorry, forget it. Carry on."

Tim and Thomas exchanged a look and raised an eyebrow apiece before turning back to the computer.

"When I say social," Tim tried again, "I mean that they hunted and killed together. It's entirely probable that the younger, quicker animals ran the prey beasts down while the older, larger members of the group provided the muscle and devastating bite power. There's actually compelling evidence among large, flesh-eating dinosaur remains, that their leg proportions may even have changed with age.

"In essence, the lower leg of the younger animals – the bit that would be from the ball of the foot to the heel, in a human – could be proportionally longer than in the same breed at a more advanced age. They were also lighter too, of course. When we encounter them, the adolescents may lack *some* of the awesome power of their elders, but they are likely to be *rapid*," Tim chattered away excitedly.

"Picture yourself as a large herbivorous dinosaur being chased by these terrors. They catch up with you, shocking you with bite after bite, bleeding you to bring you down... then you hear the slower thud, thud, thud, thud!" Tim marched the words out with his fists for emphasis. "This is the sound of the pack elders running more slowly towards you in order to deliver the colossal death blow. Just imagine the terror of those final moments."

"You are *way* too into this stuff, dude," mumbled Woodsey, shaking his head.

Tim did not hear his comment, lost as he was in the vision he had conjured.

"They almost certainly fought with one another too," he continued, "as predators from our own time do. Many fossils have been found with teeth marks from their own kind on their faces."

"Sounds like a Saturday night out in Wellington," mused Thomas, thinking of his home in New Zealand.

"What's the third animal, there?" Woodsey pointed at the screen.

"Ah, this handsome devil is Irritator Challengeri, of the Spinosaurid family," Tim explained.

"Irritator? Did he have eczema or something?"

Tim gave him a look of sufferance.

Woodsey grinned.

"Irritator," Tim continued, "was probably an opportunist predator but with a preference, indeed a specialism, for catching fish. A piscivore, if you will."

"Does that mean that he couldn't help—" Woodsey tried to ask.

"No, it doesn't!" Tim interrupted him, thrusting a thumb towards his friend. "I'm sorry, Tom. I'd better pick up the pace because the children are clearly getting bored!

"Irritator Challengeri was named for Professor Challenger, a fictional character in Sir Arthur Conan Doyle's classic novel *The Lost World*. I think we should rename him Irritator Woodseri! Anyway, as I was saying, this chap was a lot smaller than his cousin, Spinosaurus, but was still eight metres long and over a ton in weight. So, in summary: best avoided."

"So that's the worst of it?" asked Thomas, hopefully.

"Yes and no," replied Tim ambiguously. "In terms of knocking hell's bells out of your machinery, that should be the worst of it – apart from the crocodiles, of course. However—"

"There's always a however," said Woodsey.

"Well, yes," said Tim, "and in this case it will be very important to any people we send out on the ground. The small predators are likely to be, in a way, much more dangerous."

"How so?" asked Thomas.

"Dromaeosaurids have great speed and agility," said Tim, simply. "Deinonychids and raptors are probably the most widely known, but predominantly lived, or will live, later in the Cretaceous," he added for clarification.

It did not clarify so he tried again. "These animals are famous for their North American origins but they will almost certainly have had cousins or sports, with shared ancestry at least, in the South."

"Who doesn't have cousins in the Deep South," quipped Woodsey, "sport."

"Not cousins like these, believe me." Tim spoke seriously as he called up images, statistics and animations to reinforce his point.

"These are the ones any people stepping outside the ship will have to watch out for. At least our improved vehicles should offer protection here though, so it's horses for courses I suppose."

The men watched a simulation showing a pack of late Cretaceous Deinonychids brutally attacking a much larger Hadrosaur – an animal a hundred times their mass. It was a short animation but the shiver down the spine remained a while.

"It's believed that Dromaeosaurids trace their ancestry back all the way to Pangaea, before the breakup, before there was a Gondwana or any other specifically southern continent. If that's correct, then there must surely be raptors where we're going!

"I know for a fact that Buitreraptor remains were found here. They were found in a rock strata laid down, well, roughly, now. If we see one, Buitreraptor will be small but extremely fast and, very likely, shorts-soilingly vicious!"

Tim shook his head. His passion for dinosaurs was all consuming but even he looked momentarily afraid. "And where there's one raptor, there will almost certainly be more. Still, maybe I will get to discover and name a new species of raptor, too, eh?" he added, brightening slightly.

"Let's hope that's not the last thing you do, and what do you mean, 'too'?" asked Woodsey.

"Oh, I was just thinking about Tyrann— never mind. There is *some* good news, though," Tim added cheerfully, trying to dispel the atmosphere, or one could say atmos*fear*. "There should be plenty of smaller herbivores which will provide us with meat. Animals like Hypsilophodontids, young Hadrosaurids, known as duck-billed dinosaurs, and the omnipresent Iguanodonts. These must have been among the most successful families in the later Mesozoic and although there's not an exhaustive record of their presence in South America, I wouldn't be surprised if we find them in good numbers.

"Of course, they're still likely to be aggressive when threatened and most will be able to easily outrun us on foot too – or run us down, depending on how annoyed they are – there will be very few easy meals for us when we land, I'm afraid."

"But plenty of fast food!" Woodsey could not resist.

Thomas exhaled deeply, trying not to imagine his son being caught by these nightmares. "Did you mention crocodiles as well?" he asked.

"Yes," replied Tim seriously. "In this time they are diverse and, in some cases, huge! Well over twice the length and many times the size of the largest saltwater crocodile. I would suggest the drivers of your altered vehicles stay away from any river shores, beds or deltas."

Thomas nodded slowly, wearing a look of concern. "Thanks, Tim. At least that gives me some idea of what we're up against. I think I'd better get back to adapting this plant and equipment," he said. "I need a nice maths puzzle to take my mind off these clips you've shown me or I won't sleep tonight! Maybe you'd like to see what we're working on?"

"Yeah, definitely," Tim replied, eagerly.

"Right," said Thomas, breaking the link between his wall monitor and Tim's comm. "Take a look at these technical schematics. This is one of the people carriers we have on board. Now, I'm thinking that if we can keep the structural rigidity of the cabin but lighten where possible, we should be able to make them less lumbering."

Engineering puzzles eased Thomas' mind of real-world concerns, always had. Whenever the walls were closing in, he could always disappear into a realm of equations, where all was beauty and balance. He smiled slightly, without realising, as he drew Tim into *his* world.

"Obviously this will be a quick fix and we'll probably need to develop new vehicles over time, but it's a start. We're going to need the diggers, lorries and personnel carriers first. So, we've a lot to do."

"Has a strategy been devised for when we land then?" asked Tim.

Thomas nodded. "You'll hear more about it at the council meeting tomorrow, but in a nutshell this is the plan..."

Later that evening, Tim sat alone in the bar waiting for Woodsey and Hank to show. He had thoroughly enjoyed his afternoon spent with Thomas Wood and now passed the time re-familiarising himself with the suspected climatic conditions for the late Albian stage of the Cretaceous Period. He had collected so much information throughout his childhood that he felt sure he could build an advance picture of the world they would soon call home – hopefully before they had to face it for real.

Digging a little deeper, he was able to localise the data for Patagonia specifically. Tim felt sure he had read somewhere that geological and paleontological evidence suggested temperate conditions and, as far as 22nd century understanding was concerned, he seemed to be on the money.

He read on. They would likely encounter wide prairies covered with ferns, cycads and myriad scrub. Also, there would be broad forests in what would one day be Argentina. They should also find deciduous and even early flowering plant life.

If he understood correctly, Lieutenant Singh had chosen a landing zone well to the south, so they would probably be close to where the South Andean Mountains would one day stand, as the landmass narrowed towards the southern tip. This latitude may be slightly warmer than 22nd century Patagonia, but should nonetheless provide fairly comfortable living conditions. The continent would become more tropical the further north you travelled towards the equator – as it would in the future.

Tim sat back, the beginnings of a contented smile tugging at the corners of his mouth; the Andes... a little piece of home. Maybe the world they raced towards would not be so alien as many feared. Of course, the longest mountain range on the Earth in which Tim had grown up would not be as mankind had known it. He found an article in which a prominent geologist postulated that the Andean Mountains began to form in the late Triassic Period, fairly early in the Mesozoic Era and a time of extraordinary tectonic movement, roughly 200 million years before man. Although it was widely held that the Andes of the modern era began to rise around forty million years before man, during the Eocene Epoch of the Palaeogene Period, there had been several pre-Andean orogenies[3] throughout the Mesozoic and Cenozoic Eras.

Despite his fascination, it occurred to Tim that he was going to have to break this down and simplify for his crash course in Cretaceous living. The people attending would not need, and if he was honest, probably would not *want* to know about uplifting, folding and faulting rock formations sliding over the ancient Amazonian craton[4]. Indeed, if he even spoke that sentence aloud in the presence of Woodsey, his life would not be worth living. So he searched for an appropriate summary and found three key pieces of information which he thought people would wish to know.

Firstly, geologists believed that during the Cretaceous, the pre-Andean deformations and convergences began to take on a similar form and composition to the Andean Mountains everyone would be familiar with.

---

[3]   Almost 100 million years in the future, the word 'orogen' would be coined to describe the crumpling of a continental plate, an action which pushes up a mountain range; sometimes more than one range.

[4]   A craton is a large, stable block of the earth's crust; often surviving the merging and rifting of continents intact, they are generally found within a continent's interior. Almost 100 million years ago, these would simply be understood as the best places to stand.

Secondly, the rocks should contain iron ore in vast quantities. *That might come in handy if we need to build anything,* Tim thought. Thirdly, and most worryingly, the place in which they were about to land was a region of near constant instability – or at least, it suffered many *phases* of instability. "Fantastic," he muttered under his breath. "That means earthquakes and, joy of joys, volcanoes – great!"

He sighed, thinking, *I hope you know what you're doing, Lieutenant Singh. I'm really not sure we should be landing here.* Tim knew that mountain ranges were always in motion, despite appearances, but to land in a known subduction zone within a landscape populated by dinosaurs, with no support, seemed foolhardy to put it mildly. "And all this just to save fuel? But what do I know, I'm just a kid, right?" he rhetoricised anxiously.

However, simply being able to pin a contemporary name on this ancient landscape lifted Tim's spirits a little. He sensed the permanent connection, the through-line and proof of *belonging* with a world which in turn belonged to every creature born to it.

Home... but there would be differences.

Leaving aside any possible 'cataclysmic events' which might overtake them, there would be other environmental distinctions too; some of them potentially huge and yet easily taken for granted. A related article opened in a new window on Tim's screen. It discussed coprolites discovered in the early 21st century which were found to contain grass minerals dating from the late Cretaceous. Further evidence of grass had been revealed in Egypt, going back perhaps another twenty million years still. However, from the unique viewpoint of Tim and his fellow castaways, grass would probably not be widespread globally for millions of years to come.

He looked up from his notes, trying to imagine a world without grass. Elements of the robust Poaceae plant family were among the few that still thrived unassisted in the polluted 22nd century. Yet it was entirely likely that there would be none at all where they were heading. He would be willing to bet that this ancient world would be stuffed full of other oddities too, not to mention many new animals, all waiting to be discovered by the *New World*'s crew. He accepted that his might be a lonely perspective, but he really could not wait to find out – despite his misgivings about Patagonia. If you had to be all alone in the universe, this really was the only way to travel.

He linked into the ship's chrono for a moment: 2004 hours. His mum would be in her meeting on the bridge by now. She had really put in some hours with Dr Wright, attempting to wring further evidence from the bomb sites. The buzz about ship suggested that one of the engineers was being held for questioning. Everyone was gossiping about it. Tim had been told in confidence that both sites were clean; *suspiciously* clean. So naturally, the rumour mill was in full turn, producing tales to plug any inconvenient gaps in the evidence.

He looked around expectantly. *Talking of gossips*, he thought, *Woodsey and Hank should be here any minute.*

No sign yet.

Part of him was glad as he returned to his notes, his mind once more flying with giant Pterosaurs over the Pre-Andean Mountains, his eyes half closed in contented rapture. *I could give the Pre-Andes a name,* he thought suddenly. *Something a little more imaginative than 'Pre', perhaps?* This led to mulling and pondering, even musing. *Andes Mountains, Andes, Andes...* Andy's? *Who the hell is Andy – no! Who was* before *Andy? That's the question. Erm...* Peter? *Yes, Peter! Saint Peter was the older brother of Andrew, I think – I'd better look it up, ah, here we go, yes! That's it – roll fanfare – I'll call them,* The Petes! *Now, that's a good day's work and did I get all smug about it? Never fear! I'm sure to be in the history books or at least the prehistory books for that one.* He pondered some more. *'Prehistory* books', *there's something wrong with that phrase, I think. Never mind, the details can be worked out later. All I really need to do now is be the first to set foot on the Petes when we land, and stick some kind of a flag in the ground with 'Tim was 'ere' on it and—*

"Ahem," a female voice shattered the vision. "Excuse me, is anyone sitting here?"

Tim, mildly irritated by the interruption, looked up into an entirely different vision. "What? I mean... erm," he stammered nervously. "I mean no, no it's not taken." His face burned as he fought the urge to hide under the table. What was her name, Rose? "Sorry," he tried again, "I was expecting somebody else."

"So the seat *is* taken then?" asked Rose, enjoying the clumsy embarrassment she elicited from most boys her age, especially the less popular boys – that is, when she deigned to speak to them at all.

"No, I mean it is, but I mean it isn't *yet*," Tim spluttered. "Erm… would you like to sit?"

"OK." Rose took the proffered seat, giving him a blinding smile that could have started a war.

Tim stared for a long moment, then realised he was staring and briefly experimented with looking away. Realising he was now being weird, he finally remembered his computer and looked down with relief.

After a quick mental check, he realised that by asking her to sit, he had actually used up his entire repertoire with girls. He decided saying nothing more might be safest. It could have been worse; at least he had not stepped on this girl's foot.

Rose stared at him. He appeared to be concentrating just a little too hard on whatever he was reading. Eventually she accepted that he was not going to speak to her. "It's Tim, isn't it?" she tried again.

Tim was so surprised he looked up. "Yes," he answered mechanically. Another silence…

"You're not much for conversation, are you?" Rose asked, smiling.

Her smile dazzled him. Unable to stand it, he cracked. "What do you want?" he blurted out. He had no intention of saying that and, closing his eyes, he cursed himself profusely and profanely on the inside.

A small cloud drifted across Rose's expression. She had expected him to be clumsy, of course, even awestruck; that was her effect on boys. However, this one was either extraordinarily nervous or he really did not like her.

"Well, I'm sorry to have bothered you," she said, rising.

"No, I'm sorry! Don't go," Tim sputtered, wishing he could take back the last few minutes and hit reset. *Why can't you just restart people when they screw up*, he thought angrily, *like you can with computers?* "Could we start again, perhaps? How can I help you?"

Rose sat, slowly. "My father said that if I wanted to learn about the world we're going back to, no one knows more about it than you do. Could you teach me? Please? A little?"

Tim blanched, draining all the way from tomato red.

"Er, me? T-teach you?" he stuttered.

"Please," Rose answered, genuinely. "I know I've a lot to learn, probably more than anyone else on this ship." She frowned a moment, thinking on that. "Well, apart from my mother anyway. But I really want to learn. I know my old life's over and I want to be useful. I *need* to be useful. Not just taken care of by cleverer people with…" she sought for the word, "*skills.*"

Tim once again felt obliged to stick to his policy of saying nothing. He let her continue.

"I'm hoping to turn something good out of all this. At least if I can learn to be a part of this crew, then…" She spoke haltingly, finally running out of words altogether.

Making sure she had finished, he gave her an appraising look. *Maybe there's more to this one than first meets the eye*, he thought. *Or maybe the eye likes what it sees and stops looking.* "What would you like to know?" he asked evenly.

It was Rose's turn to look uncomfortable. "I could do with a little of everything, to begin with at least, starting with the basics." She sighed, exasperated by the time she had squandered in the shallows of her past. "I suppose I was something of a school mascot, in danger of qualifying as a career trophy wife, like my mum! Although, I doubt Dad sees her that way. He thinks he won the prize, bless his socks. Anyway, that future has utterly derailed and a big part of me is glad, I think."

"Really?" Tim asked, fascinated by this reversal. "From our first meeting, I doubted you'd talk to me, even if I was the last man alive," he could not help remarking.

"You almost are," she replied with a girlish giggle that had torpedoed many an ego. He looked crestfallen so she quickly added, "Sorry, I didn't mean that quite the way it sounded."

Tim sighed. "No, you're right though, if it wasn't for this crisis we're in you'd never have noticed my existence. Hardly anyone ever did."

"Well, what might have been doesn't really matter for any of us anymore, does it?" Rose pointed out. "Can we agree that it's what we do from here on that counts?" she asked, holding out her hand. "Friends?"

"Friends," replied Tim, smiling as he took it. "So who is your dad then?"

"Jim Miller, the chemist in charge of the manufacturing team for the Mars Mission." She paused, repeating, "The Mars Mission. Until just, I never gave a second thought to how incredible that sounds and now here we are, going somewhere even more astounding!" She shook her head in awe.

"I know, mad isn't it?"

"And I only found out we were going on this mission a few days ago. No one told me!"

Tim looked surprised. "How did that happen?" he asked.

"It all happened so fast and Dad was called away to NASA while I was still in school. He worked away a lot, so I never gave it much thought. Although, thinking about it now, it will be great to spend more time with him. Anyway, he left a message for me explaining everything but Mum forgot to give it to me. Long story short, I found out on my last day at school. The place was crawling with press!"

"Oh," said Tim, quietly.

Rose frowned. "Tim?"

"It's nothing, really. It's just that the media didn't come to see me, even though my mum and my teachers were expecting it. I don't think I fitted their *profile*." He gave her a rueful grin. "Still, can't say I blame them. Between the two of us, I know where I'd point my camera!" He chuckled and then flushed bright red, realising he may have just over-shared.

Rose was used to boys turning to sponge in her presence, so she barely noticed. "I didn't even know what my father did until after the bomb," she admitted, feeling slightly ashamed.

"Really?" asked Tim, genuinely astonished. "I like to try and keep up with whatever my mum is working on, as much as I can understand anyway. She *is* a bit brilliant," he added, glowing with pride.

"Your mum is Dr Patricia Norris, isn't she?"

"The same," Tim acknowledged. "I'm only here because she's so clever."

"I suppose you get your brains from her? I wish I'd paid more attention to my dad over the years," Rose admitted with a measure of regret.

"Actually, I'm adopted."

"Oh, sorry." She was suddenly embarrassed. "I've put my foot in it again, haven't I?"

"Don't be and not at all," Tim replied brightly. "My real parents died when I was two. Unfortunately, I don't know much about them as I don't have any other natural family. As far as I know anyway. My adoptive parents were just the best, though. I count myself very lucky."

"*Were* the best?" asked Rose, noticing his tense. She seemed to be noticing a lot of things just lately.

"My adoptive dad was killed in a works accident when I was twelve," said Tim, resentment crossing his young face. "Actually it wasn't an accident. 'Act-negligent' would be more precise, a calculated and deliberate act of bone idleness by a complete bottom-feeder!"

"What happened?" asked Rose. "I mean, if you want to talk about it?"

The young man's eyes bore a faraway look. After a moment's introspection he pinched the bridge of his nose to relieve pressure. "I suppose I've been both lucky and unlucky with parents," he began, slowly. "My real parents were killed by a terrorist bomb in the recycling factory where they worked. The killers justified the bombing by saying that recycling sanitary towels, lavatory paper and many other secret little necessities – which are pretty crucial when nearly fifty *billion* of us all live within a few metres of one another – was offensive to several denominations of God. Apparently, they vouched safe that these little *intimate* perks of our civilisation, the things we all take for granted, should only be used once. They reckoned that recycling and reintegrating them for a second or third outing to other *places where the sun doesn't shine*, was tantamount to deviance!"

He laughed but his bitterness was clear.

"I've always wondered if God could really be interested in such small earthly, let alone earthy, matters, what with running the universe and everything. Surely He's got enough on His plate already." He shook his head with honest bewilderment. "So many crackpot sects like that have surfaced in recent decades. Damned if I can understand any of it."

Rose felt sad and a little confused. She was a little confused that she felt sad – for *someone else*. In her own mind she thought, *Am I starting to care? Is it because almost everyone I've ever known is gone and I need to hang on to the people I have left?* What she *said* was, "You're very deep, aren't you, Tim?"

"Well, it's not all doom and gloom," he continued with a brittle smile. "Not long after I was orphaned, I was fortunate enough to be adopted by a couple of young scientists. Mum told me, when I was old enough, that they couldn't have a child of their own. So, instead of artificially creating another person in that crazy, crowded place, they thought it larger of spirit to give a home to one whom the world had discarded. Enter me – ta da!

"Whatever else had happened, I know I was very lucky to be taken in and loved by such great people."

His brief smile faded, the lump in his throat preventing him from talking for a moment.

"You OK?" asked Rose.

Tim sipped his drink. Nodding bravely he continued, "When I was twelve…" He stopped, took a breath, trying a different tack.

"One day we got this comm call from Dad's work," he shook his head sadly. "I'll never forget it. The call was actually from the police stating there had been an accident and asking Mum to make her way to the hospital. They offered to collect her but it would have taken thirty-six hours to schedule a police vehicle and counsellor, twice as long as for an *emergency* call, so she made her way as quickly as she could on the tube.

"Dad had been killed by a crane in the factory where he carried out his research in metallurgy."

Rose looked blank for a moment so Tim supplied, "The study of metals. He specialised in the development of super-light, super-strong alloys. I've no doubt that he would also have made it here on merit if…" He trailed off, his teenaged Adam's apple bobbing, swallowing his emotions.

"What was his name?" Rose asked, cautiously.

"Dr Ted Norris," Tim replied proudly. "Like Mum, he was a superb scientist. Just like Mum," he repeated quietly, shaking his head in sad memoriam.

"Sounds like he was a great guy," Rose spoke to cover Tim's discomfort. She would hardly have noticed someone else's pain, let alone cared about it, a week ago. Pondering these little changes, she was learning to like them. *I feel like I'm… more*, she realised.

"He was, he really was," Tim answered. "Obviously, the accident rocked Mum's world. Mine too. What made it even worse was that it could so easily have been avoided."

Rose was horrified by the view from the other side of the fence. "What happened?" she asked.

Tim snorted with derision. "Well, the story goes that one of the factory crane operatives, in a hurry to attend a strike demonstration over some perceived slight to his lifestyle and his right to have rights, rushed out without locking his machine down first." He looked away, reliving the memory.

"The court case was a nightmare. When that *man* was questioned, he unashamedly stated that he hadn't parked the crane because, as he'd been technically on strike, he wouldn't have been paid to press the final button which would have allowed the crane to park *itself*. So he'd left it for 'them' – whoever 'they' were – to sort out!"

He looked down at his hands, unable to meet her eye. "And so our world was smashed apart."

Rose wiped an unexpected tear from her cheek. "You won the court case though, surely?" she asked, not knowing what else to say.

"No." Tim shook his head wretchedly, still looking away. "Compensation wouldn't have brought him back anyway. And Dad hadn't been able to afford life insurance on his salary, so there was no help there, either.

"Dad's boss *tried* to help. He was a good man to be fair. He spent a lot of time with us explaining the whole situation and the processes we would have to go through. It didn't help really but just the same, he didn't have to do it – it wasn't his fault. He lost everything too. You see, the company was still punitively fined under the government's latest employment policy, but *we* never saw any of it."

He laughed harshly.

"I don't know whether this will make you laugh or cry, but the *reason* the owner of the company lost his shirt, was for failing to have a sign on the crane stating, 'In the event of a strike, please be sure to lock all plant into a safe position and switch off, *before* abandoning your post.'

"He covered a few months' rent for us, whilst Mum found her feet again. All paid from what was left of the smoking ruin of his life's endeavour, because the courts shut the company down soon after."

Tim shrugged sadly. "I suppose it often happens during hard times. Instead of being content to have a job when so many haven't, some people still have to push for more and this time everyone lost everything... and

I lost my dad. The only dad I'd ever known anyway," he finished in a small voice.

Rose was shocked and appalled by the hardships visited upon Tim and Patricia.

"Weren't the *company* insured though?" she couldn't help asking.

"Ah, well, that's another story, right there. Apparently, the company had recently lost so much money due to all manner of taxes and permits, increased labour costs, strike actions, power outages and another massive hike in employer's National Insurance – most people don't even know what that is – that the company's bank account had been too overdrawn to cover that month's grotesque insurance payment. What's worse is that, if it hadn't been for the recent strike actions, they would have met a delivery deadline and received a large payment before the direct debit was due.

"The insurers did send a letter, though. We received a copy of it. That's something else I'll never forget! It *said*: We were very sorry to learn of the death of Mr Edward Norris. However, a missed payment by the claimant puts them very clearly in breach of contract. Subsequently, there can be no possibility of an insurance payout to cover the loss."

Tim shook his head in disgust.

"They hadn't even noticed that he was *Doctor* Edward Norris." He let out a shuddering sigh.

"Lastly, and probably worst of all, his killer was not a viable target for litigation. He was worth little or nothing personally but more significantly, because he was just a lowly employee, he was not deemed responsible for his actions whilst on the *company's* time. So he was protected from criminal prosecution by the law! Mum was devastated.

"I remember thinking, even then, that within our ever more litigious society there's always someone who can be held *accountable* for just about anything that happens. Trouble is, they're less and less likely to be the person at the scene who actually *caused* the thing that happened! Still, I suppose none of that matters anymore, given our current predicament."

Rose leaned forward, squeezing Tim's hand. *I'm not surprised he seems pessimistic*, she thought. She spoke softly, "I'm really sorry, Tim. You've had a rough time so far, haven't you? And I've been so lucky and didn't appreciate it, didn't even know it."

The young man took a deep breath, exhaling some of the pain. "Anyway, we're here now and this is certainly a new start. So where did you grow up, what sort of things did you like to do before all this?" He gestured around them.

Rose felt embarrassed and not a little ashamed as she remembered her own upbringing. Particularly when she recalled some of the things she used to regard as important. Her reply was circumspect.

"Well, I'm just starting to realise that I had it pretty easy. Still, things have changed now, haven't they? I think I have too. Dad knows lots of brilliant people on board. I'm hoping to try and pick up as much stuff as I can from them, so that I can explore the crustacean!" she finished with relish.

"You mean the Cretaceous!" Tim corrected, laughing heartily, relieving some of the tightness in his chest.

Rose began laughing too, at herself, something *else* new. "Well, I told you I needed your help!" she replied.

"I like your dad," said Tim, still smiling. "He seems a really nice guy, and clever too."

"My dad's amazing, I didn't appreciate just how special he was until all this," Rose added awkwardly. "He deserves better than my mum, I realise that now!"

"That's harsh."

"That's *true*. Have you met her?"

"No," Tim admitted. "I saw her, though. She's very, erm…"

"Gorgeous?" asked Rose, smiling knowingly at the teenaged boy sitting opposite her. "Oh, she's that all right, but I don't want to talk about her. I need to know about the Creta—" she floundered.

"—ceous." Tim finished for her.

"Yeah, that." Rose smiled her dazzling smile once more.

Tim was suitably bedazzled.

"So tell me what got you into all this stuff?" she asked him.

"Huh?" he grunted. "Oh, the erm, yeah."

Rose squeezed Tim's hand again, making his temperature gauge spike again, which led to his cheeks starting to burn, *again*.

"Dinosaurs, right," he said, pulling himself together. "Well, I think my true love has always been life, really. I mean, not the love of life that

163

makes people jump off bridges attached to a rubber band or dive off a mountain strapped to a kite!"

Rose laughed and Tim enjoyed this unaccustomed female attention.

"I always thought that sort of 'loving life' was hard to understand and probably even harder to sustain!" he continued. "No, I'm just in love with the mystery of life itself, from the very beginnings of the life on Earth which we all share. From over three billion years ago, all the way through to what we've left of the natural world back home.

"I suppose that with almost fifty billion of us, well, it just breaks my heart to know that in the last hundred years the unchecked proliferation of mankind has led to the extinction of more than half of the mammals, birds, reptiles, amphibians and fish on the planet. Did you know that?"

Rose shook her head, realising that despite growing up in a city state, she had somehow lived in isolation from the real world.

"The devastation wrought has been just as bad for the plant life too," Tim continued. "The only creatures in our own time which seem to have profited by the mess we've made are some of the insects and similar invertebrates such as arachnids. They seem to be not only thriving but, in some places, quite literally colonising! All except the bees anyway. When *they* almost became extinct, we had to begin building nanotech bugs to assist with cross-pollination – then that technology began to self-replicate in ways beyond our control and—" Tim noticed that his audience was beginning to politely glaze over and returned to topic. "Anyway, it's been theorised for many years that the next dominant species on Earth will be from the insect kingdom – it's their hardiness to pollution and radiation, et cetera, you see."

He sighed with feeling. "Maybe we were living through the beginning of that phase of Earth's evolution, back home – or perhaps we've given birth to the nano-monster and all life will be *replaced*. Who needs asteroids with us around?" he mumbled to himself.

"If we do get back, do you think we're almost out of time? Humans, I mean?" asked Rose, intently.

"No one can say for sure but it's not good, is it? I believe that our numbers should be in sync with the natural world's ability to keep us. It's pretty ironic that in our 'there's-sod-all-left' world, politicians use the word 'sustainable' in connection with just about everything *but* the numbers of people!

"And you've got to admit, now everything's recycled and reused, even food and drink, it's made life for the vast majority of people pretty grim. The apartment I shared with Mum consisted of four rooms, of which the largest was 2.5 metres by 2.5 metres by 2.2 metres high. The food processor served the same grey slime protein, enzymes and supplements every day. In fact, last month, just before we left, Mum hadn't even been able to afford flavourings, thanks to another increase in public transport costs. Unfortunately for us, that meant that the grey, processed mush from the machine stopped us from dying of starvation, but that's all it did."

Now it was Rose's turn to blush, remembering their full fridge and larder back home. She thought it best not to mention it, but the more she found out about this extraordinary young man, the more she could see why Tim was such a deep thinker for his age.

"That's why I can't wait to see the world of nature we're returning to, completely unspoiled!" Tim allowed some of the excitement he always felt when discussing his favourite topic to brim to the surface.

"My dad loved the natural world too. I grew up on old television broadcasts by a 20th and 21st century writer and documentarian named David Attenborough. He was a real visionary. I think he still holds the record for the most honorary doctorates – a remarkable man and a real gentleman too, by all contemporary accounts. I would love to have met him.

"Growing up around scientists with a passion for natural history, I was hooked when mankind created an opportunity to transport life to another planet for a fresh start, as I'm sure you can imagine. We all were. Since then, we've followed the newsfeeds on the Mars Programme avidly. When mum got the chance to apply for a place on the Mars Mission itself, I was blown away! Obviously, I pushed really hard for her to go for it.

"Not to mention it got us out of that dreadful place and away from all the bad memories. You know, whatever happens next, I'm glad I'm here!"

They fell silent for a few moments, considering all that had transpired to drop them into this place and time. Eventually Rose spoke, gently. "I'm sorry you've had to deal with so much loss, Tim. Maybe this new life will be what we both need, eh?"

The forest provided thick cover. Little, bird-like Buitreraptor hopped lightly onto a low branch, making it sway gently. Its tail countered the movement naturally, its poise, perfect. Saliva dripped from its long, ravenous jaws, onto the face of one of its brethren below. The animal made a tiny, rattling growl of disapproval and shook its head, spraying spit over its pack mates. Knee-high to a man, the pride of seven were easily chased away from their last kill by a larger predator, having done all the work. Now they were hungry and they were angry.

The young man had no idea he was being stalked as he chopped wood to make a fire. A fire would keep animals away once lit, but at the moment he was vulnerable. He swung the hand axe back to strike again and cried out in shock and pain as Buitreraptor leapt from the branch, clamping its jaws around his arm like a set of serrated shears.

Screaming in agony now, the youth flailed and failed to break the predator's grip. The tiny hunter hung on, going to work with its other weapons. Grasping its victim's shoulder and neck with its clawed forearms, it ragged great, bloody furrows in the boy's side with the enlarged, sickle-shaped claws on the second toe of each foot. A crimson spray hit the other attackers in the face as they came on, working them into a frenzy.

Thomas could not move, terror paralysing him completely. As the lad turned, he realised he was looking into the terrified, screaming face of his only child. "CHRISTIAN!"

"What?" asked Woodsey, wearing an expression of mild surprise as he held out a cup of coffee.

Thomas was drenched in sweat. It had been a very long day and he had fallen asleep at his desk. He wiped a sleeve across his face, taking the proffered cup.

Woodsey nodded to himself. "Fell asleep? I thought you were sagging, that's why I went for coffee. I was getting tired too, but I think for me it was just boredom." He grinned. "I said I'd meet the guys this evening. I think I'll go after I've finished my drink."

Thomas nodded. "Those damned dinosaur movies," he muttered, taking a long draught of caffeine. He stood and pulled his boy to him, thanking his lucky stars. *His boy* naturally found this all very irritating.

Chapter 7 | Getting The Band Together

"What kind of a link?" asked Douglas.

Baines opened her mouth to explain about Sargo Lemelisk and his possible connection to their chief engineer when the door chimed.

Letting out an exasperated sigh, Douglas tried to keep the irritation from his voice as he called, "Enter."

Lieutenant Singh appeared at the door. "The councillors and the department heads are all here, Captain. Shall I show them in?"

Douglas looked back to Baines. "This will have to wait until later," he told her quietly, taking his seat at the head of the table as Captain. "Show them in please, Lieutenant."

Mother Sarah Fellows took her usual seat on Douglas' left with Dr Satnam Patel to the right. The officers and team leaders took the remaining seats as they had on previous occasions.

"Thank you for coming, everyone," Douglas greeted them. "We know you're all enormously busy at the moment." Glancing to his fellow councillors on either side he added, "And we're very grateful for all your efforts."

He waited for everyone to be seated and for Crewman Mary Hutchins to serve drinks and dispense a few plates of nibbles.

"Firstly," he continued, "we would like to start with an issue that's been on all our minds lately." He looked to Patricia Norris, "Doctor, did your examination of the forensic evidence from the crime scenes turn anything up?"

Patricia linked her fingers together and placed her hands on the table as she spoke. "I'm sorry, Captain. We found only a small amount of Lieutenant Lloyd's DNA on the wormhole drive mounting brackets, as collected by the EVA team." She appeared uncomfortable for a moment and continued delicately. "Dr Wright did find some evidence of Crewman Baccini on the walls, as residue from the blast, but no fingerprints."

Norris shrugged. "After such a powerful explosion this is perhaps not surprising."

"So it's as we thought, then?" asked Baines. "Mario didn't touch anything prior to the blast?"

"Not as far as we can tell," replied Norris. "We found nothing *at all* in the core reactor. The only thing which stands out about this is that the whole area should have the fingerprints and DNA of at least six engineers all over it. The complete lack of... well, anything, has to be classed as suspicious to put it mildly, but that's all we have I'm afraid. Our only evidence of foul play is the *lack* of evidence."

Douglas shared a secret, uncomfortable look with Baines. "Thank you for your hard work and diligence, Doctor. This wasn't unexpected, but we had to try," he said simply.

Major White put his hand up to interject, "Captain?"

"Ford?" replied Douglas, inviting the major to speak.

"Just a small point I would like to make about this evidence, or deficit. Firstly, two bomb sites but only one has any incriminating evidence around it – why would that be?

"Secondly, the only suspect we have can't easily be placed at the second bomb site at all! Now, assuming we even have the right guy, does this mean that he made a careless mistake at the first site and pulled himself together for the second one, or does it mean we have two criminals working in tandem? One of whom is more, shall we say, professional than the other? Or, and this may be even more scary folks, do we have two criminals working separately with two entirely separate agendas?"

The silence greeting this statement fairly rocked the room. Baines and Douglas shared an even more uncomfortable look, both measuring the major's description against *both* of the engineers potentially incriminated.

Baines cleared her throat. "If that's a small point, Ford, please be sure to warn me if you ever want to make a big one. I might want to get to a lifeboat or something."

A nervous titter circulated but the tension remained.

Douglas looked at Major White. "Ford, that's a pretty terrifying prospect and Ah'm sure my colleagues will agree with me when Ah say, we can't ignore the possibility you might be onto something. Can you take this on?

"For those of you who don't know," he addressed the gathering, "we are fortunate in that Major White has an ex copper on his strength, a detective no less."

He looked back to White. "Can you get Rick Drummond to start sniffing about and see what he can turn up by walking back through the thirty-six hour period between take-off and the explosion, please?"

White nodded, making a note on his pad. "Of course, Captain, I'll talk to him as soon as we're done here."

"The next item on the agenda is weapons. Dr Patel's team have been working with Major White's security force to come up with some new toys, we understand," said Douglas, nodding for Patel to continue.

"Yes," Patel began. "Together we've re-engineered some of our stun rifles into something more powerful. We upgraded all of the power cells, transformers and conductors to produce a weapon capable of delivering almost fifty times more punch than the original was capable of."

Baines whistled. "Impressive. Will that be enough, or too much perhaps, depending on what we find on the ground?"

"You may well ask, Commander," Patel nodded, acceding to her point. "We are not really sure what we will find but as these weapons can now kill – us at least – great care will be required in their use. Training will be made available for the crew and passengers as we bring more of them online. I know arming everyone isn't ideal but it may be a fact of life soon, for anyone leaving the ship. Although, I'm sure the Americans among us will feel right at home," he added with a wry smile. "It will be like a very, *very* Wild West!"

"I'll unpack my chaps." White offered his customary lopsided grin.

"The guidance of Mr Norris has been invaluable to our preparations," continued Patel. "We would have been completely in the dark otherwise, having no other experts in this field aboard." He nodded his appreciation to Tim's mother, Patricia.

"However, it would be folly to rely on one man alone, so I strongly suggest we *all* try and learn as much as we can about this time, this world. The ship's library has some information and Mr Norris has copied his personal data onto the network for anyone to view. He is also working on a 'Cretaceous Induction Course', so that we can spend a few quality hours with him in the schoolroom in small groups over the next few days. Hopefully, this will help every one of us to get to grips with what we face.

"Now, moving back to the rifles, we have fitted a dial controlling the power setting to each one. At the moment, these are gaffer-taped to the stock of each weapon. They may look a little – what is the phrase, 'Jerry-rigged'? – but they work.

"At minimum setting they may still be used in an anti-personnel capacity. As Major White has rather worryingly suggested, there may still be an enemy in our midst. These weapons will stun an adult human easily.

"Our hope is that, when set to maximum, these stun-rifles will give even the biggest animals a nasty enough shock to make them leave us alone." He looked directly at Mother Sarah. "Most importantly, they will provide us with defence but also with alternatives to killing."

"That's encouraging," said Douglas. "How many do we have?"

"Just seven at the moment, Captain," interjected White, "but we and Doc Patel's team are working with Jim Miller's people to begin production of new rifles and side arms using this technology, as we speak. However, for now, our taped-together 'Heath Rifle-sons' as we call 'em, should at least give us an edge."

"Weren't you working on some kind of grenades as well?" asked Douglas.

Patel answered, "We *are* working on a stun grenade which will be capable of emanating a subsonic frequency. It is our hope that a blast of infrasound will stun or at least scare away any animals which may threaten us. However, we've hit a snag in that regard."

"Oh?" asked Douglas.

"Yes, thanks to the information provided, again by Tim Norris, we now understand that some of the larger animals may possibly use these very low frequencies to communicate. Rather in the way that elephants used to, before they were driven to extinction in our own time," Patel looked slightly abashed.

"And?" prompted Baines mischievously, sensing his discomfiture.

Patel loosened his collar uncomfortably. "It's possible they may use infrasound as part of their mating call and ritual," he finished, awkwardly.

Baines burst out laughing.

Ford White joined in the merriment asking, "I guess we'd better be careful what message we're sending them then, huh?"

"And hope to God they don't RSVP!" quipped Baines.

Patel smiled weakly, his dark face flushing with embarrassment. "Let's just say we'll need to work on it after we've managed to run tests on the ground. If we can isolate a frequency they use to signify a warning, that would of course be preferable to one they use to, erm… well, I'm sure there will be quite a bit of trial and error. As we shall be dealing with such large animals, they, er…" he realised he was digging a hole. "Anyway, we do have a temporary fix for this problem in the shape of a device created by Captain Gleeson, our explosives expert. Major White knows more about them than I."

Patel gestured open-handed for White to continue the briefing, gratefully sitting back in his seat.

"Captain Gleeson," said White, taking up the baton, "has created a grenade which has very limited explosive power but makes one hell of a bang! It's kinda like an electronically operated firework."

He gave his best imitation of the Australian, "Ya throw the switch and then ya throw the stick – as Gleeson puts it. Throw it as far as you can in five seconds and – Bang!" White mimed the explosion with his hands.

"Gleeson calls them his 'dingo wingers' because he says they'll put just about any wild critter to flight. Oh, and he reckons they're beaut'!" the major finished, eliciting smiles around the table. The Australian seemed to be very popular despite his outspoken, occasionally coarse ways; perhaps because of them.

"That's a very positive start, thank you," commended Douglas. "Now we move on to the vehicles. How are we progressing, Doctors?" He aimed this question at Dr Samantha Portree and Dr Sam Burton.

Burton spoke first. "My people have been working with elements of Dr Portree's team, specifically her expert welders, to lighten and reinforce some of the vehicles for reconnaissance. My fellow Kiwi, Dr Tom Wood and I have put our heads together to begin shedding weight from a couple of large, four-wheel-drive people carriers.

"Tom's still working on the details but we've already begun the prototypes. Hollow box-lattice struts will provide more structural strength and support than the vehicles had originally. They aren't pretty but they should protect the drivers and passengers.

"We can't increase the power output at this short notice, that would require extensive upgrades to the motors, so we've opted for a structural solution to the problem. The introduction of crumple zones should improve their ability to handle a pounding without passing the shock through to the people inside – which is, of course, our primary concern.

"Again, Patricia's son has been showing us images, animations and fact files illustrating the types of threats we're likely to face. He terrified poor Tom half to death," he added, chuckling.

"You should try being his mother," said Patricia. "When he was younger, the books I read to him at bedtime used to keep *me* awake!"

"Well, with the help of Mr Norris' shock tactics, we now have two vehicles undergoing the process and we expect to have them ready by tomorrow," Burton continued. "We should be able to bring a couple of lorries with cranes online soon after. We'll need them to carry any loads we may need to move – timber and such. After that we're going to need to alter the diggers and other equipment as soon as possible for the next stage of our plan. I'll let Samantha explain that, as our construction and mining expert."

"Thank you," Portree acknowledged. The large screen, built into the glass wall at the far end of the meeting table, shimmered to life as the American linked it to her tablet. Calling up diagrammatical representations showing the *New World* on the ground, she explained her plan for ringed enclosures.

"We see it like this: One of the first priorities upon landing will be to create a small 'D' shaped enclosure against the ship to provide a safe area outside for our personnel. Once complete, we can begin work on a much larger perimeter earthwork, to protect the ship from damage by large animals. The hull plating is pretty tough but despite over a century and a half of sci-fi movies to draw on, we still haven't invented shields yet!"

Mother Sarah leaned forward, speaking for the first time. "Is the ship likely to be in danger once we've landed?" she asked. "It seems amazing that something so huge could be threatened by animals?"

"It could possibly be damaged by a stampede of eighty ton sauropods or even by a concentrated attack from some of the huge pack hunters that terrorise these times," answered Portree, seriously.

"If animals glimpse us through any of the windows or portholes, they may react aggressively. The *New World* is not a war ship. She was designed to meet only the very specific stresses and strains of flight, landing and cargo haulage.

"I'm sure the engineers amongst us will agree with me when I say that, although she's a behemoth, she's also fragile in many ways. Anyhow, our plan is to use the diggers, load-lifters and lorries we have – once they're adapted – to create an earthwork around the ship. We even have a bulldozer we can deploy if necessary. Although bringing all of these vehicles into service will take time if we are to guarantee the safety of operatives and passengers."

"When you say earthwork, are you suggesting something like a hill fort?" asked Douglas, thinking of the myriad forts atop the Cheviot Mountains and Eildon Hills near where he grew up.

"Exactly, Captain," answered Portree. "Once we have our ditch and earthwork, we'll begin tree-felling to produce a palisaded stockade with gates. We may also need to redirect a stream through our compound for fresh water, if there's no spring. We'll just have to see how the land lies when we get there.

"If we do have to redirect a stream into the first ever man-made reservoir and let it out again, we can easily weld together a couple of steel grills to keep the wildlife out of the watercourse. However, I think it's only fair to mention that after speaking with Tim, I strongly suggest that no one goes swimming!"

Major White took up the baton, "As more vehicles become available, my team will patrol the site offering protection for the workforce. There's even talk of building some dirt-bikes to aid travel through the rough terrain we're likely to find.

"The vehicles we have will initially be needed for foraging and mapping expeditions in conjunction with the shuttle, and I think I'm right in saying," he looked to Burton and Singh for confirmation, "that the *New World*'s escape pods can, with a little modification, be pressed into service as small reconnaissance craft?"

White took a drink whilst Burton and Singh voiced their agreement.

"This will leave the shuttle free for more heavy duty assignments, Captain.

"Fortunately, the fuel used by the lifeboats is the same as the shuttlecraft and we have reasonable supplies of this. As some of you may be aware, we were scheduled to deliver a large consignment of shuttle fuel to *Township 4* on Mars."

White smiled wryly. "I'll bet the chief quartermaster was bouncing when we didn't show. It won't be helpin' their logistics any. He must be out there *right now*, cussin'..." Ford tailed off thoughtfully.

An introspective moment followed, as everyone considered all that must somehow still be going on in their own century. Even for the extraordinary minds sat around the briefing table, this was a very difficult concept for any mortal to grasp across such a breadth of time.

They had left these people and their lives behind just a few days ago, but now none of them would exist for almost a hundred million years; possibly not even then if the *New World*'s crew messed things up in their subjective *now*.

"Ah think 'right now' is a loaded term these days, Major," Douglas noted calmly, calling everyone home. "Anyway, what's the timescale for all this?"

"Tentatively, six months?" replied Portree, looking around the table for any contradictions. None came. "That's best guess anyway, Captain," she concluded.

"Thank you, Doc—" in the middle of his reply, Douglas' comm beeped persistently. "My apologies," he said, activating the device. "Douglas here."

"*Captain, Sergeant Jackson, sir.*" In the background Douglas could hear what sounded like an altercation.

"We're in council at the moment, Sarge, is this urgent?"

"*I'm sorry, Captain, but I would have to say that it is. We have a very serious situation down in engineering and I really think you need to double down here, sir.*"

"Very good, Sarge, Ah'm on my way – Douglas out," he said, rising to leave. "Sorry everyone, this sounds important. Commander Baines will take over for me until Ah can return. Thank you."

Baines flashed him a look of concern.

"Ah'll be in touch. Carry on, Commander."

The vast bulk of the USS *New World* shone brilliant white, drenched in the light of her star. The Earth, from which she was made, was close now. She was almost home, but the previous owners were still in residence, with no intention to sell for a *very* long time. Tim Norris was the only person aboard who really understood what awaited her crew, but at the moment he was more concerned about a girl – a girl holding his hand, across a table, in a bar.

After spilling his life story and revealing so much of himself, he began to feel a little self-conscious. Realising he was still holding hands with Rose, he felt a little more so. When Woodsey finally walked in, he got the hat trick.

"Oi, Oi! How long's this been going on?" shouted the young New Zealander. "Hey SOCA, get a look at this," he called across the room to Hank Burnstein Jnr, also approaching them with the face of the rising grin.

"Way d'go, dude!" Hank added appreciatively.

Tim released Rose's hand quickly. "Trust you two to barge in—" he stopped, looking puzzled. "*SOCA?*" he asked, looking to Woodsey for explanation.

Woodsey, already laughing, jabbed a thumb over his shoulder towards Hank. "Son of Captain America. It's like son of Godzilla, but the suits are even bigger!"

"Dick!" said Hank, play punching his shoulder. Laughing and pushing each other around boisterously, they made their way to the bar.

Woodsey turned back. "Hey Tim, what are you two drinking? A nice bubbly, perhaps? Would you like me to arrange some candles for the table? Maybe an Italian waiter? Roses? A violinist?" he shouted, completely unabashed.

"No," Tim rejoindered. "Just pi—" he jumped ship, "pint please, just the usual, thank you."

Hank and Woodsey continued to laugh raucously at Tim's discomfort.

"Hey, don't get too sloshed," Woodsey called back. "We've got some important business to discuss tonight – this dump still needs a name!"

Rose was also enjoying Tim's embarrassment but hid her grin behind her hand. She was really growing quite fond of him but, like a bolt of lightning, she realised that she liked Hank, the quintessential tall, square jawed, all American boy, *a lot*.

The four teenagers sat around the table.

Hank sat next to Rose. She could not help wondering if this was intentional. "Tim, when we get back to Earth, will there be any cavemen?" she asked

Hank smiled indulgently as Tim and Woodsey looked at one another.

"You're joking, right?" asked Woodsey.

Rose merely frowned in puzzlement.

"Haha!" he laughed loudly. "The 1970s live!"

Rose's frown went double or nothing. "Eh?" she asked.

"What Woodsey means," offered Tim, "in his obliquely insolent way, is that in some fairly deadly ancient movies, they used to show cavemen and dinosaurs together, thinking that the public wouldn't know any better. There may have also been a 'human-centric' angle too – nothing could possibly have existed before us – that kind of thing."

Woodsey was still sniggering and Tim elbowed him in the ribs.

"Of course, people were less well educated then," he added, delicately.

"Unlike *now*," laughed Woodsey, sarcastically.

"Well, things do change," Hank noted, politically.

Rose said, "Yeah, totally."

Douglas entered engineering fully expecting to find some kind of a fracas in progress, but despite his preparedness he was still shocked.

Chief Engineer Hiro Nassaki stood to one side, using a console for support while nursing a bleeding lip and a respectable *shiner*. Sergeant Jackson, a little out of his comfort zone, attempted to offer tender support by asking Nassaki if he still had his wits.

In the opposite corner, completely out of control, Crewman Georgio Baccini kicked and scrambled in vain against the hydraulic strength of Private Jones' neck lock. Jones was clearly trying not to damage the young man, which left him open to minor injuries himself as the engineer flailed like a mad thing, completely incensed. Of course, hitting the nail-hard Jones was as likely to hurt the hitter as the hittee and, as the adage went, Baccini's actions were only hurting himself.

"WHAT THE *HELL* IS GOING ON HERE?" bellowed Douglas in a quite uncharacteristic flash of temper.

The Sarge snapped around and to attention in one lightning movement.

"Sir!" he said. "We were making one of our regular duty tours of the ship when Private Jones and myself heard what sounded like a heated argument in process. We doubled into the room and found Mr Nassaki on the floor with Mr Baccini about to launch himself on to him. We wrestled Mr Baccini away and I commed you immediately.

"I wouldn't normally have interrupted your meeting, Captain, but as our two remaining engineers were going at it – just a day or so before we have to land a damaged ship on a hostile planet – I didn't think it could wait, sir," he finished.

Douglas rubbed his hand down his face in disbelief. *It's all unravelling*, he thought, but kept it to himself. "Quite right, Sarge. At ease," he said.

He walked over to where Georgio was still writhing, but the energy of anger was beginning to leave him.

"Thank you, Dewi, release him please."

Private Jones relaxed some of the pressure, waiting to see how Baccini would respond before letting him go completely. The young man suddenly found his mojo again and launched himself at the chief, but Douglas was ready for it and caught him.

"Stop!" he commanded.

Baccini, panting heavily with anger and the onset of exhaustion, stopped struggling. Douglas drew his attention, looking him in the eye.

"Now Ah want you to sit in that chair and then *calmly* explain to me the meaning of all this." He pointed to the seat at Baccini's usual station.

"But, Captain," the young man shouted, moving forward again.

"That's an order, Crewman!" snapped Douglas, louder and with steel in his voice.

Baccini sat.

"Now what's all this about, Georgio? Why would you possibly want to hurt Hiro?"

"He did it, Captain! He killed Mario! Tried to kill all of us!" the young engineer spat out, his voice rising.

"Whoa!" said Douglas. "Calm *down*. Now tell me – from the beginning – what makes you believe that?"

Nassaki was shaking his head in disbelief. "He just flew at me!" he said from behind the captain. "I was working under that console, as I stood and turned he was there and, and, he hit me with that *box*! The next thing I knew—"

Douglas turned to face the chief, raising his hands placatingly. "Alright, Hiro, Ah know you're upset but you'll get your turn," he said. "Please, you need to go and get that face looked at."

Hiro looked genuinely shocked and outraged. Eventually, mumbling his assent, he left. Douglas nodded after him saying, "Go with him, Sarge, and stay with him. Bring him back when he's fixed up, please."

"Are you sure you'll be OK, sir?" asked The Sarge.

"I've got a soldier next to me who's the size of a horse. I'll be fine, Sarge."

Jackson saluted and strode out after the chief engineer. Jones stood behind Baccini, ready to act should the engineer lose control again.

"Now, start at the beginning, Georgie," said Douglas, his more usual kindly manner restored.

Baccini sniffed, wiping his eyes. "Lieutenant Nassaki asked me to fetch a multi-meter he'd left in his quarters last night, so I went to get it."

"Was Hiro's door locked?" Douglas interrupted.

"No, Captain, Hiro never locks his door. The only things he owns, other than what he stands up in, are usually to do with the ship and her workings, anyway. You know what he's like."

Douglas nodded, considering his one-track-minded engineer. "Ah do," he said.

"Well, I *thought* I did too!" snapped Baccini vehemently. "When I entered his quarters I started to look for the meter. Hiro keeps engineering spotless and woe betide anyone who leaves one of his tools out of place, but his quarters are a nightmare of half-finished electrical projects and spare parts."

Douglas' expression softened slightly, as he imagined how the most committed workaholic on the crew must spend his *spare* time. "Continue," he urged softly.

"Well, I couldn't find it at first but then I noticed the red probe of a meter sticking out from under his bed. I knelt down and there it was," said Baccini, looking meaningfully at the captain.

"The meter?" asked Douglas.

"Yes, the meter," he said, waving a hand distractedly, "but also that box."

Now he pointed to a small, black, mild steel container with one side completely caved in. *Probably from contact with the chief's head*, Douglas mused.

"The box was open on its side under his bed and inside it..." He stood and walked across to the box. Private Jones made a move to restrain Baccini but Douglas held up a hand, forestalling him. "Inside it was this remote," the engineer said, returning to his seat and passing the box to Douglas.

"I wasn't sure what it was at first. I mean, clearly it's a remote controller of some sort."

Douglas looked at the inoffensive little item in the box. *Clearly*, he thought drily, not having a clue what he was looking at.

"I don't know why I did it," continued Baccini, "but I thought, I'll put the meter across it and see what frequency it sends out. When I did, I couldn't help but notice that the frequency was 60,174.138792 Hertz."

The Captain waited but nothing more seemed to be forthcoming, so he prompted the young engineer, "Georgio, you're going to have to make allowances for us non-geniuses and explain a little further, please?"

"But that's the exact frequency, Captain, the one used by the bomb Captain Gleeson disarmed. If you recall, I was asked to inspect the unit, after it had been made safe, to see if there might be any clues in its manufacture as to where it may have come from or who made it. I scanned the operational frequency of the unit at 60,174.138792 Hertz myself, not two days ago," he said, as though this should be obvious, even to a child. "There was a memo, sir."

Douglas sat back, all amusement fading from his eyes. He suddenly felt twenty years older. "Are you sure about this?" he asked eventually.

In response the younger man merely nodded, not breaking eye contact.

"You should have brought this straight to *me*, Georgie," Douglas admonished, trying not to let too much irritation show in his voice. The young man was clearly already in the emotional red zone and nodding vigorously, still charged on nervous energy.

"I know, Captain," he replied, "but I didn't know a quarter of an hour ago. I didn't know anything then, other than I was holding the thing that was meant to kill us and it was hidden in the quarters of one of my best friends. The bomb which killed Mario must have been made by the same person. Or if not he, then he must have had something to do with it. I knew nothing other than that, sir, and I went mad!"

Baccini began to sob gently, his last vestiges of composure collapsing. "Why, Captain?" his voice cracked. "Why would Hiro kill Mario? Why would he want to hurt any of us?" The young Italian put his head in his hands. "*Mio fratello*, my poor, poor brother."

The name Sargo Lemelisk sprang into the captain's mind unbidden and would not be shunted aside. *Questions, questions, damned questions without answers*, he thought. He leaned forward to place a fatherly arm around the young engineer.

"Ah know, son, Ah know. Let it out," he soothed, as tears ran down Georgio's face. "But we've nothing conclusive yet. Ah know it looks bad for Hiro at the moment but there are still many questions."

He released Baccini, holding him at arm's length. "For starters, why would Hiro leave something that damning lying around in his *unlocked* quarters? Eh? The man's no fool. Let's hang on to that. Ah'll find the person who killed your brother, Georgie, Ah promise ye, but Ah'm not going to give up on Hiro yet. It's hard, but can you try and keep an open mind? Until we know for sure. Like you pointed out to me, Mario would never want us to blame the wrong man for this, would he?"

Georgio sniffed and wiped his eyes, fixing the captain with a stare loaded with a much older man's sadness and jade. "I can't think anymore. Prove me wrong about this, Captain, *please.*"

Douglas left Baccini with Private Jones, asking him to take the engineer to the bar for a stiff drink. "Needless to say, don't get him squaddie legless," he waved a finger.

Jones smiled slightly in his grim way. "Yes, sir."

Baines broke up the meeting with the councillors and department heads roughly an hour after Douglas left. She was keen to get down to the captain and find out what had happened. The comm call, with background accompaniment of violence, had really taken the fire out of the discussion as everyone began worrying about this latest calamity.

"I'm starting to feel like I'm on one of those ill-fated, cursed sailing ships from days of yore," Burton commented on his way out. He smiled to cover his unease but Baines understood the sentiment well enough.

"You *wish*," she said, attempting to lift their spirits. "Some of those guys got to go to Bermuda!"

He laughed and nodded, "Night, Commander."

"Night, Sam."

Douglas had changed his mind on the way back to the bridge meeting room, instead redirecting The Sarge and Hiro to apartment two of the *New World*'s guest quarters.

The three now sat on comfortable sofas around the suite's coffee table. Douglas studied his chief engineer and, it had to be said, one of his closest friends.

After an abrupt and rather unsympathetic check up, Hiro had been dismissed from sickbay by Dr Schultz and bundled to this alternate venue by the chief of security. The black eye Baccini had given him was blossoming beautifully now, and if he was not already at maximum truculence, then he was certainly on a steep approach vector.

Douglas could fairly commiserate with the engineer, if he was indeed innocent.

All of the *New World*'s crew, with the possible exception of Lieutenant Lloyd, were like family to the captain and he loved each one of them in his way. He felt like his home was being torn apart and there did not seem to be a damned thing he could do about it.

"Can you tell me anything about all this, Hiro?" he asked quietly, hardly needing to state what he was referring to.

The chief looked down at the floor sadly before answering. "Nothing, sir," he admitted wretchedly. "I just don't know what got into him. We've never had so much as a cross word since Georgio and Mario joined us eighteen months ago. His work's first rate and we've always gotten along fine, better than fine. He's one of my closest friends, Captain." He shook his head, confusion giving way to emotion. "But I know it's hard to lose a brother," he added, heavily. "Do you remember when I lost my own three years ago, Captain?"

"Aye, Ah do, Hiro." Douglas nodded with understanding. He remembered how long it had taken for Hiro to seem like himself again. It was about the only time the engineer had taken any leave without being forced. Strangely, it was the Italian twins joining the crew which put the spark of the living back into the chief. The brothers clearly loved one another, despite the usual ribbing of siblings, but rather than being jealous of their relationship, Hiro had been nourished by it.

Douglas thought back to that time. He had marvelled at the Japanese engineer's largeness of spirit, recognising that, despite his hopeless interpersonal skills, Hiro was a genuinely good man.

"You've really no idea what sent him off?" he asked eventually.

Nassaki shook his head miserably, so Douglas told him about the device Baccini found in his quarters.

Baines compiled her meeting notes for the captain after the last of the department heads had left. Her work complete, she hailed Douglas to request an update. He invited her to join the gathering in guest apartment two, but along the way, a comm call redirected her down to the Pod. She was yet to receive any details of what had transpired in engineering and subsequently, this second incident took her rather by surprise.

The door to guest apartment two chimed.

"Come," said Douglas.

Baines entered the room to find Douglas, The Sarge and Hiro seated on easy sofas with drinks before them on the coffee table.

"Ah, bad luck. You've just missed Mary delivering the refreshments," Douglas stated, mischievously.

"*Au contraire, mon capitaine*," retorted Baines. "I just nabbed her down the corridor on her way out. My order will already be en route by now, if I know Mary and her high speed choccy trolley."

"Serves me right for underestimating the cunning of a woman where coffee and chocolates are concerned, eh?" Douglas quipped. "Ah'm glad you're here."

"Sorry for the delay, Captain. I was called to a disturbance in the bar, down in the Pod," replied Baines.

Douglas gave her a quizzical look of concern. "What *now?*" he asked.

Baines looked amused. "Well, it turns out that young Mr Baccini had taken a drink or two with Dewi Jones."

The Sarge put his head in his hands. "What have they done?" he asked.

"Actually, this may have been my fault," admitted the captain, with a slightly pained expression. "Ah told Dewi to take Georgio down to the bar for a stiff drink and to look after him."

"You told a squaddie to take an emotionally unstable young man to a pub and look after him, sir?" asked The Sarge, with absolutely enough said.

Douglas smiled weakly. "Maybe not my best command decision to date," he admitted, looking at Baines. "What have they gotten up to?"

"Nothing bad, but the singing was quite loud. Apparently, some of the other patrons were a little put out by the lyrics," she said.

"Why, what were they singing about?" asked The Sarge, concerned. "Please tell me it wasn't the one about the wellingtons?"

Baines smirked. "No idea, you know I don't speak a word of Italian and I've never even *met* anyone other than Dewi who speaks Cymraeg, but the gestures were pre-Babel – I got those! Anyway, Dewi is assisting the poor lad back to his quarters now. I said I'd talk to them both in the morning, but maybe I'll let it slip my mind."

"A *better* command decision," Douglas stated ruefully, nodding his tacit consent.

Baines seated herself comfortably, leaning forward towards The Sarge. "Wellingtons?" she asked innocently, before noticing Hiro's face. "What the hell's happened to you?" she burst out.

Douglas explained the earlier situation and Baccini's revelation about the items found in Hiro's quarters.

"Ah've asked Drs Wright and Norris to make this new evidence their top priority," he said tiredly. "Hopefully the forensics may show something up this time, but Ah know for a fact that Georgie touched it and even my dabs will be on the box. We can but hope."

"Chief Nassaki was just about to tell us about Sargo Lemelisk. So much has happened in such rapid succession that I've been chasing on the tail of the information," said The Sarge, his manner as always when admonishing his superiors, exquisitely polite.

Baines could not help but notice that the Sarge's body language towards Hiro was subtly changed, too. More like a cat watching a mouse; he made no move, but should that mouse venture too far...

"Yes," said Douglas, cutting into her thoughts, "Ah'm sorry Sarge, as security chief you should have been made aware of any new information or suspicions straight away. It's just been so damned frantic, putting out one fire after another. There hasn't been a moment to get together."

The Sarge nodded magnanimously.

Baines looked back to Hiro. "So, what can you tell us about Sargo Lemelisk?" she asked, indirectly. She wondered how the engineer's story would tally with her own research, gathered earlier in the day.

Hiro looked into his coffee cup but saw only the past. "Sargo Lemelisk was…" he paused, looking for the right translation, distastefully deciding on, "an *acquaintance* of my brother, Aito. I think he was Russian but I couldn't swear to that. I only met him once and we conversed in English. He seemed like a lunatic to be honest. The two hours I spent with him – actually I'll rephrase that, spent with my brother in his presence – he did nothing but rant."

"Rant about what?" asked Baines.

"You know, communistical, hard left fanaticisms or fantasies, if you'd prefer. He was very much for the total capitulation of the Capitalist West, which considering his birthright is probably no great surprise, I suppose. What he was doing in Japan though—" Hiro sat up straight, puffing his chest out a little, "a proud nation of free enterprise, who knows? But there was something more about him, something dangerous, insidious even. I remember thinking at the time that this man, who talks so casually about killing the men of the West, might possibly do more than talk. If you placed a gun in his hand and a convenient row of innocent bystanders for target practice, then watch out."

"He wanted to kill?" asked Douglas.

"Who knows for sure? Many of his sort can be all windy trousers, but I have to say, he gave me the creeps," replied Hiro. His mangling a couple of British metaphors brought the twitch of a smile to Douglas' face for the briefest instant.

"My father owned some very large business interests, Captain, and through them had a lot of dealings with leading politicians across the spectrum. I suppose growing up around this may have sent my brother towards a love of politics. I don't know. It sent me towards engineering – my girl has never lied to me," he said, gesturing all around, intimating the ship which carried them faithfully through the stars.

"She always lets me know exactly what she wants," he continued. "My older sister, Himari, runs my father's business empire now. I never wanted it and my brother, well, that's another story. Anyway, after what my father described as the tipping of democracy into chaos last century, back in our own time that is," he corrected, his analytical mind not able to let the statement lie, "I was brought up to believe that extremism in anything political is inherently suspect, and that extreme left policies are every bit as dangerous as anything from the extreme right. He used to tell my brother and I that exponents of the far left seemed even worse to him, somehow, always imagining themselves on some sort of moral high-ground.

"Needless to say, Aito disagreed but I never forgot the way father described it to me. He likened this kind of politics to a *nouveau* religious intolerance for the modern age. So convinced of their righteousness, the noisier types can't be reasoned with and are capable of all manner of atrocities against any who disagree with their, often insane, ideals. They may even seek to bring down their own nation, if they don't get what they want. Often they operate well outside the boundaries of self-interest or even self-preservation, with concepts of law and democracy meaning little to them, unless it suits their purposes at that moment. It seems the proof is still with us, even when you throw man into the Mesozoic – lunatics!

"I think Lemelisk was such a man. I still hope we can prove that Geoff Lloyd is not." He looked down at his hands, slumping further into his seat.

"My brother bought into the beliefs of the group he'd fallen in with at university. Father was convinced he would grow out of it, but of course, he never got the chance."

Hiro paused again, struggling against weariness and painful memories. He continued, "Hard right schism, division and hierarchical bullying without conscience represent one form of evil, but are usually based in self-interest. All politics aside, self-interest is something most of us can understand deep down, to a degree at least – whether we like to admit it to ourselves or not and if you understand something, you can fight it, out in the world or within yourself.

"Father told me that good men open their minds and drive these primitive, base desires from their hearts." Hiro smiled to himself. "*I do my best, Father*," he added quietly in Japanese. "But when someone's political agendas make no sense," he continued in English, "are perhaps even self-destructive, you can really find yourself at sea."

He drank to ease his throat; he could not remember the last time he had talked this much. "We may have no idea what kind of insanity we're up against here – or who's really pushing the buttons. My father's companies supplied much material for the Mars Programme and this may have been the reason my brother came to Lemelisk's notice, given recent events. Father would never have given him the time of day.

"Growing up, I remember the ceaseless political manoeuvring around this mission. I couldn't understand why anyone would put the importance of money or politics before the saving of our entire race. By the time I got to university – this was still before my brother met Lemelisk – I think I had just started to work out for myself that the pendulum never stops in the middle. Sensible men are rarely militant men. Casting their votes quietly, they make little noise – even though their numbers are usually greater. People like Sargo Lemelisk slavishly follow leaders who lie or preach this and that, but whose only real interests are themselves and their own power. Although maybe I'm underestimating him there, perhaps he just bought into the ranting to get a slice of the power for himself."

The anger on the engineer's face was replaced with sadness as he drifted back to conversations and days gone by with his father and brother.

"When I met Lemelisk, I remember feeling dirty, almost tainted, just being around the guy. The way he spoke about people, simply because their beliefs differed from his, was contemptible. It was like his understanding was absolute and we were merely fascists. As is often the case with his type, the *facts* he touted wouldn't have convinced a child. As long as they are kept from power or responsibility, they're laughable really. He was a fool and I would have walked straight out the door had it not been such a while since I'd seen Aito and I'd been really looking forward to spending time with him." He sighed. "Anyway, long story short, my brother became more and more involved with Lemelisk who, in turn, seemed to become ever more radical and dangerous. I believe this association may have been what got Aito killed."

"I'm sorry to ask, but how did your brother die?" enquired Baines, gently.

Hiro tugged at his ear, again, a faraway look in his eyes. The tension in the room was palpable as he gathered his thoughts. He opened his mouth to answer but was interrupted as the door chimed.

"Come," said Douglas.

A large border collie barrelled into the room, followed by a tea trolley and further back, by a red-cheeked Mary Hutchins.

"I'm sorry, he followed me up here," she puffed. "I just came for your empties. Would anyone like a top-up while I'm here?"

The dog made an exuberant round of the seated two-legs, slamming chair and human legs alike with his tail. He finally settled next to Hiro with his back to the sofa leaning slightly against the engineer's shin, occasionally glancing up over his right shoulder into Hiro's face. Hiro had little experience with animals but felt strangely comforted by this.

"He knows you're upset," said Baines, thinking of a dog she had known as a child. It belonged to one of her English cousins. How she had wished for one of her own but moon base *New Florida* did not allow animals in those early days. "If you're ill or feeling low they sense it or smell it or whatever they do, but they know. They're really good at sensing people's character, too. He seems to have acquitted you. Now all we need is the evidence to back it up," she finished, her eyes twinkling at the pair. "Or should I say, bark it up."

Douglas gave her a patient look of sufferance but Mary spoke before he could answer. "I'm real sorry," she said, clearly embarrassed. "He belongs to Dr Natalie Pearson." She tried to get the dog to move. "Come on, boy, come *on!*"

Reiver appeared to have lost all of his hearing. When Hutchins stood in front of him he looked away, studying a fascinating chair in the corner of the room.

Baines laughed at the dog's impudence. "Don't worry, Mary. Tell Natalie I'll bring him back down to the Pod later."

She watched the young engineer stroking the dog's head awkwardly and being rewarded with a look of guileless friendship. Hiro was smiling as he looked down into Reiver's innocent and yet uncannily wise brown eyes. Reiver reciprocated his smile in that distinctively border collie, white teeth and lolling tongue kind of way, as he tolerated the clumsy affection of a new two-leg friend, not yet fully trained.

"Tell her that Reiver's presence is required at a top-level staff meeting," Baines said jovially. "Sometimes animals can tell us all we need to know about each other," she added, glancing meaningfully at Douglas who caught her implication. As for The Sarge, perhaps he would have been more open to doggy charm had he not still been in full cat mode.

"Ah suggest we continue this conversation tomorrow after we've slept," said Douglas. "We're all exhausted and it's not like Lemelisk is a priority for us out here." He waited for Mary to leave before continuing quietly. "Look, Hiro, the evidence against you may be circumstantial and far from conclusive, but it is alarming. We'll have to treat it with the utmost seriousness."

He raised his hand to forestall any comments. "Although as captain, Ah've got to look into this rigorously for the sake of all the souls aboard this ship, speaking as your friend, Ah don't believe any of it."

Hiro's relief was palpable. "Thank you, Captain. I can't tell you how much that means to me. I would never knowingly hurt anyone, especially not my friends on this ship."

"Ah yes," said Douglas, "and that's the rub right there."

"Captain?" asked Baines.

Douglas looked at Hiro for a long moment before speaking. "We'll go through all this tomorrow but, very simply, we may not believe that Hiro would cause harm to this ship or this crew knowingly, but what if there are other forces at work here?"

"At the risk of repeating myself – *Captain*?" she asked again.

Douglas gave her a half smile. "We were all at Canaveral for weeks before our launch. If someone managed to smuggle a bomb on board – and we know that Captain Gleeson's mining explosives havenae been tampered with, Ah checked with Gleeson and then double checked with the Pod's quartermaster who works under Burton, just in case Gleeson might be under suspicion himself – if someone could get a bomb on board then what else could they do to us whilst we were swanning around civvy street, eh?"

"You thought Gleeson might be a suspect?" asked Baines, surprised.

"Yes, if a rather obvious one, given his background in explosives," replied Douglas.

"But he risked his life disarming a bomb and saved us all."

"Yes, but who's to say he didnae plant it *to* disarm it? It was found and disarmed in very short order and we've only his word that it was ever live."

Baines whistled. "Remind me never to play poker with you."

He gave her a tight smile. "You'll lose."

"I don't doubt it," Baines confessed, a little taken aback.

"Don't worry, Commander," replied Douglas, calmly. "Ah believe that Captain Gleeson is the real deal. But that's exactly my point, given a fistful of facts and a whole lot of people who don't know each other very well, you could point anything at anybody. However, that's not going to happen here. We know Hiro *very* well and the sort of man that he is. Ah believe you knew nothing of this," said Douglas, looking directly at the engineer.

"Thank you, Captain," Hiro replied seriously.

"Is there a 'but' peeking around the corner here?" asked Baines.

Douglas sighed. "Ah'm sorry but there is," he admitted. "When we were living at Canaveral, the terrorists who plotted the attack on our ship may have been able to get to us. Ah'm sorry, Hiro, but what if you were drugged or manipulated, for God's sake, hypnotised! Who knows for sure?" he said, throwing his hands in the air.

An uncomfortable silence fell.

"Do you think that I… that I did it, but don't remember, Captain?" asked Hiro, his nervousness obvious from the quiver in his voice. Reiver snuggled closer, looking up, scanning equipment as sensitive as anything imagined by the genius of man spotting the change in his new friend instantly.

"Ah'm *saying*," Douglas said, carefully, "that it's no' impossible."

Hiro nodded thoughtfully. "I don't believe I've done anything wrong, Captain, but I understand your position. What do you suggest we do?"

"Well, Ah'm not going to chuck you in the brig with Lloyd, if that's what you're asking. The truth is we cannae say with any certainty how that remote detonator came to be in your quarters yet, but to be on the safe side Ah'm going to ask you to stay in *these* quarters under guard for the time being."

"Captain?" Hiro pleaded.

"Sorry, Lieutenant, but Ah'm responsible for all the lives on this ship, including yours. The commander will arrange to have some of your things brought up here tonight. You'll have to remain here until this is over."

"Can't I at least stay in my own quarters, Captain?"

Douglas' expression was a mixture of sadness and discomfort as he answered, "Hiro, we need to search your quarters with a full forensic sweep. You must see that?"

The engineer deflated further. "I understand, Captain. I won't make a fuss," he acquiesced in a small voice.

Douglas looked at his friend, feeling his heart break. He almost wished the man would rail against him. "Ah hate this, Hiro, but it's only until we can get the situation cleared up. However, that leads me onto our next problem," he sat upright. "The *New World* is damaged," he held his hand out flat, tilting it left and right, "aerodynamically, despite running simulations, we're not really sure how she's going to behave in atmosphere."

Hiro nodded assent.

"Also," Douglas counted on his fingers, "we've got one ship's engineer in the brig, my chief is confined to quarters, a third who is bent all out of shape with grief and worst of all, one deceased." As he spoke, his voice broke with exhaustion.

"We have two stand-in engineers from the Pod – sterling fellows Ah don't doubt – but with only a rudimentary knowledge of the ship's architecture and systems. Despite having a first-rate pilot in Sandip, we are likely to have to monitor, adjust and repair, literally on the fly as we descend. We're going to be fighting to stop the ship from being atomised on entry – and we'll worry about the entry/re-entry tense later – and all without an engineering staff! The truth is," Douglas held his hands open, palms up to the room, "Ah'm not sure we can land this bird the way things are."

0812 hours - the bridge

With Earth looming closer every hour, Captain Douglas and Lieutenant Singh huddled around the pilot's console checking systems and planning their eventual descent.

Commander Baines entered the bridge looking bleary eyed.

Douglas turned to her. "Sleep well, Commander?" he asked wryly.

"Sorry I'm late, guys, I was dead to the world and managed to sleep straight through the alarm. I'd better have the computer make it louder from now on."

"Don't have it too loud, Jill," replied Douglas. "Ah'd rather you were late than arrive on a crash cart. Besides, your quarters are next to mine and Ah dinnae want ye disturbing me!" He took a sip of coffee and grimaced. "Och! And Sandip has tried to poison me!"

Sandip looked up from the console. "Sorry, Captain, I'm a tea man, you know that."

Baines looked from one man to the other with mild exasperation. "Thank you for your concern, gentlemen, but there was really no need to send out the search party! And for your information, Captain, Sandy only makes coffee radioactive so that you *don't ask* him to make it."

"It was an emergency. Ye hadnae turned in to make me a proper one."

Singh's grin broadened. "And I'm no poet, but that's slander, Commander."

"Oh, *very* good," replied Baines, tousling the pilot's hair affectionately. "So what do we know, gentlemen?"

"Ah know Ah need another coffee before we have this conversation," Douglas chuntered moodily.

"That good, eh?" replied Baines. "I'd better put the kettle on. I could use a shot in the arm myself."

"You do know that we don't use kettles anymore, right, Commander?" offered Singh, helpfully. "Has it been that long since it was your round?"

"Har har," she replied sarcastically. "My mum was English. You can't break that kind of indoctrination!"

Once the senior staff had their hands wrapped around a caffeine fix, Douglas stated, "We need to continue our conversation with Hiro this morning, but at 0845 Ah'm joining the lecture in the Pod's school room with Tim Norris."

"Is it 'meet the captain day' again?" asked Baines sweetly.

"Nice," said Douglas. "As you *well* know, Mr Norris has worked hard putting together a briefing for the whole crew and staff, to give everyone more of an idea about what we'll likely face when we land. Sarah and Satnam have already sat through it and both said it was helpful – if a little worrying. As captain, it would be remiss of me to no-show."

"I've booked a seat for the 1300 hours class," said Singh. "Have you sat in yet, Commander?"

"I haven't," she looked at Douglas, "but if you can spare me this afternoon for a while, I wouldn't mind tagging along with Sandy?"

"Aye, Jill," said Douglas. "We should all make the time. God knows we could use any edge at all right now."

Douglas entered the school room aboard the Pod at 0850 hours to find the briefing already in session. Tim and ten seated adults all turned to look at the late arrival.

Douglas disliked tardiness in others and was slightly embarrassed. "Sorry Ah'm late, Mr Norris."

This instigated a mild titter of amusement as the sixteen-year-old magnanimously accepted an apology from the seasoned ship's captain.

"I thought you'd been caught up in something, Captain, so I gave your seat away. Sorry. Can you manage at the back?" Tim asked.

"Aye, Ah'll be fine, my fault. Forgive the interruption, please continue," Douglas said, leaning against the rear wall.

Turning back to the large screen at the front of the small classroom, Tim scrolled through a plethora of information using a combination of hand movements through the air and touch icons. The main display showed a vista of subtropical forest and rolling fern plains with smaller pages arranged radially around the focal image. "We were only just getting started, Captain, so you haven't missed much," he said. "As most of us know by now, I'm sure, we find ourselves about to land back on the Earth but during the late Albian Stage of the Cretaceous Period of the Mesozoic Era – that's about 99.2 million years ago in English," he added, smiling mildly at the looks of confusion.

"Don't worry, from here on in this briefing will be in plain language excepting a few Latin animal and plant names.

"We're expecting to put down in Patagonia. What we believe of this place in this period, is that the climate was warm – *is* warm and fairly humid. Sorry, keeping our tenses straight is a problem we are experiencing a *lot.*"

A ripple of laughter and agreement went around the room.

Tim continued, "We can expect lots of forest, scrub and fern prairie, rivers, lakes, valleys and mountains. If we are correct, and with a little bit of luck, it should look like a paradise compared with the Earth we left a few days ago. Indeed, we should be landing very close to what would be the Southern Andes in our own time, if not actually within the foothills."

"Will the Andes exist?" a woman asked out. "I thought the continents were very different in this period."

"That's perceptive," Tim answered kindly, "and technically you're right. However, the tectonic plate movement which, shall we say, laid the foundations for the Andes began around 100 million years before we find ourselves now. Due to the geology of this region, I still expect us to find mountainous areas. Science has imaginatively dubbed these early ranges as the *Pre-Andes*." He decided not to unveil his plans to rename them '*The Petes*' at this juncture, especially while in danger of being raked over the coals in public by Woodsey.

"As we're landing in the Americas, can we call them the '*New Andes*' then?" asked Woodsey.

Tim sighed. *It begins*, he thought. "That would be one school of irony, certainly. However, Old Andes would probably be more accurate."

"Oldan days?" asked Woodsey, upright and alert in his seat, as if expecting praise.

"Oh, *God*," Tim mumbled under his breath. "*So*, we expect to land on a vast savannah quite near to an impressive, if as yet, *unnamed* mountain range," he glared pointedly at Woodsey. "Of course, there will be many differences from the world we're used to, but I'm sure it will be majestic. What we may find a little strange is that there will probably be no grass, not for millions of years, in all likelihood."

A man at the back of the room put a hand up. "If there's no grass what do the large herbivores eat?" he asked.

"The herbivorous animals, particularly the large herd animals, eat the full range of ground foliage up to, in the case of the very large animals, whatever happens to be growing in the tops of the trees."

"Do you mean flying animals?" the man asked again.

"Well, not exactly," said Tim. "We'll have those too, but I was referring to animals that can graze twenty metres or more in the air –

that's sixty-five feet if you're from one of the states that still use imperial measurement. Think giraffe, only eighty tons and possibly over 130 feet, forty metres long."

The same man whistled in awe. Tim was finding this to be a common reaction. Everyone had seen movies and documentaries but there would be nothing abstract about actually standing in the shadow of such a force of nature. The reality of their situation was clearly beginning to dawn on his audience.

"We'll come on to the animals in more detail later. The first thing I wish to explain is that we are about to join an ecosystem in which mammals have barely made any impact, yet. Our ancestors were, sorry, *are* mostly small rodent-like creatures living in holes. They probably fed," Tim sighed, "*feed*, on nuts, cones and seeds, maybe worms and small insects as well, as they do today." He stopped again. "As they did last week," he gestured with a hand, "back in our own time – or should I say forward?" He laughed ruefully. "I hope this is all making sense?"

Sympathetic laughter tinkled through the group.

The man who asked the previous questions had one more. "So if most of the plants are not, as far as we know, being consumed by our ancestors, will *we* be able to consume them?"

"Now, *that* is an excellent question," Tim replied, "and unfortunately we've no way of knowing until we get down there to take samples, but you've pre-empted my next point which is this: Don't eat anything you find down there until we know what's what."

Hank Burnstein Snr read his family the riot act red-faced. There was nothing actually new about this but for the first time in his life, and within this changed reality, Hank Jnr was just beginning to think, *I don't have to take this crap anymore! So what? He'll cut me off? Cut me off from what? Everything we own is a hundred million years from here!* He remembered the promise made to himself, just before leaving home, that one day he would stand up to his father. His anger simmered just below the surface.

This latest tirade was angled at him and Clarissa, Hank's younger sister, especially.

"I saw you making eyes at that British kid," Burnstein battered on, staring his daughter down. "You're not getting involved with someone that far down the food chain, Missy!"

Missy was the nickname that Clarissa's father used. Needless to say, she hated it and Burnstein knew it.

"Tim's brilliant," Hank Jnr tried reasonably, despite his exasperation. "His mother is one of the leading minds aboard this ship."

Burnstein rounded on him. "I'll tell you when you can speak you little *som*bitch!" Barely pausing for breath he spat out derisively, "*Scientists!* What the hell do they know about makin' money? And don't think I haven't seen you with that cute little blonde chick either! Her daddy may have businesses back home, but no way are they in our league. You have your fun with her if you gotta, but don't get involved and don't dare bring any problems to my door."

"Problems?" Hank Jnr asked in disbelief.

"You know what I'm talkin' about, God-damn-it! I can't get that sort of problem fixed all the way out here," snarled Burnstein.

"Fixed?!" snapped Hank Jnr, standing up and growing red in the face himself.

"But Tim and me, we're just friends, Daddy," Clarissa argued tearfully. She looked to their mother for support but found only her usual sympathy.

"Now, now darlin'," said Chelsea in her placating manner. "I'm sure your daddy's right."

"*Friends*," laughed Burnstein nastily. "What the hell do you know about friends? You don't know squat! I know what teenage boys are after and it ain't friends, you stoopid kid. If he comes near you I'll have him on a sex offenders list!"

"He's only sixteen, Daddy, I'm nearly fifteen," Clarissa tried again in vain.

"Exactly! He's old enough and you ain't – I'll ruin him!"

"I've had enough of this. Leave her alone, Dad!" shouted Hank Jnr, for the first time in his life allowing his anger towards his father to show.

He shook with distress, but also with pent-up rage. "We have no voice, we have no choice – it's always the same! Your way or the highway! You've no respect for anyone else – none whatsoever! Never even so much as knocked before entering our rooms! If Clarrie and Tim are friends, that's great and if they become more than that, over time, good for them. I'd welcome Tim Norris as a brother-in-law. But as usual, you've made up your mind without even bothering to get any of the facts!

"Tim's a great guy and he's not leching over Clarrie, they just get on. Besides, there's no sex offender list in the age of the dinosaurs – you're unbalanced!"

Hank saw his father's colour darken in wrath but refused to back down. "You didn't even tell Mum we were leaving the planet, Dad – leaving the *planet*!"

Chelsea looked away.

"Why don't you stand up to him, Ma?"

Chelsea Burnstein appeared weary well beyond her years. "Your father only did what he believes is best for us, Hank."

"He's doing what's best for him, just like always! You know that. He treats us, *you*, like he treats the help – disgracefully!" Hank looked away, his face burning. "One day, Ma."

Chelsea stood now, shaking her head nervously. "No, Hank. It's our duty to obey him, whilst we're under his roof, remember that."

"We're *not* under his roof, Ma. He saw to that himself and now here we are!" He looked back to his father, who looked as if he were about to explode. "Shut up and obey or what? You gonna beat on us? Again?" The young man could not remember ever being so angry in all his life. He strode up to his father. "Damn your money! I'd like to take those towers you built, all around the world, and shove 'em up your—"

"Hank!" Chelsea called to her son.

He tried his best to let some of the steam out of his temper, for his mother's sake, but Burnstein Snr chose that exact moment to go off.

"You ungrateful little sonofabitch!" He grabbed his son roughly by the scruff of the neck and balled his other fist.

"Go on, Dad! Hit me again!" the younger man screamed back. "Better make it a good one because haven't you noticed I'm gettin' bigger and you're gettin' older, huh? And where's your army of sycophants and security now?

Or are you gonna disinherit me like you keep threatenin' to do? Disinherit me from what? Huh? We've got nothin', Dad. You've got nothin' – you *are* nothin'!" He spat the last words, eyes brimming with tears.

"I am one of the most powerful men in the world!" bellowed Burnstein. "*You're* nothin' and you're no son o' mine you li'l—"

"*Most powerful men in the world!*" Hank laughed, mocking his father's tone as tears streamed down his cheeks. "What world! There is no *world*! It's all gone!"

The laughter, crazed though it was, proved to be too much for Burnstein and he pulled back his fist once more, his face furious. "Don't you back-answer me you little bast—"

"Nooo!" screamed Chelsea, desperately trying to force herself in front of her son.

The door chimed and continued insistently, interrupting Burnstein's reprisal. For a moment the three of them froze as if time had stopped, but outside the door the universe was still counting and the chime was soon replaced by loud, repetitive banging.

Clarrie sobbed inconsolably as Hank Jnr wiped his face on his shirt and strode to the door, hitting the open button angrily. He was surprised to see ship's security in the doorway. "*Bore da*, Mr Burnstein," Private Dewi Jones greeted, lapsing into his native Welsh. He stood with one of the major's men, in his shadow, as it were.

"Private Jones?" Hank Jnr blinked. "Good morning. Can I help you?"

Jones looked behind Hank, observing the two women back on the sofa, both in tears, and Hank Snr on his feet, looking like he was about to birth a buffalo. "We've had a complaint about a disturbance on this floor. Is everything alright, sir?"

"A complaint by whom?" shouted Burnstein.

Jones looked at him blankly. "Just a complaint about a disturbance, sir," he answered, tonelessly non-committal.

"Well, tell whichever busybody it was, to mind their own *goddamned* business! And that goes for you two as well!" bellowed Burnstein at the security men. "If I was back home, I'd have you busted for intruding on my private apartments, soldier!"

Jones scrutinised him with little emotion, tilting his head back just slightly.

Hank Jnr saw the danger signs. "Dad, just cool it will ya, you're gonna get us into a whole bunch o' trouble."

Burnstein grabbed his son's arm and pulled him around with force, throwing him down on to the sofa with his mother and sister. "Nobody tells me what to do! You got that?" he shouted.

Jones tapped him on the shoulder. "Please calm down, sir," he said. He had a strangely high voice for such a huge man and his lack of concern coupled with his Welsh accent made the request sound almost comedic.

"Don't tell me to calm down! Don't tell me anything you bottom-feeding S.O.B!" shouted Burnstein furiously.

"Right, very well," said Jones calmly, laying hand to Burnstein's shoulder now. "Come with me please, sir."

"Get your *goddamned* hands off me, loser!" bawled Burnstein. Chelsea ran to her husband trying to pull him back into their quarters, but Jones had Burnstein by the arm and was moving away like a man o' war under full sail. Eventually he looked around, surprised to find a woman alternately hanging on and beating him with her small fists. Hank and Clarissa grabbed at their mother and pulled her away.

"I'm real sorry about this, Private," said Hank Jnr, getting control of his mother. "I'm sorry for all of it."

Jones nodded to the younger man, sympathy in his eyes. "Will the lady be alright, sir?" he asked politely. "I believe we have a counsellor on board should any of you need to talk with someone?"

"We don't need no *goddamned* shrink!" bellowed Burnstein the elder. "If I want a psych evaluation on my family, I'll pay for one! And the trick-cyclist will say whatever I *damned well* tell him to!"

"I can see that's worked out well so far, sir," replied Jones, unemotionally.

Burnstein kicked out. "Let me go you son of a bitch!"

This time Jones spun him around, his arm up his back, nose squashed into the wall. Burnstein was a big man but the strength of the Welshman was appalling. "You can walk, sir, or you can be cuffed and dragged – choose," he stated calmly.

"I'll walk," Burnstein acquiesced, seethingly.

Jones increased the pressure on Burnstein's arm to show that he meant it.

"I said I'll walk, *damnit!*"

"Very well, sir." Jones released the pressure, turning Burnstein back in the direction they were heading.

"But your superiors are gonna hear about this, this *victimisation*, damn you!" sputtered Burnstein.

"Very good, sir," Jones replied impassively. "You can put it all in writing for Sergeant Jackson, I believe you've already met him? You'll have plenty of time to write him a nice little letter from your cell in the brig, sir. He'll be glad to help I'm sure."

"That limey douche bag? I'm not dealing with that *som*bitch!"

"I'll be glad to pass that along, sir. I'm sure he'll understand," Jones acknowledged courteously. "Although, The Sarge is probably the only person on this ship who frightens me, so on second thoughts, I think I'll let you tell him that yourself, isn'it."

Hank Jnr watched as his father was carted away, contempt on his young face. Ushering the women back into their quarters, he closed the door. "Why do you always side with him, Ma?" he asked. "He treats us like property, and not property of value."

"You know why, honey," she said, looking meaningfully at her son. "We have to obey him. We have to stay together, the three of us are all we have."

"But don't ya see? He has no power over us anymore," Hank tried, but Chelsea was already locked into her usual abused spousal excuses for Clarrie's benefit. Hank was not willing to listen anymore. Having lived in a cocoon of his father's making, where all the rules were laid out and God help anyone who disobeyed, any kernel of rebellion quashed before it could form, he had had enough. It was the same all across the Burnstein empire, but now all was changed and so was Hank Jnr, he could feel it. The young man realised that, without his trillion dollar corporations, bodyguards and bands of toadies, his father was... what was he? Just some bad tempered middle-aged guy. Like a superannuated spoilt kid, willing to ruin all around him if he did not get his own way. Hank realised that his fear of his father had always been *only* that; fear, never respect and now even that was gone.

He felt both sad and free; freedom without elation.

After calming his sister, he decided to go and find his friends. The *New World* would attempt a landing very soon now. If anything went wrong, this could be their last day in this life. He knew Tim and Woodsey were busy in the schoolhouse, so he would find Rose.

Woodsey put his hand up for teacher. "Sir, please sir, can I ask a question, sir?"

Tim sighed, leaning on the desk at the front of the classroom. With emphasised patience he smiled, inviting his friend to speak, "Mr Wood?"

"Will we recognise the animals or will there be stuff with three heads or something?" asked Woodsey.

"Thank you for that well conceived and concisely worded question. No, we're well past fractal life-forms," Tim replied patiently. "We're not lost in the pre-Cambrian. Every creature we encounter should be of the normal bilateral symmetrical design. Just like the birds and the bees or you and I. The larger fauna having four limbs, a head, a mouth and a butt. Only *you* have those last two the wrong way round!"

Woodsey laughed, raising his hand again.

Tim groaned inwardly. "Yes?"

"A philosophical fist fight between Giganoses and Mapuwossnames – who wins?"

"Do you know, I was asked that exact question by another passenger only yesterday. Of course, he was only six years old and he did at least get the animals' names right," answered Tim, arching an eyebrow.

"So who would win?" Woodsey pressed.

Tim shrugged. "I haven't the foggiest. You'll have to ask Del Bond if it's the result of a 'philosophical fight' you're after, won't you?"

Others groaned at the mention of Derek and his dubious philosophies. "Are there any questions?" Tim asked in conclusion.

"Clever clogs," muttered Woodsey.

"No, if I was being clever," answered Tim, sweetly, "I would have pointed out that they can't 'fist fight' as they don't have any fists. No thumbs, you see?" Tim looked away from his friend to the other members of his audience, adding, "The halfwit has, albeit accidentally, raised another valid point though—"

"Hey!"

"—and this may actually be useful to know. It has long been the belief of palaeontologists that many large carnivores would have avoided full-on physical violence with one another, both within their own kind or interspecies conflict with other predators, as much as possible. You see, in the Cretaceous, a serious injury – especially if it affected an animal's ability to walk or run – would almost certainly have meant death. It's more likely that most confrontations were more about making noise and posturing." He gestured to his friend, "I believe that Mr Wood is running a master class on this subject down the corridor and who knows, it may even help you in the lunch queue if things get really tight!

"Are there any final questions?" Tim asked one last time.

Woodsey raised his hand once more and when he was ignored, straightened up in feigned desperation.

Tim looked at him. "Are there any *other* questions?" he added pointedly.

There was a general scraping of chairs as the briefing closed. Several people approached Tim, thanking him for his hard work and for sharing his knowledge. The captain was last to leave. Shaking the young man's hand he said, "That was well done, Tim. Thank you. Are there many crew left who haven't seen this yet?"

"I'm seeing everyone in groups of ten, Captain. Sorry you were in the group with the heckler, by the way. It was slow at first, but since Commander Baines sent a memo round urging everyone to sign up, it's picked up a lot. I reckon I've seen about two-thirds of the people on board over the last couple of days and I've two more classes booked for today. Hopefully, I'll have briefed most of us by the time we land. I just hope my compressed course in basic Cretaceous palaeontology is enough, sir. Who knows how close to the mark our scientific guesswork is?"

"It's all we've got, Tim, and it's a hell of a lot better than nothing. Well done," Douglas repeated heartily, and patting the young man on the shoulder, he left.

Chapter 8 | Plain Sailing

Major White looked up distractedly from the report he was typing. "Come," he said, frowning at his office door.

One of his security team entered. "Sir," he saluted.

White returned the salute. "What can I do for you, Paolo?"

"I don't think I can take this next duty shift, sir," the man replied exhaustedly.

"Why not, Private?" asked White, looking concerned. "You comin' down with somethin'?"

"I think I'm just exhausted, sir. I haven't slept in three days and I'm worried I'll make a mistake."

"Well, we're all exhausted, Paolo. It's not like I can spare anyone right now. What's your duty?" White asked.

"I've got to watch the prisoner in the brig, sir," answered Paolo, wearily.

"That's about the lightest duty we've got, Private!" the major snapped. "If you can't sleep get something from Doc Flannigan *after* your duty shift. Now, I've got a hell of a lot to take care of, OK? So don't let the door hit you on the ass on the way out!"

"Yessir," Paolo saluted and left dejectedly.

Douglas stood outside guest apartment two. Nodding to the guard, he hit the call button and waited for an answer. Within moments, the doors opened revealing Lieutenant Nassaki.

"Please come in, sir," he invited.

Following Hiro into his temporary quarters, Douglas saw Baines already seated on one of the sofas. He could not help thinking that the situation looked like a perfectly innocent coffee break in the staff canteen. Sighing, he took a seat himself. *What we've all been through this week*, he thought.

"How was Tim's briefing?" asked Baines.

"It was good," said Douglas, encouragingly. "His friend Mr Wood seems to be a handful, but Tim controlled the situation well. Despite his shyness, Ah think he's got real leadership potential. If we're stuck here, he might be the new *me*, one day."

"Praise indeed. So who'll be the new *me*?" asked Baines, hopefully.

"Probably Mr Wood!"

"Oh," Baines deflated theatrically.

Douglas chuckled. "Don't concern yourself, Commander. Long before that, you'll have enough to worry about being the *interim* me. Ah cannae go on for ever – Ah'm an auld man ye know!" he winked, making her smile. "You really must make time for Tim's course though, Jill, it's worth it."

"I will," she answered. "We've been waiting for you to arrive before continuing, Captain. Hiro was just about to speak more about Lemelisk and how he may have been involved with this mission from the shadows, and possibly with Aito's death."

Douglas looked searchingly at his chief engineer. He seemed to have slept badly and his bruised face was a fright, morning-after.

"Are you OK this morning, Hiro?" he asked kindly, glancing at his watch to confirm. "Yes, still morning, just about."

The engineer nodded tightly, saying, "I'll be better when I can get back to work, sir. I don't like twiddling my thumbs when there's so much to do."

Douglas was about to respond when Baines reached forward for her mug and kept on going... "What the hell!" she cried out in shock. Turning over in the air, she grasped the coffee table as an anchor.

"The artificial gravity generators must be offline!" Hiro echoed her alarm.

"Did you have any work planned in the bottom of the ship?" Douglas asked him, equally perturbed when suddenly his comm binged into life.

"*Sir, the artificial gravity is offline!*" Singh reported anxiously.

"We *know*, Lieutenant!" snapped the captain, probably a little more harshly than he intended. Grabbing Baines and pulling her back down, he added, "Stand by."

"No, sir," said Hiro, answering Douglas' question, whilst beginning to float above his seat. "Nothing planned. This is bad, Captain. There are two generators, one fore and one aft as you know and between them they provide artificial gravity across both the ship and the cargo."

"Of course, the Pod will be Zero G as well," Baines completed the statement, pulling herself into a near-seated position once more.

"Yes," agreed Hiro, simply. "There was never any need to give the Pods artificial gravity as they share ours for the trip and would be subject to Mars-standard once we dropped them off. The mission planners decided it would be safer for the inhabitants to get used to the weaker Martian gravity, rather than swapping between Mars and Earth-standard. The risk assessment illustrated a high possibility of disorientation or making unthinking mistakes when working."

"Yes, yes," said Douglas impatiently, "but here and now, will the temporary staff we have in engineering be able to get it back online?"

Before the engineer could answer, the whole ship shuddered. Looking out of the apartment's window, the three officers were shocked to see laterally spinning stars.

"What the hell was that?" shouted Douglas.

Hiro thought frantically for a second, before the answer came to him. "Our port engine has been disengaged, sir," he said, his concern now replaced with fear. "The ship has been sent into a flat spin, we're nose to tail!"

"OK, OK," said Douglas. "Let's calm down, it's not like we can hit anything in space."

"No, sir, you're wrong." Hiro's mind was jumping ahead. "If we're caught in Earth's gravity well, which I would expect us to be by now, our speed will continue to increase and we'll spin right into her!"

Baines looked from one man to the other. "Oh shi—"

"Ship's brig," Private Jones spoke clearly to the elevator, while opening a comm link to his superior.

"*Sarge here.*" The response was typically swift.

"Sarge, it's Jones. I'm escorting a man to the *New World*'s brig for aggressive behaviour. I thought it best to get him off the Pod for now, so that he can't distress the other passengers."

"*Who is it?*"

"Mr Burnstein. Causing a fracas, he was," explained the Welshman.

Contained within the lift, Hank Burnstein Snr had been released for a few moments to slump against the wall awkwardly.

"*Burnstein? Again? Book him into one of our nice quiet little rooms. I'll talk to him tomorrow!*"

"Yes, Sarge – Jones out."

Jones signed off just as he, White's man and Burnstein began to float away from the deck plates. The ship shook violently, stopping the lift automatically.

"Fabulous," Burnstein commented drily. "The clowns are running the circus again!"

Jones instinctively grabbed the handrails installed in all the cars and corridors to aid balance, in the event of the Pod being moved. He did this reflexively, as the *New World* also had handrails down both sides of her corridors, in case of artificial gravity failure. As a seasoned spacer with millions of miles under his belt, Jones had drilled and trained for this many times. Reaching out for his counterpart, he helped the man back towards the deck and the handrail. Burnstein, he let drift until his head connected with the ceiling before stretching out to pull him back too.

"Sorry, sir. Got away from me, you did."

Burnstein cursed.

Jones tried the doors. When nothing happened he prised them open manually. They were stuck between two floors. Bending to take a quick look, the Welshman turned back to his prisoner with a grim smile. "Ha, champion! It's your lucky day, boy. This is our floor!" He forced Burnstein through the bottom half of the hatch with a shove, before following himself.

Hands cuffed behind his back, it would have been a very unfortunate leap for the prisoner had the gravity chosen that moment to return. After the way his day had begun, Burnstein was so busy bracing for this exact outcome that he even forgot to swear at his captors. When he alighted softly, he was genuinely surprised, but before relief could even find a spark it was smothered by the sweaty blanket of misery once more.

A yelping and barking echoed down the corridor. Burnstein had never met a dog that liked him. However, always a man to steal any opportunity, he noticed that Jones, too, was distracted for a moment. Seeing his chance, he kicked out against the larger man's grasp, launching himself down the corridor. "You're not locking *me* in the tank overnight," he snarled triumphantly.

"Come now, sir," replied Jones mildly, shaking his hand and blowing on his knuckles where Burnstein's foot had caught him. "Let's not be doing anything silly."

At that moment, Reiver sprang around the corner leaping from floor to ceiling to floor, apparently having a whale of a time. Natalie Pearson attempted to follow, pulling herself along the handrails and calling after the errant collie. "Reiver! Come *back*!"

As the newcomers approached, each travelling in a bizarrely improvised manner, they saw a large, shouting man kick an even larger man in the hand. Reiver, at the zenith of his trajectory, sprang off the ceiling directly at the provocateur, grabbing a mouthful of rump on the way past.

"Aaaargh!" Burnstein screamed. "Aaaargh!"

As the collie locked his jaws on the man, his momentum carried them both down to the deck and into the waiting arms of Private Jones.

"*Da fachgen*," he whispered, patting the dog's head kindly and fussing his ears. "Good boy." Seizing Burnstein, he said, "I think I'll have to lock you up for your own safety, sir."

"You can't take me to the brig!" shouted Burnstein. "That monster has mauled me! I'm lacerated!"

"Sorry, sir, you heard The Sarge's orders," replied Jones, calmly.

"I demand to be taken to sickbay! I'm bleeding out!" Burnstein protested.

"I'm sure it's not that bad, *Hank bach*, it was only a little doggy," Jones placated.

"He's a monster! I want him destroyed! I need a doctor!" bellowed Burnstein as the two security officers gripped opposite rails and sailed him down the corridor. Reiver snapped a parting shot at his trouser leg. "Aaaargh! Get that *som*bitch off of me!"

Natalie frowned at the American in annoyance. "He can't help who his mother was, can he?" she snapped crossly.

"I'll have him put down!" cursed Burnstein, over his shoulder.

Reiver curled his lip, showing the *shouty* man a very impressive set of pearly naturals. "Reiver, *no*, come on," said Natalie, calmly but forcefully. Reiver disregarded Burnstein like the throwing of a switch, gently pushing off towards his mistress – tongue wagging at one end, tail wagging at the other.

Burnstein continued to shout and complain as he was led away. "I'm bleeding to death, damnit!" he insisted.

"Well if it's really as bad as that," said Jones, "I'll ask the lovely Dr Schultz to pay you a visit in your cell. Beautiful, she is."

Burnstein's colour drained. "No, not her."

Hiro pushed himself towards the captain, grasping his arm with the vice-like grip all engineers attain through years of tool use and tightening nuts by hand. He looked into Douglas' eyes. "Captain," he said, as calmly as he could manage, "I *need* to be in engineering!"

Douglas stared back at him for the shortest moment before returning the forearm clasp. "Save the ship, Hiro," he said. "Go!"

The engineer launched himself at the door, hitting the open button in one fluid movement. Once outside in the corridor he gripped the handrail and pulled himself onward, running along the wall on all fours like only a career space-monkey learns to do.

Douglas returned his attention to Baines. "We need to get back to the bridge," he said.

After sentencing Burnstein to a day and a night in the cooler, The Sarge continued his routine check of the *New World*'s storage hold. As he tightened a strap securing a storage container, his boots left the deck and he began to float. "Uh-oh," he said.

A moment later, the ship shook alarmingly.

"Here we go again," he continued speaking to himself, as he secured three other cargo crates as best he could. They had clearly not been lashed down after the indefinite postponement of their Mars landing.

Presently, the captain's voice boomed over the ship-wide PA. *"Please remain calm, everyone. As you will no doubt have noticed we are experiencing some difficulties with the artificial gravity. If you are on duty or working your shift, please remain at your station. For all passengers not on duty, please remain in, or carefully make your way to, your quarters until further notice. The repair teams and ship's crew will need the corridors clear. Thank you."*

Mere moments later, The Sarge's comm binged. "Sarge here," he answered automatically.

"Sarge, Douglas," said the captain's disembodied voice. *"Ah need you to take a security detail to main engineering on the double and send two men to the gravity balancing nexus, just fore of engineering. Liaise with Major White."*

"Yes, sir," replied The Sarge. "Are we under attack again, sir?"

"We don't know yet, could just be an equipment screw-up but Ah'm taking no chances. Hiro's on his way to engineering too. Watch his back, Sarge. Ah'll be on the bridge if you need me – Douglas out."

Private Jones left the Pod, steering a struggling and complaining Burnstein towards the brig located aboard the *New World* herself. Eventually they reached the locked entrance and Jones hit the door chime, waiting for a response from the duty officer.

Nothing.

He hit the chime once more.

Again, nothing.

Wearing a puzzled frown, the Welshman waited a few more seconds before typing his security override into the panel. The door slid open and all three men entered the brig, albeit one under duress. The sight which greeted them caused even Burnstein to shut his mouth.

"Oh, bloody 'ell," said Jones. "The Sarge'll do his nut, he will."

Major White pulled himself into engineering at the head of a five-man team. The Sarge turned, saluting as best he could, despite the weightless state in which they found themselves. "Thank you for responding to my call promptly, sir," he said.

"No problem, Sarge," replied White with his lopsided grin. "Runnin' around's all we seem to do these days."

"I'll just be happy if we can stop floating around, sir," replied The Sarge, nonplussed.

At that moment Hiro launched himself into the room, nodded to The Sarge and immediately got down to work, removing panels from consoles.

The Sarge's comm binged again. *"Sarge, this is Jones – got some hellish bad news, boy."*

Douglas and Baines made all possible speed towards the bridge after their abbreviated meeting with Hiro, weightlessness significantly hampering their progress. The captain's comm binged.

"Douglas," he answered.

"This is The Sarge, Captain. We've got another situation, sir."

Douglas sighed. "What in the world has happened now, Sarge?"

"Dewi just delivered a prisoner to the brig, sir—"

"A prisoner?" interrupted Douglas, excitedly.

"A minor misdemeanour, sir," continued Jackson, flicking the point aside. *"Getting no response from the duty officer, he overrode the door to get in and found one of Major White's men down, sir."*

"What? How?" asked Douglas, anxiously.

"Not yet clear, sir. The Major has taken a man with him to secure the area and I've ordered Jones to wait on station until he gets there."

"Who's been hurt?" demanded Douglas.

"His name was Paolo, Private Paolo. Poor sod's dead, sir," Jackson replied. *"Another young lad,"* he added sadly.

"Oh my God," said Douglas, closing his eyes.

"There's more, sir," The Sarge continued. *"Lloyd's gone too."*

Douglas snapped alert once more. "What! He's been sprung?"

"Again, not yet clear, sir. He's gone and there's a man dead. Those are all the facts so far, Captain."

"OK, Sarge," Douglas replied wearily. "Make sure the gravity nexus and engineering are permanently manned and you stay pinned to Hiro. And Ah mean you personally, Sarge. For God's sake don't let anything happen to him or we're all doomed!"

"Yes, sir – Sarge out."

Douglas ran his fingers through his hair, exhaling loudly. "Good God Almighty, Jill – what's happening to us?" he complained angrily.

Baines shook her head, for once at a complete loss for words.

"Ah'd better get down there," Douglas decided.

"I think I should go, Captain," Baines stopped him, finding her voice.

"What's your thinking?" he asked.

"Anything we do for poor Paolo can only be done posthumously now," she answered sadly, "and I'm sure Sandip will be in a flap – with the ship out of control. You're the better pilot, James. He may need your help to bring her about."

"Alright, but Jill," he caught her arm as she turned to leave. "Be really careful. We have at least one nut-job running around the ship, maybe two."

She nodded her understanding, "You too, Captain."

They parted.

Douglas burst onto the bridge to find his pilot and second officer was indeed in a flap – but a controlled flap overridden by years of training and discipline.

The pilot launched himself from one console to another throwing switches and calling up information. As Douglas approached, Singh turned to face him. "Thank God it's you, sir," he said, his relief obvious.

"What state are we in, Lieutenant?"

"The ship was thrown into a lateral spin. If it hadn't been for the inertial dampeners we'd all be smears across the bulkheads now, sir," Singh replied. "I've disengaged the main engines. The whole system is all over the show but I was able to use thrusters to control the spin. It took a few minutes to correct our trajectory but even so, our course is now mainly ballistic towards the Earth – we're caught in the planet's gravity well and still accelerating. I'm using the bow thrusters to slow us down as much as possible but without main drive it will be very difficult to control our point and angle of entry…" he tailed off.

Douglas nodded his understanding. If they failed to regain full control of the ship they would likely burn up in the atmosphere or worse, end as a smoking crater. Immediately after that thought flashed through his mind, another followed in hot pursuit; if they caused a huge ecological disaster, they could even alter the history of life on Earth to such a degree that the human race might never come to be.

Get a grip, Douglas, for God's sake, he told himself. *One crappy scenario at a time.*

"Hiro is working back in engineering," he said, causing Singh to look at him quizzically. "No time for doubts now, Sandy. It's do or die!"

Singh flashed a quick grin. "I never had any, Captain."

Douglas nodded his agreement and opened a comm channel to Crewman Baccini, "Georgio?"

"*Here, Captain,*" the young Italian responded, slightly breathlessly.

"Ah know you're in a bad place right now, but Ah need you to get to engineering and help save the ship, alright?" Douglas asked.

"*I'm already on my way, Captain,*" Georgio replied. "*I spotted the tell-tale signs that we were in trouble again almost at once,*" he added, drily – which was remarkable, as his next words were, "*I was in the shower!*"

Douglas snorted gently. Despite their predicament, he could not help wondering where all the water had ended up. "That's ma boy! Listen, there's something else," he paused for a moment, not sure how his news would be received. "I've released Hiro."

Silence...

"Georgie?" he prompted.

"*I'm here, Captain. You want me to work with him?*"

"No. We *need* you to work with him," Douglas stated emphatically. "The evidence against him smells of a fit-up to me and when measured against the man Ah know – *we* know... well, Ah don't buy it. Ah can walk you through it when we have the time, but for now, Ah'm asking you to trust me and trust Hiro too. Can you do that?"

A pause...

"*I'll do everything I can to save the ship, sir,*" he replied carefully. "*After that, I'll hear what he has to say.*"

"Thank you, Georgio, we have to work together to save all our lives. When we get to safety, we *will* get to the bottom of this, but first we have to land this bird – Douglas out."

Baines entered the brig with as much dignity as possible, given zero gravity, and found Major White kneeling at the side of Paolo's body. "Ford?" she asked, gently squeezing his shoulder.

White stood, slowly turning towards her, his face ashen. "This is my fault," he said dully.

"No one could have seen this coming," she answered compassionately.

"Paolo did, Jill. He came to see me just before his shift, told me he was exhausted and hadn't slept in three days." He looked down once more at the lifeless body. "He wanted to see Doc Flannigan and get somethin' to help him sleep. If I'd just given him a few hours to get help, to get himself together, if I'd just listened."

"We're all exhausted, Ford. You weren't to know it would come to this," she replied, trying to comfort him. "Even if he'd been fully rested, it may not have made any difference."

"Instead of trying to help the man," White continued, lost in his guilt, not hearing her, "I basically told him to get the hell out of my office and now this... now this." He shook his head sorrowfully.

Dr Flannigan stood up from the body and approached the commander.

"Heavy blow from behind, Jill," he stated. "Terrific force was applied with a square-edged implement."

"Dave," she nodded, acknowledging the doctor. "What sort of implement?"

"Well," replied Flannigan, scratching his chin, "I've come across similar injuries before, although this is the first fatality I've seen. If I didn't know better and that no firearms were permitted onboard, I'd say it was a pistol grip. You can just see a double mark where the clip is inserted into the handle. Post-mortem will tell us more when I've cut the hair, but make no mistake, Commander, this was deliberate deadly force. Stunning the man was never an option. It was murder, pure and simple. Maybe he saw his assailant or maybe they're just psychotic, who knows? He won't tell us now."

Baines blew out her cheeks in frustration. "So, how did Lloyd get out?" she asked.

"With Paolo's security key," answered White. "Dr Wright and Rick Drummond are on their way here to look at the scene for DNA, dabs, that kinda thing, but..."

"It's unlikely they'll turn anything up," Baines completed. "Whoever this is, they're highly trained. The disruption to the ship is expert. The question is: how involved is Lloyd?"

"*Could* Lloyd have disrupted the ship like that?" asked White.

"He's a senior engineer," replied Baines. "Maybe not in the same league as Chief Nassaki but he certainly knows his way around enough to have put this together with a little help from someone on the outside."

"Right, so this gets Hiro off the hook then, huh?" asked White.

"I certainly hope so, Ford," replied Baines, her face full of concern.

"Was there ever anything seriously against him?" asked Flannigan.

"Circumstantial," replied Baines, "quite possibly to cause further discord, but let's not talk about that here." She looked meaningfully at the doctor. "There will be time to go through absolutely everything that's happened but that time is not now."

Flannigan sighed, exasperation getting the better of him. "There are only a handful of people in the whole universe now, and we're *still* having to focus most of our resources on the prevention of crime and disorder! How did we ever get down from the trees in the first place, without being tripped or pushed to our deaths?" There was no answer to that, so no one tried to provide one. "Once Wright and Drummond have looked the scene over, I'll get this poor fella into our cold store, until we can arrange a proper burial," he said sadly.

"I hope that wasn't his preference," Baines could not help noting.

"What do you mean?" asked Flannigan.

"We'll have to cremate anyone we lose, either on the ship or on Earth," she elaborated. When Flannigan looked confused, she suggested, "Timeline?" by way of explanation. "If any 100-million-year-old human remains get found by the people in our own time, however unlikely, it could change history, start a holy war, who knows? No matter how clever 'persons' may be, 'people' will almost always do something stupid! So we'll have to do everything possible to preserve the future as best we can."

Burnstein sat in the corner looking lost in the middle of a murder scene. Baines called Jones over to her. "Get him back to his quarters, Dewi," she ordered quietly, "but tell him to keep his mouth shut and behave or he'll be back!"

Jones nodded, making for the American magnate when she called him back.

"And Dewi, take one of the security team with you – when you're done we need to sweep the ship. I want everyone in pairs as a minimum." She gestured to the body. "Whoever did this is extremely dangerous."

Jones nodded again. He and the security officer who helped bring Burnstein in, left to return him.

Baines turned back to the major. "Ford, can you tell The Sarge and all security personnel that there may be a gun on board – as well as a crazy!"

"Sure," White replied. "And what do we do when we find them?" he asked sharply.

Baines thought for a second. "We still don't know if Lloyd is behind this or being used as a blind, so minimal force until we're sure."

"And the other guy? He may not come quietly," White pushed.

Baines looked up from the corpse of the young man, her eyes flashing with anger. "Open season," she said.

Huddled on the bridge, Douglas and Singh were beginning to piece together what had caused the recent malfunctions. "So, we've been hacked," stated Douglas.

Singh nodded. With an elbow on the workstation he held his brow in frustration. "Whoever did this has inserted a relatively simple little program into the protocols controlling main drive and navigation. As you know, Captain, during normal space flight, once we're up to velocity, the engines only cut in sporadically and then only when course corrections are necessary. Navigation then fires the engines, making adjustments to trajectory with small, controlled bursts. This new program, possibly because of its simplicity, propagated through the entire operating system in moments, rewriting our original 'nav' procedures.

"It seems to work by cutting power at opportune moments. Our main engines are clustered in a diamond formation so that directional manipulation left and right is made fairly simple, with the upper and lower points of the diamond providing attitude control, up and down – straightforward. Unfortunately, all this software needs to do to send us spiralling out of control, is hijack navigation every time a course correction is required. The new program simply cuts one of the engines altogether. A split second is all it needs for the ship to be sent off course. Naturally, the more the system tries to regulate itself, the more protracted the error becomes until, within just a few seconds – a lifetime in computing terms and taking into account speeds of 50,000 kilometres per hour – the ship is in a flat spin.

"By the time I'd cut power to the engines, the Earth's gravity, already part of the equation, took us over completely.

"So we're heading straight for the planet," said Douglas, resigned.

"Yes, sir," replied Singh, rubbing his eyes exhaustedly. His night shift should have ended five hours ago but there had been no one else to man the bridge.

"Anything we can do?" he asked.

"We need to get that program out of the system," Singh replied simply.

"Can you do that?"

"Maybe, with Hiro's help, a full engineering team and a few months! The program has corrupted our operating system in a thousand tiny ways and is buried amongst millions of lines of code." He banged his fist on the console angrily. "I'm sorry, Captain. The only other solution I can think of is not good."

"It's OK, Sandy." Douglas placed a reassuring hand on the pilot's shoulder. "What d'ye have in mind?"

"We take her back to factory settings, but we'll lose all of the tweaks and improvements we've come to rely on over the last few years, sir." Singh turned his seat to face the older man. "This is not the same bird that came out of space dock. I doubt even Hiro would know exactly how many modifications we've made," he finished glumly.

Douglas was almost afraid to ask. "When you say 'rely on', might these tweaks be things we need to land a damaged ship?"

"Possibly, even probably. There's hardly a system we *haven't* altered or augmented. It's like a personal computer, sir, they all start out the same from the factory but everyone's ends up completely unique in terms of software and system architecture. If you put even someone as brilliant as Chief Nassaki on one of the other four Mars Vessels, he would certainly be a useful man to have around, but it would take him twelve months or more before he'd really have her measure."

He ran his fingers through his hair in agitation.

"And on top of that, the ship is damaged. Moreover, she's *aerodynamically* damaged and we've got to land on a planet with no airfields, no satellite navigation and no ground support!"

"If we regained basic control we could park in orbit," suggested Douglas, trying the idea out as he spoke. "We have reasonable food stocks for several weeks. We wouldn't have unlimited time, but..." he lapsed into thought.

"We also have seed stocks enough to feed thousands of people for years though, sir," said Singh. "They were meant for the hydroponics Pod on Mars, but the longer we leave it to plant them, the longer we go hungry and if we miss the season down there on the planet, we could find ourselves in a lot of trouble."

"We could take a shuttle on a foraging mission and hunt meat if nothing else," said Douglas.

"That would be brave but extremely dangerous, Captain," replied Singh. "Forgetting what's waiting down there for us for a minute, we don't even know how our shuttle's jet engines will perform in the atmosphere of the Cretaceous. If the oxygen mix is off it could make all the difference."

"But by that standard wouldn't it be even more dangerous to take the *New World* down?" asked Douglas.

Singh shook his head gently from side to side, mulling it over. "Maybe," he said, "but the *New World* relies on rocket propulsion primarily. Also, she has a lot more power, a *lot* more. She's made for hovering, while picking up or dropping off a 200,000 ton payload. Added to that, we have resources on this ship, not to mention expertise that a shuttle wouldn't have."

"So you're saying that we're better off going for it and not messing about with small scale trials?" asked the captain, surprised.

"Possibly, sir, I know that sounds crazy at first, but I'm not sure a trial with the shuttle would tell us much. The scale, even the technology and fuel sources are different. As you know, the *New World* can draw on solid fuel for 100% output and continuous burn requirements, whilst using hypergolic fuel for the control we're going to need to lower her safely and land without ending up in smoking ruin, sir.

"Even the electronically controlled air brakes and flaps which allow her to fly in atmosphere generate enormous stopping power. I don't doubt we'd have a good chance of putting down in the shuttle, if the oxygen mix in the atmosphere is similar to the world we left last week, but this ship would have to go down anyway, so there doesn't seem much to gain.

"I believe the *New World* can do it, sir. I just wish we could use the systems we have now instead of factory settings which were merely..." he searched for the word, "*adequate*," he finished distastefully. As with the chief engineer, the pilot had poured a lot of himself into the ship they loved.

The captain and pilot subsided into a thoughtful silence. When the comm binged, it made them jump. "Bridge," Singh answered.

"*Sandip, this is engineering,*" said Hiro's voice. "*I'm about to reinstall gravity control.*"

"That was quick," remarked Douglas. "Well done, Chief."

"*Well, we're still in a mess down here, sir, but it's something,*" replied the engineer. "*We need to warn the crew and passengers that the gravity is about to come back online, but also that it may go off and on for a little while. Do you remember the last time we changed the coils, Captain? The re-initialisation took time to balance out across the ship? Everyone will need to stay put for a couple of minutes, minimum, while she sorts herself out. Sir, can you make the announcement from the bridge?*"

"Of course, Hiro, Ah'm right on it," said Douglas.

"*I'm ready to go down here,*" replied the engineer's voice over the comm, "*but I'll wait for your announcement. Please state that the gravity will come back online thirty seconds after your message. That should give everyone time to get back to a secure position on the deck – preferably seated – there may be dizziness and nausea issues.*"

"Very good, Chief – making the call. Douglas out."

The captain's voice was heard in every part of the ship and Pod, giving the crew and passengers half a minute to get their feet back on the deck or to otherwise brace themselves.

Douglas and Singh pushed themselves into their seats awaiting the heaviness. Then it came, stomach lurching and was gone again. After a few more seconds it returned, this time to stay. The bridge officers waited out the mandatory two minutes ordered by the chief, just to be sure, before getting up. Luxuriating in the simple act of walking around the bridge instead of hurling himself across it, Douglas said, "Well, it's a start."

Hiro worked in the gravity control nexus near the front of the aft section of the ship, just behind the rear Pod docking clamps. The Sarge, on full alert, watched over the engineer as he stuck his head into all sorts of hatches and compartments. The chief had been banging at a jammed valve for several seconds before popping his head out to comment, "I ordered Lieutenant Lloyd to change this a fortnight ago – hopeless! He told me—"

"Sshhh," The Sarge held up his hand for silence and then they both heard it; a groaning sound.

Hiro traced the moaning to a smallish compartment. Looking around to check with The Sarge, he mimed that he was about to open it. Jackson nodded, pointing his stun rifle at the door. Hiro pulled the hatch quickly, throwing himself out of the way as Lloyd's head lolled out.

The prison-breaking engineer had been stuffed unceremoniously into an access tube, just about managing to turn himself over before being sick – everywhere. There was a nasty gash across the side and top of his head. In his condition, he clearly offered no threat, so The Sarge lowered his weapon slightly, stepping forwards. As he did so, another compartment door flew open with a force clearly intended to stun him and it would have, were it not for Jackson's lightning reflexes. He threw himself clear as the door's arc reached its zenith.

A slight figure, completely clad in black and wearing a ski mask, jumped out of the access tube aiming a kick at Jackson's head before he regained his posture. The force of the kick would surely have broken his neck had he not managed to roll with it. As it was, he fell back towards the exit, dropping his weapon as he fought for balance. He shook his head once to clear it and in lightning retaliation, jumped up to kick full force at the masked figure, connecting with his attacker's midriff, to the left, lower ribcage.

He expected his assailant to fly across the room winded, possibly with a couple of broken ribs, but they merely crumpled. All the energy sapped from the blow, the masked figure continued their backwards roll in a single fluid movement. Recovering with extraordinary grace and dexterity, they crouched and spun, taking The Sarge's legs from under him. Using the angular momentum of this savage arc, The Sarge's adversary seemed to pirouette up into the air, fairly dancing over the prone soldier to run away down the corridor.

"What the—" The Sarge hit his comm, shouting, "All security staff: Intruder alert, aft gravity control nexus. Figure in black wearing a ski mask – do not engage hand to hand, repeat, do *not* engage hand to hand – shoot on sight!"

Jumping to his feet, he ran to the door, rifle in hand, but the corridor was already empty. "Turkish delight!" he spat, shaken.

Hiro opened a channel to sickbay, "Chief to Dr Flannigan."

"*Go ahead, Hiro,*" the doctor's voice responded.

"Dave, we've found Lieutenant Lloyd, but he's injured – a head trauma. Please attend the aft gravity control nexus. I don't want to move him in case it causes more harm, but please come quickly – I really need him to stop throwing up on the gravity balancing controls!"

Douglas stood at the head of the table in the bridge meeting room, leaning on his knuckles and looking seriously at his fellow councillors and senior staff. "We're six hours from Earth," he said. "The ship's operating system has been compromised and we're coming in hot! Sandip has come up with a, shall we say unpalatable but necessary, plan to prevent us from smashing into the planet at 50,000 kph."

He sat, gesturing for Singh to elucidate his plan, which involved resetting the whole of the ship's navigational array and operating system back to factory standard.

"Of course," the pilot concluded after a brief explanation, "if that doesn't work, re-entry will kill us. Or should I say *entry* as we won't have left for 99.2 million years."

Douglas cleared his throat and gave him a look to stay on topic.

"However, if we reinitialise successfully," the pilot continued, nervously, "we should be able to limp down, as long as the atmospheric flight controls can compensate for the damage we sustained in the initial bomb blast. If not, the ship might break up, which will kill us. But if we do manage to land and assuming that the substrate we land *on* is stable enough to support the ship, we should be alright. If it's not, the ship might break in half, which might kill us."

"Good pep talk, Sandy," Baines commented drily as he finished. "I can't wait to get started! What do *you* think Hiro, is this the only way? As I understand it, we'll lose all our custom mods?"

Hiro nodded once. "It's certainly our only option within the time we have left. We must bear in mind that we have to power down, reinitialise the whole ship, get to grips with the old system and get control back before entering atmosphere. I can't see any way of doing that quicker than Sandip's plan."

The engineer wore a sullen expression. "We'll be lucky if we're even done in time. I just hope we're not reaching for systems we've come to rely on but won't have anymore."

He looked to Douglas. "Captain, if we're going to make this work we must move *now*! Even if everything goes our way, it will feel like someone's stolen half the spanners from our toolbox and the chances are, when we reach Earth, we'll be approaching at well over the recommended velocity."

"So we won't be able to maintain orbit?" asked Douglas.

"Sir, we'll be lucky if we are even down to re-entry speed by the time we get there. There most certainly won't be time to stop."

"But I packed my camera!" said Baines.

Mother Sarah smiled at the commander. "You're always trying to keep our spirits up, aren't you, Jill?" she said.

"But we really need to get this ship down!" Satnam Patel stated acerbically. "Hiro, is there anything at all my team can do to help?"

Hiro thought for a moment but it was Singh who supplied an answer. "We could use our entire engineering and science staff as spotters at key locations!" he said animatedly. "I should be able to talk them through the basic re-initialisation process for each station. That might give Hiro and Georgio time to focus on the big problems."

Hiro stood. "That's a good idea. If nothing else, it will save travelling time around the ship. At 550 metres she's a big girl and we can't be everywhere at once. If Sandip can organise that, I really do need to make a start, Captain."

"Dismissed, Lieutenant," he stood too, offering his hand to the engineer, "and good luck – to us all."

Hiro shook it and left the room at a jog. The Sarge, who was waiting by the door, silently fell in behind him.

Douglas turned back to the remaining crew and councillors. "Ah know this sounds crazy but we simply haven't got time to discuss the murderer we have on the loose. Just make sure that we all take extra care. Everyone not involved with the effort to reinitialise the ship should lock themselves in their quarters until further notice. No one should go anywhere alone." He looked at Sarah and Satnam. "You are, of course, both welcome to stay on the bridge for the duration of the emergency."

Sarah nodded. "Thank you, James."

Patel shook his head. "I will work with Lieutenant Singh and see what I can do to help around the ship."

"Very good," said Douglas.

"Just before we all split up," asked Sarah, "what is the condition of Mr Lloyd?"

Baines answered, "A cracked head – again, and another concussion. Doc Flannigan expects a full recovery but, as ever, we've got to tie up a security officer to keep watch over him and at a time when we need them all so badly." She shook her head, clearly irritated.

"However, on the plus side, several members of the Pod crew have volunteered to act as special security officers. Many of them are ex-military and can bring useful skills to bear but, let's face it, we need everyone we've got, whether they are up to it or not."

"Has Mr Lloyd spoken?" asked Sarah again.

"No," replied Baines. "We still don't know where we stand for sure with the man. He could be up to his ar— up to his *armpits* in this, *or* he may actually be an innocent patsy. Part of me hopes he's our ma— *one* of our men. Just so we can maroon him somewhere! But who knows?" she finished with a sigh.

"If we are going in hot, as we've heard," said Sam Burton, "shouldn't we aim for the ocean?"

"If we don't get the velocity in check it won't matter," Singh answered. "Even hitting the sea will be like slamming into concrete – concrete full of monsters."

"No curious dolphins or dewy eyed seals then?" asked Baines.

"Ask Tim," replied the pilot.

"And on that note," said Douglas, "we'd better all be about our business."

Dr Flannigan ran himself and his medical team ragged. Along with Dr Heidi Schultz and Nurse Justin Smyth, he travelled the whole ship handing out a cocktail of 'pick-me-up' drugs to the engineers, scientists and security personnel drafted in to help with the crisis. Everyone was dead on their feet and it occurred to Flannigan that he would pretty soon have to dose himself, because when they reached Earth…

He could not even finish the thought. Instead, he tried to focus his tired mind on the man in front of him.

"When was the last time you slept?" he asked

"Twenty-two hours," the security operative replied.

"Well just take one of these now and another when we reach Earth." He gave the man two pills, watching him swallow the first. "We're all going to need to be wide awake for that kick off!"

Hiro burst into engineering with The Sarge at his back and ran straight into Georgio Baccini. The two stepped back staring intently at one another. After a long moment both men spoke at once. Hiro bowed slightly saying, "You first, please."

Georgio thought for a moment before looking sideways at the chief. Tiredly he asked, "Was it you? Did you kill Mario?"

Hiro shook his head and stepped closer to the younger man. "No, Georgio. No," he said, clasping both of Baccini's arms. "I swear I would never do anything to harm any of my friends on this ship and I would never harm the *New World* on purpose, Mario knew that. I hope you can believe it too."

Georgio moved quickly. Grabbing the chief in a bear hug, he squeezed tight with his head on Hiro's shoulder. "I'm sorry," he cried softly. "I'm sorry."

Hiro recovered swiftly, also throwing his arms around his friend. "There's nothing to be sorry for. I understand how it looked." Hiro broke the embrace. "But now we've got to save everyone. Do you know what's happening?"

Georgio nodded. "We're pointed towards Earth at messy death speed!"

The Japanese engineer grinned at his Italian friend. Outlining Singh's plan, he also explained that the killer had shown but not revealed themselves and Lloyd was unconscious again but still not in the clear.

"So it's down to us to orchestrate this miracle," he looked behind him to The Sarge, "and The Sarge will make sure we live long enough to carry it out, or at least," he added sardonically, "until we all go splat!"

Baccini clasped his friend's hand in his right and took the Sarge's hand in his left. "Let's do it!" he said.

Roughly four hours remained before the *New World* careered into the old world with extreme prejudice. Hank Jnr made his way along a corridor in the residential area of the Pod as stealthily as possible. He had failed to catch up with Rose earlier in the day and was determined to find her now, before the clock ran down entirely. Even so, he was nervous. The captain had recently ordered everyone to remain in their quarters and Hank knew it. Rounding a corner, he saw a dark man and a blonde woman at the far end of another, shorter corridor. He stepped back, glancing around sneakily to see what was going on.

His teenaged hormones could not fail to notice that the female was young and absolutely stunning – although his teenaged eyes naturally registered an absolutely stunning *older* woman, who must be *at least* mid-twenties.

Hank watched as she gave the man something; something small. He put whatever it was to his mouth and swallowed, watching her stride away. Luckily for Burnstein Jnr, the man took a moment to admire the view and continued facing away from him whilst he looked for an escape or run-around.

Damn, Hank thought. He was beginning to panic when he noticed a janitor's cupboard just down the hall, back the way he had come. Stepping like a cartoon burglar in his attempt to move silently, he arrived at the door and tried the controls, panic rising again. The door opened. Relief flooding through him, he threw himself inside, just as the man turned the corner.

The door closed, lights coming to life automatically. As he glanced around, something jarred, at odds with the otherwise orderly nature of the storage area. He was drawn, almost against his will, to a bag stuffed behind one of the shelves. Leaning forward, he pulled it out. Unable to resist, he opened it.

Inside the bag were a few hand tools of the sort an engineer might attach to his belt whilst on duty. There was also a data clip and something which made the young man's eyes widen in alarm.

Rose sat on a sofa in the Millers' quarters. Her mother was in the bathroom making sure that if she died, she would look dead good doing it. Rose, on the other hand, had opted to read through some of Tim's survival course informational handouts.

He had created a short e-zine called *Cretaceous Living* and seemed to think that the title was ironic. Rose did not understand why. Being honest with herself, something else she was trying to get a handle on, she did not get a lot of the things which made Tim and Woodsey snigger themselves into near suffocation. Her lips moved as she took a run at a long name. "Agustinia Ligabuei. What is that, Latin?" She read the footnote aloud, "Sauropod dinosaur, middle Cretaceous Period – fossils found in Argentina. I am never going to remember this stuff!

"*Hang on* a minute, I thought Tim said we were going to land in *Patagonia*?" she said, shaking her head in confusion. "If I ask him, I'm just going to feel stupid again, I just know it. Still, maybe a little embarrassment is better than being eaten by a, what was it, Agustinia. Better check what they ate. Herbivore... hmm. I think that means plant eater and he's got a kind face on this picture, so that must be right." She frowned. "Hope he doesn't have a taste for roses."

Lost deep in concentration, the door chime startled her. "Who could that be?"

Her father was on duty attempting to save the ship with the rest of the technical staff, having stated that he would not be back until, a) the ship was saved, or b) the ship was lost and they would be together for the end.

"Charming, Dad. Thanks for that," she muttered, getting out of her seat. *Everyone else is meant to be in their quarters now*, she thought. *Doors locked and, as Lara put it, 'being good and doing as they're told'.*

Rose walked to the door and, with more than a little trepidation, activated the small view screen to see who was outside. To her surprise, she knew the face well.

"Hank?" she asked in disbelief. "What are you doing out?"

"Let me in!" he said, desperately looking right and left. "Let me *in*!"

Rose hit the pad activating the door. As it slid open, Hank virtually launched himself into the room but was snatched out of the air by a burly security guard.

"What are you doing out?" the man repeated Rose's question, grasping the struggling teenager by his collar.

"I... I just needed to see my girl," Hank sputtered.

Rose looked astonished. "*Your* girl?" she asked, reflexively.

The officer, whose name badge said 'Thomas', noticed the surprise on the girl's face and was immediately suspicious. "Let's see what you've got in the bag there, lad," he said.

"No!" said Hank, more forcefully than he intended. "I mean, it's nothing – just stuff," but the damage had been done. Corporal Thomas gave a double click on his comm and within seconds the sound of booted feet rang down the corridor as his partner ran to join him.

"Hold him, Pete," said Thomas, "while I search his bag. He's out against orders and..." The man tailed off. "What's this?" he said at last, looking up at Hank in shock. "You're coming with me, matey!"

"No!" shouted Hank. "Rose! I was just coming to see you!" he called as he was being dragged away. "I just wanted to ask you out, in case we died!"

Rose was stunned – for a couple of reasons. "Hank?" she called.

"Lock the door, miss," said one of the officers as they dragged the young man away, struggling like a sack full of cats.

Rose's mother entered the lounge just as the door was closing.

"Have I missed someone?" she asked, looking disappointed. Having spent three hours in the bathroom, she was feeling the need for an audience to her magnificence.

Rose simply stood, gaping like a fish's first glimpse of sky. She closed her mouth and opened it again. Eventually she declared, "I've got to go." Activating the door control, she ran down the corridor after the guards.

Lara Miller shook her artful curls and tutted, "Kids."

"Bridge," Singh answered the comm automatically.

"This is Corporal Thomas, sir, I'm with Major White's security team," said a voice Singh did not recognise.

"Go ahead, Corporal," he replied.

"Sir, I've brought a young man to the brig. He was out of bounds, but that's not why I'm troubling you. He was carrying a black sports bag—" this caught the captain's ear and he walked to stand behind Singh, *"—and in it were a few engineers' tools, a data clip and one nine-millimetre round, sir."*

Douglas and Singh stared at one another astounded. At a loss for words to describe everything that needed his attention, Douglas seemed at sea for a moment.

Singh picked up on his hesitation. "I can hold it together here for a little while, sir. It's not crunch time yet and this could be crucial. You should go, sir."

Douglas nodded. "Good man. Ah won't be long, call me if you need to and Ah'll double back – the bridge is yours, Lieutenant!"

Rose approached the forward connecting hatch between the Pod and the ship. Naturally, there were a couple of burly security types barring her way. Before they could apprehend her for being out of her quarters, she asked, "Can I come through, please? My friend has just been carried off by a couple of guards."

The security people looked nonplussed but one of them made a call.

Douglas arrived at the brig on the run, hitting the door chime. In but a moment, the small view screen lit up, the duty guard identified him and the doors unsealed and slid open. "Captain," Thomas greeted him with a salute.

Douglas returned his salute asking, "What's all this then, Corp?"

Thomas led the captain to a cell holding a frightened looking young man.

"And who might this be?" asked Douglas.

"Hank Burnstein," replied the corporal, "*Junior.*"

Douglas' eyebrows rose. "Burnstein! Again! We should reserve your family a suite in here. Maybe your daddy would like to sponsor it? We understand he enjoys putting his name on things. The Burnstein Wing, perhaps?" he cracked.

"The bag's over there, sir," Thomas said, pointing. "Unfortunately, due to the nature of its discovery, it's been handled. We haven't searched its pockets yet. I've put a call out for Dr Wright to look it over for genetic traces but with the crisis... well, we won't be getting an answer today," he finished.

Or maybe ever, thought Douglas darkly. He nodded, striding back to the young man. "You'd better start talking and make it fast, laddie! We're properly under the gun here!" he demanded.

Hank stood and walked to the bars. "S-sir," he stammered, "I don't know anything about it."

Douglas gave him an old-fashioned scowl, leaning closer to the bars himself. "Try again, laddie," he added dangerously.

Hank swallowed. "I was afraid that we might all die soon," he blurted out, "and... and I had to tell her... well, you know?"

Douglas frowned, in confusion this time. He was not really sure what he had been expecting but this was completely out of left field. "What are you babbling about, son?"

Hank took a breath and tried again. "Rose Miller, Dr Miller's daughter," he said, as if this explained everything.

When Douglas did not respond, he tried a third time.

"Well, I just wanted to ask her out, you know, before it was too late..." he trailed off under the blaze of the captain's glare.

Douglas grabbed his shirt through the bars. "If you think Ah've just left the bridge of a ship in crisis to run doon here to listen to your teenage angst about some slip of a lassie you can think again!" he shouted, shaking the young man. "Tell me," he added slowly, "aboot that bag."

"I found it!" Hank said quickly. "In a janitor's cupboard. In the *res* area of the Pod."

He went on to explain how he had finally worked up the courage to go to Rose, reasoning that if they were all about to die, then why not? While on his way he had found the bag, panicked and ran to Rose's quarters hoping to find Dr Jim Miller in residence, so that he could hand it over to someone senior.

"It was all I could think of to do," he said desperately. "That was when I was caught out of bounds by security and, well, here I am and no one will believe me!"

Hank finished his delivery just as a young woman was ushered into the brig by a guard. She ran over to his cell before anyone could grab her, holding his hands through the bars.

"It's alright," said Douglas, waving the guards down. "So you would be Rose, Jim Miller's lassie?" he asked.

"Yes," she said.

Douglas nodded. "How did Ah guess?" he asked rhetorically.

Rose turned to him. "I wasn't talking to you. I was talking to him," she said and turning back to Hank, repeated, "Yes."

This time Hank's befuddled mind got her meaning and he whooped. The teenagers smiled at one another through the bars, temporarily alone in their world.

Douglas stared at them in turn, wondering what the hell was wrong with them.

"He's not been caught pinching pies from the church picnic here! This young man has been arrested in connection with acts of terrorism and murder!" he sputtered at last, outraged.

"He doesn't know anything about that," replied Rose, matter-of-factly.

"Oh, well if that's the case maybe Ah should just let him go, eh?" Douglas responded sarcastically. "It's alright," he continued to the room at large, "we can stand Detective Drummond down, Chief Superintendent Miller here has cleared it all up for us."

"There's no need to be so grumpy," Rose answered, in a way that no lad that age would ever have gotten away with to a senior man like the captain. "Hank was just coming to see me, that's all."

Douglas' comm binged with a message. Singh needed him back on the bridge within the next fifteen minutes.

"Right," he said, returning to the teenagers. "*You* can stay here until we are able to sort this out," he gestured towards Hank, "and *you*," he pointed a finger at Rose, "can go back to your quarters to collect your mother before heading down to embarkation with the rest of the passengers. Ah want everyone in one place and strapped in."

"No!" both of the teenagers cried in unison.

Douglas raised an eyebrow, indolently tapping a finger against his captain's insignia.

"Please, sir," said Hank, "if we're in that much danger, can't I be with my mother and my sister?"

Douglas logged the omission of Burnstein Snr from the lad's list of people he wished to spend his final moments with.

"And I want to be with Daddy," announced Rose. "If this is it, he'll need me there."

Douglas thought for a moment before answering. He spoke to Rose first. "You get your father's permission and Ah'll consider it," he said.

She turned away to comm her father.

"As for you," he continued, turning back to Hank, "Ah'm sorry laddie, but Ah cannae release you now."

"But Captain, I don't know anything about this, I just found the bag," Hank pleaded.

Douglas nodded. "And for myself, Ah believe you but Ah'm responsible for all the lives on this ship, so you must understand that Ah cannae release ye whilst there's any doubt. You're a clever young man, Ah'm sure you see it? Ah'm sorry. Really," he finished, regretfully.

"I've messaged my father, he wasn't answering his comm," said Rose. "Can I go to him now?"

"Not until we hear back," said Douglas.

"It won't be a problem, Captain," she said, smiling sweetly. "He's never said no to *me*."

"Is that a fact?" remarked Douglas, sourly. A moment later, his comm binged with a message which he scanned quickly. "It's Jim Miller," he said.

"Great," said Rose. "So I can go to him then?"

"Actually, no." Douglas looked up with a satisfied smile. "He writes: Captain, we are all under enormous pressure, as I'm sure you know, to learn these systems and bring them online in sequence with everyone else. Added to this, I am informed that a murderer is on the rampage. It will be difficult enough to focus on the task at hand without worrying about the safety of my daughter. As I cannot leave my station, I therefore entrust my wife and daughter to your care in the surety that you will have them safely delivered to embarkation with the main group prior to starting our landing cycle. Thank you – and he signs it – J. Miller, PhD Chem. That is your father, is it no'?" he asked, sweetly.

"That was succinct," Hank commented with a sheepish grin.

Both Douglas and Rose glared at him.

"Sorry," he mumbled.

"But he never says no!" Rose looked like she had been slapped across the face.

Douglas chuckled. "Looks like he's learnt more than just our engine restart protocols this afternoon then, doesn't it?"

Rose frowned. "I shouldn't have spoken to him like that," she said almost to herself, shaking her head.

"Upset the old man did ye? Made him cross?" asked Douglas.

"No, worse than that," answered Rose, thoughtfully. "I think I might have encouraged him to become..." she wore the expression of someone chewing on something disgusting as she sought the word, "*independent*," she added at last.

Douglas chuckled again, calling Corporal Thomas to him. "Corp, what's your next duty?" he asked.

"I'm due to take over security in sickbay in a little over twenty minutes, sir," replied the soldier.

"Before you do, would you take Miss Miller back to her quarters, please?" Douglas saw the look of despondency settle on Hank's face, making him seem impossibly young. "And whilst you're down in residential, could you call on the Burnsteins and invite them to spend the next few hours in the brig with their son. Make it clear they're invited as guests only," he quirked a little smile. "Don't want to give Burnstein Snr an ulcer, do we? As Mr Lloyd isn't using the other cell at the moment, two of them can stay in there – not locked in of course – and one other can stay with young Hank here in the *locked* cell."

He emphasised the word making sure that Thomas caught his meaning.

"As you will have observed already, Hank, these cells have two secure seats in each, all with safety harnesses so that any prisoners can be transported safely, yet securely, during take-off and landing manoeuvres. You and your family will be quite safe here while we attempt to land the ship."

He tried to smile kindly at Burnstein Jnr, but the thought of none of them being safe in any way whatsoever at the moment soured it a little, so that it came off as more of a grimace. "Try not to worry, laddie," he tried again with a little more success, but the young man had already brightened.

"Thank you, Captain," said Hank.

Rose looked intently at Douglas. "Captain?" she asked. "If I can't go to my father, can I stay here too?"

Douglas gave her an appraising look. "Sorry, Miss Miller," he said, "but there are only five seats, four for the Burnsteins and one for our security guard over there." He gestured to the chair Thomas had been using until the captain entered the room.

"There might be a way, Captain," suggested Hank. "I doubt my father will come."

Douglas looked genuinely surprised. "Really?" he asked. He knew Burnstein was a piece of work, but this actually shocked him.

Hank nodded.

Douglas evaluated the young man, a sad understanding registering in his eyes. "Ah have to go. Thomas, let the girl stay here for a while. If the big cheese doesn't deign to show, she can have his seat." He turned to leave when a thought struck him. "Miss Miller, what about your mother?" he asked.

"Oh, she'll be alright," Rose answered scornfully, "as long as she's got her makeup bag and most importantly, her mirror. If we die, the last person she'll see will be herself – you can be sure of that!"

Douglas raised his eyebrows again but decided not to comment. "Carry on, Corporal," he said instead. Nodding to Thomas, he walked away shaking his head.

"Yes, sir," replied Thomas.

Rose turned back to the cell. "Oh Hank, I wish these weren't here," she said, gripping the bars.

"Call me Henry," Hank Burnstein Jnr said with a sudden spontaneity. "Affiliation to my father's name used to open *every* door back home but here it only seems to close those with bars," he frowned. "It's Henry," he said again, trying out the sound of it. It was another tiny freedom from his past, like a hint of blue on a grey day, offering the promise of more. "Yes, Henry."

Hiro and Georgio ran around engineering like the beheaded hens of proverb – into everything. All the while, The Sarge kept station, trying to maintain a view of them both where possible. Speaking via a secure comm channel, Douglas quickly brought him up to speed, outlining Burnstein Jnr's finding of the bag and their subsequent conversation in the brig.

"Burnstein?!" The Sarge blurted angrily.

"*Aye, Ah know,*" Douglas sympathised. "*Stay with the engineers at all costs, Sarge. They're our lifeline.*"

Closing the channel, Jackson approached Hiro. "Lieutenant," he asked, "how long will it take to reinitialise the system?"

"Now we've powered everything down, we have to restart 236 essential systems in just four hours," Nassaki replied.

"That's one a minute," Georgio chipped in morosely.

Jackson sensed both engineers' gloom. "I can see you're worried," he said. "Forgive my ignorance but isn't any of it automated? It all sounds a bit *old school.*"

"That's the thing, Sarge," Hiro answered. "Most of the computing power on spaceships is pretty ancient. That's deliberate because the technology's simple, reliable and proven. Basically, it's about as bulletproof as computer tech can be, do you see? Unfortunately the downside is that it's unsophisticated and a bit rubbish!"

"What we have to do," Georgio said, continuing the explanation whilst Hiro stuck his head into another bulkhead in order to access some old fashioned switchgear, "is get the systems back on line, one at a time and in order. Like an electronic daisy chain. Now, this wouldn't be a problem in a normal maintenance situation. We would simply amble around the ship over the next twenty-four hours – thirty-six if the captain was too busy to notice – making sure everything came online with all overlapping systems joined up neatly. There would be plenty of time to rerun an operation should a complication or confliction arise. Unfortunately, our situation means we have to bring everything back to life in rapid succession with an extended, inexperienced team strung out all over the ship – a team who've had just a couple of hours remote training via a comm channel by the pilot!"

Be careful what you ask for, Jackson thought.

"*Bridge to engineering,*" The comm came to life with Singh's voice.

"This is Hiro, Sandip. Go ahead."

"*All our teams are in place and are...*" he paused uncomfortably, "*ready?*" he stated while asking.

"That good, eh?" Georgio observed sourly.

"*They'll do their best and their best will have to do!*" Singh assured, attempting to prop up their mood with a little optimism.

"Hey, that's pretty good," said Hiro. "You should write it down the next time we're not all about to die."

"*Thank you,*" replied Singh. "*Any idea when that might be?*"

Hiro snorted, "Alright, we're as ready as we're going to be. I'm routing a comm channel to all teams: Team one? Are you on station?"

"*Affirmative,*" said a voice which sounded like Patel.

"OK, everyone," concluded Hiro. "Let's see if we can win the prestigious 99,200,000BC Gates networking award!"

Singh monitored the engine restart process from his station on the bridge. It was frustratingly slow. Gradually, he became aware of a voice speaking his name.

"Sandy...?"

"Huh? Oh, sorry, sir. We're three minutes behind schedule after the first hour and a half," he reported to the captain.

"Thank you but that wasn't actually what Ah asked ye."

"Sir?"

"How are *you* doing, Sandy? You've been staring at that screen for over an hour without a word."

Singh took a deep breath and let it out. "I'm sorry, Captain. It's just hard to sit here, waiting for our turn, with so much going on," he said.

"Aye, Ah know what you mean, but we dare not move," replied Douglas. "Aside from periodic prompts and acceptances, when our turn comes round again, we're going to have it all to do to get back on track – but Ah dinnae have to tell *you* that."

"Yes, sir. The bridge elements of the setup are second only to engineering in terms of scope and complexity." He turned his seat to face Douglas. "Ordinarily, this operation is mind-numbingly dull and long-winded. What I wouldn't give for a little boredom now!" he added ruefully.

Mother Sarah was pacing. "And are you OK, Sarah?" asked Douglas.

"Yeah," she said. "No," she followed up immediately with a little smile. "I would like to go and see the crew, Captain, especially the passengers. My mission here is to provide comfort to people in times of trouble and I don't seem to be doing that at the moment. Would it be OK for me to make a tour of the ship? Even the restart crews, if possible – only the ones who are waiting and not immediately involved, of course," she offered, stalling his complaint. "Please, Captain. I need to be with the people who are afraid for their lives, trying to give them hope. That was my promise to God."

Douglas understood. "Trouble is, Sarah, Ah cannae spare any guards for you at the moment. They're all assigned to protect the work crews and there's still a killer out there who may have plans to stop us from saving ourselves."

"Why would the killer care about me with all these important engineers and scientists carrying out essential work?" she answered, soothingly. "I don't need an escort, James. The Lord is with me. Besides, you have so many temporary security all over the ship at the moment that I doubt I'll be able to walk thirty paces between posts."

Douglas rubbed the new stubble on his jaw uncomfortably. "OK, Sarah, if you're sure. Ah suppose we all have to do our duty and it would be unfair of me to stand in the way of yours. Ah must ask you to stay away from the teams who are working, though. They must not have their focus broken, however well intended."

"I can do that. Thank you, Captain," she nodded, leaving the bridge with a victorious smile on her lips.

Patricia and Tim Norris waited patiently at their allotted station with a female security officer named Jennifer O'Brien.

Major White had flat refused Tim's presence on the restart team at first, due to the danger of attack. He had ordered the young man down to embarkation with the other passengers until the crisis was over. Tim had argued that if his mum was in danger, he wanted to be with her and if the whole ship was going down, he wanted to be with her. This was such an unassailable logic that White had finally relented, albeit with reservations.

Patricia was glad to have her son where she could protect him – with her life if necessary. It also became clear very quickly that Tim had more of a knack with these old-fashioned style computer interfaces than his mother – scientist or no. This caused Patricia to wonder how her contemporaries were faring. Probably wishing they had a kid with them to make *them* feel slow and plodding, she mused. Few of them would have any experience with such old fashioned gear, but kids can intuit anything. She watched her son with pride as his fingers flew over the disconnected panel in one last practice run. *Yes, he's got it*, she thought.

The elevator doors near their station opened. O'Brien snapped into action instantly, placing herself in front of the Norrises, her stun rifle raised at hip height with the stock folded down to keep the weapon short, for close quarters combat.

A tea trolley trundled out of the elevator, blocking the open doorway.

O'Brien stepped cat-like to the side of the door, her weapon tucked into her chest, barrel pointed at the ceiling. She took a last breath, preparing herself to turn into the lift and fire if necessary, when a grunt followed by a massive heave sent the trolley out into the corridor.

"These wheels always get stuck in the darned step between the lift car and the deck," complained Mary Hutchins, flushed. "You'd have thought NASA would have given more thought to the supply of coffee and doughnuts, wouldn't yo— oh my…" she trailed off, staring down the barrel of the stun rifle.

O'Brien relaxed, but only slightly. "What's your business here?" she asked.

"Tea and biscuits…?" Mary offered, nervously.

"Ah, momentous!" said Tim, springing up from where he had been sitting and pushing O'Brien's rifle aside in his haste to inspect the contents of the trolley. "I'll have a Coke please."

O'Brien scowled, nonplussed.

"Er… momentous?" asked Mary.

Patricia rolled her eyes. "It's the way the kids speak at the moment, back home. Last year anything good was 'sinister', this year it's 'momentous'," she explained, shaking her head.

"Ah," Mary nodded, understanding. "Well, I don't know about momentous," she added, smiling indulgently at the teenager, "but I can rustle up a pretty awesome cup of British tea if you'd prefer something warm to keep you going?"

Tim raised an eyebrow. "*Briddish* tea? Will this one be made with brackish water too—OW!" His comment was truncated by a clack around the ear from his mother.

"Sorry," Patricia apologised. To Tim's annoyance, she was speaking to Mary, not him.

Mary laughed good-naturedly. "It's alright, Tim has a point," she said. "You should have seen the rubbish NASA tried to palm off on us, but I had a word with Captain Douglas. He told them to 'sort their act out', refusing to go anywhere without a stock of genuine Earl Grey from Northumberland. That's near where he grew up, I understand."

"That's my favourite place," said Tim wistfully. "I saw a stag and one of the last red squirrels there, when I was seven," he recalled with animation. He was about to elaborate on their family trip to The Great Cheviot Nature Reserve, one of the last green places in Britain, when all the lights went out.

Dr Dave Flannigan plodded into sickbay, exhausted. All he wanted was a five minute sit-down with a cup of black coffee. The security guard posted to watch Lieutenant Lloyd straightened and saluted as he entered.

Flannigan returned the salute. "All quiet, Corporal?" he asked.

"As the grave, sir."

"Hmm... let's not jump the gun, eh?" replied the doctor, deadpan, as he glared at Lloyd's repose. "I see sleeping beauty hasn't stirred. Has Doc Schultz or Nurse Smyth returned yet?"

"Not for a time, sir," replied Thomas. "They've both been in separately to get a stack of stimulants. Dr Schultz was the last to come and go, that would have been about ten minutes ago."

Flannigan nodded. "I suppose I'd better just check on our perennial resident. Anyone would think he was collecting coupons or somethin'," he muttered sourly.

"Is that 'care miles', sir?" asked Thomas.

Flannigan chuckled appreciatively as he walked over to Lloyd's bed. Lloyd had not fully regained consciousness since the head injury. After running all the usual scans, Flannigan had put him into a light, healing coma for forty-eight hours. "He'll miss all the fun, sleeping like a baby in here. Drifting off easily while we burn alive or waking up back on Earth, after all the terror and hard work's over!" He shook his head in annoyance.

"Of all the people aboard this ship that I would love to save from fear and danger, I get this guy! The trouble with swearing to help anyone and everyone, Corp, doing no harm, is that when all you really want to do is kick their asses, the Hippocratic Oath starts to feel more 'hypocritic'. Still, I signed on to help 'em all so I'd better do my du...ty." Flannigan was suddenly distracted, staring in puzzlement at the monitoring equipment.

"These readouts are showing diagnostic results for the machine, rather than his vitals," he continued, almost to himself as he played with the settings.

Thomas walked closer. "Doctor?" he asked.

"He's not breathing!" Flannigan shouted, as all the lights went out.

Hiro was also concerned about how long the operation was taking. They were already a few minutes behind which would be critical at the end of the process. He was just about to hand over from one restart team to another when engineering was plunged into darkness.

Georgio looked at him in surprise as the dull glow of emergency lighting came to life.

"What caused that?" asked The Sarge.

Both engineers turned back to their consoles, typing frantically.

"It's ship-wide," said Georgio. "Of all the timing!"

"This was no accidental breakdown," Hiro called across his engineering station whilst opening a channel to the bridge. "We're under attack – *again*!"

"*Douglas here*," the captain's voice returned through the speaker.

"Captain – Hiro. Someone has taken the lighting circuit offline!"

"We're on emergency too. Other than the bridge and main engineering, where else can they access those systems?" asked Douglas.

"From the very next point in our restart chain," replied Hiro, anxiously. "Sir, this is bad. Not only do we need those people online in the next sixty seconds but if our saboteur is there they could stall the entire restart program. Captain, we need guards there on the double or we've had it!"

Douglas did not need telling twice and opened a channel to Major White immediately.

"I'll need to go and sort this out," said Hiro.

"No," said Georgio. "We need you here, I'll go."

Jackson broke into the conversation. "I can't go with you and be here with the chief," he said, seriously.

"I know, Sarge, but it's not far," said Baccini. "I'm just going to have to chance it."

The Sarge gave the younger man a sideways look, clearly suggesting 'this is a bad idea'.

"No choice," the Italian stated. "Chief?"

Hiro nodded. "Go," he said. "But *be* careful!"

Baccini skidded to a halt at the station in question, panting after his jog through the ship. Fear clutched at his heart. Just fifteen seconds remained before this system had to be online, but when he saw the bodies, he froze. The flickering of an emergency light added another layer of nightmare to the scene of carnage before him. A feeling of faintness threatened to overwhelm the engineer, when running, booted feet provided a timely distraction, bringing him back from the edge.

Private Jones and Major White arrived quickly from the opposite direction, faltering as they too saw what had become of the team in charge of the area.

"What happened?" snapped the major.

"I don't know," Georgio answered. "I got here just seconds ago."

There were four bodies on the floor, all within ten metres of one another. Two were scientists from the Mars Pod, a third was a security temp, the fourth and furthest away from the group was Dr Heidi Schultz.

Jones knelt to check the neck of the two scientists. The male had a massive contusion to his lower jaw. "This one's unconscious," he said, reaching across to the female. "This one's..."

White gave him an anxious, questioning look.

Jones shook his head. "Dead, sir."

Turning the body, it was easy to see why. White was an experienced soldier but he winced all the same. The right-hand side of her face had been caved in, her eye completely crushed. Worse, the pool of blood from the head trauma was considerable and appeared black in the strobing light, suggesting death had not been immediate.

He walked to the security temp a few metres away, kneeling down. The man's head lolled at a grotesque angle. "This one's dead too," he reported sadly. "Neck's broken."

Georgio gagged, turning away.

Jones moved onto Schultz. "Sir, she's breathing!"

"Great, stay with her," replied White, whilst putting a gentle hand to the engineer's back. "You OK, son?" Baccini was far away, completely unresponsive. With no time available for mollycoddling, White grabbed him, pulling him up straight. "Get it together, Crewman! You're here to do a job, so come *on*!" he barked.

Baccini nodded. "Yes," he said, dully.

White shook him again. "Engineer!" he snapped.

This time the light came back to the young man's eyes. "Yes, Major. Sorry." Making a strenuous effort to bring himself under control, he walked towards the access panel where the science staff had been working.

Jones dragged the bodies together near the prone form of Dr Schultz, whilst the major moved the unconscious man gently out of the way too. Turning back to Baccini, White asked, "What state are we in, Crewman? I need to report to the captain immediately."

"Give me a second here," replied Baccini, struggling with a breaker. "That's it!" he said through gritted teeth, straining, and the lights came back on – everywhere.

White's comm binged. "*Major White?*" enquired the captain's voice.

"White here, Captain," he said. "Crewman Baccini is here with me, hence the lights are back. He's looking over the equipment. In the meantime I need Flannigan down here immediately. We have four crewmen down, two unconscious, including Doc Schultz and two dead."

Douglas' sigh could be heard through the comm. *"Ah'll get straight on it. Who've we lost?"* he asked, tiredly.

"Not sure yet, Captain."

"Very well. Keep me appraised, Major – Douglas out."

In his command seat, Douglas opened a channel to sickbay, rubbing his fingers hard into his eyes to relieve exhaustion. "Doctor, we've an urgent situation."

"Captain, I'm a little busy here!" answered an irate Flannigan.

"What's happening *there*?" asked Douglas, stacking incredulity atop an already tottering pile of disbelief.

"Someone's tried to kill Lloyd!" the harassed response shot back. *"Someone who knew exactly what to do, too! They switched the monitors onto a diagnostic routine so that, to the casual observer, it looked like it was working normally. The guard didn't know any better so he assumed nothing was wrong."*

"What did they do to him?" asked Douglas.

"I think they injected him with a large dose of epinephrine, that's adrenaline, and it sent him headlong into tachycardia. He was just starting to arrest when I got back here. It's a miracle he's still with us – and we all thought he had no heart! I'm just giving him a shot of vasodilator phentolamine."

"Will that save him?"

"It's what we've got! Thanks for getting the lights back on by the way, at least I can see which end I'm inserting the needle. It's largely up to him now, but I'll have to keep a close eye on him, just the same."

"Well, there's something Ah need you to do for me, Dave," said Douglas. "Get your bag and get down to Major White in corridor nine – stat!"

"I can't leave him, Captain, he's still well and truly in the woods," replied Flannigan.

"Ah'm willing to take that chance, Davey."

"But if he dies it's on me, James!"

"But if ye dinnae help the team bringing the ship back online it willnae matter! You'll be able to play Lloyd a really sad song of contrition, on the harp, from the next cloud over. If it eases your conscience, Ah can make it an order?"

"No, no need, Captain," said Flannigan, realising he had been trumped. *"I'm on my way – bag and all."*

"Oh no," said Baccini, quietly.

"What is it?" asked White, kneeling down next to the engineer.

"By shutting down this panel, they've completely screwed up the protocol," Georgio replied, exhaustedly.

"Can you fix it?" asked White.

"I don't know." Baccini closed his eyes, sitting back on his haunches.

"Well, do *something*!" White snarled.

"I *am* doing something," snapped the younger man. "I'm thinking – please shut up!" As an afterthought he added, "Sir."

"OK, my bad," said White, standing up. Patting the engineer on the shoulder, he went to check on the two survivors. "Watch his back, Jones. If I'd known this station was so important I'd have posted more men."

"Yes, sir," Jones answered. "But there's probably another dozen stations just as sensitive all down the line and all as under-protected as this one. We're spread pretty thin."

White sighed. "I don't know enough about the ship to make these calls," he said.

"If anything more could've been done, the captain would've seen to it, sir," replied the Welshman, loyally. "He's a very clever man, he is."

White nodded. "Of course, I don't speak against the captain. Over the last week I've learned to respect and trust him a lot. I just wish there was more *I* could do!"

Jones now stood with his back to the wall opposite Baccini, with a clear view both ways down the corridor. "Yes, sir," he agreed. "If it helps, I reckon half the people on this ship feel the same way right now, isn'it."

White was still kneeling next to the stricken man and woman when Dr Flannigan rounded the corner at a run. He stood to greet him. "Am I glad to see you!"

Flannigan nodded to the major. "What have we here?" he asked, bending to examine the victims.

The man with the impressive bruising began to groan. Flannigan held smelling salts under his nose, making him jump and shake his head as he came the rest of the way to.

"Wha?" he said groggily.

"Easy, son, it's Doc Flannigan. You've had a good knock on the head. Can you tell me your name?"

"Parrot, Donald Parrot," he murmured.

Unsure if the fellow was in his right mind, Flannigan raised an eyebrow to the major. White shrugged, a lopsided smile tugging at his lips – '*I don't know*,' he mouthed.

"OK, Donald," tried Flannigan kindly. "Let's see if we can get you sitting up."

"Wha' happened?" the man said, a little more clearly.

"We were hoping you could tell us," said White, kneeling once more.

The man rubbed his head again to clear it. "I heard someone approach, I turned and…" he struggled against dizziness for a moment before continuing, "a pain, a bright flash in front of my eyes and then that stink you just put under my nose. Oh God, my head. Where's Jamie?"

"Jamie?" asked Flannigan.

"Jamie Ferguson," he repeated blearily. "She was working with me at this station, is she OK?" Then he saw the bodies. "*No!*" he cried, his voice breaking wretchedly as he tried desperately to get up and cross to her but Flannigan held him gently in place.

"I'm so sorry, son," he said, with feeling. "But the whole ship's in extreme danger. Can you remember anything else?"

Tears streamed down the man's face as he gulped and spoke haltingly. "Black. A black mask. Someone slight in build – not tall. That's all, I'm sorry."

Flannigan and White shared a glance. "That sounds like the perp who attacked The Sarge," said White. He immediately turned away to report this to the bridge.

Flannigan proceeded to check on Dr Schultz. There was a deep cut on her brow but her breathing was steady. Looking around, he spotted a blood stain smudged across the bulkhead above where she had fallen. It was at roughly head-height for the German woman. It looked as though she had collided with the wall with enough force to stun her, splitting her skin. Her skull seemed intact. The blow had not been strong enough to fracture bone. "Lucky," he concluded.

Parrot reached across the corridor floor for one of Ferguson's hands, sobbing quietly.

Flannigan watched him sorrowfully for a few seconds. Sniffing and swallowing his emotion, he put his back to the grieving man, providing Parrot with a modicum of privacy. He pulled out his comm, opening a channel, "Justin, come in."

"*Smyth here, Doctor,*" the ship's nurse answered.

"Are you anywhere near sickbay?" asked Flannigan.

"*Close enough, Dave. What do you need?*"

"Good, bring a stretcher down to corridor nine please, I'll need a hand to get Heidi back to sickbay. She's OK but she's had a nasty knock on the head. See if you can rustle up a couple of helpers, too, we have casualties to move."

"*On my way – Smyth out.*"

Just a few metres further down the corridor Baccini was barking into the comm, angrily. "They knew where to hit us again! Can we change the order and come back to this station? I'm thinking somewhere around power management?"

"*We could,*" Chief Nassaki answered from engineering, after a brief pause for thought, "*but it would mean unlocking the protocols in the power regulation routines again before we can plug the application back in. It will eat a bit more of the time we don't have."*

"Got a better idea?" asked Baccini.

"Well, no," Hiro admitted honestly. *"Alright, you'd better stay on station there because I'll need to slice you in between power consumption and power conduit diagnostics control. It will be about ten minutes before it's your turn. This is the only other place we can slot that protocol in without starting again so you'll need to be ready. If we miss it, the restart schedule is a bust."*

"I know," said Georgio.

"I know you know," replied Hiro. *"What I'm saying is, good luck."*

"You too, I'll be waiting for your prompt in a little over nine minutes – Baccini out."

Help arrived quickly and White watched the medical team carry the dead and wounded away, assisted by a few hastily drafted stretcher-bearers. He heard Baccini wrapping up a heated conversation with his superior via the comm and could tell that the young man was very concerned about their situation.

The engineer closed the channel and stood, turning to White and Jones. "Gentlemen," he said seriously. "For the next nine minutes, this terminal is one of the most tempting targets on the entire ship for anyone who knows what we're doing."

White nodded his understanding. "I'll stay right here with Private Jones," he said. "We've got your back, Crewman."

"Thank you," replied Georgio and got back to work without another word.

Flannigan and Smyth laid Dr Schultz down carefully on a spare bed in sickbay. Flannigan activated a scanning device, pulling it down over her unconscious form. He talked to Corporal Thomas over his shoulder. "Did you see anyone go near Lloyd over the last half hour?" he asked.

"No, sir," said Thomas, "only you and Dr Schultz, of course."

Flannigan paused what he was doing while Smyth continued to clean the wound on Schultz's brow. "Heidi was over here?" he asked. "Did you happen to see what she did?"

"Not really, sir," said the corporal. "My attention was mainly on the entrance to sickbay, in case we were attacked by the killer. I just assumed the doctor was checking on him. She's not one for explaining herself," he added.

Flannigan raised his eyebrows briefly, tilting his head in acknowledgment of the point and then frowned in thought. After a few moments he shook it aside, continuing with the job in hand. "Not sure if she's going to be able to help us during the next couple hours but I'm gonna try and wake her. Maybe she'll surprise us. She's a tough one, sure enough."

He gave the German woman an injection. Within a few seconds her eyelashes fluttered as she regained consciousness.

Douglas opened a ship-wide channel, addressing everyone on the *New World* and the Pod simultaneously. *"This is the captain. In a little over two hours we'll be entering the Earth's atmosphere and it's likely to be a rough ride. As you know, it's standard practice for all passengers to be in the embarkation lounge during take-off and landing, and this situation will be no different."*

He paused for a moment, thinking, *Now for the unpleasant part of the message.*

"As many of you may have already heard by now, we have a killer onboard, but there should be no danger to passengers if you follow my instructions. There is no need for panic or confusion.

"My orders are as follows: All passengers will make their way to embarkation within the next thirty minutes – there will be security in the corridors for your protection. It is vital that everyone remain in as large a group as possible. No one should stray off anywhere alone.

"You will certainly be aware that our crews are extremely busy with ship's operations at the moment, so we need to rely on all of you to watch out for yourselves and for each other. Everyone please make sure that all friends and neighbours are accounted for and that no one is left behind. Once everyone is in embarkation, a couple of security guards will be left with you for your protection and the embarkation lounge will be sealed.

"Ah will make a final announcement fifteen minutes before we enter atmosphere. This fifteen-minute warning will be your last chance to strap in. Please proceed in an orderly, controlled fashion and we should come through this safely. Thank you – Douglas out."

He sat back, feeling a modicum of relief, glad that particular chore was out of the way – he just hoped that no one started a panic.

Singh was speaking with Nassaki over the comm. "Twenty seconds until Georgio's intercession," he said.

"Understood," the chief replied.

Douglas realised he was squeezing the arms of his command chair so hard that his hands were cramping.

"The power regulation protocols are unlocked," Singh was saying. "5, 4, 3, 2, 1 – Georgio, it's now or never!"

They waited…

After fifty seconds of gut-wrenching anxiety, the comm came back to life, *"Got it. Lock it down, Sandip!"*

The pilot complied immediately, exhaling his relief. "Well done, Georgie. You too, Hiro – outstanding! On with the next, we're still over three minutes behind."

"Can we do it, Sandy?" asked Douglas.

"We're still in with a chance, Captain," he said.

Douglas tried to relax; he felt like a bow string. "If we pull this together you are all getting a commendation. Ah've no idea how anyone will read it, but you're getting one anyway. Ah'd promote you if we had any jobs to promote you to!"

"I'll be more than satisfied if we escape being promoted to glory, Captain," replied Singh, his boyish grin returning fleetingly.

"Ah'll raise a dram to that," agreed Douglas.

The next couple of hours flew by, with everyone living on their nerves. The engineering staff, especially, forced themselves on to new heights of speed and accuracy, the fear of imminent death spurring them like a whip.

The USS *New World* was sixteen minutes from the top of the Earth's atmosphere and they were still nearly three minutes behind schedule – that elusive three minutes which had dogged them from the beginning of the process. The whole crew had risen to the task and performed exceptionally, especially considering their exhaustion and lack of proper training. Douglas knew the hastily cobbled together engineering teams would continue to work frenetically right up to the last second.

Well, he thought, *it's time for the final announcement. Let's hope 'final' is only relative.* He stole a brief moment to compose himself before accessing the ship-wide address system once more, making sure he was also patched into the Pod.

"This is Captain Douglas with your fifteen minute warning. Be sure to strap yourselves in and secure anything which needs securing. Please take particular care to check that children and any pets are safely strapped in too. That's fifteen minutes, people! There will not be time for any further warnings so let's all get to it!

"To all the teams working hard to bring the engines back online: We salute you and thank every one of you for your tireless dedication. Remember to clip your emergency harnesses to the wall rails.

"Good luck everyone and may God be with us all – Douglas out." He let go a juddering sigh, all too aware that the moment of truth was vaulting implacably towards them.

"Amen," Mother Sarah added simply. Douglas looked around, startled. He had not heard her return to the bridge after touring the ship. "So what happens if we don't get the systems back online in time?" she asked.

"We enter atmosphere on a ballistic course at more than three times the recommended speed," he stated flatly.

"It's alright, honey," replied Sarah, laying a hand on his shoulder. "No need to sugar-coat it for me."

"Sorry," he answered ruefully. "Ah think we're all on the limit."

"So that three minutes we're astray," she asked again, "will it make it impossible for us to land?"

"Frankly," he spoke quietly, so as not to be overheard, "Ah doubt even Sandip and Hiro know for sure how it's going to go down. All Ah can say is that we'll be pushing our luck entering atmosphere at such velocity."

He sighed again, running his fingers through his hair and back down over his stubble.

"The ship was built with tolerances, of course, but even if the *New World* were in tip-top condition, Ah wouldnae give much for our chances. With hull damage and the heat from that sort of friction..." he left the sentence unfinished.

"So we need to pray?" she asked, kindly.

"Well, Ah'm in the right company for that, eh?" he smiled. "And that may be the last and only thing that has gone right for me this week."

"Captain," Singh called urgently. "Engineering have done their best, now it's on us. I need you at science station alpha now, sir, as we discussed."

Douglas jumped up, crossing the bridge in wide strides to his station for the next little while. He began working urgently, in tandem with the pilot, to bring systems back online in order. The prompts flew from one console to the next without a human word spoken and seven frantic minutes later, Singh called engineering once more. "Hiro, back to you for the final tie up. Good luck!"

"*Got it*," Nassaki responded.

The pilot sat back exhausted, taking a deep, steadying breath. He let it out, spun his chair around and walked towards the captain with his hand outstretched. "Whatever happens next, that was one hell of a performance, sir."

Douglas stood to shake the proffered hand. "Did we claim back any time?"

"*Oh* yes." Singh was shaking his head, incredulously. "Over a minute and a half! We're only one-minute-twenty out at this stage. Hiro may be able to narrow that still further, now that Georgio is back with him. He also has Commander Baines down there, too. If they can get under the minute, our reduced deceleration time will lower the stresses on the hull by an order of magnitude."

"Great," said Douglas. "Better take your pick-me-up pill, Lieutenant. We need you sharper than you've ever been in your life for the next few minutes!"

"Yeah, I'd hate to miss the fireball!"

Douglas smiled sincerely. "You're the *best*, Sandy. You can do this."

Singh returned to his seat. They sat in silence for a little while, each contemplating the next few minutes and hoping the engineers might yet pull a rabbit from the hat.

A slight buffeting began, growing more intense with each passing second. "This is it!" Singh called out. "BUCKLE UP – WE'RE GOING IN!"

Chapter 9 | The Death Card

Come rain in anger, bend arboreal bough,
This child's reigning tantrum, a new god, for now,
Bringer of the storm, driving clamour and row,
A lost world unmade, the night the New World fell...
...excerpt from the private diary of Tim Norris

"That's it," said Wright, "now hit return and... yep." He activated his comm, "This is Wright and Gleeson, station 234, to Chief Nassaki, we're all done here – over to you."

"Thank you, Doctor and Captain – got it," Hiro replied, a tinny voice through the small speaker, followed by a click as the comm disconnected.

"So what now?" Gleeson asked.

"Now we wait on station in case it all goes to hell, I suppose," answered Wright. "They were very specific about us hanging around until the end. Doesn't inspire one, does it?"

"You're a right comfort to me, d'you know that?" Gleeson realised what he had said and chortled softly, trying to cheer himself. "A Wright comfort? Get it?"

Wright raised an eyebrow. "You're welcome, Elvis."

"Hey, there's no need for that, sport!"

"Sorry, Percy."

"You're a really unfriendly bloke, do you know that?" Gleeson commented, plaintively.

Wright grinned. "You got that… *Wright*," he said, chuckling too, not because the joke was in any way funny, it was simply laugh or cry time.

Gleeson frowned. "Do you think they can land this bucket?"

"We'll soon find out," Wright replied, holding his hand out, "Captain."

Gleeson took it and shook it. "Doctor."

"Good luck!" they said together.

Within moments, the first tremors began. They experienced weightlessness for a few seconds in the corridor where they were stationed, before being slammed back down to the deck, hard.

"Aargh! Me bladdy backside!" Gleeson bawled as Wright's head collided with the rail to which their safety harnesses were tethered. It hurt like hell, but he somehow remained conscious as blood from his brow began to obscure his vision.

"You OK, Wrighto?" Gleeson shouted with concern, above the ambient roar which was beginning to fill their world.

"I've felt better!" Wright replied miserably. The ship bucked again, throwing them sideways as well as up and down. "I wish we were in proper crash seats!"

"Don't use the 'C' word, mate!" bellowed Gleeson above the howl of wind and the now constant groan of strained metal.

Wright was feeling a little confused by the blow to the head. "I didn't, did I?" he asked, mortified.

Gleeson laughed but his levity was rewarded with another plunge. "Aargh!" he shouted again, as his buttocks struck deck once more. "I wish I'd taken that bladdy number down!" he wailed.

The buffeting grew worse, shaking them like ragdolls and Wright was struggling to remain conscious. "The number?" he managed through gritted teeth.

"The one on the back of the ship!" bellowed Gleeson – the noise was cataclysmic now.

Wright tried again, with the last of his strength shouting, "Which damned number?"

"How am I driving?!" Gleeson screamed as they descended into blackness.

Huge. Blue. Douglas' perception of planet Earth stripped to the most basic as it headed straight for him at many tens of thousands of kilometres per hour. Time seemed to dilate, natural order postponed.

Huge and blue warmed up through the oranges to red, with the supplementary, hot; red hot. Atmospheric friction scored glancing blows at first, gradually gaining purchase on the hull and causing the ship to shake with escalating violence.

Douglas felt like an observer, his unconscious mind working a side action processing sound, heat and light as ruby red seared to blinding white. Vibration numbed his whole body as white hot and white noise became one.

Later, he would be left with a vague recollection of people moving about the bridge of the *New World* and someone shouting, the voice far off. Douglas wondered who it could be, as G-forces swept him to a meta reality just this side of oblivion. The greater the force crushing him to his core, the more he stepped outside himself, outside events.

He hazily contemplated the possibility that he might be dying. As the universe raced by at impossible speeds, he seemed to have all the time in the world.

Rebecca Mawar had filled the minutes preceding their descent by seeking the advice of spirit. Lowering a small table from the back of the seat in front, she laid out the tarot cards, always her 'go-to' when personally anxious; calming her through habit. On this occasion, however, the cards offered little comfort.

For Beck, reading tarot had always been part tactile experience, part emotional connection but now... now she merely turned the cards. She understood their message intellectually, yet it meant nothing to her. It was the strangest sensation, like someone had severed a comm link whilst she continued talking to herself, eventually realising there was no one there.

However, all such concerns became secondary as the ship began her descent. The whole of embarkation seemed to rattle and shake, the passengers lurching from side to side in their crash webbing as the *New World* fought the friction; air made almost solid by speed.

The roar of fire outside was matched only by the roar of fear inside, the view ports showing nothing but white flames as a brilliant *surreality* cocooned the passengers completely. All was screams.

A thousand shades of white assaulted Beck's senses as she fought the blackness seeking her. Her consciousness was hanging by a thread when a curious sound penetrated the tunnel walls of her awareness, working inwards for her attention – a dog? While her fellow passengers alternated between blacking out and waking up screaming, the primal howling of a dog's distress cut across it all. This single constant, amid the fading in and out of human perception, gave her a focus, a connection to the world at the basic levels of instinct and emotion. She grabbed it like a lifeline.

Managing to turn her head slightly against the G-forces, she saw him. Reiver – was that his name? A harness around his shoulders was clipped into the seat's safety belt arrangement and standing behind him, from Beck's perspective, were the *people*.

She had been holding on so tightly to the deck of cards that they sprang from her grasp, flying everywhere in chaotic collusion with the madness all around her. Grappling for them, she was able to snatch just one from the air and hold on to it. Invisible forces pulled her head back, her arms down. She could not read its face.

Reiver's commentary continued, but through a haze, Beck realised it was not for her or indeed her companions – he was communicating his distress to the ethereal figures at his side, in the aisle. There were four of them, completely unaffected by the jarring motions of the ship; three men and a woman. Two were soldiers, one was middle-aged, the other fairly young. The third man looked younger still, boyish even. An expression of great sadness marred the woman's face, but she held out a hand to calm the distressed animal.

Reiver whined, crouching and conscious amid the maelstrom. Hunter's reflexes, honed through a hundred thousand fathers, kept him planted. Conversely, the rows of seated passengers were thrown back and forth in vicious synchronicity, like ears of wheat in the wind.

BANG! The whole ship rocked. Everything not tied down flew through the air. Douglas experienced the vague notion of a cup and a saucer, seeming to hover for a moment.

BANG! Time returned and he was in the middle of it. The same man was still shouting... *My God*, he thought, *it's me! Ah'm shouting!* Listening to *what* he was shouting made sense of the last few seconds.

The bridge came back into focus suddenly and sharply: his ship, his crew, surrounded by fire and clamour.

"Reverse thrusters to maximum!" he heard himself cry. Years of conditioning brought forth his next order without need of conscious interference. "Bring main engines online!"

"I'm trying!" shouted another voice. "Five seconds."

The heat was suddenly unbearable. Douglas, falling irresistibly back inside himself, could see white flames engulfing the forward viewports of the bridge. Huge and blue were gone. A console exploded somewhere off to his left. *That won't help*, he thought, peripherally.

The *New World* bucked savagely, flinging pieces of hull past the windows, all instantly vaporised on their way to oblivion.

Blackness reached for Douglas once more. Instinct told him it was the final darkness and he fought with all his remaining strength to stay in the light. When he heard the prayer he was not sure if his mind was playing tricks on him – someone was praying. Would that help? Maybe he should try it?

"Bring the engines online!" someone roared from a distance. He was disconnected again, unsure if the voice was his own.

"ENGINES ONLINE!" an answering bellow filled the bridge, followed instantly by pain.

The sudden forces pushing Douglas into his safety harness were intolerable and despite his effort of will, he blacked out, only to come round to black out again. Failure's embrace seemed to close all around him when a subtle change drew a new fate for his crew, like a drop in pressure prickling his skin. The deafening roar became merely too loud for comfort as white returned to red, gradually reintroducing blue. Huge was everywhere, he was merely too close to see it.

Cooling enveloped the battered ship like a balm, quenching the sudden nova as the last few minutes' insanity bled back to reality. Remnant ticks and pings of contraction were the only testimony to the crucible survived.

"Where are we, Lieutenant?" His voice again, good, he recognised it now as normality crashed back in their wake.

"Bringing the ship around onto our pre-calculated trajectory, sir," replied Lieutenant Singh.

"You mean we're going to make it, Sandy?" Douglas asked, afraid to believe.

The pilot flashed a quick grin over his shoulder. "Was there ever any doubt, Captain?"

"Steady as she goes, Mr Singh," said Douglas, sighing with relief. Something snagged at his memory making him look around. "Where's ma damned coffee gone? That was ma favourite cup!"

After a seemingly endless time, the ship began to calm. A healing blue gradually replaced the fires of hell at the window and with it their terrors began to subside. Despite much groaning and vomiting, a relative peace settled over embarkation.

The forces pushing Beck down relented. She lifted her head to find the ethereal woman staring directly at her. When she spoke, it was across the room as across the void, "Tell Donald it wasn't his fault and tell him that I love him. I will always love him."

Beck was left with a sense of the familiar. Sudden understanding followed: the four had found her and would remain ever near. With that realisation, a name shunted into her fore-mind – Jamie!

The apparition of Dr Jamie Ferguson flashed a last inscrutable smile, before fading from the medium's sensitivity once more.

Feeling dazed, Beck's confusion was more physical than spiritual, the belated effects of a teeth-rattling re-entry. She knew the four dead crew members had reached out to her for a reason but, at the moment, it eluded her. She closed her eyes in relief and drifted for a while, grateful that she was no longer alone among all these people...

...As the roaring outside petered away to ordinary wind noise and buffeting, Beck remembered the card still clutched in her hand. She knew in her heart that nothing would ever be the same. Almost afraid to look, she unfolded it, revealing the grinning skull of the Death card.

Roughly 99.2 million years ago, Earth, Mid-Cretaceous Period

Pre-dawn Gondwana languished in deep blue stillness, the clean night air heavy only with the scent of pine. At the edge of a vast plain, a huge neck craned over the canopy just inside the tree line, a pair of docile eyes turning gently skyward.

Sniff, sniff...

Darkness always bred fear in the forest. The nocturnal hunter, epicentre to each ripple of dread among the trees, was ever close. Of course, for some, these pygmy wars were of little consequence. For some, their natural enemies were simply too small to hurt them anymore.

BANG! The silence was ripped by a sound louder than any of the ears to hear it had ever heard. Bang, *Bang,* again. The sky was instantly smaller. Blackened and bulky, it encroached upon treetops bent double by the sudden and colossal winds tearing between them, around them, at them. Something *beyond* huge clipped, cropped and collected the topmost boughs with a rending as terrifying as it was unexpected – and then came the flames.

Shocked awake, every creature in the forest stared up into the night, fire reflecting in a thousand wide eyes. Even giants, barely able to recall fear, began to realise that size was suddenly no protection at all. A crack of lightning followed immediately by a rolling boom of thunder shook the ground, providing the final aid to memory.

The stampede was born in the white of an eye but swiftly matured into madness – **ROAR!** The panicked herd moved, unstoppable.

A sluicing rain began all at once, adding misery to turmoil as the bellows of living Titanosaurs inflated to a deafening crescendo. Driven by terror, they smashed their way through the forest's edge, each massive footfall compressing sodden ground to sucking, drowning mire; lethal traps for their much smaller neighbours, startled from slumber just moments before, only to be sent running or winging for their lives, desperate to escape the trail of death and destruction left by these gentle giants turned monstrous.

Above it all, the black, westerly sky swallowed the USS *New World* whole, completely unseeing of mankind's first ever scar upon the planet.

The bridge rang with the latest round of warnings and alarms.

"Turn that damned row off!" Douglas shouted above the din as Baines burst through the doors. She had done all she could down in engineering during entry to atmosphere. When the *New World* gained the relative calm of the lower stratosphere, she took the opportunity to return to the bridge for the final landing.

"Where are we going?" she called over the buffeting, strapping in to her seat and silencing the noise.

"Who the hell knows?" Singh shouted into the post klaxon, relative quiet, his barely checked panic palpable. "Trust us to land on the night side after all that blue sky and sunshine! Can someone call up a map? We made sensor passes days ago."

The commander called up the scans taken from a few million kilometres out and frowned with concern. "They're not very detailed. Did we manage to get anything closer?" She looked towards Douglas, hopefully.

"We didnae have the time to look around," he snapped reproachfully. "We were too busy diving at Mach 50 with the computers down!"

"I didn't say anything," she replied, holding her hands up.

"Oh no," Singh muttered.

The two senior officers snapped back around. "What?" they asked in unison.

"It's raining."

"Sandy!" shouted Baines. "You scared the hell out of me!"

"Well, when we get back I'm going to have a few choice words for the engineers at NASA!" Singh called over his shoulder.

"Why, what's wrong?" asked Douglas.

Singh turned around for the briefest second. "No bloody windscreen wipers!" he snapped. "I can't see a damned thing, but if either of you has any preference for a crash site, now would be the time to call out!"

"Dinnae crash my ship!" bellowed Douglas over the wind noise. "That's an order, Lieutenant!"

"Can't you land by instruments?" asked Baines, fear overriding rational thought for a moment.

"What, using all these handy, triangulating satellite feeds we have, you mean?" the pilot retorted.

"Oh," mumbled the digital girl lost in a pre-analogue world, adjusting quietly.

"We are also short of a few landmarks, Commander, what with no human being ever seeing this continent before!"

"Right, sorry, Sandy. Stay calm."

"Stay calm? Certainly, now it's too dark to see, maybe we should stop work and hold a poetry evening perhaps? Hmm?"

"All right, keep your hair on!" Baines rejoindered, scanning the topography ahead.

"Our proximity to the ground is becoming intimate, people!" Singh pointed out, the high-pitched edge of fear in his voice.

"Alright, *alright*. Five miles straight ahead, a large clearing in the forest with a nearby river." She glanced at Douglas. "This could work for us – for now anyway."

He nodded. "Sandip, head for that clearing and hit the brakes or we'll be drilled into the Earth!"

"No, Captain. That was Jules Verne. This is journey to the middle of God knows where, sir... Don't panic, don't panic, we're alright, we're *alright*," said Singh, fighting a war on two fronts; one against the ship, the other against himself. "If only one of the other fleet pilots were here—"

"You'll do fine, Sandy."

"—instead of me!"

"Ah."

The clearing in the forest was before them almost at once, the ground terrifyingly close. Singh gave an involuntary ululation of dread, stuttering into silence as the USS *New World* miraculously came to a full and final stop. The rain smashed off her hull, flowing down her flanks and over her wings like flying waterfalls as she hovered.

"*Well done*, Mr Singh! Ah think Ah speak for all of us when Ah say that Ah'm glad you *were* here." Douglas spoke quietly into the brand new calm. "Now set her down gently, Lieutenant."

"Yes, sir."

Singh slowly and expertly lowered the 550 metre long behemoth towards the ground, her enormous mass mocking, flicking away the natural laws of the world offering her safety and respite as if they were mere guidelines.

"One hundred metres," the pilot counted down, back in the office now, after the wild ride. "Fifty metres, twenty metres, fifteen," a slight shudder gave the impression of resistance, "ten metres, five and..."

There was no boom, nor really even a bump – squelch sort of described it, magnified by over 200,000 tons of mud displacement.

Douglas released the straps from his safety harness and cautiously walked over to the pilot. "Ye did put the landing struts down?" he asked.

Singh looked up at him. "I did, but I reckon they're probably about fifteen metres under the mud now, Captain," he answered.

"Ah, that was the—" Douglas began.

"Yes, sir," Singh cut him off, pre-empting the question.

The bridge crew breathed a collective sigh of relief.

"Are we really a hundred million years in the past?" Baines asked into what felt like an unnatural silence. There was a quaver to her voice which could have been awe or perhaps even a little hysteria after the day they had survived.

"Aye," replied Douglas, his focus out through the viewports. "We're really early. Way too early. It's just no' right." He was unsure if his eyes were playing tricks on him, but he fancied that black was paling to the blue of a rapidly approaching dawn.

"Guests who arrive too early are never welcome," Baines commented distractedly. She was still a little stunned. They all were.

"Aye," repeated Douglas, gravely, "but our situation is a wee bit more serious than merely surprising Mother Earth while she's still in her bathrobe, pushing the Hoover around."

Someone began to laugh and before they knew it they were all laughing, jumping out of their seats and slapping each other on the back. Baines even tried a little victory dance; it was not well done, but that did not stop everyone from joining in and hooting for the sheer joy of a life continued.

Mother Sarah jigged around like a novice left in charge of the keys to the communion wine on New Year's Eve. "Thank you, God," she called out in jubilation and absolute sincerity.

Douglas pulled Baines and Singh into a hug. "Ah can hardly believe it," he cried.

"We had to make it so we can leave a little something for the future," Baines replied quietly, as Singh grabbed Sarah, dancing the priest around the bridge. "Knowing about that has kinda got me through all this."

Douglas nodded his understanding and opened a channel across the whole ship. "This is the captain speaking. People, we are *down*! All stations please report."

Cheers erupted across the *New World* and the Pod. Everywhere, people released safety harnesses and jumped from their seats to hug friends and loved ones, joy pushing back any exhaustion in a willing suspension of disconsolation. A dog barked like all his tea-times had come at once, wagging his tail so hard that he and his mistress went down in a flailing of limbs, laughter and licks…

…Outside, the world wrapped up its last remaining secrets in protective darkness before the new dawn consumed them.

Within an hour of the *New World*'s arrival, the sun rose over the old world and it was magnificent. Almost five days of constant worry and tension left the crew like a dam-burst.

Eventually their exuberance calmed, as did the storm outside and anyone not hospitalised, in jail, or guarding those unfortunates, crowded around the windows in embarkation. Refugees from a world of smog, steel and concrete, they took it in turns to press their faces against the portholes, each marvelling at this completely unsullied landscape and its fantastic creatures. Theirs was a vista aglow with every green of plain, forest and mountain, while snowy caps sealed away all the emeralds of the earth from the azure touch of a brand-new sky. This was a place none of them had ever seen before. This was the planet Earth.

Douglas stood alone on his bridge, lost in thought. The crew and passengers needed a little time to take in their surroundings. He understood that. Meanwhile, he used that time to work out just what he was going to say to them. Staring through the front viewports, he found himself distracted by what he saw. How could anyone be immune to such beauty?

Whoever said blue and green should ne'er be seen had ne'er the plains of the Cretaceous been. He smiled to himself as he corrupted the old saying in his mind – perhaps not brilliantly. It was something he remembered from his childhood, back in Scotland. That had been a beautiful cloudless day too, in many ways like this one. His parents had taken him on a day-trip to Abb's Head.

He remembered his father explaining how the place derived its name from Saint Æbbe, the first abbess of the Abbey founded in the 7th century and the remarkable sister of a remarkable brother – King, and posthumously Saint, Oswald.

Here, now, he understood the yearning of his ancient forebears to seek and comprehend the face of God; to find meaning in the relentless grind of time.

He recalled the warmth of the sun on his little boy's face, as he tried to scale the rocky cliffs at Coldingham Bay, weird and otherworldly shaped. He could still picture the blueness of the North Sea, ancient beyond his imagining – until today.

What a mystery it had all seemed, and now he was lost in a past, well over 16,000 times the age of the very sea that little boy had believed was eternal. Perhaps eight or nine at the time, he recalled pulling a green sweater over his shirt, with blue jeans. His mother had told him to change it, because 'blue and green should ne'er be seen'.

The great North Sea, he mused. The sea and even the cliffs themselves, as he knew them, were once unfathomably old to human eyes. Now they all waited to be taken out of the box, brand new, but not for a mountain's age to come; possibly several.

It is remarkable how children soak up facts and names so easily. In his mind, Douglas could still hear his father reading from a plaque, "The Coldingham rock stratum may have been laid down as early as the Ordovician Period." He would not have remembered the name for five minutes now, nor Æbbe, for that matter. From *when* he stood today, those rocks had begun their long existence 350 million years ago, so that 100 million years from now, a little boy could climb them and get into trouble for tearing his jeans. He smiled again, staring down his past, hindsight all in the future.

Understanding that even the North Sea's time on this Earth would be fleeting at best, he just hoped and prayed that it would *be* at all. Everything was so mixed up, even the days. The explosion which destroyed the wormhole drive was last Sunday and now, if Singh was correct about his dates, after less than five days in space it was Sunday *again*.

His head ached. He held it in his hands, trying to massage some life back into his tired mind. Almost *anything* they did would alter *something*.

Who knew just what kind of changes might be wrought by his band of castaways.

My God, we're going to have to be so *careful*, he thought sombrely.

The enormity of their responsibility fell upon Douglas like an Acme anvil. People are fond of the expression, '…in a hundred years, who's gonna care?' and it is easy to be flippant when the future is unwritten, but he was all too aware that one balls-up here could mean there would never *be* anyone *to* care. The realisation made him feel at once old and yet like a lost child. How could he guide his people through this time and place when virtually none of his memories or experiences had even happened yet? What could he draw upon?

A wave of homesickness and despair crashed over him and it took a while for his natural determination to slowly reassert, allowing him to lock the inner little boy away in his heart for a better day. *We* are *going home*, he vowed. *Ah don't know how, but we're going home and Scotland had better damned well be there when Ah get back!*

Chapter 10 | Sundays

2206 hours, 31st July AD2112

The door chimed. This was it, the culmination of the first stage of the master design. Years of planning, work and sacrifice, all leading up to this moment.

The old man stopped pacing and turned to face the double doors leading into his private study and apartments. "Come," he commanded.

They swung open automatically, allowing his aide to enter. The woman was of highly selective stock. Blonde, tall and elegant, she was almost unnaturally beautiful. Practically all of his minions were terrified of his displeasure and she was no exception, so her confident demeanour suggested that this was going to be good news.

He relaxed a little, straightening to his full and still considerable height, despite his age.

She bowed slightly. "Good evening, sir."

"Well?" he asked tersely.

"We have just received word from our contact. NASA has satellite confirmation that the *New World* made her wormhole jump at 2000 hours, but did *not* arrive at her destination near Mars."

"Excellent," he acknowledged, stroking his chin thoughtfully. "This is good, this is very good! It will certainly take the Mars Mission staff a few months to realise what has happened to her. They will doubtless attempt some kind of rescue and we know who they will send, don't we? The USS

Newfoundland has been something of an embarrassment since Canada pulled out of the project – such a shame they are clinging to the superstition that it is bad luck to change a ship's name." He chuckled nastily. "Weak fools, they play more into my hands by the day. They will have to send Bessel. When he returns to Earth, have our operatives begin *processing* his crew. Are our Middle East assets in place?"

"Yes, sir. We have confirmation that the *Last Word* will be ready for action in approximately ninety days."

"So we're on schedule," he muttered. "Fortunately, our prize is now safely stored in the past, which gives us all the time in the world. And the fleet?"

"The *Sabre* and the *Heydrich* are approximately three to four months from completion, sir. Just a little behind the *Last Word*. The *Eisernes Kreuz*, though almost complete, developed engine problems during tests. Nevertheless, the *Kreuz* should still be ready within the next ten to fifteen days, sir."

"Very well. When we move, I do not want our prize damaged. We will *assist* NASA in their rescue attempt. Do not engage the *Last Word* unless they fail."

"Yes, sir. And, sir?"

"Yes?"

The woman clapped her hands. Presently, a maid brought a trolley into the room carrying champagne in a silver bucket loaded with ice. Taking a glass from the trolley, the aide waved the woman away. She popped the cork and poured a glass, handing it to the old man.

He smiled coldly but accepted the drink.

"Congratulations on the success of stage one, sir."

He nodded, giving her permission to pour one for herself and raised his glass in salute. "To Operation Dawn."

Clink.

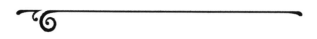

Almost 99.2 million years earlier

James Douglas, captain of the USS *New World* stepped up on to the dais at the front of the embarkation lounge. "Well, we're here," he stated confidently. "And Ah suppose you might say – we're home!"

A raucous round of applause greeted his words as a hundred souls let off steam, overjoyed just to be alive.

He raised his hands for calm. "Thankfully, despite the roughness of our descent, we've only a few cuts and bruises to show for it. Of course, now we have to think about putting our plans into action for what comes next."

The crowd quieted as people drunk on survival turned their minds back to the predicament in which they found themselves.

"However, the very first thing Ah would like us to do, is spend a minute in silence to honour our brothers and sister, lost on our epic and terrible journey from Earth to Earth: Crewman Mario Baccini; Private Andreas Paolo; Sergeant Bud O'Neill, retired; and Dr Jamie Ferguson."

The silence opened up into a void as the seconds stretched away, the quiet sobbing of the bereaved disappearing without echo or trace.

"We remember them," said Douglas, solemnly.

"It's fair to say that as of today, at least for a little while, our old lives are over and our new lives begin," he paused to let this sink in. "This is a time of change, but Ah'm sure we'll all face our new lives with hope, courage and camaraderie. There may well be one amongst us who does not belong within our new family, but as long as we work together and look out for one another, we *will* bring them to justice.

"How prophetic they were in naming this ship the *New World* to honour the founding fathers. The irony that we were all set up and on our way to *literally* colonise a new world – Mars – was lost on none of us, Ah'm sure, but this…" he gestured out of one of the view ports, "Ah think it's safe to say naebody saw this one coming."

A few nervous laughs tittered amongst the crowd.

"However, all of that is for tomorrow," he continued, in happier tones, "because today we've all earned a *holiday* and, as Lieutenant Singh assures me it's Sunday morning, a day of rest!"

Thunderous applause and calls echoed around the cavernous space. He raised his hands once more for calm, waiting and judging his moment. "We should celebrate our safe arrival and usher in a new age for our little family. Remember this everyone – we will survive!"

Cheers erupted once more and Douglas waited, letting them quiet naturally.

"And if any of you would like to join me in the bar," he let the silence build, "THE DRINKS ARE ON ME!"

He waited for another deafening roar of appreciation to abate before continuing. "Just one thing *before* we celebrate and drink to the memories of our fallen – Ah'm sorry to say that this is a critical omission which has dogged our journey from the very start."

Embarkation fell very still as people looked around nervously, wondering what else could be wrong. Eventually Douglas put them out of their misery. "What shall we call the bar?"

The sound and volume of the laughter lifted Douglas' spirits. He could not help cracking a wide grin as he said, "Surely we should name it something auspicious after the manner and place of our arrival – any ideas?"

A male voice called out, "The Mud Hole!"

Laughs and cat-calls greeted his suggestion. The captain sought out the voice in the crowd and was unsurprised to find that it belonged to the young Mr Wood. He might have known.

"Now careful," said Douglas. "That's the sort of name that might stick— oh no," he added quietly, realising what he had just said.

The passengers processed this in silence for a moment, before bursting into a storm of laughter which rang off the bulkheads. Douglas put his head in his hands, shaking it slowly. "What have Ah done?" he mumbled, but no one heard.

So off to the 'Mud Hole' they went, to drink a good deal of their supply of alcohol. Fortunately, the following hangovers would make the rationing to come, if not exactly welcome, then at least more tolerable.

Chapter 11 | Gods and Monsters

Day two on planet Earth, circa 99,200,000 BC – 0800 hours

Ship time turned out to be about eleven hours behind local time. It was also about three months in front. Before locking down his post to join the party, Singh had set the ship's computer the task of recalculating their clock and calendar to synchronise with ancient Earth, also deciding to save their own time and date for posterity. He had left it counting, feeling it was at least a notional link with home. The computer reached its conclusion quickly, updating all systems with the new time stamp. All would now be ready for when the crew resumed their duties.

The *New World* left Cape Canaveral on the 30th July, 2112, but in Late Albian, Cretaceous Gondwana, it was spring and precisely 0800 hours on the 20th April 99,198,017 BC.

Captain Douglas was alone on his bridge. He was fairly confident that it was a Monday morning – it sure as hell felt like one as he tried to force his scattered mind to focus through a dizzying hangover. At this moment Baines entered, looking *fragile*.

Douglas suddenly perked up a little. He whistled softly and began to speak, quietly of course, so that his head did not split open. He could not help noticing the sunglasses. "Shades indoors? That bad, eh?"

Baines leaned on the back of a seat, holding her free hand up in a warding motion. "I'll be just fine," she answered, delicately, "if you'll just stop shouting." Ignoring the captain's mocking grin, she vaguely became aware of something missing from the usual bridge furniture. "Where's Sandy?" she asked.

"No idea," replied Douglas, still speaking in low tones, despite Baines' protestations to the contrary. "The last Ah saw of our intrepid pilot was in the 'Mud Hole'," he chewed the name over with some distaste. "He was balancing a bar stool on his head whilst singing Bollywood's greatest hits."

Baines started to laugh but stopped, holding her head gingerly. "Oh, God..." she groaned.

"When they named that boy 'Singh', the Gods were in good humour it seems," Douglas continued.

"Bad, was it?"

"Well, considering the lad comes from a nation famous for using notes, half tones *and even quarter* notes, you'd have thought he'd be able to hit at least one of them, would ye no'?"

Baines took a sharp intake of breath, tutting, "You're a cruel man, James Douglas!"

They chuckled, eliciting further moans from each of them as they sat holding their heads.

"What were you drinking last night?" Baines asked.

"How the hell should Ah know?" said Douglas, his terse reply muffled through his hands. Looking up gently he asked, "What were *you* drinking?"

Baines looked pale. "Same as you," she answered, weakly.

"Ah said Ah didnae know."

"What's your point?"

"Ahh...," replied Douglas, his woolly mind catching up. "This just won't do. Ah need to see Dave Flannigan and get a horse pill. Ah feel like sh—"

"Now, now, Captain."

"—utting my eyes—What?"

"Oh, nothing," said Baines. "I thought you were about to say s—"

"Shutting my eyes?"

"—omething else... never mind," she finished weakly. "If you're seeing the doc, get something for me too, would you? I'll keep watch on the back of my shades until you get back."

"Ye do realise we still have a murderer out there and we have to keep the bridge locked down?" asked Douglas.

"Whoever it is won't be able to do anything for *this* headache, James. Besides, I'm all over it," she said, pressing a few buttons. She leaned back in her seat, saluting with her eyes closed.

"Jill?"

"Captain?"

"You've locked down the bridge."

"As ordered, sir."

"But Ah havenae left it yet."

Baines coughed weakly, clearing her throat. "I knew that," she said, undoing the lockdown. "Don't worry, Captain, we're parked, the handbrake's on – I'm ready for anything."

Douglas snorted, instantly regretting it as pain beat drum and cymbal against the inside of his skull. He left the bridge to journey through a ghost ship and soon found himself hoping that someone had crawled in to do a shift in sickbay. To his exquisite relief, Dr Flannigan was indeed on duty and able to offer help.

Douglas organised a senior staff meeting for 1100 hours, keeping it respectfully late in the hope that everyone would be able to sort themselves out gracefully by then. Gradually, both ship and Pod crews were coming back to life after nearly twenty-four hours 'excess all areas'. By the appointed hour, the senior staff strode, or in some cases crept, into the bridge meeting room, a little less like the walking dead.

Dr Satnam Patel had put the most work into devising a strategy for moving forward, so the three councillors agreed he should chair the meeting. "Welcome, everyone," he greeted, treating the fragile collective to a wan smile. "So this is it, and we certainly have a lot to do. We'll go through the initial issues we know of in turn, starting with a report about the prisoners. Would you care to start us off, Captain?"

Nodding to the chair, Douglas began his report. "Firstly, Lieutenant Lloyd will be kept in his healing coma for another eighteen hours or so. Once awakened, with Dr Flannigan's approval, he'll be returned to the brig and there he'll stay until we can work out exactly who's responsible for the situation we're in. Naturally, this also includes finding out who caused the deaths of our friends and comrades."

He sipped a little water, grimacing slightly as his headache took another stab at him.

"During the calamity," he continued, "when the computers were down and we were about to crash into the planet, or at least, the atmosphere, someone tried to murder Lieutenant Lloyd."

This was news to most of the gathering and a shocked silence fell as each looked from one to another.

"Lu—" what Douglas was about to say grated on him a little, but he decided it would be churlish not to continue. "*Luckily*, Dr Flannigan arrived just in time to save him. Whoever did this must have medical knowledge. They seemed to know their way around sickbay too. The adrenalin used in the attempt was stolen from Flannigan's own stock room."

"That disgusts me," Baines stated flatly.

Douglas looked at her in surprise. "Commander?"

"I'm sorry, Captain," she replied. "It just doesn't sit right with me that while so many good people have lost their lives, that creature seems to have so many."

"Well, it seems wherever we are in time, some things remain the same," the captain agreed sourly. "On a brighter note, the other prisoner, Hank Burnstein Jnr, or as he now wishes to be known, Henry – which Ah suppose makes things easier – has been released following a short but thorough investigation by Rick Drummond. Rick, as you know, is our ex-detective, who joined Major White's team as a security consultant. He could find no evidence to contradict the boy's story. It seems he really did simply find the bag, whilst dodging security on a clandestine mission to see his new girlfriend."

Douglas' exasperated smile was mirrored by others at the table. They had all been teenagers, once – excluding Tim Norris, who still was.

"The bag is being examined in more detail as we speak, by Dr Wright," Douglas continued. "We still have a known murderer and saboteur loose aboard ship. We assume this person to be the owner of said bag. Although we're unsure of the extent of Lloyd's involvement, he clearly wasn't responsible for *all* that's happened, so finding this person has to remain a top priority. That's all for now, we'll make more information available as we have it."

"Thank you, Captain," Patel resumed. "Now we'll hear from Chief Nassaki regarding the health of the ship and the project to convert the lifeboats to reconnaissance craft. Hiro, please." He invited the engineer to speak on the next point.

Hiro sat forward, the black eye inflicted by Georgio Baccini blooming like a floral pattern a few days on. "We ran a full ship-wide diagnostic this morning," he began, "and apart from the destruction caused by the explosion, and the resetting of the ship's main computer, we are otherwise fully operational. There will almost certainly be some outer hull damage due to the initial speed of our entry into the atmosphere and, as I said, we will need to close the rip in the hull caused by the bomb. To that end, later today, the captain and I will lead a team outside to look her over properly and plan a programme of repairs. Naturally, we need the ship to be in full working order in case we have to relocate in a hurry. I'll be able to put together a more thorough report after this—" Hiro paused for a moment. "I was going to say inspection, but I suppose *mission* is more appropriate?"

The concept settled within the minds of the men and women present: nothing would be straightforward from here onwards. The handful of humans would have to adapt to the basic premise that this Earth was not their Earth – not yet.

"Moving on to the lifeboats," Hiro continued. "The little ships should be perfectly usable as small orbital and atmospheric craft. The only conversion work will be to alter the docking mechanisms, so that they can recapture the pods upon their return. As the escape pods were originally designed for emergency use, the idea of uncoupling and re-docking with the ship has never really been explored.

"In a crisis, the obvious purpose of each lifeboat is to carry a maximum of ten people, either to the safety of atmosphere or at least away from a stricken vessel, keeping them alive until they can be retrieved by another capital ship. Once the evacuees are aboard, the docking bolts holding the escape pods in tight to the *New World*'s hull are..." Hiro tailed off, staring wide-eyed at Douglas.

"*Detonated*!" the two men called out together.

Their minds raced through possibilities and they continued staring dumbstruck at one another until Mother Sarah remarked, "Clearly that statement has struck a chord with you, gentlemen. Couldn't play it a little harder could ya?"

Douglas locked gazes with her, the shock of his epiphany still evident. "Hiro may have just hit on something. We've been wondering – worrying really – all the last week, how someone smuggled explosives on board to destroy the wormhole drive. There was very little trace evidence left at the bomb site and the small amount of plastic explosive attached to the Pod's reactor was unmarked and could have come from anywhere. Obviously, the only store of explosives on the ship belongs to Captain Gleeson, as part of the mining effort for Mars. Naturally, his entire inventory was checked rigorously to make sure that nothing was missing." Douglas clapped a palm to his brow. "We never considered the lifeboat release detonators and charges. Ow, ma hid!"

"I should check them straight away, sir," said the chief.

"No, wait, Hiro," said Douglas, holding up a hand whilst rubbing his forehead with the other. "This meeting is important too. Comm Georgio and get him to look into it – and make sure he takes a couple of security with him."

"Yes, sir," Hiro turned aside from the table, opening a private channel to his subordinate.

"For now," Douglas continued, "we should proceed with our meeting while this is verified."

"Very well," agreed Patel. "Next on the agenda are the funerary rites of the people we have lost. As already agreed, we must cremate the remains so as to avoid the possibility, however unlikely, of polluting the fossil record with our presence. We must observe this strictly, in order to preserve the timeline."

"As it happens," interjected Sarah, "I know that the three men, Mario, Andreas and Bud, were all Catholic, so I'll give them the full rites to comply with their faith. I've also spoken to Dr Parrot who told me that the lady, Jamie, was Christian in the wider sense, although of no specific denomination. He asked me to perform a simple, Christian ceremony on the same day.

"I hate to say it, but with the danger and all, I've been preparing a few variations on burial rites to take note of the various religions onboard.

Obviously, I'm an ordained priest but I want to respect the beliefs of everyone on the ship. I hope they will understand."

"Mother Sarah," said Douglas, kindly, "Ah'm sure everyone will agree, there's no one more qualified to take care of us in that regard."

Murmurs of assent followed his words, along with a few solemn nods of approval.

"This does present an entirely practical problem, however," stated Patel. "At the moment we have nowhere *to* cremate anyone, which brings me onto our next point. Dr Portree, would you outline your staged development plans for creating a compound, please?"

Samantha Portree sat forward in her chair, the better to take in all the faces around her. "Now we've seen the lie of the land, we've begun drawing up plans for the ditch and earthwork arrangement we discussed previously – beginning with a crescent butted against the ship. When enclosed, this will give us multiple points of egress, both pedestrian and vehicular. It will also allow people to get some air. Our small compound will be topped with a log palisade, cut to spikes to discourage climbers.

"If anyone ever built themselves a model fort when they were a kid, well that's pretty much what we're talking about. The enclosure will have to be gated for our security, or should I say 'physical safety' – I doubt the dinosaurs will try and burglarize us."

"Ahem," Tim interjected, raising a hand to speak.

"Please, Mr Norris," Patel invited.

"I don't mean to contradict anyone," the young man offered, hesitantly, "but they may actually do just that. Certainly anything remotely edible will be fair game – including us. More than that, the animals may take a great interest in our equipment and gizmos. It's impossible to say for sure, but we know that several bird species from our own time like to steal 'shiny things' and as the dinosaur is the direct ancestor of the bird..." He opened his hands, letting the words hang for a moment before adding, "In fact, we may even come across early 'true birds' in this time."

"That's a good point, Tim," Portree acknowledged. "I suppose that illustrates just how careful we'll need to be. We can no longer assume anything. Once we have the small enclosure built, we'll be able to begin construction of the much larger one we'll need to begin farming. An area of about thirty acres around the ship should do it. We'll also be able to use it for storage and exercise, perhaps even corral a few beasts, once we know what we're doing.

"We have about 150 tons of cement in our stores and many tons of structural steel, rebar and so on. Assuming we can find a source of sand, we can make concrete and begin building safe-huts around the compound, where our people will be able to take refuge from predators. This is likely to be necessary during the work *and after*, looking at some of the flying critters out there!

"We'll also need to fabricate storage facilities for grain and other crops. Simple grain stores have historically been supported off the ground – to stop small animals from stealing or spoiling our supplies. It will be the same here and now. We have huge seed stocks which were meant for the Mars hydroponics Pod. Happily they can go back into the ground and, in a little while, feed us."

Jim Miller raised a hand to comment. "Could this *introduction* of plant species, which probably don't exist yet, muddy the timeline again? Sorry," he apologised, "not trying to be obstructive, but the way plants cross-pollinate... surely messing with evolution has to be a consideration?"

"You're right, Doctor," said Douglas, "but we probably won't be able to eat much of the vegetation out there so, once again, it's do or die. Ah don't really think we have much choice on this one."

"What about the concrete and steel structures proposed?" asked Sarah. "Won't they leave traces on the landscape after we're gone?"

"Not likely," Portree answered, looking directly at the priest. "There's virtually nothing we can make that wouldn't return to its base compounds and elements within just a few thousands of years. We're so far back that that particular problem shouldn't affect us. Admittedly, it's a zillion to one chance, but our bones, and those of any animals that have travelled with us, are the only things which may survive. That's because permineralization occurs during the fossilisation process. Basically, water drains through the remains, replacing the living matter with crystallised, water-borne minerals eventually. This leaves only the shell of the bone wrapped around a core of mineralised marrow which hardens along with the sedimentary rock encasing it.

"Sorry to get technical, but knowing you guys, I'd thought I'd better revisit my college notes for a refresher! Back when I was a geology major,

I would never have guessed that I might be in danger of leaving my own bones in the ground for me to dig myself up again in a core sample!" She smiled ironically at her fellow scientists.

Hiro's comm binged, interrupting them. "Nassaki," he acknowledged.

"*Hiro,*" the voice replied through the small speaker, "*it's Georgio.*"

"Hang on," said Hiro, toggling his communicator into the room's speaker system. "Carry on Georgio, we can all hear you now."

"*OK,*" said Baccini, his voice emanating from every corner, "*I've inspected the escape pods and the four at the bow of the ship are all missing explosive charges from their launch mechanisms.*"

"What about the six aft?" asked Hiro.

"*The aft lifeboats are intact. It may be worth noting that it was near one of these that Lieutenant Lloyd was found – the first time he 'bumped his head', that is. So if he had escape on his mind, he was in the right place. That means there are four charges to factor for. One would have...*" his voice trembled slightly, trailing off. Through the comm, the listeners could hear him take a deep breath, swallowing before continuing, clearly reliving the death of his twin. "*One would have been enough to destroy the wormhole drive and...*"

"It's OK, Georgie," said Douglas, kindly. "Take your time."

"*Thank you, Captain. Well, one would have been enough. We recovered one 'de-stickered' pack from the attempt to blow the main Pod reactor, which leaves two unaccounted for.*"

Baccini's statement cut a bow wave through their thoughts. Baines leaned back, exhaling loudly into the fearful silence which crashed in after. "I thought we'd woken up from this nightmare," she muttered at last.

Mother Sarah leaned forward, taking in the professionals seated about her. "Let's just try and remember this, folks: Evil wins battles, not wars. The sneak attacks which have dogged our journey since we left Canaveral will become less easy for whoever's responsible now we're onto 'em. I say, *good luck* to anyone trying to outsmart the people in *this* room. You're as ingenious as you are courageous. It's an honour to know you and I'm proud to call you friends. Together, we'll turn this around, I have complete faith in that – and when we do, they'll be sorry they ever started this whole affair!"

Burton's and White's comms binged almost simultaneously, making several people jump. Excusing themselves, each man turned from the table to answer. After a couple of short, hushed conversations, Burton spoke first, "I hate to put a downer on such fine words, but we appear to have another problem, people. The power grid has gone down on the Pod – everything!"

"I just got the same message from one of my men," White confirmed.

"Any idea of the cause?" asked Patel.

"Not yet," replied Burton. "I'd better get down there. Could you excuse me, please?"

"Of course," said Patel.

"I'd better go with him," White added, "in case this is more than a tech failure."

Douglas nodded. "Keep us posted, please. At least a power failure isn't dangerous now we're back on terra firma."

"Actually, Captain," said Burton, turning back, "this might be a slow-burn catastrophe in the making."

"How so?" asked Sarah.

The New Zealander shook his head. "With no power, we have no air recycling. The Pod is big but with a hundred pairs of lungs pumping CO_2 into the atmosphere… well, we have to get it fixed, ASAP," he finished.

"Of course," Douglas acknowledged. "But it would take a couple of days before we were in trouble, surely?"

"True," replied Burton. "So here's hoping we've only got two days' worth of damage to repair."

"Hmm," Douglas conceded.

"Can we open the two hatches between the ship and the Pod?" asked Baines.

"Yes," agreed Burton. "Worthwhile, but of limited effectiveness, because without power we still can't control air flow."

"Erm, excuse my ignorance," said Sarah, leaning forward and putting her hand up, "but couldn't we just bring everyone onto the *New World*?"

Baines shook her head. "We couldn't sustain the population for long," she said. "The *New World*, despite her size, was designed for a crew of just thirteen and her air recycling plant is based around that sort of figure. Of course, there's plenty of redundancy, in case we need extra maintenance staff or play host to a visitor or two, but the Pod has a hundred people on board. Pretty soon the air would become unbreathable on both units."

"I guess we couldn't just open a window then, huh?" Sarah tried again, hopefully.

"You'd think it would be that simple," Douglas replied, "but needless to say, spaceships don't usually come with opening windows. Dr Burton is right though, even if we open every hatch and door the air quality in the core of the Pod would degrade as people use it. That's the trouble with living in an airtight box made up of airtight boxes – there's just no flow without the machinery to make it happen."

"More to the point," said Tim, "if you open the doors, what might stroll in?"

Burton worked two-handed, with a small torch in his mouth. He peered into a hatch containing a scramble of cables which used to make sense to him. A noise from behind made him start. He turned around quickly, slumping with relief as Captain Gleeson wheeled a large, portable CO_2 scrubber into the room with one of Burton's own engineering staff. The engineer placed it in the corner out of the way, activating the unit.

"What do you have, Burto?" asked the Australian in his usual, familiar way.

"It's a mess, mate," replied the New Zealander. "Somebody has rewired the shunt. This is the unit that controls the power flow. Obviously, we have a lot of redundant power conduits in case a system goes down, but it's all controlled from here. I'm hoping I'm wrong but it looks like it's been top and tailed."

"Top and tailed?" asked Gleeson.

"Yeah, sorry, I mean, if I was gonna sabotage this crate, I'd scramble the power so that the high power circuits fed into the low power ones and then it's frying tonight, bring a plate!"

"Surely this lot has breakers and RCCBs everywhere to stop it getting barbied?" asked the Australian, gesturing to the myriad control panels around him.

"It does, and back-ups, and back-ups to the back-ups, but if you work your way through in reverse, you can bypass them all from this room. Then, basically, the breakers are out of the loop and you can pop the lot."

"I take it you've checked the breakers?"

"Yes, and surprise, surprise, it's bad news," Burton concluded, acerbically.

"It's that easy to bagger all this up?" Gleeson asked, incredulously.

"Yeah, well it could never happen, mate, could it? Because anyone deliberately destroying this system, far from being a run of the mill saboteur, they'd have to have a death wish too," he turned to face Gleeson. "Who knew?" he asked, ironically.

Gleeson looked into the hatch over Burton's shoulder, adding his own torch light to the task. "You still use all that old fashioned cable for this stuff?" he asked, surprised.

"Yeah – spaceship," replied Burton, as if that explained everything. He turned to face Gleeson once more. "If anything breaks down and you can't breathe the air outside, you're in real trouble, mate. That's why most of what makes this place work is old tech, because we've had decades and decades to make it one hundred percent reliable."

Gleeson peered once more into the hatch and its mess of wires. "A hundred percent?" he asked.

The senior staff listened to Burton's voice booming from the speakers in the meeting room. *"The engineer in charge was found in the storage lock-up, face down with his head in a mop bucket!"* he said.

"Has the man been hurt?" asked Patel, concerned.

"He's alright, but if we'd left him much longer the rim of the bucket would have choked him. Doc Flannigan has taken him away to treat his throat and fix him up. He won't be saying much for a day or two."

Douglas felt a wave of relief. For a moment he thought he'd lost someone else. *Ah've got to find this animal soon*, he chided himself. "What can you do to get power back online, Doctor?" he asked.

"I've taken the core offline and I'm heading down to the main plant room now. If all of the safeguards in that part of the Pod are OK, I'll be able to get partial systems running again from there before I start fixing the mess in the core and power distribution bays."

"That's good news, Doctor. Please keep us appraised," replied Douglas.

"Er…" said Patel.

"Satnam?" asked Douglas.

"I think there may be more downside yet, am I right, Dr Burton?" replied Patel.

"Yeah, we can fix it, but it's gonna take at least two days just to get a basic workaround," answered the New Zealander. *"The multiple failsafes we have were meant to stop this from ever happening, but of course whoever did this bypassed all that and now it's all munted!"*

"Munted?" asked Patel.

"Yeah, it's carked it – pakaru!" Burton elaborated.

Patel looked around the table for help.

"He means it's totally cactus, mate," Gleeson's voice joined the comm link, helpfully. *"S'all rooted. The mongrel who did it's as cunning as a dunny rat too!"*

Patel simply sat back, raising his eyebrows in bafflement.

"Fully!" continued Burton. *"And after that it'll take a week or more before she'll be right. If we ever catch this…"* he sought a euphemism, "rooter, *Captain, I suggest you set 'em free."*

"Really?" asked Douglas, genuinely surprised.

"Yeah!" snapped Burton. *"Set 'em free to go and play outside for a bit."*

"Ah," said Douglas, the beginnings of a smile tugging the corners of his mouth, "Ah cannae say the idea's no' appealing, but Ah think that will have to be a discussion for another day."

"I'll get back to you when I've had a proper look around the main plant room – Burton out."

"I think," said Baines, speaking quietly into the silence which followed, "that we'll have to split those two up, if only to give the English language a chance to survive."

Life Pod, main loading bay and vehicle pool – 1300 hours

Anyone not involved with essential repairs, maintenance or security gathered in trepidation. The main bay was one of the few places on the Pod where large groups could assemble.

Captain Douglas walked to the front of the waiting crowd. "Hello, everyone. We've brought you all here because the power outage has led to problems with the environmental systems. As Ah'm sure you'll have noticed, the saboteur has struck again. Our engineers will be working around the clock to get power back as soon as possible, but unfortunately we'll likely run out of breathable air before they succeed."

A storm of panic erupted from the crowd.

Douglas held up his hands for calm which eventually came. "Sorry, sorry, that was a poor choice of words. Obviously, we have an infinite supply of breathable air just outside those hangar doors.

"Clearly our only course is to open them, which is of course what the saboteur intended. You may already be feeling a slight deterioration in air quality. The trouble is, outside is a very dangerous place for us. Naturally, we'll all have to leave the ship sooner or later but this has forced our hand and, to be brutally honest, we're no' ready."

Uproar…

"Please, please," Douglas shouted against the din, pointing at the pedestrian sized portal next to the huge hangar doors. "Ah'll be leading a small team through the personnel hatch in just a few minutes. Once we've established that there is no immediate threat, we'll be opening the main hangar doors and parking a lorry across the mouth of the cargo bay – this should at least stop anything big from getting in. We will then open the outer airlock doors to facilitate air flow around the main hangar. This will preserve the air quality, as much as possible, in other areas of the Pod for our teams of engineers."

"Captain," called a voice from the crowd. Douglas took a moment to find its source, his eye eventually alighting on Tim Norris.

"Yes, Tim?" he asked.

"Captain, I should be on the team who go with you."

Douglas scrutinised the young man – was he being brave or genuinely eager?

"I may be able to help. I have at least a basic understanding of what's out there," Tim tried again.

"That's why the answer is no, son," replied Douglas. "You're too important to risk the very first time we open the door."

"I'm not afraid, Captain."

Douglas doubted that but he smiled at the young man's courage. "Ah know, son," he replied kindly. "Soon, Ah promise, but not this time."

The captain strode toward the small hatch, nodding for The Sarge to follow with his five-man squad. One of the heavy load haulers moved to block the main vehicular hatch as ordered, but for now the doors remained resolutely closed. Its manoeuvre complete, the whine of the powerful electric motors winding down was the only sound. The tension mounted. Douglas motioned for one of his team to open the small pedestrian hatch to the right of the main doors. He, Sarge Jackson and the other four men grouped in the personnel airlock, closing the internal hatch behind them.

One of the men plugged their portable charge-pack into the outer hatch controls. Douglas stood at the threshold and, once the control panel was fully powered, turned to The Sarge. Slowly they grinned at one another. "Let's do this," he said and tapped the hatch release, inhaling deeply the warm, humid Cretaceous air.

The injured man lay in the hospital bed, a neck brace under his chin.

"Has the pain subsided any?" Nurse Justin Smyth asked, taking his pulse. The man croaked painfully and Smyth quickly held up his hand. "Forgive me, please don't try to talk just yet, just squeeze my hand for yes."

His patient did not squeeze.

"Alright, I'll give you a little more sedative to help you sleep. You'll be stiff for a few days, but a good, deep sleep now will kick-start the mending process," Smyth explained soothingly, as he reached for the syringe behind him.

It was not there.

"Where's that gone?" he muttered to himself, frowning. He turned back to the injured man saying, "I won't be a minute – must have put it down somewhere. I'll just get anoth—" Justin stopped speaking as he realised the patient was looking behind him, eyes widening in terror.

As the nurse began to turn, he felt a sudden, sharp pinch on the back of his neck and his world became sideways, collision, blackness.

Captain Douglas breathed in again, greedily. It was not just that the air was fresh, it was so *new*. Fresher and sweeter than anything he had experienced in his life, despite the humidity. *Wow*, he thought, *it's amazing how we've gotten so used to pollution – the air back home really is filthy!*

Grinning like a schoolboy, he turned to the men behind him. "This reminds me of Neil Armstrong's first step on the moon – 'a giant leap for mankind'. Being so far back in time, almost feels like Ah should step out backwards."

The men chuckled. The Sarge simply said, "I wouldn't."

Douglas saw the soldier's implacable face, and laughed appreciatively. He squared his shoulders in preparation, before taking his first ever step into the past. One step forward and then one step back, followed by three more *on* his back.

Shocked, winded and unable to cry out, he was pinned to the floor and looking up into the muzzle of a dinosaur.

The stricken man lay in his hospital bed, sedative already flowing through his veins, terror and the restrictive neck brace paralysing him as the figure in black loomed. Viewing him coldly through a ski mask, his attacker produced a needle. The prone man's wide-eyed stare followed its point, but his limbs were lead in this fully realised nightmare. The sharp sting took his breath away, oblivion his only friend now. Finally, the tunnel of his vision closed to a pair of eyes – blue eyes, beautiful eyes.

"Aaaargh!" Douglas screamed, events completely unmanning him.

The greeny-brown-skinned animal used its forelimbs to pin him to the ground, its snout snuffling around his face. The snout ended with a very dangerous looking parrot-like beak. It studied him, its eyes all browns and yellows. Douglas watched the pupils dilate, *Disney* large, in the small, semi-darkened chamber. The eyes seemed so alien and yet… and yet.

Realising that, aside from a clumsy foot in a painful place, the animal did not appear to be attacking him, he tried to enunciate this insight to his men. Unfortunately, it only came out as another shocked, "Aargh!"

Looking into the creature's eyes, he saw only clean windows to a simple soul; wide, innocent, inquisitive. Douglas calmed slightly, feeling the need to report this before anyone shot the animal. He twisted to the side opening his mouth to speak when his face disappeared behind a huge and unspeakably smelly tongue. "Aargh!" Douglas screamed again, his entire repertoire at the moment, it seemed.

The animal batted its eyelids, opening its mouth to reveal batteries of grinding teeth before letting out a squawk of indignation. Jumping up and turning with exquisite grace, the creature's powerful hind legs drove it away at an impressive lick, its head out forward, tail rigid behind.

"*Aargh?*" complained Douglas, wordlessly expressing his outrage at the men standing over him, gaping.

Eventually one man snapped out of the trance which held them. "Sorry, Captain," he said, offering the Scotsman his hand.

"Dinnae trouble yesel', Ah can manage!" spat Douglas crossly, getting to his feet. "That's no' what Ah thought was goin' te happen," he grumbled, a little incoherently.

He took a moment to centre himself, before straightening his uniform and stepping out of the ship once more, this time successfully. After walking about three paces, he stopped. "Aw Jeez," he said, wiping a hand down his cheek. "Ah stink like somebody took a wee on ma face!"

The men behind him tried and failed to muffle their laughter until The Sarge glanced their way, causing them to inspect their boots for possible lacing issues.

Jackson stepped up next to Douglas and looked around, himself breathing deeply of the past.

The captain turned to him. "Thanks for the rescue, Sarge," he noted sarcastically.

The Sarge stared stoically at his superior. "If it'd been a threat, I would have smashed its head in with my rifle butt, sir," he said simply.

"Could you no' a' stunned it?" asked Douglas.

"Would you have wanted me to, sir?" asked The Sarge, meaningfully.

Douglas looked at him askance for a moment, before the penny dropped. "Ah," he acknowledged, "electric stun rifles, right. Ah'd have received the full shunt."

"Exactly right, sir."

"Sarge? How did ye know it wasnae a threat?" asked Douglas, frowning.

"One knows another, sir," answered The Sarge, inscrutably.

The captain raised his eyebrows, nodding to himself, pointedly not asking for further explanation. He watched the animal in question rejoin its herd, near the edges of the clearing. "Ah'm gonna call that one 'The Mayor'," he said, now fully recovered from his shock and grinning in spite of himself.

Jackson simply raised an eyebrow quizzically.

"Well, he welcomed us here, did he no'?" explained the Scotsman, pulling a face after sniffing his uniform tunic. "Although, Ah think he must have gotten a little confused."

"Confused, Captain?" asked The Sarge.

"Aye," said Douglas. He wiped a hand down his shirt and sniffed it, his eyes widening in shock once more. "Ah think *this* Mayor handed me the keys to the privy!"

The cat-like figure in black ran silently through deserted, soundless corridors. Upon reaching the crew quarters they overrode the lock and broke into one of the billets. The door slid open, loud in a silence unnatural aboard a working ship. The intruder slipped inside, pulling a small, rectangular package from a belt pouch.

Just moments later the prowler re-emerged, sprinting back down the corridor and heading for sickbay, straight to the store cupboard for another syringe. Grabbing a bottle from a shelf, they filled the syringe and replaced the bottle. The black-gloved hand squirted some of the contents, leaving only the exact amount required; the quantity and timing had to be perfect…

Douglas studied the lines of his ship, gratefully. Despite some scorching, she was not too much the worse for wear. Singh had been right though, the landing struts were completely sunken into the soft earth. However, the rain had ceased a few hours after they put down and the ground was draining into the nearby river nicely.

"Will she come back out, sir?" asked one of the men.

"Aye, she's a very powerful lassie. Ah want to have a look at the explosion site," Douglas replied, striding towards the stern. "It's the other side."

Rounding the aft end of the ship, they spotted the damage at once. About twenty metres above the ground was an elongated black gash in the hull. Douglas hissed as he surveyed his wounded vessel. He shook his head, swearing in frustration.

The Sarge joined him once more. "We'll get them," he said, also looking up at the tear in the ship's flank which had cost one of their crewmen his life. Remembering young Mario, he quietly repeated, "We'll get them."

A huge, rending crash obliterated their contemplations, making the entire party jump. The Sarge merely jumped round, weapon up, as a vision from another world unfolded before their eyes. They froze, staring.

Tim and Woodsey climbed atop the lorry cab and looked out through the high-level view port above the cargo bay doors. The vista really did take some getting used to. People say, 'it was another world' but even though this was technically the same world, the saying was not other-worldly enough to describe the scene. They were besotted with what they saw.

"I can't wait to get out there!" said Woodsey.

"I can't get up there!" said a small voice from below. The lads looked down to see Clarrie, Henry's fourteen, soon to be fifteen-year-old sister, looking up at them. Woodsey jumped down onto the load bed, extending his hand to pull the girl up. Tim repeated the action down from the cab. Woodsey saw an opportunity and pushed her bum up to *help* her, winking at Tim, who scowled down at him.

"Thanks for the hand," said Clarrie, oblivious.

"Yeah, thanks a lot!" added Tim through gritted teeth.

Naturally, Woodsey laughed.

"Do you think they'll let us stay up here when the doors open?" asked Clarrie, excitedly.

"I don't think that would be a good idea," said Tim. Seeing Clarrie's disappointment, he expanded, "It could be extremely dangerous."

"But we'd be OK up here, surely?" she asked.

"Didn't you go to Tim's 'my first dinosaur' remedial class?" asked Woodsey, grinning wickedly.

"Actually, my *workshops* were called 'Cretaceous Living'," Tim corrected him, importantly.

"Dad wouldn't let me go," admitted Clarissa, glumly.

"They were really good," said Woodsey, "*honestly.*"

Tim glared at him until his friend's straight face collapsed into laughter.

"Why wouldn't your dad allow you to come to my lectures, Clarrie?" asked Tim, perplexed.

"Probably because you're not good enough for DOCA," supplied Woodsey, still grinning.

"DOCA?" asked Clarrie.

"Daughter of Cap—"

"Yes, we *know*," Tim interrupted. Woodsey laughed again, eventually infecting even Tim's scowl. "You're just a pair of ears stapled to a grin – d'you know that?" He was laughing too, now. "Anyway," he continued, looking down at Clarrie, "in answer to your question – no, we would not be safe up here. Apart from being at munching height for some of the animals out there, we may even be grabbed by something from the air."

Clarissa gasped in awe. "Giant birds?" she asked, her voice pitched just above a whisper.

"Well, maybe," said Tim, "but probably not like the birds you're thinking of. Many of the birds here are very characteristically dinosaur, with teeth and tails. There are some birds in this era – that is, what we would call 'true birds' – but we believe they were, sorry, *are* fairly small. However, the Pterosaurs are a very different story. There are some giant, flightless birds too, in the fossil record, but I'm not sure if they were here and now – I'd have to look it up."

"Yeah, I'll be sure to bring it up at *Doctor Raptor*'s next surgery," mocked Woodsey. "Hey, if there are birds here, does that mean some of the dinosaurs lost their teeth? And if so – how? Too much chocolate? Rugby? Talking when they should have been listening?"

"I love the way you can make even a sensible question sound fatuous," replied Tim. "You should get a job interviewing people in the media!"

"Now that's not an answer, Mr Norris, and I'm afraid I'm going to have to press you..." Woodsey badgered, using his most official tone.

Tim snorted. "Palaeontologists discovered evidence suggesting that some dinosaur species, although born with teeth, later lost them as their beaks grew. Through many generations, they began to need their teeth for shorter and shorter periods of their development. Eventually, they were able to do without them altogether and were born with beaks."

"Why is the word 'beak' always so funny – I love it!" interrupted Woodsey.

"*You* would," said Tim. "You like to stick yours into other people's business enough! Now I like the word 'thagomizer'."

"That doesn't surprise me at all," retorted Woodsey. "What the *hell* is a thagomizer?!"

"Look it up, it'll make your eyes water!" laughed Tim. "Anyway, back to your beloved 'beaks'. Early experiments in the 1980s provided evidence to suggest that birds, from our time, might still be able to generate teeth if their jaw tissue was artificially stimulated with the right type of molecules. It hadn't been categorically proven that birds evolved from dinosaurs then, so this was highly suggestive evidence at the time. It implied that *our birds*' ancestors would have grown teeth naturally, if you went back far enough." Tim grinned, reaching his stride. "Actually, I read a really interesting article about—"

"I wish I hadn't asked! I really do!" Woodsey cut him off.

Tim faltered, gaping slightly at his friend's obnoxiousness but Clarissa simply gazed up at him. "You know everything, Timmy. How'd you get to be so smart?" she asked with the frank and hungry adoration of a teenaged almost-woman in the presence of her latest idol.

Tim felt the need to adjust his collar uncomfortably as his temperature spiked. Woodsey bent double laughing at him. "Oh Timmy," he said as huskily as he could manage between giggles, "what a fat head you've got!"

"Will you just f—ind something else to do!" Tim snapped, the edges of his temper fraying.

Clarissa laid her head on Tim's shoulder, just staring up at him. He patted her head awkwardly.

Woodsey sissed until a roar of laughter eventually burst out of him. "I'm gonna leave you two 'love Pterosaurs' to the view before I laugh myself off the roof of this truck!" he said, sniggering as he climbed down. Tim watched him walk away laughing raucously.

"*Do* you love Pterosaurs?" Clarrie asked, dreamily.

Tim put his face in his hands, blowing out his cheeks. "No, he was just... well, never mind," he said, smiling down at her. She answered his smile with her own and turning back to the view, Tim ventured an arm around her shoulder. Nothing went wrong, so he left it there.

Douglas took a few steps forward unthinkingly. He stumbled over a tuft of earth, bringing him back to his senses, but he still could not believe what he was seeing and hearing. At the edges of the clearing some deforestation was taking place with no regard at all for the environment – when an eighty ton sauropod dinosaur pushes a tree over, it stays pushed.

It began with one giant neck pushing through the treetops, closely followed by an enormous, barrel-shaped body, but this was just the beginning. By the time the tail was revealed there were three of them, then seven and then lots. The herd smashed their way through the forest like gargantuan, slow-motion mowers. Smaller animals dashed out of the trees, running or flying off in all directions, livid about the intrusion and their impending homelessness. Once the trees were felled, their tops were stripped at an industrial rate by some seriously big eaters.

The herd must have numbered a hundred or more. The youngest were around five or six metres in length from their small heads to the tips of their swishing and flicking tails, but these were just tots compared with the forty-metre-plus adults. Their skin tone ranged from green to brown, some more brown to grey. The fifty-year-old man in Douglas' mind wondered if they changed hue with age, as the smaller ones were more 'forest coloured'. Perhaps this was a defence mechanism for the much more vulnerable young ones, allowing them to hide in the trees until they were big enough to join the herd? Those were the thoughts of the man, but the little boy in Douglas' mind just laughed for the simple joy of it all and continued to laugh until the fifty-year-old man let him out.

All six men followed his lead, some even tearfully, laughing and marvelling at the sheer wonder of this life. The force shared by every creature that has ever lived, or ever will live.

As their hearts soared and the moment owned them, reality began a dirty-tricks campaign. The trees off to their right exploded into motion, as massive animals flew out of the forest in rapid succession – ten, twelve, fifteen. They ran on hugely powerful hind legs, tails arrow-straight, perfectly balanced, the claws on their smaller forelimbs reaching and grasping in anticipation of carnage. As one, their massive jaws gaped wide, bellowing challenge and the roar was deafening, the speed alarming; screaming, the peace fell.

The six stood stock-still, shocked. The Sarge was well versed in controlling his fear but this was a test he would never forget. One of the giants ran close to the men, a huge male. It slowed, looking Douglas straight in the eye and his legs felt like water. That split-second glance was like staring into a furnace, a heart of infinite violence. The animal roared again and Douglas lost his balance, his ears ringing. Having checked them out, the creature suddenly picked up the pace once more, taking off after his brethren faster than any athlete could hope to match. The message was clear: why stoop to pick up a nugget off the floor when there's a half pounder with everything, waiting on a plate?

Douglas was not offended. His mind began to race as his body seemed to slow. He felt such pity for these wonderful, majestic, peaceful creatures, about to have their world torn apart – a vision so eerily similar to a film shown by Tim Norris just days ago. Shock dulled his mind as he struggled to process. Then he considered the *New World*, the bomb, Mario, images, connections, images. A sound began in his stomach, roared up through his lungs and tore out of his throat – "Get the bloody hell out of here!"

The spell broke. All six men ran like every demon in hell was after them, none even daring to break step long enough to check over his shoulder. After what seemed like an eternity they threw themselves into the airlock, the last man in hitting the close.

They collapsed, chests heaving and that was how Commander Baines found them as she opened the inner hatch. "I take it that didn't go well?" she asked.

"Let's just say," said Douglas, panting heavily, "that you can tell Dr Portree we've found her some logs for her palisade, but Ah wouldnae try and collect them just yet."

A little while later, Douglas and Baines observed the aftermath of the attack together, from the safety of a high-level window. The small war outside had abated, leaving wounded on both sides. One of the giant sauropods, a sub-adult, had actually been brought down by the hunting pack.

Tim was able to tentatively identify the herbivores as Argentinasaurus before the herd began to move on, more in irritation than terror, it seemed; their swishing tails and bad tempered, stamping tantrums shaking the ground. The Argentinasaurs seemed to accept the attack, and the loss, as a fact of life. Indeed, some of the hugest among them had barely glanced up from their task of knocking down trees and eating, throughout the engagement. Far from horrified, they were simply too big to even be bothered.

Prima facie, this casual attitude may have seemed ridiculous, but the Mapusaurs certainly gave them, and their falling trees, a wide berth. Any pride of hunters can be permanently divided into the experienced and the dead. The living Mapusaurs knew instinctively that one swipe of a fifteen-metre-long tail could send them, seven tons or no, flying through the air to a smash landing and slow, agonising death.

To the watching humans, it was both appalling and bizarre. To the unlucky victim the ordeal was to be hideously drawn out, a suffering more terrible than mere words can describe. Baines watched the awful spectacle through her tears as the terrified, tormented creature was eaten in stages, whilst bleeding to death. Even the thick, many-layered hull of the ship could not completely prevent the tortured screams from eating into her soul. Douglas remained rigid, but she could tell how much the ordeal was affecting him.

In contrast, the Mapusaurus pack seemed happy with their situation and showed no signs of leaving the area any time soon. The larger predators knocked the younger members away from their prey at first, whilst gorging themselves. Through it all, the cruelly fated victim still mewed and brayed tragically. Once sated, the more senior Mapusaurs began to allow the smaller animals in to feed, without ever letting them forget their place. There was a clear pecking order even among the young, leading to further snapping and posturing before everyone got to eat.

"Ah cannae stand this," said Douglas. "Ah wish to God we had guns on this ship so that we could put that poor creature out of its misery."

Baines was simply too choked to speak. A full hour since the initial attack and still the poor creature lived, its cries heartbreaking.

"We'll check back later," Douglas mumbled, wretchedly. As he turned away, his comm binged to life.

Dr Flannigan had spent the last hour checking the passengers' wellbeing and was now considering his next move. The air quality was deteriorating gradually, but they were still many, many hours from any risk of hypoxia. In all likelihood the captain would find a safe way to open the main hangar bay or get the oxygen scrubbers working again before the air became unbreathable.

Despite this, he thought it best to prepare for the worst and made his way back to sickbay for a bag full of syringes and some liquid oxygen. A rather desperate last resort, perhaps, but it would allow him to inject the solution into anyone collapsing from carbon dioxide poisoning – or hypercapnia – to keep their organs oxygenated.

Flannigan always kept good stocks of liquid oxygen, believing no space-farer should be without it. Chemically, the microparticles consisted of a single, thin layer of lipids, in this case naturally occurring fat molecules, encasing a tiny bubble of oxygen gas. An injection could buy anyone suffering from hypercapnic respiratory failure as much as half an hour without oxygen; time enough to get the patient to mechanical breathing apparatus or a supply of natural air.

The doctor walked into his sickbay humming tunelessly to himself, whilst running other precautions he might take through his mind. Lost in thought, he strode past the two patients, almost tripping over a foot sticking out from between the second and third beds.

It belonged to Justin Smyth, who was sprawled across the floor in an unnatural position. Flannigan desperately pushed the third bed aside, kneeling to check the nurse's condition. He almost laughed with relief when he found a strong pulse.

A syringe lay on the floor near Smyth, but more importantly, a discarded bottle of sedative lay on the bed he had just heaved aside.

"At least they tipped me off as to what they did to ya, kid." He stood quickly, walking to the medicine storeroom for some hydroxocobalamin, more widely known as B12b. He laid the prone man in a more natural and comfortable position on the floor, injecting him where he lay. Smyth began to regain consciousness within moments.

"Urrgghh," he said.

"You OK?" asked Flannigan, helping the young man into a sitting position against the side of the bed. "Huh?"

"I feel like I've been to a student party," Smyth stated groggily.

Flannigan chuckled. "Can you stand?"

"Maybe."

"Come on, let me help you," said Flannigan, hauling Smyth to his feet. He swayed a little and compromised by sitting on the bed. "Well, you're off the floor at least. What happened?"

"Not sure," Smyth replied, rubbing his forehead. "I was about to give this chap a little more sedative to help him sleep," he looked at Flannigan clearly now. "He was struggling with the pain. Next thing I know, I'm falling and then it was now."

Smyth looked at his watch. "I must have been out about forty minutes—" he caught his breath. "Dave! If the attacker gave him a full syringe he might be in serious trouble!" He got up more successfully this time, staggering a little as he crossed to the man with the neck injury.

Flannigan dashed around the other side of the bed, taking the man's pulse. "Thready," he said with a grimace. "I take it he got hit with the same stuff the attacker used on you? I only found one syringe and bottle."

Justin shrugged. "I assume so, but he'd already had some. If that evil sod's caused him to OD..." He looked down at the man in his care. "I'm sorry, mate. I just didn't see them coming."

Flannigan grabbed Smyth's arm across the bed. "Hey, this wasn't your fault, kid – we're dealing with an A1 wacko here! I'm gonna hit him with some B12b. Check on Lloyd, will ya? We might get lucky and free up a bed!"

"You don't mean that, Dave." Justin gave him his 'understanding' look.

"Don't I?" Flannigan sighed. "No, I suppose not, but I'm getting there."

Smyth gave him an indulgent smile and went to check on the regular patient.

"Come on, fella," said Flannigan, willing the attack victim back from the void. "Come *on...*"

Slowly the man started to move, his eyes fluttering open slightly. His voice came as the merest rasp, "That sleep went by fast. I still feel like crap!"

Flannigan laughed out loud this time, genuinely pleased that the man was OK. "Someone knocked you out before the nurse was able to give you a *nighty night.*"

"Lieutenant Lloyd is as indestructible as ever, it seems," Justin called across the room.

"Mmm, can't say as I'm surprised," drawled Flannigan. Looking back down at the man on the bed, he asked, "Do you remember what happened, before you went under?"

The man coughed, trying to rub his throat but the neck brace denied him. "It was a woman," he croaked.

Flannigan and Smyth stared at one another, incredulous. "You saw her?" asked Smyth, striding back around the bed. The man managed a small, painful nod.

"Did ya recognise her?" asked Flannigan.

In answer, he received an almost imperceptible shake of the head, followed by a whispered, "All in black with a mask. But the eyes..." He coughed again. "Blue, pretty, young," was all he could manage, the pain wracking his neck and throat.

"You take it easy, son," Flannigan soothed. "That's hugely helpful. Now try and get some proper rest, I'll check on you shortly." He nodded for Smyth to keep an eye on the man and commed Sergeant Jackson.

"Sarge here."

"Sarge, it's Doc Flannigan. Can you spare two security personnel to guard sickbay? It's urgent."

"They'll be with you on the double, sir."

"Thanks Sarge, and when you're done, can you meet me on the bridge? I need to speak to the Captain and you're gonna wanna hear it – Flannigan out."

The doctor strode over to his office. The small room was internal to the sickbay suite and therefore did not require a sealable hatch. He turned the traditional handle and managed to open the door a little way before it jammed. Pushing harder, he realised there was something on the other side preventing the door from swinging. He set his shoulder to it and the weight budged slightly, allowing him to squeeze his head through the crack. The obstruction was yet another body.

"Ah hell – Justin, get over here will ya?" he called over his shoulder.

At Flannigan's behest, Douglas, Baines, Jackson and Singh met with him on the bridge a few minutes later. "It's a woman!" snapped Flannigan, urgently.

"I don't suppose we need to ask who you mean," said Baines, "but how do you know?"

Flannigan explained the events in sickbay, describing how Burton's man and Smyth were injected with sedative and knocked out. "Smyth is OK but the other guy is lucky to be alive after the dose he got! This creature cares nothing for the lives she's destroying."

"And he's sure it was a woman?" Douglas pressed.

Flannigan nodded affirmative.

"Well, whoever this blue-eyed beauty is, her time is running out!" the captain continued, with savage satisfaction. "This is her first mistake – let's hope it's the beginning of a new trend. Jill, go through all passenger files and see how many women we have with blue eyes – Ah want to know straight away."

"On it!" Baines threw herself into a chair next to a terminal and began typing frantically.

Douglas looked at Jackson. "This is our first break, Sarge. Ah'm going to want to see them all and Ah'm going to want to know exactly where they were an hour ago, witness reports, the lot! Get Drummond, get White, get everybody to answer this shout. The commander will forward the list to you in a few minutes." He leered, quite uncharacteristically nastily, pointing through the bulkhead across the plain. "Turns out those beasties out there aren't the only ones going hunting today."

The Sarge nodded, saluted and left.

"Got them," said Baines. "We have nineteen females on board with blue eyes. Two of them are younger children, so that leaves seventeen possibles."

"Burton's laddie said that it was a *young* woman. Does that narrow it any?" Douglas asked Baines.

"Well, no one is exactly old here, Captain. This mission was hardly a day-trip to Bognor for a deckchair and an ice cream. But eight of the women are under thirty."

"He also said she was a 'looker'," Douglas supplemented.

"Beauty is in the eye of the beholder, Captain. Should we hold a pageant? Besides, NASA would never allow anyone ugly to go into space. Surely you've seen all the movies? At least, not unless they're funny and crack jokes all the time..." Baines frowned. "Oh," she finished in a small voice.

Douglas snorted, "Ha! Dinnae worry yoursel', lassie, there's always room on ma ship for people of ability."

"Oh *thanks*, Captain," said Baines, deflating. "You know just what to say to a gal. I'll just be in the next room if you need me – having my head fitted for a bag!" The three men laughed as she stood and walked back to them. "And by the way," she added, widening her eyes with exaggeration and pointing to each in turn with her index finger. "In case you were wondering – brown!"

"Do Ah need to search your quarters for blue contact lenses then?" asked Douglas, deadpan.

"Is that your poker face again, Captain?" replied Baines with indolent sweetness.

Douglas laughed, reinvigorated by this breakthrough and best of all, this time the knowledge had not cost any lives. "We'll need to see them all, but we'll start with the sixteen to thirties."

"Is that our next move, or are you planning a vacation?" asked Baines, cheekily.

"*Nice*," retorted Douglas, sarcastically.

"Are you going to check the crew too?" asked Singh.

Baines and Douglas looked at one another. "There's only Mary and Heidi—" Baines broke off, mid-sentence. "No..." she said, shaking her head, unwilling to countenance the possibility.

"They both have blue eyes, Commander," said Douglas, "so Ah reckon that puts us back up to nineteen."

"Well, it can't have been Schultz," Flannigan added, matter-of-factly.

"What do you mean?" prompted Douglas.

"Didn't I tell you?" asked the doctor, looking surprised. "I found her in my office, on the floor. She was knocked out with the sedative too."

"And you didn't think to mention that?" snapped Baines, tersely.

"Sorry, I thought I had," said Flannigan. "Look, I've just found one of my patients almost murdered and my entire medical staff on the floor unconscious – I'm on edge, OK? I only went back for supplies and a cup of coffee to pick me up, *damnit.*"

"Alright, *alright*," said Douglas. "So we're back down to eighteen suspects. What happened to Schultz, same MO as the others?"

"Yeah, sedative injection knocked her sideways. She said she saw no one and just woke up on the floor when I gave her the B12b jab." Flannigan frowned slightly. "It's odd though..." he frowned thoughtfully.

"What else did you find, Doctor?" asked Singh, intrigued by Flannigan's tone.

"Well, I didn't find anything as such," answered Flannigan, slowly. "It's just something Justin mentioned before I left – that he didn't remember Heidi being in the office before he was taken out. He could have sworn he was alone with the patients."

Flannigan's face cleared and he continued, "I guess she must have come back some time after Smyth had been rendered unconscious, meeting the killer on their way out, perhaps?"

"But you said that Schultz saw no one," Singh stated, unwilling to let the point go. Something was niggling at the back of his brain but he could not quite see it yet. "Or at least that's what she *said.*"

"OK, so we're back up to nineteen," Douglas reaffirmed. Baines looked doubtful, so he declared flatly, "We're making no more suppositions and giving no more chances to hide. We rule out no one! Whoever it is has got a lot to pay for. Then we can finally sort out where Lloyd fits into all this. He was the only one in sickbay who wasn't attacked, Ah see."

"Well, he is in a coma to be fair, James," said Flannigan. "It's not like he was gonna bear witness or hinder this woman in any way."

"Maybe, but it's yet another red mark in his ledger. Let's get these people interviewed and then we'll see if we can have our very first spring clean."

The brief meeting on the bridge broke up. The Sarge began organising a round of interviews with the blue-eyed women on Baines' list. Flannigan returned to his patients and Baines and Douglas returned to their viewport, leaving Singh alone on the bridge.

Douglas hoped to find the pack of carnivores gone. They were not. Worse still, the poor creature so horribly wounded was somehow still alive and mewing pitifully. All the officers could do was watch, praying for an end to its suffering.

As if in answer, one of the smaller Mapusaurs darted in, taking a huge, savage bite from the sauropod's chest. It received a massive kick in return from the dying animal, sending it flying, but the attacker had youth on its side and rolled back to its feet, roaring in fury. The kick was simply a spastic jerk as the bite reached the victim's heart, bringing its long anguish to a horrific conclusion.

The whole plain seemed to pause for a moment's silence, with only the shrieks of distant birds disrespecting the temporary armistice.

Douglas wiped an unaccustomed tear from his cheek. "Thank God," he said. "Thank God."

It had taken five hours for the unfortunate youngster to die. Douglas and Baines had had no choice but to keep checking in periodically. It had been an awful, excruciating death to witness, yet the carnivores were completely unmoved by the tragedy, literally or figuratively, and certainly showed no interest in leaving. Most were sunning themselves around their kill, at peace with the world, for now – unfettered by conscience.

"This really isn't our home, is it?" Douglas commented quietly, not really expecting an answer.

Baines sniffed, wiping a final tear away. "Nature has always been cruel, I guess."

"Aye. Ah suppose the concept of humanity becomes more abstract, the closer you get to the natural world. Come, we need to pick ourselves up and get planning. We cannae do anything about what's happened out there but we *can* try and make sure it disnae happen te us!

"After all, there's barely thirty-six billion days to go before we take back the planet," he replied, attempting to cheer his first officer a little. "So we need to be ready!"

"You've been working that out, haven't you?"

"O' course not!"

"Hmm. Well, when you put it like *that*, it doesn't sound so bad," replied Baines, taking a deep breath and smiling bravely in return. "We just need to remain patient and start counting down – begin some kind of tally, perhaps. We could incentivise it still further, too."

"Really? How so?"

"Think of it like an advent calendar."

Douglas frowned. "Go on," he asked tentatively.

"A chocolate behind every door would work for me."

The air on the Pod began to feel more and more lived-in as the day wore on. To relieve the situation, passengers boarded the *New World* in shifts to breathe the cleaned air, also taking turns in the escape pods, utilising their onboard life-support. These measures slowed the degradation in air quality, leaving a skeleton staff of thirty or so individuals free to work about the Pod, using a couple of portable CO_2 scrubbers in the more enclosed spaces. Slowly, they began to restore the damaged power grid, but Burton's prediction of two days' work for a basic workaround looked as though it might prove accurate; everything was indeed munted and pakaru.

Furthermore, the fifteen-strong pack of killers outside, the largest comparable in size to Tyrannosaurus Rex, were hampering their hopes of sending out excavators to begin the ditches and ramparts.

Another hour passed. "They're not going, Jill," said Douglas.

"I noticed. Should we just wait them out?"

"There must be more we can do."

"What did you have in mind? 'Cause it'll take more than a targeted leaflet campaign, I can tell you that."

"Aye," Douglas chuckled, "that it will. Let's have a word with the experts, see what they think."

"Tim?" she asked.

"Aye, there's also that zoologist, Dr... er?" he floundered.

"Pearson, Dr Natalie Pearson," supplied Baines.

"That's the one," he agreed ruefully. "The lassie with the dog. Ah really need to start memorising the passenger list."

"What, with all that spare time you've got?" she answered, raising an eyebrow. "Anyway, you can leave that to me. It'll come with time, and it looks like we're going to be with them for quite a lot of it."

Douglas looked back out of the view port. "Ah hope so," he answered, distantly. "Come on, let's go and see if we can find out how long we're likely to have our guests outside."

The Sarge and Private Jones guarded a corridor full of hatches, each of which led to one of the aft escape pods. Douglas greeted them with a nod to each. "Which lifeboats have Mr Norris and Dr Pearson in them?"

Jackson checked the small screen on his comm. "They're both in the same one, Captain. That one," he directed them down the corridor.

Douglas thanked him and walked with his first officer along to *Lifeboat 7*. As he cycled the hatch, the five people inside looked up in surprise.

"Time's up already?" asked Tim.

"No," Douglas answered, "we need some advice. Can you and Dr Pearson join us for a minute, please?"

Tim and Natalie dutifully followed the officers back onto the main ship, closing the hatch behind them. A muffled barking ensued.

Baines laughed. "You'd better let him come along too or your three friends in there will be deaf by the time you get back."

Pearson cycled the hatch once more. A crack appeared and Reiver burst through it. The collie gave one last *woof* of indignation, making plain his feelings about his mistress' thoughtlessness, and they all walked a little further down the corridor, so as not to be overheard.

"Ah take it that Tim has explained the situation we have outside, Dr Pearson?" asked Douglas.

"The Mapusaurus pack?" asked Natalie.

"The very same," Douglas replied. "We were hoping they might move along now they've—," he swallowed distastefully, "eaten."

"We don't think that's likely for some time, Captain," Tim stated.

"No," said Pearson, taking up the explanation. "Tim has been bringing me up to speed on the animals here. If large predators from our time are anything to go by – or at least the few we have left – they could be camped out there for the week. Even for such huge beasts, there must be three meals at least for each animal on that carcass. Lions, for example, will glut a vast amount of meat, blood and bone and then pretty much sleep it off for two or three days before repeating."

"Won't it have putrified after a few days in the sun?" asked Baines, wrinkling her nose in disgust.

"Putrid to our delicate sensibilities," Tim chuckled. "To them it's like adding barbeque sauce – it brings out the aroma and flavour."

"And," continued Pearson, "when the carcass has been stripped to the point where those bruisers lose interest in it, the smaller predators will descend in a bone stripping frenzy. Put it this way, after the giants get bored and wander off looking for their next meal, I wouldn't go out there if you offered me 'The Naturalist of the Year Award' and a lifetime research grant. That corpse will be alive with small killers!"

"So we're stuck then?" asked Douglas. "Bar moving the ship, which has to be a last resort due to the scarcity of our resources."

"Maybe not," said Tim, thoughtfully.

"What is it, Tim?" asked Baines.

"Well," the young man answered slowly, chewing his lip, "we can only make guesses about the behaviour of these creatures until we get to know them better, but it may be that we can put them to work *for* us."

"What, like beasts of burden?" asked Baines, again.

"Er – no," replied Tim. "That would be a very interesting strategy indeed, if only briefly. No, what I meant was, they've just eaten their fill."

"Ah," Pearson nodded her understanding, "I'm with you."

"Yes," said Tim, scratching his chin in thought before resuming his rationalisation. "We assume they're going to be pretty torpid for a day or two, now. Perhaps we could work some machines on the other side of the ship? It's a risk but as long as no one gets out of the cabs, they should be alright. The machines shouldn't attract the animals after they've gorged themselves. They won't smell enticing to them. When they get hungry again… well, who knows, but they're not at the moment. What do you think, Captain? Commander?"

"So you think they'll leave us alone and just catch a few rays over there?" asked Baines, looking doubtful.

"It's possible, even likely," agreed Pearson.

"What about if we get any other visitors to the party?" asked Douglas.

"Our movements may attract a few small, fast predators always after a quick meal, but our machines should protect us from those," replied Tim. "It's doubtful we'll see another major incursion, such as the one you witnessed earlier, Captain. Not just yet, anyway, and this is where we press our *guests* into service for us."

"How do you mean?" asked Douglas.

"Security," Tim answered simply. "The Mapusaurus pride own this clearing now, until they decide to move on. It's highly unlikely that anyone will try and take it away from them." The young man raised an eyebrow. "Would you?"

Douglas cleared his throat uncomfortably. "Ah see your point," he admitted. "So you think we might have a day or two's grace until they get hungry again?"

"We believe so, Captain," said Pearson. "When they start to get restless we can bring the machines back in. Hopefully, the power will be back by then and we'll be able to open and close the cargo bay doors quickly, as needed. Winding them closed with the geared hand wheels would be suicide if they're chasing us. That bunch raiding our cargo bay would be like the wrath of ancient gods."

Douglas felt a small shudder go down his spine; apart from reliving the spectacle witnessed outside, he also recalled just how close he had stood to a very bad tempered Mapusaurus bull. "Och, Ah'll never sleep again," he muttered.

"Captain?" asked Pearson.

"Sorry, just thinking aloud. Well, it's a plan and we have little choice it seems, thank you. Hopefully we can outwit them with our superior intellects," he added, wryly. "We've got to try something. We're over a barrel here."

"Or fish in a barrel, depending how you look at it," Tim commented, darkly.

"Mmm," agreed Douglas, "that's why we cannae risk letting anything on board. We're prisoners in here at the moment, and if it weren't enough that we've got monsters out there, we've also got a monster in here too, trying to turn us over to them."

Chapter 12 | Primedieval

Near the top of the *New World*, a hatch opened on the starboard side. The opener of the hatch dropped a large package on the deck, just inside the ship. It landed with a wet slap. The sun warmed it quickly, making it bleed. The black clad figure pulled the face from the hatch's locking control panel and began ripping out the cabling behind. Once satisfied the controls were well and truly out of commission, they walked quickly but calmly back into the heart of the vessel.

"The earthworks are going well," stated Baines, "and the animals are leaving us alone for the moment. Now, where did you want to build the castle again?"

"Ah think you mean the motte," Douglas answered in schoolmasterly tones. "What we're working on at the moment is the bailey. Did they teach ye nothing at loony school?"

'Loony' was the slang term given to people who were born on the lunar sphere.

"You know, I was always rather proud of being the first loony," replied Baines, "but the way you put that little inflection into the word makes me question the wisdom of telling anyone, ever again!"

"Glad to be of service," replied Douglas, wiggling his eyebrows. "Have they enclosed back to the ship yet?"

"Pretty much, they're just making a bit of a job of what will be the gateway, today. After that we'll need timber for the palisade and gates."

"Well, that herd of Argentinasaurus felled plenty of lumber for us. We just have to get the machinery over to it," said Douglas. "Don't suppose our friends have left yet?"

"No such luck. In fact, Natalie, who's been keeping an eye on them, as you know, has noticed they're getting a little bit rowdy again."

A shadow crossed Douglas' face. "That lot getting rowdy could make a Glaswegian bar fight look like a tea dance. Can we no' distract them? Keep them busy? Ah don't know – find them something to do?"

"They're not spaniels, James. However, it has been a couple of days since their feast. Perhaps we could send Lloyd out to barter for wood?" Baines suggested, innocently.

"Aye," said Douglas, "now he's back behind bars we need to have another chat with him. Just before Ah returned to the bridge, Ah took The Sarge and Dr Wright to search his quarters again. We haven't been in there since the first search following his initial arrest."

"He hasn't been back there though, has he?" asked Baines.

"No, it was just a hunch," said Douglas, with a crafty smile. "But guess what? We found one of the missing packs of plastic explosive from the escape pod docking bolts."

Baines looked astonished. "Really? But how…?"

"Exactly. It is remotely possible that we missed it first time around, but Ah sincerely doubt it," said Douglas, triumphantly. "This must have been the work of our mysterious blue-eyes."

"But why draw attention to the fact that she's out there?"

"The cat is well and truly out of the bag on that one, since the attack on The Sarge whilst Lloyd was there at the same time – albeit throwing up! Ah think that this move was meant to sink him, finally. Ah reckon she's thinking that, now we're here with our new, fledgling and highly unstable little society, someone will call for his blood and he'll be dealt with. Let's face it, we're hardly likely to believe a word he says, are we?"

"Do you think Lloyd knows who she is?" Baines asked thoughtfully.

"It wouldn't surprise me if he doesn't. Would you trust that sort of information to a man like him?"

"Well, no, but are we abandoning the idea that they were in it together, then?"

"Maybe." Douglas stroked his chin thoughtfully. "Maybe not. It's possible he had dealings or arranged drops with this person without knowing her identity. Wright thinks the fingerprints on the explosive are a match for Lloyd but he's checking to make sure. Ah think Lloyd's up to his neck in this, but by the same token Ah suspect he's been used too – just a fool and his vanity."

"You sound sorry for him," Baines noted with surprise.

"No – well, maybe a little," said Douglas. "He's a pretty tragic figure now. It's hard to imagine anyone ever being more alone."

Baines leaned forward. "He may have been Mario's murderer, James. I have to say, I'm not running over with sympathy."

"Ah know. Just wish we could prove it. Ah'm going to interview him again, fancy coming with?"

"Definitely. He's locked up now, isn't he?"

"Aye."

"Excellent, I'll bring the rotten fruit with stones in."

"Perfect."

Dr Wright arrived at the bridge, carrying the black sports bag found by Burnstein Jnr. He activated the door chime and waited.

The small screen next to the opening and locking controls lit up with the face of Lieutenant Singh. "How may I help you, Doctor?" he asked.

"Hello Lieutenant, I've finished with the black bag," Wright replied, holding the item up in evidence for the camera. "The captain asked me to bring him the results as soon as I had them."

The door slid open. "Come on in, Doctor. The captain and the commander are both with Lieutenant Lloyd at the moment, but you can leave the bag here with me if you like?"

"OK, Lieutenant, my report is on this data clip," said Wright, handing the items over. "You may be interested to know that the data clip we found in the bag did indeed contain the program that took over the ship's navigational systems. Georgio Baccini's checked it out and concurs. Now you have the programme, will you be able to back engineer it to fix the ship's operating system?"

"No, Doctor," Singh replied sadly. "Unfortunately, during the crisis, we had to wipe the OS and reinstall from factory settings, so we've lost ours, forever."

White nodded. "Bad luck. Oh, by the way, Georgio also identified the tool belt and tools as belonging to Lieutenant Lloyd. He's certain of it. Apparently, he and his brother, Mario, had a certain *familiarity* with Lloyd's tools."

Singh smiled sadly at the memory. "Yes, I remember some of Geoff's equipment had the unfortunate habit of going missing for days at a time. With two identical suspects and no hard evidence, it must have driven him crazy." He sobered. "Maybe it did. Are there any prints or genetic traces on any of the items?"

"Yes, all Lloyd, even the bullet."

Singh whistled. "Looks pretty black for him then."

"On the face of it, but I'm not wholly convinced."

"How so?"

"It's just that the items are completely clean apart from these very *deliberate* prints," Wright explained. "What I mean is – it's like he picked up each, pre-cleaned item, once, then put them down and never touched them again. If they'd been handled in the normal way, there would inevitably have been smudged prints all over them. What's also weird is that they're all right-hand prints."

"I believe Lloyd *is* right-handed, Doctor, so that would follow, wouldn't it?" asked Singh.

"Not necessarily. If I took a number of your personal belongings or work tools, say, and checked them for prints, would it be likely that you only touched them once? And with your right hand only? I can't help noticing that your tea cup is on the left side of your work station – are you left-handed, Lieutenant?"

Singh looked thoughtful. "No, I'm not. Now I come to think about it logically, I'd have to concede that those prints do sound a little *unnatural.* So how do you think they got onto the items if Lloyd hasn't handled them? There seems little doubt they were his."

"All I can say for certain is that each item was cleaned meticulously and *then* Lieutenant Lloyd's hands, or I should say hand, touched each of them once," answered Wright. "The how and the why are not my department."

Singh nodded. "I'd better call the captain with the main points of this while he's down there." He returned to his station to activate the comm and noticed a warning light flashing on the main pilot's console. "Looks like that's not all I've got to tell him."

His first comm message went out as an emergency call to Sergeant Jackson. "Sarge, it's Sandip. We've got an open docking airlock in corridor three, near the top of the ship. Can you get a squad up there straight away to check it out, please?"

"Aye, aye, Lieutenant."

Singh turned back to Wright, quizzically. "What the hell could have caused that? I'd better let the captain know that something else might be going on, too. He's not going to be a happy chappy."

Douglas and Baines sat opposite Lloyd's cell. When they entered, the prisoner had simply rolled his eyes and then looked away, ignoring them.

Here we go again, thought Baines. *"Déjà vu,"* she said.

Lloyd remained silent at first, but clearly a retort was bursting to get out of him. "If this is becoming repetitive, Commander, you could just try – I don't know – letting me go?" he snapped at last. "We both know you haven't got any evidence to support locking me up like this."

"No evidence?" spluttered Baines, in disbelief.

Douglas put a hand on her arm to calm her. "Unfortunately, Lieutenant, we have too much evidence on you. Our problem is trying to work out what you've done and what your partner is trying to make it look like you've done," he said.

"What partner?" asked Lloyd, frostily. "To whom exactly are you referring?"

"That's what Ah'd like to know," remarked Douglas when his comm chimed, interrupting the interrogation. "Douglas," he answered.

"Captain, Sandip. I need to talk to you in private please. Can you find a quiet corner, sir?"

"Aye, bear with me." He left the brig, sealing the door behind him. "OK, Sandy, Ah'm alone in the corridor now. Please continue."

Singh gave Douglas a quick overview of the new evidence discovered by Dr Wright's examination of the bag and contents. *"Wright thinks the dabs are suspect, sir, but he's not sure how it was done as the prints are real. It occurred to me that Lloyd has been unconscious in one way or another for a sizeable chunk of the last week and with the recent incidents in sickbay, perhaps the patients and medical staff were attacked just to get them out of the way for a while? Giving whoever it was chance to get Lloyd's prints in some way? This may even partially explain the attempts on Lloyd himself."*

"So you're suggesting," Douglas spoke slowly, working the idea through, "that whoever set this up, aside from being the most likely candidate for our killer and saboteur, is also someone who has plenty of opportunity to be in sickbay?"

"Do they need to be mutually exclusive, sir?" asked Singh, reasonably.

"You have a theory, Sandy?"

"Just that, sir, but..."

"It's OK, son, it's just between us," Douglas reassured his pilot.

"I hate saying this, Captain, but it occurred to me that the killer could have cleaned the objects and then pressed Lloyd's hand onto them while he was out of it. Also, we have someone we already know was around when Smyth was attacked, albeit with a few question marks attached – someone who has permanent access to sickbay and all of our pharmaceuticals. This person is slight, female, athletic, beautiful, and," he paused, adding weight to his summation, *"has blue eyes!"*

Douglas felt a sinking feeling in his heart. "Dr Schultz," he stated, flatly. "But don't forget she was also drugged," he added, trying to find another alternative.

"*Perhaps she dosed herself?*" Singh proposed, simply.

"But there was no syringe where she collapsed," said Douglas. "Flannigan said he only found one, under the bed by Justin. Surely she couldn't have knocked herself out in Dave's office and then moved the evidence. She was out cold, blocking the door. He couldn't even get into the room."

"*I know, Captain, but with respect, maybe you've got that the wrong way around?*"

Douglas was piqued. "Go on, Sandy, Ah'm listening."

"*What I mean, sir, is that she clearly couldn't knock herself out and then move the evidence, but perhaps she could leave the evidence before moving herself. Speaking from my own area of expertise, I often set this ship up to undertake delayed action tasks and leave her to it. Surely a medical expert could set the scene before self-administering just the right dose, allowing them to get into position before it took effect?*"

Douglas was silent for some time.

"*Captain?*"

"Ah really don't like this train of thought, Lieutenant," he admitted at last.

"*Sorry, Captain. It's just a theory.*"

"You misunderstand me, Sandip. It's possible you might have hit the nail right on the head. It's plausible, too damned plausible and Ah don't like it."

"*I don't think we can prove it though, sir.*"

"Maybe not, but perhaps we can narrow it down by verifying everyone's movements at these critical times," Douglas replied, thoughtfully. "Firstly, we need to ask Dave Flannigan if what you're suggesting is possible. Get onto that, please."

"*Certainly, sir, but there is one other thing, Captain,*" Singh added cautiously.

"Oh?" asked Douglas.

"A few minutes ago a docking hatch was opened high up, in corridor three. It may be nothing but I've had The Sarge despatch a team to investigate. They haven't reported in yet."

"What could have caused that?" asked Douglas, frowning.

"All I can tell you from here, Captain, is that it wasn't a request from the bridge or engineering. That suggests that it was opened from the local control console. Trouble is, I can't get it to handshake with the bridge computer. I've locked all the external hatches down with a security code now, so that they may only be opened with the command authority of a bridge officer or chiefs of security or engineering. When I hear back from The Sarge, I'll get Hiro onto it to find out the cause, sir."

"We should have locked those down a long time ago, damn it!" Douglas fumed.

"I know, sir, locking her from the inside once she has landed has never been a priority before. I'm sorry, sir."

"No, it's not your fault, Sandy," said Douglas. "No one thought of it. It just goes to show that we need to re-evaluate every aspect of security. Make time to go through it all with The Sarge, will you? Top to bottom, and let me know where we need new protocols. We can no longer afford to take anything for granted."

"Please stand by, Captain, I've got Private Jones on another channel."

On the bridge, Singh flicked between channels. "Go ahead, Private."

"Lieutenant, the hatch controls have been mangled, they have," reported Jones, in his sing-song Welsh accent.

Singh rubbed his eyes with tired frustration. "So it's sabotage?" he asked.

"Almost certainly, sir, but I'm more worried about the infestation, isn'it!"

"The what?!"

Baines stared at Lloyd, who affected not to care. "Come on, Geoff, who is it?" she asked.

"I'm sure I don't know *what* you're talking about," he answered, airily.

"Doesn't all this mean *anything* to you? People you've known, for years in some cases, are dying! Others too, just innocent passengers being taken to their place of work. How can you live with that?" His nonchalance was frustrating her.

"I keep telling you, it's nothing to do with me."

"Right, so when you were busted out of the brig a few days ago, you were just an innocent bystander as the ship's systems were sabotaged again?" she asked, disdainfully.

"You may recall that I was seriously injured during those events," retaliated Lloyd, "and have been in a coma for most of the time since. What do you want from me?" He spat these last words, finally showing agitation himself.

"Tell me what happened when young Paolo was murdered," Baines demanded, regaining her calm as Lloyd lost his.

"I didn't see that," he answered, sharply.

"What *did* you see?" she asked, patiently.

Lloyd took a deep breath and let it out, relaxing a little. "I was facing the other way when I heard a wet crunch and the sound of a body hitting the floor. By the time I turned around, a figure in black was bending to take the man's security key."

"Then what?"

"*Then* they came towards *me*. Surely you've got all this on camera?!" he asked, exasperated.

Baines smiled at him sardonically. "You *know* we haven't."

A flicker of confusion crossed Lloyd's face for a moment. "Cameras offline?"

"Let's get past the bit where you pretend to know nothing about that and tell me what happened next," demanded Baines.

"You think *I* disabled the security cameras from in here?" asked Lloyd, raising his eyebrows. "I didn't know you had such respect for my talents, Commander. Still, I suppose I shouldn't be too surprised really. I must seem extraordinarily gifted from your limited perspective."

"Well, you know I've always been quietly in awe of your abilities, Geoff," she answered with false civility. "By the way, the toilet is just behind you, should you need to wipe your chin or anything! Your friend really has proven themself to be rather brilliant though, it seems. Your particular skill set, on the other hand, appears to be geared more towards getting knocked out and caught. Don't get despondent, however, you've done a first rate job on your end so far! Now, please continue."

Lloyd gave her a look of absolute loathing – the arrogant man taunted. Baines smiled helpfully at him.

"What do *you* know about it?" he asked, eventually. Baines thought she heard just a hint of weakness in Lloyd's self-satisfied carapace of defence.

"Tell me about it then," she encouraged. "*Impress* me."

"What can I say?" he continued, visibly pulling himself back together, much to Baines' irritation. "Whoever it was let me out and told me to follow them."

"This person spoke to you?" she asked, leaning forward in her seat with interest. "What was their voice like? A man's? A woman's? Accented?"

"Dunno," said Lloyd, non-committally.

"Try again, skip!" said Baines, witheringly.

"Their voice was distorted electronically," he explained with a shrug.

Baines looked at him sideways for a moment, wondering if he was telling the truth about that. Her comm chimed, breaking into her thoughts. "Baines," she answered.

"*Jill, keep plugging down there,*" said Douglas' voice over the comm. "*Ah'm on my way up to the airlock in corridor three.*"

"Problem?" she asked.

"*Not sure yet, Ah'll call you when Ah am – Douglas out.*"

Lloyd sniggered nastily. "More trouble, Commander?" he asked, unpleasantly.

"Nothing for you to worry your little head about," retorted Baines, pushing her concern down. "Looks like it's just you and me," she smiled, wolfishly. "Would you like some fruit?"

Douglas ran into corridor three to find Jones and Thomas standing with rifles raised towards the open hatch. The soldiers' uniforms were torn here and there, and they sported some nasty cuts on their faces, along with what were clearly defensive wounds on their hands and arms.

The question died on Douglas' lips as he skidded to a halt, gaping at the half dozen or so bodies on the floor, all around them.

Down in one of the storage cupboards aboard the Life Pod, a robbery was taking place. The perpetrator helped themselves liberally to all manner of goods: long-life food rations, climbing equipment, a rucksack, two pairs of bicycle panniers, detergent, water containers and tarpaulin, along with a few other necessities for living rough. Once every compartment of every pack was stuffed to bursting, the thief checked their rifle over and stowed spare battery packs within a multi-pocketed waistcoat. The weapon had recently belonged to one of the extended security team, who had been forced to exchange it for a concussion. The black-clad figure nodded with satisfaction, pulling out an old, US Army, nine millimetre hand gun from a hip holster, to check that it too was loaded.

Making their way down to the vehicle pool, they swiftly set about stealing a bicycle. The bicycles were originally for use on Mars. The linked nature of the Mars Pods and other ancillary structures, such as the ore and mineral mines, made them ideal transport for the lengthy connecting tunnels, without using power. The bikes' wide wheels, designed to deal with the mixed, rugged surfaces down the mines, would also make traversing the rough ground outside the ship possible. Furthermore, the bicycle could carry or be carried, to suit the challenging terrain of a world without roads.

The thief slung the panniers over purpose-made frames mounted above the front and rear wheels. Throwing the rucksack around their shoulders, they snorted derisively – how they had made these weak people dance to every crisis.

The vehicle pool was deserted, the Pod work crews spread between the core and plant rooms, busy with repairs to the power grid. The way was clear all the way to the main pedestrian airlock hatch. From there it was a simple matter to power the control console, using the battery pack left by Douglas' first away mission, and then open the door.

Nothing happened.

They tried the process again: apply the power, build the charge and... nothing.

Hiro was alone in engineering, his security guard summoned away to help with some kind of search. He was not sure of the details, being far too busy working with the ship's operating system to be concerned with it right now. He had hated every minute since the reboot. No engineer worth his salt could put up with factory settings for long, and he was finding whole colonies of little annoyances every time he asked the computer to do anything. Tutting quietly to himself, he realised it was going to take him months to put everything back.

The opportunity this created gradually dawned on him and a grin spread across his face like butter on a bagel – it would take months to put everything back! That would be months of being able to legitimately avoid as much human contact as possible, tweaking every system as he went, and not forgetting the crowning bonus – the ship would be stationary while he worked. "I can get it all perfect," he spoke to himself in hushed tones, almost reverently. "Better than before!"

He was currently buried in an inspection chamber and began to climb out, intent on finding his work pad so that he could design a programme of restitution. Even the thought of writing the 'to do list' gave him butterflies. He could not remember the last time he felt this content. Sticking his head out of the hatch and looking around for his tablet, his eyes, alight with excitement, suddenly crossed.

This was an automatic response, enabling him to focus on the silencer attached to the barrel of the nine millimetre pistol pointed no more than ten centimetres from his nose.

Baines nonchalantly devoured an apple and some grapes as she read a comm message from Lieutenant Singh. The text file referred to the sports bag and its contents. Also appended were Dr Wright's conclusions.

Lloyd seethed in silence.

"Well, I did offer you one," Baines smirked.

"I don't want your damned apples!" snapped Lloyd. "I want to get out of here!"

"Well, in that case you'll be glad to know that if you're not forthcoming with the information I want, you may indeed be taking a trip outside. How do you like *dem* apples?"

"You wouldn't dare!" he glared at her.

"We've had this conversation before, remember? You have no law to hide behind now. It's justice really, isn't it? Like all criminals, you've stepped well outside the law and now you want the same law you contemptuously discarded, to wrap you up like a warm, soft blanket. Only problem is, we've *all* stepped outside the law now, Geoff. *Ain't no sheriff in this picture*," she said, playing up a cowboy accent as she ate another grape with great satisfaction. "So why don't you get down off your high horse and start talking? It might just save your life. For example, you could start by telling me what happened after you were busted out of here."

"Why should I help *you*?" he snarled, irritably.

"Firstly, for the reasons I've just stated and secondly, because your partner in all this has done everything possible to frame you," Baines explained calmly.

Lloyd looked slightly stunned.

"Nothing to say?" she prompted, sweetly.

"I..." he dithered for a second, "I don't have any partner. I'm innocent."

Baines exhaled deeply. "Seriously, Geoff, if you don't give me something in mitigation, sentencing is likely to be rather swift and very uncomfortable for you. The sports bag containing the data clip, the one with the worm on it which almost destroyed the ship, was also found to contain your tool belt *and* a nine millimetre round – all of which had your prints on them. Care to discuss?"

Lloyd's colour drained. "What's this? What bag? I haven't—"

"Oh, and there's also the plastic explosive," Baines continued, airily, "ditto with your prints on it *and*, did I mention the explosive was found in *your* quarters?"

"I… I…" He tried to answer but nothing coherent came.

"Whatever your relationship with this person *was*, you've been hung out to dry, Geoff. You must see that now?" She drove the point home.

"Look, I don't know what she—"

"It was a woman then, was it?" Baines interrupted.

Lloyd swallowed.

Baines, miming a gun with her hand, pointed it at Lloyd as she feigned the hammer going down with her thumb. She winked at him, *Gotcha!*

Douglas took the last few steps more slowly. "Are you boys alright?" he asked the battered men. Both soldiers nodded, so he added the supplementary, "What the hell are these?"

"Some sort of birds, sir," said Thomas.

"With damned big teeth, isn't it," added Jones.

The winged nightmares, Douglas could see there were seven of them now, were around a metre across the span with large heads, long snouts and mouths fully loaded with savage, reptilian teeth. Vicious talons adorned their feet and even their wings. Douglas studied them more closely. Their wiry, muscular little arms ended in clawed fingers, the largest of which extended all the way to the wingtip, creating the framework for the membranous wing itself. They were leathery but also had short downy feathers over their bodies; all russets and reds. He guessed these helped the creatures stay warm and display, as with birds. Clearly all the same species, each had a relatively short tail between their hind legs which in turn were webbed together at the thighs. What did Tim call them, Pterosaurs? A vague memory surfaced of the young man explaining how the early Pterosaurs had long tails, which may have been of some assistance to their aerobatics. However, the later, more aerodynamically advanced animals evolved much shorter tails. He guessed these creatures fell somewhere between the two. Their visage was terrifying, almost demonic, but there was also an undeniable, savage beauty about them.

"You managed to drop them with the Heath-Riflesons, then?" asked Douglas.

"*Eventually*, sir," said Thomas, more than a little unsettled.

"Corp?" Douglas queried.

"Well, sir, they dropped in the end, but I swear we stunned 'em hard enough to bring Jones here down. They can't weigh more than a kilo or two!" He stared down at the little creatures with horrified respect. "What's more, we found a scrap of meat on the deck that wasn't from them – or us," he added acerbically. "I think it might have been steak, sir, they were fighting over it when we arrived."

"They were *baited* in here?" asked Douglas, raising his eyebrows in astonishment.

"Looks like, sir," replied Thomas, frowning.

"With steak?!"

"I know," Thomas acknowledged. "Talk about a waste. I never even ate real meat before I joined the NASA mission, let alone steak. Well, you remember what standard fare was like back home, sir."

Douglas grunted. He remembered. "Are they dead?" he asked.

"I damned well hope so!" snapped Jones, more rattled than Douglas ever remembered seeing him.

"We had to give them a good blast, Captain," continued Thomas. "They just kept shaking it off and they were *so* fast, they were tearing into us. I know we're to try non-lethal approaches where possible, sir, but…"

"Don't worry, men," said Douglas, placatingly. "Rather them than you, eh?"

Thomas nodded and swallowed; trained soldier though he was, this was well outside his theatre of experience.

"We'd better get Dr Pearson to examine the bodies and check they're not carrying any parasites or diseases we need to be aware of. You two need to get those wounds cleaned and seen to, ASAP."

"Not yet, sir," said Jones. "At least one of them got past us and flew down the corridor. A right nasty big one as well, it was. There may have been more."

"Ah didnae see anything when Ah ran up here," stated Douglas with alarm. "It must have gone the other way."

He pulled his comm from a pocket and hailed the bridge. "Sandip, close all of the internal bulkhead hatches immediately. They don't need to be locked, just closed. We seem to have a vicious flying reptile free on the ship. Put out a ship-wide warning over the PA – include the Pod too, if their comms are up yet, just in case." He studied the control panel on the exterior hatch. "Better get Hiro up here to repair this docking hatch too, the controls have been ripped out – it's like spaghetti in there."

He turned back to the soldiers. "Sorry boys, Ah'd like to send you to sickbay but we need to guard that hatch against any more gatecrashers. Ah'll get a medic up here to dress you up at least. Once Hiro's done his thing and closed the hatch, you can take yourselves off for treatment and a full check-up. Like Ah said, we don't know what these critters might be carrying."

"Yes, sir," the men answered without hesitation.

"The lunatic who caused this might still be up here too."

The soldiers looked at one another grimly.

"So keep 'em peeled and watch your backs. Good work," Douglas tossed them a salute and left. Pulling the stun pistol he always wore these days from its belt holster, he turned the corner with caution.

As it happened, the 'lunatic' was actually down in engineering, pointing a loaded side-arm at Chief Nassaki's face. Hiro's comm binged, making him jump so badly that he almost fell back down the hatch. The black-clad figure gripped him with their empty hand, pulling him back from the edge.

"Thanks," said Hiro, automatically, before looking back down at the pistol pointing at his stomach. "Oh…" he added, glumly.

The figure motioned towards the door with their gun.

Hiro remained still for a moment. "I don't suppose that's unloaded by any chance?" he asked, attempting a friendly smile.

It took but a fraction of a second for the gun to be pointed at the floor, fired and returned to its position covering the engineer.

Hiro swallowed. The hole in the deck was about fifteen millimetres away from his foot. He nodded sideways towards the door. The figure in black nodded up and down once. Hiro walked.

"Your only chance of living out the week is to come completely clean, NOW!" shouted Baines, all humour gone.

Lloyd glared at his antagonist, breathing deeply. He was clearly steadying himself for something. "I have a request," he said at last.

Baines leaned back in her chair, looking at him askance. "Go on," she prompted, guardedly.

"A single malt, a good one, and I'll tell you all I know – everything."

"You're bargaining for a whiskey? *Now*?" she asked in frank disbelief.

"What other chance will I ever get?" he replied simply. "And make it a very large one. I'm sure that damned Scotsman will have some hidden away somewhere."

"Better spell it w-h-i-s-k-y then," she said, pulling out her comm. "Captain? Erm, it's like this…"

Within a few minutes the door to the brig slid open once more to admit Captain Douglas bearing a mature single malt, a Glencairn whisky glass and a grudge.

"Don't worry, Captain, I've got a glass," said Lloyd, waving a safety glass receptacle around smugly.

Douglas looked down at the bottle and then at Lloyd. Then down at the bottle again, then at Lloyd again.

"*Captain*," said Baines, "I know it hurts but—"

"Stop talking!" he ordered, tetchily. "We cannae torture the prisoner, but it's OK to torture me, is that it?"

Baines covered her lower face with a hand, hiding a smile which threatened to escalate into laughter. "Maybe we can set up a still when we've gotten settled…" she tried helpfully, but trailed off under the furnace of Douglas' glare.

"A *still*?" He stared at her as if she were mad. "This is fifty-year-old oak-matured! *Fifty years old!* Ah'm talking the Holy Grail and you're talking rot-gut-shine!"

Lloyd waved his glass from side to side indolently. "Do I need to rattle this on the bars or something? I'm unsure of the protocol." He was enjoying his last dig.

Douglas whished like the Flying Scotsman himself. "Of all the people Ah thought Ah'd share this dram with, Ah cannae believe that… Aarggh, ye'd better have something good for me, Lloyd, or Ah swear Ah'll put ye ootside for the neet like the damned cat for this!"

Douglas pointedly poured himself a generous measure first. Slowly, and with all the grace of a man parting with his last pennies to the taxman, he poured a little whisky into Lloyd's glass too.

"Ahem," said Lloyd, not moving the glass a millimetre.

Douglas grumbled incoherently. Grudgingly, oh so grudgingly, he poured a little more into the proffered tumbler.

"Thank you, Captain," Lloyd acknowledged. Smiling victoriously, he saluted with the tumbler and took a large swig.

Douglas sat down next to Baines, in a perfectly foul mood.

"Don't suppose you've got another tot there, have you, Captain?" she asked hopefully.

Douglas turned slowly to face his first officer. "This was your idea, wasn't it, Jill?" he asked gruffly.

"Well, I wouldn't say that. I mean, not exactly."

Douglas gave a tight, mirthless smile. "Precisely. So ye'll be needing to keep a clear head te make sure that we dinnae miss anything, will ye no'?" he said with satisfaction.

The duty guard's face crawled all over his head in an attempt to stay straight. Baines noticed and lashed out, "Eyes front, Private!"

Hiro and the masked figure made their way along eerily quiet corridors. To Hiro's dismay, the security guard between the *New World* and the Pod had already been dealt with. He sincerely hoped the condition was not permanent.

Presently, they came to the main cargo bay and motor pool. He was pushed towards the small hatch alongside the much larger cargo doors, wondering what on Earth his tormentor's plan might be.

The figure retrieved a heavily laden bicycle from behind a parked lorry, still covering Nassaki with the pistol. A brutal push sent Hiro sprawling in front of the personnel hatch.

He picked himself up, turning back to face his captor in confusion. It was his first chance to stand back and study them and he now suspected his life might be in the hands of a woman. *She* motioned towards the hatch.

"You want me to *open* it?" he asked, incredulous. "Have you seen what's out there?"

The masked head moved ever so slightly to the side as the gun raised another inch or two; the subtle movement and blue eyes speaking eloquently of patience expired.

"OK," he continued, nervously, "but we have no power to these doors. When the captain's party went out they used a power pack to open it – I don't have one."

The figure merely lifted their head slightly, a subtle movement as the eyes darted around the engineer and back. Hiro looked around, cursing inwardly as his eye alighted upon *just what he needed*. Stowed against the bulkhead, behind a mini digger, was the battery set the captain's team had used to power up the hatch.

Out of options, Hiro complied, bringing the control panel to life. "Are you sure you want me to do this?" he asked, a tremor in his voice.

The masked figure gave an economical, quick-jerk gesture with the gun, which was unmistakable.

Hiro hit the open button.

Nothing happened.

He looked around. Smiling nervously, he tried again.

Nothing...

"Erm," he said, "it *should* have worked." The gun flicked back towards him, making him throw his hands in the air. "Give me a minute, give me a minute!" he cried, turning back to the locking mechanism. It looked like the Pod's hatch had been locked down from central control; powering it up must have allowed it to receive the command wirelessly. Hiro frowned, not sure whether that was even possible with power down all across the Pod, and then he had it. "The chief of operations must have locked all ground level access points down when we landed," he said, "just in case someone opened it up by accident. I wasn't part of the first mission outside because it turned out to be a security operation, but I think I can override it."

The bulkhead portholes provided a low light, just enough to see by. Hiro tinkered with the control panel in the gloom for a few moments. When all of the overhead lighting came on, illuminating the whole cargo bay, it took them both by surprise.

The terrorist snapped their head this way and that, assessing the situation in a heartbeat, before turning back to Hiro and pointing the gun at his face.

The terrified engineer threw his hands up once more. "It wasn't me! That wasn't me!"

The black gloved hand pulled back the firing hammer, putting the weapon to Hiro's head. With their free hand they pointed at the door.

Hiro gulped, "Yes, yes, I'm on it." Using his chief of engineering security codes, he attempted to unlock the hatch and to his exquisite relief, it opened. He unplugged the power-pack, unthinkingly leaving the inner hatch open behind him, as he plugged into the external hatch at the other end of the airlock. He repeated the unlocking routine, too terrified to even look round. The hatch in front of him opened too, exposing him for the very first time to Cretaceous Gondwana. He peeked outside gingerly.

The massive earthworks the construction team had built already stood five metres tall. Directly in front of the main cargo bay doors, a hundred metres out, there was a large opening between the two ramparts and through it he could see the clearing in which the *New World* had landed. The way appeared unobstructed right up to the tree line.

Hiro's mind raced – the shock and wonder of his location suddenly real. He was about to exchange his controlled, manmade environment for the beauty and savagery of a world unadulterated. He would have loved to explore these musings and feelings more fully, but was all too aware of the clear and present danger standing right behind him. Slowly, hesitantly, he began to turn when all the lights went out again, but this time only for him.

Burton whooped. "Let there be light, dude!" he exclaimed, loudly.

Gleeson grinned as he shook the New Zealander's hand in congratulation. "It's a good start, mate."

One of the panels began to beep at them. Burton studied it, his elation fading fast. "What the hell?"

"What is it?" asked Gleeson.

"Some drongo's opened the hatch down in the cargo bay," said Burton.

The moment stretched as they stared at one another in confusion.

"Why would..." Gleeson began, then his eyes widened in sudden understanding. He turned quickly to one of the other engineers in the plant room and snapped, "Get the captain on the line! We need security down in the main cargo bay and I mean bladdy yesterday, mate!"

He grabbed his rifle and ran out with Burton hot on his tail, not altogether sure what was happening.

The two men ran into the main cargo bay, panting heavily. It appeared deserted, so they jogged across to the open pedestrian hatch, slowing with caution as they drew close. Daylight streamed in, meaning both hatches were open.

"Crap," Gleeson muttered. The Australian flattened his back to the bulkhead and warily looked around the corner. The New Zealander leaned around his colleague, mimicking the action. The sight which greeted them promised to return as a vision – each night when they closed their eyes.

"WHOOAAA!" they shouted, together, followed by, "Nasso!"

Lieutenant Hiro Nassaki lay across the threshold of the outer hatch, his body in the airlock, his head and one of his arms outside. Also outside, bent over and sniffing the prone engineer like an unfamiliar morsel at a buffet, was a huge, female Mapusaurus.

"AAARRGGHHH!" screamed the Oceanians in unison. Gleeson's body remembered he was a soldier and he automatically began shooting, the stun bolts hitting the animal's face with a percussive thump.

The Mapusaurus stepped back and grunted, shaking her head in surprise. After a moment she sneezed, hugely, and all three men were hit by the return fire. After clearing her sinuses she, too, found her voice: **ROAR**!

The magnitude of the sound almost stunned them as it bounced and rebounded in the small, metal antechamber.

"AAARRGGHHH!" the men retaliated. Gleeson fired once, twice, thrice, causing the massive beast to stagger back a little further. Burton saw his chance to undertake the bravest act he could ever wish to forget. He dove into the mêlée, dragging Hiro's feet back until he was fully inside the Pod once more.

Shaking off the stun blasts, the animal spotted the New Zealander, on his feet, near the doorway.

His whole world in slow-motion, Burton's mind treated him to a flashback – "*Bigger and often even more aggressive than the male, the female Mapusaurus...*" the voice of Tim Norris spoke with a surreal calmness – "I can't remember what he said next!" cried Burton.

"*What*?! SHUT THE BLADDY DOOR!" screamed Gleeson.

The female Mapusaurus had no such lapse in memory, she knew her business well. She opened her mouth wide and *lunged*; all rotten stink and teeth like steak knives. She was about to take Burton, when his shattered wits caught up with the situation and he dove for the close stud.

The hatch sealed quickly, knocking the creature's head to the side and deflecting its attack with barely a millisecond to spare. The New Zealander had sat through departmental accounts meetings which shot by faster than that instant. As he waited for the door to close, his legs caught up with his wits and collapsed under him. He fell on top of Hiro and they lay slumped together, against the hatch.

"Is he alive?" asked Gleeson.

"Am *I*?" asked Burton, tremulously, shock hitting him like a train.

"Come on, mate, on your feet."

Burton refused to move for a minute. He was shaken and damned well not going to be stirred.

Dr Flannigan dressed the injuries to Private Jones' face and arms. The antiseptic must have stung like hell but Jones barely flinched. Corporal Thomas was covered in plasters, with a press and bandage wrapped around his left forearm. Before Flannigan could finish with Jones, his comm binged. He raised his eyes to the ceiling. "What now?" he muttered under his breath as he answered the call.

"*Doc? It's Captain Gleeson. I need you to get down to the main cargo bay in the Pod, mate,*" said the Australian, sounding anxious.

"What's happened, Captain?"

"*Nasso's down. Step it like you're running for the dunny, Lieutenant! Gleeson out.*"

Flannigan raised his eyebrows. "Nasso?" he repeated, slightly baffled. "I think he wants me to move with alacrity. Sorry, Jones. I'll get back to you as soon as I can."

"Do you want one of us to come with you, Doctor? I mean, if there's trouble?" Thomas asked with concern.

"Nooo n-n-no," Flannigan replied quietly, in his easy-going manner. "You boys just make sure nothing else comes through that hole," he gestured towards the open hatch, gaping twenty metres above the ground. Quickly packing his equipment into a ubiquitous, leather doctor's bag, he set off at a trot, not realising that he had just made a mistake. Regret would follow on swift wings.

He ran through the ship and Pod, wondering what had befallen 'Nasso' – he assumed the Australian meant Nassaki. Progress was slow, as every hatch was closed against him. They were not actually locked, so he never thought to close them behind him, Singh's ship-wide warning completely driven from his mind in his rush to help an injured colleague.

He ran. His heart pumped blood faster and faster, powering his muscles on and on.

Two snouts sniffed, hidden in an alcove as he ran past. The doctor had dead blood on his sleeves from the soldiers' wounds and hot blood coursing just beneath his skin.

The killers released their clawed grip on an access panel and, surfing the currents left in the air by the running man, they rode his slipstream. He was just two hatches from his destination when they fell upon him from behind like javelins.

Flannigan cried out in shock as the Pterosaurs dove, knocking the forty-seven-year-old army doctor to the deck with the ferocity of their strike. The murderous reptiles answered with a screeching cry of their own, as they set about their prey with tooth and claw. Rolling onto his back, Flannigan held the bag in front of him like a shield.

Darting, diving and screaming they came on, relentless. He punched and kicked, swinging the bag wildly at every opportunity, but the little animals' reflexes were liquid lightning. Every time he managed to land bag or fist they were already somewhere else, easily shaking off his glancing blows. The creatures were only small, but Flannigan knew he was in trouble and would tire long before they did – especially if they kept bleeding him.

With a huge effort he sprang to his feet, yowling in agony as a set of tiny jaws bit deeply into the back of his neck with teeth like tacks. "You little…!" He managed to grab the smaller of the two, throwing it hard against a bulkhead before it could bite his face, but the animal merely turned in the air, barely scraping the wall. This was his last chance and he ran for his life through the hatch, ignoring the constant bites and scratches as best he could.

The final hatch was just ahead when Flannigan spun like a shot-putter – launching his bag at the *open* control ten feet away, he dove. Sprawled across the floor of the main cargo bay, he used the last wind in his lungs to scream, "HEEYYYY!"

Two of Major White's men helped Sam Burton to a seat. They left Hiro where he lay, unconscious, unwilling to move him before the doctor's arrival for fear of causing further injury. Gleeson and White stood aside, catching up quietly, when they all heard a sudden scuffle and a shout from the far end of the bay.

Seeking out the source of the commotion, they saw Flannigan on the deck, under a savage aerial attack from a pair of bird-like reptiles. The doctor covered his head as best he could, while crawling to retrieve his stout leather bag, and only protection.

"WITH MEEE!" bellowed White as he ran to help.

Gleeson followed immediately, the other two security operatives hot on his heels. It took just seconds for the four soldiers to converge on Flannigan's position, but even so, his injuries were mounting up. He screamed in agony, his strength almost gone.

White aimed a stun bolt at the larger of the two reptiles, knocking the animal back and forcing it to fly a small circuit of the area to recover. Having shaken off the effects, it came back at him like a fury, screaming hate. The whirlwind of teeth and claws targeted his face and eyes. He suffered a deep bite to his cheek and a claw across his nose before he was able to bat the creature away.

The animal easily outdistanced his ineffectual counter attack, but by circling to come again it created an opportunity, allowing one of the skirmishers to take another shot. The low power stun bolt found its mark. Deterred, the little Pterosaur flew a much larger loop creating yet more space between it and the men. The soldier dialled his Heath-Rifleson to maximum and when the next bolt struck, the pitiless, flying nightmare was reduced to scorched leather and blackened bone as it fell from the air – quite dead.

Gleeson ran in close to Flannigan as the remaining Pterosaur kept up a continual, withering attack on the weakening, unarmed doctor. The Australian caught the creature unawares with an army boot, stunning it. For a moment it lay on the deck flapping one wing ineffectually, but growing up in the bush among other vicious predators, Gleeson knew better than to give quarter. He jumped on the creature, landing double-footed on its little body and head. There was a sickly crack-pop and the fight was over.

He turned back to Flannigan, who was bleeding from a dozen nasty cuts and gashes all over his head and arms. "Er... thanks for coming so quickly, mate," was the best he could manage.

"Oh, any time," replied Flannigan, raising himself up on one elbow, unsteadily. He felt very lightheaded.

"You OK, Dave?" asked White.

"I could use a beer," he said, groaning weakly and raising his hands for assistance. "Help me up, fellas."

"Shall I get that German doctor down here?" asked Gleeson, full of concern. "You look like crap, mate."

"Good God, no, I'm not that desperate, but thanks for your diagnosis, Captain." The healing power of sarcasm boosted Flannigan's strength a little. "C'mon, let's check on Hiro."

Gleeson and White glanced at one another, shaking their heads in rueful respect for the old warhorse. Together they helped Flannigan hobble over to the engineer who, to everyone's relief, was beginning to stir all on his own.

"Help me down to him," said Flannigan.

Kneeling with a little help, he took the engineer's pulse, flicked a torch into his eyes and made all the usual checks doctors perform whilst deciding what to do with the patient – or in Hiro's case, the impatient. He attempted to rise but Flannigan held him still.

"Mmm," the doctor commented with a satisfied nod, "a small concussion, nothing too serious. How many fingers am I holding up?"

"How many fingers am *I* holding up?!" Hiro snapped, making a rude hand gesture. "Let me go!" He sat up, crossly. "I need to check the hatch. If they've broken my ship again, I'll..."

The three men, standing around the engineer, laughed as Gleeson helped him to his feet.

"Gentlemen, would you help Hiro to sickba—" began Flannigan.

"No!" Hiro interrupted. "I've got too much to d—"

"Save it, Lieutenant!" Flannigan barked, drawing on his last reserves. "Sickbay – that's an order!"

"But—"

"But nothin' – not even Douglas can overrule me on medical matters, you know that." He nodded to Major White. "Get him to sickbay, please,

Major. Call ahead and tell Smyth that Hiro will need treatment for a light concussion and that he will be staying with us OVERNIGHT," he raised his voice over the chief's futile complaining.

"You need to get there yourself, mate," advised Gleeson, looking down at the doctor now sitting on the deck with his back against a wall.

"I just need a minute," he replied, breathing heavily and wincing as he put a hand to his bleeding ear. He laughed softly as Hiro was led away, cursing in Japanese. "He's alright." Looking across to where Burton sat, he enquired, "Are you injured, Sam?"

"Just a bit shocked, I think. Feels like someone pulled the plug out of my bath tub," he replied, tiredly.

"That'll be the adrenaline fade," said Flannigan. "I'm feeling it myself. Looks like you've had quite an adventure of your own down here?"

"It's a gripping tale, mate," Burton replied wearily.

"Go on."

"I'd rather not talk about it."

Flannigan chuckled again and reached up for Gleeson to help him to his feet. "I feel like I've advanced my legs a generous bonus and now I can't get any damned work out of 'em!"

"Sorry I called you down into this, Doc," said Gleeson. "Come on, you need to get that head looked at."

"Never truer words spoken!" Flannigan snapped and he limped off grumbling.

"Hang on, mate, we'll help you." Gleeson pulled Burton to his feet and together they trotted to catch up.

Lieutenant Singh was once again the only bridge officer on duty, so Major White brought him up to speed with events in the Pod's cargo bay. Singh subsequently placed a call to the brig – so that he could pass along the worry.

"*Brig*," a soldier's unemotional voice responded.

"This is Lieutenant Singh. Is the captain there?"

"Er... well."

Singh sensed the hesitation, also hearing something else going on in the background... singing? "What the hell is going on down there, Private?" he asked, peremptorily.

"I'll get the commander for you, sir," he replied.

A moment later, Commander Baines' voice replaced him, *"Everything OK, Sandy?"*

"I need to see you, Commander. Can you and the captain meet me in sickbay please?"

"That may be a little difficult."

Baines stepped aside and activated a small camera built into the wall comm, providing Singh with a fish-eye view of the brig. He could now clearly make out the captain and Lloyd in the background, sat on the floor either side of the bars and brandishing their glasses out of time with an old army song.

"...And her legs were like the legs of a – burp! And a, OOOOHH, Ooohh, there she goes again, wearing nothing but a union flag, la la la... how's it go again?"

Baines moved back in front of the camera, rocking with suppressed laughter. *"I'll meet you there in just a minute, Sandy – Baines out."*

Singh blinked as the connection was severed. Chuckling softly, he locked the bridge down and made his way to sickbay.

Baines called the brig security guard to her. "When they've had enough, can you get Lloyd on his bunk and get the captain back to his quarters? Make sure that neither of them is left lying on their backs."

"I used to be an MP, Commander," replied the soldier with a wink. "I know the drill."

She nodded and left for sickbay.

Baines arrived just before Singh. She was still grinning, but pulled up short when she saw Nurse Smyth patching up Flannigan's myriad wounds and lacerations. Hiro lay on a bed holding an icepack to his head, with a new shiner replacing the fading one to his other eye.

Both men were clearly battered and bad tempered.

"Have you two been squabbling over table tennis again?" she asked.

"That's funny," said Flannigan, flatly.

Baines smiled sympathetically. "Sorry, Dave. What's happened now?"

Singh entered at this point to explain events in the cargo bay as he had been given them by Major White. Flannigan augmented the tale here and there, as his headache allowed, but was mostly glad to let someone else do the talking.

"I've despatched Georgio to fix the open upper hatch where the creatures entered the ship and left orders for Jones to come down here for his plasters and bandages when it's sealed," Singh reported, frowning slightly. "He said, *'I'll come down now in a minute'*. He says that a lot but I'm not sure what it means?" He shook his head in bewilderment.

"Dr Burton had the good sense to lock down the Pod's external hatches when we landed, it seems. I wish we'd thought of that on the ship before those killer birds got in. Still, I suppose it wouldn't have prevented the saboteur from kidnapping our chief engineer to unlock them again, would it?" Singh looked over towards Hiro, still lying down with his ice pack. "Or stopped Hiro from almost becoming a T Rex tuckbox for that matter."

"That was a lot funnier before it happened!" Hiro snapped, moodily.

Baines covered a smile with her hand again. "Why don't you tell us what happened, Chief?" she asked.

"I was having a really great day," Hiro began, "making a list of everything I needed to do to get Sekai well again."

"Sekai?" asked Flannigan.

"It's his pet name for the ship," Baines whispered. "Continue, Hiro, please."

"OK, so then there was this gun in my face, I nearly fell down the— oh, never mind. What matters is that it was the figure in black again, the same one who attacked The Sarge and myself a few days ago – I'm sure of it. I was route-marched down to the Pod and forced to open the hatch at gunpoint. I wasn't sure what to do at first. I mean, obviously, you'd have to be suicidal to go out there. However, they made it quite clear that this was exactly what they did want to do!"

"Did she speak to you?" asked Baines.

"No," said Hiro, pulling the icepack away from his head and inspecting the spot of blood on it. He relocated it to a slightly different position.

"Only another five minutes with that," Flannigan interjected, "then give it a rest for a couple of hours before trying it again."

Hiro nodded to the doctor but spoke to Baines, "It *was* a woman then? I thought it might be."

"Yes," she replied. "Lloyd said she used an electronic voice distorter."

"She didn't speak to me at all," Hiro continued. "She didn't need to – her eloquence with the gun was undeniable. I saw her riding away across the plain, just as I blacked out. I tried to fight it but…"

"Considering what happened while you were unconscious, you were much happier out of it – believe me," Singh muttered.

"What do you mean?" asked Hiro. "And what *do* I smell of?"

Singh scratched his stubble wondering, not for the first time, whether he should have kept his mouth shut. "Nothing to worry about really. Burton dove in and saved you from definitely being eaten by a huge flesh-eating dinosaur, that's all. Unfortunately, when Gleeson shot the animal he made it… erm… *sneeze*, apparently. Look, there's no nice way of putting this, you're covered in dinosaur snot! You know that unpleasant smell of sneeze? Well, imagine it from a snout over a metre long that has been buried in a rotting corpse left out in the sun for days – that's you now."

Hiro pulled his hands up to his chest, prissily, as if afraid to touch himself. "Dave?" he asked tremulously. "Can I have a shower please?"

"You might want to send Sam Burton a fruit basket, too, or perhaps you should 'say it with shower gel', eh?" Singh added, grinning. "I know he got blasted too and I'm pretty sure he blames you."

Ignoring the pilot's taunting, Flannigan looked serious. "Jill," he said, "I'm real worried about Heidi. I thought she'd be here to stitch me up, but we can't find her anywhere."

"You were better off with Justin, I think," Baines answered quietly.

"I know we take the, well, you know," said Flannigan, "but she's a first-rate doctor, really. I'm worried what might have happened to her."

"I think that her absence now is proof that she was a lot more than that," Baines suggested, sadly.

Hiro, Smyth and Flannigan looked from one to another, then back to the commander. "Are you saying what I think you're saying?" asked Flannigan slowly.

"We knew she was one of the nineteen *possibles* James wanted to interview, Dave—" she began.

"Yes, but—"

"No, Dave," she spoke over him, regretfully, "it all fits. Times, locations, descriptions. Drummond has been working for days on who might have been at each incident site. He's got some insanely complicated flowchart arrangement on an easel in his quarters, apparently. I had a chat with him just after I made up the 'blue eyes list'. That really tightened it up. Now the killer has left the ship, stocked up for the safari from hell and Heidi, as we see, is missing."

"Is anyone else missing?" asked Singh.

"That's worth checking, just to be on the safe side," Baines replied. "Can you get Ford onto that now? Ask him to take a register or something."

Singh nodded and made the call.

"Has anyone looked for the man who was guarding the hatch between the ship and the Pod?" asked Hiro. "I'm sorry, with everything, he slipped my mind. I hope he was only knocked out."

Baines touched Sandip lightly on the arm. "Ask Ford to find the hatch guard as well." Turning to Smyth, she asked, "Justin, can you get down there, please? The poor guy may need some first aid."

Smyth nodded, packed a few supplies into a bag and left.

"Hope that's all he needs," Hiro remarked. "That woman's a killer!"

Flannigan was staring into space.

"You OK, Dave?" asked Baines, gently.

He shook his head slowly. "All those people and all this pain. How did I not see what was right under my nose?"

"None of us did," admitted Baines, trying to comfort him. "We've got a psychologist on board who made enough money to be here, so I assume he knows something of his trade. I intend to have a chat with him when the dust settles. Try and work out what sort of mind we're dealing with. We believe we know the *who*, which is critical of course. Now I want to know the *why*. It's the only way we can fight her."

Flannigan looked up. "Fight her? I thought she was gone?"

"For now," said Baines, "but clearly there are powerful forces at work in that woman. She'll be back and we'll need to be ready because she may have other help on this ship."

"You mean Lloyd?" asked Hiro.

Baines sighed, looking uncomfortable. "Not exactly. I wasn't going to burden you with this – what with you convalescing and all, but…" she rubbed her tired eyes, releasing some of the pressure she could feel building. "Look, Lloyd has told us quite a story."

Baines and Singh left sickbay together, returning to the bridge. Singh immediately took his station, requesting updates from Baccini and Jones. Baines called Major White and Sergeant Jackson to meet with her.

White was first to arrive. "The man Schultz attacked – the guy guarding the hatch – is gonna be OK," he said as he entered. "He's had a bit of a beating, but Nurse Smyth says he'll be just fine after a few days' rest."

The Sarge entered right on his heels. "He's lucky to be alive," he said. "She's lethal. She got the better of me, I can't deny it."

"Wow! The man Schultz attacked," Baines could not help repeating. "That's the first time anyone's said her name outright – in connection with all this, I mean. Kinda brings it home, doesn't it? Where was he?"

"Shoved into a closet down the hall," answered the major. "He was still unconscious when we found him." He turned to The Sarge. "Do you think you could have stopped her?"

Jackson considered a moment. "I don't know," he replied simply. "Definitely not without cost."

"That's a sobering thought," Baines noted. "Look, boys, the reason I asked you to come here was to discuss the new reality. We may have rid ourselves of a problem but, yet again, a larger one has raised its ugly head."

"We're just not catching a break, are we?" White addressed his question to no one in particular.

Baines ushered the two soldiers towards the meeting room. "Come and grab yourselves a seat, I've made some coffee." Before following, she called across to Singh, "Sandy, you have the bridge, and Lieutenant?"

He turned his seat to face her. "Commander?"

"Keep the door locked."

Lieutenant Singh pressed the locking control to seal the bridge from his console. "Affirmative," he said, returning to his scans of the local topography. "I'm planning a route for our flyover tomorrow with the captain. Despite everything, I can't help being pretty excited about it."

Baines nodded. "Don't forget we're not only looking for resources now. *She's* out there and she's armed."

"Yes, Commander," replied Singh, dutifully. As he absorbed Baines' warning, an idea struck him and he began typing ferociously.

"But that needn't stop you from recording the journey," she added. "I thought we might show the film of your first flyover in embarkation, as a morale booster for everyone."

Singh stopped typing for a moment, looking up. "I'll let you know when it's been through my editing room." He gave her a winning smile before returning to his labours with vigour, his inner little boy already in flight.

Baines joined the other two men in the meeting room and the three officers got themselves *coffeed*.

"Alright," said Ford, "I'll ask it first: now what?"

Baines nodded, understanding the major's frustration. "We had a good long chat with Lloyd earlier," she began. "He's decided to cooperate."

White looked both impressed and quizzical. "How d'ya pull that off?"

"All it took was the captain's pride and joy to get him talking," she replied with a wink.

"Pride and joy?" asked White.

"His fifty-year-old single malt," she answered. "The one he'd been saving."

Jackson whistled.

"Yeah," she acknowledged. "He was *not* happy. Well, not at first anyway."

"Did he cheer up later?" asked Jackson, straight faced.

"About halfway down the bottle as it happens," Baines admitted. "Anyway, the captain intends to go through this in council tomorrow, but I wanted you two to know about it immediately. We may need to take steps and put measures in place."

The soldiers glanced at one another, bracing for another unwanted revelation.

"Lloyd said that he was paid a large sum of money to disrupt the ship – *disrupt*, not destroy. Obviously, the money is pointless now and, as we're the only thing standing between him and the maw of a flesh-eating dinosaur, he wisely decided to 'fess up and toe the line."

"What did he tell you?" asked White.

"Apparently, about six months ago, a terrorist group contacted him whilst on leave. They're a faction well known for being rabidly against the Mars Mission, their rhetoric stating dubious morality in an attempt to sublimate sneak attacks and violence. The main thrust of their griping is to make humanity aware that leaving Earth is against God's will or some such.

"Lloyd, for his part, didn't care what *they* believed. *He* believed that their money should be *his* money. So you see, he's not completely without a code!

"He knew the United Nations had tried to deal peacefully with this group on a number of occasions, but they did so without knowing how many layers were involved or who was really pulling the strings. The UN sent in mediators, of course, logically and systematically explaining the threat facing mankind. They drew charts and provided examples showing the positive effects of the colonisation of Mars, how it will ease the strain on our planet's resources, et cetera, et cetera.

"Lloyd said he knew no argument was possible, once religious tenets were cited. He only dealt with the group slightly, but he could make no sense of their position at all, even within the remit of their stated beliefs. Some of them may well have bought into it, some people will believe anything, but he seems to think it might all be a front for something else.

"The terrorists' response made worldwide headlines a while back, though, you may recall. 'If humanity dies out, that will be God's punishment on the wicked, but the chosen will live forever in paradise.' Remember that one?

"We can only infer that 'the wicked' means us and 'the chosen' means them. It's all crazy, like going back to the religious strife of 16th century Europe. Naturally, this latest set of nutcrackers also have all the answers – the same ones. Lloyd, however, merely hoped they had the other half of his money. He was surprisingly candid after a few whiskies.

"The bad news for us is, when they enlisted him to their cause, they told him virtually nothing of their larger plans and he'd not been stupid enough to ask. You can't blame him for that. They simply tempted him with a huge pot of money and ordered him to make a spectacle of the last Mars Mission in a very *specific* way. A spectacle that mankind would remember forever – or for as long as we persist on a used-up, sickly Earth – in all likelihood, not forever. Still, as long he spent his last years in luxury, the way he saw it, the rest of us could go to hell!"

Jackson and White simply looked at one another in disgusted silence.

"And do we trust this reversal, Commander?" asked White.

"I wouldn't trust him outside his cage, but I think he's telling us the truth now. His options are bleak, and his only real chance of staying alive is to give us whatever we need." She looked earnestly at White. "I take your point though, Ford. We certainly won't be taking everything he says as gospel without checking it out."

"And that's all?" asked The Sarge.

"Not quite," replied Baines. "I saved the worst for last, I'm afraid. His information boils down to this: apparently, there's a whole team of insurgents among us!"

The Sarge paused, with his coffee cup halfway to his lips. Eventually he asked, "I don't suppose he was kind enough to tell us who these people are?"

Baines shook her head. "He doesn't know—" she corrected herself, "*says* he doesn't know."

"Did he happen to mention how *many* they are?" The Sarge tried again.

"Could be eight, could be a dozen," she answered. "He wasn't sure."

White clunked his coffee cup down a little harder than he meant to, spilling the drink over the side a little.

Baines was slightly surprised by this show of emotion from the usually unflappable major. "You OK, Ford?" she asked.

"Sorry." He sighed, deeply. "Just look at the havoc one of them created and now there might be a dozen more?"

"I know," agreed Baines.

"And if they're all as deadly as Schultz, where does that leave us?" White continued. "Most of the people on this mission are scientists and families. The few soldiers we have aren't going to be enough – not if they're all *that* highly trained and *that* organised."

"We don't know that, sir," The Sarge broke in. "Presumably some of them will be from a technical background. That would certainly explain how they've been so damned good at hitting us in the soft parts!"

"I think you're right, Sarge," Baines concurred. "Though, they will be no less deadly for it. According to Lloyd, the plan was to hijack the ship and take it on a mission of their choosing."

"What mission?" Ford asked.

"He wasn't sure, but he thought it would be to do with Mars," explained Baines. "He suspected they intended to hold the ship to ransom, or so he says."

"You believe that's *all* he thought?" asked Jackson.

Baines looked at him. "Why, what do you think, Sarge?"

"For a start, the wormhole drive blew up near Earth. If he set that bomb, or was involved with it, he must have known we weren't never gonna reach Mars," replied The Sarge, his London accent coming to the fore.

Baines frowned. "You know, that passed me by," she said, a little shamefaced. "We've been through so much in such quick succession," she clenched her fists, "but that's no excuse."

"Also," continued Jackson, "they clearly planned to bring their own crew aboard. So at the very least, what would that have meant for all of us? Furthermore, if the ship *was* ransomed, what then? Were they planning to ask for money? They already seem to have plenty to splash about."

"So what do you think could have been their purpose?" asked White.

"Who knows?" said The Sarge, unusually animated. "A suicide run on New York? London? Berlin? Delhi? It's been done before, and wouldn't that make a nice spectacle in the media? However, my point is this: even if Lloyd didn't know the details, he must have suspected it would be chips for the rest of us!" He turned to Baines. "*Did* he plant the bomb that killed young Mario?"

His last question hit hard. Baines bit her lip and then nodded slowly. "Yes," she said, simply.

"So he was happy to murder one of our own," The Sarge stated quietly, sitting back, his expression unreadable once more.

"I don't think it was that simple, Sarge. He said that the bomb was only meant to take out that room, which it did, and stop the ship, which it also did. He expected the crew to be at their stations during the explosion. For some reason Mario was with the drive when it was engaged. He told us that had been unexpected and he wished he could take it back."

"Really?" asked Jackson, sourly. "Mario was a good kid, I liked him."

"We all did, Sarge," said Baines, "but who knows? It may have been unintentional. In fairness, in the years I've known him, that's the only time I've ever seen Lloyd look like he was in any way contrite, let alone sorry. He told us something else I thought was interesting and possibly significant, too. His explicit orders were to use a much smaller amount of explosive. He admitted to being in a rage when he planted the device – something about another request for a senior posting being denied, coupled with the twins stealing his tools again."

Another flicker of anger crossed The Sarge's face.

"Of course," Baines continued, "he may have simply bottled it! I dare say he would have been panicking about being discovered at that point – and so he strapped the whole pack, from one of the lifeboat release bolts, to the drive. He knew it was too much but also that it wasn't enough to destroy the ship, so he took the quickest route out of there – probably before he lost his nerve altogether. Apparently his contact at Canaveral had been *very* specific about the amount of explosive, so I'm guessing that the effect we experienced wasn't what was ordered."

"You're saying he had no idea we would be thrown back in time by exploding the new wormhole?" asked White.

"Apparently not," said Baines. "And on that, I believe him. I just can't see him deliberately getting himself stuck here with the rest of us, especially if he was anticipating a fat payday! It's no good to him now."

"Pity he didn't care about the consequences at the time. He sold us all out, knowing it might be our lives." There was an edge of steel to The Sarge's voice now. "But it's not my job to pass judgement – lucky for him!"

White nodded his agreement. "If he's confessed, then something's going to have to be done with him."

"With him or to him?" asked Baines.

"Either works for me," White admitted.

This time it was The Sarge who nodded agreement.

"I understand your feelings, gentlemen," said Baines, attempting to calm the growing anger, "but this is a complicated situation and we can't afford to throw away any asset at this point."

"You think he might still be useful to us?" asked Jackson.

"I think it's possible," replied Baines. "He may not be able to identify them, and frankly I'm quite happy to believe that they would have fed him only the bare minimum of information to get him on board with their scheme, but he may know other things. Perhaps even things he doesn't realise yet – it may simply be up to us to ask the right questions. He said that the black-suited, masked killer was a stranger to him. After being busted out of the brig, he was simply ordered to go with her and do as he was told, under threat of execution. They did some damage at the gravity control nexus, minor sabotage and not ship threatening – apparently, he knew nothing of the virus programme designed to crash the ship – and then she beat him unconscious. He also stated that he didn't realise it was a woman at the time because she used a vocal distortion unit."

"Blind, is he?" The Sarge interjected moodily. "He must have been working with her for several minutes. Most men find the shape of Dr Schultz distracting to the exclusion of pretty much all else!"

"Point," agreed Baines. "But setting that aside for the moment, the loss of gravity Lloyd engineered, perhaps under coercion, was clearly to keep *us* busy while the new software took hold within the ship's operating system.

As for whether she wanted Lloyd dead or not at that point, we can't be sure, maybe she was interrupted. However, the attempt on his life in sickbay was certainly suggestive that he'd outlived his usefulness as a diversion and needed silencing. Obviously, when you," she gestured to The Sarge, "and Hiro discovered that there was another saboteur on board, the cat was out of the bag. After that, there was no point leaving Lloyd around to take the blame. And just to reiterate, if Schultz wants Lloyd dead, well, there's just a chance he might know something significant."

She looked uncomfortable for a moment. "Of course, there is also another reason for keeping him alive."

"Oh?" asked White.

"Can we really afford to get rid of an experienced ship's engineer?"

A black cloud crossed The Sarge's face. "You're thinking of returning him to duty down the line?" he asked, clearly doing his best to remain polite.

"I don't know if the captain will bend to that degree," Baines offered, "but Lloyd does have value as a resource and, let's face it, every one of us is irreplaceable now. There are no more people!"

The muscles in Jackson's jaw bunched, relaxed, bunched and relaxed again. "Moving on from that point for the moment," he said, diplomatically, "we need a plan to ferret out these other insurgents, as soon as."

"Agreed," said Baines. "Trouble is – where do we start? We don't even know if our own security team can be trusted. Hell, even one of us could be involved!"

"We can't proceed like that, we'll never make it," White stated simply, in a way that brooked no contradiction. "I know it goes against all military training, but we can't fight a cold war while we're in the middle of a real one. So let's just agree to agree that it's not us and carry on from there. If we don't work together, we've lost anyway."

Silence fell. Lost in their individual thoughts and concerns, it was a while before anyone could bring themselves to speak further.

"Who else knows about this?" Jackson asked eventually.

"Douglas, Singh, Flannigan, Smyth, Nassaki and the three of us," replied Baines.

"Just crew. Good. We should keep it that way. At least until we know more," The Sarge suggested seriously.

"The captain intends to tell Mother Sarah and Dr Patel tomorrow," said Baines. "He feels that it would be wrong to deny the council."

The Sarge looked away, frustrated. "Civilians?" he asked in disbelief.

"I know, I *know*, but you know what he's like. He hates the idea of military in charge of government, or working underground, no matter how small the scale. He's such a good man, Sarge."

"He's one of the best men I've ever known," The Sarge replied, completely without rancour, "but if this leaks because of a point of honour..." He left the sentence hanging.

"The one ray of sunlight I can see throughout this crisis," said White, "is that it seems only Lloyd and Schultz have been active. This suggests that these 'sleepers' were only to be activated under certain circumstances. Dare we hope these *circumstances* can nevermore be realised, in light of our situation? Being lost in the past and all?"

"You think this might change if the captain informs the council?" asked Baines.

The major laid his hands on the table. "I'm simply saying, the more people who know that *we* know, the more dangerous the situation becomes, Commander. If this should leak, things could get real ugly, real fast. Surely, it's best to keep it quiet. Firstly, if they don't know we're onto them they won't feel the need to be so careful and, secondly, if they *do* know we're onto them, they may have a kneejerk reaction."

"You mean the sleepers might wake?"

White nodded. "And a dozen fanatics loose on this ship could end this party altogether!"

"A fair point, Ford, but let's say we can keep these sleepers sleeping - then what? We all just carry on and say no more about it?"

"No, but we really need to buy a little time, Jill – time to get to grips with everything. If we can keep them sleeping just long enough for us to turn this situation around, we might be able to stop running all over the ship putting out fires and hit back! We need to build. Between these crazies and those monsters outside, we can't even get our feet under us!"

"Can't argue with that," Baines agreed. "However, with regards to the insurgents, I don't think we can assume what they may or may not know. And I don't think we can even start unravelling this mystery, until *we* know exactly what their mission *was* and, most importantly, what the hell it is that they want now?"

"I agree with that, Commander," said The Sarge, "and it gives me an idea. I said we should keep this quiet, but on second thoughts…"

Baines and White looked at him in surprise.

"Penny for your thoughts, Sarge?" Baines prompted.

Jackson answered slowly and thoughtfully. "Hmm, maybe playing it close to our chest won't achieve anything after all. Maybe we should just ask them."

0700 hours came around very quickly for James Douglas. He raised his head off the pillow, groaned and put it back down. Taking a moment to gather himself, he tried again. This time he made it all the way to his feet, swayed a bit, and staggered into his en suite. Looking in the mirror, he could not help recalling a very similar mirror in a very similar en suite, back in his quarters at Cape Canaveral, just a fortnight ago. However, the face which stared back at him two weeks ago had presented itself rather better.

Two weeks, he thought groggily. Two weeks since their world had been turned upside down. People often use that phrase and yet, "What the hell de they know aboot it?" He spoke the thought gruffly, through a throat on fire.

After his shower, shave and er... morning preparations, he was dressed and off to work. He arrived at the bridge only to find it locked down. Despite hitting the open three times, the doors remained closed, resolute in their dumb insolence.

Labouring under his hangover and muttering under his breath about being 'locked out of his own damned ship', Douglas keyed his captain's security codes to unlock them, finally stepping onto the bridge.

As the ship was no longer in motion, a twenty-four hour duty was no longer deemed necessary and he was glad to be the first in. It would give him a few more minutes to recover before he had to face anybody.

He sat in his command chair collecting his thoughts quietly. A door behind him opened suddenly, making him jump. Commander Baines strode out of the small galley off the bridge bearing his usual first coffee.

"Ah thought Ah was first in," he said blearily.

"And *I* thought you'd need this before you see anyone else," she replied sympathetically, with just a hint of mischief in her eyes.

"How did ye know?" asked Douglas, innocently.

"Well, it occurred to me about the same time that you broke into song last night. As you made me the designated driver, and thank you for that by the way, I watched you with interest – you know, just looking out for

351

my captain. My observations went something like this: he's alright, he's alright, he's not alright, he's not alright – oh dear."

Douglas laughed in spite of himself, pulling up with a grimace. "Ooh, ma hid."

Baines indolently tapped a small box of painkillers on the arm of his chair.

"Ah knew there was a reason Ah promoted you," he said. "How come the bridge was locked down, if you were in here?"

"Yes," she replied, "sorry about that. I made it an order last night, after what Lloyd told us about *the others*. Obviously, I couldn't run it by you, as you were—"

"Off duty?" Douglas supplied, helpfully.

"That's as good a description as any!" laughed Baines. "Look, I had a meeting with White and Jackson last night and The Sarge made a suggestion. It's pretty wild but not without merit. I'd like your take on it please, James."

Baines explained Jackson's *revelation* plan.

"You're right, that *is* pretty wild," he said. "Ah'm meeting with Sarah and Satnam at 0800, Ah'll see what they have to say about it. Care to sit in?"

Douglas' meeting with Mother Sarah and Dr Patel went well. With everyone in agreement, plans were laid for the implementation of The Sarge's idea later in the day. The captain kept the meeting as short as possible because that very afternoon, he and four others had a date with Cretaceous Patagonia. Surveying their surroundings was critical to their survival, that it just might be the most exciting flight plan ever devised was hardly his fault.

Afterward, he strolled through his ship whistling cheerfully, exchanging pleasantries and even a few jokes with the people he passed. With Schultz's departure, he felt that a load had been lifted and hoped the lighter atmosphere would continue.

Making his way down to the laboratories deep within the Pod, he sought out Dr Norris. Members of her team were dissecting the small Pterosaurs which had invaded the ship. He greeted the people at their workstations with a smile, despite the gruesome spectacle. Others examined slides and samples taken from the same animals.

Regardless of the captain's fresh *bonhomie*, his hung-over, empty tummy was still in poor humour, so he moved along quickly. Eventually, his feet carried him to the door of the team leader's office where he knocked.

"Come in," he heard Norris' voice from inside.

"Good morning, Doctor," he said, popping his head around the door. "Ah hope Ah'm not disturbing you?"

"Captain," said Norris, standing up behind her desk. "Please, come in, have a seat."

"Thank you, Doctor," replied Douglas, taking the proffered chair.

"It's probably about time you started calling me Patricia."

"Only if you'll call me James," he smiled. "Ah've come to ask you a favour, Patricia."

"Oh? I'll be happy to help in any way I can."

"Well, this is no ordinary request, so don't feel pressured to acquiesce."

"You intrigue me, James."

"Ah need to borrow your son, please."

"Oh."

"Ah said it was nay ordinary request," repeated Douglas. "You see, we're going for our first flyover in the ship's shuttlecraft. Obviously, Ah don't need to ask Tim if he'd like to accompany us – Ah'm sure he'd rip my arm off for the chance!"

"Quite," agreed Norris, noncommittally.

"We don't plan to land the ship on this occasion, as it's just a look around – a brief geological survey and mapping trip, using aerial scanners only. Ah know how much Tim wants to see the animals out there, and from our perspective, his knowledge could help us gain a better understanding of what we're seeing. Naturally, Ah wanted your permission before bringing it up with the laddie. There *should* be no danger, but…" he let the caveat hang.

"But everything we do here is potentially dangerous," she completed, nodding her understanding. She thought for a moment. "I'm sure he'll be able to help you, James, so OK. More than that, if he ever got wind of this conversation and found out I'd said no, he'd probably ignore me for a month!" She smiled. "He'll be over the moon. When do you plan to leave?"

"This afternoon, 1400 hours."

"And you won't be landing?"

"Scout's honour," Douglas promised, raising two fingers to his temple.

"Very well. Could I just ask one thing, James?"

"Of course."

"Could *I* tell him? It seems like all I've been able to give him of late is bad news. This will help to make up for it, I'm sure."

"Certainly. Until later then. Thank you, Patricia."

1400 hours – shuttle bay, *USS New World*.
Captain Douglas keyed his security codes into the shuttle's access panel – about a week and a half after locking the craft down, he realised. The events immediately following the explosion and destruction of the wormhole drive came back to life in his mind; events which had scattered his crew all through the ship in the hope of preventing the bomber's escape. This was the exact spot where Singh had explained how they were lost almost 100 million years in the past. He was surprised how long ago it seemed as the hatch opened, despite the near constant panic since.

Turning to his shuttle team, he said, "This is it, lady and gentlemen. We're finally going sight-seeing. Our intention is to spend an hour or so only, on this first trip, just to get our bearings and see what's within a twenty-mile radius of our landing site. As you know our main mission is to look for mineral deposits and potential mining sites. We also need to keep an eye out for any sign of our rogue Dr Schultz. Ah know it's a needle in a haystack, a needle that will be intelligently camouflaging itself in a haystack, actually, but we'll keep them peeled nonetheless. Follow me, please."

Douglas nodded to The Sarge, who headed a six-man, armed security detail on station in the shuttle bay and stepped aboard. The small shuttle crew of four followed closely behind, Lieutenant Singh taking the helm as

Douglas sat in the co-pilot's seat. The other three stations, largely given over to myriad scanning equipment, were taken by Dr Jim Miller, Dr Samantha Portree and Tim Norris.

Miller represented the manufacturing team and would be scanning the chemical composition of the soils. Portree represented the mining and construction team; her focus would be the complex geology of the area they were about to investigate.

Lastly, Tim Norris, as the acknowledged expert on the Cretaceous Period, was in charge of Christmas morning – or that was how it felt to him. He was ecstatic and quite possibly the only member of the crew for whom life just kept getting better and better. If a low flight over a world full of prehistoric animals was not enough, earlier in the day, the captain had recruited him, along with Dr Natalie Pearson, to put together a new zoology team. To Tim's delight, Natalie's ever-present sidekick, Reiver, was also determined to be involved with this project, as in all things. He could certainly be described as a specialist in the field of bone collection, particularly with regard to testing them to destruction. True to the nature of his species, he was utterly undaunted by size.

Tim and Natalie were tasked with building a comprehensive understanding of the fauna they would all be sharing their lives with – possibly even the *rest* of their lives with – and not just the fauna. Fortunately, Patricia Norris' team also included a couple of botanists who awaited the shuttle's findings as avidly as everyone else.

The botanists' original assignment had been the adaption of Terran flora and fungi for life on Mars. They had little palaeobotanical knowledge, but the opportunity to observe life from a completely remote, previously inaccessible age was irresistible. How could any scientist fail to be excited by the prospect, despite everything? When the crew's attention turned to planting and rearing crops, their knowledge would become invaluable.

Once the initial shock of their predicament ebbed, the impressive minds aboard the *New World* soon realised that a complex model could now be constructed. By using knowledge gained in the 22nd century, alongside hints left in the fossil and geological records, added to observations from the *actual* past, as now seen, they could piece together a unique picture of evolution.

When not fearing for their lives, the scientists were lost in a sort of intellectual euphoria, already plotting ways of extrapolating the whole story-arc of life on Earth from these two unique reference points in time. For many of the science staff, this 'evolution unravelled' was mesmerising. Who could have ever believed they would have the chance to combine the knowledge of an ancient past from a long-lost future, compare and corroborate that knowledge with observations taken in the 'now' that *used* to be 'then', to hopefully complete a puzzle mankind had barely found the edges to, until now. Although, it might be argued that 'now' *is* actually 'then', but of course, you have to expect a little paradox every now and then.

However, paradox did not end there. Their strategy would have provided 'the dream assignment' for most of the staff, had their predicament not been such a nightmare.

Douglas activated the shuttle's communications console, opening a channel to the bridge of the *New World*. "Commander, we're good to go." He motioned for Singh to open the bay doors remotely from his pilot's console.

"*God speed, Captain,*" Baines' voice came through the speakers hidden around the shuttle's small bridge. "*Pick me up a stick of rock.*"

"Ah'll have a word with the geologist," Douglas replied, lightning fast.

"*Too much coffee today, Captain?*" asked Baines.

Douglas smiled. "See you in one hour, Commander. Hold the fort and keep the drawbridge up."

"*We'll have you on scanners. Good luck, everyone – enjoy yourselves.*"

The bay doors were now fully open and, after the Pterosaur incursion, the security team were on high alert. Happily, the skies around the ship were clear on this occasion. Singh raised the shuttle gently on thrusters, easing the little vessel forwards with great care. He kept the manoeuvre tight and smooth, the power low; the safety of the men behind them his primary concern.

Once outside the shuttle bay, they hovered fifteen metres in the air. The height gave them a superb view of the incomplete defensive earthworks, so quickly excavated behind the backs of the Mapusaurus pack. Singh slowly fed power into the jet turbines, gently turning the little craft away from her mothership.

Commander Baines sat alone on the bridge of the *New World*, watching the shuttle grow smaller in the monitor. "Come back in one piece," she muttered quietly.

Chapter 13 | It Shouldn't Happen to a Vet!

Dr Patel and Mother Sarah seated themselves around the conference table. "Thank you for coming," said Baines. "The captain was keen for this meeting to go forward, even though he couldn't attend personally."

"Have you heard from the shuttle yet?" asked Sarah.

"No comm traffic, but I'm keeping a close eye on them with the ship's sensors." She waved a hand over the table top and a screen popped up. Swivelling it, so that Patel and Sarah could see, she pointed out the icon representing the shuttle. It travelled across a simplistic, virtual simulacrum of the lands outside the *New World*. They were fascinated by the way the area around the shuttle was fleshed out on the fly, becoming highly detailed before their eyes.

"Wow!" said Sarah. "I've never seen that before."

"The shuttle is processing the results of the survey as it gathers them and sending back full telemetry. The scanning computers – which I'm happy to say are far more sophisticated than the *New World*'s core system – are building an electronic model of the world around us. Look," she tapped an area on the touch-screen, in the wake of the shuttle. A second window opened, listing soil and geological compositions alongside types and disposition of flora and fauna.

Photographic records were also appended, supporting each element of the survey. Baines tapped a link to activate a brief video which showed a small group of sauropod younglings through a gap in the forest canopy. Hidden away in their little crèche among the trees, they lived within a brief envelope of security. Already aloof to the diminutive predators of the forest, they were, for now, still small enough themselves to hide from the huge killers prowling the plains.

"That's truly amazing," Sarah added, still lost in wonder.

Patel watched the readings scroll up the screen with the eye of a scientist, but even he could not help but marvel at the lost world opening up before them.

"Quite," said Baines, in a slightly miffed tone. "I'm sure they're like little boys in a toyshop out there, but if I could return you to *our* agenda, I think it will become apparent why the captain wanted this meeting to continue in his absence."

"Are you intimating that our illustrious captain wanted to dodge this meeting?" asked Patel.

"I would *never.*" Baines' outrage was entirely unconvincing.

The councillors laughed.

"I wondered why he'd insisted this morning's meeting be kept so short. We barely discussed the highlights of Lloyd's confession," Sarah admitted. "Now I begin to see."

"Indeed," Baines acknowledged. "Right, here we go. Given our situation, we'll all need to draw from ship's supplies for food, drink, et cetera. Obviously, money is no good here and as we need all the help we can get, everyone will have to work, too. Especially when we begin farming for our subsistence once the defence perimeter is complete. The captain thought that some kind of work-related 'token' system might be the way forward? These tokens, earned by labour, will allow us to *buy* the things we need, whilst making sure we all do our bit."

Patel whistled softly. "Captain Douglas is flying around in a space shuttle looking at dinosaurs and we have to develop a *fiscal* strategy?"

"That's about the size of it, yes," Baines agreed sulkily. "What do you think?"

"I think," Patel replied slowly, "that I have always admired the captain's skill as an organiser, but now I am in awe of him."

"Welcome to my world," said Baines.

"But I don't know anything about economics!" interrupted Sarah, slightly taken aback.

Baines linked her fingers and twiddled her thumbs. "That *is* kind of the point," she said. "James doesn't want greed and corruption to take over our lives here as it did back home. There just aren't enough of us to carry any deadwood. He wants a system that is simple, obvious and fair for all."

"What if someone *can't* work? Due to injury or illness, perhaps?" asked Sarah. "Do we let them starve?"

Baines laughed. "Is that the viewpoint of the modern Church, Sarah? How delightfully Dickensian! No, our numbers are so small that any special cases can easily be remedied, I'm sure. It's a start anyway. If it needs to become more sophisticated later, well, we'll just have to cross that headache when the beer runs out." She smiled at the councillors.

Patel and Fellows looked at one another, Patel asking, "And just who was James going to nominate to explain this new 'currency' to Mr Burnstein? Do you think *he* will be happy to earn food tokens by cleaning, what does that most eloquent Captain Gleeson call them, *the dunnies?*"

Baines suddenly brightened. "I hadn't considered that, but now you come to mention it, I can't imagine anyone more suited to a new career in public convenience!"

"I don't wish to speak out of turn, Jill," Sarah cut in, almost apologetically, "but I think dear Jim Miller may be about to have a few problems at home too, if this is gonna be the new way."

"Well, at least he'll get advance warning, Sarah – he'll be in charge of making the tokens."

For the sake of professionalism, they tried not to smirk at the idea of Mr Burnstein and Mrs Miller being introduced to the concepts of physical labour and rationing.

"Everyone will *have* to work," stated Patel, more seriously. "We won't be able to carry anyone who is capable of contributing but won't. Even the children will have to help. We'll need absolutely every able body, if we're to get through this. It will be like going back – or forward, I should say – to the Neolithic or the Bronze Age, with everyone doing their bit for the group."

"Child labour too?" asked Baines, in mock surprise. "*The good old days!*"

Patel quirked a half-smile. "Are you one of those 'unreconstructed females' who rose to dominance in the mid-21st century, Commander?"

"Phwoar! You should have met my mother," Baines' eyes twinkled. "My dad was frightened to argue with her. No wonder he spent so much of his time back home moon walking!"

"You've never mentioned your parents, Jill. Do they still live on the moon? I've always wanted to visit but never got around to it. I bet it's romantic, huh?" asked Sarah.

"The views are beyond description, Sarah, the Earth hanging in the sky..." She smiled in remembrance. "Maybe we could take a shuttle one day and I'll show you. The moon is still there after all. Here we are in *your* home 100 million years ago – I'd love to see mine too. See how *it's* changed, you know? My father's American and was an early settler on the moon-base, New Florida. He met my mother while visiting relatives in England. After queuing for what seemed like an age for a loaf of bread – that's what the British have always done apparently, according to Mum – a rather attractive young woman, also stranded in line, caught his eye.

"Anyway, they got to talking and Dad explained how he lived on New Florida and my mum asked if that was the base named after the location of a medieval monastery in Mid Wales. Blissfully unaware that he'd been reeled in, because so many US place names are transplanted from Britain, Dad set about explaining that Florida was actually a state in America. Apparently his reward had been a mocking grin."

Patel's eyes began to glaze over, so he rubbed his left temple in an attempt to revive himself while Mother Sarah encouraged Baines to continue.

"They began a long-distance relationship but that wasn't good enough for my mother – oh no! She moved to the moon to keep an eye on him. Then little *me* came along – the first loony! Dad has always told me how dismayed he was that I inherited Mum's mocking grin. I've simply no *idea* what he could possibly mean." She grinned to the contrary.

Sarah chuckled. "With all we've been through, any kind of a grin is most welcome!"

"Yes," said Baines, thinking wistfully of home. With a resigned sigh, she continued, "But unfortunately the next item on our agenda is less of a laughing matter, I'm afraid."

"Oh good," said Patel, without thinking. Clearing his throat awkwardly, he added, "I mean... *good*, erm... it's good that we're getting to the heart of the matter. You were saying, Commander?"

His *faux pas* was greeted with silence.

"*Right*," said Baines, evenly. "Next on the list is Lieutenant Lloyd and what's to be done with him, now that he's confessed."

They brooded for a little while.

"What are our options?" asked Patel, eventually.

Baines took a moment before replying. "They all seem rather prosaic to me. Some people are vying for execution or exile, which amounts to the same thing really. Some advocate imprisonment and others, if not many, have even suggested reformation and reintegration." She took a sip of her coffee. "All these opinions seem overly simplistic, lacking any detail. As for reformation, where on Earth would you start with that, in our situation? And who would want to work themselves ragged to keep him fed and watered in a comfy cell while he *reforms?*"

Sarah tugged at her ear in discomfiture. "The other thing is the little matter of a fair trial. This also needs to be discussed and that said, perhaps we shouldn't really be exploring the sentence before it has even taken place?"

Baines looked surprised. "A trial? Fair?"

"Of course, surely we need to hold one?" replied Sarah, reasonably. "A public one too, I would suggest. After all, we've *all* been landed here against our will."

Baines was taken still further aback. "Public—" she sputtered, eyes widening. "And just how are we meant to set that up?" she asked finally.

"Well, I've spent quite a bit of time reading up on everyone's files over the last few days," replied Sarah. "I think it's important to know as much as possible about everyone in order to represent their needs as a councillor. I see it as my *mission*, no pun intended, to know everyone, because Satnam and James are so busy with their other duties. One thing I *can* tell you is that we have two people on board with legal experience."

"And who might they be?" Baines was not thrilled by this new direction.

"There's a lady," Sarah continued, "one of the paid seats, if you will – not that any of *that* matters anymore – who used to be a defence attorney back in Seattle. Her name is Liz Barton-Frehly, Frehly being her maiden name. Her husband's name is Dick."

Baines looked at Patel raising an eyebrow. "*Is* it?" she asked.

"Yes," continued Sarah, oblivious. "Apparently, she used to represent defendants from deprived backgrounds who couldn't afford legal counsel. Although that description hardly fits Mr Lloyd, I wondered if it would be worth asking her to take the case?"

"A poor man's lawyer then," stated Baines. "How did she afford a seat?"

"Her husband owns one of the last oil fields in South America, although they lived in Seattle." The priest looked uncomfortable once more. "I'm not in any position to pass judgement, but I think she chose to work as she did to compensate, at least in a small way, for her husband's corporate *excesses*?"

"Talking about judgement," Baines replied pointedly. "In this impromptu courtroom of yours, who are you measuring up for that chair?"

"I thought the captain, maybe...?" Sarah tailed off when she caught the commander's expression.

"Have you mentioned any of this to James?" Baines asked cautiously.

"Not yet, I thought you mi—"

"Oooh no," Baines cut her off, "you can leave me out of *that* conversation, please."

"You think the captain will object, Jill?" asked Patel.

"I can only guess at his reaction, Satnam, because when you ask him, I'll be busy checking on something or other. Quite possibly at the other end of the ship, I shouldn't wonder."

"Well, who then?" Sarah enquired. "Surely James is the best man aboard for the job? He *is* the captain."

Baines nodded. "I absolutely agree. I'm just not going to be the one to ask him!"

"Do you think he will refuse?" asked Patel.

The commander puffed out her cheeks. "Let me tell you something about Captain James Douglas. He's a man of achievement, a true veteran. He rightly deserves his commission to captain the *New World* but that's *all* he's ever wanted. He hates the idea of military-in-government. We've already pushed him into a role he never sought. He doesn't want power, which of course makes him ideal for the job, but *he* doesn't see it that way. He is a truly honourable man. Is James a leader? Definitely. Is he a ruler? Not so much. A judge? Never. He will really hate that, if you force it on him. He agonises about having too much power placed in his hands as it is. He'll blow a fuse if you try and make him a judge!"

Patel nodded his understanding. "I think you're right about the captain, Jill. He is a good man. So who should do it then? Lloyd is military after all, what about you?"

Baines sat back like a giant spider had just landed on the table in front of her. "*Me?*"

"Yeees," Sarah acknowledged slowly, mulling the idea over. "I think that the captain would completely endorse that choice, don't you, Satnam? You clearly have his trust, Commander, and ours. In fact we all believe you to be a woman of honour, a true vet yourself, one might say. So why not?"

"Look," Baines backpedalled, "let's not jump to any conclusions here. I mean, we haven't actually *asked* James yet…"

Patel and Fellows laughed.

"I think we can call that settled then," said Sarah.

Baines slumped. "I don't know anything about legal procedure," she said, plaintively. "Talk about a kangaroo court!"

"I don't know anything about economics," replied Sarah, with a tight smile. "We all have our little problems today, don't we?"

"All you will need to do is listen, impartially, to the learned counsel," added Patel, reasonably.

"What about a jury?" asked Baines.

"I'm sure we can choose twelve respectable, fair-minded individuals at random from the roster without too much difficulty," replied Sarah.

"No we can't," said Baines, flatly. "Have you forgotten that our crew is, apparently, liberally salted with hidden terrorists now?"

"Ah," said the priest.

"Exactly," a vengeful light flickered in Baines' eyes. "Fortunately, I have an idea which might cut through that problem, though."

"Go on," Satnam prompted, guardedly.

"You three!" Baines exclaimed, triumphantly. "A balanced perspective if ever I knew one: the scientist, the soldier and the priest. Who could argue with that?"

Fellows and Patel looked at one another uncomfortably.

Patel tried first, "Well, as you say, the captain probably won't want to be asked—"

"Oh, don't worry," Baines cut him off. "I'll be happy to tell him what *you've* decided!"

"Well, I... er," he tried again.

"We... er," seconded Sarah.

"So! I think we can call *that* settled then." Baines smiled unpleasantly, echoing Sarah's earlier assertion. After enjoying the moment, her smile turned to a frown. "By the way, who *are* the learned counsel? You mentioned that Frehly woman, who's the other?"

"Ah, I might have a little surprise for you there," said Mother Sarah, a glint in her eye. "Do you remember, a few moments ago, you mentioned a kangaroo court?"

Singh brought the shuttle through a wide turn into a steep sided valley. The mountains, so massive from the *New World*, were vast almost beyond seeing, up close. He could not help thinking that this brought them into scale with everything else in these parts.

The video they were capturing would be epic and jaw dropping, a real treat for the folks back on the ship. Huge herds of dinosaurs flocked and marched across the plains, or skirted the forest edges. Stupendous waterfalls thousands of feet high, separated into rainbows, coalesced and smashed into the rocks below. Brilliantly coloured flying reptiles whirled and glided all around them, some further across the wing than the twelve-metre shuttle was long.

The vistas were stunning, the snow-capped peaks breathtaking. The canopy below them could only be described as being like a blanket of crushed velvet. The similes springing from nature's palette could have picked every poet's pockets without spending a word. Each picture may be worth a thousand, but as the shuttle crew pondered the cost, their attention was very suddenly, and very fully, grabbed.

"What is it, Lieutenant?" asked Douglas.

The shuttle hovered above what appeared to be just another small, innocuous clearing. The computers continued scanning quietly in the background, freeing the crew to marvel at everything within their field of vision. They would have moved on, but a constant beeping from one of the sensors demanded attention.

"That's the *special* search algorithm I programmed yesterday, sir," replied Singh, showing just a little concern. "As the second part of our mission is to look for a *missing person*," he said diplomatically, with a small sideways nod for emphasis, "I programmed the ship's sensors to look for anything which appeared manmade."

Douglas was impressed. "Sandy, there's no one Ah'd rather be lost a hundred million years ago with," he said.

"Thank you, Captain," said Singh. "The feeling's mutual. Well, apart from that leggy brunette who works for Tim's mum, perhaps."

A brilliant smile flashed across his dark face and Tim's laughter rang from the back of the cabin.

Douglas grinned too. "Ah'll try not to take it to heart. What have ye found?"

Singh looked completely bewildered. "It looks like tyre tracks, sir."

"Excellent! That'll be the bike she filched from our stores," he explained for the benefit of the other crew.

"No, sir," said Singh, heavily. He turned to Douglas looking thunderstruck.

"OK. Let's hear it," Douglas prompted, guardedly.

"You'd better see this." Singh routed the feed onto the main screen and, in a huddle, they viewed the unimaginable.

Beck ambled through her private quarters to see who was at the door. The tiny screen showed a young man outside. Studying his features more closely, she caught her breath. "Can I help you?" she asked, cautiously.

"*Hello, Miss Mawar*," his voice was projected through the small speaker set into the door console. "*I wonder if I might ask a favour of you, please?*"

Beck saw no reason to deny the young man. "Sure," she answered, opening the door and inviting him in.

Once inside with the hatch closed behind them, the young man approached her, offering his hand enthusiastically. "I'm Georgio," he said.

"Hi, Georgio," she answered, slightly dazed – she *knew* that face, how was this possible?

"Are you OK, miss? Is this a bad time?"

"Er... no, I'm fine," she managed. "You just look a little familiar."

"I dare say you've seen me about the ship, I'm one of the *New World*'s engineers," he replied proudly.

"No. Well, yeah – maybe." She offered Georgio a seat, still holding a half empty glass in her hand. When she turned around, she emptied the other half, all over the carpet. Standing in front of her, smiling broadly, was a carbon copy of the man who was sitting behind her.

"Whoa! Are you sure you're OK, miss?" Georgio got out of his seat to help her to pick up the glass. "Can I get something to clean it up, perhaps?"

"It's OK, it's only water," she answered dreamily. "Your brother is here."

This time Georgio dropped the glass. They reached an unspoken decision to leave the receptacle where it was clearly destined to be and fell back into opposing seats around Beck's coffee table.

"You..." Georgio hesitated, "you knew Mario?"

"No, but I saw him once, the night we landed here."

Georgio opened and closed his mouth a few times but to no avail. All he could do was stare.

"Maybe we could use glasses with more than water in them," said Beck, getting to her feet. Moments later she returned from the kitchen bearing a couple of brandies. Both men were still there, so she gave the drink to the one for whom it would do the most good.

"I..." Georgio tried again.

"You came to see me about your brother," she said – it wasn't a question. "His name was Mario, did you say?"

She felt a little more relaxed after the brandy stiffener. Georgio merely nodded.

"He's here, now," she admitted, glancing at the ethereal double of the man seated in front of her. "Do you have a message for Georgio?" she asked the shade. The figure nodded and began to speak.

The door chimed. Hiro slept. Dr Flannigan had forced him to take another day off and, although he hated to admit it, he was absolutely exhausted after his recent trials.

The door chimed again. It could not possibly be for him, he registered blearily; he was merely dreaming.

The third chime was followed by banging and someone shouting, "Hiro! Let me in!"

The engineer groaned, pulling the duvet of denial up over his head, but this only led to more banging and shouting. "HIRO!"

After this last cannonade on his door, he let go a long string of invective in his native Japanese. "What is it?" the engineer managed to call out at last. He was now irrevocably awake and far enough back into the real world to recognise the voice as Georgio's.

"Let me in!" Despite being muffled by the door, Hiro could clearly tell his colleague was agitated or excited about something.

Wrapping the duvet around his body like a comfort blanket, he staggered towards the door, stepping on some nameless object left on the floor as he went. His wordless primal cry gradually coalesced into another stream of oaths as he hopped the last few steps to admit his friend. The door had barely begun to slide open when Georgio flew past him through the crack.

"What the hell is it?" the chief snapped, crossly. His foul temper was completely wasted on the exuberant Italian, however. So much so, that he began to wonder if his only remaining subordinate may have been imbibing.

Finally, Georgio calmed down enough to speak. "Hiro! I've spoken to him! Well, he's spoken to me anyway."

"That's fantastic," replied Hiro, sourly. "Put it in a full report and give it to me, I don't know, next year or something," he added, rubbing sleep out of his eyes.

"No, you don't understand," cried Georgio, laughing. "It was Mario!"

"Eh?" asked Hiro, becoming concerned.

Georgio was nodding vigorously now. "Mario! He spoke to me!" He grabbed his friend and superior officer, dancing him around in circles. Hiro had a simple choice, keep hold of his duvet and end up on the floor in a heap, or let it go and be danced around in his boxers. He can hardly be said to have made the dignified choice, but at least he remained on his feet.

"Wha-a-a-t a-a-re yo-u-u-u t-t-talk-k-king abo-u-u-u-t?" he stammered as he was bounced around the room. "Sto-o-o-p, stop! Let me get my trousers and then we can sit down and you can tell me what's happened."

A minute later, they faced one another across the small dining table in the chief's quarters. "I'd offer you a drink, but that would only encourage you to stay. Well, tell me then?" Hiro asked, terse and red eyed, doing his best to ignore the elephant Georgio had introduced into the room.

"I went to see Beck." Hiro looked blank, so Georgio tried again. "Beck? The medium?"

"Medium what?"

"Ha ha, that's a-really funny. The old ones are a-always the best, no?" laughed Georgio, his giddiness emphasising his slight accent.

"Funny?" asked Hiro, mystified.

"Oh, you're serious," said Georgio, his enthusiasm slipping slightly. "Beck is a medium – you know, talks to ghosts and spirits, yes?" he explained, waving his hands around, gesturing spookily.

Hiro stared at his friend, askance. "Have you been hitting the bottle again? I know it's been hard for yo—"

"NO!" Georgio laughed again. "It was really him, Hiro. He spoke to me, through her."

"*Really*," remarked Hiro, doubtfully, his misgiving so forceful that it shoved the elephant back outside, "and what did he say?"

Georgio waved away his friend's suspicions. "Mario told me that you were his very dear friend and that I should put any doubts aside that you had anything to do with what happened to him," he imparted, a little more seriously.

Hiro raised his eyebrows, completely taken aback. "Really?"

Georgio nodded earnestly. "He also said that Geoff genuinely didn't intend what happened." For the first time, a shadow crossed the young man's face. "He said I should forgive him, as *he's* forgiven him. That Geoff's been really upset about causing Mario's death, he just can't show it – he doesn't know how."

"You really believe this?" asked Hiro, his scepticism impossible to hide.

"Yes, of course. Don't you?" Georgio looked disappointed.

Hiro simply stared in silence for a moment, chewing his lip.

"I know that look," said Georgio. "Doubting like Thomas as the English say. Yes?"

"Actually, at the moment I think I could teach Thomas a thing or two. Look Georgie, I know it's been hard. I remember when I lost my brother, Aito. But this—"

"No, no, listen, there's more," continued Georgio. "He told me I *must* forgive Geoff. It's important. He said it was really important to my future."

"What's that supposed to mean?"

"I don't know."

"Can you do it?"

"Do what?"

"Forgive him?"

Georgio sat in silence, searching for the answer. "I can try," he acknowledged at last. "If it was an accident, I mean. I suppose I must try, if Mario tells me I need to."

"If it was an *accident*?" Hiro repeated, angrily, slamming his fist down on the table. "He blew our damned ship up!"

"But he didn't intend to hurt anyone, Hiro."

Hiro blew out his cheeks, re-inflating the elephant between them which subsequently began trumpeting around the room again. Despite this, he could commiserate with his friend's state of mind, from personal experience, so he spoke carefully. "I'm very happy for you, if you can find forgiveness for that man, Georgie," he began gently, "but *I* still don't trust him – will *never* trust him again. He killed one of my best friends, hurt Sekai and tried to blame it all on me! As for all this with Mario... well, I just don't know."

"Geoff is going to do something important, Hiro." Baccini studied his superior officer and best friend in the whole *New World* for a moment, adding solemnly, "I know he is. Mario told me."

Hiro wore an expression of sympathy, but decided the situation needed nipping in the bud, before it turned the younger man's head altogether. "So what, you think he's going to save us all? Do something wildly heroic, in spite of himself, at the very end? From a prison cell?" Hiro could feel his exasperation rising, so he tried again, putting it in the terms that one geek might use to another. "Georgie, he's bad news, bad all the way to the end. This is Geoff we're talking about, not Gollum!"

"Can ye tell me what Ah'm seeing? 'Cause Ah know what it looks like but Ah cannae believe it!"

Singh turned to his captain in awe. "The computer has cross-referenced everything we have in our library from the fossil record – everything! Including the much more 'in-depth' research notes from Tim's personal files." He placed his hands together, almost prayer like as he pondered. "It's not a couple of parallel millipede tracks, I *can* tell you that," he said at last. "In fact *Michelin* tracks might be closer to the mark."

"But..." tried Jim Miller.

"They are fossilised in stone, yes," Singh finished the sentence for him.

"It must be some sort of weird geological anomaly," Portree chipped in, "surely?"

"You ever seen anything like this before?" asked Singh, turning to face her.

"No," she admitted weakly.

"These are *very old* tyre tracks from an off-road vehicle," Singh continued. "Certainly not a bicycle either. From the size of the tracks, the depth and the gauge it was probably from a two or three ton machine – something about the size of an Erotic Violence, perhaps."

The captain's ears channelled the words into his mind where they ran a search through his memory, finally picketing just outside his understanding. "A what?!" he *askclaimed.*

Singh nodded matter-of-factly. "Yes, haven't you been home for a while, Captain? Most people can't afford to drive anymore and the roads are jammed anyway. However, in India we still know how to build automatically piloted 4x4s for the British executive classes. Market research over the last hundred years has led us to give successive models ever more evocative names, making them sound more cred, more *sexy.*"

"*Really,*" Douglas commented, with about as much interest as one might expect to find accruing in a young, working adult's savings account.

"Of course, that's progress! Although, I don't really see what's sexy about a two ton off-roader myself..." he added thoughtfully. "But it's amazing what imagery you can conjure up if you buy an empty-headed celebrity and put their name to your product," he rallied. "Perhaps give them a flashy title like 'design consultant' and bang! You've got another winner. We've been doing it for years. The new 'Erotic Violence Allroad' has sold off-the-scale, apparently. A *yaar* of mine heads the worldwide sales team, you see? His name is Bhupati, and he's a jolly good chap."

Douglas leaned back in his chair and slowly rubbed a hand down his face, holding on to his chin as he sighed patiently.

"It's very clever stuff, this micromarketing," Singh prattled on, distracted, as he often did when skirting the delivery of worrying news. "Did you know that in the north of England it was going to be re-badged as the 'Erotic Violence *Anyroad*'? Bhupati really knows his stuff! Apparently that campaign failed in the north, though. It transpired that they weren't all that interested in the automatic drinks dispenser or the 'drive me to a five-star restaurant' feature. All they seemed to care about was 'wull it start in t' cold mornings and wull it pull t' beast out t' bog?' Being a *yaar*, he got me a great deal on some shares. In fact, I remember Bhupati saying—"

Douglas felt the need to break in before his sanity unravelled altogether. "Your little asides always fascinate me, Sandip, but what the hell was it doing HERE!?" he said, working himself up from a snipe to a bawl as he jabbed his finger at the display. He calmed again, adding thoughtfully, "And *when?*"

"And where could this vehicle have possibly come from?" added Portree.

Singh opened his mouth to answer but Douglas cut him off crossly. "If you say Surrey, so help me..."

"No, Captain," Singh held his hands up. "I was going to say, it came from the past. Hard to say for sure how far back, using remote scans, anyway. We'll need to get down there and take samples to be precise. However, the initial sensor analysis suggests the mud-stone, in which the tracks are fossilised, is around twenty *million* years old."

"Well, that puts the cat well and truly amongst the Pterosaurs," Miller remarked. "Doesn't it?"

They looked from one to another for a moment, each hoping that someone, anyone, would have at least a theory which might begin to explain all this.

The shuttle hovered on autopilot, allowing Singh to query the computer, the sudden, wordless silence broken only by the manic clatter of fingers across a keyboard. Eventually he sat back, rubbing his chin.

"Sandy?" Douglas prompted.

"Hmm, there's something else, sir," he said, quietly contemplative. "I've focused our full scanning suite on the area of interest. Just below the surface of the rock I'm reading bones – fossilised bones, naturally."

"Bones will have been getting themselves fossilised for hundreds of millions of years before the Cretaceous," Douglas stated, looking to Tim for confirmation, "surely?"

"Quite right, Captain," Tim agreed. "Finding fossilised bones in this period should be no surprise – all waiting to be discovered by us a hundred million years from now."

"So," Singh countered, turning in his seat once more to face Tim directly, "just out of curiosity, would you expect *human* remains from a death occurring approximately *120 million years* before man to turn up here, then?"

Douglas took the shuttle crew to the bridge of the *New World* immediately upon their return and called a meeting with Baines, Patel and Mother Sarah. Singh ran through their findings, quickly leading up to their shocking discovery. Douglas edited with a nudge back on track here and there. At last, they all sat in silence, attempting to digest what they had learned.

Samantha Portree was first to speak, "Clearly someone has been here before us. The geology can't lie."

"But how's that possible?" asked Baines. "Wasn't it a zillion to one chance that brought *us* here?"

"Ah think," said Douglas, wearily, "that we may have to send a team out there to dig the site and bring the remains back to our labs. Perhaps we'll know more then. Clearly, being lost a hundred million years ago is *not* as weird as it gets – turns out, there's more!"

"Can we do that, James?" asked Sarah. "Wouldn't it be dangerous to have people on the ground out there?"

"Aye, it would," replied Douglas, "but Ah think we have to chance it. We've no idea what this could mean – what the ramifications might be. Fortunately, most of the animals ran from the sound of the shuttle as we approached, so hopefully we can use that to keep them away. Also, the creatures we saw in the forest appeared a wee bit more manageable, in terms of size at least. We'll take an armed team and plenty of those, what did Gleeson call them, 'Dingo Wingers'?"

"It seems the larger predators stick to the plains and forest edges," said Tim. "I expected that to be the case. The denser foliage, further in, would restrict their movement too much. We'd be very unlucky to find any larger animals so deep, Captain, but we must take great care, nevertheless. Some of the hunters in the forest could still be deadly to us, even poisonous for all we know."

"What can you tell us about the smaller predators?" asked Baines. "Dromeo…?"

"Dromeosaurids," Tim provided, helpfully. "Very good, Commander. Those or other, similar dinosaur families may well be here, but I'm guessing."

"So there might be nothing like that here?" asked Douglas, hopefully.

"I doubt that, Captain," said Tim. "If there's a niche, an animal will rise to fill it. That's Darwinism 101, really. I recommend we prepare for the worst. Our ground team should expect small, extremely fast and very aggressive predators, sir – quite deadly. I suggest Kevlar suits, Heath-Riflesons, stun grenades, everything we have to throw at them, and then just pray we don't need any of it," he finished, quietly.

"I was thinking," chipped in Jim Miller. "We can very quickly and easily knock together some riot shields as well, Captain. I can set the machine up to make a mould and have them with you in, say, a couple of hours?"

Douglas nodded. "That's good thinking. Any other ideas?" he asked, looking around the table.

Tim raised a hand. Douglas nodded for him to speak.

"Just a thought," the young man spoke hesitantly, "but couldn't we make a shield to cover the entire dig?"

"That's interesting, Tim," acknowledged Miller. "What did you have in mind?"

"What about something like a large, reinforced tent?" Tim asked, continuing with a little more confidence. "It could even have steel reinforcement bands moulded into walls made from a polymer that's clear one way, opaque the other? That would allow the people to see out but not let the animals see in, providing fewer disturbances. It would possibly cut down on UV too, wouldn't it? So the diggers don't get cooked? Add ventilation points and… well, that's it really." He waited for their reaction.

"Ah can tell you're Patricia's laddie," Douglas remarked appreciatively. He looked back to Miller. "Ah'm guessing this will take a wee bit longer, Jim?"

Miller nodded assent. "Probably four or five days to design and build, Captain, but we can do it," he stated, assuredly. "We have all the plant and supplies we need for this."

"Excellent," said Douglas. "Now, we can't land there, so everything's going to have to go up and down on ropes and pulleys through the shuttle's belly-hatch. There will certainly be an element of peril, but Ah hope that the roar of the engines will scare away most of the wildlife – at least during the most dangerous times of loading and unloading. The shuttle will have to drop the team and retreat to the *New World*, for safety. Ah don't think we dare put down out there. We just don't know enough about what we're up against yet and should the shuttle be damaged or destroyed it would be an irreplaceable loss."

The comm binged for attention. Douglas activated it from a flush control panel set within the conference table.

"*Captain, it's Jackson*," the voice came from all points via sound plates built into the fabric of the meeting room.

"Go ahead, Sarge."

"*Sir, I received a report of a large smokestack to the north. As we've got teams outside in diggers, I've stationed myself by one of the high-level viewports to take a look and there does indeed appear to be a large forest fire some miles off. I don't know whether this will be a threat to the ship, but I thought I'd better let you know.*"

"Thank you, Sarge. Could you guess at the distance?" asked Douglas.

"*Four, maybe five miles, sir,*"

"Stay on the channel, Sarge." Douglas swapped his attention to the people around the table. "Could this be a threat to us, do you think?"

"I suppose it would depend on the size of the blaze, the direction of the wind, that type of thing," hazarded Patel, cautiously. "A major forest fire could engulf the entire region. The weather is hot and there has been no further rainfall since the night of our arrival."

"Do we know if this dry spell is set to continue?" asked Baines.

"The *New World* has a basic atmospheric and meteorological suite," said Singh. "Shall I go next door and pull up the results?"

Douglas nodded for Singh to leave, saying, "Jim, Satnam, if we are going to be here for a while, would it be possible to build a wee satellite and send it up into a geosynchronous orbit to keep an eye on things for us? We could always move it if we relocate?"

Patel and Miller nodded to one another. "That sounds sensible, James," said Patel. "We can borrow a lot of the design from the systems built into this ship. With a full sensor suite as well, it could be very useful indeed. Perhaps it could even spot signs of Schultz."

"Actually, I may have some very good news on that front," said Miller. "We have a small communications satellite on board, already."

"Really?" asked Douglas, pleased to receive positive news for a change.

"Yes, Mars has—had? Will have?" Miller smiled, confusing his tenses and himself. "I'll start again. When we left, Mars had a satellite in orbit already. The problem was, with four townships spread around the planet, the coverage wasn't great and the residents were getting pretty cheesed off with the constant comms black-outs. NASA very kindly gave Sam Burton a second one, which is safely packed away in the Pod cargo bay. With a few additions like cameras, extra sensors and a meteorological suite, we should be good to go. Probably take about a week or so to prep it, I'm guessing. Then the shuttle can run it up into orbit and Bob's your uncle!"

"Mankind's finest hour," said Baines, darkly.

"Jill?" asked Douglas.

"We've been here all of a few days, and we're building a spy-satellite."

"Think of it as a weather balloon," replied Douglas, wryly, "with teeth!"

"*That could be a great asset, Captain,*" The Sarge's voice came through the speakers again. "*And would really help us keep track of everybody, as we start to send out exploration teams, I mean.*"

"See?" Douglas winked at Baines. "It's search and rescue now as well, just like a big cuddly teddy bear in the sky!"

"I don't know what sort of a teddy bear you were given as a baby," retorted Baines. "Mine was called Flopsy, and he would have made a rubbish spy."

"How so?" asked Douglas, taking the bait.

"He only had one ear."

The Sarge coughed politely and said, "*About this fire, sir.*"

"Quite right, Sarge," Douglas acknowledged. "What do we think, people?"

"Captain?"

"Yes, Tim."

"When we came back in the shuttle, I couldn't help noticing the digger drivers were out again."

"That's right," Baines answered. "Natalie reported that the Mapusaurs had made another kill and were sleeping it off. The construction team were keen to go and as Dr Portree was with you, they came to me for permission to take the machinery out. Why, do you see a problem?"

Tim thought for a moment. "Sergeant Jackson?" he asked.

"*Yes, Mr Norris?*"

"Would you say that the fire is heading this way?"

"*The wind is blowing the stack this way, yes. It's difficult to say whether the fire has grown as such, please bear with me a second.*" The channel went still for a few heartbeats. "*I'm just looking through my electro-binoculars and... yes, it does seem to have grown a little. I'm not sure if that means it's bigger or closer, though.*"

"And the wind is blowing it towards the ship?" asked Tim, to clarify.

"*Yes, sir. It appears so.*"

Tim frowned, contemplating, not noticing the soldier's courtesy to a civilian – even a young one. "Captain," he said at last, "I would recall those digger crews immediately."

"What's your thinking, Tim?" asked Douglas.

"Whether the fire is a threat to us or not, it may flush the animals this way. As we saw from the shuttle, there are some huge plains out there, much bigger than the clearing we landed in. All separated by bits of forest and interconnected by many animal thoroughfares."

"What are you saying?" asked Baines.

"I'm saying," Tim clarified, "that who knows what might come flying out of those trees in panic? If they run straight into our digger teams... look, I don't know anything for sure, but terrified animals are best given a wide berth, that's all."

"Especially if they can knock earthmovers over without breaking step," Baines could not help but jump to the logical conclusion.

"Tim's right," agreed Douglas, recalling his own close encounter with a running Mapusaurus bull. "Call them back in, Jill, and tell them to hurry. Ah don't want to take any chances. Maybe we can carry on with the building tomorrow."

"Captain," said Singh, stepping back into the meeting room. "There's a large weather system forming to the east, out at sea. We've got no real way of knowing whether it will come this way or disperse altogether, though. We'll have to keep an eye on it. As far as we can see for now, the weather on top of us looks fairly stable."

"No rain to put the fire out, then?" asked Douglas.

"Doesn't look like it, Captain," Singh replied. "But it could still change quickly. In fact, it might get pretty wild here. We don't have enough information to build any kind of picture yet."

"Perhaps our new satellite will help with that," stated Douglas, with satisfaction.

"Satellite?" asked the pilot, optimistically jumping ahead to triangulate his future. "Can we have two?"

Woodsey, Rose, Clarissa and Henry, until so recently known as Hank, waited in the *Mud Hole* for the intrepid explorer's return. The shuttle had docked with the *New World* over an hour ago but still no Tim.

"Do you think he's alright?" Clarissa worried. "He could have been eaten!"

Woodsey feigned concern. "Hey, you're right, Clarrie," he agreed. "It could take days before they find enough remains to hold a funeral."

"OMG! What d'ya mean?" Clarissa cried out, covering her mouth with her hands in shock.

"Well, the T Rex will have to digest him first, and I've noticed there's quite a lotta bone on that kid. Then it'll have to go to the dunny, won't it?" grinned Woodsey.

"Eek!" squeaked Clarissa.

"Don't listen to him, Clarrie," big-brother-Henry came to the rescue. "Tim's just done something momentous. There's bound to be some kind of debriefing procedure or somethin'."

"Really?" asked Woodsey, innocently. "They'll be taking his kecks off?"

Rose laughed. "You're terrible!" she accused Woodsey. "What do you think they've found?"

Woodsey looked around, making sure they were not overheard as he drew everyone in close and secret. "Well, there was talk," he whispered, "about buried treasure."

Rose took a sharp intake of breath. "Really?" she asked, wide-eyed. "Like gold in the rocks or the river?"

"Woodsey, will you cut it out!" snapped Henry.

Woodsey burst out laughing. "Y'know, you're getting old before your time, mate. There are too many women in your life!"

"Well, with your pick-up lines, that's never gonna happen to you, is it?" Henry retorted, making them all laugh. "I wish he'd hurry though, I'm dyin' to know what they've seen."

"Yeah," said Woodsey, "I can't wait to see the film they've promised us. I mean, we've all seen monster movies, but to have it all just outside the door – Wow!"

"Do you think they'll ever let *us* outside?" asked Rose.

"Of course they will," said Henry, "when it's safe."

"I don't wanna go out," said Clarissa. "Not with monsters out there!"

Henry gave Woodsey a thump on the shoulder. "See what you done now?"

"Hey!" Woodsey cried out, scandalised. "It's not my fault! I didn't put 'em out there!"

"You're the one calling 'em monsters, putting a stoopid idea into her head!" Henry said, hotly.

"Putting an idea into her head?" Woodsey threw the words back, eyebrows shooting up in disbelief. "Well, someone had to put one in, mate – it's hardly standing-room-only in there, is it?"

"Look," said Henry. "I—"

"Look!" said Rose, pointing.

"It's Tim!" shouted Clarissa and the squabble completely evaporated as they jumped out of their usual seats to surround the conquering hero, assaulting him with questions.

Eight vehicles worked the defensive ramparts. Two thirty-ton excavators were assigned to Manufacturing Pod Four's vehicle pool and both were outside moving huge bucketfuls of earth around and dumping it into two tipper lorries. Such powerful machines made short work of the movement, their massive, toothed buckets carving up the land like cheesecake in a New York Deli. The lorries drove the spoil back inside the earthworks and up the ramps formed at the rear, depositing it on top to be layered and levelled later.

A pair of smaller, ten-ton excavators worked behind the larger machines, using their spreader buckets to neaten up the sides of the steep-sided ditches in a smoothing, tamping action. At the top of the rampart, two comparatively tiny, three-ton machines worked to level the surface before trenching for the timber palisades.

The teams split into two, with four machines working each side of the 'D' shaped rampart, separated by the gap left for the proposed gateway at the centre. They were working well, everyone eager after a frustrating couple of days' inactivity due to, of all things, dinosaurs on the site.[5]

Glad to recommence work, the only thing the drivers had left to complain about was the lack of any radio stations. Almost 100 million years would pass before commercials gained keyless entry into homes and workplaces – paying their way in with the occasional song. Undistracted, the drivers noticed the smokestack sometime before they were recalled to the ship, watching it steadily approach. At such a distance, it had caused little concern, but orders were orders. Both of the mini-diggers at the top of the banks began their descent, their progress painfully slow, despite the fully ramped and trafficable nature of the enclosure's inner face.

The crews manning the larger machines near the stern of the *New World* also dutifully stopped work and started back towards the Pod's main cargo bay. The bow team were a little ahead of schedule and reluctant to lose ground. The three remaining drivers took a vote, deciding that another few minutes would enable them to complete their task. This, in

---

[5] Despite the inarguable validity of their work, archaeologists and palaeontologists can be the construction worker's worst nightmare. However, the *New World*'s digging crews circumnavigated this whole issue, deriving literally 'massive' delays straight from source, in the form of *living* fossils.

turn, would allow them to relax indoors until the go-ahead was given for work to commence on the palisade.

They pressed on and within a few minutes were indeed finished ahead of schedule, happily bantering across the airwaves and giving themselves a pat on the back for a tidy job.

The lorry easily outpaced the excavators, leaving them behind. It soon made its way through the cargo bay doors, huge tyres throwing clumps of mud and soil everywhere. Unfortunately, the tracked machines were still outside the unfinished compound when the ground began to shake.

"What did you see, Timmy? You're so brave to have gone out there." Adoration was written all over Clarissa's young face as she gazed up at him.

"Erm—" Tim began.

Before he could find an appropriate answer, Woodsey butted in. "Oh yes, please do tell us, Timmy. Please, *please*," he simpered. "You're my hero, Timmy!"

"Stop calling me Timmy!" Tim snapped crossly.

"You don't get offended by Clarrie calling you Timmy!" Woodsey bit back.

"Everything *you* say is calculated to offend!"

Rose let out a bark of laughter.

Grinning broadly, Henry prompted, "Ahh come on, Tim, we're dyin' to know."

Tim recounted his flight over Cretaceous Gondwana, describing all of its mysteries and miracles. He talked of the animals he had seen, the huge Pterosaurs circling around them whenever they slowed or hovered, the extraordinary beauty of the mountains and the refracted colours of the waterfalls. Reliving it in his mind, he was numbed by the enormity of all he had experienced and the sheer privilege he had been granted.

"I can't believe it," he said finally, almost breathless.

"Can't believe what?" asked Rose.

Tim shook his head ruefully. "Take your pick. We also found some fossil remains on the ground."

"You landed?" asked Woodsey, looking impressed.

"No, no, we weren't allowed to do that."

"You had the captain with you, dude," remarked Woodsey. "Who could have stopped you?"

"You don't know my mum! The captain promised her we wouldn't set down on the first trip and wisely kept his word."

"What were the fossils?" asked Henry.

Tim looked uncomfortable. "I can't tell you, sorry."

"*What*?!" the other teenagers chorused.

"I'm sorry, really." Trying to wave down their annoyance, he explained, "I was in a secret council meeting. I can't tell anybody about it."

"You're having a giraffe, mate! We're not just anybody!" Woodsey blurted.

"I'm sorry, I've been placed in a position of trust and I'm not going to let the captain down," Tim replied seriously.

"Wow!" exclaimed Clarissa in hushed tones, completely awestruck.

"Ah c'mon!" tried Woodsey again.

"Look," said Tim, "Lieutenant Singh is going to prepare the footage we recorded for a public viewing tomorrow evening. It's going to be awesome! The captain will tell everybody what we've found and if he decides to make it common knowledge then I'll answer any questions you have – deal?"

"*Deal*," the four thoroughly disappointed teenagers replied lifelessly.

"Well, the least you can do is get a round in, *Timmy*!" chided Woodsey.

"Will you stop the 'Timmy' thing?" asked Tim wearily, knowing he was wasting his breath.

Rose looked thoughtful. "What are we going to buy drinks *with*, when the money runs out?" she asked.

"Huh?" asked Henry.

"Well, it's not like we can make or earn any more, is it? How will we buy things?" Rose asked again.

Tim looked impressed. "You know what, Rose? That's very perceptive, that is. I don't know – never even thought about it, to be honest."

"Your dad's minted though, isn't he?" Woodsey asked Rose. "It'll be a while before you run out of mints, surely?"

"We were—" she stopped speaking, allowing new Rose to take over, "*comfortable*," she hedged.

Woodsey sniggered at her.

"But that was before the disaster and everything. Surely, it's all different now?" she added, frowning in thought. "Well, isn't it?"

"Look, I've already thought about all that, and planned for it," Woodsey expounded, confidently.

"Oh?" asked Henry. "What are *you* going to do for money then?"

"I'm gonna rob your dad!" laughed the New Zealander.

The Sarge saw them coming from his vantage point near the top of the ship and activated his analogue radio, shouting into the receiver, "Digger crew: Get back to the Pod now! Move it!" He stole a quick look through his electro-binoculars. "Your position is about to be overrun! Repeat: You are about to be overrun. Get out of there!"

He watched as the diggers became even more jerky and awkward in their movements, which probably meant they were flat-out. Unfortunately, this only equated to the speed of a fairly slow jog – not nearly enough.

The clearing where the *New World* slept suddenly erupted as a terrifying menagerie broiled out of the forest. From The Sarge's bird's-eye perspective, it bore all the chaos and madness of an early mosh pit, but there were no friendly faces or helping hands to pick up the fallen from this dance. The downed stayed down and the crushed remained crushed. As creatures of all shapes and sizes barged their way into the clearing, the noise was almost stupefying, with every individual battling frantically to place as much distance as possible between themselves and the oldest of all enemies: fire.

The stampede broke about the enormous edifice of the ship like a heavy tide; a forced divergence around the world of man. This changed landscape saw the unlucky cast into the new ditch or crushed blindly against its rampart.

Fortunately for mankind, the construction teams had just about done enough. Now fully encircled by the surge, their massive earthwork protected the *New World* from the rush and smash of thousands of tons of terror on the run.

Although the rampart held, the ditch below it writhed with bodies, all attempting to scramble back out at any cost. The tide had stalled. Any animals that made it around the ship now faced a new challenge.

Despite taking their ease for the last day or so, the Mapusaurus pack had become increasingly agitated as they too scented smoke...

The Sarge's radio crackled to life, "*Sarge, this is Natalie. They're moving – all of them!*"

He had taken the earlier precaution of tasking Dr Pearson with keeping vigil *their* side of the ship, for this very reason, while he watched over the digger crews working *his* side. The veteran soldier intended to be ready, just in case they were forced to display the better part of valour, and in a hurry. He had been right.

"Oh, Turkish Delight!" Jackson spat vehemently. He toggled the talk-back switch. "Understood – Sarge out."

The Mapusaurs were a marauding pack of killers, no doubt, but scavenging was also well within their scope. The indiscriminate, mostly accidental killing taking place all around sent them into a blood-frenzy. It was *Mappy* hour.

These terrible, beautiful, incredible creatures belonged to the family of carnivorous dinosaurs known as Carcharodontosaurs. The Latin name Carcharodontosaurus literally meaning 'shark toothed lizard', and almost too good for metaphor, the sharks were circling today. However, as they fought their way around the obstacle represented by the *New World*, they encountered threats even to their majesty. The first was the deadly crush which took the lives of three of their number; the second was a rival pack of Giganotosaurus, flushed out of their own territory by fire and set on a collision course. They converged exactly where the hapless digger drivers attempted their escape.

Giganotosaurus was a larger cousin of the deadly Mapusaurus. Ideally, they would have avoided one another where at all possible, hunting separate domains to circumvent the sort of injuries which might result from a direct confrontation. However, as the digger drivers caught up in the mêlée were becoming all too aware, this day was not shaping up ideally for anybody.

Terror drove the men almost out of their minds, whereas the wall of flesh, teeth and claws pursuing them was *fuelled* by it; a demonic horde on the trail of two interloping apes, lost in a past they barely understood.

Battered and shaken, they gambled everything on a final, valiant effort, all the while praying not to be overturned. Though their machines moved with excruciating slowness, the world outside seemed to leap, lunge and scream by the drivers' windows as if on fast-forward. As the tractors rattled and juddered over rough ground, and even a few bodies, the drivers were able to summon the last of their wits to spin their cabs through 180 degrees. Although still at a crawl, travelling in reverse made sense, enabling them to both face the onslaught and raise their huge buckets as deadly, defensive weapons.

Just in front, and feeling like a man making harbour in a storm, the driver of the smaller excavator eventually pierced the incomplete gateway. He was now inside the ramparts and reaching for the safety of the cargo bay. The new earth walls were being tested, but so far they stood resolute, deflecting the stampede around him, and the entire *New World*, in waves.

The operator of the larger machine found himself in a less favourable circumstance. Bringing up the rear, he trundled over the massively oversized causeway created to carry plant across the ditch and into the enclosure. Eventually, this earthen bridge would be narrowed and the sides battered[6] to prevent slippage and create a more defensible entrance, but the builders had simply not been granted the time necessary to undertake this stage of construction yet. In its current state – almost fifteen metres wide and with naturally sloping edges – the planned 'defensible causeway' actually provided the ideal platform for an assault on the gateway.

---

[6] A batter is a backward leaning slope created to retain a bank, or in this case, the sides of an earthen bridge. However, almost 100 million years into the future, the word 'battered' will become more commonly associated with fish and chips.

Giganotosaurus and Mapusaurus, masters of their respective domains, faced off like warring clans at the gates to the *New World*. With each adult averaging between twelve and fifteen metres in length, they completely straddled the land-bridge behind the plodding earthmover and covered quite a sizeable area around it. The gently inclined edges offered no protection at all from the sides.

Carnivorous theropod dinosaurs were in no way subtle. They filled up their space, and at that moment, the stranded machine operator began to feel them filling up his, too. Some of the most dangerous animals the world has ever bred faced this last man in the middle. *He* faced his death. A giant yellow earthmover on a bridge, travelling more slowly than any other object within theatre, was more than a little disadvantaged in terms of camouflage. So, there was nothing for it but to keep moving and hope their 'cousins' reunion' remained more distracting than his retreat. Without armaments, his chances of surviving the serrated savagery of those jaws were slim, especially en masse. Assuming he made it as far as the gateway, he could only trust that, in the end, his thirty-tonner might just prove the last word in blunt instruments.

Both packs needed to defend the area from their competition. Even in the throes of terror, the stampede attempted to avoid the impending bloodbath, causing an outgoing compression wave. The general chaos escalated still further as a large group of enormous sauropod dinosaurs finally caught up with the retreat and began shoving into the herd from the rear. Their strategy of hiding among the crowd was deeply flawed – about as successful as a man trying to hide in a puddle – but the forces they brought to bear were unstoppable.

It was the worst possible moment for a clash to break out between the giant carnivores and the ensuing violence shocked the driver to his core, his predicament made all the worse by the realisation that if he drove his machine all the way through the gateway, the battle would spill into their new enclosure.

He stopped his tracks in their tracks, at the halfway point, blocking the entrance between the two ramparts. It was all he could do. Out of options now, he made a stand. Terrified and alone, he truly saw Death at work, praying fervently that this metaphor would not soon appear directly under his name – in his obituary. His only solace was the fact that his colleague would now reach the safety of the ship, thanks to the blocked entrance he now provided.

The wholesale slaughter distracted most of the predators away from the petrified driver. However, there still remained enough animals at the sides of the engagement to press a partial attack on the monstrous, bright yellow invader, with a view to cracking open the tempting snack inside. Massive bodies flung one another against the walls of the gateway. As he swung the bucket threateningly, the man could not help noticing that the edges were beginning to crumble in some areas, despite their twenty-metre depth.

The killers came on. Sandwiched between rough earthen walls of his own making, the man felt like a quarry in his own quarry, but he could not flee. If he moved, others would die. His body shook uncontrollably, as courage alone fought the overpowering impulse to get out of his cab and run like hell.

The Sarge reached for his comm, once more opening a channel to the captain.

"*Douglas here.*" The captain was back on his bridge and in his command chair.

"Sir, we've got a man in serious trouble out there. One excavator didn't make it back. He's trying to hold the gateway, fighting the dinosaurs off with the digger's bucket – it's bizarre! Those monsters are fighting a war and that poor sod's right in the middle of it."

"*But the commander ordered them in several minutes ago!*" The astonishment in Douglas' voice rang clear, even through the comm.

"And most of 'em did as they were told, Captain, but for a couple of stragglers – clever Herberts – who thought they knew better. The lucky one of the two is just entering the airlock now. Sir, can you send Lieutenant Singh out in the shuttle? Maybe he can *buzz* the animals, using the noise of the jets to back them off? Like you suggested earlier?"

A short moment passed as The Sarge waited for a response.

"*He's on his way, Sarge, good thinking. Ah hope he's in time to help. Can you order a team to watch the skies when the shuttle bay doors open, please? We've got enough trouble by all accounts, without having the ship invaded.*"

"They're already en route, sir. I took the initiative."
"Glad you did, Sarge."

Captain Gleeson stood with Major White at the threshold of the cargo bay's main vehicular hatch, watching the horror show. Each was armed with a Heath-Rifleson and a bandolier of Dingo Wingers.

A few smaller animals milled about the compound, having slipped in more by accident than judgement, before the gateway was blocked by the excavators. None of them appeared threatening; rather, they looked lost, wandering along the base of the rampart searching for a way out.

The driver of the smaller digger had just achieved the relative safety of the cargo bay. He was clearly terrified, possibly even in shock, but White barked orders at him, showing no mercy.

"Crank this goddamn thing back around and guard the door!" he bellowed at the shell-shocked driver. When he did not respond, the major grabbed the man's shirt, shaking him. "You've already caused enough trouble, mister. So help now! DO IT!"

White jumped down from the machine, allowing the traumatised driver to manoeuvre into a defensive position, at least partially blocking the bay doors. The ten-ton excavator now faced forwards, with its backfill blade on the deck for added stability and its two metre wide spreading bucket raised high to meet any possible challenge. Although the spreader had no teeth, the awesome hydraulic strength of the machine still made it a brutal bludgeoner and the leading edge a lethal cutter.

White returned to Gleeson. "Ready to play hero again, Elvis?" he shouted above the din.

Gleeson wore his most sarcastic expression. "Uh huh," he answered, simply.

The giant, toothed bucket of the thirty tonner swung across the mouth of the ramparts in graceful arcs as the arm hinged and straightened, pushed and twisted, craning in a fashion almost as birdlike as the dinosaurs themselves. Defending the bottleneck of the gateway, it put Gleeson in mind of an avenging swan from hell. The two soldiers shook hands and, steeling themselves, ran towards the fray.

The animals attacked the digger completely without fear, but quickly learned respect after a few side swipes sent them tumbling. A full grown

Giganotosaurus slipped under the arm of the machine making a beeline for the driver, but one devastating drop of the massive bucket, made deadlier still by gravity, cut the creature almost completely in two. Blood and entrails sprayed all across the gateway and the excavator, the sudden splatter entirely blocking the driver's view. The cab's windscreen wiper activated automatically and there was a surreal moment where the driver's three-cubic-metre, one-man-universe was filled by the sound of an electric pump delivering washer fluid. However, claret curtains soon parted to reveal a killing corridor, where monsters, driven berserk by the stench of gore, indulged a savage, wide-eyed bloodlust.

Two Mapusaurs remained within the pinch-point between the ramparts. As one, they secured the corpse of the Giganotosaurus with a taloned hind foot, while chomping huge mouthfuls of flesh. Snouts livid red, teeth clogged with shredded meat, dripping with nameless fluids and mucus, they shared the unexpected repast for a moment only, before turning on each other.

The machine operator watched in horrified fascination. Clearly the pack's allegiance during the hunt shifted with the wind, possibly breaking down entirely after the kill; a behaviour equating to little more than guidelines, it seemed.

Regaining his senses, he backed his machine away a little further. He stayed within the twenty-metre-long gateway, but creeping even a few metres back towards the *New World* made him feel better.

Outside the manmade enclosure, on the land-bridge, much of the fire appeared to be leaving the greater skirmish. Both sides seemed to sense the threat of mutually assured destruction and began to take a step back. Excepting opportunistic snaps at anything close, the giant theropods slowly retreated into a shouting contest, battle lines redrawn. The Mapusaurs outnumbered the Giganotosaurs but the latter's greater size and strength levelled the playing field and so the fighting degenerated into a contest of wills and nerve for the spoils.

Within the gateway, the brief spat between the Mapusaurs came to an abrupt end as one of the animals gave one last roar of indignation before limping away. The victor glutted itself before any others showed an interest in the digger's kill. Despite the sudden surplus, the giant still had a greedy eye for the man, just out of reach inside his hastily reinforced container, becoming emboldened each time the digger came to rest. The operator could only defend from one direction, but against a single adversary this was achievable. Especially as the creature was currently the sole beneficiary of an unexpected banquet.

If the driver continued to reverse his machine back out of the bottleneck, he would leave the dinosaurs a clear run at the open cargo bay behind his position.

Stalemate…

He also had another pressing concern; after the big push on the ramparts, and all his self-defence *diggering*, the massive batteries which drove his machine were almost depleted.

He breathed deeply, using this lull in combat to contemplate his next move while he wiped sweat from his brow. His name was Red and he had joined the Mars Mission with his younger brother to find excitement. His brother had been on the other crew, the ones smart enough to obey their orders and get back inside the ship.

As he pondered his mistake, a pair of adolescent Giganotosaurs stalked cautiously into the gateway. It was clear hunting behaviour and, any second, the feasting adult Mapusaurus would be bound to notice.

"You're a bladdy drongo!" Red cursed himself, returning his hand to the controls quickly. The sudden movement caused a minor draught to circulate around his cab and for the first time he noticed that the air was beginning to feel *lived-in*.

He sniffed his armpit… *Could be worse*, he thought. When the *crack-boom* of explosions erupted to either side of him, it nearly was. His hands, holding the control joysticks in a death grip, jumped, sending the bucket up and to the side. The 'house' of the machine spun quickly in a completely unpredictable movement that caught one of the youngsters by surprise, launching him into his pack-mate. The pack-mate was so unhappy about it that she attacked the victim back in his face.

Other animals were beginning to explore the opposite end of the gateway and the whole chaos seemed primed to erupt once more, when two men came out of nowhere, running left and right of the heavy machine. They were soldiers, but despite shouting insults at the top of their lungs, they nevertheless appeared impossibly small and fragile, scaled as they were against the blood-spattered earthmover and its huge adversaries.

Gleeson and White threw small stick-grenades at the giants, sending deafening bangs echoing around the narrow gateway. The beasts were certainly spooked by this turn of events. White and Gleeson hoped the bangs would scatter them, perhaps even create a stampede in the opposite direction, as one might expect from a herd of cattle. It was fifty/fifty, but luck was not on their side and their shooing tactics failed. The situation was more akin to wading through a pack of wild dogs, than cattle. Kicking out and shouting, one hopes, to cow them, whilst always running the risk of making them angrier still. Ultimately, what really made the situation worse was that these were not dogs.

The *ROAR* was ear-splitting. As one, they charged.

"Whoaoaoaaaa!" Elvis sang out.

"*RUUUNN!*" White bellowed.

The giant predators slammed into the excavator. Despite the driver's heroic attempt to stabilise his machine by turning and dropping the bucket, it was too late and the digger went over with a terrible *groan* and *clang*. Still strapped into his harness, Red decided his only choice was to stay put, play dead and hope Tom Wood's protective cage would save him.

As the combined forces of this new super-pack scrambled over the stricken earthmover, the two soldiers began what must surely have been a contender for the longest run in history, or prehistory. Gleeson looked over his shoulder into a vision from darkest Revelation, terrible gnashing of teeth and all. With more than sixty metres still to cover, the monsters bore down on them.

Everything changed in a heartbeat as a sonic blast, so loud it knocked White and Gleeson to the ground, reverberated around the enclosure. They rolled onto their backs, expecting the end, only to find themselves looking up at the belly of the shuttle, jet thrusters throttled wide open.

All was noise and dust. Something smacked White in the face and he knocked it reflexively aside before realising it was a rope. Communication was not possible, so he slapped a piece of it into Gleeson's hand, wrapping the piece he had around his wrist. The rope began to rise and rise faster as the ship climbed vertically. In an action somewhere between that of a rope trick and a yoyo, the two men popped from the top of the dust cloud coughing heartily into a clear sky.

"Bladdy lucky that wasn't a diesel," shouted Gleeson, looking down at the toppled digger and trying to distract himself out of his panic.

"Why?" White shouted back. "Would it have exploded?"

"Naow," drawled the Australian. "He's turned it over, mate. He'd have never got it going again!"

White's response to this invaluable titbit was lost, however, because at that moment they were both hauled through the cargo hatch of the craft. White's men simply grabbed them by whatever they could reach, launching the pair quite unceremoniously into the hold behind them. Considering the alternative fate they had avoided by a hair's breadth, the officers were not overly put out by this rough treatment.

One of the men shouted above the engine noise, "Just the two of you, sir?"

White and Gleeson glanced at one another before looking down from the hatch. "The driver's still in the middle of all that," yelled Gleeson.

All four men now peered through the dust at the turmoil below them, dismayed.

"There's nothing we can do," acknowledged White, sadly. "We'll lose the whole ship if we go down there."

Gleeson's colour drained. "The ship!" he shouted.

White caught on immediately, turning to his men, "Call the pilot and get him to order the Pod cargo hatch closed!"

The driver of the smaller digger remained on guard at the threshold of the Pod's main doors. He saw his workmate's machine go over and the running soldiers fall. As the deafening sound of powerful jet engines filled the enclosure, his view was obscured by a blinding dust cloud, and out of that dust, came the attack.

A young adult Mapusaurus burst past the digger before the man at the controls could react. A soldier standing in the path of the creature screamed – a scream which cut off almost immediately.

Feeling like he was in a dream state, his movements slowed, the operator turned his machine in an attempt to bat the animal away. Unfortunately, this only propelled the creature at even greater speed in the direction it had already decided to take.

News of the emergency had spread quickly and temporary security personnel, recalled to service, were approaching from all sides to prop up the established team. These men and women plunged into the fray with stun rifles or anything they could lay their hands on, hoping to bring the dinosaur down. Unfortunately, the sudden influx of people meant their weapons could only be used at low power, causing no more than minor irritation to the giant in their midst. The whole hangar was in chaos, which only served to feed the fear and therefore the aggression of the beast.

Corporal Thomas had been standing just inside the outer hatch, next to the smaller excavator, when the animal tore past, forcing him to dive out of the way. Now back on his feet, he could see other carnivores skirmishing still, near the edges of the compound outside. They were getting accustomed to the noise of the shuttle's engines. He prayed the distraction would hold a little longer as he shouted for the digger driver to creep his machine back over the threshold and retreat inside.

The pair of young Giganotosaurs skirted the fracas, still working in tandem. Corporal Thomas spotted them at once. They moved more purposefully than the other animals out there and seemed to have already shaken off any surprise caused by the noisy jet engines. Probably no more than three years old and barely half-grown, they were already the weight of bull elephants and they were *fast* – more than that, they were heading his way. They locked eyes on the soldier and charged immediately.

"Oh, crap! Jonesy, close the outer hatch! CLOSE IT *NOW!*" he bellowed urgently.

Luckily Private Jones was attentive to his post at the cargo bay door controls, despite his near brush with the huge Mapusaurus which raged past him just seconds before. The hatch sealed with a teeth-jarring clang. The echo rang loudly around the vehicular airlock, but it was hardly the note of safety Corporal Thomas had been hoping for. They now had a much larger predatory dinosaur trapped in the ship *with* them. He ushered the machine operator back towards the inner hatch. Already rolling, the driver rotated the house of the excavator once more, to face the latest threat.

Inside the cargo bay, the Mapusaurus was also spinning around, furiously, taunted by little creatures it did not recognise or understand. Its senses were bombarded with strange, unnatural sights, smells and sounds.

Although enormous, the animal was also afraid and knew only one way to express its distress. It lunged.

Although surrounded by a ring of antagonists, they were mere mouthfuls. It would require at least five of them to provide a decent meal. However this time, the lethal jaws snapped on nothing but air – its five a day would have to wait.

The people encircling the dinosaur were also afraid and had frustrations of their own. They could harass and confuse, but no one dared risk hitting one of their fellows with 500,000 volts. Their continuous feints with low-power stun bolts merely compounded the animal's growing fear of entrapment, with each taunt and trick adding to its ferocity.

When the digger hove into view, the beast recognised a worthy opponent at last. Lowering its head, it charged. The resulting clash was almost fantastic, a million to one chance impossible to repeat. As the creature leapt, the driver was just able to rotate the house of the machine in sync with the movement. Bringing the boom and dipper around in a graceful arc, with sublime timing and almost surreal gentleness, he deposited the enraged Mapusaurus back into the voluminous airlock from which it had sprinted, just moments before.

Akin to kicking-out-time on a crisp December evening, the dinosaur skated across the metal deck like a drunk on ice, swaying and flailing but somehow keeping its feet – all the while roaring in fury. The considerable force of its own momentum slammed it hard against the closed outer hatch, stunning it momentarily.

"SHUT THE INNER HATCH!" someone screamed.

"I'm doing it, I am!" Jones bawled in reply.

The Mapusaurus rallied, turning to take another run at these vexatious little creatures it could not quite bring to bay. The digger drove right up to the hatch, the driver swinging the bucket wildly. The threat kept the animal back, its head bobbing and tail swishing angrily, looking for an opening – but the doors were closing. Its roar of frustration was deafening within the enclosed space, when with a final, resounding *clang* the hatch sealed and all fell still.

Jones activated the airlock camera, watching the feed on a small screen set into the door controls. The animal paced around its impromptu cell, striking the walls lividly with its tail.

"Tidy," the Welshman commented, satisfied.

Captain Douglas arrived during the aftermath, jogging over to view Jones' catch. The men watched the caged animal, mesmerised. "Is there any movement from the man still outside in the other machine?" he asked eventually.

Jones summoned a separate feed from the external camera above the main hatch. The digger was on its side with no movement around it. "Not that I can see, sir."

Douglas shook his head sadly. "OK, let it go," he said quietly.

Jones opened the outer hatch and the dinosaur ran towards freedom, still roaring defiance.

Singh hovered above what now looked very much like a warzone. White and Gleeson joined him on the shuttle's small bridge. As the dust began to clear they saw the animal burst from the Pod cargo bay, retracing its steps to the enclosure's gateway. From there, it ran to find its family; no longer a monster, just a frightened animal seeking the comfort of its kin.

The Mapusaurs and Giganotosaurs were now separated by several hundred metres. As that distance increased, they wound down the ostentation of their aggressive display proportionally. The conflict had reduced both sides and many of the survivors were visibly wounded. Within moments, they had disappeared from the clearing altogether, once again in pursuit of the migrants from the fire, but both sides the poorer for their exchange. Each pack instinctively chose a different route, thus completing the inevitable cycle of diplomacy-war-diplomacy.

Singh shook his head sadly as he viewed the broken remains of so many creatures caught in the wrong place at the wrong time. "What a mess," he said, "and what a waste." He activated the comm. "Singh to the *New World.*"

"*Jill here, Sandy. Go ahead.*"

"Commander, we're all clear now. Please send out a rescue team, quickly. The digger driver may have survived.

"*Understood. Bring her home, Lieutenant. I'm opening the shuttle bay hatch for you now.*"

Douglas watched in silence as the remains of the fallen soldier were collected from the cargo bay floor. The body parts were wrapped with as much dignity and respect as possible and removed to the cold storage facility in sickbay – now most definitely a morgue.

As the stretcher was lifted, he ordered all servicemen and women to attention, holding his salute until the bearers were gone.

Natalie Pearson also waited respectfully for them to leave before approaching the captain. He was facing away from her so she stepped alongside him, gently touching his elbow.

"Dr Pearson," he acknowledged, sadly. "How can Ah help you?"

"I know this is a bad time, Captain," she apologised, "but it can't wait."

Douglas took a deep steadying breath. "Of course, Doctor. Please continue?"

"We need to send a work crew out there straight away, sir."

"Why, Doctor? The digger driver has been retrieved, mercifully alive, no less. What else is there to do?"

"The bodies, Captain," she said. "They have to be piled and burned, and I'm sorry, sir, but I don't mean tomorrow."

"The dead animals?"

"Yes, sir. If we leave them, this clearing will be a free buffet for every predator within a ten mile radius. The smell of fire and charred bodies will also help to keep the animals away." She gave Douglas an intent look. "We must act while those creatures are spooked and on the run from here. They won't be for long."

Douglas nodded. "Of course. Thank you for the heads-up. Ah'll get Sergeant Jackson to liaise with Dr Portree straight away and get a crew onto it."

When Natalie did not leave, Douglas asked, "Is there something else, Doctor?"

"It's a bit unsavoury, Captain." She rubbed her eyes and smiled wearily. "That wasn't a pun. We should, perhaps, gather some food. In a world of 'eat or be eaten', it might be wise to use this opportunity and find out what's good and what's not, so to speak. I suggest we select from the herbivores – I should be able to advise the teams out there, no need to risk Tim Norris."

Douglas bowed to the logic of the zoologist's proposal and nodded his acceptance. He gave The Sarge his orders and walked over to where Dr Flannigan checked on the two fortunate digger operators.

Flannigan, his arm still in a sling and his head bandaged, turned as he approached. "Captain," he greeted.

Douglas stopped, looking the walking-wounded doctor up and down, managing a half smile. "Are you the best we had to send?" he asked.

Flannigan chuckled. "You can't put me down that easily, James. Just don't ask me for an arm wrestle right now, OK?"

Douglas' smile warmed as he patted the doctor on his good shoulder, but faded quickly as he focused his attention on the drivers. "You were ordered to bring your machines back inside. What happened?" he asked, coldly.

The men looked at one another guiltily, swallowing without speaking. There really was nothing to be said.

"We lost a brave soldier today," Douglas tore into them. "His name was Jack Dorset. Remember him. And the next time you get an order from me or from ma staff – obey!"

One of the men opened his mouth to speak but Douglas cut him off.

"The only reason you two are not in the *brig* right now, is because what you did afterwards was incredibly brave and selfless. If you hadnae caused this crisis, Ah'd be pinning a medal on ye – but ye *did* cause it."

Regret was plain on the men's faces as they looked down at the deck.

"However," he continued, glaring at the driver of the larger machine, which had been turned over, "if ye'd bottled it and run, hadn't stood your ground out there, we'd have had an army of those things in here, doubtless losing many lives and probably a significant portion of the Pod. It was a brave thing to do. And you," he turned, pointing at the other man. "It was bad enough that we lost Jack, but if you hadn't defended the cargo bay hatch, we may have lost many of these people here to that monster."

He took a deep breath. "Ah cannae congratulate ye. Ah simply ask ye to remember and learn from this. *Everything* we do here, *every* situation we come across can be potentially deadly. One loose cannon deciding to go their own way could bring disaster down on us all.

"Well, that's all Ah've got to say. Carry on, Doctor." He nodded to Flannigan and strode away to check on the clear up operation.

Chapter 14 | All in the Past

"The construction work is moving apace now the animals are giving us a wide berth," Baines pronounced as she shared a simple lunch with Douglas in the meeting room off the bridge. "We've had no serious wildlife issues for nearly four days now. Not since the stampede."

"Is there much timber still to cut?" asked Douglas.

"Yes, a great deal. Those Argentinasaurus really did us a solid, when they knocked all those trees down. Of course, when you step out into the clearing, it's like a gong farmer's Elysium out there. Naturally, Patricia Norris thinks this is all some sort of wonderful bonus. Apparently all the poop and ashes will do us the power of good when we come to plant the area."

Baines shook her head in rueful memory. "Life seemed a lot easier on the moon, planting in hydroponics glasshouses. When you get over to the lumber site, though, it all kinda feels so normal, just workers cutting trees and trimming branches."

"We could all do with a touch of normalcy in our lives just now."

"Yes, but of course, that's before you notice the circle of armed security personnel and the armoured people carriers parked for the crews to retreat to, if they get company. There's also the ring of explosives Gleeson set up around the site to greet unwanted guests. Not to mention the Kevlar suits everyone's wearing under their lumberjack shirts, and the fact that all the construction workers are armed as well. But apart from *all that*, it feels pretty normal. Alright there's no site hut, with nude calendars on the wall and no blaring radio but—"

"Aye, Ah get it!" laughed Douglas. "By the way, what's a gong farmer?"

Baines laughed too. "Did they no' teach ye anything in Scottie school?" she said, returning the captain's 'loony' taunt from a few days earlier. "Let's just say that Tudor England is a place I am very happy I'll never see!"

Douglas laughed again. "What was that accent?" he enquired. "Scandinavian? It was quite convincing."

"Har har," Baines retorted. "Oh, by the way, there's another piece of good news, too. They managed to save the big digger – the one knocked over in the attack?"

"Good," replied Douglas. "Very good. We cannae afford to lose plant and equipment like that."

"Indeed," Baines continued. "They turned it the right way up using a couple of the other diggers. There was some damage to one of the tracks and a few hydraulic hoses needed changing, but largely it was fine, bar a little scratched paint and the need for a damned good wash down." She grinned. "Apparently, it's really lucky that the power plant is an electric motor and not a diesel engine."

"Oh?" enquired Douglas.

"Yes, ask Major White about it when you see him. I'm sure he'll be pleased to explain it the way he was given it," she finished, mischievously.

Douglas looked at her sideways. "Ah see."

He used his napkin and pushed his plate aside. "Do you know, virtually *nothing* has happened in four days?" he said. "No one has been hurt, nothing has been blown up, no one has sabotaged anything, none of my engineers have tried to kill anyone," he paused for a moment. "Do ye think we just might be through the worst of it now that *she's* gone?"

"I wouldn't like to bet on it, Captain. We still don't have the first clue who the others are or what their play is."

"We've only Lloyd's word that they even exist, though," Douglas pointed out.

"That's true, but it does make sense. We certainly can't sit on our laurels."

Douglas sighed. "Aye, Ah suppose."

Baines looked at him with concern. "Are you OK, James?"

"Aye, Ah just cannae help wondering if Ah could have averted all this with nothing more than a few kind words and an attempt to care more about a man under ma command."

"Lloyd, you mean?"

"Aye."

"He was vile to everyone around him. What could you have done to change that?"

Douglas looked anguished. "Ah could have tried, Jill. That drink Ah had with him the other night was the first and only time Ah've ever shared more than the shortest possible moment with the man."

"Well, I do have to refer you to my last comment, James. It was hardly your fault. He drove everyone away."

"Aye, but maybe he wouldn't have taken such drastic action if Ah'd just tried to include him a little more. He was genuinely upset about Mario. Once he'd decided to confess it all came out. He's so alone, Jill, more alone than anyone in the world right now."

"Apart from Heidi, perhaps," suggested Baines. "But then she still has her mates on board among us. Captain, you can't blame yourself for Lloyd's actions. Who could have possibly foreseen that a serving officer on the Mars fleet would have taken up with a bunch of terrorists? Besides," she smiled understandingly, "after half a bottle of fifty-year-old single-malt, I'd have been in tears too, confessing to whatever you've got!"

Douglas' return smile was fleeting. "And, in a couple of days we have the trial," he stated wearily.

"Well, I can't say I'm excited about that, either."

"Ah think a good many are though, Jill." He gave her an intent look. "Ah'm worried it's going to be a circus. People are *looking forward* to it!"

"Do you think I could push a few toffee apples? In the crowd, maybe?" asked Baines, brightly.

Douglas gave her a long-suffering look.

"Sorry, Captain. Everyone on this ship has been wronged. I think it's only natural to want to see the man who caused it all, getting his."

"Aye, that's just it though," Douglas retorted crossly. "He didnae cause it all. Not all of it. He was just a cog in the machine. A fool who was bought by the right words whispered in his ear."

"And a boat load of cash! Let's not romanticise this, James. He caused the death of a brilliant young man, ruined the lives of many others, and the ball *he* set in motion may yet cause the end of us all."

"But—" Douglas tried.

"*And*, Captain," Baines cut him off, unwilling to be deflected, "one wrong move here and the human race may never even exist. I can't help thinking that he needs to take quite a lot of the blame for all this!"

Douglas slumped slightly in his seat and sighed, nodding gently.

Baines eyed him sympathetically. "You're such a good man, James. Don't try and shoulder his blame. You carry weight enough already and you don't deserve it."

Douglas smiled wanly. "Ah'll try not to," he said. "Thanks, Mum."

Baines grinned. "Oh, by the way, I've asked the 'learned counsel'," she pressed the inverted comma bunnies back into service, "*not* to call Georgio."

"Doesn't he want to give evidence?" Douglas asked in surprise.

"Yes, he does. That's the problem."

The captain frowned questioningly.

She sighed. "Have you heard that he went to see Rebecca Mawar?"

"Mawar? Refresh my memory again?"

"She's the rich spiritualist medium, from the paid seats."

"Oh. And...?"

"I understand grief must run its course, but I think she's filled his head with..." she shrugged, confounded. "I don't know what. Apparently, there are stories of his brother coming back to visit him, bringing messages from the *other side*. She's convinced him that Lloyd didn't mean to cause Mario's death. Allegedly, Mario has told him that Lloyd is very sorry, and should be forgiven."

"And you don't think that this will be taken completely seriously in court?" asked Douglas, raising an eyebrow.

"Let's just say," Baines replied patiently, "that I think Lloyd has enough people wanting to see him fall, without having his backside kicked by Banquo!"

"Maybe Mario has a point though?"

"*Ohh*, Captain – you're not buying any of that?"

"No. Well, not the messages from beyond the grave. It's just the sentiment which rings true for me. Maybe we do need to forgive him. As you once said to me, Jill, not very long ago, we're all we have now. Can we afford grudges with everything else we face?"

Baines sat back, giving Douglas a look somewhere between exasperation and devotion. Eventually, she leaned forward again, grasping his hand across the table. "James, I don't think that approach will garner much support from the passengers. They need to see some form of justice to help them make sense of this crazy hand we've been dealt."

Before Douglas could answer, the door chimed. He sighed. "Come."

Mary Hutchins followed her refreshments trolley into the room. "Hi folks," she greeted. "Just wondered if you'd finished with your lunch and whether you'd like coffee?"

"Ooh, yes please, Mary, and do you have anything else for me?" asked Baines, hopefully.

Mary leaned down to the seated commander, confidentially. "Double chocolate muffins," she whispered.

"YAY!" Baines exclaimed, punching the air.

"Also," Mary continued, "Mother Sarah and Dr Patel are on the bridge. They're just saying hi to Sandip, shall I invite them in?"

"Please," replied Douglas.

Douglas and Baines rose to greet the councillors as they entered.

"The commander was just updating me about the sawing and milling operation over the way," said Douglas. "Ah'm sure she'll be happy to bring you up to speed, but first Ah'd like to talk about this trial in a couple of days."

Douglas gave the two women and the man an appraising look.

"Since Ah left the organisation of this wee courtroom gathering to the three of you, Ah was rather surprised to learn that Ah'm going to be back in the middle of it! Ah was doubly surprised when it was advertised as a public event. Maybe we should celebrate it annually, as a holiday perhaps?"

He stared them down for a moment, gradually raising an eyebrow in amusement. "Ah was yet *more* surprised, although gratified, to learn that you've also tied each other up in this.

"So, it seems we have to come up with a plan for punishment, should the man be found guilty – which Ah have to say is pretty likely. And if that wasn't enough, it seems Ah need a strategy preventing the three of you from ever being left alone together again, too!"

Sarah smiled. "We always look to the captain for wise counsel," she said, humbly.

"Yes," said Patel. "It would also have been useful if you had warned us about the cunning of Commander Baines, Captain."

"And I always thought she was such a nice girl," seconded Sarah.

"I'm still here, you know," mumbled Baines.

Douglas chuckled. "Right, so, guilty verdict, what comes next?"

"He may not be found guilty," suggested Sarah.

"True," said Baines, "but we don't really need to plan for saying 'you can go', do we?"

"Do you think not?" asked Patel, seriously.

"Fair point," she admitted. "I'd better knobble the jury then! I'm guessing that Mother Sarah might be receptive to a bribe? Half of this double chocolate muffin perhaps?"

"We're skirting the issue here," said Douglas.

Baines nodded agreement. "Actually, Captain, we're marching off in the opposite direction from it."

"Indeed," he concurred. "So the choices are: banishment, imprisonment, or...? We have no way of readjusting the man, and Ah cannae bring myself to order the death penalty."

"No," agreed Sarah. "Surely we've evolved beyond that, even here."

"I wouldn't want to carry the order out myself," added Patel, "so I can hardly insist that someone else do it."

"Banishment amounts to the same thing, you know," Baines pointed out, inconveniently. "I don't think we can wash our consciences clean by simply kicking him outside and pretending we didn't kill him."

"So it's imprisonment then?" asked Sarah.

Douglas and Patel nodded.

"OK. Devil's advocate, what if that's not enough for the mob?" asked Baines. "What if they don't feel they should *have* to work their backsides off to keep him in a nice safe cell on three squares? Especially since *he* caused all this, yet *they* will be the ones out there risking their lives planting, harvesting and gathering!"

Douglas, Sarah and Patel eyed one another uncomfortably.

"Are you saying," Douglas asked carefully, "that you would want to order the death penalty?"

"I wouldn't want to, Captain," replied Baines, "but I may have to consider it. From a resource perspective alone he would be a liability, and it may cause all kinds of unrest among the people. *People* who are looking to us to protect them from what he and his compatriots have done – may still be doing, for that matter. We should also consider that sending the strongest kind of message like this might help us with these same compatriots in the future."

Douglas sighed with great sadness. "We'll leave it to your best judgement, Jill," he said, quietly. "But if you don't want the responsibility, Ah'll do it."

"I can't let you shoulder this too, Captain. I just need some time to consider my best course."

"Well, knock off early then. Go and take a little R and R," said Douglas. "By the way," he added, brightening a little, "they're putting that damned sign up tonight, at the bar. There'll be a bit of a do on. Maybe you'd like to go? Perhaps we all should? The ceremony will make it official – it's the Mud Hole, and yes, it's stuck!"

Baines appreciated the captain's attempt to cheer her. "Well, I should really go back out to check on the defensive works and the lumber treatment, Captain."

"Don't worry, Jill, Ah'll do that," replied Douglas. "It's about time Ah went and saw it all, anyway."

"You won't have to, Captain. They have a whole team out there," she replied, seriously.

"Won't have to what?"

"Saw it all."

Sarah burst out laughing, shaking her head, completely tickled.

Douglas blew out his cheeks. "Jill, Ah just gave you the afternoon off so why don't you, ahem, make like a tree!"

Baines groaned, rising from her seat. "Ooh, you did not just say that."

"He did!" laughed Sarah.

"I *wood* never have believed it," Baines rejoindered.

Douglas stood up, pointing at the door. "Will ye get out of here!" he laughed.

After a few moments the giggles came to a natural end. Sarah wiped her eyes and called Baines back. "Just before you go, Jill, do we have a completion date for the first stage of the fortifications outside? A few folks have asked when they might be able to leave the ship and I'm still mindful that we need to put those poor people we have in the morgue to rest, too. Maybe their funerals will bring a little closure to the bad times, for the people they left behind."

"It's close now, Sarah. Most of the palisade is already on top of the ramparts. The crews are bringing lumber for the gates and walkways into the new compound to work on it, making things much safer. We'll only need to defend the narrow gateway soon."

"And the skies, of course," added Patel, darkly.

"Yes, once we've completed the fort, for want of a better description, that will be our biggest concern for people outside," Baines agreed. "At the moment, all we've got is helmets and Kevlar armour. Maybe we'll be able to manufacture a glass dome or something? If the geology boffins can find enough of the right kind of silicates and a source of crude oil to begin developing polymers from scratch." She shook her head ruefully. "Not a tall order at all."

"So, what you're saying is, our people will be working the land and riding out of the fort in suits of armour?" asked Sarah.

"How delightfully *primedieval*!" Patel contributed one of his extremely rare puns.

"Apart from the 'riding'," agreed Baines. "Our Dobbins are a little thin on the ground."

"Not necessarily," replied Douglas, with a knowing smile.

"We've got rides?" asked Baines, sitting back down excitedly. "Tell me more!"

"Hiro's been pottering, strictly when off duty of course," he said.

After a moment's pause, Baines blurted, "Go on then!" She laughed, frustrated by the captain holding in his secrets.

"Well, he's fitted a rather powerful electric motor and battery to one of the runabout bicycles we have down in the Pod cargo bay. He says it'll have a 1600 kilometre range and will do about 160 kilometres per hour! With the terrain in these parts that should prove very interesting on cycle suspension. Maybe he should have fitted it with wings?" he added wryly.

"Hiro!" He shook his head with amusement and then suddenly pointed a warning finger at Baines. "Don't give him any ideas about the wings, Ah was only joking!

"Apparently, like the rifles, it's all a bit 'Heath Robinson' at the moment, but Ah daresay he'll soon be selling them with satellite navigation and custom paint jobs, if Ah know my chief engineer."

"WOW! Where do I sign up for one?" asked Baines. "Can I have flames down the sides?"

"How did Ah know that would be your reaction?" said Douglas.

"Wouldn't mind one myself!" Mother Sarah stated, striking everyone dumb for a moment.

"Are you going out to start the dig at the fossil site tomorrow, Captain?" asked Patel, after a pause.

"Yes, Jim Miller's team have finished everything we need in record time," replied Douglas. "It'll be good to get some answers. Maybe it will even provide distraction from the bloodlust everyone seems to have for Lloyd."

"May I come with you?" asked Patel. "I'm due a rest day, and I would be fascinated to see everything out there."

"Of course," Douglas replied. "It would be useful to have you there, Ah'm sure."

"Thank you." Patel rubbed his hands together excitedly. "If that's everything for now, I'll go and clear today's job list and get ready for my daytrip! Until tomorrow then, Captain. Ladies."

0800 hours. Captain Douglas strode into the Pod's manufacturing bay looking for Jim Miller. He found him giving instructions to the driver of a telehandler, about to lift what had become known as the 'dig-tent'. He waited for the operation to finish before distracting them. "Good morning, Jim," he greeted at last. "Is she ready?"

"Ah, Captain," replied Miller. "Good morning – STEADY THERE – sorry about that," Jim apologised, after his interjection to the driver. "Don't want to lose her before she's seen any action, do we?"

The driver held his hand up, a little embarrassed by his own jerky manoeuvre.

"Are you ready for the shuttle?" asked Douglas.

"Yes, I think now would be a good time, please."

Douglas opened a channel to Lieutenant Singh on his personal comm, "Sandip?"

"*Yes, sir,*" Singh's voice came through the little speaker, distorting slightly.

"We're ready for the shuttle – outside the Pod cargo doors, please."

"*Aye, aye, Captain. I've already run through all the pre-flight system checks this morning. I just need to summon my guards, to stop any 'birdlife' from getting in as we open the shuttle bay doors, then I'll be with you directly.*"

Douglas smiled at the excitement in Singh's voice. "That boy was born to fly," he confided to Miller.

"I hope so, Captain. He's going to have to hold the shuttle absolutely steady whilst we place the dig-tent on the ground," he gestured towards the giant polymer shell. "Not to mention whilst we lower everything, and *everyone*, down."

"Never fear, Jim," assured Douglas, watching the telehandler drive through the large bulkhead doors separating the manufacturing bay from the main cargo bay. "We can trust Sandy. After bringing the *New World* into atmosphere, damaged, at three times the recommended speed *and* managing to set her down, intact, without instruments, this should be a walk in the park!"

Jim smiled sardonically. "Can't think what sort of a park would be full of dinosaurs, Captain."

The roar of the shuttle's engines filled the compound as it came in to land just outside the main cargo hatch.

Douglas and Miller left the manufacturing bay, following in the wake of the telehandler. Crossing into the main cargo hold, they were greeted by a scene which bordered on bedlam. Men and women ran errands, shouted orders, busied themselves carrying and checking things, all within the landscape of a mechanised ants' nest. Nevertheless, during the short time it took the two men to cross the main hangar, the apparent chaos had coalesced into cohesion and all at once, everything was ready.

The enormous, steel bulkhead doors split at the centre, sliding away from one another to reveal the twenty-five-metre-deep vehicular airlock, and everything moved on a stage. The hangar bay hatch closed behind them. Once sealed, the outer airlock doors began to slide open with a hydraulic hiss, allowing bright daylight to pour in through the widening crack. Not far from the opening was the *New World*'s shuttle, glistening white in the morning sunshine.

As Douglas and Miller approached the little craft, a friendly voice hailed them from behind.

"Good morning, Captain and Dr Jim."

They turned to see Dr Satnam Patel approaching their position from the guarded, and very much smaller, pedestrian airlock. He seemed uncharacteristically cheerful and carried a small rucksack, thrown casually over one shoulder.

"Good morning!" the men called back.

"What have ye there?" asked Douglas. "Are ye planning on camping out?"

"What, *this*?" replied Patel, shrugging slightly to indicate his pack. "Have you brought field rations to eat whilst you're out there today?"

"Aye," said Douglas. "Of course, we could be gone for most of the day."

"Well," Patel continued, clearly pleased with himself, "*I* haven't!" He pulled the bag from around his shoulder, opening the top slightly. The aroma of fresh, Indian home cooking caressed their nostrils like a lager-lout's lover.

"Ooh," the two men chorused.

"I don't suppose," asked Miller, hopefully, "that you could stretch that a little… perhaps?"

"Don't worry," Patel answered, knowingly. "It occurred to me, while I was preparing this, that you British would never forgive me if I didn't bring enough curry to go round!"

The dig crew gathered around the shuttle's cargo hatch. After a few moments it opened to reveal Lieutenant Singh, who beckoned them aboard.

Douglas gestured for Patel to lead the way. "After you, Satnam, we'll just follow ye like a couple o' Bisto Kids."

Most of the loading team made their way back into the Pod via the pedestrian hatch. Only a couple of men and a few guards remained behind, standing ready to link up the dig-tent to the winch cables that would be lowered from the shuttle, once airborne.

The captain exchanged nods, smiles and greetings with everyone as he passed them on his way up through the little ship. Leaving the cargo hold, centre aft, he strode through the small passenger area, centre forward, finally arriving at the craft's small bridge. Miller and Patel followed him. Singh and Natalie Pearson were already at their stations.

"You got roped into this as well, Natalie?" asked Douglas, cheerfully.

"We've no expert diggers, no field palaeontologists or archaeologists, so here I am," she stated. "I've very little experience, but I did spend a week on a dig in Arizona when I was a student. We were looking for dinosaur fossils! Can you believe that? And now here I am in the time of the dinosaurs digging up human remains. Does anyone else feel that we may have simply been drugged, and this is just one almighty psychotic episode?"

"Ah wake up every morning hoping for that to be the case, lassie," Douglas replied, kindly.

"We also have one of our historians aboard," Pearson continued. "He's strapped into one of the passenger seats behind us." She put her hand to the side of her mouth, conspiratorially. "He doesn't like flying," she whispered.

"So he caught a spaceship to Mars?" exclaimed Douglas, jovially.

"Well, I did mention that point, Captain, and he said that after a lifetime of reading history, he thought it would be rather nice to *make* some."

"Fair play," Douglas acknowledged, "but why's he here *now*?"

"As I said, Captain, our experience in digging archaeology is very sketchy. Apart from a week in the desert I've only ever studied living specimens. At least, the only ones that weren't, were fresh on the autopsy table," explained Pearson.

"So presumably he has the *right* sort of experience?" asked Douglas, hopefully.

Pearson winced slightly. "Not exactly, Captain. When he was a kid he spent a summer at Vindolanda, digging. He said it was that which got him interested in archaeology. However, it also threw into sharp relief his preference for indoor work which didn't get him dirty or make him sweat. Hence, he went the History route instead," she finished, with a chuckle.

Douglas pinched his nose to ease the pressure headache he could feel coming on. "Great," he said, trying not to look too forlorn. "So, what's our armchair historian's name?"

"Thomas Beckett," replied Natalie, showing her amusement.

Douglas pulled back, raising his eyebrows. "Our historian is Thomas à Becket?" he asked, disbelieving.

"I know," she laughed. "But he swears he's no relation. Luckily, he's happy with just plain old Thomas – *never* Tom!" she added sternly.

Douglas rubbed a hand down his face, shaking his head slightly. "Ah'm with you, Natalie, this has to be a drugged-up hallucination!"

"We're ready to take off, Captain," Singh cut in.

"OK," said Douglas. "Make the announcements."

"O-oh, sir," Singh retorted, like a disappointed schoolboy.

Douglas snorted. "It's the drugs, it must be. Ah cannae believe any of you lot are real!" He strapped into the co-pilot's seat. "Alright," he said, "if it makes ye happy, then it cannae be that bad!"

The pilot sat back in contentment. Natalie, Jim and Satnam simply looked from one to another in bemused bafflement.

Then Douglas spoke. "Good morning, this is your captain speaking…"

The crew and passengers elsewhere on the little ship were slightly bewildered, as the captain's 'fasten your seatbelts' message was accompanied by hoots of laughter from the bridge.

Commander Baines sat alone on the bridge of the *New World*, typing up a report on the construction team's progress. The captain was adamant that all their actions be fully documented, in case they ever found a way back.

"We're lost a hundred million years ago and I still have to fill out reports," she addressed the air. "Still, I suppose it would make a hell of a read, if anyone ever believed a word of it."

Her musings were interrupted as the bridge comm binged for her attention. "Commander Baines here."

"*Commander,*" replied a disembodied, male voice. "*This is Dr Klaus Fischer. Would it be possible to interrupt the captain for a moment, please?*"

Frowning momentarily, she eventually placed the accent, just a hint of German to the otherwise excellent English. "I'm afraid he's not on the ship right now, Doctor. May I be of service?"

"*Certainly, Commander. Could we meet, please? Just briefly?*"

"Of course, Doctor. I assume you're in the biology labs? I'll meet you there."

Baines made sure her work was saved, while feeling guilty about being saved from her work.

A few minutes later, she walked into Patricia Norris' domain, deep within the Pod. The biologists were all hard at work, early it seemed, although Patricia appeared to be involved in an animated discussion with her son. Words such as *beer* and *shouting* and *graffiti* and *Woodsey* floated across the room. Grinning at the normalcy of the little domestic, betwixt teen and parent, Baines continued past them.

Dr Klaus Fischer strode across the lab to greet her with an unexpected cup of coffee, for which she thanked him.

"It is only NASA's finest, I'm afraid," the German biologist apologised. "Thank you for seeing me so quickly, Commander. If you would kindly follow me, please – Dr Norris has graciously offered me the use of her office for our chat." He ushered Baines into the office, offering her a seat.

"So, Doctor," she said. "How can I help?"

"Commander, there are five German nationals on this ship," he stated. Clearly embarrassed he added, "As you know, there used to be six."

"Ah," said Baines, seeing where this was going, "and you feel... *associated*? *Implicated*?"

"Perhaps. In a way, Commander," Fischer acknowledged haltingly. "We just don't want the captain, or indeed anyone, to think we are in any way linked with the actions of that young woman."

Baines smiled sympathetically. "Try not to worry, Doctor. I don't think people would believe that you were. I know it hasn't even crossed the captain's mind, if that's any comfort?"

Fischer relaxed a little. "I— *we* are very relieved to hear that, Commander," he said. "However, it may have crossed other people's minds, I'm afraid."

Baines expression darkened. "What's happened?"

"Nothing much to speak of," Fischer held up a placating hand. "We did hear Mr Burnstein whispering, 'the Krauts are at it again' loud enough for all to hear in the Mud Hole, last night."

"Burnstein? Again?" exploded Baines. "As if we don't have enough to deal with!"

"Well, not just him I'm afraid." Fischer looked genuinely sorry to have troubled her.

"What else has happened?" she asked, quietly.

"As I said, nothing has *happened* exactly," continued Fischer. "We are just finding that, more and more, we are sitting in one another's company, you see?"

"Please explain, precisely, Doctor."

"I simply mean that a few of the other crew, and I must stress *only* a few, seem to want to move away from us. I'm sorry to burden you with something so trivial, Commander," he apologised.

"Not at all, Doctor, nor do I think this is trivial," she replied, thoughtfully. "I'll have a word with the captain and see what he'd like to do. I will also impress upon everyone the importance of inclusivity."

"Dr Schultz was," Fischer sought the right phrase, "rather *outspoken*, when it came to certain points of view."

"Hmm, it's fair to say that Heidi possessed a strong sense of nationalistic pride. I didn't think it was any more than that. Was it?"

"I'm not completely sure, Commander," he said, also looking thoughtful. "It has been over a century and a half since the Holocaust. Since then the German people have been absolutely adamant that the sort of extremist faction who dominated our nation during that era, never be allowed to rise again."

"I understand, Doctor," Baines acknowledged. "Recent history has borne this out fully. You have nothing to apologise for. My father was American and my mother was English but I was born on the moon, so I'm fortunate in that I don't feel tied to *anybody's* past mistakes or excesses, really. Not that anyone should ever be accountable for the actions of previous generations. I believe it's what *we* do that counts."

She smiled at the scientist sitting across the desk.

"The British, particularly the English, have been blamed for just about everything you can think of. I know history is always in danger of being repeated, but I think most of them believe in moving forward on merit now, rather than at someone else's expense. They also have much in their long, long history to be proud of though, and rightly so. Is it not the same with Germany? A great nation of many extraordinary people, mostly committed to a better future?"

"I would certainly hope so."

"History is naturally weighted towards great and especially terrible events. We should certainly remember these lessons, but it seems to me we can learn far more about people from the way they fight to put things right, than from hanging onto past prejudices and mistakes made by the powerful few."

Fischer smiled. "Thank you, Commander, that's kind of you. However, in all nations, there are always the hangers-on to the bad-old-days and the bad-old-ways, it seems."

"You think that Schultz was some species of Nazi?" asked Baines, her concern growing.

"I'm not sure. Sometimes she just made people feel *schwach*, erm, forgive me," he searched his memory for the translation, "*weak*. The way she looked at people gave some of us, as the Americans say, the creeps." He shook his head. "She occasionally mentioned her grandfather, more in the way that she would say, 'My grandfather would never tolerate this or that, or *these* people'. It made the rest of us very uneasy. We had only known her a very short time and so tried to remain on friendly terms, as you do in such close proximity, but it was difficult."

"Yes, well, *we* were saddled with her *and* Lloyd on this ship. Imagine how much fun that was."

Fischer smiled politely.

"Thank you for bringing all this to my attention, Doctor. Now, if you will excuse me, I'm feeling an overwhelming urge to interrupt Mr Burnstein's breakfast!"

The shuttle flew over the forests of Gondwana. The day was so sunny and the view so stupendous that any lyricist worth his salt could have found fame on the basis of a morning's work. All things seemed possible as Lieutenant Singh brought the ship in to hover above the place the crew now called *Fossil Rock*.

The rock itself formed a steep-sided promontory buried under thick vegetation. The fortuitous clearing, which allowed the first shuttle mission to identify their extraordinary find, was situated at the top of these cliffs. The drop was not sheer, nor was it huge, maybe fifteen or twenty metres, but it would be enough to make things difficult and potentially dangerous for the dig team.

The Sarge viewed their landing zone with the calculating mind of a military strategist. The topography did offer one obvious benefit. The continuity of the crag around two sides of the proposed dig site would offer some defence from these directions, against predators on the ground. If push came to shove, it would also mean there were fewer directions in which to run, of course – and then there was always attack from the air to worry about.

The shuttle's engines seemed to put flight to the local wildlife, for a little while at least. The Sarge stood ready at the edge of the belly hatch tallying his pros and cons. Captain Douglas would not be derailed from this course, so he was in a make-do-and-mend situation. Ultimately, he could only ensure that the immediate vicinity was safe briefly, while they unloaded everyone. After that, it would be in the lap of the gods. He led a security team of eight, including himself. They were of mixed ability and experience, but he would have to push that point aside too, for the next few minutes. His was the vital task of coordinating with the pilot in order to help him lower the dig-tent into position.

The protective enclosure, far too big to fit into the shuttle's hold, was currently suspended by steel cables from the bottom of the ship, like a giant plate cloche.

In order to avoid damaging the archaeology, their plan was to lower the heavy structure and initially set it down adjacent to the dig site. The Sarge gave what appeared to be an innocent little dell one more visual sweep from the safety of the air, before calling Singh with the all clear.

The dig-tent *whomped* gently onto the ferns, sending a flurry of insect life into the air. Jackson sighed. *Not just giants to worry about, then,* he thought. There was very little rainforest left in the world he had known, but he had visited some of it. They were not his fondest memories.

Singh held the shuttle steady for the loading crew to begin winching the first security down. The soldiers stepped onto the raft-like cradle they would use to lower all personnel and equipment, in stages. It carried four men easily, so fortunately, no one had to go down alone.

The Sarge descended with the first group. The moment he had boots on the ground, he split the advance group into two pairs and quickly reconnoitred for hidden threats. Once satisfied, he radioed back up to the ship, reporting the immediate area safe and clearing the second armed detail to follow them down.

With the area as secure as possible, the first diggers came next. The dig team were a group of six, including Natalie Pearson and Thomas Beckett. Beckett was furious about his manner of evacuation from the shuttle.

"I would never have gone along with this if I'd known you weren't going to land!" he railed.

"We have no choice," Natalie shouted back over the noise of the engines. "Cables and pulleys are all we've got!"

"I want to go back!" Beckett retorted. "I'm a historian, not Tarzan!"

"Sorry," said Natalie in his ear. "What I meant is – *you've* got no choice. We're the only people on this expedition who have even *seen* a dig, so get out!"

Beckett stumbled out onto the raft with all the poise of a man drunk in charge of a punt, his profanities lost to the wind and the roar of the engines.

Eventually the diggers were all down and working within the perimeter of soldiers to examine the site. Their first task was to ensure the dig-tent could be located without damaging anything of significance. Presently, Natalie asked The Sarge to radio the pilot and request that he lift the dig-tent once more, ready for repositioning.

Several nail-biting minutes later, the dig-tent was placed near the edge of the cliff and over the archaeology. A small entrance hatch at the end was opened, allowing the team to scramble inside with their equipment. The structure was about twelve metres long and seven in width; roomy enough for everyone and all their gear. The Sarge secured the hatch behind them, ordering his men to pop the ventilation flaps. There was barely a breath of wind, but at least they were safe for the moment.

Douglas ordered Singh back to the *New World* and with the shuttle's departure there returned a relative silence to the clearing.

"Wow!" Natalie spoke quietly. "We're really alone now, aren't we?"

"Thank you for that little comfort!" snapped Beckett. The ride down on the hoist had upset him badly. He was still shaking.

Although inside the protective structure, The Sarge set his guards at all points of the compass, while the civilians set about unpacking everything. The Captain and Patel scrutinised the fossilised tyre tracks, marvelling at the detail which remained.

Despite the lack of a breeze, the materials used in the dig-tent's manufacture made it fairly cool and airy inside. Opaque from the outside, the structure afforded the people inside a reasonable view of the surrounding forest, through the walls. As the swell of the shuttle's engines died away down the valley, some of the braver, or more inquisitive, animals began to return and the tiny glade filled once more with the chirruping and buzzing of small, forest life. Far from threatening, it was idyllic.

Only The Sarge remained unimpressed. High above them, a flash of sunlight reflected from the top of a rocky escarpment. It caught his attention immediately. He stared hard at the area, finally tearing open a pocket within his combat jacket to retrieve a small pair of field glasses, but whatever the cause, it was not to be repeated.

Douglas moved to stand next to his chief of security. "What is it, Sarge?" he asked softly, taking care to keep his posture relaxed.

Without looking away from the escarpment, The Sarge leaned close. "It's just possible we're being observed, sir," he whispered.

Tim may have missed out on the archaeology, but he was very pleased with the consolation prize. Natalie knew how disappointed he had been. To make up for it, she had approached him with a most solemn request: to take care of someone she loved, while she was away. More than that, if anything happened to her, she wanted to know that he would receive all the love and attention he needed, for the rest of his days.

Being of a fairly serious and diligent nature, Tim had accepted the responsibility at once and with sobriety. However, once Natalie had left, he lost no time in taking his temporary charge for exercise and, most importantly, playtime.

Reiver found the gymnasium a place of great entertainment. The young man ran around with his friend until he collapsed, panting. Realising that the collie showed no such signs of fatigue, or even calming down, it was up to him to develop a new strategy which would allow the game to continue. So, he now commanded the field from astride an exercise horse – his new game: 'obstacle course fetch'.

Tim was practically bursting with news he was really not meant to tell anyone, while Reiver was *actually* bursting balls he was really not meant to be playing with. *Pop!* – another one. Dimly aware that he should probably stop taking them from the games cupboard and that further mum-related aggravation could be a distinct possibility in his future, Tim tried to think of a solution.

However, he had so much more on his mind at that moment. Although he had not been allowed to go with them, his imagination was nevertheless fully engaged in the mystery unfolding for the pseudo-archaeologists. Baffling did not even begin to describe the situation and being sworn to secrecy made matters even worse. At least he could rely on Reiver not to blab.

Pop! – Oops, how many is that now? Tim pondered and then with a metaphorical 'pop' an idea occurred to him. A possible way to overt, or at least offset, his mother's wrath. When Rose's father, Jim, returned, he would ask if he could possibly manufacture a couple of dog-proof balls from the Pod's polymer stocks. Tim had never owned a dog of his own; their tiny housing cell had simply not allowed for one. Subsequently, he was unaware that, even in the 22nd century, a successful platform for the dog-proof toy continued to elude man's grasp. Despite his ignorance in this regard, he *was* aware that if they ever wanted to play any sports again, a ground breaking design might soon prove mission critical.

The repetition of throwing a ball over and over allowed his mind to drift elsewhere to the rhythm of the collie continuum. Reiver had no idea that his constant, untiring circuit was helping Tim to think, but he did understand that this particular two-leg was very generous with the bouncy pop things – he would have been in trouble long ago had mummy been there.

Both boys were content in their own little worlds.

Hiro sat alone in the Mud Hole, eating a light lunch before his afternoon shift began. A man walked by his table, smiling in friendly greeting. Hiro did not know his name, so he nodded in return but did not speak.

"Hiro," the stranger acknowledged as he passed.

The engineer frowned slightly, turning to watch the figure walk away. He was fairly sure the man was unknown to him, although he would be the first to admit that his own facial recognition skills were poor. People confused him, wandering around without serial numbers the way they did, but there was *something* familiar about this fellow – a man who, to the best of his knowledge, he had never met before but who clearly knew, or at least recognised, him.

He wrestled with recollection a moment longer. "Must be someone I've seen around the ship," he muttered to himself, eventually. As a senior officer, it was not so strange for the passengers to know his name by now.

He tried to shrug it off, but there was something, just an itch at the back of his mind that he could not quite reach.

Oh well. A problem for another day, he thought, pushing his plate away purposefully and gulping the last of his drink. *No time to ponder it now, Sekai needs me.*

Mother Sarah sat on a couch in her private quarters. She was concerned about the details of a military funeral. In fact, she had not given any kind of ceremony for a while. Her growing seniority within the church had pushed her evermore towards the role of administrator rather than priest.

Major White sat across her coffee table on the opposite couch, sipping his drink. The three deceased soldiers were under his direct command, so she sought the major's advice to make sure she was on the right lines. Determined to do justice to the fallen, the responsibility weighed on her, and not just the military aspects. These were the first funerals she would conduct here and she needed, even more than usual, to start the healing process so the people left behind could face what lay ahead. With a heavy heart she suspected these would be merely the first of many.

She pushed that thought down, focusing on the details. The major was calm and considerate as always, but she could tell that he too really needed a lift. Naturally, he blamed himself for the loss of his men. As a senior military man he would never dream of admitting to his burden, but she knew, and it increased her determination to get it right for all concerned, which of course led to even more pressure for her.

Her own father had served a twelve-year tour in the army during his younger days. A warmth spread through her chest as she remembered him, the embryo of a smile tugging at her lips as his favourite phrase leapt into her mind.

White gave her a quizzical look. "Sarah?"

"Sorry, Ford. I was just thinking about my dad. He had a saying—" She deepened her voice in imitation. "When it comes to the army, Sarah, every problem shared is a problem doubled!" She sighed. "It was always his way to make light of bad situations. How I wish he was with me now."

"Sounds like the sorta guy we could all use on the team," White answered kindly. "I can't pretend to fill in for your daddy, Sarah, but I've picked up a few adages about military life myself over the years." He chuckled, then sobered. "You know if you ever need support, you can call on me. Anytime. We're all feelin' it, now and then, right?"

Mother Sarah smiled affectionately at him. "And that's just one of the things that keeps me going, Ford. Thank you. Despite this whole situation, we're all in it together, or at least most of us are. I'm learning to admire and love the folks on this boat. We've all been shoved so far outside of our comfort zone that it seems like pure science fiction sometimes. But I guess the personal and interpersonal problems we face are common enough. All I know for sure is that I, like all my new friends, no, like my new *family*, will not shrink from my duty."

"I'm not digging that up!" snapped Thomas Beckett, outraged.

"What did you think you were going to be doing here?" asked Natalie, equally outraged.

"I see my role as purely supervisory," the historian pronounced pompously.

"Oh, *really*," replied Pearson. "So, you see yourself in the role of overseer do you? Perhaps you should watch us dig while you document and catalogue the finds? Pack them up nicely, that sort of thing?"

"Exactly," Beckett agreed, pleased this tiresome, energetic type was finally beginning to understand the subtle nuances of the role he had carved out for himself.

"I totally agree," said Pearson.

"You do? Of *course* you do." He was clearly warming to his new standing within the community.

"*Absolutely*," she stated with conviction. Then she pressed a shovel hard against his waist-coated chest, almost smashing his gold pocket watch. Beckett stepped back in surprise, grappling with the implement to stop it from falling. "As soon as we *have* some finds, you can analyse and document to your heart's content. Until then you dig!"

"But I…" he sputtered.

"Do you want to survive this little field trip?" she asked. Clearly this pampered, patch-elbow-jacketed, library loafer needed the facts of life on safari explained to him.

"Well, I—" he tried again.

"The longer we stay out here, the more chance there is of something going wrong *out there*." Natalie pointed through the walls of the dig-tent. "Animals are easily spooked, but before long they will become inquisitive. Knowing the sort of animals we are dealing with, do you think this would be a good thing?"

"Well, of course, I wouldn't want to—"

"Dig then!" Natalie barked. "We can't afford any passengers on this trip and every minute counts. Anyway," she added, smiling sweetly, "think of it as good practice for when you have to help out with the planting of spuds and cabbages when the compound is complete."

"I'm a historian, not a farmer!"

"It seems there's no end to the things you're not, Thomas."

"I'll tell you what I'm not! I'm not even being paid for this, that's what I'm not!"

"Paid? I thought historians were used to working and studying all hours for little or no reward? Well, if all this is simply about invoicing, once you've dug the cabbage patch, feel free to submit an agrarian reform *bill* at your leisure. Now, *come on*, Thomas!"

Before he could bluster any more, she shoved him towards the tiny excavation already underway, courtesy of some of Samantha Portree's construction workers. Even Dr Patel was down on hands and knees, scraping away with a pointing trowel in his hand and a look of beatific pleasure on his face.

By the middle of the afternoon they had managed to lift a section of the fossilised tyre tracks out of the ground, packaging them safely into one of the storage containers brought from the ship. Other team members had managed to retrieve a skull with the top dentition almost intact along with half of the lower jaw, a few ribs, some lower vertebrae and most of the pelvis.

Were this an ordinary archaeological dig and the remains those of some long-forgotten Saxon farmer, for example, it would have been a very poignant moment for all concerned. As with all archaeology, the idea and the mystery of touching the past, finding out about people *just like us*, is always fascinating, always thought provoking. Imagination takes flight when attempting to reconstruct the daily routines of someone as they built, farmed and played; separated from us by time alone, a surreal barrier so thin that it stretches forever, without ever letting us touch. At least that was what the team used to believe.

The surrealism on this dig was of a different sort, however. Here, the bizarre was compounded with paradox, overbuilt by the impossible and sported a side order of *what the hell?* It was unfathomable to all, yet lost on no one.

Their portable scanning equipment located further finds. Originally intended for mineral surveys on Mars, the tried and tested ground penetrating radar and soil-resistance suite built into the little machine was an absolute gift for their purposes. Accordingly, the very first protagonists in the brand new field of Cretaceous archaeological anthropology were astounded by the results it provided.

The little unit's frantic beeping naturally attracted the attention of the other diggers. Natalie peeked at the readings on the device's flat screen, whistling softly.

Douglas and Patel also wandered over to investigate. "Something interesting, Doctor?" asked the captain.

"I'll say," Natalie replied. "Let me plug this into the desktop holo-projector." She walked over to the finds table, where Beckett had managed to wangle the job of packing things up for transport. She had to admit, the man's fastidious attention to his immaculate dress appeared to make him the ideal choice for wrapping up other things too. "That's a neat job, Thomas," she encouraged, attempting to rebuild the broken bridge between them.

"Mmph," Beckett grunted, non-committal.

She plugged the scanner into the desktop device and tried again. "You might want to see this, Thomas."

A partial representation of the dig site sprang into being, constructed from nothing more than controlled incoherent light. The three-dimensional model displayed two cubic metres of the excavation from ground level, shown at the top of the cube, down to two metres below ground level. What it displayed made everyone gasp in wonder. Locked within the rock were many human bones, slightly disarticulated, but still resting in the approximate shape of a human skeleton. Viewing the representation in three dimensions this way, Natalie guessed that a survey of the next virtual cube might reveal even more. However, even this first slice through the geology held further intrigue for the ad hoc archaeologists, for it clearly showed *two* sets of earthly remains entombed within the mudstone.

"That's amazing," Natalie gasped. The full ramifications of this find, even the clear and ever-present danger, were temporarily driven from her mind by the wonder of discovery. "From the remains already uncovered, I'm pretty sure the first skeleton is male. You can tell by the cranial ridges and from the shape of the pelvis," she explained to the men and women crowding around the display. "Not sure about this other one, though. Until we actually excavate, it'll be hard to say for sure. It could be a woman or possibly an adolescent. We'll see."

Douglas checked his watch. "We'd better start packing up, people. The shuttle will be back for us in the next quarter of an hour." He turned to The Sarge. "It looks like this will go on for a wee while. We'll need to drive the steel split-pins into the ground outside. When Sandip shoos the wildlife away with rocket noise, take care of it, Sarge, while we get everything back up to the ship."

"Yes, sir," Jackson acknowledged.

"Do we need to take all of the equipment, Captain? If we are planning a return tomorrow?" asked Natalie.

"Ah'm afraid so," said Douglas, seriously. "We cannae afford to lose any of this gear either to rampaging animals or—"

When Douglas did not finish the statement Natalie hazarded, "Schultz?"

Douglas shrugged. "She's out there somewhere and Ah'm no' giving her any more matériel to add to the gear she nicked from us!" he spat, still deeply affronted by the larceny aboard his ship.

By the time the dig team heard the roar, a huge shadow was already over them. Douglas looked up at the underbelly of his shuttle as he pressed the comm's *speak* button. "Pushing it a bit weren't we, Mr Singh?"

"*Must have been the direction of the wind, sir,*" the pilot answered.

Douglas raised an eyebrow slightly. "How about dropping us a rope, Lieutenant?"

"*The boys in the cargo hold are already on it, Captain – sending the cradle down now.*"

Douglas nodded to The Sarge and the soldiers climbed out through the hatch to set up a perimeter around the cradle's landing site. The shuttle engines appeared to have cleared the area of wildlife once more. Douglas wondered whether the animals might get used to this and adjust. A disturbing thought.

Once The Sarge gave the all-clear, the dig crew moved quickly, loading their pre-packed finds and equipment back onto the hoist cradle. After a few trips up and down, it was the turn of the diggers themselves. Finally, the soldiers came up in two lifts, bringing the operation full-circle as the belly hatch sealed. Douglas, Pearson, Patel and Miller made their way back to their bridge stations while the passengers strapped themselves in. With everyone and everything secured, Lieutenant Singh *proceeded* away, in a calm, textbook manner towards the *New World*.

The flight was short, the shuttle landing in its berth smoothly. Singh gently powered down the engines.

"Was that *cautious* piece of flying for me or the tourists?" Douglas asked his pilot.

"Sir?"

Douglas winked. "Thanks for the lift, Sandy." He unstrapped and, along with everyone else, made his way to the main hatch. Within moments, the shuttle bay security team, who had become known as the 'birdwatchers', gave way to Pod engineering and handling staff, as the finds were taken down to the labs for close examination.

"You can leave the equipment," said Douglas. "We'll need it all again tomorrow and the shuttle will be locked down for the night."

Tim and Woodsey were in Patricia's lab already when the technicians began unpacking the finds. By this stage, word had got around that the shuttle team had found something and that something was top secret. Naturally, due to the sensitive nature of this information, many people already knew about it and others perpetuated rumours which were actually nowhere near as wild as the truth.

"Mr Wood," Douglas greeted. "Ah dinnae remember inviting you to be a part of this project."

"Oh, I, erm…" stuttered Woodsey.

Tim butted in before anyone else could speak. "I didn't tell anyone, Captain, honestly," he said, full of concern.

Douglas put a hand gently to the young man's shoulder. "Ah didnae think for one minute that you had, Mr Norris. You see, on board a ship – any ship – when the crew is ordered to absolute secrecy, everyone usually knows all about it by the time the captain's finished ordering everyone to absolute secrecy."

"Can I ask what you've found, Captain?" ventured Tim, cautiously.

"Aye, Ah'll let your friend Natalie explain. Ah see you've been looking after her dog," Douglas bent down to tousle the animal's ears.

"Yes," Tim replied, ruefully. "Mum's already told me off for bringing him into the lab, but I reckon he's as curious as I am."

Reiver, his fur neatly brushed, sat dutifully to attention, paw raised in proper greeting. He remained completely motionless apart from the propeller at his rear, which smacked the deck like a grounded outboard.

The captain smiled, shaking the proffered limb. "Very smartly turned out, laddie. Very smart indeed."

Tim frowned. He and Woodsey could remain on sufferance, compliments all the way for the dog. He could have sworn Reiver looked smug as he glanced up with a "*Chuff!*" Tim was beginning to understand that this soft bark, depending on the situation, was the collie's way of saying either, 'look at me, I'm awesome – *see* me being good!' or 'Oi! I want something!' Such a tiny vocabulary and yet dogs had managed, over millennia, to train the human race to do almost everything for them.

The young man's musings on just what 'it's a dog's life' actually entailed were interrupted as his mother and her team gathered around for Dr Natalie Pearson's briefing.

The group were rapt by the dig's findings so far and Natalie's short disclosure was greeted by a protracted silence while everyone grappled with this latest twist.

"There's little doubt as to the age of your finds, then?" asked Patricia.

"The shuttle's scans gave a reasonable ball-park," replied Natalie. "I'll send one of the core samples we cut from the rock, and a bone fragment, down to Dr Portree. She has some fairly heavy duty radiocarbon dating equipment amongst her mining gear."

"Dr Pearson, how long do you expect it to take before we get results back?" asked Douglas.

"An in-depth study will take weeks but we should be able to put the highlights together this evening, Captain. It may give us a bit more direction for tomorrow's dig."

"Very good, Doctors, Ah'll leave it with you." Douglas tossed them a casual salute and left the scientists to their intellectual frenzy.

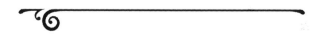

Sitting alone in his quarters later that evening, Douglas mulled over a long and very eventful day. The peace and solitude soon became soporific and he began to nod. "Time to turn in for the night, Ah think," he yawned. Barely had the words left his lips when the door chimed. He sighed. "So much for that!" he muttered, walking to the door and activating the small screen built into the locking control panel; no one could afford to be complacent these days.

The screen lit up to show Dr Pearson, waiting patiently in the corridor. Douglas pressed 'open' and smiled in greeting. "Natalie, come in, please."

She looked tired but determined. "Hello, Captain. I'm sorry to disturb you so late, but I thought you'd want to know what we've found.

I didn't want to spring it on you tomorrow. I'm sure you'll have some thinking to do."

Douglas frowned slightly. "That sounds ominous. Please have a seat, Doctor." He offered his guest a drink, pouring them both a 'wee dram' as a nightcap.

Natalie accepted the tumbler gratefully. "Thank you."

"So, what is it you've found?" he asked.

"Something that's almost beyond belief, Captain, to be honest," she said. "I mean, even more than usual around here."

"Go on," he encouraged.

"The radiocarbon dating analysis came back and the initial prediction, of about twenty million years old, seems to have been borne out. However, what's even more extraordinary is that Patricia Norris thinks she's identified the man."

Douglas stared for a moment. "Come again?"

"I *know*." Pearson sighed, exhaustedly. "You may want to top your glass up before you hear the rest, Captain."

Douglas thought it would be remiss to disobey doctor's orders. He topped the zoologist's glass up too; she looked like she needed it.

"Thanks. As we saved nearly three-quarters of the teeth in the skull," said Pearson, taking a scotch livener, "Patricia came up with the idea of cross-checking them with Mars Mission personnel records in the ship's computer. Which sounded crazy at first, but then digging up the fossilised bones of a man who died 120 million years *before* man, isn't what you'd call normal. So we thought, why not?"

"And what did ye find?" asked Douglas, unsure whether he wanted to know.

"I'm sorry to break this to you, Captain, but the man we found was a friend of yours." Natalie paused. Perceiving that Douglas was either unwilling to ask, or was perhaps incapable of asking, who it was, she regretfully let the hammer fall. "Forgive me, but we're fairly sure that the bones we found were the fossilised remains of Captain Bessel."

The news hit Douglas like a gut-punch. "Arnold Bessel?" he managed eventually.

She nodded sympathetically. "I'm so sorry, Captain."

"You're sure? There's no doubt?" asked Douglas, unwilling to believe.

"As sure as we can be," she shrugged apologetically. "It's not just the dental records. We shaved off sections of bone, it's mostly fossilised, but there are still some traces of DNA in the shards. It's on the limits of our technology given the age, but we ran it past Dr Wright who cross-referenced the DNA samples, once again, with Mars Mission personnel records. He said there was a close match with the DNA sample we have on record for Captain Bessel – close enough to be familial. Add the fact that Captain Bessel had no family working within the Mars Mission, or NASA, to the dental records, and it seems fairly conclusive." She took a breath to continue but faltered, looking uncomfortable.

"There's more?" asked Douglas, picking up on her reticence.

"Possibly, Captain," she admitted. "You must understand though, this is more conjectural than the evidence we have for Captain Bessel."

"Go on, Doctor," Douglas prompted, stoically.

"We've analysed the scans of the other body. Fortunately, they were both pretty well preserved and we seem to have another semi-complete dentition. Obviously, we haven't excavated the second skeleton yet, but from the initial scans – and the resolution on that scanning equipment is superb – we think we have another match. Lieutenant Audrey Jansen."

"Audrey," Douglas repeated, morosely. "She was Arnold's pilot. They were both friends of mine – fine officers."

"Yes, Captain, I'm sorry. The fact that the two sets of remains were so closely connected also adds to the likelihood of the match, I'm afraid."

"Of course, thank you, Doctor, you've done a remarkable job." He sighed and took another drink. "Ah'd better tell Lieutenant Lloyd about this, too."

"Really?" asked Pearson, too surprised to be courteous. "Sorry, Captain. I didn't mean to pry."

Douglas smiled sadly. "No need for apology, Natalie. Lloyd and Audrey had a thing going some years back. He mentioned her during our little chat the other night."

"Is he still holding a candle for her?"

"One in each hand. He'd never admit to that outwardly, of course, but Ah think Ah should let him know. It's the least Ah can do." He frowned in thought. "Do we have any idea how they came to be here?"

Pearson raised a wry eyebrow. "That might take a little longer to work out. The only theory we have so far is for some kind of a rescue mission, mounted after we disappeared," she shrugged. "It could have taken them months to figure out what happened to us. If they managed to find a way to replicate the effects of the disaster, presumably without blowing a massive hole in the side of their ship, and follow a wormhole back here..." she tailed off, considering the possibility. "All I can say is, if that's what they did, it was incredibly brave, Captain. They could have ended up anywhere or any*when*!"

"So, they left after we did and arrived twenty million years before us?" asked Douglas in disbelief.

"It's just a theory," she shrugged again. "They and their ship, the USS *Newfoundland*, were all safe on Earth when we departed. We left first and they arrived first, I've no idea how the hare and the tortoise figure in this story."

Her expression became uncomfortable once more. "The thing is, Captain, they must have been fully kitted out for a rescue mission. You see, unlike us, they knew where and when they were going, more or less."

"That makes sense," agreed Douglas. "What's your point?"

"Simply that they arrived twenty million years ago and clearly never left. Now, you can bet NASA called in the top minds in the world to prepare them for this period," she stated. "However, despite almost certainly being as prepared as anyone could possibly be, they..." she faltered.

"Died?" asked Douglas.

Natalie nodded awkwardly.

"So what chance do *we* have of surviving? Is that what you're saying?" he asked again, sagging slightly. "Poor Arnold, poor all of them – but what courage, Natalie, what courage to have done that," his voice was hoarse with admiration. "Ah've known Arnold Bessel most of my life – since we were children. His father was American Air Force, based in Scotland for a few years. We stayed in touch from then on. His influence helped get me this post, in fact." He put his head in his hands and sighed deeply.

"I'm sorry, Captain." Natalie stood, placing a hand on Douglas' shoulder. "I'd better leave you. I'll see you in the morning."

Douglas got to his feet, wearily. "Thank you, Natalie. Ah'll see you in the shuttle bay at 0800, and well done," he added seriously. "Ah may not like your findings, but that's outstanding work."

"Thank you, Captain. I *am* sorry," she repeated gently. "However, just before I go, there's one piece of news which is a *little* more hopeful, perhaps."

"Oh?" asked Douglas, lifting slightly.

"Yes, Dr Satnam Patel was with us when we made these discoveries. He said it gave him some new ideas about how to think about our problem. If they managed to deliberately manipulate a wormhole to travel back here, then he just might have the beginnings of an idea to take us home. Although, he did say that, theoretically, time travel is easier backwards because of the maximum speed of photons and, er... well, perhaps it would be best if Satnam explained it."

"Aye," replied Douglas, chuckling softly, "but Ah doubt it would help!"

It was a milestone day for the teenagers. Gathered in the embarkation lounge, they positively chomped at the bit, because today, Tim, Woodsey, Henry and Rose were going outside. All were sixteen or over and under the new ruling, they had reached their majority and subsequently, the decision was theirs – all except Clarissa, who was not happy.

Henry tried to placate his younger sister. It seemed that Burnstein Snr had chosen today to become a concerned parent, refusing her permission to go out with the others. He had tried to stop Henry too, but Henry had decided that on this 'new world' he would make his own decisions. He was eighteen and older than the others anyhow, so not going out with them would have shamed him.

"I'm sorry, Clarrie. I'd take you if I could," he explained gently.

"Can't I go and just not tell Dad?" she asked, plaintively.

He smiled patiently. "Y'know we can't do that. Without authorisation from a parent or guardian you can't go outside. I'm real sorry, Clarrie, but it's only for now. You'll be able to go out soon. We'll *all* have to go out soon."

"But today's the first time and Timmy's going too!" She fought back tears of frustration. Henry attempted a hug but she pulled away. "You could try and talk Ma around?" she asked, giving it one last try.

"Ma will just do whatever *he* says," said Henry, trying to keep the bitterness out of his voice. "You know that."

"Try Pa again, then!"

He looked down at her sadly. "When I tried, it just made him worse. You know he was still spittin' nails about that chewin' out Commander Baines gave him about the Germans. Look, I promise I'll take you out with me as soon as I can, OK? Huh?"

Clarissa slumped and turned away. Henry pulled at Tim's sleeve. "Try and cheer her up a bit before we go, will ya?"

Tim nodded and caught up with Clarrie as she set off on her *slow walk*.

Rose and Woodsey were laughing about something, so Henry went to investigate. "Hey! What's with you two?" he asked.

Rose gave Woodsey a shove. "It *will* get big again!"

Henry raised an eyebrow wondering what on Earth the New Zealander had told her this time.

Rose looked to him. "Tell him, Henry!"

"Tell him what?" he asked, mystified.

"I've told her about the effects of wearing a Kevlar helmet, mate," Woodsey admitted, grinning broadly. "The *long-term* effects, that is."

"And what would those be?" asked Henry.

"Kevlar chemically bonds with human hair at the molecular level, causing permanent flattening," Woodsey explained, sagely. "They use it as a cure for people with frizzy hair."

Henry immediately saw where this was going, so he adopted a serious expression. "Yeah, I'd heard that," he agreed. "Apparently, it's irreversible too." He looked at Rose's voluminous blonde locks, shaking his head and sucking his teeth with concern. "I doubt you'll ever get it back like that again," he postulated sadly.

"No!" squeaked Rose, putting a hand to her hair. "Surely my lifting gel will get it back?" she asked, really worried now.

"Well, you might get away with it the first time," replied Henry, "but the effects are cumulative, or so I've heard."

Woodsey was nodding vigorously, loving it. "Yeah, that's right. More than once though, and you'll have to join the flat-head society," he added for good measure.

Rose squeaked again in alarm, which fortuitously covered the snort of laughter which burst out of Henry before he could get himself back under control.

"By the way," asked Woodsey, frowning slightly with interest. "How much hair product do you have and what are you going to do after it's gone?"

Rose blanched. "I've got to go," she said.

"What? Why?" asked Henry, troubled by this new direction his carefully planned morning had just taken.

"Because if Mum realises that our hair and makeup products will come to an end, she'll hide them all!"

Woodsey and Henry burst out laughing. "What are you going to do?" asked Henry. "Divvy them up and stash your half?"

"No!" Rose retorted. "I'm going to steal most of it and hide it!"

The boys laughed again. "Surely that can wait?" asked Woodsey. "We *are* about to step outside onto prehistoric Earth!"

Rose shook her head. "No, it can't. If Lara gets there first, I won't see any of it!"

"Well, she hasn't tried to hide it so far, has she?" asked Henry, trying to placate her.

"That's because no one's told her it's going to run out!" snapped Rose.

"Surely she's worked that out already?" asked Woodsey in disbelief.

"Have you met Mrs Miller?" Henry gave him a secret look.

Woodsey nodded, looking thoughtful. "When I realised she was Rose's mum, I tried to say hello once."

"Tried to? What happened?" asked Rose.

"I was almost knocked out by her personal armada of remote 'selfie' cameras, buzzing about to catch her best sides." He shrugged. "Still, I'm sure you'll be alright. The dinosaurs *were* known for having great hair – no, *wait!*"

Henry was grinning but Rose was becoming more annoyed; an annoyance sure to make its way his way shortly. He held his hands up, trying not to laugh and reached a gentle arm around her shoulder. "Don't sweat it. With or without makeup or any other products you'll always be crazy hot!" He smiled his most ingratiating smile.

Rose did not return it. Instead she replied, "If all the beauty products run out, I'm going to look haggard, like I'm about twenty-five or something!" She waited to be corrected, a vain hope which turned into *a vain hope.*

"I'm sure it'll be fine, honey. It's only for an hour or so," Henry tried, inexperience causing him to completely miss his cue.

"Yeah," Woodsey chipped in, all concern, "so *you* say! But what if she gets back and Old Mother Hubbard has already raided the cupboard?"

"Not *helping*," replied Henry, in a singsong voice through a tight smile.

"I've got to go!" Rose pulled away, adamantly this time. "I don't want to join the fat-heads, it's not worth it!"

"Flat-heads," Woodsey called after her. "I said flat-heads."

"Will you pipe down?!" Henry complained, getting wound up by both sides.

"Let me *go!*" the ghost of old Rose flashed, possessing the body of the new.

By the time Tim returned, all three were shouting at one another. Whilst he tried to find out what in the world they were bickering about, they were drowned out by the roar of the shuttle's engines opening up as the dig team made their way back to *Fossil Rock.* The teenagers ran as one to a porthole, watching them go.

"Great!" Tim cried, excitedly. "Commander Baines said we could go and get ourselves kitted-up in the security office, once the dig team were away. Let's go!"

"Do we have to wear helmets?" asked Rose.

"Of course, you don't want one of those carnivorous Pterosaurs to scalp you, do you?" asked Tim, reasonably.

Rose touched her hair again, anxious, yet undecided.

"It's not true about Kevlar, Rose," said Henry, kindly. "Woodsey was just makin' it up." He turned to his friend, demanding a lifeline out of the hole he had dug for himself. "Well, tell her!"

Woodsey gave Rose a look of absolute sincerity. "The Kevlar thing's all gospel, mate," he vouched, unhelpfully.

"See, I told you!" Rose shouted at Henry.

"He's lying!"

"Not me, mate."

"You just don't care about what happens to me!"

"*I* don't care?"

"She's right, mate. If my girl's hair was gonna fall out—"

"Save it will ya!"

"Even your friend cares more about me than you do!"

"*Does* he?"

"Well, I wouldn't tell any Sheila to keep her hair on, but…"

"Will you shut yer damned mouth!"

"Don't tell him to shut up! This is all *your* fault!"

"Well, there's no need to give the bloke a hard time. Maybe you could use an umbrella or something?"

"Save it!"

"Shut up!"

Tim was halfway across the large chamber when Rose called. "Where are you going, Tim?"

"I thought I'd get suited up and have a walk outside," he called over his shoulder. "Maybe even climb up to the new walkway along the palisade and see the amazing views over the plains, forests and mountains. Perhaps study the incredible prehistoric animals out there. You never know, this miraculous chance to see what no human being has ever seen before might be worth a look, but don't let me interrupt you. Bye."

The suddenly muted trio looked from one to another, before shouting in unison, "*Wait for me!*"

Major White was already in the security office, checking everyone's equipment personally. He was not happy that the first group of sightseers were all kids and would accompany them first time out. His small squad of armed security personnel were also preparing for their walk outside.

When White expressed his concerns to Commander Baines, she had told him that they all had to go out sooner or later and if they did get into trouble, at least teenagers would be better able to make a run for it.

White had misgivings, but despite them, he greeted the young men and woman warmly as they entered. "Hey kids! Looking forward to your first walk out?"

"Yes, sir!" said Tim, his face alight with excitement. "That is, as long as these three *squabblers* cut it out." He pointed at his friends with a thumb over the shoulder.

"Hey, I was just an innocent *squabblee*, mate," muttered Woodsey.

"Are you kidding? You started it all!" Henry snapped back, scandalised.

"It was *you* who told me the effects of Kevlar were Cumberland!" Rose chipped in, still seething.

"Cumulative," Henry remarked. "I said they were cumulative."

"Don't correct me!"

"I didn't!"

"You *did*!"

"Yeah, I know how she feels, mate."

The security officers watched with mild amusement until White shouted, "Enough!"

Tim was already getting into a Kevlar suit as the major continued, "Out there is a dangerous place. Very dangerous, so we'll have no messin' around, OK?"

"Yes, sir," said three, rather quieter, voices.

White blew out his cheeks to calm himself. "Right, now put these on," he said, shaking his head.

"Major White, can I ask you about the helmets?" asked Rose.

Woodsey snorted and Henry looked away to hide his smirk. White looked levelly at her. "Well?" he asked eventually.

"Will it flatten my hair?"

White rubbed a hand down his face slowly, to buy some time while he waited for patience to arrive. "Probably," he admitted, wearily.

"Eek! I can't go then!"

White was at a loss. He opened his mouth to speak but Tim placed a gentle hand on his arm. "Major, may I say something, please?"

The major, stuck between bafflement and impatience, gave him the floor. "Knock yourself out, kid."

"Rose," Tim began, "Kevlar will not chemically bond with your hair, nor will it give you a flat head. Check with your dad if you don't believe me. Those two were just winding you up. In fact don't believe anything Woodsey ever tells you and you'll be just fine, OK? Now can we go outside, please?"

The outer airlock opened and five soldiers stepped outside. After checking the immediate vicinity for threats, White gave the all clear and the four youths followed them, looking rather like a hockey team without the sticks.

The outer palisade was now complete and stood five metres high atop the earthwork ramparts, making the whole construct around ten metres tall. The front of the earthwork was shored up and held back with further tree trunks, raked at such an angle as to make it much too steep for a large animal to climb, but still with enough lean to create a batter, countering the thrust of the retained embankment and preventing slippage.

The tree trunks were tall enough to give the builders plenty of options with regards to cutting and dressing. The five-metre timber walls both extended another two metres underground, deeper in some places. The workmen used trenches, dug by the smaller machinery, to situate the trunks. Heavier plant then drove them still further into the earth before backfilling.

From outside the enclosure, the whole structure appeared as a massive ditch with a slightly sloping timber wall behind it and another vertical timber wall on top of that. The primitive walls were a monument to human ingenuity. Indeed, in a very real sense, they were *the* monument – the solid archetype and very first unnatural thing ever actually *constructed* upon the Earth.

The lower wall held back thousands of tons of soil and stones, which was ramped neatly at the rear and stitched with a criss-cross of small roads and accessways. The construction team had even completed some of the 'high walk' which, although built primarily for security, would soon allow people to stroll along the walls for a breathtaking view of their new world.

With the massive gates now in place, the compound was locked down and safe – at least from any land-based incursion. Secured by two draw bars, made from tree trunks stripped of their bark, the gates could not be opened quickly, but at eight metres tall, they were immensely strong.

Regardless of their 'tall as necessary, small as possible' design, they could only be opened by machine, each brace weighing a couple of tons in its own right.

The gaggle of teenagers ambled across the enclosure, unsure where to investigate first. However, aside from the weirdness of a pseudo Iron Age rampart and palisade, snuggled up against the belly of a vast spaceship, they all kept at least one eye on the skies. The story of Dr Flannigan's brush with vicious, flying reptiles had spread through the crew like a celebrity liaison on social media – complete with biting commentary and obligatory clawing. In fact, many of the passengers were deeply afraid to leave the ship, in some cases expressing a desire *never* to do so.

Tim did not feel that way. Indeed, he suspected that part of the reason they had been permitted to take this little stroll outside, was because their leaders saw this growing fear of leaving the ship as a problem in the making. By allowing a bunch of kids to go outside – albeit with an armed escort – they were trying to illustrate that it was in fact child's play.

For Tim, it was just about seeing a dinosaur – a real one, in the real world. Not on a screen, not behind glass – *real*. However, being interested in almost everything does have its drawbacks, being easily distracted chief among them, and his attention was suddenly drawn up towards the team working on the wall-walk. They were driving a second, inner row of posts into the top of the rampart, parallel to the main wall. These were spaced at roughly 1200mm intervals and cross-braced to the outer leaf. The cross-bracing timbers were cut for purpose and connected using large, if basic, dovetail joints. This locked-together, out-rigger framework provided the main skeleton on which the walkway would sit.

In the fathomless, far flung future, armies of men would work for months or even years to accomplish similar security systems. All with basic tools of wood, bone, stone and later, metal. A few moments more into the future would, of course, see man create machines capable of working a thousand man-hours in a day. Knowing that no one would build a JCB digger for almost a hundred million years, Tim could not help but smile as he watched just such a machine push a huge tree trunk into the Cretaceous soil, with no obvious sign of effort.

He recognised the construction principles as basically Roman and was sure he had read somewhere that even they may have pinched the idea. It allowed a very solid, very strong structure to be assembled very quickly and here they were, *re*-using it before it had even been invented – he would be willing to lay money that the Romans' work was tidier though. After a moment his smile turned to a frown.

Time…

"Hey, Tim, wassup?" asked Henry, breaking into his thoughts.

"Oh, nothing really," Tim answered, slowly returning from his reverie. "I was just thinking that we've ruined our world back home. We've over-consumed and over-bred ourselves to the brink of our own demise and now we're *here*. Now, we've even broken time, too. I wonder what price we, or *someone*, will have to pay for it."

Henry chuckled. "You are one cheerful S.O.B, d'ya know that?"

Tim laughed. "Hey, someone needs to keep you on the ground," he retorted. "You've been floating around with that stupid grin on your face since Rose agreed to put up with you!"

"Oh, and what about you and my kid sister?" asked Henry, archly.

"That… that's completely different," Tim backpedalled.

"*Really*," Henry mocked, hitting Tim on the shoulder. "So you don't think she's hot then, huh?"

"Of course not," Tim replied, rubbing his upper arm. "I would say she's sweetly pretty, you crass American!"

They laughed together, but reaching the top of the rampart, both fell silent; awe, for once, without shock.

"That is truly momentous," said Tim.

"Awesome," agreed Henry.

"The work crews have done an incredible job putting all this together so quickly," said Tim. "Even with heavy machinery, this is a *lot* of work. I know there's still much to do but even so, fair play."

"Yeah," agreed Henry. "It was a good idea to keep a permanent fire going out here, from the cutting waste. Keeping the animals at arms' length has really moved the work on. I always look when I go past a window – haven't seen anything monstrous in the clearing for days now. I heard that was your idea, huh?"

"Well, it was just something I *sort of* discussed with Natalie a few days ago," Tim replied, a little awkwardly. "Smoke will normally frighten animals away, you know? But she filled in all the details really."

"You and your English modesty," chuckled Henry, ruffling the younger boy's hair in a friendly, if boisterous, manner. "I can see why you've got my kid sister hooked – you're embarrassing me!"

"Oi!" Tim cried out, batting the bigger lad off as best he could. They both laughed again before returning to the miracle before their eyes. Such beauty and such peace; the only sounds those of Woodsey and Rose squabbling a little way off.

"I hope they let the fires go out soon," said Tim, distantly. "I want my dinosaurs back."

"Hmm," Henry answered without really listening and they lapsed into a contented silence once more.

The moment was only slightly marred by the loud, hollow slap and cry of, "Owww!" as Rose carried out a surprise durability test on the New Zealander's Kevlar helmet for him.

Henry and Tim ignored them. "Hey, Tim."

"Yeah?" Tim replied, barely able to tear his eyes away from the view.

"This is all so incredible," Henry continued mildly, "and things have been going pretty well for days now, haven't they?"

"They have," Tim agreed, smiling dreamily now. "It's like we're starting again – all brand new," he added, gesturing with a sweep of his arm.

"So," Henry pressed on, doggedly, "how long do you think it will be before it all goes to crap again?"

The monsters may have been keeping their distance but the gods were listening. A deafening *CRACK* and *BOOM* rolled across plain and forest. Tim ducked in surprise, seeing Henry do likewise. They turned around sharply to see vast, blacker than black clouds amassing behind them. While their focus had been fixed on the sweeping vista to the west, a storm front had rolled in from the baby Atlantic, fifty miles east. It drove inland towards them with almost supernatural speed. BANG! Lightning struck the *New World*. The leviathan just sat there and took it stolidly, as the super-high voltage worked its way down her flanks harmlessly into the ground.

"Any second now it's going to—" Tim may as well have mimed the rest of his comment. The rain did not start so much as it just happened. There was nothing and then there was deluge, enveloping them like liquid shrink wrap. The water, it could hardly be called rain, bounced off the young men's body armour with the sound and thrash intensity of a blast-beat.

Tim turned to Henry, streams shelving off his helmet and shoulder pads. "You know the next time you want to ask me something?" he cried above the sudden, accompanying wind.

"Yeah?"

"Don't."

Natalie knelt in the pit at *Fossil Rock*, studying the two fossilised skeletons partially revealed at the centre of the excavation. The diggers were barely amateur archaeologists, but regardless, the whole team had shown the utmost respect for the remains from the beginning. Now their identities were known, there was a real sense of reverence as the finds from the former NASA officers were handled and cleaned. It was like laying out family.

They were down to the second skull, but there remained much stone still to clear around the female. The work demanded great care and to fully expose her, without damage, would certainly take more time than they had today.

Her, Natalie thought. *When did* that *happen?* Yesterday, these remains were just a collection of bone-shaped stones, mere representations of lives long extinguished. Now, they not only had noun, but personal pronoun and even proper noun. Added to that, when the *New World* left home, a little over a fortnight ago, these people were alive and well and safely on base at Canaveral.

Natalie wiped her brow, taking a moment to consider... *And now they're twenty million years dead! Leaving aside that they died 120 million years before either of them were born for a moment, how do we even begin to work through that intellectually, let alone spiritually?* She sighed, deciding it might be best to record what they had at this stage. Hopefully, viewing the excavation with a more empirical eye might help her shrug off some of the insanity which seemed to have become their lives, at least for a little while. Besides, if they continued down they might run out of time.

Before she could say as much to her dig mate, communication became almost impossible.

The explosive white noise was immediate and deafening, but seemed to roll in and out to even greater severity. Everyone reacted by covering their ears involuntarily as they watched the light outside fall black as night. The trees, bent double by the sudden violence of the storm, began to shed almost at once, bombarding the dig-tent with frightening force.

Natalie climbed out of her trench and walked across to The Sarge. Comforted by his silent unflappability, she yelled, "WHERE THE HELL DID THAT COME FROM?" above the din.

"I DON'T KNOW," he bellowed back, "BUT I HOPE IT DOESN'T STAY OVER US!"

"I KNOW, IT'S KILLING MY EARS!" she shouted, still covering them.

Jackson shook his head and pointed up. "THEY WON'T BE ABLE TO FLY IN THIS. WE'RE STUCK HERE UNTIL THIS BLOWS OVER!"

"Oh, crap!" she cursed; a comparative whisper when compared with the roar outside.

Douglas had decided against visiting *Fossil Rock* with the others that morning, choosing instead to meet with Lloyd. Delivering the news of bereavement to family and loved ones was every commanding officer's worst nightmare. He had done his best, but the situation with Lloyd added another layer of complex discomfiture. Lloyd had taken it quietly enough, for his own part. Of course, it was hard to know how bad it was underneath.

He left the brig with a sigh of relief and set off for the bridge, barely travelling three steps before his comm sounded. "Douglas," he answered.

"Captain, it's Jill. We've been hit by an enormous weather front. No warning, just blat!"

"We have *got* to get that satellite up!" Douglas remonstrated aloud.

"Yes, sir, but the immediate issue is, we can't go out or fly. This is a big one!"

"Are the construction crews back in?"

"Yes, Captain, wet, cold and thoroughly disgruntled, but they're fine."

"And the kids? Are they back inside?"

"Affirmative."

"Surely Sandip's back with the shuttle by now?"

"Yes, he's been back a while."

"Is there a 'but' or a 'however' about to break into this conversation, Commander?"

"Yes, sir, it's the dig team. We're not sure when we'll be able to reach them in this."

"Aah, crap!"

Douglas strode onto his bridge. "So, what do we have?" he asked directly.

"A storm from hell," replied Baines.

"And it's getting worse, Captain," Singh added. "Hurricane force winds on the way."

"Och, surely it's just April showers," said Douglas. "These squalls always caught ye by surprise, even back home."

"We've got 150 mile an hour gusts!" Singh reported. "Bit rougher than Bonnie Scotland, Captain."

"Oh, Ah don't know. It gets pretty fierce up in the highlands, laddie."

"The compound is beginning to flood too," continued Singh, "which will make it difficult to go out at ground level, until it subsides. Not without flooding the Pod cargo bay, anyway."

"Oh," Baines commented, quietly.

Both men turned to look at her. "Jill?" asked Douglas.

"Erm... of course, you know our water stocks are finite, Captain," Baines sidled adroitly up to the bombshell she was about to drop. "That's why we chose this clearing, because of its proximity to the river, yes?"

The men waited for more, completely unwilling to help her out.

"Well," she tried again, "I was speaking with Satnam Patel about a way of refreshing our supplies. Obviously, building a pipeline from the river is out of the question at the moment. So we came up with the idea of taking one of the shipping containers we have down in the cargo hold, welding the doors shut and reinforcing them. They're already made to fit on our lorries, so transport to the river and back should be no problem.

"Satnam had some welders cut the top off the container, using the steel to build baffles along its length to prevent the build up of wave pressure along the tank. Apparently, this might destabilise the truck or even turn it over. The baffles were fitted leaving spaces at the top and bottom so that the tank can still be filled and drained easily."

Douglas waited patiently for his first officer to finish, sighing heavily as he put his head in his hands. "That was a hell of a story, Jill. Now, why don't we skip to the crappy ending?" he asked.

"Captain?" she ventured, innocently.

"Oh, aye," confirmed Douglas. "Ah've developed a nose for these things. Let's have it!"

"I know we don't have *many* lorries," Baines soldiered on, "but I thought, you know, a bit of rain couldn't hurt, could it?"

"What've ye done?"

"I ordered them to drive the new water tank outside to catch some rain water. Naturally, it made sense to leave it on the lorry for ease of moving it… later…" she trailed off.

"Can we bring it back in?" Douglas asked Singh.

Singh shook his head. "This flash flood is like nothing I've ever seen, sir, even in the Indian monsoon season. Unfortunately the new compound is rather keeping the water in, too. It's probably up to the wheel arches by now. The river's up over its banks, you see, so it's likely to get worse – and quickly." He turned to face his superiors. "The groundworks and palisade were constructed with extraordinary speed out of a necessity to keep the wildlife out. I don't think we can blame anyone for leaving drainage for another day."

"No, we cannae blame those hardworking boys," said Douglas, "but what about our wee lorry out there?"

"All I can say is – it hasn't floated off *yet*, sir," Singh reported, calling up a feed from one of the external cams.

"Are we going to lose it, Sandy?" Baines asked, looking slightly green in the gills.

The pilot checked his instruments. "It's been raining for an hour, Commander. If it continues overnight, the truck will be under water. The weight of the water tank on its back should keep it in place as it fills but, as for the electrics…"

"Wait a minute, aren't the trucks airtight and subsequently watertight?" asked Douglas. "They were built for Mars, after all. Aren't they basically spaceships without flight capability?"

"Yes, sir, but only their cabins and crew spaces are 'spaceships', as you say. The rest of the vehicle is basically just a lorry. It's insulated against extreme cold and the workings are protected for heavy duty, but that's all. Although we *were* effecting weather changes on Mars, flooding wasn't a projected issue for some years, possibly not even within the expected working life of these vehicles. I mean, they're OK in the rain, but..." he looked at Baines apologetically. "Neither our technicians who adapted the vehicles, nor the original builders, anticipated anyone taking them on any *amphibious* manoeuvres."

"And the levels are too high to open the Pod hatch? Even if we're quick?" asked Douglas.

"If we opened the outer airlock, it would flood to at least a metre depth. I could check with Hiro or Sam Burton, but I'd be concerned about how the electronics would—" Singh stalled, interrupted by a massive rending grumble as the ship lurched. The movement was momentary but a slight pitch in the floor could now be felt.

"What the hell was that?" cried Douglas, hanging on to the back of his chair, in case it came again.

"Oh my God! We're sinking!" Baines called out, checking her instrument panel.

"Captain," Singh spoke as calmly as he could manage, "I'm afraid I'm going to have to recommend against opening any of the hatches just at the moment!"

"We're going to drown!" Thomas Beckett shouted over the deafening roar of torrential rain and constant ballistic barrage. As the ground outside became oversaturated, rivulets of water began to run under the sides of the dig-tent.

"Don't be silly, Thomas," Natalie called back. "We're on the top of a cliff. There's no immediate danger to us."

"Life is less than peaches for us, though, missus!" one of the diggers yelled out from the trench.

"Hmm, so I see," she was forced to acknowledge. "Can we use the industrial vacuum cleaner to pump it out?"

"EH?"

"I SAID – can we use the industrial vacuum cleaner *to pump it out*?" Natalie shouted.

The man cupped his hands, calling back in a broad Australian accent, "I don't know if it's a 'wet and dry' machine. Mars is mostly bone dry on the surface, so I doubt it made the specifier's wish list!"

"You don't have the manual with you?" she asked, hopefully.

The Australian gave her a look and climbed out of the trench. "Did I bring the instructions for a *vacuum cleaner* on an archaeological dig a hundred million years ago?"

She smiled apologetically. "I'm guessing not?" she called into his ear.

"Right," he said. "That hole's full of dirt, grit, sand and water. It'd be like supping Pommy lager! You really think it's worth carking the machine for? It's not like the Sheila's gonna drown, is it?"

"Good point," Natalie conceded. "Well, apart from the lager, obviously." She turned to take in the whole team. "BUCKETS!" she bawled.

One of the crew grabbed a battery powered breaker, smashing a small culvert into the rock at the edge of the tent to fashion a rough chute. The rest of the diggers set about throwing the water, bucket at a time, through the new hole, to make its way down the rockface outside.

The chain was hard at it when a wrenching, tearing sound cut straight through the white noise of the rain, vibrating their tympanic membranes at the precise frequency of fear. The bailing stopped immediately, as the team searched one another's faces for any scrap of comfort.

"GRAB THE BLADDY TENT!" bellowed The Sarge, barrow-boy genetics storming to the fore with uncouth, but undeniable, practicality.

Everyone leapt for a handhold on the steel framework which gave the polymerised structure its rigidity. One of the eighteen steel split-pins, driven into the earth and stone with a handheld, hydraulic hammer just yesterday, had ripped free and others were developing a disconcerting wobble.

The dig-tent weighed over a ton but was so big that it was like trying to pin down a sail.

"CAN WE TIE IT OFF TO A TREE?" shouted someone.

"OPEN THAT HATCH AND WE'RE ALL GONE – OVER THE EDGE!" The Sarge roared above the increased wind noise, as the edge of the tent began to lift. "EVERYONE GET OVER HERE! THE WIND IS COMING FROM THIS DIRECTION. *MOVE IT*!"

The diggers and soldiers pounced as one, all grabbing a piece of the side as it began to rise. They managed to balance the force of the hurricane winds – barely. Only Beckett stayed where he was, looking shocked by the events unfolding around him. The Sarge noticed and felt obliged to speak out, "GET OVER HERE, BECKETT! BEFORE I GET OVER THERE, YOU PILLOCK!"

Beckett snapped out of his trance, moving to stand at the opposite end of the group from Sergeant Jackson, but he added his weight, nonetheless. They were essentially trapped inside a giant, vibrating shuttlecock. The noise and the buffeting were terrifying. The fourteen human beings had no more control over their destiny than a paper boat in a rip current, so they dug in and grabbed the dig-tent like their lives depended on it – *because* their lives depended on it.

Beckett was on the cusp of panic, his only conscious thought: *It's bad enough being lost in a world in which I don't belong, but being lost over a cliff in a world in which I don't belong, would just be the limit! I should never have left my library!*

They hung on, they held fast, to the tent, to each other – to life.

"Do you think they'll come for us?" shouted Natalie, hope taking flight.

"I hope not," The Sarge shot it down. "If they do, it won't help us and it certainly won't help them. We've got to ride it out."

There was a bang and a buck and a *BANG*. The dig-tent lifted, tearing many of the steel pins out at once. "LET IT GO!" The Sarge bellowed. "LET IT *GOOOOO*!" He dropped to the ground hoping the others had heard him.

Any hopes of their protective enclosure staying earthbound were torn away, as the whole structure was snatched into the air. An instant of relative high pressure under the tent allowed the team to hit the ground and stay there, as their world flew apart. Once raised, the dig-tent began turning over, allowing the full force of the hurricane to reach beneath. In a blink, it took off as if fired from a gun, ripping through the trees at the edge of the cliff, collecting others as it flew.

The Sarge fell on his back, watching in wide-eyed horror as the twelve-metre-long structure shot down the valley at incredible speed.

"CRAWL FOR THE TREES! CRAWL FOR THE TREES!" he roared above the storm and the rain. He grabbed Natalie by the straps on her denim work dungarees, dragging her after him.

Miraculously, everyone made it to the tree line, despite being drenched, breathless and terrified. This was fortunate, but the trees themselves were also under attack from the winds. Stooped over, some cracked, while others lost limbs alarmingly. The refugees from the dig clung desperately onto the trunks and to each other. Now fully in the clutches of the hurricane, they prayed for it all to stop.

Climbing up and down ladders for things one has forgotten is always tiresome. In order to save time, Hiro extended just past his comfortable reach.

The ship lurched at that moment, tipping him over the edge and down the access tube. He was wedged tight in the small maintenance shaft, having banged his head off the wall on the way down. He tried to move but his clothing had snagged a socket driver in the fall, jamming it into some switch gear. Hearing a subtle scraping noise from above, he twisted to look up and was just in time to see the handheld terminal he had left at the rim of the hatch fall towards him, also striking his head.

Georgio fared a little better. Nevertheless, the movement had thrown him off balance so that he bumped his hip hard against a console near his workstation. He looked around for his colleague to express his natural outrage, but only saw only a pair of legs kicking and struggling from the top of an access hatch – the one his friend had so lately been peering down. What he *heard*, were muffled words – mostly unprintable ones.

He hobbled over to help Hiro by pulling at his legs. This did little to release the engineer but it certainly released another string of invective. Hiro was so far down the hatch that Georgio could only reach just past his knees.

"Sorry," he said. "Hang on." Kneeling over the hatch, he managed to straighten Hiro's legs, pulling them into his chest. Adjusting the angle so that he could apply his strength, he tugged again.

"Mmphagmph!" Sounds of annoyance found their way around the stuck form of the chief.

Georgio apologised once more and tried again, this time pushing Hiro down further into the hatch.

"MMPHAGMPH!" Sounds of alarm found their way around the stuck form of the chief.

"What can I do?" Georgio called down the shaft.

"MMPHAGMPHOFF!"

"There's no need to be like that!"

"Mmphullnowph."

"*Che cosa*?"

"MMPHULLNOW!"

"Pull now?"

"Mphyes."

"Oh," Georgio chuckled, "I could have sworn you said—"

"**MMPHULLNOWWWWW!**"

"Sorry, yes, of course." Georgio obliged and a red-faced, ruffled chief popped out of the bottleneck like a bad vintage.

"Thanks for hurrying!" he griped, after rubbing his chest and taking a few breaths. "What happened?"

"You fell down the—"

"TO THE SHIP!"

"Oh, it lurched," replied Georgio, checking readouts. "Uh-oh, I think we're sinking."

Hiro looked thoughtfully at his younger colleague. "Hmm," he said. "In that case I'd better call the captain."

"Why? I'm sure he would have felt it."

"In case the bridge crew get any crazy ideas about blasting us out of here. With our landing struts and belly sucked into the mud it could rip us apart!"

"Could we *blast* our way out of here?" asked Baines.

Douglas and Singh looked at one another and both shrugged, unsure how to answer, when the comm binged.

"Bridge," Singh answered.

"Sandip, it's Hiro."

"Go ahead, Hiro, the captain and the commander are here also."

"Are we sinking?"

"Yes."

"Are you thinking about blasting us out of here?"

The three bridge officers exchanged glances. "Of course not," Singh lied shamelessly.

"Good, don't. It could rip us apart," said the chief, brooking no argument. *"At what rate are we sinking?"*

"We've capsized more than actually sunk," Singh reported. "We're about a metre lower to starboard and about a metre up to port. Unfortunately, the main cargo and vehicle access is on the starboard side, so we'll have to dig our way out before any vehicles will be able to leave the Pod. That's after the flooding's gone down, of course."

"We're flooding?" asked Hiro, fearing even worse news.

"No, all hatches well and truly battened, I'm glad to report. Now, *obviously* we can't blast our way out of here," Singh raised a wry eyebrow to his colleagues once more, "so, how are we to right the ship?"

"Well, firstly, I suggest we don't try and move her in the middle of a hurricane. Secondly, if we build a support structure to hold a quarter of the ship, we can retract the landing struts one at a time. Then, using the heavy diggers, we excavate underneath each strut and build a rubble-concrete pile. When it's cured, we lower the strut just enough to take the weight and repeat for the other three struts. When all four struts have a foundation we

can lift Sekai and lock her off at whatever level we need to, up to the full height of the landing gear, should we need to protect her."

The bridge officers nodded to one another, impressed.

"That's brilliant, Hiro," said Douglas. "Did ye just come up with that off the hoof?"

"No, sir, I put the plan together when we landed, but building the enclosure took priority, as there were concerns about missing the crop planting season."

"Ah see. Ah take it there's not a lot we can do about the situation right now, then?" asked Douglas.

"No, sir," replied the engineer, *"not unless it's the absolute last resort before the end. If it became an emergency, we could uncouple the ship from the Pod and attempt a liftoff without the payload. I suppose we could then reattach using the grapplers and pull the Pod back into position from the air, but that would be really risky, sir – suicidal in this weather. "*

"Understood. So what, then? We just keep sinking?" asked Douglas, looking around for ideas.

"We must wait for the weather to change and hope we don't capsize past the point where my plan can work, sir," Hiro answered. *"I did argue with Doctors Norris, Patel and Portree at the time that, although the earthworks are very important, I believe building a foundation for the ship to sit upon is just as important, sir. In the event of extreme weather, for example, where floods might destabilise the ground."*

Hiro did not finish his sentence with an exclamation mark but they all heard it.

"Well, as it turns out, Hiro, you were absolutely right," Douglas flashed a pained look towards his fellow bridge officers. "Ah think we're all agreed, here, that your plan should be the very first thing we do, once this situation has blown over. Now, can you put your brilliant mind to work on another problem for us, please?"

"What's that, sir?" the chief asked, completely immune to flattery.

"We have fourteen terrified people out there in all this. So, how the hell can we get them back without smashing the shuttle into the ground?"

"I'll think on it, sir – engineering out."

The comm fell silent.

"That's us told, then," said Baines.

The wind ripped at the trees, constantly peppering the people hanging on to them with organic missiles. The exposed team, already terrified, were now freezing too, each wondering how long their death grip on the tree trunks could be maintained. Their equipment and finds flew either into the forest or over the edge of the tree-strewn cliff to the river below. They watched them go, powerless to do anything else.

Their tables were long gone. All that remained was a small case, bobbing, still earthbound against all the odds. Eventually the battle was lost and it too flew off into the unknown with just about everything else.

"Noooo!" shouted Beckett.

"What's the matter, mate?" the Australian construction worker called over the howl of the wind.

"All my sandwiches were in there, and my tea flask!" wailed Beckett.

The Australian laughed, despite everything. Beckett looked bereft as he hung on for dear life.

"There must be something we can do!" snapped Douglas, angrily. "What's the wind speed now?"

"No change, sir," Singh provided. "According to the ship's scanners, it appears the eye of the storm is about an hour from us. Looks like it will pass through here, unless it changes course in the meantime."

"Can we use that?" asked Baines. "How big is it?"

"About twenty miles in diameter," replied Singh, turning to face them. "This is a *big* storm."

"So it will be clear skies for about…" Douglas calculated for a second, "eight minutes?"

"In theory, sir," Singh replied, "but what can we do in *that* time? We could get the shuttle launched and get to them certainly, but there's no way we could get them all aboard and make it back here – even if we left all their equipment behind. We'd be smashed to pieces, trying to dock with the *New World* upon our return. If we put down on the plain we might weather the storm, as long as we don't float off down the river – it's a lake out there now! And one flying tree could destroy the shuttle."

The three officers fell silent again, wracking their brains for a rescue plan.

"Well, could we no' get to them overland?" asked Douglas, exasperated.

"Even in fine weather that would be an eight hour route march, Captain," said Baines. "*Each* way. And then what could you do even if you found them? You'd just be another team lost out in that!" She pointed at the ferocious storm through the viewports. "Of course, that's if you manage to avoid drowning in the floods."

"What if we chanced getting a vehicle out?" the captain tried again, willing to consider anything at this stage. "The ground rises away from here towards *Fossil Rock* and those big, all-wheel-drive trucks we have should be able to wade a metre, surely? We could always pump the water out of the airlock—"

"Hey!" Baines interrupted. "We've already got a vehicle out there, a thirty-two-tonner with eight-wheel-drive, no less!"

Douglas snapped his fingers. "Of course!" he exclaimed. "The lorry you abandoned to the storm!"

"*Hey*," Baines repeated, plaintively.

"All we need to do is reach it," continued Douglas, oblivious, "and if it's got a partial load of water on back, so much the better for weight." Grasping for any solution, his mind worked quickly now. "Perhaps we could lower ourselves down from a high-level hatch."

Baines shook her head, the excitement ebbing quickly as her second thoughts trounced the captain's plan. "Captain, whoever goes out there will be blown all over the place and smashed against the ship in these winds."

"Ah'm willing to risk it!" Douglas slapped his right fist into his left palm with determination.

"But then what?" Baines asked in disbelief. "They're thirty miles away – alright twenty, as the Pterodactyl flies, but by the time you've travelled a couple of miles, *at best*, the hurricane will be on you again."

"True," Douglas admitted, "but when it catches us, we'll have more chance in a huge truck like that than on foot. They can travel home in the back, once we've ditched the water.

"When we flew to *Fossil Rock* the first time, we followed a game trail that wended its way through the forests between the plains. It took us most of the way there. It would be slow but Ah believe that beastie outside could make it."

"Captain," said Baines, trying to calm the situation, "that game trail may not even be there anymore – these winds could have filled any trails or tracks with dead trees by now, for all we know!"

"Ah've got to try, Jill," Douglas replied, distress evident in his voice, "Ah sent those people out there for a completely nonessential purpose. Ah cannae just abandon them to their fate."

"You weren't to know this storm was coming in, James," Baines argued, her face colouring as she grew more nervous of what the captain's guilt might force him to try. "No one could."

"Er…" Singh interrupted, mildly, "there's also the matter of the gates."

"What?" Douglas and Baines asked together.

"The gates," he repeated, patiently. "They're shut and barred. The bars weigh a couple of tons each, I've been told. We can only move them with one of the diggers, remember? And we can't get the diggers out."

"Exactly! Thank you, Sandy." Placing her hope in reason, Baines hammered her point home. "There's no way of getting that lorry out of there."

The captain felt as though his colleagues were ganging up on him and was now looking mutinous, no mean feat on his own ship. "Doesnae the lorry have a crane?" he enquired, jutting out his chin.

"Captain," Baines pleaded, "you're talking about stepping out of a high-level hatch, abseiling down the hull of the ship, getting into the lorry, driving it across the compound – if it will even move – getting out of the lorry in water and muck up to your waist, putting the crane legs out onto soft mud, operating the crane to swing a couple of large tree trunks out of their hoops, dragging the gates open and driving away! And all that in 150 mile an hour winds!" She took a deep breath. "James, *please*! We all want to save those people but if I'd suggested that, you'd lock me in the brig – you know you would. I mean, do you even know how to work a HIAB?"

"Ah'm nae going te abandon those people and Ah cannae risk anyone else, Jill," said Douglas, getting stubbornly to his feet. "Ah'm the captain, it's ma duty to try anything which might save them – anything! No matter how long the odds."

"Yes, you're the captain," Baines restated, also rising and laying a placating hand on his shoulder. "That's exactly why we can't afford to lose you. As much as we want to save them, James, we need our captain too!"

"So what de ye suggest Ah do?" asked Douglas, wretchedly.

"*I* suggest that we need to calm down and think about this logically. Maybe we could—"

Singh coughed politely, interrupting them. "Excuse me, but I think I have a solution. Hopefully one we can all survive."

Douglas and Baines turned to the pilot. "Spit it out, laddie!" Douglas barked impatiently.

Singh flashed them his perfect white grin. "We use the shuttle."

"Has something changed and I've missed it?" asked Baines, wearily.

"We use the *space* shuttle," Singh clarified and tried again. "We prep for a rescue mission and wait in the shuttle bay for our window in the storm. Once the eye is over us, we zoom out towards *Fossil Rock* and retrieve the dig crew."

"But," Baines could not help but notice the obvious flaw in the plan, "you won't get back in time to dock with the ship before the hurricane—"

"Aha," Sandip cut her off to reveal his trick. "We don't try and beat the storm back."

"But, as we've already said, setting down outside might lose us the shuttle too," Douglas joined in, not sure where his pilot was going with this. "Ah mean, if it's a choice between keeping the shuttle safe and those people's lives, then of course—"

"We won't set down!" Sandip cut across him, triumphantly. "We shoot straight up through the eye! The shuttle can easily get above the storm to wait it out. I suggest heading for space. We don't know how long the storm might cover us here and once in a geosynchronous orbit we'll use very little fuel. Not to mention that it would be much safer than landing elsewhere, what with giant ferocious dinosaurs all over the place. No, we just wait up there, in perfect tranquillity, for the battering down here to blow itself out. Then we just pop home – simple."

A moment's silence…

"OK, so that's brilliant. When do we get started?" asked Baines.

Douglas moved to stand behind Singh, giving him a pat on the shoulder. "That's very good thinking, Sandy. It could be the chance we've been hoping for. Well done. It'll be damned dangerous though."

He leaned over to view the pilot's instruments. "Right, whilst we've been *discussing* our options," he continued diplomatically, "we've lost quarter of an hour or more. Is the eye of the storm still heading for us, about forty minutes out?"

"As far as I can tell, sir," Singh acknowledged. "Obviously, before the storm hit, we were only expecting a short hop, so we'll need to refuel the shuttle and give her a full check over before we try something like this."

Douglas nodded. "We'd better be about it, then."

Singh stood and they walked towards the door, discussing their preparations.

"Captain? Sandy? Aren't you forgetting something?" asked Baines.

They turned, waiting for her to elaborate.

"Your prep of the shuttle is vital, of course, but how long do you think you'll be up there?" she asked.

"Not really sure," replied Singh.

"What's your point?" asked Douglas.

"Well, if you're up there for a day or two, you might need *a sandwich or two*, perhaps? And let's not forget those poor wretches out there are going to be freezing as well as starving, and *that's* assuming you find them in one piece. You're going to need food, blankets, dry clothes and a doctor."

"Well, *of course* we'll need those! That's why you're such an exemplary first officer, Jill. You allow me to keep ma eye on the big picture, ye ken?" Douglas created a frame with his hands, grinning at her through it.

"*Right,*" she replied. "Well, you two go and set up your easels and I'll stick to joining the dots."

Douglas gave her his most charming smile – the one that sank her every time – before tossing a casual salute as they turned to leave.

"Captain," she called them back. "Don't get banged up – we're all out of shuttle paint!"

"Mind the shop, Commander," he countered with a wink.

Baines watched them go with concern, muttering, "Please be careful, James."

The dig team were reaching the limits of endurance. Some suffered more than others as rain lashed and fatigue gnawed at them. Despite the warm climate, they were soaked through to the skin and the ferocity of the wind was freezing them. Beckett had lost his grip some time ago, his energy completely drained. A couple of construction workers held on to him courageously, but the effort was sapping their remaining strength as well.

Natalie faced the realisation that, with no end in sight, she could hold on no longer. Her hands began to slip. The Sarge saw that she was in trouble and reached for her, losing his own grip in the process. The wind claimed them like a momentary buoyancy at first, lifting them gently off the ground. They waited for the violent tug, certain the end was upon them, when incredibly it was all over. As quickly as they were lifted, they were discarded, both sagging into a surreal calm. Dropping just a few inches onto the wet earth, they were left cramped and panting.

The effect around them was virtually instantaneous, as if a huge fan had been unplugged. The trees straightened, their limbs creaking back to natural positions and there was localised silence; the sudden tranquillity disturbed only by the *drip, drip* of water from the leaves above them. Within moments, the roar of the hurricane sounded far off, leaving behind a primal freshness and a smell not dissimilar to freshly mown grass.

The team's arms and legs were locked into position around the anchor points they had found. They were so stiff that it took a while for them to release their grip. Gradually, they experimented with movement, eventually managing to stand and congratulate one another on their survival. There were even a few hoots of laughter as people found themselves alive against all odds.

Natalie waved them down. "We must be *quiet*," she hissed, little more than a whisper but just loud enough to make it through the group. "Any animals that have remained in the locale will also be coming back to their senses. They'll be scared and they'll be angry and we don't want to attract their attention – especially as we've lost our protection. Do any of you still have your weapons?"

The Sarge and two others had retained their rifles but the other weapons had clearly disappeared off and beyond. He gave the weaponless men and women a look of disappointment and reproof, but did not want to come down too hard on them.

The recent emergencies had forced them to extend their security contingent once more. Many of the new recruits were ex or non-combat military, but even so, their field experience was patchy and variable. However, they were willing to stand up and be counted, so Major White had accepted them into the fold gratefully, if a little reluctantly, as a sort of 'home guard'.

Before The Sarge was able to say anything, a deafening roar split the air. Looking up in surprise, he felt a surge of relief. Hovering above them, against all hope, was the shuttle, with the cradle already on its way down. Jackson was not a man usually given to emotional display or lyricism, but at that moment, it seemed like the most beautiful thing he had ever seen or heard in his life.

His radio crackled with a man's voice. "*Sarge, send 'em up five at a time, as quickly as you can, we'll have to chance the extra weight.*"

The Sarge could see the man mouthing the words above him, could see the urgency in his expression. He wasted no time on questions and simply pushed the first five people onto the cradle immediately. Once the first team were on their way up, he radioed back. "I take it we're fighting the clock?"

"*Yes, Sarge,*" the man replied from the belly hatch above. "*We're in the eye of the storm. Any minute now, all hell's gonna break loose again and if it catches the shuttle, we'll all be landowners!*"

"Understood," The Sarge answered as he watched the cradle deposit its first load of passengers to begin another, agonisingly slow descent. "Come *on!*" he muttered under his breath.

The second team jumped quickly aboard and the hoist repeated the operation. Only the Sarge and three others remained now. Of the three, two had retained their weapons, which automatically qualified them for the worst job – that of watching everyone's back before getting to safety themselves.

The Sarge observed them eyeing one another cynically; clearly they had worked this out for themselves. "Sorry, fellas, this is the reward for showing competence," he said, with a wink to demonstrate his confidence in them.

The cradle descended for the final time. Not waiting for it to land, The Sarge hustled his men aboard as soon as it reached chest height. Taking a last three-sixty view of the glade, he satisfied himself that nothing was poised to pounce before jumping up after them.

They were almost up to the winch when the storm returned. It struck the little ship like a hammer blow, batting it sideways before the pilot could mount any kind of defence to counter the colossal forces working against him.

"HANG ON!" The Sarge screamed at his men as they drew within two metres of the ship. The crew in the cargo hatch leaned out courageously, straining against their harnesses with arms outstretched to help. The wind was deafening as debris flew at them and around them once more. The shuttle bucked like a wild bull, sending the cradle flailing violently. The vibration and brutality of the movement caused one of its four steel cables to snap free. It whipped one of The Sarge's men fully across the chest, breaking his grip. He was out cold and would have certainly been thrown to his death were it not for his flak jacket.

One of the men reaching from the shuttle caught its straps in an iron grip, tearing his own shoulder. Nevertheless, he held on to the unconscious man, screaming, "HELP *MEEE!*" as the very live dead weight flew around like a ragdoll.

The cradle snapped and spun through crazy angles on its three remaining tethers, caught in a micro-maelstrom between storm and ship. The three conscious men hung on a tether each, with every ounce of determination left to them. Just a few more seconds would see them within reach of help, but they would feel every passing fractal of those terrifying seconds, before welcome hands dragged them up through the hatch.

One, one thousand...

The most savage gust yet twisted the cradle upside-down, spilling all three men. They hung from their cables desperately, two of them one-handed. With almost superhuman will they caught themselves, just as the wind changed direction throwing their legs out horizontally. The Sarge felt the impact of a boot in the face – had he not focused every ounce of his being on keeping his hands tight around the cable, the shock might have sent him twisting and thrashing into the maw of the mini cyclone which had spun their platform.

Two, one thousand...

The cradle slammed downwards, snapping hard against its ties, further stressing them as it spun the three men around. The Sarge and one other landed back in the cradle, screaming against fate and tortured tendons. The third man was hit by the cradle's handrail as it flipped back violently. He closed his eyes as blood streamed down his face, unable to do anything more than close a fist tight around the cable to which he clung for his life.

Three, one thousand...

The unconscious man flipped almost 180 degrees, making his rescuer scream in torment as he slammed headfirst into The Sarge, who heard, more than felt, the sickening crack, so focused was he on his grip. Had they been bareheaded, both men's skulls would have split wide open. Consciousness was beginning to fade, the three men outside in the storm simply having little more to give – courage had brought them this far, but hope was failing them.

Four, one thousand...

The wind and buffeting seemed to weaken. The Sarge knew this had to be subjective; he had stared death in the face more than once and recognised *the calm*. After the last few hours it came as something of a relief. *So this is it*, he thought. He could sense rather than feel himself being pulled from pillar to post. It was like movement *described* rather than experienced. *I expected there to be more pain...* The words formed themselves in his mind, which despite everything seemed to be working at light speed, although he wasn't exactly sure who '*I*' was anymore.

Five, one thousand...

Noise returned, the howling of a hurricane, the screams of the injured, and he was back in the middle of it. "Oh, Turkish Delight!" he said, realising that the pulling and tugging he was experiencing was not the storm tearing him apart, it was the rescue team dragging him bodily into the shuttle.

The man with the torn shoulder had blacked out from pain but not before the last of the soldiers had been saved and the cradle cut free from the winch.

Six, one thousand...

Fully awake and very much alive, The Sarge saw it glance off the side of the shuttle, rocketing away down the valley with all the other flying debris as the belly hatch closed. In those last moments the pressure increased around the closing doors, turning the roar of the wind into an ear-splitting shriek. "GET US OUT OF HERE!" he screamed above it all.

Singh did not need the radio. He could hear the sounds of a bad situation and the shouts for help from below with his own ears. Fully committed to preventing the ship from crashing into the forest or the side of the valley below, his concentration was absolute, so Douglas toggled the ship's intercom.

"Get everyone strapped down immediately, repeat, *immediately!* We have to leave *NOW!*"

Singh gave them twenty seconds to comply, barely avoiding disaster three times in that short window. "It's now or never, Captain!"

"Do it!" Douglas shouted.

"Here we *gooo!*" Singh called. He pointed the little ship back towards the eye of the storm, pouring on the power. Flying with the wind, rather than battling to remain stationary against it, took some of the anger out of the fight, but the buffeting was still teeth-rattling. The wind speeds were now in excess of 300 kilometres per hour and time appeared to dilate for everyone on board as they hunkered down, completely powerless to do anything but place all their faith in the one man who could save them.

Singh let out an involuntary primal scream as the storm spat the remains of their own cradle back at them once more. It came out of nowhere, from his right. Before he could even gather his wits, muscle memory and instinct had already pushed the stick forward, taking the shuttle down steeply, allowing the crumpled steel frame to fly across his field of vision, diagonally up and left, missing the shuttle's nose by the thickness of a paintjob.

He heard screams from the passenger compartment behind but could pay them no heed, as he fought the vicious currents determined to smash them into the ground. He pulled up, hearing something heavy clang off the hull. The shuttle responded sluggishly against the awesome power ranged against it and for a moment he thought they had taken damage. Before he could contemplate what the collision with the unknown object may have broken, the whole ship jumped wildly to the left with bone-jarring ferocity. Singh almost blacked out from the sudden, lateral G-forces and before he knew it he was fighting his own over-steer, because the shuttle had popped out of the black Hadesian sky into brilliant blue clarity and calm. They were once more in *the eye.*

He did not waste any time on the view, but pointed the ship straight up towards space, praying their recent manoeuvres had not smeared any of his passengers across the bulkheads.

Baines' heart alternated between her mouth and her shoes. She had no way of getting a signal through the storm. She could only wait and hope.

Just minutes after the shuttle left, black storm replaced blue sky once more. She watched the hurricane reassert control through the bridge viewports. It happened so fast, it felt like being buried.

She brooded…

Presently, the doors to the bridge chimed. Activating the screen on her console, she saw Mother Sarah waiting in the corridor outside. She opened the doors, allowing Sarah to enter and was pleasantly surprised to see Mary Hutchins follow with her trolley in tow, and behind her, a furry presence capable of banishing almost any frown.

"We thought you could use some quality company," said the priest.

Reiver, despite his wildly oscillating rear, somehow made a beeline for Baines. His wag began somewhere near the base of his ribcage and surged all through his hind quarters before arriving at last at the tip of his tail.

"Reiver!" Baines cried, kneeling down and pulling him into a hug.

"Tim suggested I bring him along," explained Mary. "He thought, as you both have people you care about out there, you might like to wait it out together. Do you mind?"

"No," replied Baines, smiling, her eyes bright with moisture. "I don't mind at all. Please thank Tim for his kindness, if you see him before I do. I know how much he loves spending time with Reiver – just a pity about the circumstances."

"I assume you won't mind the medicinal coffee and chocolate truffles we brought, either?" asked Sarah.

The shuttle soon left the troposphere behind. Safe from the storm, it headed on up through the stratosphere. At the top of the stratosphere, with ninety-five percent of the Earth's atmosphere behind it, the little ship powered on through the mesosphere and the mesopause. From here on, up into the thermosphere, the temperature on the hull actually increased slightly as it began to absorb almost direct radiation from the sun; all buffeting and wind noise forgotten in the silence of space.

Singh stayed on the power, breaking the immediate hold of Earth's gravity and flying into a geosynchronous orbit, a little over 22,000 miles above the surface of the planet. Once at pace with the location of the *New World* below, he programmed the autopilot.

The colossal speed required, due to the angular momentum created by the distance between the shuttle and the mothership down on the surface, was astonishing and yet in the black velvet of space it was as if they, and the planet spinning beneath them, were barely moving at all.

Douglas unstrapped from his seat and shot aft to check on everyone. As he ran through the passenger area towards the cargo hold, he was relieved to see all crew and evacuees strapped down in some fashion or other.

Every member of the rescued dig team was a mess of cuts and bruises, still shivering from the storm or shock, or both. Despite this, they were clearly very happy to be alive.

As Douglas passed Thomas Beckett, still strapped into a passenger seat, the historian caught his sleeve saying, "Thank you for saving our lives, Captain."

"You're welcome, Mr Beckett," replied Douglas.

"However, I knew as a boy that I didn't want to be an archaeologist and you have most definitely failed to change my mind on the subject!"

Douglas was a little put out at first, but gradually it dawned on him that this was probably a fair point. He cracked an exasperated smile. "Well, Ah dare say that reading the history we are creating here could be," he searched for a euphemism, "*entertaining*. Living through it is a whole different kettle of fish. From here onwards, may you live in boring times, Mr Beckett."

"Likewise, Captain," replied the historian with a battered, tired smile, "and, Captain, thank you for coming for us."

Douglas nodded and continued through to the cargo hold.

As soon as Dr Flannigan saw Douglas, he released his own harness and jumped up to examine the unconscious soldier who had been whipped by the cable. The man was still out, but his vitals were strong.

He turned to the crewman with the dislocated shoulder, who had come round during their flight and was whimpering as bravely as he could. "That was a hell of thing you did back there, son. You definitely saved that guy's life," he said.

The man just nodded through gritted teeth.

"Hold him, James," said Flannigan, roping Douglas into helping. "This is gonna hurt a lot, son. I'll count down from five. Brace yourself."

Flannigan shoved the shoulder back into its socket on 'three' – it was an old trick and it caused the man to cry out in shock, allowing some of the pain to sneak under the radar. The injured winch operator sagged back against the hull of the ship, the sweat of agony pouring down his face.

"You OK?" asked Flannigan.

The young man just nodded, breathing hard.

"I'll give you something for the pain." The doctor pulled a syringe and a small bottle from his bag. After giving the injection, he manufactured a sling for the man's arm from some ubiquitous medical-cotton sheet.

Content he had done all he could for him for now, he moved on to the injured soldier who was still unconscious. Flannigan checked him over as best he could. "He's got two or three cracked ribs," he looked up at Douglas. "He'll know about those tomorrow, but I think the blow just knocked the wind, and probably everything else, out of him," he grinned, reaching for his smelling salts.

He brought the man round, making sure he was fully conscious and otherwise OK before administering anything for the pain. He checked for pupil responses, whilst explaining how the young man opposite had reached out of the ship, plucking the soldier from certain death, with a miraculous catch. The story helped take the injured man's mind off the pain and he insisted on thanking his heroic rescuer before the mild sedative took him irresistibly back to sleep, a natural sleep this time.

"How are *you* holding up, Dave?" asked Douglas. "The last time Ah saw you, you didn't look much better than these guys," he gestured towards the injured men.

"Ah, that was then," said Flannigan, brushing the captain's concern away. "James, I need to talk to you after I've cleaned up all these cuts and scratches."

Douglas nodded his assent.

Whilst Flannigan did his rounds, Douglas worked with the shuttle crew to hand out blankets and dry fatigues for everyone. "Ah'm afraid there wasnae time to worry about getting shoes from your quarters," he said to the group at large. "You'll just have to put your boots by the air circulators to dry them and wander around in your stockinged feet for the day. At least that'll save my carpets, looking at the state of ye all!"

"You don't want these beauties near the air recyc, mate," said the Australian construction worker. Raucous assent from his co-workers filled the cabin, attesting the point.

Douglas smiled at their spirit, despite everything. "Well, maybe *ye* could wait 'til we get back and hang 'em outside, laddie," he said.

After a few minutes, Flannigan sought Douglas out once more, speaking quietly. "I'm gonna need some help, James."

Douglas nodded agreement. "Aye, in a place as dangerous as this, one doctor's no' enough."

"Heidi was a brilliant surgeon, too, better than me in that regard, if I'm honest," said Flannigan. "I need to replace her by training someone else."

"Who'd ye have in mind?" asked Douglas.

Flannigan glanced over to where Natalie sat, looking tired and bruised. He nodded for Douglas to follow him as he approached her.

"How are you feelin', Natalie?" he asked.

"Oh, I'll live," she smiled wearily up at them, "thanks to all of you."

"Actually, most of the credit goes to Lieutenant Singh," said Douglas. "It was his idea which allowed us to pull you out of there and his extraordinary, if daredevil, flying that saved our lives just now."

"Tell him I owe him a..." she thought for a second, "whatever that Indian lager is, that he likes." She smiled again.

"Natalie," said Flannigan, kneeling down to sit with her, "I need to talk to you about something."

"Oh? This isn't about the mess my hair's in, is it?"

"Er, no," Flannigan chuckled and then frowned. "Since we—" he paused uncomfortably. "Since we *lost* Dr Schultz, I'm concerned that I may not be able to keep up with the medical needs of the crew – especially as we're in such a dangerous predicament."

Natalie nodded. "Are you going to give Justin extra training?" she asked.

"Yeah," he admitted. "The kid didn't wanna be a doctor but it looks like I'm gonna have to force the issue. Unfortunately, that's gonna take time – even though he's a great nurse and a great student. What I'm most concerned about is this: if something were to happen to me, it could leave everyone in a mess the next time we get an emergency. Hell, I might need a physician myself!"

"And emergencies have been a regular part of our daily routine just lately," Douglas added.

"Indeed," Flannigan agreed. "Now, I've been doing some digging through people's files over the last few days, while I've been feeling sorry for myself in sickbay," he added with chagrin. "There are one or two biologists among Doc Norris' team who have appropriate knowledge and I will be talking to them as soon as I can – trouble is though, they've no surgical experience to speak of. Maybe a few animal autopsies, but..." he shrugged.

"But?" asked Natalie, smelling a trap.

"Well, yeah," Flannigan acknowledged, busted. "I couldn't help noticing on your record that you have considerable experience with surgical procedures."

"Veterinary procedures!" Natalie exclaimed, wide eyed. "I've never treated a person!"

"Surely we're all just mammals," said Douglas, "and Ah'm sure Mother Sarah would tell you that we're all God's creatures, too."

"Absolutely," said Natalie, "and if you had a rabbit with a trichobezoar or a myopathic horse I'd be happy to render any assistance I could, but operating on *people*?"

"What can I say? I need all the help I can get and you're it!" Flannigan affirmed. "Look, I'm not talking about leaving you to sink or swim – I just need you to work with me. You have the closest skill set to what I need for a surgeon, but I'll have to train others, too. Will you help?"

Natalie put her head in her hands, exhaling loudly. "Of course I'll help," she said, quietly. "I suppose, if everyone is going to have to work at least two jobs, it will feel more like home, anyway." She gave Flannigan a sideways glance. "I hope your department has great insurance cover!"

"Don't sweat it, we should be safe from malpractice lawyers here," he replied with a wink. "I hope."

Douglas raised an eyebrow. "Clearly you haven't spent much time with Mr Burnstein. Anyway, Ah'll give you *doctors* some space to discuss the details."

He stood to leave and then changed his mind. "Natalie," he said, "Ah've been meaning to ask you about the skeleton of Audrey Jansen."

"Yes, Captain?"

Douglas frowned in puzzlement. "It's just that Arnold's skeleton was near the surface when we discovered him. If they died together, shouldn't they have been at the same..." he sought for the word, "same level? In the stone, Ah mean?"

"You're quite right, Captain," replied Natalie. "Technically they were. The mud stone buried them together, at the same time – the stratigraphy leaves us in no doubt about that. As the sediments were laid down, over the millions of years since their passing, the mud and sand turned to stone and that stone was subject to ground heave at some point. In fact that may very well be a process which is still ongoing, albeit geologically slowly, literally. In a nutshell, what we discovered was a stratigraphy canted over by about thirty degrees. The stone and soil, et cetera, we cleared to reach Audrey, was all laid down after whatever incident overtook them both. The stone and strata surrounding the remains of Captain Bessel were simply eroded off the top as the landscape changed."

"So it's certain we're only dealing with one incident? They definitely died together?" clarified Douglas.

"As certain as we can be. It's highly likely they were both laid down and stratified within a very short window. The fact that some of the bones were slightly disarticulated and mixed up makes it entirely possible they went together, perhaps even sharing the same fate."

Natalie's scientific interest in the puzzle left her feeling slightly guilty as she remembered these *long dead* individuals were actually the captain's friends; people he may well have been sharing a drink and a chat with, just a few weeks ago. "Sorry, Captain," she felt the need to add.

He smiled sadly at her. "Ah can understand the fascination, Natalie," he allowed. "It's a remarkable story. Ah'm just a little too close to it." He nodded to the doctors and made his way back to the shuttle's small bridge.

Lieutenant Sandip Singh was lost in a study of impossible perspective as he looked down upon the Earth. He loved this view of home from orbit, although of course, this Earth was not the home of his childhood. All the continents were just a little *off*, but there were certainly recognisable patterns. India was still thousands of miles south of the rest of Asia, but nowhere near as far from home as one of her sons. Despite the beauty and awe, a twinge of homesickness clutched at his heart – he missed Fang too and hoped she had been taken in by one of his cat-loving friends back at Canaveral.

He pulled away from his sorrows, deciding it was best to focus on just how lucky he was to see such things. What always amazed him was just how big a planet was. There was nowhere you could place yourself to adequately understand its size. From space they were just perfect circles of this colour or that, almost abstract. Of course, were he any closer, he would be down upon it, which would provide no perspective at all.

He decided his favourite view was from here, from orbit. Maybe it was the vibrant blues and greens, dusted with white caps and draped with clouds, all beautifully lit against the starscape beyond. Or perhaps it was the way the sphere's majestic curve disappeared just around the corner, forever, no matter how hard you chased it – truly a *god's-eye* view, though even this could not fully reveal the scale. After all, when a mountain becomes so small it can barely be singled out, what does one measure against?

Completely lost, Lieutenant Singh sighed in exquisite agony. Thoughts as far away as his home, he linked his hands behind his head and leaned back contentedly.

"Everything OK, Sandy?" asked Douglas.

Singh jumped, so markedly that playing cool was never an option.

Douglas chuckled. "Sorry, laddie, did Ah surprise ye?"

"I was away with the angels, Captain," the pilot replied ruefully, before a frown of concern crossed his face. "Is everyone OK back there?"

"Aye, nothing that won't mend and it's all thanks to you. Well done, Lieutenant – really." Douglas patted the younger officer companionably on the shoulder.

"We were lucky, sir."

"Well, we knew the plan was dangerous, but we were desperate," Douglas acknowledged. "All those people back there owe you their lives and that's a fact. Ah doubt that any of them would have survived that storm much longer without shelter or protection. But most importantly, *we made it*."

He took a long look out of the viewport before continuing. "We didnae get the chance to take this in when we arrived last week. Ah've absolute faith in you as a pilot, Sandy, never doubt that, but the speed we came in…" He shook his head, whistling softly. "Ah've got to admit Ah thought we'd had it. Ah cannae believe it was just last week."

"I know," Singh agreed, gesturing towards the Earth. "We were only heading *away* from her a fortnight ago – everything fine, just another day at the office."

"Aye, and the speed that hurricane came in, knocking everything sideways, was like an allegory for what happened next – and since," Douglas remarked, frowning. "That weather system really caught us with our trousers round our ankles today. We *must* get that satellite up here. Pity we haven't got it on board now, in fact."

They lapsed into a thoughtful, companionable silence, each lost in the view for a moment before Douglas continued. "Aye, there's nothing for it, we'll have to come back up here again."

Singh caught Douglas' reflection in the viewport. "Oh *no*," he replied, deadpan.

They both laughed, forcing their recent stress and fear to recede a little.

"It's beautiful – home but not home," remarked Douglas. "Maybe we should let others come up here with the satellite. Give someone else the chance to see these wonders, eh? What do ye think?"

Singh continued to laugh quietly. "With respect, Captain, I disagree!"

Chapter 15 | Redemption and Sacrifice

Baines felt nervous and self-conscious before the hundred or more souls in the embarkation lounge, now hastily rearranged to double as a courtroom. Up on the dais she sat behind the 'bench'.

At the 'bar', to her front and right sat Liz Barton-Frehly; front and left, Captain Elvis Percival Gleeson.

Lloyd sat to Barton-Frehly's left, looking disgruntled. When offered legal aid, he had strenuously protested, preferring to represent himself rather than trust anyone else to get it right. In the end, Douglas had insisted he accept counsel, to ensure the trial was conducted as fairly as possible. After all, *The People* were watching.

Baines found Lloyd's attitude comforting in a way. Repentant Lloyd was a wholly unholy thing – just another anomaly on a ship already turned upside-down.

The captain's forced exile in orbit had delayed the trial by a couple of days, but now it was upon them, Baines could see that all involved looked uncomfortable: Patel, Fellows, Douglas, Gleeson; *me*, she thought. The only people who did not appear overly concerned, irritatingly, were the Defence.

Barton-Frehly was obviously used to this sort of thing, although the circumstances and the surroundings might have given her pause. Lloyd, on the other hand, simply wore his usual look of annoyance – appearing more irritated than afraid. This in turn annoyed Baines. *He could at least have the decency to look more nervous than I feel,* she thought. *Who's on trial here, for goodness sakes?*

She sighed. She was doing a lot of that this morning, and could not help wondering if they could really do this. She felt like they were just making stuff up. *Still, there's no backing out now,* she thought. *So I might as well get the show on the road.*

It was perhaps unsurprising that NASA neglected to furnish the *New World* with a gavel, so Baines had improvised by borrowing a two and a half pound lump hammer and some steel plate from the construction department.

She struck the plate twice, wincing guiltily at the loud *clack*. Concerned for the safety of the electronics within the podium, she checked under the plate, making a mental note to bring the hammer down more gently next time.

The Sarge, on cue shouted, "ORDER!" His usual way of bringing about order was to shout, 'SHUT UP!' or '*SHAT IT!*' in his salt-of-the-earth cockney accent. A sergeant-at-law he was not and Baines was secretly amused by the veteran's attempt at formality.

She allowed a few moments more for the gathering to calm completely, before asking Gleeson to set out the case for the prosecution.

Gleeson, for his part, had been even less enthusiastic about his involvement than the others drafted. His education in the law came as something of a surprise to everyone. His was an old legal family, controlling a substantial and longstanding practice down under. His father had pressured him into the University of Law, where Gleeson achieved a good degree and looked all set for a successful career within the firm. He stuck it out for another two years, but having barely finished his training contract, he left – practically running away – to join the army and escape both his father, and the law.

In the military he learned his true vocation and found that he really loved 'blowing stuff up'. Subsequently, he re-trained, re-qualified and the rest should have been history. Unfortunately, recent events seemed to have placed *the rest* millions of years in his future.

When asked to perform the task of lead prosecutor, Gleeson had firstly refused, railing against the imposition with accompanying hand gestures. "There are three types of people in the law: the ones looking for wealth," he had stated, holding up his pinkie, "the ones looking for justice," holding up his third finger, "and the ones looking for the exit!" This last was illustrated quite pointedly with his second finger and might even have been mistaken for a middle finger gesture.

"If you need to blow a hole through a rockface, I'm your man. If you need to legislate against a blow-hole, I'm gone! I never told anybody I was even trained in law! Bladdy computers! Everything you've ever achieved held on record, waiting to be trotted out and used against you in a court of law!"

Despite Lloyd's and Gleeson's reluctance to follow procedure, Captain Douglas had been insistent that all possible steps be taken to make sure the trial was carried out as fairly and professionally as possible, considering their circumstances. Gleeson and Barton-Frehly were the only qualified people on board with direct legal experience, so there was little choice in who the advocates should be – especially in the face of the captain's strenuous *request*. Eventually Gleeson had calmed down, agreeing to assist with the caveat – no pun intended – that he would *not* defend 'that dunny-brained Pommy rooter who landed us here!'

Gleeson rose to stand behind his desk. He shuffled his notes and cleared his throat in preparation for his opening statement. "The counsel for the prosecution intends to prove, beyond reasonable doubt, that on the 31st of July AD2112, Lieutenant Geoffrey Lloyd did knowingly assist and take part in a terrorist attack upon the USS *New World*. This attack led directly to the death of Crewman Mario Baccini, who was killed by a bomb placed within the casing of the wormhole drive itself, while carrying out his duties.

"Lieutenant Lloyd has already confessed to planting this bomb. He used his position—"

A protracted "*Oooh*" washed over the public gallery in gentle waves, interrupting him.

"Order," said Baines, moderately. "Please continue, Captain Gleeson."

Gleeson nodded. "He used his position as a senior officer within the Mars fleet to kill and cause destruction to internationally held property. Further charges include: Collusion with a terrorist organisation with intent to cause harm to the state, to property, and to endanger life; conspiracy with a murderer and saboteur, known to the defendant, upon this ship;

and lastly, attempting to pervert the course of justice by falsely accusing another officer of the fleet while withholding information."

He set his notes aside, referring to his tablet before adding, "The Prosecution intends to indict, primarily, for murder."

Gleeson sat.

"Thank you, Captain Gleeson," said Baines. "Mrs Barton-Frehly, I will now hear your opening remarks for the Defence, please."

Barton-Frehly rose to address the court. "Thank you, Your Honour, lady and gentlemen of the jury. The Defence intends to prove that, with regards to the intentions of the terrorist organisation, Lieutenant Geoffrey Lloyd was not in possession of the full facts. We also intend to prove that there was certainly never any intention to commit murder. My client admits to the act of sabotage and intentionally damaging the wormhole drive, for which he is truly repentant—" Uproar and catcalls cut across the rest of her statement.

Baines dropped the lump hammer again but nothing short of smashing the podium would have regained the crowd's attention at that point. She gestured to The Sarge.

"SHUT UP!" he bellowed.

Baines was comforted by Jackson's return to his roots, hoping that other things would soon return to some sort of normality after the trial, too. However, even The Sarge was not completely successful this time and his order was merely followed by a disgruntled quiet*ish*.

Baines addressed the public gallery once a little decorum had been restored. "I understand that feelings are running high, given our predicament and what has happened to us, but I must insist that both Prosecution *and* Defence be given a fair hearing. Please continue, Mrs Barton-Frehly."

"Thank you, Your Honour," replied the lawyer. "The defendant admits to causing the explosion that damaged the wormhole drive—"

"*Damaged?*" someone shouted from the crowd in anger and disbelief. "There's nothing left of it!"

Baines used her 'gavel on steroids' once more to call for quiet.

Barton-Frehly continued patiently, "*damaged* the wormhole drive, but his belief at the time of the offence was that the area would be clear of all personnel. Obviously, no one could have foreseen the unfortunate turn of events which was to follow. There was no *mens rea*, no intention to cause physical harm to any person or persons. As the sabotage was designed to be localised, my client did not expect the main ship to be placed in danger and certainly had no intention of harming the crew. We respectfully request that the court consider the alternative charges of criminal damage and reckless endangerment." Barton-Frehly sat down as the public gallery blew up.

It took a little while to restore some semblance of decorum. Eventually, Gleeson rose once more to address the court.

Baines recognised the Defence, inviting him to speak.

The Australian turned to his learned colleague, tasking her with a couple of questions. "What evidence have you been *looking* at? Are your eyes painted on?"

The public gallery roared with delight.

Baines closed her eyes, kneading her brow. When the selection of Gleeson to this role had first been speculated, she had voiced some concerns. Now, her misgivings had scored a direct hit and she knew this was going to be a very long day.

Not everyone attended the trial. Dr Aabid Hussain walked among the parked lorries in the Pod vehicle pool and cargo bay. He reached underneath one of the eight-wheelers to confirm his readings. As a chemist working under Jim Miller, he was well qualified to bring any chemical anomalies to the attention of the 'powers that be'.

He nodded, satisfied. Just one more task to undertake and he would be able to bring this to the attention of Commander Baines at an opportune moment – a time he hoped would be sooner, rather than later.

The Defence's strategy did not succeed and Lloyd entered a plea of 'not guilty' to murder. The Prosecution called a number of professional witnesses, each describing the effects of the incident, the crime scenes' evidence and the trail which subsequently led to Lieutenant Lloyd's arrest, escape and ultimate re-arrest.

After a short recess, it was time to call the witnesses for the Defence. Surprisingly, there were three. However, Barton-Frehly decided that only one should give evidence in court.

Lieutenant Dave Flannigan, in his capacity as ship's doctor, gave evidence stating that three separate attacks, possibly even attempts on Lloyd's life, had occurred since the bombing. He also attested to the varying degrees of injury Lloyd sustained on each occasion.

"The first occurred as the defendant attempted to flee the ship in a lifeboat that he didn't quite reach," he began.

"Objection," said Barton-Frehly, standing.

"Your reason for objecting to your own witness, Mrs Barton-Frehly?" asked Baines.

"The use of the term 'flee the ship' is entirely derogatory, intended to cast my client in a negative light. As we have already stated, my client had no reason to suspect that the ship would be in any danger from his act of sabotage. I request that the court treats this witness as hostile and strikes that particular comment from the record, Your Honour."

"Quiet, in the public gallery!" Baines snapped, before the hubbub could escalate once more. "I think, Mrs Barton-Frehly, that having planted a bomb on the ship, which was far more powerful than his mission required – as demonstrated by his own confession – we can assume that 'fleeing' was *exactly* what your client was about. Overruled!"

Baines gestured for Flannigan to resume his testimony.

"The second injury the defendant sustained came from the severe beating he received from Dr Schultz—"

This announcement actually drew a cheer from the gallery.

Flannigan waited patiently for the noise and jeering to subside before continuing, "The third injury, also inflicted by Dr Schultz, was almost certainly an attempt on Lieutenant Lloyd's life, whilst he was in a medically induced coma."

The public erupted into further applause, some even going so far as to give a standing ovation.

Flannigan tried his best to be impartial, pointing out that the terrorists themselves were the ones who tried to kill Lloyd, but the mood of the people marooned was not sympathetic.

The next man willing to give evidence on Lloyd's behalf was actually the brother of his unintended victim, Georgio Baccini. Georgio, obsessing about messages from *the beyond*, had visited Beck Mawar daily ever since her first revelation. The Defence counsel suspected this might not go over too well in court, graciously refusing his very earnest offer of help and forgiveness.

The only other person willing to stand up and discuss the character of Lieutenant Lloyd, as it pertained to the character of all of mankind within a framework of existentialism, was Del Bond, the philosopher. Counsel for the Defence decided that a character witness from Del Bond might provoke a riot, carrying the further possibility that neither man would survive long enough to hear the jury's verdict.

After very brief closing speeches from both counsels, largely reiterating the opening statements, the jury retired to discuss the evidence they had heard.

Baines suspected that the worst was yet to come. While attempting to quiet her nerves privately in her quarters, she was passed a request from the jury for her assistance on a point of procedure. She acknowledged the message wearily. The jury were in session in the bridge meeting room and as she made her way to them, she could not help feeling slightly annoyed that her brief respite had been interrupted. "A real judge would have them running to her," she muttered moodily.

As she walked through the ship, Barton-Frehly's words came back to her – '*No one could have foreseen the unfortunate turn of events which was to follow*'. She remembered saying more or less the same thing to the captain about a week ago and that conversation, almost disregarded at the time, haunted her now. "This story began a hundred million years ago and yet that artefact is still to be laid in the earth. It might even be me who discards it!"

She arrived on the bridge with a sense of almost indestructible inevitability weighing her down. At this moment she and the jury held the fate of one man completely in their hands, but did that really matter? Whatever she, or they, did next, somehow it had already happened.

"Thank you for coming, Jill." Sarah cut through her thoughts. "You look like you're carrying the whole world on your shoulders."

Baines sat tiredly. "Let's just say time's arrow seems a little less predictable than it once did. Perhaps you could put in a word for a few repairs with the great fletcher in the sky?"

Sarah frowned in puzzlement.

"Forgive me, Sarah," Baines explained. "I get a little grouchy when I'm beat."

"You did well, Jill," said Douglas. "That could have degenerated into a complete circus out there."

"And it would have," Baines noted, "if we'd let the clowns take the stand."

Patel chuckled. "You don't think Mr Bond's testimony would have helped proceedings then?"

"Who *knows* how that could have ended," replied Baines, honestly.

"Look, Jill," Douglas cut to the chase, "when we give the verdict out there, we need to know how severely you intend to sentence him."

Baines looked taken aback. "Is this ethical?"

The council and pressed jury looked uncomfortable. Eventually, Douglas shrugged. "No," he admitted simply, "probably not. It's just that *if* we find him guilty—"

"*If?*"

"—then, will that mean the death sentence? We really don't want that, Jill. We can't justify it."

"So, just to be clear, James, you would pronounce him innocent to avoid that judgement?"

The triumvirate eyed one another awkwardly. Douglas shrugged again. "Possibly," he said.

Baines studied him for a moment. "And you'd watch our whole society, such as it is, tear itself apart, all to save that man's life – the man who did this to us?"

"We're not savages, Jill," said Sarah.

"And we should be better than the man we are sentencing," added Patel.

Baines raised her eyebrows, staring at Douglas, waiting for his two penn'orth.

The captain looked extremely uncomfortable but did not speak.

"And you think we can afford this kind of sentiment?" asked Baines. "All one hundred of us? One hundred million years from home, with no one but ourselves to rely on? You don't think the people out there – the people who are *trusting* us to make the right decision, by the way – will be disgusted if he simply walks away? And walks to where, incidentally?"

No one answered, so she continued. "You see, we've had this conversation before, but you still haven't given me any answers, let alone options!" She addressed her last question to the captain directly, "If I let him go what do you really think will happen, James?"

"Ah'm damned if Ah know," Douglas acknowledged irritably, "but *execution*?"

"It would be kinder than exile," answered Baines.

"Jill—" said Douglas.

"No, James," Baines cut him off. "I understand the dilemma and the weight of conscience, I really do, but we are supposed to be representing a system of justice here – and justice for all, not just Lloyd. We are behaving like some kind of secret cabal, making deals, trying to obtain outcomes without risk to ourselves." She breathed heavily, looking angry now.

"I suggest that no one, right now, feels the weight of this more than I do, but I agreed to take on this role so that the council wouldn't have to. So that any blame down the line wouldn't affect *your* ability to rule." She stood, facing the triumvirate across the conference table. "Speaking not as commander of this ship, but as the judge *you* made me, I *instruct* you to carry out your duty and deliver your verdict. Your verdict should, furthermore, be based on the weight of evidence you have heard, without fear or favour! I will carry out the duty you have asked of me, to the best of my ability."

She looked each of the three councillors in the eye, one at a time. "You *will* either trust me or replace me. I'll be in my quarters. Please let me know when you have either a decision or a verdict."

Sarah and Satnam looked like they had received a smack in the face.

Douglas stared for a while and then smiled slowly, not with humour, but with pride. "Ah apologise, Your Honour," he said, with a glint in his eye. "You'll have our verdict presently. And Jill," Douglas stood, "if anything ever happens to me, Ah'll have no worries about leaving this mission in your hands." He saluted her.

Events had left Baines a little at sea, but she saluted the captain and strode from the room without another word.

The court resumed its session a little under two hours later. Baines was really feeling the burden of judgement now. She looked at the jury of three and cleared her throat to speak. "Mr Foreman, have you reached a verdict?"

Douglas stood. "We have, Your Honour."

"And was that verdict unanimous?"

"No, Your Honour – two to one in favour."

"Very well. In a case as serious as this one, I would prefer a unanimous verdict before proceeding with sentencing. I suspect your difficulty stems from the fact that, although there seems virtually no doubt Lieutenant Lloyd committed this terrible act, there is little direct evidence that he intended to *murder* Crewman Mario Baccini. If I permitted a charge of manslaughter, would that enable you to draw a concurrence?"

Douglas, Fellows and Patel huddled for a few moments.

While they discussed this new direction, Lloyd's situation seemed to finally bear down on him. Already prepared for the worst, this development may have created an opportunity for a lighter sentence, but looking at the attitude of the crowd – the mob – he doubted it. This was going to be bad, and with that realisation came a strange kind of peace.

Always a scornful man teetering on the edge of anger, his last breath seemed to expel it all as he arrived at a second realisation; acceptance was all he had left. *Maybe this is what dying will feel like*, he thought. *I know I've done terrible things, things I can't put right – being a military officer in a position of trust only makes my crime all the more damning. Maybe a quick, humane end would be for the best? Maybe the only thing I can do for the people I have stranded here is give them a sense of justice, or at least revenge?*

Captain Douglas stood once more and all Lloyd's thoughts seemed to jam, his breath caught and his stomach lurched. It was time.

"Your Honour, we can now give a unanimous verdict," he pronounced.

Baines nodded. "Very good. Mr Foreman, for the crime of *murder*, do you find Lieutenant Geoffrey Lloyd guilty or not guilty?" she asked.

"Not guilty," Douglas stated clearly.

A second, much louder "*OOOH!*" gusted through the public gallery.

Baines brought the hammer down again for quiet. "For the crime of *manslaughter*, do you find Lieutenant Geoffrey Lloyd guilty or not guilty?"

There was absolute silence as Douglas swallowed, looking Lloyd in the eye. "Guilty."

A slow clap came from somewhere near the back of the tiered seats, but was soon overpowered as people began shouting, "*Not enough!*"

However, before the passengers' outrage could really get going, Baines stood, shouting, "SILENCE!" She glared at what she could not help feeling was more *audience* than *concerned populace*. "This is not a game! This is not to entertain *you*! One more word or sound from the gallery and I will have you *all* removed! Is that *clear*?" The build up to this moment had stripped all her usual affability and she stood red-in-the-face furious. Few people had ever seen this side of her and silence fell immediately.

"Lieutenant Lloyd," she continued, retaking her seat. Her voice, measured once more, filled the silence following her outburst. "You have heard the verdict of the jury. Before I pass sentence, do you or your counsel wish to offer any words of mitigation?"

"Hah! Mitigation!" Hank Burnstein Snr called out scornfully.

Baines went puce. "Sergeant Jackson," she bellowed. "Remove that man immediately!"

"Hey, who the hell d' you think you are, lady?" Burnstein bawled across the cavernous room as the soldiers grabbed him.

Baines' temper was scathing as she quietly, but within the hearing of everyone, snarled, "One more *syllable* out of you, Burnstein, and it'll be the brig again, *damn you*! And next stop after that will be outside with the dinosaurs – so bite your lip!"

Burnstein was manhandled away, stunned and speechless, as Baines turned back to the Defence. "I apologise for the disruption, Lieutenant Lloyd. Do you or your counsel wish to speak?" she asked with cold calm.

Liz Barton-Frehly made to stand but Lloyd gently pushed her back down, standing himself. "I wish to speak, Your Honour, please," he stated, evenly.

Baines nodded. "Please," she invited.

Lloyd took a deep breath. "I didn't want this trial," he said, an unusual introduction for mitigation, but everyone listened in silence. "The reason I didn't want it was because it was not necessary. I understand why the council needed a show of fairness and justice for you all, so that this little society can hold together. If I can help with this last act, then I am content. However, the trial was not necessary because I *am* guilty of killing that young man, Mario Baccini, and whether I intended to or not is beside the point now.

"My actions have led us all to the predicament in which we now find ourselves. I was selfish.

"I could offer in mitigation all kinds of excuses for my behaviour. My failures, the way everything has always seemed to go wrong for me, but what would be the point? If things had gone as I intended, the ship would have stalled, I would have escaped, been paid a king's ransom and what? Lived happily ever after?" He left the question hanging for a moment.

"Perhaps... I don't know. All I do know is that my choices led to the death of a very special, very clever young man and irrevocably hurt his twin brother." He laughed quietly, a curious mixture of ruefulness and utter despair.

"A twin brother, who has not only found the capacity to forgive me for the terrible mistake I made, but who was also willing to stand up in this court to ask for clemency on my behalf!" He wiped a shaking hand down his face to remove perspiration and relieve some of his nervous exhaustion. His face carried a look of abject disgust, but this time, it was all directed inwards.

"There are three things I would like to say," he continued. "The first is that, whatever punishment you feel I deserve, I will bear without complaint. I deserve it and," he looked Baines in the eye, pointedly, "you should not feel guilty for passing your judgement. The guilt is mine and mine alone.

"The second thing I would like to say is actually a request. I would beg of the court that I be allowed to visit the grave of Lieutenant Audrey Jansen before my sentence is carried out. In truth my time with her is pretty much the only thing that I *don't* regret, now, at the end.

"Thirdly, I simply wish to say to all of you here, for everything I have done and everything I have caused to happen, I'm sorry."

He sat and no one said anything for a long, long moment.

Eventually Baines straightened in her seat, taking a deep breath. She could not bring herself to look at Douglas or the jury, or anyone but Lloyd. For that instant, it was as if they were alone. *Damn the man*, she thought. *That's just about the best speech he could have made and just about the last thing I needed to hear right now.*

She nodded to The Sarge who asked the prisoner to stand.

"Lieutenant Geoffrey Lloyd, you have been found guilty of the manslaughter of Crewman Mario Baccini.

"We are living through very exceptional circumstances here, in every way. For our society to function we must have rules and punishment for breaking them, and there can be no more serious offence than the unlawful killing of another.

"Although you may not have intended to cause the death of Mario Baccini, you deliberately manufactured a situation where such a thing was possible, with no regard for anyone or anything other than your own agenda and enrichment through criminal activity.

"But as I said, these are times without parallel and our options for punishment, due to our situation, are limited. It seems that I can only choose between exile, which will almost certainly mean your death, execution, which many here believe you deserve, or imprisonment, which we can ill afford.

"You have compounded one bad situation on top of another with your actions. However, we need absolutely every person we have in this time, in this world, and throwing an experienced engineer away will not help our circumstances. However, you *are* the reason we're all here and the reason Mario is not."

She took several steadying breaths, staring down at Lloyd. Whatever she did now was going to upset someone, so she chose what she hoped would prove the most useful and least damaging course for the future.

"We are all balancing on a knife edge," she continued. "Any action against the safety of our people must be followed up with swift retribution or *we will not survive!*" She tapped her finger on the bench in time, emphasising each word. "Sometimes, that may well mean an eye for an eye, or a tooth for tooth. We cannot afford leniency or weakness when we are fighting for our very existence, every day. Our survival will only be possible if we can trust one another and laws are an important part of that trust.

"Some are saying that the conditions in which we must now live should dictate our responses, and that a premeditated criminal act leading to the death of another should also carry the sentence of death – the difference between premeditated unlawful killing and murder being little more than semantic. *Your* actions, Lieutenant Lloyd, have gone still further beyond this crime, by starting a chain of events which have led to the deaths of others and, it's possible, may even lead to the very end of human life altogether!

"Less than two centuries ago, back in our own time, you would have simply been court-martialled and shot for what you have done!"

Lloyd closed his eyes and lowered his head. The room was absolutely silent now.

"However, as I have already stated, these are completely unprecedented times. From the evidence we have heard here today and from the words of remorse out of your own mouth, I don't believe it was your *intention* to kill Mario Baccini, or indeed cause the level of damage which came from your actions, but this most certainly does not exonerate you." She paused to let her meaning sink in.

"So the sentence will be as follows: You will be stripped of your rank, and all the privileges thereof, with immediate effect. You will serve six months in the brig, with the possibility of one short reprieve to visit the grave of Lieutenant Jansen, at Captain Douglas' pleasure and discretion. Lieutenant Jansen was a fine officer and should be mourned by *all* who knew her.

"In your time alone, I hope you will consider your future as part of this crew, as part of this society. I hope you will also consider all of the things you can do to earn the life that has been given back to you. Sergeant Jackson, take him down."

As Lloyd was led across the floor, he paused in front of the bench, giving Baines a simple nod. It was a salute, it was a thank you, it was an apology; it was all that could not be said.

Baines waited for the excitement to quiet before rising one final time to speak. "If you would all remain seated, please, Captain Douglas has an important announcement to make."

She stood behind 'the bench', bowed to the court and walked to the side of the stage, stepping down with relief. Douglas passed her on his way to the front of the auditorium, giving her just the ghost of a wink.

Baines moved away from the group, finding a quiet place to lean against a wall, out of the way. She heaved a huge, shuddering sigh as she let some of the tension of the last few days escape. Her legs suddenly felt likely to give way, so she bent her knees, keeping her back straight against the wall. The run up to the trial and the anxiety of the event had weighed more heavily than she realised, but for better or worse, it was over now and there was nothing else to do but pray she had made the right call and would never have to do anything like it ever again.

Mother Sarah approached her. The priest did not speak, but merely knelt to give the commander's hand a companionable squeeze. After sharing a brief look of understanding with the younger woman, she returned to her seat next to Patel, who also looked towards Baines. Catching her eye, he too nodded his approval.

An undercurrent of low murmuring struck up as Douglas made his way to the podium. The renewed disquiet seemed to flutter among the tiered seats like nervous birds in a dovecote. Today had already proved full of drama and captain's announcements were rare, and often serious.

He looked around, taking in the faces of the people for whom he was now responsible. "Ah know it's been a fairly harrowing day for us all, but whilst we're together there's something else you should know."

Right, now for some more bad news, he thought to himself, taking a deep breath. "We've recently been given compelling testimony which suggests that we have a small team of terrorist insurgents among us."

A gale of incoherent chatter tore through the passengers. Douglas understood their concern well enough and allowed a few moments for the first wave of shock to dissipate before proceeding. He raised his hands for calm and the crowd quieted quickly.

"It seems there was a plan in place to hijack the *New World*, rather than destroy it," he admitted.

The grumbling outrage of over a hundred people resumed immediately and Douglas waved his hands once more, waiting for it to ebb. Eventually a brittle silence returned, everyone leaning forward to hear more clearly.

"We know, or suspect, there may be as many as a dozen people potentially still working with Dr Schultz to take our ship away from us. We don't know whether they wanted to take hostages after their attack, or whether it was simply the ship they were after. We *do* know Schultz wasn't alone. Indeed, had it not been for Lieutenant Lloyd's eventual assistance, we might never have realised the full extent of the danger we're in, even now – at least, not until it was too late."

Uproar forced him to stop again, as angry voices railed once more against the leniency the prisoner had received. Clearly these people, stranded in a nightmare world 100 million years away from their friends and families, considered Lloyd's change of heart rather too little too late.

He waited once more for the noise to abate before continuing, "Please try and stay calm. Ah can understand your anger but you *need* to hear this."

Douglas took a moment to decide how best to play things. He could feel the crowd's anger, but he could not spare them this knowledge – all their lives might depend upon it, so he pressed on. "Whatever their agenda or plan was, must surely be irrelevant now. As far as we know, none of these people have yet raised a hand against us or the ship. Now, Ah'm not expecting anyone to stand up and confess here, but surely we can agree that we are all in this together from here onwards. Ah speak to the people who are part of this insurgency group directly now: Whatever your intentions were, this is a chance for a clean slate – for all of us to simply work together and get on with our lives. Our circumstances are uniquely difficult and so Ah ask ye, we all ask ye, to be a part of this family now. We are the only human beings alive in the universe – what can we *possibly* have to fight about?!"

Despite expecting it, Douglas was saddened by what happened next. The suspicion he feared rolled through the crowd like a Mexican wave, as one face turned to another in doubt.

"Please, everyone!" Douglas raised his voice. "The last thing we need now is to be casting suspicion and blame around randomly, especially without proof! Division itself will surely bring us down if we give in to that. As far as we can tell, there is no longer any reason for these people to act against us. We are *so* far removed from the world of politics, wealth, greed or religious intolerance now – there's nothing left but us. This is the shocking truth: we are *all* we have!

"Although our physicists will not give up on trying to find a way home, we must build a *new* home right here.

"Now, this is important. The reasons we've brought this out into the light are manifold. Firstly, Ah want the insurgents to know that *we* know you're here now, and we'll be watching.

"Secondly, and more importantly, we implore anyone associated with this terrorist movement to simply realise that this is our reality now, this is our new world, and we must surely work together if we are to keep it and survive.

"Thirdly, no one can defend against something of which they are ignorant. So, just in case we can't make these people see sense, it is vital that everyone is aware of the situation. We must all be on our guard for anything suspicious.

"Lastly, there's a chance some or any of you may witness something. Ah must stress here, that keeping your wits about you, does not mean throwing around accusations or attacking your fellows! If you have any suspicions at all, or witness anything which seems odd, report it to either Major White or Sergeant Jackson, quickly and *quietly*.

"Remember, most of the people on this ship have nothing to do with this conspiracy, so don't lose heart! Ah'm hopeful the people we are talking about – to – will accept this situation and simply become, what they have so far only seemed to be, valued comrades and members of our tiny family of humanity. Let me repeat, none of these people have done anything wrong, as far as we know, *yet*."

Only silence greeted Douglas' words.

"Right, so, assuming no one wants to own up," he asked, half joking, half hoping, "then that's all, thank you." He turned away from the podium and stepped down from the small stage. Baines, Patel and Fellows fell in behind as he bade them follow him back to the bridge.

The four of them sat in the meeting room as Mary dispensed tea and coffee. Baines was utterly drained.

Douglas gave her a warm but appraising look. "Was it always your intention to sentence Lloyd the way you did, Jill, throwing us the lifeline of manslaughter?" he asked.

Baines placed her elbow on the table, supporting her head wearily with her right hand. "I'm sure it would be improper for me to answer that question, Captain," she answered with just a twinkle of usual humour.

"Quite right," agreed Douglas.

"I would have done whatever I had to do and expected no less from the jury," she added, hoarsely. She relaxed a little. "But I have spent the last few days trying to find an answer, any answer which might at least partially serve all ends, and serve our future. Six months was not nearly enough for the things he's done and caused to happen, but we're simply not in a position where we can incarcerate him for years. I just hope it's long enough to take the edge off the bloodlust and the hatred. We've lost enough. As long as Lloyd plays the part I hope he will, we may all just get through this incident without too many scars."

"You did a remarkable job," admitted Patel. "Not just out there, but in here too. You shamed us and you were right to do so." He looked to his co-councillors. "It's a lesson we should never forget."

"Luckily," said Douglas, stretching languidly as the tension ebbed from his body, "Ah've got a first officer who keeps me honest."

They all smiled at that.

"Your courage saved a man's life today, Jill," Sarah added. "The compromise you struck may have saved our society from tearing itself apart, before it even had chance to get started, too. Hopefully, we can *all* move forward now, without a stain on our consciences. Well done, Jill. Really, well done."

"As long as Lloyd doesn't let me down," said Baines, a shadow of concern in her already dark eyes.

"Do you know," Douglas remarked, brightly, "Ah don't think he will. Ah'm taking a team out to *Fossil Rock* tomorrow in the hope of salvaging the wreckage of our equipment. Ah don't know if we'll find anything, but we have to try. Ah'll take Lloyd with us so that he can say his goodbyes – we're not risking the trip twice. Ah've decided to take the remains of Arnold back there, too."

A flicker of sadness crossed his face. "Captain Arnold Bessel and Lieutenant Audrey Jansen," he murmured. "They've been together so long, Ah cannae bring myself to separate them now. It seems wrong." He turned to the priest. "Maybe you would come with us and say a few words, Sarah?"

"I'd be happy to, James. I haven't been outside the ship since we boarded at Canaveral. It would do me no harm to take in a little fresh air."

"Georgio wants to come as well," said Douglas. "Obviously, when Ah said yes, Ah didn't know that Lloyd would be coming with us. Ah'll have to warn him and see what he says. As we've promised Lloyd, officially, that he can visit her grave, it would be a poor show to renege now. Apparently, Georgio and Mario both knew Audrey too. Ah didnae realise until all this. It promises to be an interesting little trip," he concluded sardonically.

They finished their drinks and turned in for the night, all spent, after an emotionally exhausting day; a day which, just possibly, had not turned out too badly in the end.

The giant spaceship dominated the clearing, despite the only natural illumination coming from a quarter moon. Through the darkness, hundreds of windows twinkled with the light of controlled electricity, a force never before seen on this world.

The eyes of the night watched the ship. One pair in particular studied the vessel, patiently waiting at the edge of the clearing – intelligent eyes, blue eyes.

Their patience was rewarded presently, as a white light began flashing rhythmically, sending very deliberate, syncopated patterns out into the night. One creature alone in the entire outside world was able to decipher this complex message represented in light, and understand its meaning.

Dr Heidi Schultz waited for the Morse code to cease before kneeling to ignite the small fire she had prepared earlier. She came to the same spot at the same time each night, but tonight was different. Tonight there was a message.

She could not risk sending a return, in case it was spotted by the wrong people. Whether understood or not, it would advertise her presence. She waited for the fire to establish itself before pouring stolen disinfectant onto the flames. This action was not to douse them, but to add the boric acid the chemical contained to the tiny conflagration.

The flames flared bright green as Schultz ran away through the forest, finding her way using infrared goggles, also lifted from the ship's stores. Her message, a completely oblique will-o'-the-wisp to all but the one for whom it was intended, was received.

She continued to run all the way around the *New World*, to the opposite side of the clearing from her little fire. The green tinge had not lasted long, the fire itself burning out some minutes later. She waited in the darkness. Once satisfied that no response would come from her enemies, she used the topography for cover where possible, making her way toward the ship. The *New World* had capsized slightly during the storm and she was able to find a tuck underneath the port side. Now all she had to do was wait for the appointed hour.

Morning brought the promise of a fresh, sunny day. Strapped into the passenger seats aboard the shuttle, a small team of nine waited to depart for *Fossil Rock*. Dr Natalie Pearson, Mother Sarah Fellows and Georgio Baccini fidgeted impatiently. The red-haired Australian construction worker, whose name, rather surprisingly but almost inevitably, turned out to be Bluey, scanned listlessly through an inventory of missing items on his tablet. Geoff Lloyd sat subdued, under the watchful and completely expressionless gazes of The Sarge and three other security personnel.

Douglas and Singh ran final pre-flight checks on the shuttle's small bridge, bringing the total complement to eleven. The 'birdwatchers' were armed and ready, waiting for the bay doors to open.

The mood was sombre and Singh resisted the urge to ask the Captain to make the usual announcements. The launch cycle was significantly shorter in atmosphere. Without need to decompress the shuttle bay, the large doors opened directly, flooding the chamber with bright sunlight. Even so, Natalie continued to feel stifled by the doldrums radiating from the crew. She hoped their humour would lighten once they took flight, to see again the majesty of the world outside.

The little ship left its berth slowly, gently turning towards their destination. Once the *New World* was safely behind them, the pilot opened up the engines and they accelerated rapidly away, but the atmosphere pervading the group stayed with them. However, a question had been niggling at Natalie for a little while, so she attempted to strike up a conversation, hoping to brighten the journey.

"Bluey? Why do they call you 'Bluey'?"

"S'me name," the Australian replied unhelpfully, not looking up from his tablet.

"Yes, I see that, but why not – I don't know – 'Red', perhaps?"

The Australian looked completely blank. "Why would they call me that?" he asked, puzzled.

Natalie felt her face warm and knew it had flushed as red as Bluey's mop of hair. "Erm, your hair?" she tried, squirming awkwardly.

Bluey continued to stare blankly back at her. "Why would anybody want to call *me* Red?" he asked again.

Feeling a little tongue-tied, Natalie fervently wished she had kept her mouth shut. This was not the trench she had expected to find herself in today. Unwilling to place further trust in words, she merely gave an embarrassed shrug.

"Me brother's called Red. That would just confuse everybody," stated Bluey, ending all debate.

Natalie's eyebrows shot up. "Of course, how silly of me," she acknowledged, reversing out of the conversation. Fortunately, she only had to endure the awkward silence for a few more moments. To her immense relief they were soon hovering over *Fossil Rock* once more.

The soldiers descended first, to secure the area. In the movies, this usually meant jumping out of some kind of vehicle, draped with machine guns, spinning around and loudly declaring, 'The area's secured!' Invariably this happens mere moments before an attack is launched from around a corner which turns out not to have been.

Natalie hoped the real world would yield a little more attention to detail, whilst praying their security team was not salted with 'red shirts'. Luckily, The Sarge was first on the ground. There could be no guarantees, but she had learned to trust him. In fact, lately she began to feel strangely drawn to the rugged, no nonsense solider. Perhaps it was because he had saved her life, perhaps more. She forced herself to focus on the site below.

The forest canopy had intruded much further into the clearing during their previous missions, making landing unnecessarily risky. However, the storm had flattened many of the trees surrounding the small glade, so many in fact that once sure the coast was clear of predators, Lieutenant Singh confirmed that he could now land.

The Sarge gave the thumbs-up and Singh brought the little ship down onto a soft bed of storm-smashed vegetation – for the very first time, directly onto prehistoric soil.

Bluey and Natalie set to work immediately, searching for their lost equipment. Memories of the hurricane were very much centre and forward in their minds, as they were for everyone returning to the *locus in quo*. Their terrifying brush with one of Mother Nature's most violent tantrums had certainly left its mark on the survivors, as it had on the ground. Even the indestructible Sarge still had an angry bruise on his cheek from a boot in the face received during their rescue. The feeling was unsettling, even for first-time visitors.

Natalie stared balefully at the tree trunk she had held onto throughout the storm. In a very real sense, it had saved her life. The Sarge, keeping an eye on everyone, noticed her unease and stepped over, placing a comforting hand at her elbow.

"Are you thinking we owe that tree?" he asked, ruefully.

"How did you guess?"

"Oh, it crossed my mind."

Natalie turned to him. "I never thanked you for saving my life either, did I? Twice, in fact. I'm sorry. Thank you, Sarge."

"Not necessary, Doctor. It was, and is, my job to protect you, all of you."

"Yes, but when I lost my grip, you grabbed me for a second time and in trying to save me, lost your own. If the wind hadn't dropped that instant, it would have killed you." Tears welled at the corners of her eyes and she wiped them away irritably. She did not want this man to think her weak.

The Sarge looked down at her, a mischievous twinkle in his eye. "But it didn't," he said simply.

"Thank you," she repeated, "and please, call me Natalie."

"You're welcome, *Natalie*. Now, if it's all the same to you, I'd quite like to get what's left of this gear packed into the ship, before we all get ate."

Natalie smiled warmly at him. "I can do that," she said, returning to her task with a positive step.

Fortunately, most of their tools and apparatus were packed into protective flight cases as soon as the severity of the storm had been realised, so there remained some hope. They just needed to find where the wind had deposited everything.

There was not much hope for equipment carried over the craggy drop cutting away the northern and western edges of the clearing. It would simply be too dangerous to climb down to the valley floor away from the group, looking for lost boxes in the middle of a Cretaceous forest. However, on the top of the plateau, they soon began to discover finds – rather more modern finds than the ones previously sought at *Fossil Rock*.

The table-top holo-projector was first to be found. It was damaged but probably fixable. The all-in-one soil-resistance and ground penetrating radar machine was found between the splintered boughs of a tree, some five metres above the ground. With some very careful climbing and extrication, it was retrieved miraculously unharmed. Other smaller items like shovels, picks, hammers, torches, et cetera were also turning up within ten or twenty metres of the dig site, many caught in the branches of trees descending the cliff. They saved everything they could reach safely but had no preconceptions about reclaiming everything.

From the debris dispersal patterns, they discerned how the shape of the valley, whipping the hurricane winds into a frenzy, had created eddies which flung wreckage and foliage in all directions. The revelation led them to begin searching the forest behind the dig too, contrary to the main direction of the wind, and sure enough their efforts paid dividends.

"Ah'm surprised we've recovered so much," said Douglas. "Looks like we've been lucky, eh?"

"Nah, mate. I can't find Blossom," Bluey commented, moodily.

"Blossom?"

"She's me favourite breaker – only eight kilograms but with a 2000 blow per minute, 300 joule kick and a no-shock grip. I get a full day's work out of her batteries, too. Yeah, she's a real beauty." The Australian heaved a massive sigh, "I'm devvo." With that, he strode off to resume his quest to rescue 'Blossom'.

"Have we been lucky?" asked The Sarge, overhearing the brief exchange.

Douglas looked at him quizzically.

"We lost five rifles, sir. None have been found when so much other stuff has. I think there's been more than chance at work here, Captain."

Douglas frowned. "You think they've been picked up?"

"There's only one person out here," The Sarge replied, looking up into the hills, "but that's the one person I really wouldn't want to take possession, sir."

"How could she possibly have found this site?" asked Douglas, sceptically.

Jackson pointed up towards a shelf above them, on the side of a nearby mountain. "That's where I'd camp, if I were her. Somewhere up there, sir.

Remember? Where we caught that flash of reflected sunlight? From there she could keep an eye on the *New World*, the plains and any moves we might make." He shrugged. "She was probably tracking us with her stolen binoculars from the moment the shuttle left base. It's what I'd do, anyway."

Douglas nodded. "Let's hope the rifles turn up. Ah cannae believe she's survived out here all alone," he said, adding to himself, "just when Ah thought things were going well. Keep your mouth shut, Douglas."

"She's just one more deadly predator, sir," The Sarge replied, philosophically. "If the others can eke out a living, then why not Dr Schultz? She's certainly got the skills and probably has more brainpower than all of the other predators combined."

"Aye, you're right," Douglas admitted. "It's just that when she left Ah thought, well, Ah hoped it would all... och, damnit!" he cursed, non-directionally.

The Sarge nodded. He understood Douglas' frustration. "We used to believe that nothing short of an asteroid could tumble the dominion of the dinosaurs. Now we'll see how much Turkish Delight a handful of monkeys can bring down on their heads. I can't help feeling sorry for 'em," he finished sourly.

Lloyd knelt in the trench, next to the last earthly remains of Lieutenant Audrey Jansen. She was as the dig team had left her, once they had cleared the scattered foliage and debris. Her skull still peeked out of the stone, revealing most of her face. He leaned down, running a finger around the eye and down the cheek in the way that he had in life.

Smiling sadly, he spoke, little more than a whisper for no one else to hear. "I always knew you'd leave, but I didn't think you'd go this far to be rid of me," he said, letting out a shuddering breath. "Goodbye, my love."

He stood over the grave one last time, before stepping out of the trench.

As Lloyd moved aside, Natalie moved in, respectfully replacing the bones of Captain Arnold Bessel. Satisfied they were laid out correctly, she jumped back out of the trench as Mother Sarah began to say a few words of closure and comfort for the long, long departed but by the most bizarre quirk of fate, not forgotten, man and woman.

Lloyd watched the process with dull detachment. Wiping a single tear from his cheek, he glanced up at young Georgio Baccini, standing opposite him across the trench and his eyes widened in horror.

Baines was enjoying a little time out. Earlier that morning, she had spent a constructive hour with the chief engineer, discussing the planned underpinning operation beneath the ship and the repairs to the tear in her side. Assuming the current fair weather held, it would be several days before the soil dried sufficiently for groundworks. The storm and flood waters had not yet fully subsided, but Hiro was anxious to have everything in place ready. After all, they had been fortunate once, but if the ship continued to cant further, they might yet have real problems on their hands.

Baines reran the engineer's proposal through her mind, sharing his concern after the way the hurricane had surprised them. *22nd century man is just not accustomed to being taken so completely unawares by the weather... and neither is 22nd century woman, apparently*, she thought ruefully. At least the lorry had survived the storm. Had it been wrecked, she would never have heard the end it.

She made an effort to push her worries aside for a while. All was well at the moment and she was at her leisure for the first time in a *very* long time. After making a pot of coffee and surrounding herself with snacks, she asked the computer to play a selection of pastoral classical music. Nothing too dynamic, that might suddenly scare the pants off her if she nodded off. *Yes, today is a good day*, she thought, curling up with a real book borrowed from Lieutenant Singh.

Sandy had a whole library of them, always talking about how much more relaxing the reading experience could be with paper, ink and binding. Baines had read very few physical books until this voyage. With all the choice in the world available at a voice command or the touch of a button, she hardly saw the point. However, back on the first day of their journey, which seemed so long ago now, she had taken him up on his longstanding offer. Apparently, the book was a classic and like so many classics, everyone knew of it but hardly anyone had actually *read* it. She chuckled softly to herself. Only Sandip could set off on a voyage to Mars and lend her a space opera to read 'to take her mind off things'.

She removed what was apparently called a *bookmark,* or a 'quitter strip' as Sandy referred to them, and sighed contentedly as she continued the saga. She had to admit, the book conferred a certain tactile pleasure that was winning her over and the escapism of the story was also proving anaesthetic to her real-world concerns. There really was nothing quite like sitting in safety and comfort while reading about someone else's crappy day full of monsters, space disasters and psychopaths.

Chief Nassaki had the bridge, so operations were in safe hands should any issues arise at the dig site. Hiro had offered to take the shift, suggesting she take the rest of the day. It was a rare event to see the chief on bridge duty, but he had a lot of diagnostic work to run on the bridge computers, apparently, and would be constantly flitting from one workstation to another.

Baines was touched by his concern, although she suspected that he probably just wanted her out of the way whilst he was talking to his 'Sekai'. She smiled, stretched and luxuriated on her sofa. Whatever the reason, she was just glad to find a little time for herself.

"Now, where was I? Ah, yes – that's no moon, it's a space sta— aargh!" she exclaimed in frustration as her comm binged. Sighing deeply, she answered, "Baines."

"I'm sorry, Commander," Hiro's voice called through the small speaker. *"I've just had a very 'energetic' conversation with one of Dr Miller's chemists, a Dr Aabid Hussain. Apparently, he's found some strange chemical traces on one of the lorries in the Pod cargo hold. I told him the captain would be back before long but he was insistent that this couldn't wait."*

"Did he tell you any more than that?" asked Baines.

"No, but he was very agitated. When I offered to go myself, he pointed out that his findings were a matter of ship's security. I informed him that I have the highest clearance, to which he replied that he would call me, like a shot, if the vending machine on his level broke down, but this was above my pay grade!"

Baines laughed. "The cheeky sod!"

"Well, I expect we'll have a lot of this type of thing now, with a ship full of twitchy scientists – each more qualified than the last. It's not overly surprising, after the captain's speech yesterday. Although, I think we should look into it, Commander. Would you like me to go down there anyway? I can lock the bridge?"

"No, it's OK," said Baines, resigned. "I'll go. In the Pod cargo bay, you say?"

"Yes, Commander."

"On my way."

Baines arrived in the main cargo bay a few minutes later. She spotted Hussain at the far end of the vast chamber. Although they had not spoken directly, she recognised him from his photograph in the passenger files.

"Good morning, Dr Hussain," she greeted. "How can I help you?"

Hussain nodded brusquely. "The samples I took are in there, Commander." He guided her to one of the smaller storage areas leading off the main bay. "But I'd like to show you where I found them first."

He walked her around a couple of the lorries, which did not really clarify anything, but she humoured him politely. Finally he marched her back to the storage room. "After you, Commander," he said, courteous for the first time.

Baines thanked him and walked into a darkened room. She turned, only to see the door closing behind her. "Hey!" she shouted, scrabbling around to find the door controls in the total blackout. Deep, masculine laughter from the darkness behind made her stop. The laughter, she could hardly fail to note, was of the unpleasant sort. She turned to face the stranger, but before her eyes could fully adjust, hard, white light struck her and she was blinded all over again.

"Thank you for coming down here, Commander," said a rich, aristocratic voice.

"Did they teach you this little routine in *baddie school*?" Baines asked snarkily, shielding her aching eyes.

The laughter resumed.

"And Dr Hussain? One of your merry men, is he?" she added.

"Oh, *yes*," the deep voice replied. "Dr Hussain has proven himself *very* useful, for now. I wouldn't be the least bit surprised if he didn't prove himself to be more useful still, before this little costume party is over."

"Who *are* you?" asked Baines, more bravely than she felt. She could hear other noises now, scuffs of movement around the room. It seemed they were not alone. *Oh, crap*, she thought.

"Commander, I'm offended. You, who diligently knows everyone's name so you can constantly prompt that Scottish oaf, you of all people, I would expect to know who I am."

The voice was smarmy and guano slick treacherous, but there *was* just a quality to it that Baines thought she might recognise. She squinted against the light, not quite willing to believe, but she had to ask, "*Del Bond?*"

Georgio stood very near the edge of the crag, looking down into the grave as Mother Sarah spoke. He glanced up to see Geoff staring at him, terror etched into his every feature. Before he could speak, Lloyd launched himself across the pit at him, but missed.

Georgio spun out of the way, convinced the reflexes of youth had saved him.

It was actually Lloyd who had saved him, by throwing his entire weight at the dinosaur leaping from the trees behind and to the right of him.

The young Mapusaurus was probably no more than two or three years old but already several hundred kilos in weight. Lloyd was lucky, or perhaps unlucky, because he caught the animal off balance with just one clawed foot on the ground and they went over the edge, together. The crag was very steep-sided but tree studded and everyone heard the crashing as the two fell, screaming and roaring after their fashion, as they disappeared from view.

It was over in the bridge of a second. The others woke to the danger quickly, but too late to help. In any case, they had their own problems – the animal was not hunting alone.

The door behind Baines slid open once more. She spun around quickly, hoping for a chance to leap back through it, but her way was blocked. Dr Aabid Hussain had returned with another.

Baines gaped for a second, before stepping back further into the room as the newcomer pointed a nine millimetre pistol at her midriff. They entered, sealing the door behind them. This time, as the door closed, the lights came on fully to compensate and Baines could see that they carried at least five rifles slung over their shoulders.

"*Schultz*," she breathed the name like a curse.

The blonde doctor merely curled a lip in recognition.

"Welcome back, Doctor," Del Bond greeted. "Clearly, you got my message?"

Schultz merely nodded at the man but her focus never left Baines.

"When you nicked all that stuff," Baines pointed out, with bottomless bravado, "you seem to have forgotten to pinch a hairbrush!"

Schultz just sneered.

Baines turned back to Bond. "What do you want from me?" she asked. "Whatever it is, you can shove it up your backside and use it as a trumpet!"

Bond laughed again. "Delightful," he said, mocking her courage.

Baines was completely surrounded now. Including herself, there were nine people in the room. "The bridge crew know where I am, you know. It won't take long for a team to get down here," she said, seriously hoping for the best. She knew that by 'crew' she meant 'Hiro' and if he glanced up from underneath one of the consoles he was pulling apart, it would be a miracle.

"Oh, you think so?" asked Bond in his unctuous way. "We took the liberty of recording your short conversation and walkabout outside, with Dr Hussain, playing it back for the cargo bay cameras – on loop. I dare say the ingenious Mr Nassaki will eventually spot the deception for what it is, but I doubt he will notice for quite some time."

Baines stared at him, wishing with all her might that James or The Sarge were on the bridge, but this situation had obviously been orchestrated to take full advantage of both men's absence. With Private Jones and Major White also busy about their daily routines, and with no reason to suspect what was happening, her wish bank was all tapped out. She had no intention of confirming these facts for the enemy, however, so she changed the subject. "You know, I couldn't stand you when you were a philosopher, but now I've really gone off you."

"Ha ha, marvellous," replied Bond, clapping his hands together foppishly.

"And where did that posh accent come from?" asked Baines, playing for time. "I thought you were from Milton Keynes?"

"Oh come, Commander, you didn't really think a *philosopher* could afford to buy a ticket for this ride, did you?" he asked.

"I suppose not. It was a rubbish cover story," Baines retorted.

"Precisely," Bond agreed. "So ridiculous it had to be true! Oh dear, Commander, do you mind if I call you Jill? You did make it all rather easy."

Jill frowned, as an idea struck her. "Do you really not like being called Derek, then?" she asked.

A tiny cloud fluttered across Bond's blue sky and Baines caught the slight tell. "Well, here we are," she said. "So what do you want, *Derek*?"

"From you?" asked Bond, in mock surprise. "Oh, nothing from you, Jill."

"OK. What next, *Derek*?" She enjoyed the slight tic that twitched his face each time she spoke his name. "Do we just hang around until we get hungry, or...?" She shrugged.

"No, my dear, we hang around until Daddy gets home." Bond's smile slipped up a notch on its own oil. "I'm sure the valiant Captain Douglas will be only too pleased to help me."

Baines laughed without humour. "You're dreaming, Derek! The only thing you'll get from the captain is what you deserve!"

"Oh, I do hope so. I've worked so terribly hard to get this far, you see?" he smiled again. "I may not know how to play the trumpet, which you so kindly proffered, but when the good captain arrives, I'll bet I can play *you*, like a flute!" His disgusting *bonhomie* dropped into a snarl.

A second Mapusaurus roared, launching itself from the tree line. The people dove and scattered, leaving the animal temporarily confused. While it snapped around wildly, unsure whom to follow, Natalie searched for signs of a larger pack. She found none, which was a *semi*-comfort – at least, from the backhanded perspective of a woman lost in the jungle, who finds herself standing next to *just the one* tiger.

At least the dense forest did not afford the sort of room adults of the species required. She guessed the pair had lost or quite possibly been abandoned by their mother and were not yet fully trained in the art of hunting.

Douglas did not care. "SHOOT HIM!" he bellowed.

"He's only a baby!" Natalie shouted, her love of animals driving out some of her fear.

"Are you serious?" cried Bluey.

Even without training, these animals were hard-coded killers and they were really quick, but if Natalie's theory was correct, it would explain the youngsters' retreat to the forest for safety. Here they could learn from a school of slightly less hard knocks.

Sergeant Jackson levelled his rifle at the funeral crasher, intent on beginning lesson one immediately, but there were just too many people around. There were plenty of clear shots but no clear backgrounds. He looked about him for inspiration and then saw it. Between two low branches in a nearby tree, he spotted a metal container left by the storm. He picked up a good sized stick and began to beat it noisily.

The young dinosaur spun around, giving this strange din its utmost attention. It leaned forward, snarling with menace, clawed hands clenching and unclenching in anticipation of the kill.

Douglas had seen this behaviour before, having had a narrow escape with a full grown bull Mapusaurus the very first time he stepped outside the ship. He realised The Sarge's game, aimed his pistol at the animal's side and fired a low-powered stun bolt.

The shock enraged the juvenile further, making it turn towards Douglas. The animal lowered its head, about to charge, when Bluey made a throaty, yodelling sound. The unfamiliar cry made the animal snap round yet again.

During the fracas, Lieutenant Singh ran for the ship. Throwing himself into the pilot's seat, he bypassed everything he could to get the engines fired up as quickly as possible.

The human beings stood in a circle around the dinosaur. No one dared take a shot from one of the Heath-Riflesons because a high power shot would kill any person it touched. Even a low power hit would stun them, in all likelihood turning them into Mapu chow.

One of the soldiers stood at the edge of the cliff, jumping and flapping his arms about while shouting obscenities. Turning one final time, the young Mapusaurus took the bait, committing to a charge.

"Watch out!" shouted Bluey. "He'll have you over the side."

"I've got it," the man shouted back, bouncing from side to side on the balls of his feet, to keep the animal guessing. "I'm floating like a butterfly!"

"Yeah, well this bee's got a chainsaw for a face – *RUN!*"

The charge felt like an age for a man both metaphorically and very literally on the edge, but he waited bravely until the last possible moment. The creature leapt across the funereal trench as the soldier rolled into it, hunkering down, praying he was fast enough.

The dinosaur flew over him, preying. His fast was over.

Everyone else, who could, fired.

Douglas heard the crunch of broken bones from the pit, as the man scrambled to save himself and cried out in directionless anger at the desecration, while firing rapidly towards the predator.

With lightning reflexes, the Mapusaurus skidded to the edge, avoiding a deadly fall by shouldering into a tree. Its tail swished rapidly, movements which proved so unpredictable that the recovery team's shots went wide. Regaining its balance in a heartbeat, the creature turned with terrifying speed, about to take the head of the man climbing from the dig trench, when a honking, animal cry rang through the forest.

The soldier got to his feet and ran as only a man being chased by a carnivorous dinosaur can. Everyone stopped firing, no longer able to get a clear shot. The predator paused, confused, sniffing the air for an instant, before charging at Douglas, who screamed.

The sound of that scream triggered a recognition response in another small reptilian mind and the owner of the honking call ran out of the forest, also heading for the captain.

The latecomer was less impressive than the Mapusaurus but as Douglas watched them both approach from separate directions he knew he could not hope to match their speed.

The Mapusaurus, fixated on Douglas, was slow to take notice of the other, smaller creature and it crashed into the predator's side using its head like a ram. The Mapusaurus fell but sprang almost immediately back to its feet. Douglas fancied he recognised the little dinosaur that had interrupted the predator's charge. It screamed in terror as the young predator turned to face this new threat and screamed in pain as the Mapusaurus attacked. The adversaries went down in a bundle, the smaller animal shrieking as a huge *ROAR* tore through the glade.

The Mapusaurus gave up its advantage instantly and shot off, back into the forest.

The men and women collapsed, panting, bathed in a symphony of rocket noise as Singh opened up the shuttle's engines. He brought the little ship back down near the centre of the clearing.

Douglas and The Sarge rallied everyone quickly to begin loading the salvaged equipment into the cargo hold.

"He's coming with us," said Douglas, pointing at the wounded animal. It mewed pathetically as it tried and failed to get to its feet. Unable to run from the engine roar, the creature was clearly terrified.

"Are you sure, Captain?" asked Natalie.

"Of course Ah'm sure," snapped Douglas, impatiently. "That's the Mayor! And he saved my life. We're no' leaving him here to get eaten by that thing and that's final! Help me get him in."

Many heads were shaken in disbelief and misgiving, but the crew did as ordered, carefully carrying the creature aboard the shuttle.

"What about Geoff?" asked Georgio.

With the fight for their lives, Douglas had temporarily forgotten about Lloyd. "He went over the cliff, laddie, with that evil thing's evil twin. Ah'm sorry," he added sympathetically.

Georgio looked bleakly at the spot where Lloyd had fallen from the edge. "He saved my life," he said, quietly.

"Aye," Douglas agreed, sadly. "If it helps, Ah genuinely think he wanted redemption. It was too late and he knew it, but saving your life, well, in the scheme of things, Ah dinnae think that anyone could have asked any more of the man."

Georgio nodded slightly. "Mario was right, it was important that I forgave him while I had the chance."

Douglas guided the young and very confused engineer through the hatch with kindness. Once safely inside the shuttle, he sealed it behind them.

Natalie and Bluey strapped themselves in as best they could within the small cargo hold, wishing to stay with the wounded animal while the shuttle flew back to the *New World*.

"Do you know what it is yet?" asked Bluey.

"No," Natalie admitted, "but I bet I know a man who will."

Bluey nodded. "So, are you gonna tell Beckett or am I?"

Natalie frowned. "Tell him what?"

Bluey laughed. "That The Sarge stoved the side of his beloved tucker box in, with a piece of green lumber!"

The shuttle docked in its berth aboard the *New World* without incident. Douglas unstrapped and walked down to the cargo bay, slowing as he reached Mother Sarah. "How are you, Sarah?" he asked.

"That was quite an adventure," she admitted shakily. "But I'm fine, James, don't worry. We priests have always gone to battle, you know."

"Aye, true enough," agreed Douglas. He patted her companionably on the shoulder and continued further down the ship to check on his wounded saviour.

As he entered the cargo hold, he saw The Mayor lying on his side, panting heavily with a large, blood-soaked compress taped onto his hip.

"How is he?" asked Douglas, kneeling down to stroke the animal's head, gently. "Ah assume he's a he?"

"He is a boy. One who's lost a lot of blood, unfortunately," replied Natalie. "That was a *big* bite. He's in shock. Still, the wound's already coagulating nicely and as long as we can keep it clean he should make it – providing he'll eat and take fluids. Animals have an extraordinary healing capacity."

Douglas looked into the innocent eyes of the creature. "You'll be OK, laddie, and thank ye," he added gently. "Dr Pearson will soon get you back on your feet. You're in good hands."

He turned back to Natalie. "He saved my life, and when Ah think of all the names Ah called him when he knocked me flat on my backside the first time Ah stepped off the ship." He smiled fondly at the creature. "Do you think he remembered me? Is that why he came when I called?"

"Ahem, *called*, Captain?" Natalie asked, innocently.

Douglas frowned at her. "Alright, *screamed* then. You remind me of Commander Baines!" he remarked tetchily.

Natalie laughed. "It's possible. We believe many dinosaurs had superior senses. He may have recognised your voice or your smell—"

"*Smell?*" Douglas cut in, raising his eyebrows.

"Scent," Natalie laughed again, "your *scent*, Captain."

Douglas laughed too. "Do we know what sort of animal he is?"

"I don't. When you described your first encounter, Tim thought he might be some kind of Iguanodont – a smaller descendant of Iguanodon or a proto-Hadrosaur, perhaps. Apparently there haven't been, or *won't be*, many finds of this sort in South America, according to Tim anyway. He says the giant sauropods dominated here. But, hey, who knows? The fossil record we have is only a fraction of a percent of all that has lived throughout the history of life on Earth, so who can guess what we'll find while we're here?"

"Or what will find us," Douglas added, darkly.

"Well, if Tim can't identify him exactly, then I think we should call him *Mayor Dougli Salvator*," Natalie proposed.

"Hey, now just go easy with the naming things," said Douglas. "Stuff like that has a habit of sticking around here!"

"Right, Captain," Natalie replied, seriously.

Douglas left her, but as he walked towards the doors which led back into the ship, he heard her call loudly across the shuttle bay, "Can someone get me a trolley to carry *Mayor Dougli Salvator* down to the biology labs, please?"

Douglas stopped, tilting his head back slightly as he closed his eyes and sighed. After a moment he simply lowered his head and trudged on.

Douglas waited patiently for Commander Baines to open the bridge doors. It was a surprise to find Hiro on station instead.

"Hiro? Where's the commander?" he asked.

"She was here earlier, sir," replied Hiro, "but she looked exhausted. As I had to work on the bridge anyway today, I sort of *encouraged* her to take some time for herself, while I remained on station here until you returned."

"Aye," agreed Douglas. "She's been through it the last few days. Well done, Lieutenant."

"Hmm, unfortunately, it didn't exactly turn out as we'd hoped, sir," Hiro admitted.

As he viewed a video feed from the Pod, his expression changed to one of concern. Turning back to Douglas, he spoke quickly. "Sir, we had an irate call from a Dr Aabid Hussain, saying that he'd found some strange chemical traces on one of the lorries. I offered to go down there but he insisted it was a security matter and demanded to see the commander."

"What did they find?" asked Douglas, picking up on the concern suddenly emanating from his chief engineer.

"I don't know, sir," Hiro replied, nervously. "I've been so tied up, I lost track of the time. She must have been down there an hour and a half now, at least. That wouldn't concern me particularly, but I've just spotted this."

He beckoned Douglas, who looked at the screen over his shoulder. The video feed clearly showed Baines walking around the cargo bay with Hussain. Nothing untoward there, but suddenly, the people appeared to jump a couple of metres to the left, beginning their walk around all over again.

"What are we looking at?" asked Douglas. "A fault with the camera?"

Hiro selected multiple cameras and the screen divided. The commander and the doctor were shown walking around the main cargo hold from eight different perspectives. Every one of them jumped at the same time.

"That's on loop!" Hiro shouted, turning to Douglas. "The cameras have been tampered with, sir! She went in there and hasn't come back out!"

"Get me a comm link to Sergeant Jackson and Major White, *now*," ordered Douglas, pointing at Hiro's console.

Hiro quickly did as instructed, receiving a response straight away.

"Ford, Sarge, this is Douglas. Ah need everybody who knows which end of a gun goes bang, to be armed and doubled down to the Pod cargo bay *immediately*. Everyone you can find, Jill's in trouble! Ah'm on my way down – Douglas out!"

"I'm sorry, sir," said Hiro. "It all looked normal at a glance."

"Not your fault, Lieutenant. Hold the fort," said Douglas, striding towards the door. "And Hiro," he said, turning around, "keep the bridge locked down!"

Douglas ran into the Pod's main cargo hold followed by Singh, The Sarge and twelve other crew, all armed with Heath-Riflesons. He skidded to a stop, unable to believe his eyes. Just five metres away, Dr Heidi Schultz stood bold as brass, with a group of armed men and women at her back.

Slowly, two opposing lines formed. Baines was held around the neck by two of Schultz's minions.

"So you worked it out in the end, old man," Schultz sneered nastily, a look which marred her considerable beauty; her English, as always, harshly accented with Bavarian V-Ws.

Douglas assessed the situation instantly. It was bad. "Let her go," he said, simply.

"Predictable," replied Schultz contemptuously. "Predictable and weak, and that is why you will always lose. Just back from reburying our long dead friends, are we? I suppose you have also worked Captain Bessel and Lieutenant Jansen up into great heroes, yes? Travelling across time to save you?"

She continued with an expression of mocking sorrow. "But they got it wrong by twenty million years and died bravely." Smiling nastily again, she added, "You should know that Bessel was one of us. He was a *true* believer."

"Liar!" Douglas spat.

"*Nein, Kapitän.*" Schultz was clearly enjoying Douglas' outrage. "I assure you this is quite true. We were meant to go back just 100,000 years to start over again with a new, handpicked human race. We would have trained the ancient people, using their pressed labour to build a better, stronger, *purer* civilisation. All would have worked perfectly had that idiot Lloyd not panicked, laying too much explosive within the wormhole drive. Another weak little man," she sighed. "I will have to kill him too, when I see him next, I think," she added, almost apologetically.

"Too late, Schultz," Douglas replied tersely, disgusted by this woman he used to think of as a colleague. "He's already dead."

Schultz smiled in genuine surprise. "You have killed him? Well done, *Kapitän*. There might be hope for you yet."

"No!" Douglas snarled. "The man died a hero's death, saving a life, and that's the way we will all remember him." He looked around the assembled crew behind him, brooking no argument. "He was no longer your pawn when it mattered. When it mattered, he did the right thing. That is why scum like you will never *vin!*" he spat, mocking her Germanic accent. "No' in the end!"

"Never mind," Schultz allowed, unconcerned. "Was your other *friend* 'doing the right thing' too? When he tried to reinforce us? Bessel was to bring our backup, you see. He failed, but this is of no consequence."

"Ah don't believe you," Douglas dismissed her. "And Ah'll no' allow you and your *animals* to soil his memory!" he added, with a nod to the people ranged behind her.

"More weakness, *Kapitän*," Schultz repeated, simply. "You are *all* so weak. You will not be required in the new world."

"Humanity doesnae make a person weak," retorted Douglas. "The courage of mankind to do the right thing has echoed down throughout our history. It's what gives us the strength to face any setback, any obstacle standing in our path, and win through. If ye cannae see that, then you're blind and ye willnae see your end, when it comes, either."

"Enough!" Schultz spat, ending the debate. "Here is how it will be. You will get your pathetic, mongrel menagerie off this ship and hand over all of the security codes to me or," she turned to Baines, "she dies."

"If she dies," Douglas retorted dangerously, "you will be the very next body to hit the deck – that Ah promise ye!"

"You think I won't do it?" the beautiful monster asked, arching a delicate eyebrow in amusement.

"If you want to die right here, right now, just say the word." Douglas spoke quietly, radiating freezing cold fury.

The sounds of running feet erupted from the passageway behind him as Major White and Captain Gleeson led seven others, all armed, into the cargo bay. They quickly joined Douglas' ranks, levelling their rifles and tilting the odds almost three to one in favour of the *New World*'s crew. The captain turned back to Schultz once more, smiling nastily. "Just say the word," he repeated.

"A stand-off," Schultz noted, without obvious concern, "but I still hold most of the aces I think." She picked out Dr Klaus Fischer from the late arrivals. The German biologist was acting as an emergency security operative alongside many others. "Klaus," she said. "Why don't you join me and help rebuild what was stolen from our people?"

Fischer gave her a look of disgust. "I want nothing to do with you or your sick cause," he spoke levelly but the anger was clear in his eyes, "and neither does our modern *Deutschland*. We turned our back on your kind long ago. We should have stamped you out, but don't confuse kindness with weakness, Heidi. We *will* stop you!"

"*Schwach dummkopf!*" Schultz spat at him with contempt. "Such beautiful English, you even sound like them!"

"*I love my country*," Fischer replied in German, "*and I'm proud of my heritage, with perhaps one or two exceptions.*" He switched back to English so that everyone could understand where he stood. "Your ways should forever be remembered, but only so that we *never* repeat them!"

"You will die with your *friends* then? Yes? That is fine with me." She cut Fischer off, returning her gaze to Douglas. "Get your people off the ship and give me the security codes. Do this, and I will not have to kill any more of your pets."

Douglas glared for a long moment, running scenarios through his mind.

"No, Captain," said Baines. She could see he was considering Schultz's demands. "It's one life for a hundred. You can't do it, you know you can't."

Douglas ignored her, his eyes boring into Heidi's. "One life for a hundred," he repeated, distractedly. "The commander is right – as she so often is."

"You will sacrifice her?" asked Schultz, with obvious surprise.

"No," said Douglas, doggedly. "Ah'll make ye a new offer."

Schultz sighed theatrically. "Well?" she asked.

"Ah'll give you and your band of, of *scum*, ma shuttle," he replied at last.

"And we take the commander too, yes?"

"No – just the shuttle, you will release Commander Baines."

"So you can lock me out of it by remote? *Kapitän*, please," Schultz answered, disdainfully. "It looks like I will have to make an example after all." She turned to give one of her henchman the order to fire.

"Wait!" snapped Douglas.

She held up a hand for the man to wait. "Well, *Kapitän*?"

"You will not be locked out of the shuttle," he explained.

"And I'm supposed to trust your word on that?" She looked at him like he was a fool. "I don't think so. I weary of this." She turned again.

"Ye'll no' be locked out of the shuttle," Douglas spoke quickly, the tension in his voice obvious, "because *Ah'll* be going with ye!"

"NO!" Baines shouted, fearfully.

Again, Douglas ignored her, glaring only at Schultz, who tilted her head to one side in thought.

"Very well," she answered slowly, "but I want the shuttle brought down to the enclosure outside, here." She pointed towards the hangar doors behind her. "I'm not walking through the ship's corridors so you can ambush me."

"Fine," agreed Douglas.

"No, Captain," Baines tried again. This time Schultz struck the prisoner in the stomach with her pistol grip. Baines, taken by surprise, crumpled, coughing. Being restrained by the neck was all that prevented her from going down.

Douglas gave Schultz a look of absolute loathing. "She's an unarmed prisoner, and restrained, you coward!"

"Ha!" Schultz laughed in his face. "Live out there for a few days with the monsters and then call me that, *Kapitän*. I have the strength to do whatever must be done – strength your kind entirely lack. I will not let my people become extinct simply to pander to fools like you!"

"Ah've heard enough!" spat Douglas, his voice thick with anger. "*Singh*, bring ma shuttle down outside, *now*!"

"Yes sir." The pilot cast one last look at Baines before running for the exit.

Schultz directed one of her followers towards the hangar doors behind them, with a nod.

A tear ran down Baines' cheek as she stared at Douglas, shaking her head in silent desperation. For a long moment, the two sides faced one another without moving. Eventually Schultz spoke once more.

"Bessel's attempt to find us may have failed, *Kapitän*. This is perhaps no surprise as he was a friend of *yours*, but others will come – others true to *mein Großvater's* cause." She curled her lip into another unpleasant smile, her eyes burning with a strange light. "Such genius. All this from a *bierdose*, a beer can ring-pull!"

Douglas' jaw dropped.

"Ah, I see you know what I'm talking about, *Kapitän*. Do you still doubt our reach? Our ability to bend everything and everyone to our will? We control government, military, media – everything. Can you imagine the intricacies of the planning required to make all this possible? The *brilliance* of its conception?"

"Grandpa Schultz sounds like a bladdy fruitcake in charge of the bladdy picnic," muttered Gleeson.

Schultz's look of wonder turned to spite. "When our support arrives, you will be overrun and exterminated and just in case you doubt us, I will make our position plain."

She took a step towards Dr Aabid Hussain. "We also use terrorists, political and religious fanatics, all manner of sects and dissident groups to do our dirty work. We fund their little schemes to further our much larger ones. Their petty causes often sow discord but are always engineered to serve ours. Of course, the perpetrators never realise this. Despite his dual US citizenship, Dr Hussain here is a representative of one of the groups we encourage in the Middle East. He has served our interests well, although he believed he was serving his own."

Hussain looked at her askance for the first time.

She stopped, looking back towards Douglas. "But now we are here, I will *show* you how the new world will be."

With that, she aimed her nine millimetre pistol at Douglas. He braced for the pain, but at the last moment, she turned and shot Hussain in the temple. The man collapsed like a sack of dirty laundry.

The echo of the gunshot died away to be replaced by the roar of atmospheric jet engines from outside. While Schultz taunted the crew, even to the point of murdering a man in cold blood, another of her people had opened the inner and outer hangar doors, ready for their escape.

A storm of debris devils erupted in the compound, now visible through the large opening as the shuttle landed.

Captain Douglas stared at the dead man with a soldier's dispassion. Intellectually, he may have been relieved that the enemy was a man down, but he still carried a human being's natural horror at Schultz's contempt for life. He had extended the olive branch after Lloyd's court case in the hope that the insurgents would see reason, and now this. He was more affected by the death of an enemy than she was by the murder of an accomplice – it was inconceivable.

Captain Gleeson broke the shocked silence. "Now, how about carking the others, then we can have the rest of the day off, ya psycho mare!"

Schultz narrowed her eyes at the Australian for a moment but otherwise ignored him. "You will now load extra fuel and food supplies into the shuttle's hold," she said, cutting into Douglas' reverie. "Aviation *and* hypergolic fuel, and, *Kapitän*," she paused, smiling a huntress smile, "*Captain*, don't keep me waiting." To make her point, she waved her pistol indolently in Commander Baines' direction once more.

Douglas swallowed and nodded to some of his people to make it happen.

"Let the Commander go," he demanded.

"Certainly," agreed Schultz, "and you will join us over here – *please*."

Her courtesy was merely a sarcastic device, but Douglas knew he had only two options. He could allow Jill Baines to die or surrender his weapon to the man next to him and walk towards the enemy. It was no choice. He crossed the space between the two sides as Baines was shoved, hard, back towards the *New World*'s crew.

Parity restored, Schultz casually holstered her pistol. "Welcome to the winning side, *Kapitän*."

"Captain!" cried Baines, wretchedly.

Singh returned through the open main airlock, walking back to the crew's side of the lines. "She's gassed up and ready to go, Captain," he said, quietly.

The men loading the shuttle with extra fuel and containers full of supplies returned presently, nodding to Douglas that their task was complete.

"Thank you, Sandip," he said, looking the lieutenant in the eye. He glanced around the rest of the gathered crew. "Thank you all, for everything."

"I *say*," drawled Del Bond. "Isn't this delicious? *Such* drama!"

Douglas looked the erstwhile philosopher up and down. "Do ye know what, Derek, dinnae look too deeply for the meaning o' this," he said, landing Bond an uppercut to the jaw, which removed a couple of teeth and a pound of pride when he hit the deck.

"Ha!" barked Gleeson. "What a humdinger! He won't need to ask why that happened!"

A rumble and a clatter of something being knocked over sounded from the corner of the bay, behind Schultz's team. She looked around quickly, drawing her gun once more, but could see nothing untoward.

The scene was now being watched from under a tarpaulin by a new pair of eyes, inquisitive eyes, *brown* eyes.

Eventually, Schultz disregarded the noise as natural and glared down at Bond, contemptuously. He was still down on the deck. She nodded to a man and a woman near him. "You two, pick him up," she ordered.

There followed an awkward silence as everyone recovered their bearings after successive distractions.

"After we were sent back in time, why did you keep attacking us? Ah mean, if you wanted the ship intact?" Douglas asked Schultz.

Schultz was unreadable, eventually saying, "I had reasons, but plans change."

"James," Baines spoke into the exchange, her voice breaking. "Don't do this."

For the first time Douglas looked at her, looked deep into her eyes; everything he wanted to say in that gaze. Then he straightened. Standing smartly to attention, he saluted her. "Good luck, *Captain* Baines."

"NO!" Baines cried out, her eyes wide, her legs almost giving way.

Douglas was impassive, the full military bearing. "Do Ah stand relieved, Captain?" he asked.

Baines mouthed no, no, *no* soundlessly as tears streamed down her cheeks.

"Captain?" Douglas snapped, rigidly.

Baines straightened and batted her tears away, standing as tall as she could. "You—" her voice cracked, forcing her to gulp a deep breath before trying again. "You stand relieved, sir." She saluted.

Douglas maintained the salute a while longer. Eventually, he smiled warmly at her and winked. Lowering the salute, he turned and strode out of the cargo bay, across the compound and into the waiting shuttle with Schultz's guards struggling to keep pace.

The crew members present followed irresistibly outside.

The terrorists kept a wary eye on them, falling back by sections, also making their way across the compound.

Bond lagged behind. He was cursing roundly and shouting about how much he was going to make Douglas pay, when a crash sounded from inside the Pod cargo bay. The noise was like a stack of pots and pans smashing to the floor, followed by a skittering.

Everyone turned in surprise to see Reiver shoot out from under the blue tarpaulin near the main hatch. He must have been travelling at thirty miles an hour by the time he collected Bond, taking him down for the second time in as many minutes. The man screamed as the dog pinned him to the ground.

Captain Douglas had disappeared into the shuttle by now, along with the insurgency team. Only Schultz remained outside for one last look around. She curled her lip in disgust as she watched Bond try, ineffectually, to defend himself from his attacker. She was about to leave when someone called her name.

"Schultz!" Baines shouted, striding to within a few paces.

The two women faced one another. Dr Heidi Schultz raised her head, looking haughtily down her nose at her antagonist.

Captain Jill Baines raised her arm, pointing directly at her enemy. Her eyes burned with almost demented hatred and pain as she snarled, "I'll be coming for you… *bitch*!"

The shuttle's engines roared to life.

Schultz stared at Baines just a moment longer, expressionless, before turning on her heel. The hatch closed behind her as she entered the craft. Within moments they lifted from the ground, gaining height gradually to hover fifteen metres above the top of the earthworks.

The crew of the *New World* stood in an arc around Baines, all gazing up at the rising ship in disbelief and despair.

The shuttle put her stern to the mothership and accelerated away once more.

Baines ran up onto the new palisade walkway to watch the little ship grow smaller and smaller in her sight, until at last, it was gone altogether. The air smelt of exhaust fumes as she took a deep, shuddering breath, her exhalation carrying a single word on the wind to follow in the shuttle's wake.

"James," she said.